THE C...
OF
MALCOLM HARRIS

VOLUME SEVEN
DESCENT INTO DARKNESS:
AUTOBIOGRAPHY
OF A VAMPIRE

A NOVEL BY
TERRANCE KILPATRICK

As always, I dedicate this book to my first and greatest fan, my wife, Debra. I would also like to extend my deepest appreciation to all my early fans, Patricia, Sandy, Kerry, Pat and especially my sister Karen and my mother, Gladys.

"Be sober, be vigilant; because your adversary the devil, as a roaring lion, walketh about, seeking whom he may devour"

1 Peter, 5:8

AUTHOR'S NOTE

Due to many reader's requests, I felt compelled to write this book. I wanted to explore how a character like Tayla could move them to experience such things as pity, praise, and admiration, even to condemnation. All in all, I wanted to emphasize the dual nature of this character. This book is the third and last of three prequels to the Chronicles of Malcolm Harris. It may seem confusing to the reader if this is their first introduction to the character of Tayla Elisabeta Rokosovich, Queen of the *Order of the Clan of the Red Velvet*. She is a stunning character, a villain and heroine, complex and rich with emotion, yet a paradox all at the same time. If she confuses you, I suggest you read *Fear No Evil* to gain a point of reference. Often, she is speaking directly to Malcolm Harris, usually at the beginning of a chapter for she wrote this account specifically for him.

I centered the first part of the story to illustrate the relationship between Tayla's mother and father. My story starts out at the Battle of Varna. While approaching the port city of Varna, Prince Vladis of Wallachia meets a camp follower whom he finds so attractive, he falls deeply in love with her. It was close, very intimate, and nearly indestructible. The same was true for her father's love for his children was beyond reproach, which makes this story tragic for the nature of vampirism causes him to betray himself and destroy that which he loves. I am aware that readers of my first book, "Deliver Us from Evil" will recall that Tayla tells Malcolm a different story entirely about her family and the tragedy that befalls them. I have made statements about a vampire's memory in that they remember everything except that which a source of power does not want them to remember. The loss of her fondest memories has been her curse for nearly eight hundred years.

The second part illustrates how Tayla's father's ex-wife was nothing more than an evil woman by her own nature. This evil is particularly important as she shows what one woman can do if she hates enough. It is the tale of how a lowly peasant girl can be born into a set of circumstances and rise above her station. And she does it tragically.

The third part tells of how she defends her new nature, creates a race of beings like herself and organizes those like her into clans.

The fourth part illustrates the struggles the children go through to establish themselves as a dominate predator of the species and establishing the rule of each child's clan. Tayla declares herself a Queen and challenges the *Order of the Dragons of Set*. To have a Papal edict regarding heresy, especially against vampires, she eliminates the *Order of the Dragons of Set*. This frees her from their meddling and allows her to establish her kingdom.

The fifth and final part is about her entry into the New World, that of the North Americas and her journey across a young nation. It describes her hand in shaping history, and intervention at times to produce the outcomes we now know as the history of America. Her final chapter is the details of how she built her empire, not only as a vampire queen, but her financial and real estate empires as well. It entails all the developments that the readers have come to know as the Upper and Lower Estates, the familiars that were with her in the first accounts, and finally her meeting with her most treasured relationship of all, that of Malcolm and his family.

Throughout this book, I hoped the reader will get a firm grasp of the emotional capabilities of my main character, Tayla. She is courageous, relentless, wise due to her longevity and can turn her usual benevolence to those she likes into anger quickly. Her first and foremost instinct is that of survival. She is compassionate and is very sentimental. She desired all the blessings of mortality but instead was given the curses of loneliness, of doom, and sadness. She does not live in a paradise on Earth but rather in a world of regret.

PROLOGUE

The dimly lit chamber was deep within the lower levels of the castle. It was the deepest one could go. The castle, long abandoned by the former occupants, now belonged to the undead, the rightful heirs to it. The dungeon was old, the air stale and dank. The smell of mold mixed with the smell of charcoal left a malodourous smell in the room. The only light was that of the torches and the brazier full of branding irons. Without that light, would have been in utter darkness, without any sound.

The vampiress had waited for a long time for this moment. Her victory was in the making. The priest, Father Joachim, had followed her carcfully laid out trail and fell into her trap. He alone survived her ambush. She had taken him captive to extract information from him. She wanted to know why this war between the siblings and the church had gotten to this point. The vampires wanted no war. They only wanted to survive. The church would not tolerate their existence. She had to know why.

The priest who had been unconscious began to stir, showing signs of coming back into awareness. When he opened his eyes, he got the shock of his life.

She tightened the noose around the priest's neck as his labored respirations became even louder and more strained. No matter how much she had tried to give the church a wide berth, it had not worked. The enemy she had not wanted placed her and her kind at the top of its enemies list. She had the priest just where she wanted him: On a rack, bound and naked. The look in her vampire eyes inspired fear into the priest that he had never known or had even seen in his parishioners. He could see into the brazier sitting next to the rack. The firebrands glowed red as they sat in the fire. The heat in the chamber caused the priest to sweat profusely.

Tayla hissed and spat out her feelings. "My anger has had years in which to build its foundation upon. The endless cavalcade of persecution, with the shadow of damnation hanging over my head has tested my patience long enough. Now, you will pay, as will your family and their offspring as well. I shall wipe out your name from the earth, as you and yours planned to extinguish mine."

She had all the instruments of torture that Father Joachim had come to know and use to extract information from her familiars to track down and kill her spawn. The vampire Queen, Queen Tayla of the *Order of the Clan of the Red Velvet* told him what she had planned for him. She planned to separate not only his connection to this world, but that no one would ever know he had been born. "This blade shall sever you and all that you have done from the history of this world. The world shall remember you no more. Only I, Tayla, Queen of the *Clan of the Order of the Red Velvet* will know of your fate. No one will know where your remains will lie, or the fate that put them there. To kill a mother's children is to bring out maternal instincts of anger and revenge that many think not possible. You know the tears of a mother who has lost her children. If you do that to a vampire's children, you invite retribution more terrible than you could imagine. Dominican, you have done exactly that."

"Not true, thou foulest of creatures," cried out the priest. "I know your ways, your propensity for evil. I also knew you would eventually find out who is at the source of your torment. Yes! I have killed your spawn. I tracked them down and slew them in the name of the Almighty God. It is His commands I obey, and He commands that you all be put to the stake, to the flame for purging, and delivered up to eternal damnation!"

The priest, though a rope was about his neck, taut and constricting his airway, was defiant though he knew he was damned to his fate. He told her of his mission, as it was his crusade to extinguish her kind from the earth. "Your soul is beyond hope, and it is damned, do you hear? Damned! You may kill me, and you may be able to make me cry out pitifully, but you will never persuade me to betray my faith in Christ. You are the devil's agent, Tayla. The devil's agent! He uses you, and

6

through you he multiplies his legions of agents. His army is being born because of you and your wickedness. To save the earth from you and those like you, I was compelled by the will of God to destroy you!"

Ahhhhh!" he cried out in pain.

No family of his would survive this world. They were all marked. Marked with the edict of death that the undead monarch could give, and all vampires were bound to fulfill. His family, his existence would not even be a memory. It would be as if neither he nor his family had ever existed. He would be forgotten.

"I have done no harm to you. I left you and the church alone. What did that reward me? It rewarded me not. And from whom do you take these orders to murder and persecute, priest?"

"The Dominican Order has orders from Rome," he panted as his pain increased and his airway was compromised, "to expunge all heresy from the church and any agents of Satan who encourage and preach it. You and your kind are placed at the top of the order in which we must do this. Any of your familiars whom you have placed under your spell are targets and their confessions have led us to the colonies of your evil spawn. It is my mission in life to destroy you and your kind. From the beginning, your kind has been the enemy of my God!"

The vampire Queen had suffered the loss of too many faithful and obedient servants. The Dominicans and their inquisition had also murdered many innocent believers in their endeavors to stamp out the heresy of vampyria. It was not as if she had had a choice. This madness of persecution and the pursuit of survival had forced her and her brothers and sister to react.

Tayla knew of the Dominican's policy for torture. They could use any means necessary that did not draw blood. Therefore, the use of the rack, the firebrand, and crushing weights and water to inflict pain, done with such skill that any mortal would sing like a bird allowed them to obtain confessions, most of which were doubtful. The Vatican had told the order that she and her kind were as a plague upon the earth, and that they were to destroy them. The Vatican along with all the cardinals and bishops of Europe were convinced she was the agent of the devil and her spawn was to be Satan's army. From what source did the church receive this information?

"You fool! You cannot even abide by your own edicts of blood. You torture my familiars and then draw the blood of my kind. Which is it? Blood or no Blood? Well, I can think of many endless ways of exacting the most pain from a miserable creature such as yourself, but I think I will just give you what you give us. What was it you said? The stake, the flame and damnation? Tell me how the stake feels!"

"No, wait! Please!! Aaaaahhhhhhhhhhhhh! Oh, forgive me Father!"

Tayla had decided to give the same fate to him that he had given to her kind: the stake into the chest, piercing the heart. As she drove the stake into his heart, he cried out in utter terror. As she finished him, cutting off his head, she raised his head to look him in the face. His blood poured out upon the stony floor.

"Since you told me your orders were from Rome, then to Rome I will have to go," she said softly, with a gleam in her now violet eyes. She intended to confront the Pope himself.

TABLE OF CONTENTS

Character Glossary

A glossary defining the characters mentioned in this book and a description of the role they play.

CHAPTER ONE

A SPECIAL SEAL

2017

Malcolm Harris was surprised at how long the manuscript regarding the Dragon's involvement in the Roman Empire turned out to be. It was incredibly long and the more he read, it seemed as if he was reading Tolstoy's *"War and Peace"* for the details of so much history in so many different parts of Europe must have involved quite a lot of traveling to gather detailed information. The labor that Queen Tayla must have expended had to be nothing less than monumental. Few mortal authors would have attempted such a feat. Then again, she was not mortal and certainly not ordinary.

Nonetheless, she felt that Malcolm needed to know this as she must have certainly felt it relevant to the history of her kind. "Indeed," Malcolm thought as he stored it away along with the other manuscripts. He had no proper place to store them. Therefore, he needed to create an environment that would be conducive to the safekeeping of parchment documents. Time and the elements would be their biggest enemy. Since this was an area close to that of which Dr. Martha Rivera McAllister was familiar with, he had contacted her for names of firms that specialized in environmentally friendly storage of aged documents.

She had cautioned him against anyone having actual access to the manuscripts as that could set off a chain of events. The *Order of the Blue Velvet* still survived. Her warning was that the

Blue Velvet Clan would certainly have something to say about the existence of their kind being revealed to the world without their expressed permission.

Malcolm knew there would never be any "expressed permission" given and rightfully so. He felt that someone else would have to deal with that, perhaps in another generation and time. He did not want anyone he knew, family or otherwise to have that burden to carry.

Anubis, who had stayed on as the manager of Malcolm's business affairs, had also started reading the manuscripts. Suffice it to say that he too was intrigued with the material he read. He lamented that this account, which he termed a personal masterpiece of history, could not be shared with the rest of the world. Agreeing wholeheartedly with Dr. McAllister's view, he volunteered to take on the responsibility of having a storage facility built on the premises.

Malcolm went down to the vault once again to explore Queen Tayla's treasures. He found one more remaining manuscript. It was an extremely large one. Strangely, he had not seen it before when he found the others. Was there a spell put upon them? Did they only appear when the one before it had been read? It did occur to Malcolm that perhaps this was Queen Tayla's intentions all along. This account, like the others had a seal placed upon it. This seal was different than the others as it showed the heraldry of Tayla's coat of arms. The personal seal must have some significance. He did not break it but carefully removed it from the vault. It too, was wrapped in heavy leather binding but this leather seemed much fresher than the others had. The thought of the seal was on his mind the entire time it took him to find his way back to the Upper Estate. Before he approached the Gates of Hell, it occurred to him that this could be her autobiography. The thought of that excited him and he could not wait to read the contents of the manuscript if indeed that was its subject.

He wondered if it was written in English. Were there exact dates along with names of people involved? A million more questions rushed through his mind as the elevator made its ascent upwards to the mansion.

It was evening when he arrived topside. Rachel was waiting for him, eager to introduce to him the resumes of new applicants for the house butler and several maids positions. The former house butler Mortis had been gone for several years and the upkeep of the house was tremendous.

Anubis had been outsourcing the positions on a temporary basis as he did not want anyone becoming too familiar with Malcolm's and Rachel's affairs. Though all but one of the clans were gone, their existence must remain hidden from the world.

Anubis aka Whitman Bauer trusted only the familiars who served Queen Tayla to staff the estate. Where are they now? As the Harris' business manager, he ran their financial empire. But running the estate was no longer his job.

Often, Martha and Sean McAllister would visit for long periods between expeditions and her teaching at Boston College. During the Christmas holidays, all the familiars would visit for nearly a week of festivities. When the familiars were away, the house seemed empty without the camaraderie they had all shared. Those holidays were a special time. There was always room for one more as families grew and their children became like family to the Harris'.

Rachel knew the upkeep of the estate was an impossible job for one housewife, and therefore eagerly relented to have temporary help take over some of those duties. The children were all grown and off on their own. In short, the estate was far too large for just the two of them, along with Paul Vetter and Shade (Sally Kensington Vetter) to take care of. Paul pastored a church not too far from the estate, so he and Sally still lived with the Harris'.

Now, Rachel wanted to staff full time positions to keep the palatial home in pristine condition. Malcolm was far too distracted to take a serious interest in reading a resume. Rachel was insistent. Reluctantly, he relented and read them.

All the applicants had excellent qualifications, experience, and an inexhaustible list of references. As he read them, he wondered who could be trusted in a house with as many secrets to divulge as this one did. All great resumes and references aside, the primary criteria would be a relationship with an employee

14

built on trust. He had that while they fought the clans. They all had a stake in the fight. But now, there was no compelling reason to have help there except to keep a clean house and handsome grounds. When would it be safe to feel relaxed around them and not worry about arousing suspicions or curiosities?

He had settled on three, two maid applicants and a butler applicant. He decided to interview them and if possible, start them off immediately as he knew the house was in dire need of domestic help. Both maid applicants were in their forties, mildly frumpish in appearance and seemingly very professional.

Rachel checked out their references while Malcolm interviewed them on the phone. All three seemed perfect for the job and Malcolm asked them if they could come to the estate for a weekend and see if the estate was a place they could learn to call home. Later, he would hire someone to replace Moon and Leech.

When he had managed to find time to open the seal of the latest leather binder of parchment, another hand-written note in all too familiar handwriting slid out and landed upon his desk. Opening it, he sat down to read.

Upon a document of parchment, written in ink of a familiar handwriting, her words came alive to him as if she were there speaking to him.

"Dearest Malcolm, now that you have found the last of my stories, I wish you to read them often. As promised, I give to you the gift of my race's history, my history. I think you will find many things to learn, even if you did not comprehend them the first time. I wanted to write this story as told by me. However, the memories written here are not necessarily my own, as they are the memories of the things that witnessed them, even when I was not there to remember them. Therefore, I wrote this in the third person, as a neutral bystander with no personal interest in portraying events to coincide with my wishes. I have no wishes other than I wish the truth to be told. The same questions as before have the same answers as now. Yes, my own hand, my own story plus the memories of those things that were there at the time, even when I was not. There will be sad times when you read, and there will be times when you may be standing upon

15

your desk cheering. I ask that you remember not to take sides. This is merely history. Nothing can change it. We can only learn from it.

This was the way it was when I was a mortal. But I am not mortal. Therefore, as a vampire, I am not inside the realm governed by time. I started writing this account before meeting you for the first time. I met you long before you would have remembered so. You do not recall that night. I was able to write it quickly as my recall of events seemed to be much sharper, more accurate with details. Later, I told you about my father, who I described as a tyrant. That was not altogether true. When I was mortal, my recollections of him were of such a nature. Mortal memory is flawed. It is based on perception, not fact and therefore it is faulty at times. My process of recalling from inanimate objects what occurred tells a different story. I wished many nights that I could confront him and demand answers. I wished I could tell him how much he meant to me as a father to his child. The memory from the stones of his castle did tell me of his pain and his love. I only wished I could have known then what I know now. Another virtue of being a vampire…regret. Regret begets sadness.

The curse of being a vampire, is that it seems you are doomed to live with your memories, especially the bad ones. When I said I had forgotten how my mother looked and sounded, it was only when I went back and went through her things that I recalled all of it. What you do as a vampire stays with you for an eternity. That which we did as mortals you are more likely to forget. Forgetfulness begets forgiveness. Such is the blessing of mortality.

I wanted this last manuscript to be the one that you not only read, but study. The history I tell here will contradict some of what you and the rest of the world have come to accept as truth, or as the phrase goes, "most scholars believe…" Just because we believe something does not necessarily make it true. Much of the world is considering the possibility of that. My place will be determined by the simple fact that I believed something as true. I have witnessed and sometimes, even shaped history. The Dragon watched me, manipulated me, all the while remaining in the shadows, undetected. As my history unfolds before you, I learned about who and what I was by taking slow, small steps. I taught it to my brothers and sister. The Dragon did not come to us right away, but stayed in the shadows, watching my siblings and me. He knew we hated him. For he was responsible for my father's destruction. He and my father's wife, Illona.

Again, I congratulate you and your team on your victory over the Dragon. Yes, I saw that coming too. Even now, he remains imprisoned in the tomb you put him in, guarded by angelic sentries. I have never seen such evil and destruction come about as I had seen in his hand's involvement. I wrote this account you are about to read because I know of your desire to know me better. We would have had to talk many a night before my fireplace for me to tell all that I must say. There are some things that I cannot say to you.

Enjoy my words again, Malcolm. I can almost envision you reading it. I can imagine your yearning that I be there when you read. I know you want to remember my voice, and my scent. You want to sit in your chair by the fireplace, close your eyes and listen to my voice repeating the words. That will not be possible as before. Your memory of me will have to suffice. Although it is a very romantic and touching dream, I will be in a place I know you have dreamed of already. In spirit and memory, I shall always be with you."

He knew that as a man, he had become the closest resemblance of a love interest she had ever had in her whole, long-lasting life. At least, the only one who had never betrayed her or left her in her world alone. Folding the letter carefully and placing it back into its envelope, he stared at her portrait at the far end of the library. She was right. He did want to sit in that chair he sat in so many nights listening to an enchanting voice. For now, he only had the memory of her voice. He hoped he would never forget it. Her words alone would whisk him away to a world he could only dream of, existing long ago.

PART ONE

ANNARA AND VLADIS

1201 AD

CHAPTER TWO

THE BATTLE FOR VARNA

The battle had gone on since the night before. It was a March night, with no moon and the sky was overcast. The snow had not disappeared on the mountain slopes yet, but another month would change that. The air was damp and cold. A light rain mixed with fog enveloped the battlefield such that the sounds of battle were much more easily discernible than the sight of men in combat.

At the beginning, one could hear thundering hooves as cavalry formations began to charge the flanks of the enemy's formation. Next, the commands to nock, draw and release came before the whoosh and thud of arrows hitting their targets.

A knight outfitted in Frankish black armor gave the archery commander the direction to shoot and when to release. Time after time, the commands to shoot massive volleys of arrows were repeated. Light infantry, who were in the lead, died under waves of arrows they could not see. There was shouting, snarling, screaming and the sounds of men clad in various combinations of armor crashing against walls of soldiers holding up shields. The sound of metal blades striking against armor and shields, lances splitting, from close combat filled the night air. The shouting of commands, men crying out in agony as they died or were wounded, horses neighing when wounded blended in making the sound of the night a roaring symphony of carnage and chaos.

Another heavily armored cavalier on a large black warhorse appeared to be leading the battle, calling out commands from behind his armored visor. The core of the cavalry consisted of armored Boyars and Bulgar horse archers supplemented by Vlach cavalry and Cuman horse archers.

He had led a charge into the enemy's left flank causing disarray amongst the foot soldier force. The enemy cavalry did a countercharge and the melee was on.

In fog-shrouded darkness, the enemy could barely see. The troops of the other side did not enjoy any ability to see their enemies either. Some enemy soldiers carried torches to keep formations together. This tactic worked against them as the cavalier in black directed his cavalry force to attack them from behind, the side and then from the front. They were confused and tried to withdraw.

They were cut off by the Vlach cavalry and forced to fight. This proved to be disastrous as horse archers shot their horses through with arrows and they became dismounted or trapped under their horses. Annihilation came quickly.

The black knight dismounted, pulling out a mace from behind his saddle and approached an opposing warrior who had been thrown from his horse. The enemy warrior had chain mail and thick leather scale armor, much lighter than the metal skin used by the dismounted knight. The other warrior moved quickly to engage the knight in armor, knowing his opponent's vision was impaired and his freedom of movement was limited. However, much to the unarmored warrior's dismay, the knight in black was much more skilled and agile in his metal skin than anyone would have thought.

The warrior in chain mail and leather was armed with sword and shield and as he raised his blade, the knight in black parried with his mace, causing the sword to miss. The knight prepared to counter the blow. Blood spattered across the armored warrior's helmet as his mace came down on the unprotected adversary's head. It split his opponent's head. The man fell upon the already soaked ground as the life had already left his body.

On another part of the battlefield, the other knight in full black armor had led a charge of mounted cavalry and the process of decimating the enemy formation began. The fighting lasted until just before dawn. The black knights began to fall back as their victory had been assured. Many prisoners had been taken. The losses to the enemy were devastating.

They approached the Bulgarian Emperor, Kaloyan who along with many nobles and princes, had remained in the rear. Emperor Kaloyan, crowned only four years before, was the youngest of three brothers to be crowned Emperor of the Bulgarian Empire. This early morning, he was flexing his muscle and letting his enemies, as well as his nobility know that he was not to be trifled with regarding what he thought was his and what was not. He knew he had their full support, but a show of his resolve would cement that relationship.

Their generals and captains came in one by one. Many had declared victory with many prisoners in custody. It was still dark when the two knights bade their employers to take their leave. The two knights never revealed their faces to the Emperor or his court. Kaloyan normally would have been insulted and would have demanded they remove their helmets. Vladis, a commander of troops loyal to the Wallachian lands, intervened on their behalf, stating that the knight's identities must be kept secret as they were wanted in other lands. Kaloyan thanked them, offering them a reward of their choosing.

One prince noticed that the horse (destrier) of the larger of the two knights was wounded. He offered his own horse as gratitude for the victory over the Byzantines. The Byzantines had been invading their lands for years, demanding tribute and captives to serve in their armies in exchange for peace. Most of the time, the Bulgarian and Balkan kingdoms had bargained for peace, paying a steep price for it. The Byzantines were now demanding more and more each year until finally, the people of that region had had enough of their demands. They would either be free, or they would die at the hands of their enemies.

The knight took the horse of the prince and both knights left the field. Within an hour, the fog allowed limited visibility and the rain had ceased. Later, after the fog had burned off, the entire battlefield was visible. A cold wind began to blow across the fields of carnage. What a sight! Nearly five thousand enemy, many of the Varna defenders, lie dead or dying on the blood-soaked ground. The losses to the Balkan kingdoms were light to moderate, but the victory was priceless to them. It was now possible that the siege against Varna could be victorious as a large force of Byzantines had left the city to engage the Bulgarian forces.

*   *   *

Three days before the battle, a stranger came into the tent of the generals and princes of the Bulgarian and Balkan kingdoms alliance. Every warlord and prince who could say he was a man of means or had a castle was there. All had sworn allegiance to the Emperor Kaloyan of the Bulgarian Empire. The Emperor was scheduled to be there as he was traveling with the Bishop of Tarnovo. Remnants of different kingdom's armies allied with Kaloyan were coming into the camp each day to join forces with those already encamped there. They were waiting for the Bishop of Tarnovo to arrive to give his blessing before combat commenced.

The Balkans had been provinces of the Eastern Roman Empire. This was the year 1201 AD and for nearly two centuries, the Byzantine Empire had threatened the Bulgarian corner of Europe. Following the collapse of the First Bulgarian Empire the country came under increasing oppressive Byzantine rule. The oppression usually came in the form of exacting new and higher taxes from the Bulgarian people.

At the turn of the new century the Bulgarian Emperor Kaloyan seized the strong castle of Constancia (near modern Simeonovgrad) and then struck in the opposite direction and besieged the last Byzantine stronghold to the north of the Balkan Mountains, the port city of Varna.

Up to this point, the Balkan forces had not been able to stop the ravaging forces of the Byzantine empire. The city of Varna, on the Bulgarian Black sea coast, was less than fifteen miles away from camp.

The stranger had undergone the utmost of scrutinization to determine whether he was an agent for the Byzantines or even Hungary, or a man who sought to help the Balkan kingdoms against the current invasion. The only reason they allowed him

22

to stay and speak to the Balkan chiefs was because he had already approached one whose ear, he had gained favor with.

"We must conclude this business before the Bishop arrives!" the Wallachian prince whispered to the stranger. "He must not know of your involvement. Not only will he not give his blessing before the battle, I will be excommunicated for involving you and your companions."

"Do not worry, Prince Vladis, I know what I am doing. My knights will bring about the victory you seek. You just put them up front with your lead chargers and you will see. I will have them come to your camp just after nightfall three days from hence. It is best for them to fight at night, as you can see, the enemy will not see them until they are upon them. After you have taken Varna, I will come to see you at your castle and accept payment. Until then, I bid you farewell." The stranger who was clad in mail over a tunic of black leather, with a large cape of bearskin across his shoulders, mounted a large black horse and rode off.

As the Wallachian noble watched the stranger ride off, another nobleman, Kajal came out of the tent and observed. "Who was that, Vladis?"

"Our guarantee of victory!"

"Ha! Well, we could certainly use that! A guarantee of victory, you say. I do appreciate your optimism, though we are facing overwhelming odds and you speak of victory already?" He laughed.

Then he turned, saying, "I think you and I should get drunk, rut with the finest girls here, and die like men when the time comes!"

The prince knew he was right. Men had been searching for ways to guarantee victory since warfare had begun. Nothing worked, not even overwhelming odds against your adversary. The only thing "guaranteed" was that death would certainly follow, and for many, that ghastly hand of death would tap many on the shoulder in the upcoming battle.

"Nothing lasts forever, my friend!" Vladis said out to his friend just before they entered the tent. His friend turned and smiled. They embraced in friendship and entered the large tent.

A makeshift tavern was what it had become, to include strong drink and camp followers. For a fee, a man could forget that death was only around the corner and enjoy the embrace of a woman who was eager to satisfy a man's desires, to assist in his efforts to forget or even find courage. The tent was full of men at arms, and many wanton women, some fully dressed and others partially clothed. Some were serfs sent there while others were outright slaves, captured from enemy forces. One female, barely old enough to be a woman, whose hair was an array of dark chestnut brown, appeared as though she did not belong there. As were all the women of that time, her face bore the look of exposure to a harsh environment. Still, she had beautiful features, clear brown eyes, and unblemished skin but for dirt and soot from fires. Her clothing, nothing more than a heavy woolen tunic, was plain, with minimal patches for repair and wore no jewelry. Footwear to keep her feet warm consisted of leather with fur towards the skin, laced up with leather thongs. Her hair was tied behind her head, so it flowed down her back and left her face well exposed. She seemed to be very observant of those patrons willing to spend their gold and silver for her company and when any man began to approach her, she quickly looked away in shyness.

The Prince of Wallachia smiled as he knew she was a novice at this trade. Vladis immediately approached her and struck up a conversation with her. She seemed frightened, as she found it hard to look directly at him. Vladis could tell this girl had never been in such a situation before, and most likely was a virgin. Her shyness attracted him.

As his friend got very drunk, Vladis lost complete track of time conversing with this young girl. He ordered drink but had only one drink of strong wine. The Prince was lost in a room full of people, as the woman began to relax in his presence and before long, she talked with ease. Her voice calmed him as the sight of her face soothed his raging desires. They seemed so enchanted with each other's company that no one interrupted them. Hours passed, and knowing what she was there for, she reluctantly led him away to a more private place. It was magic for him though she was trembling.

"Where are you from?" he asked, gazing into her dark eyes.

"I am from Walachia, across the Danube," she replied looking upward from beneath him.

"Walachia? I am Vladis, the Prince from the southern region of Walachia."

"Oh, my Lord! I mean really, my Lord. You are MY prince! I came here to accompany our troops in the field, per your orders."

"Yes, I do remember giving that order. I believe I asked for thirty girls to provide comfort to our soldiers. I had no idea you were one of those girls. This must be fate."

"My Lord Vladis, what do you mean? You could have ordered me to give myself to you and I would have no recourse."

"Yes, but you might not have been willing to do so. I know women of your station are whatever I say you will be. Here I am, lying next to you, yet I feel strangely out of place here. You seem to be something of much more value than I can describe. Being here with you makes me happy. I will not just be satisfied that I will have taken your virtue from you, but feel as though I should treasure this moment, even wish that I enjoyed it more being with you than I had ever wanted to be with anyone else."

"My Lord Vladis, I am sure you have had many women in your life, and I know you have a wife. I hear she is beautiful, and high born. When you leave this tent, I know you will think no more of me."

"No, that is not true. My marriage is one of arrangement between our fathers. Our families are tied together for the purposes of political and financial convenience. She rarely talks or dines with me. Her hate for me translates into never sleeping with me. Therefore, I will most likely not have any heirs. I am convinced she hates me as I was not her choice. To be honest, I think she hopes that I do not survive the battle. If that happens, then she by right inherits all that I own, even my title. She remains a princess, and I die childless."

The tone of his last sentence sounded like a last desperate plea for the man to leave a legacy in this world. She was moved by his sad revelation to her. What could she do to ease that pain of hopelessness? At this moment, only one thing, the obvious thing, seemed to be the only solution to an impossible situation. "Perhaps I can help with your loneliness." She pulled him in closer to her, as her lips embraced his in a rare moment of complete passion and surrender.

*   *   *

The Byzantines outnumbered those in the camp at this moment three to one. Reinforcements were on their way, but then, so were many more enemy soldiers still ready to defend Varna. Scouts counted them at least a day away from their camp. Their confidence in a victorious outcome was all that was keeping them from attacking even now.

The stranger in black camped at an abandoned dwelling several miles away. Inside the dwelling were several boxes. Two contained creatures of immense power and capabilities the world had rarely seen. Two more contained sand. Not just any sand, but sand from Egypt. In this part of the world, they had never seen such creatures. But in the centuries to come, this land would become famous for the existence of such beings, even being named as the origin of their existence.

The stranger, Vojislav Rekvas, was the current embodiment of the Dragon, the vessel in which the evil entity Set dwelled within. Three days before, he and his party set out on a journey to Varna and observed the fortifications of the port city. He sent this information to scouts waiting at the camp of the Emperor Kaloyan. The first to receive this information was Prince Vladis of Walachia. He asked to meet with Vojislav to confirm the intelligence gathered on his trip to Varna. Vladis, traveling with an escort to the abandoned dwelling met the Dragon. The meeting went well.

"Prince Vladis, I am honored. I apologize for us having to meet here, but there is no way I can be vetted to enter your camp as I am not known by anyone there. We have much to discuss." They entered the remnants of a dwelling made of stone whose hearth was still functioning. The fire had cooked a pot of stew made from venison. It was hot and there was plenty to go around. Vojislav ensured that the prince's escort were fed as well.

The two men discussed military intelligence over a plate of the stew. "Outside the walls of the city, past the moat, I saw thousands of troops getting ready to march. I do not think they are going home. My instincts tell me they are marching here. In fact, I am certain of it. The field trains are minimal, indicating they are not planning on marching a long way. I believe they know of your staging area and plan to attack it early before all your troops arrive."

"What you say makes for good logic and sound reason. I might add, your stew is very hearty and tasty. I have not eaten as well as this since I left my castle in Walachia. I thank you for your generosity and your support. My scouts will advise me on their progress when they decide to move in our direction. This way we can be ready. Why do you share such valuable information? Are you loyal to the Emperor Kaloyan? I will verify this information first, so I can know I should trust you."

"Of course, Prince Vladis. I would expect nothing less. When you can verify it, share it with the other field commanders so you can formulate a battle plan."

Of all the information discussed, the most important pieces of information he gave to Vladis was that the Byzantines were fully aware of the existence of the gathering of armies to the camp where Kaloyan would launch his attack on Varna. Vladis knew this meant there were either spies in camp or there were scouts close by to observe and report.

The two men agreed the Byzantine strategy was to strike first via surprise during a nighttime attack to interdict the Bulgarians plans on Varna. They would not do that if they did not realize the Emperor Kaloyan's forces were a legitimate threat.

"If they know where we are then they know about our siege engine. They know of its size and how it will breach the moat. This is most likely why they are coming to attack us first," the Wallachian prince stated.

Vojislav agreed. "Once the army is complete, pieces of the siege engine will be transported to Varna and assembled just out of sight of the city's walls." It was the main key to the assault on Varna.

Vladis stated with enthusiasm, "Then this attack upon our camp must be won at all costs, for the siege is dependent upon the siege engine and its deployment against Varna!"

"I could not agree more. This, Prince Vladis, is why you need me and my help. I can guarantee victory when they attack your encampment. You will be ready, and I will send my knights to lead your troops in battle. You only need to discuss this with your troops to trust my knights and victory will follow."

*   *   *

It was the evening of the day of the battle. Reports had been coming in all day to give final tallies of the dead and wounded, the number of soldiers captured, and the amount of material lost and captured. A post battle council was scheduled for that evening to give time for commanders to gather information and report it to the Emperor.

The port city of Varna was located on the western coast of the Black Sea. The city was a busy port and key to the invasion of Bulgaria. The Byzantines held it with a large garrison. Some of the best soldiers of the Byzantine army, western mercenaries, were members of that garrison. They had not been part of the army that had marched out to intercept the Bulgarian army. After the first taste of battle against the Byzantines, many commanders had lost their nerve and wanted to retreat, back across the Danube or the Morava rivers. The Emperor wanted no part of retreat and publicly shamed anyone who talked of such things.

Though the Bulgarians had won the first battle for Varna, the siege had not even begun. The Bulgarian forces could still lose Varna and the Byzantines could still take Bulgaria back into its empire.

Prince Vladis knew this, and during the post-battle council, he said so to the Emperor Kaloyan. "The time to march on Varna is now! I am certain that survivors of last night's victory have made their way back to Varna and the city's defenders know that the winds of favor have changed. Will they be content with the way things are now? Of course not. They will know the siege engine is intact and is coming. They will prepare for its employment against them. Reinforcements will be on their way to strengthen the garrison. The longer we delay, the more blood will be spilled, most likely our own." He sat down at his place in the tent.

Kaloyan, still a young man, seemed deep in thought. He had heard all of Vladis's words, as he had heard those of his other nobles and captains. Wisdom and patience allowed him to focus on the important aspects of the campaign without letting emotions cloud his judgment. He mourned the loss of his troops, although they were minimal compared to the losses incurred by the Byzantine forces. Still, he knew he would need them to take Varna. The Emperor took a long drink of ale before he expressed his opinion.

"Prince Vladis is right. We were fortunate in that we were forewarned of their impending attack. What was supposed to be a surprise attack against us turned out to be an important victory. I have no doubts regarding of what is being discussed in Varna at this moment. They will say the devil was with us. They will say he rode a black horse, dressed in black armor and was able to be in two places at once. Let them fear us, I say. If the devil is relentless, then let us be relentless. Let us move on Varna at once, and strike while the winds favor us. The reinforcements are still coming in, to replace our losses. They can join us at Varna as easily. It will take some time to reassemble the siege engine. The quicker the better. Prince Vladis, you are one of my most able commanders. Ready your troops to move as you will be our lead element."

Vladis did not expect to receive the Emperor's support so enthusiastically but as soon as he had finished, the rest of the nobles and captains joined in a loud chorus of approval. His friend came up to him.

"Now you have done it! Now we are the lead in the column and surely, we will be ambushed along the road to Varna if not engaged directly at the fortress. I thought we would have been killed last night. How inaccurate could I have been? I must have rutted with four, maybe five girls and drank until I could barely stand up. By the time I was sober and fit for battle, I was sitting on my horse, dressed for combat wondering how I got there because I do not remember preparing for it. You were mounted beside me, telling me as you poured icy water down my neck that if I just kept close to you, I would be fine. Do you remember that?"

"Yes, Kajil, I remember that," replied Vladis.

"I also remember you telling me that we were guaranteed victory. Do you remember that part as well?"

"Yes, and after that you wanted to rut and drink to your heart's content for you were certain we were going to die in that battle. We did not die. We were victorious. Why? We both had something to live for. You had your drink and women. I found something that I cannot describe, and I want very much to get back to it as soon as I can."

"Oh, yes, I remember that much. I seem to remember a certain woman who must have put a spell on you. And, she was not your wife, I might add." Kajil giggled after he said it. It was not uncommon for noblemen to have mistresses they cared more for than a lawful wife, even if she was of convenience.

"Kajil, someday, maybe, you might be so fortunate that you may find a woman who mystifies you so much that she will seem to be the only woman in the world. No one will come even close to the joy she may give to you."

"I do not care for such women. As long as they give to me what I want…"

Vladis interrupted him. "What you want is for them to serve you. Cook this, clean that, lay down or bend over for me and take care of me when I need you to! All my life I have had such women. And I can say, I enjoyed them. But this woman I met; she is different. How she is different, I cannot say. But the joy is in the mystery and it draws me to her like a bee to a flower. Tell me, Kajil, has it ever occurred to you that there might be something a woman wants from you other than to mount her like cattle or horses do? I thought not," he said as the expression did not change on the fellow warrior's face.

Kajil looked at him as if he wondered who had stolen his friend's body and was now in possession of it. "You have an insight into the hearts and minds of women. I do not. That, my friend, is a simple truth I have come to accept. It gives me one less thing to keep me awake at night."

*   *   *

The next morning, Vladis awoke from inside the woman's tent. They had slept in each other's company all night. Several had come looking for her to buy her company and time, but upon seeing that Prince Vladis was being "attended to", they promptly left and did not come back.

"The army moves on Varna today. We should be within sight of her walls by nightfall. I am ordered to be the lead unit on the march to the city. It will be dangerous as they know we are coming and probably will do anything to stop or slow us down. The weaker we are when we arrive, the better they can withstand us."

The young woman with long, chestnut brown hair and dark eyes closed her eyes and fought back tears. She had dressed by this time and was helping the prince put his clothing on which included some light armor.

"You serve a prince well," he told her. "I will return, my lady."

"My Prince, I am not a lady. I am of low station and birth. I am your property and my feelings and wishes are not of your concern. I exist because of your grace and protection. That is all."

"I see. Well, all that may be true, but it is not all. I do have concerns for you. I cannot act on them now for I have a war to fight, but this war cannot last forever. I should send you back this day to my lands north of the river. That way I do not have to wonder how many of this army's soldiers will lie with you or want to lie with you. I do not want to share you with another. I want you exclusively for me."

"I know that I may have your heart at this moment, but tomorrow or the next day, I may lose you. I must go on living. Send me back if you wish. I will lie with no other, as I am not married, nor has any suitor approached me."

"No one has ever asked for your hand?" he asked.

31

"No, my lord. My Father asks for a high price for my dowry, such that none in our village can afford me. He says it is his way of keeping me safe. He was furious that I was sent here to provide company for the soldiers."

"Go home. Tell your father he need not worry about suitors for his daughter. He is right to ask for more than anyone can afford. I think you are worth it."

"And my low born caste? Does this not bother you? And you are married? How will your wife feel when she finds out you would rather be in my arms than hers?"

Vladis could see that the woman was emotional and passionate. It was something he was not used to as Illona was cold and calculating, always looking to better her station in life. "I told you about my wife. Illona is a wife in name only. She is of Anatolian descent. Long ago, our marriage was arranged by our fathers. She resents it as much as I do. She probably has her own lovers to dally with. If she does, then I do not have any guilt about what we are doing. Either way, I shall ask the Bishop for an annulment. If he grants it, I will pay that dowry and your father will be richer than he could imagine. You, Annara, could be a princess." By this time, he was dressed.

"Tell your father that I sent you home. Tell him your chastity is untouched. Tell him you have the eye and the heart of Prince Vladis and speak of this to no one else, and he is to speak to no one of it. I will come to speak with him after this battle is done. Now, pack your things. You are going home."

He gave her a horse, some money, and a letter with his seal upon it to back up her story when she saw her father again. She left, smiling yet fighting back her tears as she was sure she would never see him again. It was a long way back to Wallachia.

*   *   *

For the most part, it was the siege engine that brought down the fortress at Varna. Pieces of the siege engine were transported by wagon and reassembled out of sight from the defenders. It did not matter, for the defenders of the city already knew about the device and its ability to breach the walls of the city. Varna was surrounded on the eastern side by thick, high stone walls which also had a sizeable moat in front of them. Crossing the moat by foot was nearly impossible for infantry, totally impossible for cavalry, and only a siege engine built to bridge the moat would be successful. That is exactly what the Balkan forces had going for them. They only had to breach the wall successfully at one point and the rest of the army could follow across. The third day of the siege, 24 March 1201 AD, the Bulgarian army crossed the moat breaching the walls of the city. The losses the Bulgarians and Balkan allies suffered at the hands of a smaller garrison angered the Emperor Kaloyan so much, the nobles saw a side of him they had rarely seen. The young emperor killed all the remaining defenders, as well as those civilians who had collaborated, even though they had surrendered and knowing it was Easter. He had them thrown in the moat and buried alive. Then, he commenced to having the city walls destroyed.

The Bishop of Tarnovo was still close by to observe the battle. Word reached the Bishop of the Emperor's conduct. It angered the Bishop so much he immediately threatened to excommunicate him if he did not immediately return to Tarnovo.

Varna was now in the hands of the Bulgarian Emperor Kaloyan. His destruction of the Byzantium garrison and the fortress that guarded it was complete. Leaving a garrison of his own there to hold it against a possible counterattack, he reluctantly returned to Tarnovo to face the wrath of the Bishop.

Prince Vladis regretted sending Annara back to his lands in the north. He had not even sent her away with an escort. He thought to himself as he rode away from Varna, "How stupid of a prince I am! I find something that makes me happy, gives me a purpose and a joy for living, even made me fight harder so I could return to her and I treated her like this! God forgive me!"

*   *   *

Annara had gotten about five miles from the camp and stopped. She thought, "I have not nearly enough food to last the trip back. I am alone and at the mercy of any wild beast, robber, or murderer in these forests. I have no knowledge of defending myself nor of finding my way home." She decided to wait upon the return of her Prince Vladis. She would stay back at the camp, now abandoned, and wait for the army to return. Hopefully, she thought her prince might see the reason for her disobedience and forgive her, but better to risk that than not ever seeing any familiar face again. There was little left to scavenge from in terms of food or other supplies.

After a few days, she heard the advance of a caravan of wagons and horses. It was the entourage of the Bishop of Tarnovo. She stood to watch them pass her by. Calling out to them, she inquired of any news of the battle. She cried out, "Are we victorious or is all lost?" The wagon carrying the Bishop passed by her slowly and the cleric inside heard her cries. He commanded his wagon to stop.

He opened the door and was assisted out, so he could stretch his legs and see who it was, crying out for answers. He saw Annara, a young, beautiful girl, nearly in tears.

"My Lord Bishop, your grace, please tell me are we victorious at Varna?"

He answered in a dignified voice, restraining his anger for how the victory was achieved, "My child, we are victorious. Varna is back in the hands of the Bulgarian Empire. It was at great cost, but the price was paid."

"Any word as to the fate of Prince Vladis, your Grace?"

"My child, I have no word as to the fate of Prince Vladis. I know of whom you speak. He is a great man, full of life and promise to be a great prince of his land. Are you in his service? What is your name?"

"Yes, my Lord Bishop, I am in his service and I am called Annara. I was sent here as part of a company of women to provide service and comfort to the Prince's men at arms. Yet, the Prince saw me and kept me from contact with any of those men. He felt as though I should be kept away from such things as that. I met the Prince for the first time only a few days ago, yet I feel as though God has something special in mind for it. He sent me home, but I have little to sustain me for the trip and no escort for protection. I hope he forgives me for my disobedience, but I came back here to await his return in hopes that we may join company again."

He smiled saying, "Oh, yes, I see it all now. You are in love with the Prince. It is obvious even to an old man such as me, someone who has not felt such feelings in this heart for ages. I gave my heart to God years ago, but I am still a man, and I have a memory. If it pleases you, I can escort you to Tarnovo, for that is where I am going. After that, my escort can be your escort to the castle of Prince Vladis. Besides, I need a fresh face to talk to, one that can remind me that even I, an old man of God, still has a purpose in this world regarding this thing we call love."

She hesitated, wondering if her Prince would come by here at all. He expected to see her back in Wallachia. If he should take another way home, and she was not there, what would he think? The decision was easy.

"If my Lord Bishop's Grace will have me, I should be honored to accompany you to your city of Tarnovo."

"Excellent. Gather your things and ride here in my coach with me." He looked upwards to the sky, smiling, and said, "Lord, add this to my list of good deeds."

CHAPTER THREE

PETITIONING THE BISHOP

As Annara correctly assumed the possibility that he would, Prince Vladis did go home by a different route from Varna. Annara seemed to be on his mind frequently. The young Prince was conflicted. He knew he must petition the Bishop for a writ of annulment of marriage. His father was now deceased as was his wife's father. The marriage was a sham. The lands her father had left her would support her, even though most of them were currently in the hands of her brothers. The marriage was arranged to ensure mutual security, in case their lands came under attack, the family and forces of Prince Vladis and Wallachia would come to their aid. All he knew was that as far as his marriage was concerned, he was miserable, lonely, and empty.

He rode at the head of his troops, many of which were horsemen, while several companies of his men were foot soldiers and archers. The journey home to Wallachia would take a few weeks. He also knew the stranger would soon arrive at his castle for payment for the use of his seemingly invincible knights. It was true the knights were very instrumental in their victory in the night battle outside Varna. Neither the Emperor Kaloyan nor the Bishop of Tarnovo were aware of them.

Each night they made camp, Vladis's mind was on Annara. He knew the chances of getting the annulment was slim at best. Still, it was a chance to be happy. If his wife Illona, wanted to be happy, then certainly she might be inclined to also petition the Bishop for an annulment. Of course, there might be the possibility that the Bishop might defer to the Bishop in Constantinople.

He decided to ask Kajil, even though he probably knew even less of how the Holy Church would see his circumstances than the Prince would. "Kajil, you know my marriage is difficult as well as embarrassing to talk about, but you are my friend. I have to tell you, I have no one to talk to about it."

"Not even the girl you spent the night with before the battle?"

"I am sorry, but you are right to say what you said. She is on my mind constantly, yet I am powerless to do anything regarding her or my status. I can only say that I regret marrying Illona. You know her. She is something of a curse to me. I find no redeeming qualities in our continued marriage, so I want to submit a writ of dissolution of marriage to the Bishop of Tarnovo. He may disallow it, he may grant it, or he may defer to the Holy See. What do you think?"

"I think that if you do not follow through on your idea to write to the Bishop for an annulment, the answer will always be no. You will live your life in misery, while that girl will be only as far as your memory can take you. Of course, you can order her to be your mistress, but I can see, my friend, that would not do for you. You want to be with her, legally, and every other way as well, most of all, you want her to want to be with you. Until you get that divorce and Illona goes back to where she came from, you will never realize your dream and you, my friend who has changed over the week, will be hard to live with, be it the battlefield or at court."

*   *   *

The Bishop's column could see the gates of Tarnovo as they crested the top of the hill. It was close to midday when they could see the spires of the Cathedral of Tarnovo. Annara had never been more than a few miles away from the castle of Prince Vladis. That was only because she accompanied her father to the forest to assist in cutting wood and gathering of firewood. It was also the way her father kept such a strict eye on her. He knew she was young, pretty and most of all, naive. She had no formal education, for most people of that time in history could neither read nor write. She was a very impressionable girl and her father was certain that she could easily be taken advantage of by any man, low or high born. She had no brothers, so she was very much ignorant when it came to the thoughts of males in general. Her only Christian upbringing had come at the hands of the priests of the church such that she understood the purpose of the church and the personages of God, Jesus, and Mary, the mother of Jesus. She knew there was far more that she did not know or understand than the amount she did.

The Bishop's party arrived in Tarnovo, very tired and eager to dismount. The Bishop lived in fortified quarters adjacent to a monastery which was close to the cathedral in Tarnovo. As they disembarked the coach, the Bishop asked Annara if she wanted to leave for Wallachia immediately or rest and leave for home the following morning. She chose to leave immediately.

He gave her his blessing, arranging for fresh soldiers and a nun to accompany her to Prince Vladis's castle. She had enjoyed conversing with the Bishop while traveling. He had explained many things to her, answering her many questions. He watched her mount her horse, accompanied by the soldiers and the sister from a nearby convent. The Bishop prayed he had not made a mistake in letting her go so early.

*   *   *

Illona, wife of Prince Vladis, stood close to the window of her chambers looking out across the landscape. From her window, she could see the road leading to the entrance to the castle. She had not seen anyone approach for days.

She was not worried, though. In fact, she was worried if he showed. It would mean that he had survived the campaign to secure Varna. It would mean she was still married to the man she had been forced to marry. She had resented so much being forced to marry Vladis. Her dislike of his family equaled her dislike of her husband. They had not much in common and her pride, not to mention the violation of her sheer will and independence caused such a resentment in her heart, it was inconceivable there

38

could be any warmth or affection between the two of them. She had not desired a husband and felt she could handle the wealth and power of her family far better than her brothers. Only now, she had no power or wealth she could call her own. It was all Vladis's and all she had was a title. If he had been killed, then all would be hers. She had even considered assassination as a last resort. Either way, she was not happy being married to Prince Vladis, and wanted out of the marriage. She desired this so much, she had already petitioned the Bishop for an annulment of the marriage soon after Vladis had left for the campaign to secure Varna.

*   *   *

The Bishop had dined and retired for the evening. Annara was on his mind. He thought fondly towards her. He was impressed with her curiosity, her innocence, and her desire to learn more about God. He prayed for her safety and the good conduct of the soldiers he had provided for her security. Normally, he would not have done such a thing for a peasant girl. However, he knew Vladis. If Vladis thought of her as something special, then there was something worth honoring about her.

The Bishop of Tarnovo awoke early that morning as usual. He went to chapel before his breakfast. He could hear some chants coming from the monastic congregation next door as they began to sing. The morning bells were not due to ring for quite some time. While at chapel, he prayed before the altar. He prayed his usual, ritual prayers for the things that he wanted to make the day as perfect as possible. And when he was finished with those prayers, he said another prayer aloud, saying he wanted to have wisdom flow within his spirit, for he knew this was the day when his decisions would have a most profound effect on his flock. After prayers, he went to his study where monks brought his breakfast to him. He ate alone, while slipping into a daydream where he would be free of the trappings of rituals he was expected to perform. Being a bishop had become quite boring to him at times. The routines of listening, trying to give advice, counseling, and being pious all the while trying to

39

convince everyone else that he was happy bored him. It was exhausting for him.

His servant brought him a collection of papers and petitions sent from all the areas for which he had jurisdiction over. The messages addressed to the Bishop of Tarnovo came to his study at different times of the day. Most of them were letters of requests from all parts of his authority. Some were request for attendance of baptism, of marriage, of funerals, et cetera. Others were questions of religious nature, clarifying the stance the Church had taken regarding matters of sensitive natures. Some were requests to be passed on such as for dispensations and support for candidates to fill positions within the empire, whether it be political or religious. Then, there were the requests for annulments. These matters required diligent investigations if the criteria were met and if so, both parties had to agree.

One of those messages was the petition for annulment of marriage between the wife, Princess Illona of Moldavia, and Prince Vladis of Wallachia. The criteria listed was that upon solemn and sworn oath, the Prince had not consummated the marriage in any way that would form the basis of marriage as recognized by the Holy Church. The Princess was willing to provide sworn testimony by no less than three witnesses. The petition had been sent while the Prince of Wallachia had been campaigning in the south against Varna in service to the Emperor Kayolan.

He had had several conversations with Prince Vladis during the campaign to secure Varna. One of those conversations was at the coronation of Emperor Kayolan. He reminisced about that time. His memory was not as good as his age had advanced. The Bishop recalled some information the Prince had shared with him, which came rolling back to him easily, like thunder in a storm. It was a storm that was discussed between an unhappy man, who wanted to do the proper and honorable thing and a man of God who could offer a means to mediate between them. He had met Illona only once, and after that encounter, it was obvious why, if it were true, the reasons for her petition were born of her own nature.

"Ah, yes. This marriage is a disaster. Kajil has already told me of it." He grabbed a plumed pen, dipped it into the inkwell, and began to write his approval. He had expected a petition of this nature for when Vladis' friend, Kajil had come to him for confession before battle, he learned of the entire tragic affair of Vladis and his wife.

Kajil knew his divulging of Vladis's source of torment would be kept confidential. Vladis had often talked about his joke of a marriage, but never acted out on his wishes to petition for an annulment. Moldavia was currently not in any danger he knew of, so the arranged marriage was not necessary. Besides, he thought, if needed, of course Wallachia would come to the aid of Moldavia.

The Bishop took little time to consider the criteria necessary to validate an annulment. Kajil had already sworn and testified, in confession, of the true nature of Vladis's wife. He wrote his approval of the annulment, feeling confident of his decision based upon the obvious intent of both parties.

"How convenient it is that I should receive this after speaking with the young girl, Annara," he told his servant. "I should really speak with Prince Vladis before granting such a request. However, prior conversations have revealed to me that this annulment is what he desires as well. She has made compelling claims as to why I should grant such a request, but her reasons are of her own doing. This woman is cold. Her heart cannot be of anything but stone. Still, I must listen to her plea, as I am bound by duty to do so. I will send a message to the castle of Prince Vladis, for his eyes only, that he may address these concerns on behalf of his wife. If they are true, then I shall grant them, but if they are not, what would the Prince desire that I do? Give me pen and paper so that I might write my message to the Prince! I will also write my approval of the annulment of their marriage. I think this will satisfy both parties." The servant left to procure the items necessary to write a message.

*   *   *

Annara and her party had already spent one night in the forest. The next day, the party crossed the Danube river at a common ferry often used. The captain knew of a landing where a boat served as a ferry carrying passengers from bank to bank. Because of melting snows, the current was swift. It was a wide river, unfordable at any place and served as the border between Bulgaria and Wallachia. They crossed with ease and were now in Wallachia, Annara's home. A toll was asked of the party and the captain of her escort paid it, informing the ferry master that he traveled in the name of the Bishop of Tarnovo.

Annara rode in silence as did her escort. Her hands and feet were chilled. Her woolen tunic shielded her from bitterly cold winds, but she had no boots nor mittens. The nun who rode closest to her had not said a word the entire time to her. Annara noticed the nun had coverage for her head. It was just as well, for the nun's hair had been shorn. The nun had an extra cover for her head but declined to use it and gave it to Annara instead. It was a welcomed gesture.

The sun was no longer overhead. It was late afternoon, and soon they would be making camp to spend the night in the forest. Annara remained observant, despite the silence. She thought it best to maintain vigilance if robbers or worse should present itself. The escort needed to be ready to defend and if needed, she would need to escape the clutches of whoever would assault them.

Fortunately, nothing happened the entire trip. They made camp, and Annara tasked herself to collect firewood. She had wrapped her blanket around her to keep warm. The time was early spring, so the temperatures were still cold in the forest. The escorting soldiers built a large fire and the party quickly warmed themselves. A supper of bread and beans, with some cheese was shared by all. Soon, most began to retire for the evening, struggling to stay warm during the night.

Morning came with the light of a new day. The usual routine of breaking camp initiated itself with preparations to move further northeast. Annara ate a crust of bread for breakfast. She mounted Vladis' horse with all her possessions strapped behind her saddle and left the makeshift camp.

Later that day, she soon recognized familiar landscapes. It teased her that home might be nearby, but she was not. She was still miles from home and soon, it was time to make camp again. Two days later, in the late afternoon they were in sight of the castle of Prince Vladis. It was also the home of Princess Illona. They crossed a smaller river at a guardhouse on the road to the castle.

Annara was excited about getting home. She hoped she would be allowed to go directly to her home in the village of serfs and peasants without having to pass before the Princess Illona. Still, she wondered if the Prince had already arrived home and if not, when would he arrive?

She bid her escort farewell and left the group to go home. The party continued to the castle to seek refuge for a night and begin the journey home to Tarnovo the next morning. Her father was excited to see her alive, and even more so, her virtue intact. Annara presented the letter with Vladis's seal upon it. Alas, neither could read but the friar assigned to the region could. He would take the letter to him.

The escort of soldiers and the nun spent the night as guests of the Princess Illona as Prince Vladis had not arrived home yet. Princess Illona was a woman who loved style. She was all about appearances. Wearing one of her best gowns, a dark red velvet one with ermine trim at the cuffs and the lowcut neckline she played host to the Bishop's detachment of guards. During the evening meal, the curiosity of the Princess got the best of her.

"You say the Bishop sent you as escorts for a peasant girl who was left behind by my husband before the siege of Varna began? It would seem my husband deems the worth of this girl to be substantial enough to return her to the home of her master."

"Aye, my lady," said the captain of the escort. "She must have made an impression upon the Bishop for he stopped on our way back from Varna and saw her still at the camp. She inquired about the outcome at Varna. We told her, and the Bishop ordered us to stop. He asked who she was. She said she belonged to the estate of Prince Vladis. The Bishop asked if she wanted to accompany us to Tarnovo, which she agreed to. The next thing I knew was I was ordered to bring her here."

"Sister Magda, this is true?" asked Princess Illona.

"It is, Princess. I was asked to provide the company of a chaperone to the girl."

"This girl, what is her name? I should like to ask her what her relationship to my husband is and how she managed to find him in the camp of the Emperor Kayolan."

The captain of the soldiers answered, "My lady, her name is Annara. She is a peasant girl, one of those your husband sent with a band of camp followers to the camp outside of Varna."

Princess Illona smiled inwardly. Her mind swirled with ideas, scheming with ways to use this information to her advantage. Immediately, she thought the worst. Another woman, a peasant girl of all things, had caught the eye of her husband. Normally, she would not care. However, to be set aside for the affections of a young, ignorant girl who was so low born that she could not be of any less significance if she tried, this infuriated her. Why, she wondered, would she feel threatened by someone she would not give a second glance, even less a first glance to who might think she could take her husband from her? A Prince, no less! The more she thought of it, the angrier she became.

"My husband sent a group of women to the Emperor's camp for servicing the soldiers?" She called a servant to her end of the table, whispering something inaudible to the servant's ear.

The nun, Sister Magda, sat at the other end of the table. She looked extremely uncomfortable with the subject being discussed and could tell the Prince's wife would no doubt keep asking questions until she got the answers she wanted. In her heart, she lamented for the captain, for she knew he was a simpleton who did not know he was being manipulated for information.

"Sister Magda, were you there in the Emperor's camp?" Illona knew that if she had accompanied the Bishop to the camp, then it was condoned by the Bishop.

"Princess Illona, I was not there. I had never seen the peasant girl, Annara, until the Bishop ordered me to accompany her to this castle, to return a serf of yours and your husbands to these lands. I do not approve of young women being anywhere near a battle, especially for that purpose. It goes against the church's teachings as well as God's."

Illona continued to pry information from the soldier. "Captain, the purpose of these women, can you state them to me? Why so many?"

The soldier wanted to respond candidly but knew better. He tried to make his response seem measured and artful. "My Lady, these women, low born they may be, provide a service to the men who are away from home. Most of the time, it is someone to talk to. Other times, especially if they are not married, an opportunity to find comfort and affection, even if from a stranger. My Lady, my men and I are in the service of the Bishop of Tarnovo. We are sworn to watch over him and protect him. Therefore, it would be difficult for any of us to be attended to by any of those girls. However, they are paid and paid well for their trouble. It is a common practice in campaigns of warfare. I have seen it many times. As to how many, I should say the women could number between thirty and seventy. The size of the army dictates how many. Also, it depends on the noblemen and the availability of the women. Remember, someone has to care for them while they are pressed into service."

His answers only infuriated the Princess more. "Women should never be for the sole purpose of being a man's enjoyment!"

CHAPTER FOUR

THE EYES AND EARS OF PETER

It was three days later. The soldiers and nun who escorted Annara home had left the castle and were on their way back to the Bishop at Tarnovo. Vladis appeared on the road just before arriving at the guardhouse across the river. He was at the head of the column of soldiers whose oaths of fealty to him were sworn long before the campaign against the Byzantines. Most of his soldiers had survived. The few who had been wounded were helped along by fellow men at arms or were mounted on horses. Vladis had suffered a few cuts and bruises, but mostly he was exhausted. Sleep had been a rare, and costly commodity. A few marauding bands of Byzantine mercenaries who had deserted before Varna fell had raided or ambushed isolated units. Everyone had to be vigilant. Even though many of his men were mounted, many were also on foot and could not move at a mounted speed. The unit could only move as fast as its slowest members. Crossing the Danube back into Wallachia had taken more than a day as his troops far exceeded the amount of ferries available to expedite them across the river. Some men fell overboard from the crowded boats and sank due to their armor.

Vladis stopped at the small stone bridge. He wanted all his men to catch up and cross the river at the same time. It would ensure unity and the loyalty of his men. As he waited, a messenger was sent ahead to make ready for the largest part of his garrison to be quartered, fed and re-equipped. Vladis knew the battle may have been over, but sooner or later, another battle would be right around the corner. His castle was located just across the Danube near a place that would be called in modern times, Giurgiu.

As for Illona, he felt the message would reach her eventually, but he did not feel as though she would be waiting at the front entrance to the castle to congratulate him on his victory. Returning home held little promise for him regarding coming home to a grateful wife. He had no illusions about that. However, the possibility of seeing Annara again held a brightly lit flame in his otherwise dark world.

When his troops arrived at the castle entrance, many of the inhabitants cheered loudly for them. Some were family members of his soldiers. Naturally, they were jubilant for their safe return.

Princess Illona sat in her chambers, crying for her situation was intolerable. She had a callous nature towards her husband for she was terribly mean and cruel. Though her complete lack of interaction with her husband was of her own doing, she felt like a prisoner in the castle. It was she who refused to consummate the marriage. Vladis had been willing to honor their fathers dictates of marriage to each other. She had not been so willing. Before her father had died, she cursed him to his face for being such a brute as to force her to marry someone who was not only a stranger, but someone who she had nothing in common with but a title and money. They had never even met each other before they were forced into marriage The concept of arranged marriages so disgusted her that she vowed she would never submit to her husband, no matter how kind or civil he was to her.

One of his servants came up to Vladis to offer wine to drink. Vladis gladly took the cup, swallowed the entire amount, then asked if his wife was aware that he had returned.

"Yes, my Lord, she is. She is currently in her chambers with the door secured from the inside. I think she is afraid that you might seek her out and do that which she is afraid to do."

Vladis laughed out loud. "What? She thinks I am going to run up there in that tower and break down the door and force my wife to have sex with me?" He looked up to the tower. He knew if he were to yell, she would probably hear him. "Have no fear, Illona! I am not coming up!"

47

Muttering under his breath, he looked at his servant to pour him another cup's worth of wine. "I would not go up there if she were the last woman on earth."

"Draw me a bath with fresh robes. I want to be presentable when I feast tonight with my troops."

*   *   *

Annara heard from her father that troops had arrived at the castle. A large celebration was to be held in their honor that evening. Of course, the peasants would not be invited, but still Annara felt that if she were to show up, she would not be refused. Her father heard her say this and when she did, he chuckled to himself. She was barely a woman and already in love with someone she could never have. There was hardly anyone in the village who could afford his asking price for marrying his daughter. He knew it was selfish, but he knew it would still be a while before she was ready for marriage.

A boy who had been a childhood friend came to the door that evening. He asked if he could speak to Annara. His name was Peter and he was a year younger than she. He was the closest child to resemble a brother to Annara she would ever see.

"Did you hear about the soldiers coming home?" he asked.

"Yes, my father told me. Was Prince Vladis among them?" she asked of her friend.

"Oh, yes! He was at the head of the column. He looked good though. I could see no wounds."

"You saw him?" Her excitement grew.

"Oh, yes, I saw him. He looked tired, but he was in good health."

"Peter, I thank you for telling me. You are the closest person to me, like a brother. How close can you get inside the castle? I mean, can you get close to the prince, enough to hear what he says?"

"I guess so. Nobody cares what I do, besides my father works inside the castle, so they know my father and they know me. Why do you ask such things?"

"Peter, I met the Prince when I went down south for the campaign against Varna. The Prince had ordered that a group of young, single women be sent as camp followers to keep soldiers happy. I was one of those sent. My father argued against it, saying I was just a child. But I am close to the age that I should marry. My aunts and uncles have agreed that it is true. Well, my father's price for me to any suitor is too high, and because of that, he says my virtue is intact, whatever that means. I know I am naïve in the ways of the world. My father shelters me as if I were a personal treasure that he wants no one to know that he possesses. I met the Prince and he found favor in me. He talked with me, listened to me, and he did not violate me or use me in any way at all. I sensed he respected me and perhaps, maybe even something more. He told me about his wife. She is cruel and seems to hate him for being forced to marry him. He told me he wanted an annulment from the church regarding his marriage. Peter, you must promise me you will not say anything about this to anyone. No one! Not your father or mother, not your friends and especially the Prince's wife! I only want to know if he mentions me to anyone else and especially if the Princess finds out about me. I may not be educated but I know if she finds out about the Prince and I, one of two things may happen. She will be happy I have caught his eye and will become his mistress, or she will be angry and lash out at him, me, or both of us. I just want you to listen. Do not ask questions, or indicate you know of anything. Do not even let on that you know of me. Understand?"

Peter agreed and swore an oath of secrecy. He liked Annara as he had only brothers and no sisters. He also had both parents to live with. As he walked away, he smiled. His friend had found a sweetheart and it was no other than the Lord of the estate, a Prince no less! Perhaps he could benefit from this if all worked out well. He knew he just had to watch his tongue and keep his ears open.

Because a young boy of his age seemed insignificant to adults, few paid him any attention. If he was with his father, they seemed to see only his father and not him. It was exactly the way he wanted it, for he now considered it his full-time job to watch out for Annara. He was familiar with all the stories about Illona, wife of Prince Vladis, and never doubted any of them.

His brothers had told him things, terrible things about the Princess of the castle. He was in fear they might be true, but then, the thought of all of it excited him, as well as fed his insatiable curiosity. Each day, he would meet with Annara to tell her of his observations. Each day he had but little to tell her.

She had been home nearly a month when Prince Vladis saw the boy and his father. He noticed they both were in the castle often. He stopped Peter's father and asked, "Your boy, what is his age?"

Peter's father bowed before the Prince, saying, "My Prince, my son, Peter is thirteen years of age. I count the Christmas', so I know. He was born the day before Christmas, so I can keep track of his age that way."

Prince Vladis stood tall before Peter, who had not quite yet come into puberty. Peter had never been so close to the Prince as he was now. The attire of the Prince impressed the young lad. He was clad in a hauberk, with robes of red and black over it. A hauberk is a shirt of mail. The term is used to describe a shirt reaching at least to mid-thigh and including sleeves. His crest was emblazoned upon the front of his chest upon the tunic that he wore over the mail. Greaves of armor protected his legs as well as his arms. He held his gauntlets in one hand and reached out to Peter with the other.

"Tell me lad...do you get any time to play with the other children of the village?"

"Well, uhmm, yes my Lord, sometimes I do. Not too much for I help my father with his work."

"That is good. I was wondering if you might know a girl about the age of fourteen or so, maybe fifteen, who is called Annara? And if you do, could you tell me where I might find her?"

Peter knew this was his moment. Annara would want him to tell her where to find her. He wondered in that split second of time he hesitated to give the prince his response if his response would put Annara in danger. The look on Annara's face when she would talk about the prince told him what to do.

50

"Sire, I do know who she is. She is one of my best friends. Do you need to see her?"

"I would like to see her father first if I may. Can you show me where they dwell?"

"Yes, sire, as you wish! Follow me!" Peter had not even looked up at his father for approval or recognition as to what to say to his master. He just did it.

He left immediately with the Prince in tow, right behind him. He led him to the hut that Annara and her father lived in. Annara and her father were not at home but in the forest cutting wood. As they were about to turn and leave the hut, Annara and her father appeared on the road with an ox-drawn cart full of wood for the fires of the castle. Vladis was about to continue on the road leading up to the castle when Peter said aloud, "Sire, she comes this way even now, with her father. See the cart of wood? That is Annara and her father."

"Thank you, boy, I will speak to her father alone. Return to your father, now."

Peter did as he was told.

CHAPTER FIVE

THE ANNULMENT

Annara could see Peter leaving the front of her hut and traveling back towards the castle. It was afternoon and she and her father were transporting firewood. Her father looked at his daughter, immediately seeing the light in her eyes shine and a smile he rarely saw break out across her face. He could tell this was the reason for her joy and her sadness.

Her father, Josef, had little to offer his daughter to counter her sadness. Aside from her aunts, she had no woman to emulate. It seemed as if she were caught between being a young girl and a woman. He knew he was a poor candidate for showing his beloved daughter how to be a woman, one who was fully aware of her abilities and her disadvantages. Most of all, he could not show her how to make up for those disadvantages. Her aunts were not available much of the time as they worked the fields.

Now, as he looked at his daughter, practically dressed in beggar's clothing, she had caught the eye of a prince, the Lord of the estate, no less. As the noble drew closer, Josef could see the same look of joy and excitement in his face. It was then he knew.

Josef halted the cart and bowed before the nobleman. Annara did as her father did.

"A woodcutter I surmise?" asked Vladis.

"Yes, my Lord. I am a woodcutter. I am Josef, and this is my daughter, Annara."

"I have met your daughter. I trust she has told you the details of our encounter just before the battle of Varna. May we confer in your hut?"

"As you wish my Lord. I have little to offer in terms of drink or food."

"I am not here to drink or eat. I am here to discuss the hand of your daughter. I must confess, I am quite taken with her. I am an honorable man and would not presume to take advantage of you or her."

They reached the hut and went inside. The door consisted of wooden planks held together with crossed planks and pegs. Thongs of leather served as hinges. Outside, a large stack of firewood served to heat the dwelling. It appears the entire hut was centered around a large fireplace. The floor was composed of some planking and a lot of straw. Under the straw was mere dirt. There were some flat stones laid in front of the fireplace. Several rough- hewn beams held in place with some pegging and lashed together with leather thongs formed the basis of the roof. Thickly thatched straw covered the woven network of small limbs to hold up the ceiling. Some shelving could be found, which contained mostly kitchen utensils and dishes. The woodcutter lit a candle as the hut had but one window. The two sat down together at a small table, rough-hewn wooden planks also held together with pegs and leather binding. The table sat in front of the hearth, with a large empty kettle hanging by a chain from a bar with a hinge so that the kettle could be pulled away from the fire. Inside the one room hut were two cots, each with adequate amounts of bedding. Their chairs were merely stools, with no backs to them. The extreme poverty was evident throughout the hut.

Josef said to Prince Vladis, "I do the best I can under the conditions. The war has left me with fewer customers to sell to.

Prince Vladis began, "I met Annara down south during the campaign. The circumstances one meets true love under is strange, do you not think? Annara is beautiful. If I could have her as a wife, she would be my treasure. I have lived long enough without the affection of a woman who freely gives in return what I am so willing to bestow upon such a woman. I give you my word, upon my honor, that her chastity is intact. I saw no one else with her during the campaign and I gave orders that she was not to be touched by anyone."

Josef was impressed. The prince went straight to the heart of the matter. The thought that an actual prince would be interested in his daughter was enough to excite him, for he knew his daughter's happiness was at stake, not to mention that Prince Vladis could pay the asking price for her hand.

Vladis felt embarrassed that he was so inept at asking a father for his daughter's hand in marriage, especially since he was already married. He was sure that Josef was unaware of his wife's capacity to be unkind and outright cruel.

"I must petition the Bishop for a writ of annulment of marriage from Illona. I know that this must be done before any relationship can begin between myself and Annara." He produced a letter. "This is my show of good faith. I will have this sent to the Bishop in Tarnovo as soon as possible. When my answer comes from the Bishop, I will come again to ask for her hand. I have thought long and hard about my decision. I know this is all highly irregular. My birth may have been of high status, but her effect on me raises me to the stars. Annara is different from most young girls. I am older than she, but she still has my eye and my heart. I honestly believe she always will."

Josef took time with his response. Finally, he said, "I have never imagined that a man such as yourself would come to my house, even less to ask for my daughter's hand in marriage. I am honored that you would consider her. That you are in my hut is such an honor. My daughter is all I have. My brothers and their wives and children are the cause of my envy as they have each other. Their families are intact. Annara's mother died when she was young. It was the hardest, most painful experience of my life. I have tried my best to raise her, but she needs a woman to teach her how to be a woman. I am but a poor woodcutter who loves his daughter. I have only love to give her, and I have taught her to love others. This world is a cruel one, so cruel as to take away her mother at such a young age. I see her becoming more like her as she grows. It is difficult to think that she may leave me one day and then, I will be alone."

"She will not be leaving you. She will be up on that hill in that castle, where you can come and visit her every day. And, she will still be your daughter." Prince Vladis rose from his chair and patted the woodcutter on his broad shoulder. "I will return when I have received notice from the Bishop, until then, you live under my protection." The noblemen in red and black left the hut.

Josef looked at his daughter, Annara, who stood silently and embarrassed, yet happy inside that she did not need to keep a secret from her father. He smiled, saying, "Annara, you have done well! Very well, my child."

*   *   *

As Annara had her spy in her friend, Peter, so did Illona. The princess noticed a change in her husband. He was no longer sullen and sad. He had appeared as though he had a large burden lifted from his shoulders and seemed to anticipate good news each day. She wondered why the change in him. What was he up to? She would find out. She had three maids who served her. Two were from Moldavia. They had traveled with her to meet her new husband as part of the bride's wedding party. The third, a maid who had long been part of the Prince's household, was from Wallachia. Of these three, she consulted the most with the one from Wallachia.

"This custom of sending women to the camps of the soldiers, how long has this been going on?" she inquired.

The maid, Katarina, a young pretty woman in her late teens with red hair and sparkling blue eyes, answered, "My Lady, I have seen men go to war many times. Often, nearly every time, women would travel with them to provide their bodies for the men's entertainment and pleasure. Often, the men would pay for their services. The women would bring the money home and it would provide for the family. Women of all types, and backgrounds would be there. I was fortunate that I never was pressed into that kind of service. I suppose it was better them than I."

"Do you think my husband found love in one of these women's arms?"

Katarina answered, "You yourself have told me, as well as Magda and Portia, that you refuse to consummate your marriage with Prince Vladis. Does it really matter to you that his needs are met by a lowly peasant whore instead of you? After all, it is better for that woman to be the scabbard for his sword than you, no?"

"I suppose, but knowing he is even the slightest bit merry annoys me. If I find out he has been rutting with one of those dirty women, I will be terribly angry. It is bad enough I must be his wife, but to be made a fool of by someone who has nothing to offer other than her body and a lustful appetite, that I cannot accept. I will not tolerate it!"

Katarina asked, "Suppose he has found someone he fancies, and orders her to lie still while he thrusts into her. What choice does the poor thing have? Face his wrath or face yours?"

Illona replied, an evil smirk upon her cold face, "It matters not. I want all of you to watch him. Follow him when he leaves the castle. If you cannot do this, have another who is close to him watch him. Bribe them if you can, even sleep with them if you must but I want to know every move and every place my husband goes. Most of all, find out who he is seeing. If he is seeing someone else, bring her to me."

Portia interjected, "My Lady, what of the petition for annulment you have sent to the Bishop of Tarnovo?

Illona stopped dead in her tracks. She had forgotten all about the petition she had sent to the Bishop! For the first few seconds, she had wished the Bishop had not received the letter, but she knew surely, he had received it by now, perhaps even had responded to it. Then, she hoped he had responded, though stating that he refused to grant the annulment. Then a whirlwind of emotions flew through her like a winter's blizzard. She asked herself why she was in the marriage in the first place. Her anger and resentment stemmed from her father for forcing her to marry Vladis. He had been the cause of her hatred for her husband. Vladis was merely the conduit for her anger. Hating him and making his life miserable had become her hobby, because she could not make a dead man feel her wrath for being in a non-functioning marriage. If the Bishop had granted her an annulment, then Vladis could no longer be the object of her torment. How could she let go of her favorite passion...hating her husband?

"It seems so long ago that I wrote my request, right after Vladis went on campaign against Varna. That was weeks ago. Has everything changed so much? I still hate him. He means nothing to me."

Portia asked again, "If the Bishop grants the annulment, he will find out and we all will be sent back to Moldavia...in shame. Who will want you then?"

"Plenty of desirable men, men who want a woman with money and a title, that is who will want her!" answered Katarina.

"I care not if any man desires me. I have not found love here, nor will I find it at home. My father has done this to me!"

Magda walked in but responded as if she had been listening the entire time. "You speak the truth, my lady. Your father has done this to you, not Prince Vladis. Let him go if the Bishop grants your request. An annulment is not the same as a divorce. It only means it was a mistake. No consummation took place and your chastity remains pure."

"I see only one path to take here. We must travel to see the Bishop and perhaps intercept his letter if need be. I will convince him that this marriage is indeed consummated and you three will swear to the fact that you have indeed witnessed the act yourselves. Swear it!" she cried out.

All three maidens nodded in affirmation, saying "We swear it!"

*   *   *

Illona and her maidens traveled by wagon to Tarnovo for the sole purpose of lying to the Bishop of Tarnovo, the leading clergy of Wallachia. The voyage took over a week but travel in those days was generally slow, even if wheels were involved. Roads were in disrepair for the Romans had built most of the main roads, but the Romans, though marvelous engineers, had faded into history long ago.

Finally, the afternoon came when the party arrived in Tarnovo. They immediately sought out the Bishop, finding him in his office across from the monastery where he usually was at this time of day. Illona's servant sought an audience with the Bishop who normally would have turned them away for he had many appointments already. The name of the petitioner startled the Bishop. He allowed the party an audience.

Into his office strode the Princess Illona, along with the three maidens, Katarina, Magda, and Portia. The armed escort and her butler stayed outside in a waiting area. All three were well dressed for the visit and the matter of the visit greatly concerned the Bishop.

The Bishop, dressed in the black and white robes of his office, sat in a heavy, ornate chair of carved wood. His arms rested upon the chair's wooden arms. His back was supported by a red velvet cloth cover on the back of the chair. A large, gaudy chain supporting a heavy cross of gold hung from his neck and shoulders. In front of him was a heavy table, cluttered with many manuscripts and scrolls upon it. He offered wine to them.

"Princess Illona, welcome to my humble dwelling. As you can see, even I, a lowly officer of the Lord, am destined to humble accommodations. To what honor do I owe this visit to, your Grace?"

Illona quickly went to the point. "Some time ago, I petitioned you for an annulment of my marriage to Prince Vladis of Wallachia. I must confess, I did so in haste. My husband had left me to pursue glory on the battlefield. I thought I would not see him alive again. But God was merciful and brought him home to me again. Now, my petition for an annulment would be a lie."

The Bishop listened closely, asking, "And why would your request be a lie? Is it made upon false pretenses?"

The Princess Illona answered, "Yes, my Lord Bishop. It is upon false pretenses. My husband has consummated this marriage with me. Though I was against this marriage from the start, it is hard for a man to not desire a woman, especially his woman, though I did not desire him. Upon his arrival home, he took me in a fit of passion and lust, not love, and made me unfit to be married to any other man. I am violated now. I cannot marry any other man for I am ashamed. I feel the only way I can remedy the shame of my husband's rape of me is to stay married to him to retain my honor as a woman and a wife."

The Bishop was astonished. It seemed so much had happened since Varna. "You say Prince Vladis raped you? How can a man rape his wife? Is he not entitled to her? Was this not part of the wedding vows, that you two should be joined not only in spirit and in matrimony, which included conjugal relations between a man and a woman? Why was this made now and not when you were married? I remember when you were married. I was there, performing the ceremony. The look of anger and resentment was on your face even then if I remember correctly. If I close my eyes, I am sure I could still recall it."

"Your grace, I beg you not to grant the annulment. I could not bear the shame!"

"Princess, what of your husband's shame? A petition came from him barely a few weeks after receiving yours. I granted both petitions. I have heard testimony already of the state of your marriage. And, I know Prince Vladis. He would not lie to me. Unless, you can give proof that the Prince's claim is untrue, I cannot rescind my declaration of annulment of your marriage."

The Bishop was steadfast in his position. The resolve in his answer to the Princess stirred her to a deep state of anger. The Bishop could see the emotions churning in her like a sudden storm upon the sea. He knew his answer had been the right one, for her shame was nothing more than an attempt to protect her vanity and her pride.

Katarina spoke up, "Your Grace, all three of us are prepared to swear we have witnessed the act ourselves. We heard the sounds of lust and rape come from their room with our own ears."

"All three of you? You heard the sounds? And what are those sounds? I may be the Bishop, but I was a man before I was the Bishop! A man in love may make those sounds as well and I know for sure a woman who is in the throes of passion may make those sounds as well. I think you will have to do much better than that, ladies. My decision stands."

Illona was indignant of the Bishop. He had barely listened to her lies while already having his mind made up. The entire trip was a wasted effort. She turned and left the room with her maidens and gathered her party for the return trip to the castle north of the Danube.

*   *   *

Prince Vladis was happy his wife had gone away. He had not known at the time she had petitioned the Bishop for an annulment while he was fighting at Varna. The day after she left, two letters from the Bishop arrived. He managed to obtain them, though one was addressed to the Princess. After reading the Bishop's answer to him, he leaped for joy.

The Bishop's letter read, "To the Noble Prince and humble servant of the Holy Church, Prince Vladis of Wallachia, I, the Bishop of Tarnovo, have received and heard your wife's petition for annulment of your marriage. I have no doubt that her conditions required for annulment have been met. The marriage is without consummation and there is no love between the two of you. The hope that a true marriage can grow from your union seems impossible. I have it on good faith from sources I cannot reveal, your marriage indeed meets the requirements for annulment. Only the both of you contesting my decision could convince me to rescind it and declare you both still married. In these days of constant war, and scarcity of peace, we find we must do what we can to find happiness in our lives, be they short or long-lived. I wish you well in your search for happiness, as well as her search, though I doubt she will find it unless she has a change of heart and a mood of repentance. My son, keep your honor, maintain your nobility, and follow your heart if it is after God. Go in peace. Your friend, Stanzylch, Bishop of Tarnovo."

His marriage to her was over! He could barely control himself. He asked for his friar to write a response to the Bishop immediately confirming her reasons for the annulment were true and that he was more than agreeable to the Bishops decision. The friar took the dictation of Prince Vladis.

"To the Honorable and Most Reverent, His Grace and Bishop of Tarnovo, I, Prince Vladis respond to the inquiry of your letter to me. I agree that the marriage has never been consummated, though I wanted to make this a true marriage, it has not been and

60

never will be upon the desire and determination of the Princess Illona to become a wife in the truest sense of matrimony to include conjugal rights bestowed upon both wife and husband. This I swear before Almighty God. I understand that upon receipt of this letter you will know that the marriage of myself and the Princess Illona is hereby dissolved and annulled before God and all witnesses. The Princess shall be returned immediately back to her home in Moldavia, her fortune, her virtue, and her title intact. Always your humble servant and friend, Prince Vladis"

Vladis sealed the letter using a stamp of wax with the seal of his title, Prince of Wallachia. The letter was dispatched immediately by special courier to reach the Bishop as soon as possible.

Immediately, he went in search of Annara and her father, with the Bishop's letter in hand. On his way, he stopped and gathered his local priest from the local chapel and requested he perform a marriage ceremony soon.

The news of the Bishop's granting of an annulment spread like wildfire throughout the castle. Some members of the household broke down in tears while others were jubilant. It was clear whose loyalty she had and did not have.

Vladis arrived at Annara and Josef's hut in haste. They had just sat down to eat their evening meal that Annara had spent most of the afternoon making. Josef heard the Prince's horse arrive, whinnying and neighing as if it too were jubilant.

He opened the door to see the Prince tying his horse to a post. "My Lord, to what honor do we owe this visit?" he asked as he bowed before the Prince.

"Josef, I have great news. My wife, the Princess Illona, had petitioned the Bishop of Tarnovo for an annulment while I was campaigning against Varna. He has granted it! I can scarcely believe it myself. I have it right here in my hand the key to my freedom…and Annara's future. If she will have me, and with your permission, I would like to marry your daughter soon."

Josef could hardly believe his ears. It was true, the Prince had a letter, even though Josef could not read, it had a seal upon it that signified it came from the Holy Church.

Annara had not said a word. Instead, she kept quiet, restraining her jubilation that her Prince had come for her as he had promised. When Josef looked towards his daughter for her answer, her radiant smile said all he needed to know. Josef agreed to Vladis' proposal of marriage.

*   *   *

Illona was not used to being refused the things she wished. As soon as she was outside the Bishop's house, she gathered her entourage and declared the party would travel to whomever held the Bishop accountable for his decisions and would petition them for an audience.

"Your Grace, who would that be?" asked her butler.

"How about the Patriarch of Constantinople? He should be high enough to reverse the Bishop's decision. The Bishop has no other save the Patriarch of Constantinople."

"That is in the land of our enemies. Is that where we must travel? And, pray we are successful in getting there, will he grant you an audience, and even less, a reversal of the Bishop's decision?"

The butler replied, "Princess, the Patriarch has no authority or jurisdiction outside Byzantium or the Byzantine empire. Rome will not recognize his authority. And there is the issue of Constantinople being at war with us. I am afraid we are out of options."

Illona looked at the butler with fire in her eyes. "I am never out of options." She pulled forth from a pocket sewn into her gown, a stamp used to indent the sign of the Bishop's authority into the wax seal of letters. "This is my option and I intend to use it. I will make a false document, stating that the Bishop has reversed his decision, and show it to my husband. If he has plans of remarrying, he will be heartbroken to hear his plans will never come to pass." She giggled, and then the mirth left her face. The vengeful woman replaced it with an evil and nasty expression.

In those days, as were many days before and many more since, not everyone could be trusted, for an honest man, one of integrity and reliability was hard to find. Illona knew this all too well. She knew more of the ways of the wicked world than her husband did. She was counting that she was correct in her assessment of human nature.

They set to work forging a document by bribing a monk, then threatening him with his life to obtain a letter of the Bishop's handwriting. The butler then had him practice the writing until he was able to match the pen to the paper with the same style. The Princess told the monk what to say. Within a few days, they had the document completed along with the wax seal of the Bishop to make it seem authentic. They paid the monk and had him return the stamp back to the Bishop's office without his noticing it. The monk then sent the letter back to the castle via courier so that the Prince would be able to receive it as official mail. Ilona's mission was accomplished.

*   *   *

No one at the castle, including Prince Vladis, missed Princess Illona. It was not known exactly where the Princess Illona had traveled. She had not divulged the exact location, but every clue indicated she had traveled south across the Danube to Tarnovo. If this were true, Vladis surmised it would mean she had gone to the Bishop. For what purpose, he could only imagine. He had the Bishop's response to his request for annulment and that was all he cared about. He couldn't care less if she did not come back.

CHAPTER SIX

THE LETTER

The Princess Illona and her entourage returned to the castle not saying much to anyone. The less anyone said, the less lies needed to be told. The company seemed very somber. The only one who seemed normal was Illona. She was in her usual, bitter mood and when she approached Vladis, she could tell something was different. There was a change over him that she could only suspect that he had received the letters the Bishop had referred to when they had conversed.

Vladis emerged from the large front door of the castle to meet her. It was near complete darkness, and the evening drizzle was about to turn into a complete downpour. A torch burned in a sconce just outside the door. He stood with his arms folded, his stance was one of authority, and his face was somber. She dismounted her carriage along with her maids. A servant helped them step down.

"Nice of you to tell me where you were going. Seems you have been gone over two weeks. I suppose I was to worry about you, but since you gave no destination, I could not send any patrol out to find you and ensure your well-being."

"I took my own security with me. I cannot say I trust anyone you would appoint to watch over me. They probably would be the very ones to murder me!"

"I am afraid that is a tactic to which you would stoop. I see the change of scenery has not changed your demeanor towards me. Just as well, as few things you do these days surprise me. I suspect you have gone to see the Bishop of Tarnovo. How is he these days? I have not seen him since the Varna campaign."

"Since you must know," she said contemptibly, "I did see the Bishop. I had written a petition towards him for an annulment of our marriage. He said he received it, and answered it, which you may have already taken receipt of it. I convinced him that our marriage is beyond that of annulment and now he is considering rescinding his decision. That is all." She passed by him, smug in her ruse, knowing she had him so upset he became speechless. "No one gets the upper hand on me", she thought to herself. Her ladies followed her into the castle, barely acknowledging the Prince. The contempt they felt was tangible.

The news of this stunned Vladis. He knew something was foul here and he was determined to get to the bottom of it. Could the Bishop have rescinded his decision? Was it even possible?

At this time, Vladis needed a friend, a good friend. The only one he could think of was Kajil. He sent a messenger to find him and invite him to come to the castle. It was to be a long, cold, sleepless night. He wished he could take Annara to his bed on such a night, but it would not be proper. When could he give notice to Illona that the marriage was over, and the annulment was official? He thought it best to not act in haste.

The morning came, and first light was nothing more than a gray continuation of the mist that had covered the castle the night before. Everywhere was damp and cold. He ordered his breakfast brought to him. He ate alone, as usual re-reading the letters. The friar had taught him basic reading and writing while he was yet a boy, a skill he had kept to himself all these years. He thought it best that his enemies do not know his intellect or the extent of education he had undergone. The Bishop's words rang in his mind as if they had been spoken to him by the mouth of the Bishop himself.

"To my friend and humble servant, Prince Vladis of Wallachia, I, the Bishop of Tarnovo have received, and read the petitions for annulment of the marriage between yourself and the Princess of Moldavia. I know from the testimony of others and yourself that this marriage is a complete and utter failure. For whatever the reason it has not been consummated, the fact that neither of you have given in to your base desires, and that your contempt for each other far outweighs any desire to consummate this marriage, I have hereby granted the annulment. There is much to tell and advise you about, my friend. I am aware that there is another that may have captured your heart. If you value this person's life, beyond simple love but with the compassion of Christ, do not let Princess Illona know of her existence until after this marriage dissolution has taken place. I fear greatly for her safety. Go with God, my son, and heed my warnings about the terrible vengeance of your wife."

The Bishop was warning him, the Prince of Wallachia about the vengeance of his wife, Illona. He smiled to himself, thinking that he above anyone who walked this earth, should know the extent of vengeance the Princess would enact should she find out about Annara. This letter would have to be hidden or destroyed such that Illona would not be able to learn of the Bishops warning. He decided to destroy it, so he burned it in the fire, making sure that every part of the parchment was consumed by the flames.

That week, another message from the Bishop came to the castle. It was delivered by special courier from Tarnovo, but it was not just one, but two. One was addressed to Princess Illona, while the other was addressed to Prince Vladis.

At first, both were brought to Vladis. Vladis sat down at the long table in the dining hall. A few ministers and wardens were present, including the friar. He picked up the one addressed to Princess Illona and prepared to open it. Before he could, she appeared at the door and saw him with mailed documents. It was not uncommon for him to see his wife's mail before giving it to her. She did not need the friar to read her mail to her. She too had received education while still quite young from monks and friars in Moldavia. Most of the nobility and nearly all the common peasants and workers of the Middle Ages were illiterate. Only those within the Holy Church possessed the ability to read and write, unless they had been taught by those who made it their business that reading, and writing were preserved from the Dark Ages.

"Stop!" she commanded. "Whose mail is that in your hands, husband?"

"I believe this one is addressed to you, wife. Shall I open it? It is from the Bishop. I trust the letter is regarding your petition for annulment."

"I will read for myself," she said defiantly. She approached him, taking the letter from his hand. She sat down at a chair some considerable distance from him. It was clear she could not be close to him. Her real reason was that she did not want him to be able to see the handwriting style on the parchment for he might be able to detect forgery.

He picked up the other letter and broke the seal upon it. He expected the subject of his letter to also confirm the decision of the Bishop regarding the annulment. Instead, it read something quite different.

She dropped the letter into her lap and looked up at her husband nearly twenty feet away. Putting on her best act of disappointment, she began to form tears in her dark eyes. "Husband, we are still married. Our annulment has been denied. She feigned breaking down and sobbing. In a fit of acting heartbroken, she ran out of the room and to her chambers.

Vladis was stunned. A servant picked up the letter which had fallen to the wooden floor. The friar, dressed in his usual dark brown robes, read it aloud, confirming the Bishop's decision. He too was stunned and saddened. Now, he could not marry Annara. He was trapped into a hellacious marriage to a woman who not only did not love him but hated him with every fiber of her being.

He was near despondency. The friar, placed the letter in front of him, knowing the Prince could read. Vladis still had the other letter in his hand. Slowly, he brought the other letter up to his face and finished opening it, fully expecting the letter to confirm or repeat what Ilona's letter had said regarding the Bishop's decision. Instead, it read, "Vladis, Prince of Wallachia and humble servant to the Bishop of Tarnovo, I salute you for your enduring patience and steadfastness to do the right thing. In a visit from your wife, she has spoken to me personally regarding the petition for annulment. She came to me with an entourage, including three maidens prepared to swear before the Almighty that your marriage had indeed been consummated. I felt in my heart that these women were only being loyal to their mistress, and their testimony would be false. I denied their request to rescind my decision. Your marriage is indeed annulled and no longer in effect. Send this woman away from you immediately while you can. The same day she came to me, my signature stamp was missing for nearly three days. Then, it miraculously reappeared. The same day it was found was the same day the Princess' entourage began the journey home. I suspect that if you receive a message with my official stamp, it is a forgery stating that I have changed course and your marriage is still in effect. You are right not to trust her. I have sent this message out the same day as my stamp took its usual place upon my desk. May this letter find you well and gives to you the joy you so richly deserve."

He quickly dismissed everyone in the hall, except for the friar. "Friar Phillipe, you have known me nearly all of my life. You have served me, my house, and the church faithfully all these years. Tell me, to whom is your first loyalty?"

"My Lord, you should know, I serve the Lord God Almighty and His church first. You are a part of that church; therefore, I serve you as well. That is my calling."

"Phillipe, you have answered well. I need to know who I can trust and those who I cannot. I know where my wife stands and those who follow her, well, the answer is obvious. I have a task for you. Come with me!"

Friar Phillipe followed Vladis to his chambers and watched him take out a collection of letters. He brought forth several which were from the Bishop of Tarnovo.

"Sit at that desk and use my looking glass to read these letters." The friar did as he was instructed.

"Do you notice anything different between the two letters, not accounting for the content of them, but the writing styles of each. The letters of the alphabet specifically are what I want you to take special notice of."

After several minutes of reading and comparison, the friar looked up. Vladis placed the letter that Illona had just received from the Bishop in front of him. "Compare the letters of this letter to the one I had you just read."

It took a while, but the friar seemed to know exactly what Vladis wanted to know. He took his time comparing the same words and letters often used by the Bishop. Sometime later, the friar looked up at him, stating, "My Lord, I know what you are looking for. I do find discrepancies in certain words and letters. I suspect these letters are a copy and if they are, then I further suspect that this entire letter addressed to your wife is a forgery. I cannot be exactly sure beyond a doubt, but I suspect the nature of the situation has dictated that drastic measures have been enacted to keep your marriage intact. That is all I can say."

Vladis smiled and allowed Friar Phillipe to read the letter he had just received from the Bishop. Friar Phillipe was speechless. "Phillipe, you are one of the most trusted of my court. I thank you for being such an honest man. They are hard to find these days."

Vladis left him and went to Illona's chambers. He could hear laughter and conversation coming from her room. As he approached, the laughter was coming from several women. "You should have seen his face!" he heard his wife saying, though the door was closed. He put his ear to the door and continued to listen to the voice of his wife telling her maids how their ruse of deception had worked as planned. Just then, he heard footsteps behind him. The friar had followed him, as if suspecting all along what his Prince was about to find out.

Friar Phillipe replied, "It is hard to keep secrets when they are shared by others." His face was grim, indicating his great disappointment in the Princess and her maids. Justice was about to knock on her door.

CHAPTER SEVEN

THE MARRIAGE

Vladis pushed open the door to his wife's chambers with great force. After finding out about her deception and lying, he could have torn the door off its hinges. His posture accompanied by his clenched fists revealed his wrath at being deceived. The limit to his patience and his reasoning had been crossed. One look at his face and Illona knew she had been caught in her lie.

The other women quickly left the room, even without being ordered to do so. The friar entered the room after they left. Friar Phillipe was of calm and rational demeanor.

"My Lord, please do not do anything rash. I think you know the right thing to do," he begged his master.

"I do," said Vladis. His face was red with anger, his voice nearly choked for his teeth were clenched. Finally, with great deliberation, he said, "Friar Phillipe, please tell this woman the truth regarding our marriage."

The friar stood between the woman and the man as a means of preventing them from going to blows. He had never seen it happen between the two but there was a first time for everything and now certainly had the potential to be one of those times.

"Princess Illona, there is a situation here that I must bring to your attention. You have a letter and your husband has a letter. Both are from the Bishop. Both were sent out on the same day you left the monastery in Tarnovo. I think you know the conclusion we have come to. There is a forgery and I think the one who is responsible for it is you. We think this is true because the Bishop thinks it is. What do you have to say for yourself? I know I speak on the behalf of your husband for I read both letters. Upon my examination of those letters, I have determined there are distinct differences in his usual writing styles and letters made by his hand. The one addressed to you is a forgery. The one addressed to him is by the hand of the Bishop. Your marriage is indeed annulled. You are no longer the Princess of Wallachia."

Illona was so angry at being caught red-handed she burst into tears and told them both to get out of her room and locked the door behind them. She then proceeded to throw everything not nailed down at the door, screaming she would have vengeance on the two of them.

*   *   *

During the evening, a trio of riders approached the castle. Dressed in black, the three rode upon black horses and seemed familiar to some of the soldiers garrisoned at the guardhouse. The time since the siege of Varna had been nearly six weeks. Vojislav Rekvas, the current embodiment of the Dragon, also known as the Son of Set, led the other two riders and approached the guardhouse. The guardhouse was merely a stone cottage meant to house guards before they crossed the wooden bridge leading to the castle. It was not meant to be a part of the castle's defenses, but merely a clearing point for guests, messengers and travelers seeking shelter without having to enter the castle. It had an extension which also served as a tavern for those who passed by.

The torches in the sconces outside on the guardhouse cottage wall burned brightly. The night was cold and damp, though it was nearly May. A fog seemed to have accompanied the riders, rolling in quite suddenly. His companions were still dressed in the armor they had worn during the night battle before marching on Varna.

Still mounted, Vojislav approached the guard holding a torch in his hand. He then dismounted, taking off his hooded cloak of black, revealing his face. "I am Vojislav Rekvas, a comrade in arms to your master, Prince Vladis. We were at Varna together.

Tell your master I wait for his invitation to enter his castle to complete our business. He will know who I am."

The soldier immediately left to deliver the message to the castle, whose foundation was on higher ground, some two hundred yards away. A pair of small rivers winding past the isthmus upon which the castle sat, served as a natural defense against an assault on its walls. The message came back that the Prince of Wallachia would receive the trio.

The Prince's hall was not as large as other noble's halls, but it was more than enough to accommodate the guests he was used to receiving. He could house fifty to sixty guests at long tables to feast at. His kitchens could turn out enough food to feed such a large crowd. The dining hall was heated by a large hearth, whose fire seemed to burn bright at any time of day. His lands were vast enough to supply food in terms of grain, vegetables, and meat for the Prince's table. Many of his troops had either fallen in battle against the Byzantines or had left to join the crusades in the Holy Land. He currently had about two hundred soldiers to garrison his castle and the neighboring countryside. If needed, he could raise more troops, but it would take time. The emperor had found favor in the Prince and therefore supplied him with favors and the backing of Imperial troops if needed to defend his lands.

Within an hour, the Prince had prepared a meal and arranged for quarters for the three guests. Vladis knew he owed Vojislav a good sum of gold for his services and aid rendered during the Varna campaign. He was an honorable man and intended to keep that bargain.

The four of them, Vladis, Vojislav along with the two vampires, Nefertiti and Akhenaten sat at the table. Vladis and Vojislav ate and drank while the other two, still dressed in armor of black, sat quietly and watched. It made Vladis nervous that the other two seemed so quiet and ominous, never speaking, never showing reaction to any conversation.

"Never mind about those two. I know they seem strange to you," Vojislav said as he drank wine.

Vladis did not mean to insult, but his curiosity got the best of him. "The smaller one, is that a …"

72

"A woman? Yes, you are quite observant. Believe me, she has a long history. They both do. You would not believe me if I told you the tale. All you need to know is they follow me, obey me, and protect me. They enforce my will and guarantee that no harm comes to me."

"Vojislav, you should know you have nothing to fear from me. We had a bargain, and before you, in those chests are payment as agreed upon for your services at Varna."

"That is good. You have nothing to fear from me as well. I would not turn on such a trustworthy client. Besides, I need the money."

"Where do you go from here?" asked Vladis.

"I suppose we will join the crusaders. They need my services and most of all, they have a lot of gold to acquire. They took it from someone and now I will take it from them. I have already arranged passage to their coast within the month. And what of your plans? Still married to the woman I hear you cannot stand the sight of. Or is it she cannot stand the site of you?" He laughed, as he lifted his chalice to drink.

"Seems you may have heard about my wife. Terrible woman, she is. I have recently learned I have acquired an annulment from the Bishop of Tarnovo. She is to be returned to Moldavia within a month. As of now, she is up in her chambers sulking, plotting no doubt as to how she can prevent me from removing her from my house. She is evil, and I pity the man who will have her when I have removed her from here."

"Evil you say? That is most interesting. As warriors, I and my companions know something of evil. War is evil. Men are evil. I find it evil that men who mean well, commit evil to achieve an end that is good. I believe the word for that is hypocrisy. After giving it some fair amount of thought, it seems to me that is what these crusades are about. The Holy Church has guaranteed salvation to those miserable and evil creatures who have no other vocation than to slit another's throat if the throat they slit is one who has a different faith. Have many of your men left to join the crusades?"

Vladis replied, "Unfortunately, yes. I guess they felt they could get more if they joined those evil ones you just mentioned.

I wish them luck and would welcome them back if it did not satisfy their whims at fortune and conquest. Loyalty means more to me than those things."

"I understand very well the importance of loyalty and trust. This woman you are no longer married to, when does she leave for her homeland?"

Vladis smiled, saying, "When her mind becomes rational again and she sees the futility of trying to keep that which does not belong to her anymore, I suspect she will be gone within a month. I will be happy when she leaves for then I will marry the one I genuinely love and finally be happy."

"Is that one you truly love the one you met before the night battle against Varna?"

"How do you know of her? I never mentioned her to you. In fact, you had already left camp before I had met her. So, nothing I do is a secret to you?" Vladis asked.

"My friend, little gets past me. I have eyes and ears everywhere. This is how I have survived for so long."

Vladis found Vojislav fascinating. "My friend, you are a mystery to me. I know truly little about you, but I owe a great deal to you, regarding my success in battle. The Emperor wanted me to guarantee him a victory."

As he tore off a piece of meat from a drumstick, he said, "And you did so! The Emperor finds favor in you and so do I. Let us eat and drink, in victory, in success, in conquest. Soon I will be going to the Holy lands, not for a pilgrimage but for the pure joy of conquering it. It is what makes me happy." He turned and looked at his companions, quiet and reserved. "Trust me, it makes them happy as well."

*   *   *

Vladis paid Vojislav Rekvas and sent him and his mysterious companions on their way. As far as he knew, they were heading south and east to join the crusades. They would probably fall to the Turks or to the Saracens. He had heard the numbers of enemy soldiers were too many for the European armies to defend against. He was glad he had not decided to join the crusaders effort to retake the Holy Lands. The decision not to participate had irritated Illona greatly. Her reasons why it did so were obvious.

Illona had left the castle, angry and sullen, vowing to get revenge on him and others who had exposed her scheme to remain married to the Prince of Wallachia. Now, she would return to the country to the north, Moldavia. Her father, now deceased, would not be there to welcome her. Her mother had passed long ago. Her brothers now ruled those lands. They would not be as welcoming to her if she had been more cordial to them. In short, she would be coming home to nothing but a cold reception.

After she had left, Vladis had Annara prepare for a wedding. He would marry in secret, for he did not want to give an improper reflection upon his house and his status. After all, this was the Middle Ages and these times called for proper observances of one's station. Her aunts gave the young and beautiful girl a bath, cleaned and fixed her hair such that she was twice as beautiful as before.

One week later, the maiden, born into poverty and low born as one could be, became the legal wife of Vladis Rokosovich, Prince of Wallachia. He stood in his chapel, within his castle walls, dressed in his finest armor and robes. Friar Phillipe would perform the ceremony. His friend, Kajil had arrived only two days before. He would serve as the witness for the Prince while Annara's aunt served as her witness.

Annara looked radiant in her wedding gown, with a wreath of flowers sitting atop her groomed dark hair, measuring down her back, and a matching bouquet of flowers in her hands. A simple gown of white woolen fabric with embroidered hems and borders showed off her femininity and youth very well.

The heart and mind of the Prince was immediately captured upon seeing his bride. Her father led her to him and stood behind her as the friar began to perform the ceremony. Her aunts and uncles were there to attend the event.

For the first time in her poverty-stricken life, Annara felt as though she were something special. She became aware of her worth. Often, she had wondered where her life would take her.

Now, the young peasant girl would realize a dream she had never told anyone about. It was not about changing her station in life. It was not about making her father proud of her. It was that she would be remembered and known long after she was gone. She knew she would have children by the Prince. She was willing to do that without marriage for having the children of a prince…that would be her legacy, her offspring. Her role would be a mother, being a wife was extra. The man who would make this happen was standing beside her, ready to take a most solemn oath before all these witnesses and before God.

No one in the village was aware of this wedding taking place, save the relatives. Josef did not want them to know for the attention would turn to envy against Annara. He did not want that for his only child.

At a local tavern, a private dinner would be held for the family outside the castle, one that Vladis and Kajil would both be proud to attend. There was dancing and minstrels who played while bards told stories. Vladis had no other brothers or sisters so he did not have to explain why he had married one of his serfs to no one. Still, he made the proper observances.

Kajil was glad to see his noble friend and prince happy for the first time in a long time. Vladis was relaxed, joyous and near giddy at the idea that he would finally be spending the night with a beautiful girl, one that he would not have to sleep with one eye open. He could see joy and excitement on all the faces of the young girl's relatives, especially her father's face. The dancing was light, but there were few people sitting when the music started. When the dancing stopped, and the feast started, the merriment seemed tangible to him. He had not seen such a festive atmosphere since last Christmas at his own castle.

Vladis could hardly take his eyes off his new bride, as he wanted to bed her as soon as possible. If there were improprieties being taken, lines of social standing being crossed, he did not care at all.

She was proud to be his and wanted only his acknowledgement for she cared not for the approval of others, but the one she loved. The festivities and celebration went on into the night. It was late when Vladis finally took Annara into his bed at the inn. The bed was warm, for her aunts had placed bed warmers under the covers. They wanted her first night to be special. Special oils were placed around the room to give off pleasing aromas. Her new husband had his own linens brought to the inn to ensure her comfort. Guards were posted outside to ensure safety and privacy. It was the first time Annara had slept in a real bed.

CHAPTER EIGHT

FOR THE SAKE OF ANYTHING BUT LOVE

Annara awoke the next morning surprised to find that breakfast was waiting for her. She had never known any man until last night. Vladis, knowledgeable in the ways of the world and savvy in the carnality of it, taught her the way a man should lie with a wife. It was a wonderful experience for Annara, as she did not feel pain, or embarrassment. She knew she did not know or understand but trusted her new husband to teach her all that she would need to know. She was a woman now in every sense of the word. She gazed at the food prepared for her as she was not used to having someone else prepare food. She was a peasant, a lowly serf, born into a world of poverty and servitude. Socially, she was a slave to the master and owner of the land but last night seemed to have changed all of that.

She laughed, sighed, and giggled while watching her husband make faces. It was as though she were living a dream…a dream that was too good to be true.

For the next few weeks, she maintained her residence at the hut. This was being done while all traces of Illona's presence was erased from the castle. The Princess' servants and attendees were dismissed.

Within a month, Annara began to experience what all women have come to know as "morning sickness". She had it for nearly a week before her father finally noticed his daughter sick and with an appetite. Her father had seen his wife come down with it before Annara was born. He called for his sister to come and attend to Annara while he worked in the forest.

The aunt came immediately and after a while noticed there was a glow about her. She knew the truth and told Annara she was now not just a wife, but an expectant mother. The aunt rejoiced that her niece was expecting a child, but Annara became very frightened. She began to cry, and tears rolled down her kind face.

"Child," her aunt said calmingly, "this is a blessing. A child on the first night of your marriage. It is a good sign. You will be fruitful and above all, our Lord and master has planted his seed in you and will continue to do so such that you will be blessed with more children. I would be so happy if I were you. Your mother would be pleased. When will you tell the Prince?"

*   *   *

Illona's caravan traveled many miles to the north to arrive at the family castle in Moldavia. It was an uncomfortable journey as the Romans had not built as good of roads to the north as they had in the south. The weather did not treat her very kindly either. Rain, accompanied by cold, added further misery to going home in shame and disappointment. She traveled through familiar territory, noticing that nothing had changed. It too added to her disappointment. She longed for change. Something different, anything different would satisfy her. Up to this moment, her life had been exceptionally dull. The dullness and boredom, along with a deep-seated resentment had forged her familiar but serpentine personality. Her resentment came from feeling cheated out of her inheritance. The fact that she was powerless to do anything about it caused her constant sullenness.

Although she traveled with her three maidens, her companions did not bring about any change to her sour outlook. For the longest time, the conversation seemed to focus on who would be the suitor who could melt her heart. Katarina, Portia, and Magda talked incessantly about how they felt when they found love, or at least when it felt like it was love. However, Illona had a heart of stone, and a will of iron. After leaving Wallachia, it would take quite a man to break her into dissolving her hatred of men who she could not control.

She did not look forward to meeting with her older brother, now considered the patriarch of their family. The idea of her having to come to him for support bit her like the fangs of a serpent. It evoked even more hatred of her former husband.

The caravan rode through the peasant village. It too had not changed. Inside the carriage, the women could hear the gates of her brother's castle opening. The wagon stopped in the open space inside the walls by the front door of the keep. She had arrived at the castle to be met by her brother and sister-in-law. Word had already reached his household that she was now an unmarried and unsullied woman. To him, it held a position of shame and insult. He was angry with Prince Vladis for the treatment of his sister. He wanted his sister to remain married and stay in Wallachia. He knew she had a reputation for maneuver, intrigue, and manipulation. Trust was not one of her virtues. Besides, he was married and there was little room in the castle for both women.

His meeting with Illona was stiff but cordial. It was not the heartfelt welcome home any other woman in her situation might expect. She knew she should not expect any warmth from her brother. Illona had never been close to either of her brothers. Her parents had an order of who was the favorite and the eldest brother was at the top of that order. She was not the second favorite child either. Perhaps that was the reason for her instinct for survival. She had been raised in an environment where she knew she could expect to be given little. What she did manage to receive, she obtained with her own means. Her brother received her and agreed to house her until another suitor could be found for her. After all, she was untouched and unsullied. It was as if the marriage had never been.

Her brother's wife followed her to her room. It was the room she had grown up in. Little had changed in that room. It brought back many memories of childhood disappointments and terrors. "Will your old chambers be sufficient, sister-in-law?"

"I suppose they will have to be, will they not?" she replied.

"Illona, you are not welcome here anymore," the wife said softly but sternly. "Your brother receives you because it is the right thing to do. You, Illona, have never been about doing the right thing, and I know it. That is why I tell you, I want you out of this castle and on your way, wherever that may be, as soon as possible. I hold none of my feelings back. I know you are trouble. You were trouble before your marriage to Prince Vladis and you are trouble even now. I know you will find no suitor that will tolerate you. You love only yourself and that I can doubt as well. No harm shall come to you, but if you cause any problems here in my family, you shall pay for it. Do you understand me?"

"Yes, sister-in-law. I understand. I understand you have no idea of the things I grew up with, that made the fire that forged me into what I am. I do not expect you to understand how one can be so betrayed by their father, to be left with nothing of what they were entitled to, forsaken by a marriage to a stranger in a foreign land. I understand, but you do not."

"My husband will send you on your way, with enough to get you by, but after that, you are on your own."

That was fine with Illona except that she had been outsmarted by one who she had always felt was inept and incapable of matching wits with her. Vladis had beaten her at her own game of deceit. He had used truth. She despised that and vowed revenge. She had one card left to play.

That night, at dinner, she watched the family of her brother. They ate together, spent time with each other and no politics, or any other stressful subject came up. In short, she could see her brother was happy, as he had a family, money, position, and a home. He had much to lose if an invader should come across the border to the north. Moldavia was dependent on aid to come from Wallachia, on the pretense that Wallachia would be next on the invader's path to conquest. Now that arrangement was in jeopardy. The security of Moldavia was not assured.

After dinner, Illona talked with her brother and sister-in-law. She continuously brought up the subject of the arranged alliance between the two countries. Before the night was to be early morning, she had wormed her way into her brother's heart and mind, with the idea that his homeland might be in danger.

Before he retired, he sat at his desk and wrote a letter by candlelight to the Bishop of Tarnovo, along with another letter to the Emperor Kayolan. He would "fix" this problem once and for all.

He asked both Bishop and Emperor to put pressure on Prince Vladis to accept his sister Illona back into the marriage. He emphasized that the security of his domain was vital to the Bulgarian Empire and that the marriage was the foundation to that security arrangement. He cared nothing of whether Vladis had fallen in love with another. It was inconsequential to him that his sister felt humiliated and someone else might be enjoying Vladis's bed. He felt his sister probably already knew of it and already accepted it. If he would not accept Illona back, perhaps he could arrange for one of his daughters to be wed to the Prince, though his daughters were not anywhere near the age for matrimony. After a moment of reasoning, he thought better of it, for if Illona hated their father for arranging a marriage, how would his own daughter feel if he did the same? The letters went out by courier the next morning.

*　　　　　*　　　　　*

Nearly a month passed before the letters responding to Illona's brother, the Prince of Moldavia, returned. He had thought the letters may have gotten lost or the recipients refused to get involved. However, because this could turn into a matter of security not just for Moldavia but for the Bulgarian Empire, responding letters returned. The first came from the Emperor Kayolan himself. He had conferred with the Bishop of Tarnovo regarding the matter and the letter read, "Gunter, Prince of Moldavia, greetings from your Emperor. I have received your letter stating the issues of your predicament. It is indeed a delicate matter of which I am not used to intervening upon. However, the security of our state and empire is my utmost responsibility. The Bishop of Tarnovo tells me that Prince Vladis has already married again after granting an annulment which I understand both parties wanted. Now, your sister has had a change of heart. This is indeed uncommon. If all that matters to you is the preservation of the alliance between Wallachia and Moldavia, I am sure some compromise can be reached. But it must be done quickly and quietly. If Vladis has remarried, then he must put her away quietly if he can. Illona must be brought to heel, as she is the price for the alliance. If Vladis takes her back within his castle, back to the marriage bed, they must consummate this marriage, or I must act upon my own accord to achieve the peace and the security of my eastern borders. Speak with the Bishop." The letter bore the Imperial stamp.

There were a lot of hidden meanings to the words in the letter. Gunter knew he must convince Vladis to take Illona back on his own or the Emperor would act. If he acted, it meant that troops might be involved. He needed to speak with Vladis himself. If Vladis would receive him, perhaps he would receive the Bishop as well. He opened the letter from the Bishop. It read, "Greetings to you Prince Gunter. I hope this letter finds you well in spirit and health. I have heard of this debacle between Prince Vladis and Illona, who I now know is among your household again. I know the marriage between the two of them was a mistake from the very start. A simple agreement, signed by both of you, pledging support and alliance should warfare come to either of you should have been enough. Instead, lives are being ruined for the sake of anything but love which is what the marriage should have been about to begin with. Now, I see I must go to Prince Vladis and plead with him to take back within his walls and house the very thing that has plagued him for these last few years. I shall leave and be there by the beginning of August. If you should like to meet me there, perhaps, we can finally resolve this matter. My best to you and your family." The letter was signed with his signature and his seal. He decided to meet the Bishop at Prince Vladis's castle. Illona would come along too, for if he could convince Vladis to at least quarter her in his castle, he would be satisfied. He would do anything to get her away from his family and castle, because he knew his sister all too well.

CHAPTER NINE

THE NAME ABOVE THE DOOR

The castle was humming with excitement. A meeting with great anticipation was occurring and many of the Prince's court wanted to be inside the hall to witness the negotiations. It was an interesting collection of events bringing the three individuals together. All three brought baggage of the humankind with them. Gunter brought Illona along with her personal entourage. The Bishop brought with him the monk who was bribed by Illona to forge the letter regarding the refusal of annulment of marriage. Finally, there was Vladis. His new wife and his friend, Kajil were at both his sides.

Gunter sat across from the Prince of Wallachia with Illona at his side. Gunter produced the letter from the Emperor which basically stated for them to work this out or the Emperor would be involved. Neither wanted that. Illona, her eyes like daggers, stared an evil stare at Annara.

Annara, because she was so much prettier than Illona, felt she did not need to stare back. She merely looked at her husband with adoring eyes from time to time, which she knew would infuriate Illona even more.

The Bishop watched this dynamic exchange of feminine warfare. He had seen a lot in his time as an agent of the Church. He knew this was not going to turn out well for Vladis or Annara.

"What is important here is that the alliance be spared and continue to go on, with or without the marriage," said Gunter in his opening statement. "My sister, though she treated you badly, and she knows it all too well," he looked at her with accusing eyes, "needs the appearances of a marriage in order to hide the scandal of having been put away. Will you not take her back, even in name only?"

"Prince Gunter, that is what we had before. In name only was the entire marriage. There was no love, no contact and certainly, no relations performed during the entire duration of it. Besides, I am married again, this time for real, with having already consummated this marriage. As you can see, my wife is already with child. And, for once, I am happy to have her by my side. What kind of man would I be if I put her away to take back your sister, the most cold and hateful woman I have ever known into my house?"

"You would be the kindest of men, the most honorable of men, to take a woman who has endured the shame of rejection, who has such remorse for the ways she has treated you, and entreat her with kindness, if not pity, that she keeps her honor and not suffer further shame."

Vladis could barely contain a laugh upon hearing Gunter's pleading with him to take back the source of his pain. "Remorse you say. Let her say it with her own lips and tongue, that I may remember it always. I am surprised she would want to come back here to me. Is she willing to merely be the name above the door and not the wife inside the house? I am not a spiteful nor vindictive man. I treat all those in my circle with equal respect and favor. As for my wife, I will not put her away. She carries my child inside her. I put life inside her, and I must admit, she has put life inside me."

Gunter leaned over and whispered something to Illona. She nodded her head, though her face was red, and her eyes were tearing up. He looked back towards Vladis, Annara, and Kajil. "Prince Vladis, she is willing to endure the shame and humiliation of being the name above the door and not the wife inside. That is painful enough. If you will do so, the alliance will remain intact and the Emperor will be satisfied."

"Uh Hmmm! I have something to say regarding this," interjected the Bishop. "This is most extraordinary. Never have I seen a man living under the same roof with two women, both of whom have been legally in the marriage bed of the man. It is not lawful for such things to happen. Therefore, I must make an amendment to this arrangement. I am authorized by the Emperor to sanction this arrangement, but before I do, let me introduce someone to you. Neither of you know my monk who accompanies me, with perhaps the exception of one. That would be you, Princess Illona. My cleric tells me that you bribed him to forge a letter bearing my signature and stole my seal stamp to seal a letter that was an outright lie. I want to confront you about this, here and now. What you did was wrong! Therefore, I have no qualm regarding you and your shame. You deserve every bit of it, as I question your repentance. Your motives were deceitful. I expect an apology."

Illona knew what she must do. Even though the meeting was her ultimate defeat, her shaming and humiliation, she knew all she had to do was wait. Vengeance on all those who sat at this table would be hers, she vowed to herself. Until then, she was willing to agree to anything.

"My most humble apologies, your grace. What you have said is the truth. I was deceitful and hateful. My pride, my vanity, my arrogance, all were the source of my actions against my husband. He has done nothing to deserve this. I harbor no ill will against him for my actions warranted his retribution and therefore, I deserve nothing. Vladis, if you will accept me back into your house, you may have as little to do with me as you like. Your misery will no longer be my purpose. I am broken in spirit, in pride and will."

The Bishop replied, "I accept your apology. The Emperor is interested in appearances. Therefore, if she stays, she stays here in the castle. Annara shall stay in the village. Neither women are to speak or see each other after this. Understood? Good, for the Emperor must not be forced to intervene. Go in peace."

Up to this point, Annara nor Kajil had not said any words. Neither had the forger monk. The two princes stared at each other across the large table in the feasting hall. Finally, Vladis shook his head, "Very well, you may stay here. Your name will be above the door. But my marriage bed will only have Annara in it."

He called for a steward to pour wine for them all, and drinking to the agreement, he was satisfied to put the matter to rest. Vladis had saved the alliance, satisfied the Emperor, bowed to the church while keeping his wife and appearing kind to the evil former wife. He was exhausted yet elated at his many gains and few losses.

His first act was to build Annara a new house, one fit for the wife of a prince now that his marriage to her was no longer secret. He would not have his child be born into abject poverty nor would it not know its father. He wanted to take an active part in the raising of the child. Dreaming of the many things he could do with a new son, it never occurred to him that his first child with Annara might just be a girl.

Within a few months, the house was complete. Annara's father, Josef, was happy for his daughter and excited for the arrival of his first grandchild. Life was good for both.

The summer months passed. Annara's belly grew with her child. Each night she would sing to her unborn, while sewing clothing for the child. Josef cared for her when she could not move about so easily. Peace was in the land for the time being and as autumn began to creep in, the peasants collected the abundant harvests. The land grew rich and fat as Annara did with her child.

Then, one December night of 1202 AD, a stunning pain hit Annara, like a spear to her belly. Vladis was sent for and came as soon as he could. Her water broke but fortunately, one of her aunts was a good midwife and gently attended to her, until she gave birth to a beautiful, crying girl. He took the child in his arms and gave thanks to God for the delivery of his first child. He did not express any regrets that the child was a girl. He would love this child more than anything. The girl child was strong, and healthy. She could not think of a good name for her, but wanted a name that would be special. She decided to name her Tayla Elisabeta. Her hair was dark, and her eyes would turn brown after a time. When she would be fully grown, he knew she would turn the heads of anyone who would call himself a man.

PART TWO

A FUTURE QUEEN

1205 AD

CHAPTER TEN

THE DRAGON RETURNS

Annara was determined that her daughter would have the best the circumstances could offer. After all, she was the daughter of a prince. Annara was happy, although she was used to the poorest conditions of living. Modest accommodations were an improvement in her lifestyle, though it pained Vladis to not be able to have her in the castle with him. He was faithful to the agreement that Annara not enter the castle and Illona kept her agreement not to enter the village or any countryside near it. He made frequent trips to the villa he had built for her.

Illona stayed in the castle, carrying on relations with her butler when she felt her needs for affection were too much for her to ignore. Discretion was observed. No one talked about it, nor did they use it against each other. If Vladis ever knew, he did not talk about it. He decided if she were having relations with whomever, that was her business. After all, she was not his wife anymore. She was free to pursue her interests if they remained discreet.

Vladis visited Annara every day. They both were happy, and devoted themselves to raising their baby, Tayla. He spent a great deal of time at the villa, going home late in the afternoon to tend to the business of a prince. Sometimes he would not arrive until later in the mornings. Rarely would he not see Annara or his child, Tayla. The people knew of the charade of matrimony with his former wife, the truth of his heart and the love he had for Annara and their child, and the burden of secrecy he carried during those early years of Tayla's life. Everyone knew not to talk about it. They all prospered because of it. Because of his devotion to Annara, he made no more demands on the fathers of pretty peasant girls which before, he had quenched his lustful thirst upon. All the peasants of the estate were in happy agreement that Annara's marriage to the Prince was the best thing to happen to them. They lived in peace, enjoying the justice and protection of the prince.

Once in a great while a visitor or a stranger would come to the inn next to the bridge leading to the gatehouse. This night, a familiar face showed up at the inn. He always had two companions with him who rarely said a word. Vojislav Rekvas had returned from the Holy Lands and the city of Jerusalem. Both he and his companions appeared fatigued and weary as they entered the inn. A young boy was paid with gold to tend to their horses. A maiden brought them ale and some food. Only Vojislav ate the food and partook of the ale. His vampires had already dined. The maiden took the plate back when he had finished but before she could leave the table, his arm, dressed in mail and armor upon it, grabbed her. It startled her, such that she gasped in fear. "Have no fear, girl, for I do not seek my pleasure from the likes of you. I wish to inquire if one here knows of the Prince who resides in that castle. Is it still Prince Vladis?"

The young maid nodded yes. He let her go. "Good. I am glad. Inform his grace, the Prince that an old friend of his has arrived and wishes an audience with him. I am Vojislav Rekvas."

The girl sent word to the guard post that Vojislav Rekvas had returned from the crusades and wanted to speak with the Prince. Word came back immediately that Vladis would receive him. The three left the inn and proceeded to the castle.

Vladis was uneasy receiving the seasoned soldier. However, he was very curious about the crusaders exploits so he tried to dismiss the aura of mystery about him. No matter how hard he did so, he could not forget how the mysterious knight and his companions guaranteed victory at Varna when the odds against them were overwhelming. "It was a lost cause to take them on, but we did it," he whispered to himself before Rekvas came into the room. As Vojislav entered his hall, Vladis marveled at the mystery surrounding the man. His companions followed him into the room. They were silent, as their armor made no sounds when they moved. Vojislav was dressed in light armor as a knight and warrior. His coat of arms emblazoned upon his tunic which covered his breast of chain mail. It was two dragons connected at the tail, circling around a moon and fire.

Vladis had not seen this crest upon any noblemen's livery. He had not seen it as any knight's colors or standard. It was as if Vojislav Rekvas was the only knight who identified with it. "Welcome to my home, my old friend. It has been four years since we saw each other." He stood up to greet his guest.

"Prince Vladis, my old friend, not too many years, I hope. I traveled back from the Holy Lands, for it is a lost cause, I fear. I know many will disagree with me and many were sad to see me leave. On the other hand, many were extremely glad to see me leave with my companions. Either way, I left with that which I came for." He chuckled as he looked over to them. They were expressionless and still, like human statues. "I tend to frighten people, my enemies and allies alike. A bad habit for sure, but in this line of work, it being war, it instills a fear that comes in handy very frequently. I think I sometimes frighten even you."

"I am not afraid. I have given you no cause to wish me harm. Respect, aid, and comfort have always been extended to you. If I had offended you, I might consider myself in danger of incurring your wrath. As of this moment, I have not."

"This is true, Vladis, this is true. You need not fear me. I need only a warm bed, perhaps someone to share it with, and a hot meal in the morning. Then, I will be on my way. Can your hospitality afford that to an old friend?"

"And for your companions?" Vladis asked.

"Oh, for them, they usually find their own accommodations. But a comfortable room will do nicely if you can provide it."

"It shall be done." Vladis called for his servant, with instructions given that food and lodging be provided. He also gave instructions that their mounts be cared for as well.

The two talked more. Rekvas informed the prince, "The Byzantine Emperor, Alexius of Constantinople, was removed and in turn, his successor was also assassinated for his attempts to submit the Byzantine church to the rule of the Church of Rome.

After the Franks left Greece, the Crusaders were decisively defeated by Emperor Kaloyan at Adrianople that same year."

"What? Another war? Why was I not asked to join in?" asked Vladis.

"I suppose there was not time enough to raise a larger army. An uprising occurred at Adrianople. Here, the Greek revolt found the aid of the Bulgarian forces. Your immediate superior, King Johannes, had immediately gone to their aid. Johannes met Baldwin, decisively decimated his army and killed him."

"Baldwin is dead? The Byzantine emperor is dead?" Vladis was astonished at the news he had not been privy to.

"An army of crusaders has captured Thessalonica, and traveling at its head is Boniface, Marquis of Montferrat. He is married to Margaret, daughter of the King of Hungary. Hungary, you remember, was a former enemy of the Bulgarian Empire. I have been summoned by the King of Hungary for business I currently am not at liberty to discuss. However, I can say that Boniface will be dead within two years."

It was then that Illona walked into the room. She immediately caught Vojislav's eye. He watched with a longing gaze at her as she took a seat at the table.

Vladis knew that Illona and Vojislav had met before. It was when the knight had come for payment promised for his services at Varna's battle.

In a low voice, Vojislav said, "I hear your wife has always been a wife in name only. I know you love another. Is this not true?"

"It is true. Absolutely true," replied the prince.

"Then I must tell you, since I think you will not be offended by my saying, that I have been attracted to her since I met her those few years ago. Does this anger you?"

Vladis smiled. "No, it does not. She has hated me since I have known her, and I think she still does, perhaps even more so now. Yes, I am married to another, not just legally, but I love her, and it is a real marriage. Illona is here to keep appearances for the sake of an alliance between Moldavia and Wallachia. Nothing more, nothing less."

"Then I propose that should I convince her to share a bed with me, you would not think it rude or find it offensive should she accept my offer?"

"The agreement between me and Illona is that we both occupy this castle with the appearance of man and wife. It does not have to be real. There is no love lost between me and her. If you find her desirable, then by all means, take her if she wishes to submit to you. I only ask that you respect her and not treat her like a common whore."

Illona sat quietly at the end of the table. Though the two conversed in low tones, Illona's hearing was acute. She could discern the words spoken by both. It was Vladis' words that surprised her. That he asked that she be respected and not be treated like a common whore impressed her. Her husband, though he was not truly her husband, still wanted respect given to her. The decision to sleep with his friend, though she was free to do so, was strictly up to her.

"I shall leave you both to your reacquainting, and perhaps later, your vices." As he rose from the table, he looked down at the end where Illona sat quietly. Her nod met his nod at precisely the same time, indicating both agreed that no boundaries were being crossed.

The next morning came and with it, a light shower. The skies were grey, and light was at a minimum. Breakfast was served in the dining hall where only the night before the Prince of the castle sat and talked with the strangest knight who ever put on a full set of armor. By the time Vladis arrived to partake in the morning meal, he was informed that Vojislav Rekvas and his companions had already taken leave of the castle. In a way, Vladis was relieved that his guest was gone, but he missed the interesting conversations, particularly the updates on current events. He did not miss the two mysterious companions who followed him. Vladis would go directly to Annara after breakfast.

CHAPTER ELEVEN

THE BROOD

Few of the villagers had ever seen a child so beautiful. It was easily seen that she favored her mother. This was not only in her looks but her personality. The girl child, Tayla, was now three years old. She had been walking and talking for quite some time now. As she grew taller, she was slender, poised with a charming smile. Her features were angelic, accompanied with long brown hair and large dark eyes.

Tayla was emotional and expressed herself well, not only in vocabulary but also in her body language. She seemed to have an ability to read people's character, even at an early age. Like many children, her innocence forced her to wear her heart on her sleeve for all to see. One could never tell if she would be strong emotionally or fragile, easily hurt and discouraged. Fortunately, because of her father, she knew little disappointment during her formative years. It was for this reason that she would grow up as a kind, courageous girl, crusading for the welfare of others not so fortunate and oppressed. She was repulsed by any act of cruelty, whether deserved or not.

By the time she would become a young woman, her courage and intellect earned her respect amongst the other serfs in the village. Though they belonged to the estate, much like the stock and the crops, she always treated them with kindness and respect. She never felt she was better than them. Her position as the daughter of a prince made her keenly aware of her duty to champion the plight of those less privileged.

Prince Vladis was proud like a peacock when she would run up to him, arms outstretched for him to pick her up. She recognized her father each time he walked through the door of her mother's new house. The hearth was always blazing brightly with food cooking, so warmth was always available. Grandfather Josef was getting older and was given leave to fend for his family, cutting wood and securing food. Both he and Annara tended a small garden out in the back of the villa. She learned to weave and sew from her aunts and began to make clothes for her baby daughter.

Vladis saw Annara nearly every day. Loving her was the easiest thing he had ever done. It came naturally as if it were meant to be. He was comfortable and joyful. Contentment met him at her door when he came to the villa. Each day, she seemed lovelier than before, if that were possible. Her aunts noticed a familiar countenance about her. It was then that a new revelation came to these wise women. She was pregnant again!

Rascha was born nine months later. She was blessed with an easy pregnancy for she had no complications. The birth of a son pleased Vladis very much. A future prince suited him well. No sooner had Annara had Rascha, she was pregnant again. This child would be known as Othar. He too entered the world as a loved son of the Prince of Wallachia. Annara had her hands full, raising her brood as a proud mother. The three grew strong and healthy, as they were much loved. Their parents and grandfather insured they never knew hunger. Basic needs were always met. Their grandfather spent a great deal of time with them. By the time Tayla was five, she began to spend time helping her mother. The boys learned chores from their grandfather.

Annara could see her first child was special. Her intelligence matched her beauty. The demeanor of the little girl was one of obedience, curiosity, courage, and loving trust. The innocence of her young life impressed her father.

Her brothers were something of a different sort. Rascha seemed stubborn, impulsive, possessive and it could be assumed that he could be aggressive if threatened. He tended to be independent, but still looked up to his sister. His audacity to test his parents, to go where his siblings would not, differentiated him from the others. As Rascha grew up, one great quality that Rascha did display was loyalty to his family. If his sister or his brother were threatened, Rascha was ready to fight. It would be that way for the rest of their mortal lives. Often, Rascha would be quick to jump to conclusions that were not based on fact but often on preconceived notions that the world was against him. This accounted for the frequent fights he got into even at a young age. Sometimes he would be excluded from certain games because of his violent temper. He sometimes lacked a sense of fair play but was bold, courageous, and loyal to his family.

Othar was of a milder sort as he was a follower whereas Rascha seemed to be a leader. He was intelligent, much more so than his brother for he was far more analytical. He was a thinker, a planner who would proceed cautiously. This was in great contrast to Rascha. The boys would engage in games, competing against each other and soon, against other boys in the village. Othar would lose often but never gave up until he found a way to win. He did this by studying his opponent, locating his weaknesses, and then exploiting them. He was willing to lose until he could win.

By the time Tayla was seven, Annara had given birth to Prieta. The name meant dark in Spanish. The friar had said so when he baptized the baby. It was because of her near black hair and dark eyes. They were darker than Tayla's eyes. She would be the last of Annara's brood. The family was now complete. The children would help care for their baby sister.

Prieta grew up in the shadows of her siblings. Their protective natures and her inner shyness kept her there. She was a follower of her sister and older brother as soon as she was able to walk. She loved her mother knowing the nurturing nature of her mother and father. Her grandfather seemed to favor her above all the other three. She grew up pretty, shy, and much aware that she found herself subordinate to her older siblings. She too was protective of her brothers and sister and always stood ready to defend them if needed.

Their mother was not educated and therefore could not offer to pass on any knowledge to her children. Only her skills and talents as a mother could she pass on to Tayla and Prieta. Josef was without education also but talented in skills needed to survive the bitter winters and to provide for families in need of shelter and food. This he passed on to Rascha and Othar. They both became excellent hunters and trappers, even as children. Skills with the axe and saw were bestowed upon them.

Maternal instincts ran deep in Tayla. Since she was the oldest, she looked out for her brothers and sister often. They all looked up to her for protection and guidance. Annara watched over her brood as they grew. Her boys listened to their father and grandfather while Tayla and Prieta followed their mother, hanging on every word she said and action she performed. They learned how to be polite, courteous, and feminine. As their mother taught them, they excelled in the female practices of domestic duties. By the time Tayla was seven years old, she noticed her father began to change. Of course, there was a reason for this. These were times where change came about usually in a violent way. Social changes were usually the result of a political or military victory.

Her father began to come around a little less frequently. When he did come around, he seemed sad. He never stayed long for he always felt someone might be watching. His actions said that his coming to see her mother might be forbidden and that if caught, it might put them in danger. Of course, the children did not and could not understand the forces that were at work with terrible catastrophic results placed upon them all.

One night, he came to see them. He was dressed in full armor, ready for battle or at least a campaign it seemed. He held their mother very tightly and for a long time, as if he never wanted to let go. Vladis was quiet around the children. Annara was sobbing quietly, while Josef lowered his head in sadness. As for the children, he held them, kissed them on their foreheads and tucked them into bed before leaving for the castle. Then, he did not come around at all for a while. When he finally returned, he was different. Hugely different.

CHAPTER TWELVE

THE DRAGON'S NATURE

The Emperor Kaloyan had died under mysterious circumstances during the siege of Thessalonica in 1207. The Prince had been called by the new emperor, Boril, to fight for the Bulgarian Empire. Vladis would have opted for sitting out this next war, but his obligations to the Emperor would not allow for it. He regretted deeply having to leave the woman he loved and his children behind. Boril did not know Vladis nor was he aware of the arrangement worked out by his predecessor and the Bishop of Tarnovo. Vladis feared that his actions might betray his emotions regarding the new Emperor such that his loyalty might be called into question. Therefore, he had to keep his thoughts and feelings regarding this war a secret. To be certain, his heart was not committed to fighting at this time. He felt there was no need for this conflict as he was certain that diplomacy could resolve the issue. However, he had to go, so with his troops pledged to the Emperor, he left the castle to take part in the campaign.

Before he left, Vojislav Rekvas, visited Illona more often than Vladis was aware. Often, she would leave the castle and rendezvous with him at locations far away from prying eyes. Vladis never gave it a second thought. After all, their relationship did not allow for emotional involvement. He had given it more of a chance than it had deserved.

Vojislav rarely stayed more than a few days in one place. He knew he had enemies but that was not the reason for his suspicion and paranoia. He had two mouths, full of fangs and bellies hungry for blood, for which he was responsible for. Moving about kept the suspicions of murder at a minimum. Vojislav knew that the fear his vampires instilled upon onlookers would stir up vigilantism against them. At this time, no one knew who or what they were. All they knew was that when the two mysterious beings came around, the stench of death and destruction of lives came with them.

His reputation was one of a dark nature and many people feared him. The only one who did not was Vladis. Perhaps this was because Rekvas had helped him win the battle at Varna. Their relationship had been built on trust and mutual respect. However, Vladis was completely unaware of just who Vojislav Rekvas really was. He would not find this out until much later.

The Dragon's liaisons with Illona did not cause alarm to Vladis. He was aware of the Dragon's interest in her, but as said before, not to the extent it was. The most harm was done with Vladis's subject's full knowledge of the meetings and improper relationship. This, of course became known also to Annara and her father.

One night, the two were in the presence of a clearing in the forest. They were alone, with no attendants or vampires present. They had their mounts, and bedrolls should they decide to lay upon the ground for such frolic as they wished to indulge in. But, Illona had other ideas for entertainment that evening. She wanted to learn about what the Dragon had hinted regarding his capabilities.

"You have knowledge, forbidden knowledge and I want to learn of it," she whispered into his ears as he pawed her with his hands upon and under her clothing. "Tell me of it and I will give all I have to you."

"You know nothing of what you ask, my sweet. Can you handle such power?"

"Teach me the things you know!" she whispered passionately to him.

When evil meets good, it is neither pure evil nor pure good that comes from it. However, if evil meets evil, then the evil is twice as bad. This is what the Dragon wanted all along. He knew the true nature of Illona. Reading her like a signpost, he surmised

99

her heart was as evil as his. He also knew that in her youth, she consulted with astrologers, soothsayers, and the like. As time went on, she began to consult with practitioners of black magic. She herself had been interested in such practices since she was a child. This was one reason she had been cut off from her father's wealth. Her father had observed his daughter making inquiries regarding such things and felt she would be leaning towards the darkest of magic.

The Moldavian prince's efforts to reach out to the church resulted in punitive treatment of her and he resented the church taking such a harsh view of her. After all, Illona was his daughter. Her father was aware of her coarse and rebellious personality, and abrasiveness towards her parents and siblings. Her brothers felt she was possessed by evil as she was always contentious and eager to confront on the pettiest of issues. Either way, Vojislav knew he had found the woman he was meant to be with.

The company she kept were people of immoral and iniquitous character. Scheming, manipulative courtesans and potential suitors she used in a masterful way. When she could not find any use for them, she dismissed them rough and abruptly. For this, she had many enemies. She had always been drawn to the darkest of natures and the characteristics of shadows. Perhaps this was the reason for the attraction between the two.

"I admire you for being the person you choose to be. Because of that, I offer my tutorship to you, giving you the chance of attaining real, dark power."

Such an offer seemed irresistible to someone of Illona's character. "I did ask for it. Am I worthy of such a privilege? I am willing to pay that price for the knowledge."

The Dragon asked, "Once you attain that kind of power, what will you do with it? Who will you serve? My master or yourself? It is the most important question you will ever be asked."

"Tell me of your master. I do not know of him," she replied.

Vojislav was amazed that she was so willing and so trusting of him to lead her into a world of dark power. He knew he was making a great sacrifice in allowing an outsider to come into his world, willing as she was, for it could cost the Order more than it could afford. He felt so much for her and was sure she was his perfect match, that he felt this was the moment to put his identity at stake.

"I believe you have already been serving him for as long as you can remember. You just have not been formally introduced. Let me tell you my story and then you can decide if this is the path you want to follow. If you decide to follow, there is no turning back. You cannot change your mind. Do you understand?"

She reached out to him, pulling his head towards hers. Their mouths met, and she embraced him in a long and passionate kiss. Then, she dropped her cloak and her dress followed soon after. Soon she was naked in the moonlight, ready to offer herself to the Dragon. The air was chilling but she was exhilarated to know her life was about to change forever.

The Dragon took her in his arms and proceeded to tell her the most fascinating story by whispering it into her ear. He would let Set tell the story to her. He had appeared to every Dragon since the high priestess Abinosekhat had given birth to the first one. He felt certain Set was eager to portray himself and would make his presence known to her. As his voice spoke into her ears, she drifted off into a trance, visualizing time spinning backwards, to a place in ancient Egypt, to a night when a high priestess performed a ritual bringing about the physical manifestation of evil in its most pure form. Soon, her body became limp, so Vojislav eased her down to the ground. He wrapped her in her cloak and covered her with his. The night air was cold. Illona fell into a dream. He would stay with her until Set was finished with her. The night was a long one, with a cold wind blowing.

He built a fire to keep himself warm and this woman for whom he had made a sacrifice of his identity to bring into the dark fold of Set. Staring into the fire while Set dealt with Illona, he thought of the Order and what had happened to it. The *Order of the Dragons of Set* had dwindled down to a bare few. Most of them were still headquartered in Rome. He had not been in contact with them in several years. Perhaps, it was time to venture home to Rome.

101

A while back, there had been a certain amount of instability between the members of the Order. Many of them had been long established members who were quite set in their ways. Vojislav felt he was quite capable of carrying out Set's wishes on his own. The Order turned their back on him for a time such that he left and went eastward. That is how he came to be in this land.

Time passed slowly. Eventually, the dawn's faint light began to show through the forest of trees. The fire had died down to just mere red and orange embers. They still gave off plenty of heat to warm his hands and feet. Illona still lay fast asleep.

Vojislav had been awake the entire night. Fatigue had not affected him. He did not want Illona to wake yet until Set was finished with her. Therefore, he left his cloak upon her. Cloak or no cloak, she had to be cold, though she did not wake.

When the dawn came, he knew the sun would soon begin warming the air. He looked forward to it and considered adding wood to the fire. It was at that moment Set began to appear to him as the morning mist began to unfold. Vojislav fell to his knees, reverent to his god. The thick black smoke surrounded him and Illona, still asleep on the ground. Finally, the familiar black monolithic shape set itself before him.

"Is this the one you have chosen for your consort? Your mate? I have wondered about you Vojislav for quite some time. It is time you chose a mate but why did you choose this one? She likes to lead, not follow. You need a follower, not someone to compete with you for power. Now that she knows who you are, and more importantly, who I am, will you trust her to carry out my will, or trust her to carry out her own?"

"Master," said Vojislav in a low voice, "She complements me in all my shortcomings. She shows strength where I have weakness, and hardness where I am soft. I think she is perfect for me. If we produce an heir, he will be of the perfect union to be the next Dragon, should she raise him."

"You think your wisdom to be sound. I knew you would feel this way. You want her to be yours, but she must be watched closely. She desires power and will be ruthless to attain it. This woman will not submit herself to you or me."

"If it pleases you, Master, I am the Dragon and no one, especially this woman is going to change that. She shall meet my needs and serve my purpose and your will. Of this, I swear to you."

"She is not the one I had picked for you. I have given you a wide path to follow, and now you seem to desire to deviate from it. There will be a cost for she will not prove to be in accordance to my wishes and my will."

Eventually, Illona woke shivering and discovered her nakedness. She clung to both cloaks until the Dragon managed to help her dress and then and only then would she give up his cloak to him.

"I am a selfish woman, Vojislav. I have always been so. But, after your story revealed itself to me, I now see the world as it really is. You are powerful! More than powerful, you are chosen! I know I can never be chosen, but I can be the mother of the one chosen to succeed you. If you will have me."

The Dragon spoke. "We have some obstacles in front of us. You are considered married to the Prince, Vladis. You would have to do one of two things. Renounce him before the Bishop and the Emperor, so you can have the annulment. Or...," he paused.

"Yes, continue Vojislav..." she said.

"Vladis will have to die. This will make you a widow, and no one will blame you for remarrying. This option is the most convenient and certainly serves both our purposes."

"And what of your two attack dogs you control. Set told me of them and their natures. What of them? How will they fit into our plans?"

"Attack dogs? They are beloved to me and come with me. We are bonded together. I would never part with them. They will not harm you, for you will come to know them and they you. They are like family to me. Do you still want to marry me, have my son, and follow Set?"

She buttoned up her brocade dress pulled her cloak around her to get warm, then looked him in the eye. "Yes, I do. That should settle everything. Let us leave this place. I am sure I will be missed."

103

They rode back through the forest in the early morning. When they came to the check point to cross the bridge, they parted ways. She knew he was going to ensure the vampires were safely tucked away from the sun's rays. She did not know where and she did not care.

Her dream had given her the forbidden knowledge regarding the Dragon, the cult of Set and the *Order of the Dragons of Set*. She was aware of the history starting all the way back to Egypt and all its secrets. She was changed now. Being resented, hated, unloved, and cast away was hard when she always felt she should have been as privileged as her brothers   No one had given her any understanding or answers as to why she was hateful and mad at the world. Now, all was clear, and her evil nature now had purpose. It was not just about her selfishness and her penchant for discord. There was a reason for her nature. It was to match that of the Dragon, Vojislav Rekvas! She also knew there was no turning back, but she had no regrets.

CHAPTER THIRTEEN

OF DOUBT AND FEAR

Two women, Princess Illona and her confidant, Katerina, conversed in the princess' chambers. Seamstress' had delivered a few new gowns for Illona to try on and have fitted. Illona was her usual self, but suddenly, her mood changed. She sat down in front of a large mirror, picked up her hairbrush and let down her long dark hair. It was nearly waist length, clean, beautiful, and full of body. She handed the brush to Katerina.

"I have decided to end this charade of a marriage," Illona passively said to her handmaiden, Katarina. "It is dishonest to both me and Prince Vladis and the sooner this ends the better."

Katarina, brushing the princess' hair with an ornate brush made with a mother-of-pearl handle, was so shocked when she heard this statement, she nearly dropped the expensive hairbrush. "What?! Why? You have nearly everything you want. The title, the husband to be miserable and most of all, the lands, and the fortune! What else could persuade you to give all this up?"

Illona sighed. "Love... In one word, I can give you the explanation you seek. I am in love, finally, with someone. I find myself challenged to be able to even explain it, but I know in my heart, he is the one I should have been with all along."

Katarina stopped brushing and came around to face Illona. "Think of what you are about to do. If you seek an annulment again, think of what the Emperor may do. He may disavow both of you. No lands, no titles, and no fortune to take with you. You will both be banished from the kingdom, maybe, if you are lucky.

The Bishop was clear about this when he met with you and Prince Vladis, was he not?"

"I believe he said, 'forced to intervene'. That could mean any number of things. Besides, if Vladis were to fall in battle all my troubles will be put to rest and neither the Bishop nor the Emperor will have cause to intervene against me."

Katerina put her hands on her hips and said, "Well, now we are getting somewhere. What are the chances of that happening? Fairly good or maybe not at all? Or are you thinking like you usually do and are conspiring to make things happen? And this person you have fallen in love with…Vojislav? Can he make this happen should you wish it to be so?"

Princess Illona smiled and looked Katerina in the eyes.

"I think he would do anything for me, whether I asked it or not. It is like he can read my mind sometimes. He knows me so well, maybe better than I know myself."

"Last time I took account of you, you knew yourself pretty well, and if I remember correctly, you like yourself the way you are. I think it is just your nature. Is it his nature, as well? If so, then maybe you two are a match. Perhaps, you should commission the dress maker to make a wedding dress."

"Not yet."

*   *   *

Prince Vladis was exhausted. He had spent the entire day in the saddle. This day was exactly like the day before. Constantly moving towards the enemy or away from them. At least he was not on foot. He wished he could see where the enemy was and then attack and get the business of war over with. He was tired of fighting. In his younger days, his spirit was far more aggressive and bolder than it was now. He was married, with children. He longed to see them, to hold them and tell them how much he missed them. It was this thing called war that kept him from them. When he was young, fighting, drinking, whoring, and gambling with not just his money but his life as well were his pastimes. But now, those times were in the past. He had responsibilities not just to the Emperor but to his family. It made him think of all the times he had taken husbands and fathers on campaigns, away from their families. He knew the resentment of fighting someone else's war. Still, he had no choice. It was expected and demanded that his allegiance to the Emperor be shown with troops ready for battle.

He traveled with his friend, Kajil. Kajil noticed the changes in Vladis. He knew it was because of Annara and the children. He had seen her when they left Vladis's castle for the campaign. Though he felt she was beautiful and knew she was quite a catch, he felt no envy at all. He was happy for Vladis for he knew she had made his friend happy and content.

Kajil, on the other hand, was single. His father was another nobleman in another part of the empire. Kajil was happy to spread his wild oats everywhere, and always wondered if he had any illegitimate children out there somewhere. At least his friend, Prince Vladis did not have to wonder.

It had taken nearly two weeks for Vladis's troops to catch up with the Emperor's army. Word had gone out to all the territories in the empire that the campaign season was upon them and the Byzantines were ready to invade again. Everyone wondered if the Battle of Varna would be fought over again. And if so, would they be able to draw them out like they did last time. Vojislav was nowhere to be found and it seemed that he either had joined the crusades in the Holy Land or was he avoiding this fight altogether. Before Vladis had left, he had confirmation that Illona and Vojislav were intimately involved. Vladis had not confronted him nor Illona regarding it for their agreement did not forbid any relationship if it was done discreetly and quietly. Those requirements had been met as far as Vladis was concerned. He did not hear of it through any serf or peasant or even his wife. The illusion of a marriage of convenience was also one of political necessity. Illona herself had disclosed it to him. She also told him that since he was about to resume campaigning for the Emperor, Vojislav thought it best to go away for a while so as not to embarrass his friend or to bring shame upon his household. To Vladis, that was not an unreasonable statement to make. It seemed an honorable thing to do.

Finally, the destination of the long march was made known. It was not Varna. Vladis seemed relieved. The rumors were ruse, to confuse enemy spies by the direction the army traveled in. Vladis had been on this route before as had many of his men. Soon, they made camp on the same location as before. Ironically, the weather seemed as if it had not changed. It was spring, the month of April. History seemed poised as if to repeat itself. Vladis had doubts and ill feelings about this trip. He wished he had not come but he had been given no choice. So, here he was, about to either kill the enemy or be killed by the enemy. Only, he was not sure who the enemy was or where they were. All he knew for sure was that he was part of an army on the move, but to where?

They made camp amongst the trees. A simple lean-to shelter kept the dew and rain off the Prince. He had camped in such a primitive setting before and therefore he was no stranger to the life and hardships of being a soldier. Vladis had brought no camp followers this time. He did not believe in doing such things anymore and therefore broke tradition by leaving the young girls at home with their families. The fathers certainly appreciated this, knowing their daughter's virginities would be left intact and if violated, it would not be by the wanton lust of lonely soldiers.

Campfires were difficult to start that night for the light rain and dew made a fire nearly impossible. With no fire, there was little warmth. The men were tired and therefore needed to rest. Campfires and camp followers would not be the priority that night. Most of the men managed to build even the most rudimentary type of shelter. Only a few slept out in the intermittent showers throughout the night.

Dawn came and soon men began to stir trying to light up fires to cook with. Only a few were able to get started and most men began to search for wood that might be dry enough to ignite. They broke camp by mid-morning and resumed the trek southwest instead of east. The army was in the vicinity of Ovech. Word began to spread within the marching column that scouts who had gone forward towards the city of Varna and the three fortresses had returned to report the city still in the hands of the Bulgarians. This was good news.

108

So where was the army headed? There was a town known by the Bulgarians as Boruj or Boruy. In modern times, it would be known as Stara Zagora. This was the objective of their advance towards the southwestern part of Thrace, part of the Bulgarian Empire.

Later that night, Boril called for a meeting of all his commanders and nobles to inform them of the situation. The Greek noblemen of eastern Thrace had risen and sought assistance from the Latin Empire already during the reign of Kaloyan. Kaloyan was dead now and therefore the nobles sought assistance from the Latin Empire, notably the Byzantines. Boril wanted to reconquer the region and secure it for his empire. The purpose of their long march was to perform a scheme of maneuver designed to fool the Byzantines that they would head for Varna. Instead, they were coming straight for the Byzantine army in Thrace. The army moved slowly, for rains had turned the roads into quagmires. Finally, they met on the battlefield outside of Boruy.

It was June of 1208. During the night, the Bulgarians under Emperor Boril maneuvered towards the unfortificd camp of the Byzantines. At dawn, they suddenly attacked and the soldiers on duty put up a fierce fight to gain some time for the rest to prepare for battle. While the Latins were still forming their squads, they suffered heavy casualties, specially by the hands of the numerous and well-experienced Bulgarian archers, who shot those still without their armor. In the meantime, the Bulgarian cavalry circumvented the Latin flanks and managed to attack their main body. Boril's army outnumbered the Byzantines but the Byzantine army was personally led by Henry, Emperor of Constantinople. Boril won the day but after a twelve-day retreat, the Byzantines stopped near Phillippopolis and accepted battle on better ground to favor the Byzantine army.

Surprisingly, Boril's army was defeated and forced to withdraw. Many were captured. Of those, Prince Vladis of Wallachia was amongst them. His friend, Kajil had been killed in combat. Vladis had gone to his aid only to be turned back by other mounted knights. He could not reach his friend and watched him die at the hands of the murderous Byzantine infantry. They pulled him from his mount, and he went down swinging his sword in every direction at his enemies. Vladis could see he was surrounded by at least eight soldiers. He fought valiantly but the odds were not in his favor to extricate himself from such a calamity.

Prince Vladis on the other hand, was dressed as a nobleman, and those knights who surrounded him recognized him as such. They pressed him to surrender at the point of many lances. He thought of Annara and his children. "Better to be captured and ransomed than to die on this cursed battlefield," he thought. He hadn't wanted to fight this campaign anyway and now his friend had died bravely and honorably, but dead, nonetheless.

Demoralized, he threw down his sword and dismounted.

*   *   *

Meanwhile, back at home on Prince Vladis's estate, word finally reached home that Boril's forces had been defeated in a large battle in the south, near Phillippopolis. Word spread like wildfire and all sorts of rumors and suspicions arose concerning the disposition of the Prince. Was he alive, or wounded? Perhaps he was captured. If so, would he be ransomed as was customary for soldiers of nobility?

Annara was practically hysterical with doubt and fear. If her husband was dead, then Illona would move to inherit everything and she would be left with nothing, especially for her children. Their birthright was in danger and now that Vladis was nowhere to be found, it could only be surmised that he might have been killed in the battle in the south.

Annara was angry that he had left her at the request of the Emperor. After all, he had fought in many campaigns only to come back a slightly more fractured Prince than before. How many times must a man prove his worth, his courage and loyalty before one can say, "Enough!" She wondered often, questioning her father who could not say for he had not been a soldier. Tonight, she wondered alone.

Illona was overjoyed for now she could reassume her title as Princess of Wallachia if Prince Vladis were dead now. Even more, she would also be free to marry Vojislav, when he returned. She had not seen him lately as well and wondered if he might have joined in the action near Plovdiv.

Annara's children, Tayla and Rascha were old enough to understand the predicament they were in. To make matters worse, the Bishop of Tarnovo, the kind, elderly gentleman of God had died in his sleep. Not an uncommon occurrence for a man of his years. The odd part of these troublesome times was that the friar who had performed the ceremony of marrying Annara and Vladis as man and wife also died that same day. Aside from the guests at the wedding, there were no officials either of the church or the magistrate that could vouch that Annara and Prince Vladis of Wallachia were ever legally married. The Prince's witness, Kajil, had been killed which only left Annara's aunt to witness the legality of the marriage. Annara feared for her aunt's safety.

CHAPTER FOURTEEN

JANOS OF PLOVDIV

It was a rainy, dark night when the stranger's coach arrived at the monastery in Tarnovo. A few guards on horseback accompanied him. The coachmen dismounted, opening the coach's door while a middle-aged man in clerical robes dismounted from the steps rapidly and retreated to the shelter of an overhanging roof at the front door. Another man, seemingly unimportant, banged upon the heavy wooden door with the hilt of a sword.

"Open up, I say! Open up in the name of the Bishop of Tarnovo!"

The door opened slowly to reveal a monk standing with a lantern in one hand, while his head bowed in reverence to the man in the robes of an important official of the church. A new Bishop of Tarnovo, Janos of Plovdiv, had been appointed by the Archbishop of Constantinople. Prior to this appointment, he had been the abbot of the Rila Monastery. He had spent many years there, starting out as a monk and eventually becoming the abbot of the monastery.

When he had arrived in Tarnovo to assume his office, the deceased Bishop's monk who clerked for him, quickly moved to enact his master's last will and testament. It was the former's wish that the monk be able to continue to clerk for the new Bishop. He was also to give a letter to the new Bishop, signed personally by the now-deceased yet still celebrated man of God.

The new cleric took to his new office with vigor, eager to perform his duties as the new Bishop. Janos was much younger than his predecessor. He brought energy, will and a fresh approach to a seemingly stale spiritual environment. Once there, he met Brother Bartholomew, the old Bishop's clerk. The monk greeted the new Bishop cordially and produced the letter from his old master. The new Bishop opened it and read it aloud.

"To my successor, whomever the blessed Archbishop of Constantinople shall designate, I give my final salutations and my sincerest farewell. I have foreseen my death and even now, our Lord sends his angels to carry me home. I embrace my soon to be departure.

I have instructed my clerk, Brother Bartholomew, a fine lad whose love for our Lord has exceeded his vices which he has left behind since taking his vows. Listed below are instructions for my final disposition. Most importantly I wish to make known my wishes and secrets which I trust you will keep close to your heart.

There are things of which you must know. The church has enemies in this land. Fierce and terrible enemies of which only the wisdom of our Lord can guide us such that we may prevail against them. An agent of Satan lives amongst us. I have no proof, nor can I say his name by which he travels under, but he is here, nonetheless. Bartholomew alone can assist you and for this reason, I ask, perhaps implore you to keep him on as your assistant and clerk. He is trustworthy and knows the secrets for which I am about to entrust you with. First, beware of the Princess Illona. She will tell you that she is married to Prince Vladis of Wallachia, but she is not. I have granted an annulment to that empty marriage. However, the Prince is legally and properly married to a peasant girl, Annara, who has since bore four children to him. The campaign that is underway shall no doubt find many a child fatherless and many a wife a widow. If it finds Annara a widow and Prince Vladis's children fatherless, keep in mind that Annara is the rightful heir to the Prince's estate. Do not allow this evil woman to disinherit these humble people from what may be due them. Protecting such innocence is my final mission from our Lord."

The Bishop stopped reading. He looked up from the letter to see Bartholomew standing, his hands folded behind his back and looking downwards at the floor of stone.

"This is the seal of this office upon this document. Are you sure you did not write this yourself?"

Bartholomew answered, "No your grace. I would never do such a thing."

"But you have in the past. The Bishop told me of it quite a while ago. He had since forgiven you, but how can I be sure you have not done such a thing again?"

"I owe the Bishop many things, to include restoring my honor to its rightful place. He asked me, after I had such a moment of weakness, the truth about that matter. I felt such remorse that I came to tell the truth and have always done so since that day. It is not for my benefit that you believe my testimony but that of the Bishop's. A great lapse of justice may take place and it was his wish that you prevent it."

"Very well," replied the new Bishop. "I will honor his wish and keep you on. Regarding this marriage to a serf, this is a matter that must be addressed immediately. Have you actually met this woman?"

"Yes, your grace. I was with the Bishop when he was dispatched by the Emperor himself to solve this matter. The marriage to the Princess Illona was merely a matter of politics, your grace. It united the kingdoms of Wallachia and that of Moldavia. It provided for a security pact between the two kingdoms."

"I see. So, this woman dislikes her husband enough to sue for an annulment meaning the marriage was never consummated. But she still lives on inside the castle as if they were still married? That is outrageous! It is sinful. It goes against God's law regarding marriage. And he is legally married to a peasant girl who has already given four children to him?"

Bartholomew replied, "That is correct, your grace. The wife Annara lives in a villa outside the castle. Before Princess Illona can declare her husband dead, she will try to establish legitimacy as his only heir. I fear she has moved in that direction already with the help of the one the Bishop mentions in his letter. He is

114

the enemy of our Lord. I have observed him from far off. He is usually in the company of two knights, dressed all in black. They are only seen at night. Never in the daylight."

Janos knew of Prince Vladis because of the stories told by warriors at the dining tables of many noblemen that Prince Vladis was the hero of the Battle of Varna. These stories reached the ears of the newly appointed Bishop while he was a guest of some of these noblemen who had campaigned with the Emperor. It was tales of his daring and his bravery, his chivalry and his humanity towards others that impressed the new Bishop.

After a few moments of being deep in thought, the Bishop spoke to the monk. "Brother Bartholomew, I have a job for you. You shall go to this estate and replace the friar. I shall write the letters authorizing you to be the replacement. You shall be my eyes and ears for the time being. I shall write documentation stating that the two in question are married and no such disinheriting shall occur. You shall carry these letters but do not reveal them to the Princess. Do you understand? You shall remain there until the matter is resolved, meaning, Prince Vladis comes home alive, or Annara is given title to the estate per the rights of a legal and recognized spouse."

"Yes, your grace. As your eyes and your ears, I shall go and report anything significant back to you, your grace."

"Go in peace, my son."

Bartholomew responded, "I shall do so with my utmost ability. I will make personal contact with the wife of the Prince and inquire diligently of his disposition: missing, killed or captured. May it be the latter."

"If you should meet with the legal wife, be sure to not let the Princess Illona know of it. There may be a price to pay for it. I fear this may have been the fate of the last friar. If so, she is not above treachery of the worst kind. Perhaps this is the enemy of God that my predecessor talked about."

"I understand." The monk left to prepare to travel.

*   *   *

From the moment Brother Bartholomew arrived at the chapel from which he would carry out his duties, he knew his life was in danger. His mission was not to investigate the circumstances under which his predecessor had died but to assume and fulfill his duties as his successor. He wondered if the Princess Illona would see it that way. The monk carried letters as directed by the Bishop. One was the letter designating the Bishops decision to install the monk as the new friar. Another was the letter certifying Annara and her children as the legal heirs to the Prince's title and lands due to her legal and lawful marriage to Prince Vladis, while another stated the legal and permanent annulment of the marriage between Illona and Vladis.

He had written down a copy of the letter to the successor that the now-deceased Bishop of Tarnovo dictated before he died. And, there was something else… a letter to Annara. Brother Bartholomew had taken the liberty to have read it before sealing it with the seal of the Bishop. It was the only copy and he was determined to give it to Annara when he was finally able to meet her. Unfortunately, the opportunity had not presented itself. The letter was in a safe place for he knew he must not let it fall into the wrong hands.

For the first few weeks, his stay was uneventful. Villagers came to him for the usual reasons, mostly for confession or for the sacrament. Word got out rather quickly that the estate had another friar to conduct religious services for the peasants as well as others above that station. Soon, he had his hands full. The last thing he expected was a call from the Princess requesting his presence for an urgent matter.

He had not had the opportunity to visit Annara or her children. He wondered if she would remember him. He hoped the Princess would not for if she did, no doubt she would consider him dangerous to her cause as he could easily foil her plans to eliminate Prince Vlad's true heirs.

He arrived at the guardhouse next to the bridge, only to be met by a guard posted. His horse was a borrowed mare as he currently had no means of transportation of his own. Friars rarely had any personal effects and certainly a horse was far more than a man of his occupation could afford. He was escorted into the walls of the castle and prepared to enter the hall of the Prince. He saw a plaque of wood nailed above the door, with Annara's name inscribed upon it. The thought of the arrangement that was made years ago made him smile. If only Prince Vladis were here, he thought.

Eventually, he was met by the Princess Illona in a room that was normally meant for receiving guests of importance. He, being a lowly man of the cloth, was certainly not one of any great importance but he did have something no one else did…knowledge of the "arrangement".

Illona, dressed in a gown of fine wool, trimmed in fine ermine fur, walked into the room. She took a seat and motioned to the new friar that he should take a seat as well. When he had sat down on a wooden stool with no back to it, she began to speak.

"Friar, I believe my husband is dead. He has not returned from the war against the Byzantines. I cannot be sure, but I fear it deep down in my heart."

Brother Bartholomew could barely contain himself as he could see through her emotional charade immediately. Instead, he wanted her to verbally trap herself by revealing her true intentions regarding this visit. She asked if it were possible that she could take communion as it had been a long time since she had participated in the rite.

"Princess, I am instructed to give the sacrament of communion to those who ask for it. I would hear your confession as well."

"Very well, Friar, it has been many months since my last confession. Bless me father for I have sinned."

"Tell me of your sin, Princess, that I may absolve you of your deeds."

She began to tell him of many things she had done, to include jealousy and scheming against her husband that she feared dead. Her remorse came for she had not asked for his forgiveness causing her great sorrow. This sudden change of heart caused Brother Bartholomew to seriously wonder if she was sincere. When she had finished, he told her of her penance, and she agreed. Then, he left. He wanted out of there as fast as his legs could carry him. Something told him that the spirit inside her was not her own. His thoughts swirled in his head as he made his way out of the castle. She did not appear to be the same woman he had seen humbled by the Bishop and the Prince years ago. What alarmed him the most was that she did not let on that she might have recognized him. If she did, then she would know that he knew the true "arrangement" of their marriage and immediately move to silence him.

He remembered what the deceased Bishop had told him about one who was as close to the devil as if he wore the same clothes. There was only one he could think of that matched that description and his name was Rekvas. Tales of murder and disappearances of entire families had spread throughout the region and the superstitious country folk only spread the rumors faster than the wind could carry them. To Brother Bartholomew, there was only one question in his mind…what was the truth?

*   *   *

For weeks, Vladis had not seen the sun's light nor felt the wind of cool fresh air upon his face. As a prisoner of war, captured in battle, he felt despondent to the point of hopelessness. Even the time of the year was unknown to him. He knew it must be Autumn, for the air was beginning to grow cold. If he could but get word to someone informing them of his dire circumstances, perhaps his captors would be willing to negotiate for his release, paying a customary ransom. He was not chained nor shackled but his small cell with a window which allowed a small amount of cold, fresh air to trickle in if the wind was right, allowed him his only respite from the stench of human filth. As a soldier, he had endured many hardships, but as a prince, he had never been so abased as he was at this hour.

He was fed once a day, watered twice a day, but not allowed out of his cell. A small lamp afforded him his only light. His jailer was a mute and therefore could not engage in any conversation. He knew not of his captor or his name, nor did he know of where he was imprisoned. Occasionally, a few soldiers would come to his cell, and strike him repeatedly, questioning him about his knowledge of the Emperor Boril's plans.

118

Finally, after what seemed a lengthy collection of days of suffering, a stranger accompanied the jailer to his cell door. The stranger held a sprig of mint to his nose to counter the smell of what seemed the first level of hell itself. The lamp finally gave illumination to the face of his captor. The man, dressed in the armor of a noblemen, smiled as he began to speak to Vladis.

"I am the Baron Regevaks Descondes of Plovdiv. You, Prince Vladis, are my prisoner. I apologize that I have not come to you sooner. I only learned of your identity a few days ago. It is a pity you should end up in this place. I reserve it only for the worst of the worst. Criminals, condemned men, those accused of sorcery and witchcraft, traitors… you know the sort. But you! Well, you are none of that. An honorable man, who fought well, I might add. But your army lost the battle on that day. The day was ours and now you are here. Is there someone I can get word to so that you may have your release negotiated for? I hear there is a wife, a Princess Illona who awaits word of you?"

"She is not my wife, and she would like nothing more to hear that I rot in this cell. At least she is not my legal wife. She occupies the castle with her treacherous lot, but she has no access to my fortune."

The Baron sighed. The lamp was growing dim for it needed more oil to burn. The air was beginning to affect the Baron, a man of large build and stature. He wore his armor, even in his own castle perhaps because he did not trust those of his court or that his castle was poorly heated. He pulled a flask from his belt and shared a drink with Prince Vladis. Vladis was grateful for the drink of something that did not taste of sewer water, stale, and foul. Finally, he said, "Then who does?"

"I and I alone can negotiate for my release. What are your terms?"

*   *   *

The terms of the ransom for Prince Vladis were discussed and agreed upon. Two chests of silver and one of gold would be payment enough, and an oath to not take arms against the Baron. Prince Vladis could afford it but not much more. Financially, it

119

almost ruined him but better to live poorer than to die richer. He did not care as much for the lifestyle of a prince as he did to be a father and a husband for someone he genuinely loved. All the money in the kingdom could not satisfy him or make him want to be married to Illona, legal or not. He was tired of the charade of marriage to someone for the simple use of a security agreement.

The Baron sent troops with him to escort him home and receive the ransom payment. Normally, this was not done this way. The Baron also attached a condition to the agreement. Should Prince Vladis default upon the conditions, his family would be taken instead. Prince Vladis told the Baron that should he release him, he would throw in Princess Illona as a gift. He knew the sooner he was rid of her, the better for everyone, especially his family. Security pact or not, nothing was worth the misery she inflicted just by being under his roof.

Regevaks Descondes had habits that would have made barbarians squeamish. He loved power and the abuse it entitled him satiated his desire to inflict damaging pain and humiliation upon his victims. When he told Vladis about his cell, he lied. He had put many a man and woman inside those walls of rock, for the imagined crimes he spoke of. The Baron had heard of Princess Illona and was curious about her. To take a woman of privilege and break her down was a rare opportunity. He welcomed the idea of having the wife of a prince but did not seriously expect Prince Vladis to just hand her over nor would she volunteer to come to the Baron. If she arrived at his castle, he fully expected her to be in chains. And for him, that was the equivalent of being gift-wrapped.

CHAPTER FIFTEEN

RETURN OF THE PRINCE

The soldiers of the Baron Regevaks Descondes escorted Vladis home. Clad in cloaks of green and white, they were soldiers of a slightly different kind. They were well fed, equipped, disciplined and loyal to their master. Vladis had no doubt they would carry out their master's wishes should he refuse to uphold his end of the bargain regarding the ransom.

Though the weather was not yet cold, as it was well into the autumn of the year, the journey was excruciatingly difficult, as Vladis' health was poor. He coughed constantly and ran fevers while he rode. He had no doubt that he had caught the condition we know today as pneumonia, but he did not complain. His pride saw to that. He essentially was a broken man, with only one reason to live…family.

Upon arrival at his castle, the Baron's escort waited outside while he made ready to pay his own ransom. He had no garrison to protect him or his family. They were still with Emperor Boril's army if they were still alive. As of now, his life was full of assumptions. He assumed his soldiers may have pledged fealty to a nobleman who survived, or that perhaps they might have deserted and tried to make their way back to the castle here to swear loyalty to the Princess Illona. The unknown is a fearsome monster.

He approached the few sentries still on duty. To them, he was nearly unrecognizable. When they did recognize him, they began to sound the bell alerting all those in the castle the master and Prince of Wallachia had come home. He had not come home under his own flag or standard. This was one reason his sentries did not recognize him. Also, he was emaciated beyond their belief, for nearly being starved. It would take some time to restore him back to his health. He wondered what the Princess Illona would think. It was his profound belief that she would be disappointed that he had returned. Would she prevent him from paying the ransom, assuming she had as much right to the princely treasure as he did, forgetting they were not married anymore? A million questions raced through his mind. He knew where his money was hidden. It was a practice his father had taught him that he and he alone should oversee the financial side of his title. He hoped she had not discovered it before he was able to lay his own hands upon it. More than anything, he could not wait to see Annara and his children again.

Vladis collapsed just inside his hall. Servants ran to his aid and carried him to his chambers. When Vladis came to, he asked for his most trusted aid. Johannes, a man well into his years, came to him. Vladis motioned him to come close to him as he could only whisper. Illona had not reached him yet.

"Pay my ransom, two chests of silver and one of gold to the Baron's men outside. Do it now before it is too late!" His voice was barely discernible, but Johannes understood him and the importance of doing it quickly. He knew Illona and hated her as much as Vladis did. Perhaps more because he had personally heard and seen her deviousness.

Johannes quickly moved to the place where the Princes' treasure room was located. It was a secret room unknown to nearly all the castle staff. Only Johannes knew of it outside the Prince.

Illona came into the room, pale and expressionless, to see that the Prince seemed to be lying on his deathbed. In disbelief, she nearly broke down. Not for any sentimentality she might have held for him, but that her plans were now in serious jeopardy. Regaining her composure, she called for Brother Bartholomew to attend to him, as she anxiously awaited his passing.

Johannes delivered the silver and gold, without the knowledge of Illona and sent the troops on their way. But, before the captain of this detachment left, he turned to say, "My master, the Baron Descondes, wants to know if your Prince was serious about sending the Princess Illona to him as a gift. I understand their marriage was annulled long ago. If so, send her out."

Johannes was shocked. Here was a perfect chance to rid himself of the evilest of women he had ever known. He replied to the captain, "I shall inquire of my lord if he so desires it. He is not well, and I fear that he may not recover from his captivity. If so, my personal feeling is that you shall have her, and do with her whatever you wish."

Johannes eagerly approached Vladis, still lying on his bed in a feverous condition, wheezing and coughing. A physician had been sent for along with the friar, Bartholomew. The physician arrived first, and began to make a poultice, thinking the device would draw out the inflammation from his lungs. Warm soup was brought to him and helped him regain his strength. When the time was right, Johannes asked his master the question the captain asked. Would Vladis give up his former wife to his captor? Even in his tormented condition, Vladis could not bring himself to do it. "No, she stays."

"Master, my Prince, I beg you to reconsider. She is a stone around your neck. Think of Annara and your children. She has been plotting to usurp their birthright and to destroy all witness to your marriage to Annara. Please, send this woman away!"

At this time, Brother Bartholomew arrived. He prepared to give last rites to the Prince. But, Vladis had other ideas. He had no intention of dying. "Everyone out, except Johannes and Bartholomew."

Everyone else left and closed the door behind them. Now, it was just the three of them. Vladis's breathing returned to a calmer, more even rate. "I do not know of you. What happened to the friar that married my wife Annara and I?"

"Forgive me, my Prince, but I am Brother Bartholomew. I was here when the Bishop of Tarnovo came here and negotiated a truce between you and your former wife."

Vladis smiled. "I knew you looked familiar. Thank God someone is alive who remembers the truth!"

"Sire, you are in great danger as are your wife and children are as well. You know your former spouse better than anyone here. She has been plotting to take complete control of your estate, title, and fortune since you left for war. I bear letters from the new Bishop of Tarnovo. The other Bishop died while you were on campaign in the south. God rest his soul, for he was such a wise man, kind and gentle. He left instructions for me and the new Bishop of Tarnovo, Janos of Plovdiv. He is aware of your true marital circumstances and wishes me to monitor all developments concerning it. He wishes that you not live under the same roof unmarried to a woman as evil as this one. I concur that you should send the Princess Illona away as soon as possible. Your servant, Johannes, is right."

Johannes chimed in, "If the Bishop of Tarnovo wishes it, it must be God's will that it be done. Do this speedily for she no doubt will resist with all determination."

With a weak nod of his feverish head, he relented. Within the hour, the Princess Illona was escorted by the troops of the Baron Regevaks Descondes out of Vladis's castle. She screamed and fought against them, but they had her bound and her ladies in waiting were with her, but they were not bound. The captain of the detachment came to Vladis to complete the transaction. He looked out the window at the procession of females taken against their will to accompany the troops back to the castle of the Baron. He smiled. "I cannot imagine what the Baron will say when he actually lays eyes on your former wife."

Mustering all of his strength, Vladis interrupted, saying, "Pray he does not go blind for she is the medusa herself. I cannot stand the sight of her for I see no beauty in her. Perhaps outward, but she is a seductress, full of evil, and darkness. He will not be happy with her. He will take more pleasure from her attendants I am sure of that."

"Prince Vladis, you have upheld your end of the bargain. It is here that I must bid you farewell, and hope we never meet again, especially on the battlefield." He turned and left the room.

Brother Bartholomew and Johannes watched him through the window of the Prince's chambers as he exited the castle. The mounted troops carried the women in the Princess' carriage. A cart loaded with their baggage followed behind. The soldiers headed south, in the direction from whence they had come.

Johannes breathed a sigh of relief. He was so happy and ecstatic with joy he could hardly contain himself. "She is gone. Forever, she is gone! Can you believe it? This is such a great day for our master and Prince has come home to us, delivered from his enemies while the evil of this house had left us never to return."

Bartholomew, smiling, asked the Prince, "Shall I send for your wife and children. I don't think they know you have returned from the war."

Still weak, Vladis answered, "No, they must not see me this way. Let me recover so that they will never remember seeing me near death this way. I must regain my health. Say nothing to anyone.

However, word that Prince Vladis had returned from the war and the Princess Illona had been taken away by his captors and was part of the ransom payment spread quickly. Soon, the news reached Annara. She immediately made her way to the castle, alone.

She was granted admittance for they recognized her to be the real wife. She found Johannes and asked him directly if the rumors were true. Reluctantly, he told her the truth and admitted her to see her husband. She nearly broke down in sobs to see her husband in such dire straits, near death with a fever and breathing so shallow. She immediately began to care for him, nursing him back to health. She told Johannes to send word to her father to look after the children while she took care of her husband.

*　　　　*　　　　*

Josef watched his grandchildren with the greatest of care. He wanted them to never to be out of his sight. He had good reason to care, especially when the sun disappeared from the blue sky at night. He only felt truly safe during the daylight hours.

The rumors were growing, always traveling with travelers, tales of death and murder, of evil spirits who rode horses and wore black armor. He could feel the cold winds in the autumn air and knew it would be a hard winter. His bones in his arthritic joints told him that winter would be especially tough this year as the harvests had not been what they had expected. They would get them through the winter, but not leave much to spare. Annara was gone to the castle while Josef watched her children. He was puzzled why she did not want them there. Perhaps it was because of the evil Princess Illona. Seeing Vladis' children might cause her to snap in jealousy and send her mind over the edge, making her evil unpredictable. Tayla, Rascha, Othar and little Prieta often asked about their mother but Josef could only reassure them she would return. Still the feeling of uneasiness remained in his consciousness.

Tayla, being the oldest, took up where her mother left off. She was now fourteen. Already, her grandfather spurned away any boy close to her age. Tayla was barely interested in boys as she was to learn things about life. She wanted an education.

A few days later, Brother Bartholomew came to the villa to check in on them. With his arrival, he brought news of their mother. With her permission, he told them what had happened and that soon, they would be joining their mother and father. They would be leaving the villa and joining their mother and the Prince in the castle.

Tayla, a poor girl, born to a peasant woman, fathered by the Prince of Wallachia, tried to imagine herself as a future princess. She could not. She knew if she did become this nearly impossible dream, it could only happen if she received the proper education and training only a lady of fine upbringing should have. It was her wish and dream to have such a thing. Of such a noble wish, would the making of a future Queen be made.

PART THREE

DEATH COMES TO US ALL

1214 AD

CHAPTER SIXTEEN

AN INTOLERABLE LOSS

It was a sound, hardly a whisper but loud enough to resonate in Princess Illona's dreams to wake her. It was the dead of night, all quiet and still. There was no wind, no breeze, not even insects making their usual sounds of the night. Every so often, drops of dew would land on leaves or grass, breaking the nearly impenetrable silence. Only silence, married with the extreme darkness, pervaded the night. She heard it again, whispering her name. Her eyes opened, and she remembered she was sleeping upon the ground, shackled next to her carriage along with her attending ladies. The shackles were cold around her wrists and ankles. She found herself lying amongst her ladies, huddled together amongst blankets under and over them. A fire that once blazed next to them had dwindled down to glowing embers. The autumn night was cold enough with the fire.

Illona sat up, trying to be as quiet as possible to ascertain where the whispers were coming from. The darkness was nearly impenetrable as the other campfires also had dwindled to embers and coals.

Soon, she could make out a shape walking amongst the sleeping soldiers. She could only watch, seeing no other movement. The shape seemed alone, moving silently amongst the bodies of those who slept. Soon, it came to her, and then, she recognized the entity...Vojislav Rekvas. It was the Dragon, reappearing to his already declared love as she found herself in the most desperate of circumstances.

"I have come to rescue you, my sweet. Fear not for these

men are not of sufficient force to keep me from you. I have been watching from afar, always ready to come to your aid. That time is now, for your former husband has now given me the opportunity to take you from him and your would-be abuser, the Baron Regevaks Descondes. He would not love and care for you like I would. I know the man's propensity for violence against women. He has no honor, nor chivalry. He is as the wolf, a predator in the world amongst the sheep, giving in to his most basic desires."

"My love, I have waited for so long. I was beginning to give up hope of anyone rescuing me. My ladies, will they be given the same care as I?"

"Of course, my dear. I could not think of any other way to deal with this tragedy but to give aid and comfort to all those involved. My knights will have dispatched those of the Baron's forces before dawn. Rest assured, we will have you and your ladies safe before the sunrise."

"I want to go home. But", she paused despondently, "I cannot go home. Vladis has returned to the castle, these men came with him to claim the ransom, and Vladis gave me and my women as part of that ransom. I objected against that, but it was futile."

"My dear, we can remedy that, but we have to rid you of your captors first. I will take care of the Baron as well, so he will not send more troops after you. I understand he has a sizable garrison of which I must deal with before we have the situation in hand."

"What will you do?" she asked.

"Have no fear, my love. I wish you to go back to sleep, resting assured that when that sun rises, you will be free."

She nodded her understanding, then reclined back and pulled the blankets over her. She knew blood was about to be shed and she did not want to witness it. She thought of herself and how she got to this point. Her former husband had given her away, but she could not blame him. She had given up on him and was prepared to take his title, his fortune and cut out his legally begotten children and wife out of their inheritance. To imagine that he would have forgiven her of her evil plans would have been wishful thinking at best. Because she had found feelings for

129

Rekvas she never had for Vladis, her hatred of Vladis seemed to have waxed cold. She felt that the title, the fortune, and the castle did not seem to mean as much to her. Things had changed so much in the last forty-eight hours.

The silence continued until she drifted off to sleep again. The next thing she knew, the dawn had come. Her attending ladies were stirring, and the one thing that seemed wrong was there was no soldiers to be found. The camp was empty, save for the traces of personal armor and weapons, some tents, and horses tied to lines between trees. Campfires were smoldering, giving off little heat but none were attended to. Illona rose to find her shackles had been removed. Her attending ladies' restraints were also gone. The chill in the autumn air occupied their senses, leaving them shivering in the morning cold.

Illona scanned the camp for any trace of the Dragon, Vojislav Rekvas. She could not find him. Katarina, Magda, and Portia by appearance, looked disheveled, but otherwise were unharmed. No one had been violated by their captors, but they all knew that was to come later when they would arrive at the Baron's castle.

"Check the wagons, look for food. One of you attempt to restart this fire, for we may be here for a while. I will look for our rescuer for I know who is responsible for our freedom. Have no fear for he will return to us," stated Princess Illona. As she turned to look toward the wood line now visible, she muttered to herself, "My love, where are you?"

She wandered along the edge of the clearing where they had camped, looking for the Dragon or looking for the remains of their captors, for she was certain they all had been killed. If so, where were the bodies of soldiers?

As she was deep in thought about such issues, the sound of one approaching through the woods reached her. She stopped, alarmed, yet hopeful it was Vojislav. It was as she hoped. Vojislav hurried his pace, approaching her with outspread arms and embraced the Princess, holding her in an affectionate embrace.

"There were a few who ran from us. They were the ones who carried the ransom chests. I have recovered those along with enough horses for us to return. Light your fire, have your breakfast. Then, you and your ladies will return from whence you came. My knights have unfinished business with the Baron. Once that is complete, I will join you at your castle and then we will finalize the business with your ex-husband. I trust you slept well after we spoke last night?"

Princess Illona, still dazzled by the abilities of her beloved, smiled, nodding her answer that she had. "I trust in your words, my love. The things you say, the acts you do, amaze me, and bedazzle me. It is difficult for me to understand."

"Someday, after we are married, you will understand completely. And you will know we were meant for each other," the Dragon replied.

$$*\qquad*\qquad*$$

It was several days later. The Dragon had tracked several survivors of the Baron's troop escort back to his castle. The castle was a large one, old and well-fortified. It had seen many a battle and rarely had its walls been breached. It had few weaknesses and many strengths. Hundreds of souls had dashed themselves upon its stone walls, only to have done so in vain. The Dragon would wait until the sun had vanished from the sky. It was then that he would have the advantage. He surveyed the castle and decided that he should take the castle and occupy it for himself and the bride he would have in Princess Illona. But to do so, meant that he would have to defeat the Baron in mortal combat such that by tradition, his castle would be forfeited to him as the spoils of victory. It would be the perfect place to house his knights, the vampires Akhenaten and Nefertiti. Its location in the southern part of the Bulgarian empire gave him a tremendous strategic advantage.

When the night fell, the Dragon and his minions went on full assault. His vampires, transforming themselves into beings capable of flight, carried Rekvas over the ramparts and walls of the castle onto a balcony for which they could enter undetected into the castle. Soon, Rekvas found himself in the hall of the Baron, interrupting his nightly supper. Two knights clad in polished black armor, their faces hidden yet brandishing weapons of the finest craftmanship available stood on each side of him. The Baron dined with only a few others of his immediate inner circle. It was not known if the Baron was married, but if he was, he was not in the company of any of his family.

In a loud and powerful voice, the Dragon, Vojislav Rekvas shouted, "Behold, Baron Descondes, I bring tidings of fear and alarm unto you and your household. Beware of me for I am known as the Dragon, and I have been watching you for quite some time. I know your ways; I know your sins. And, the time for reckoning has come for you all."

The Baron looked up, dropped his leg of chicken into his plate, took a long drink of wine from his goblet, then wiped his mouth with the sleeve of his tunic. He might have seemed shocked if he had not smiled and said, "Vojislav Rekvas, I was wondering when you were going to show up. I was almost disappointed. But here you are. Yes, you have killed many of my soldiers, but not all. You retrieved my ransom money and it still is in the hands of an evil woman both of us know, but that is not my concern. The fact that you are here is my concern. It is a moment for which I have waited for since hearing from the *Order of the Dragons of Set* in Rome. They have given me some instructions and I want so much to carry them out."

The Dragon, who was caught off guard by the Baron's remarks, asked, "What are you talking about?"

"I am talking about the Order, Vojislav. You have been gone too long, Dragon. I too am a member. If you had maintained regular contact with the Order, you would know this. Instead, you forsook the Order to chase after a woman that you know Set has told you was not his choice for you. You knew of my reputation, but you did not know me. I know more about you than you do of me. I am surprised that you showed this moment of weakness and error. You disobeyed Set. Did he not tell you there would be a price to pay? Well, you are here to pay that price. Have no fear, we will not harm the Princess Illona. She is not part of this."

"So, I am to pay a price, am I?"

The Baron took another drink from his goblet. "No, not you. Them," he said, pointing to the vampires in black armor. "They will pay it for you."

"They are immortal. They cannot die."

The Baron shouted out, "Guards!" Several archers appeared with crossbows, loaded, and pointed at the vampires. The Baron gave the order, "Loose!'

Crossbow bolts, tipped with silver points and fletched with white feathers, plunged into the armor of the vampires, piercing the steel and mail to enter their hearts. They both staggered and fell to their knees.

"Father, what is happening to us?" cried Akhenaten.

Nefertiti, in awful pain, cried out, "Help us!" Both clutched at the bolts protruding from their chests, desperately trying to pull them out.

The Dragon, shocked that such a thing was possible, took a cup from the Baron's table and seemed determined to catch the blood from each vampire's chest wound. He knew their blood was precious and he was determined not to waste any of it. It must be replenished for them to survive as it has since the beginning.

"Do not waste your time and efforts, Vojislav. They are dying. It is their second death. Set revealed to us the nature of their weakness and their vulnerability. Everyone has a weakness, even you. Perhaps you even more for you are in a human body." The Baron stood up and walked around from his table. The two vampires, were dying a slow death, bleeding out from their hearts which had not beat a single time in several thousand years.

"Father help us! We have served you faithfully!" cried the beautiful Nefertiti. The Dragon bent down on one knee and removed her helmet. Her perfect skin, smooth and unblemished, grew paler by the minute. He wanted to let her drink her own blood from the cup to stay the inevitable. "I am sorry, so sorry for my mistake. This is my fault," he whispered to her, holding her head in his hands.

The Baron approached Akhenaten and removed his helmet as well. "Yes, great king of Egypt, you did serve the master, the Dragon, faithfully, but he has not been faithful to his master. He put another before our master. Set has decreed that a price be paid for his disobedience and disloyalty. And you, Akhenaten, firstborn of all vampires, are the one to pay for the sin of your master, Vojislav Rekvas, the Dragon."

When he had finished talking, he took hold of the crossbow bolt, and in one swift move, he pushed it into the vampire's body, further piercing its heart. Akhenaten cried out a final time and collapse as a corpse on the floor.

The corpse of the vampire began to deteriorate rapidly, until there was only ash and bone inside the armor. His armor began to fall apart as there was no structure to hold its shape.

Nefertiti, in tears of sorrow and pain, asked the Dragon, "Father, send me after my husband. Wherever he goes, I wish to go also. We loved you and all those who came before you. Please, I beg you!"

To honor Nefertiti's wishes, the Dragon did as the Baron had done to Akhenaten. He took the end of the bolt and pushed it all the way through the armor until it came through to the other side. After her last gasp from blood which she began to choke upon, she died in his arms. Within seconds, she too began to decompose, leaving only a pile of ash and bone under her armor.

For the first time in his life, the Dragon felt such sadness that he cried. He had lost his two companions. These nocturnal companions who fought for him, protected him, enabled him, and carried out his orders were like his arms. He was able to do so much because of them. Now, he felt powerless. It was as if Set had stripped him of his most priceless possession, his vampires. He looked up at the Baron. Anger was in his eye. He immediately wanted revenge for he felt murder in his heart. He pulled his sword.

As soon as his intentions were made known, the Baron said, "I would not do that. My guards will cut you down the moment you raise that sword. If those crossbows can kill that which we all believed to be immortal, imagine what they can do to you? You cannot risk it. You have no heir to assume the spirit of Set. That, I am to inform you is now your most pressing responsibility. Find the suitable woman, the one Set will reveal to you and marry, have the child, raise it, teach it, prepare it. For it will be the continuation of Set in this world. Illona will not share you. She will be jealous of your relationship with Set and of the vampires. Think of it, Vojislav! If Set has no use for her, why should you?"

Vojislav was devastated. All he had ever held dear to him was gone in only a few minutes. His vampires, his love, his hope, and dreams…gone.

"I wish you to leave my castle and return to Rome immediately. It is there you shall find direction. Perhaps, you will meet the woman you were intended to marry. But…she is not here." He returned to his table to finish his meal.

The Baron did not have to ask twice for the Dragon to leave. He left the castle, despondent beyond comprehension, and returned to where his horse was secured. The horses of his companions were not there. Instead, there was a pile of ash and bones left behind as the horses died when their riders did. Perhaps they were not of this world either. Either way, the Dragon mounted his horse and began his trip back to the castle of Prince Vladis to say goodbye to Princess Illona. He still carried the cup of blood from Nefertiti's wound. Perhaps it was sentimentality that drove him to do such a thing. The Dragon looked at it after a while as the sun began to rise. The blood had coagulated on the inside surface of the vessel. He noticed the sunlight influenced it. He quickly put it away after he realized it may have power.

Throughout the trip, the Dragon was thinking about his vampires. The Baron had given him an intolerable loss. He needed his vampires back. How could he create what took so much time and effort to do so the first time? How could he recreate the ceremony of the "Opening of the Mouth"? He would have to use the cup and the blood of Nefertiti in it. If it could have sustained the life of a vampire, perhaps it could also create it as well. While he rode to Prince Vladis's estate, he plotted how he could kill the Baron and the rest of the Order of the Dragon of Set. He was angry beyond description. Revenge was at the forefront of his mind. The loss had taken away his ability for super reasoning, the one characteristic the Dragon had always been known for. They had taken away not just his companions but something he considered a family heirloom. For over two millennia, the vampires had accompanied every Dragon to fulfill his decrees, to carry out their orders, and to protect the Dragon always against enemies of the Order. Now the Order seemed to be turning against him.

The dark knights, the vampires, they were his source of knowledge for he learned so much from them. This was something he understood to be power. Now, he was vulnerable. It was time he used his power as the Dragon.

Within a few days, he made his way to Vladis's castle. What he walked into was nothing short of a tempest. Illona had returned, tried to throw Annara out, and had made everyone miserable. She was still the same Illona as always. He found that Illona had hidden the ransom money and refused to give it up unless everything returned to the way it was. With one exception…she had not mentioned anything about being with Vojislav. The Order seemed to be correct in their assessment of Illona.

*   *   *

"Annara will not leave my castle. I forbid it! You are no longer my wife and you were never a wife to me! I could not be happier that you are out of my life. The Baron wanted you, why in God's name I do not understand, but I sent you to him. I would have hoped you would have been happier with him as you are understandably not happy with me. But, how could you be?"

Vladis was angry that Illona would make demands upon him, especially demands that he could not in his heart agree to. Since she had a good part of his fortune, she was in a position of strength to negotiate her demands. The demand that she wanted him to agree to was that he leave his castle, renounce his title and fortune to her. She knew her demand was completely unreasonable, but she had to give an impossible demand so that she could get what she really wanted. She was already a princess, and she could get a castle simply by marrying. Her real ambition was to amass a fortune so that she and Vojislav Rekvas would be able to start a new life together without the prospects of starting out in poverty. Except she had not discussed any of this with Vojislav.

"It is true, Vladis. I was never happy with you. Give me most of what fortune you have left, and I will leave you forever. I will relinquish all claims to your household, your name, title, and estate. You shall see me no more. Do we agree?"

"You have two chests of silver, one of gold. Do you not think this is enough? If not, then your greed is meant to punish me."

"I grow tired of your stubbornness. I will retire to my chambers and you may give me an answer when you have come to your senses." She arose and left the room. Annara was at his side when the discussion had taken place. She was appalled at the brazenness of the woman who hated her husband.

The Dragon had arrived shortly after this discussion took place. Vladis was tired, angry, and short tempered. Still, Vladis was happy he had arrived, for he had feared he too was a casualty at Phillippopolis. Prince Vladis was a cordial and gracious host and would never turn a friend away especially if it was Vojislav Rekvas.

"Vojislav, I apologize for the mess you have walked into. Please, sit by my fire. Warm yourself. Drink your fill of my wine."

Vojislav accepted his hospitality, taking off his gauntlets and warming himself next to the blazing fire.

"I have been informed that it was you that rescued my former wife. She is someone I know you are very fond of, if not close to. I am happy that no harm came to her or her ladies attending. As you might have heard, the chests of silver and gold have been absconded with and only the Princess knows of their location. I only thought I was poor when I paid the ransom the Baron Descondes demanded. My former wife is demanding I give her nearly all the rest in exchange for leaving the castle. What am I to do?"

"I only came to make sure she and her ladies made it back to this castle safe and unharmed. I had no idea of what she would do once she had arrived. I did not tell her to take your fortune. I went on to the Baron's castle to deal with him." He thought to himself that she had done that all on her own.

"And tell me, friend, what was his reaction to the loss of his ransom?" asked the Prince.

137

A moment of silence passed before Vojislav would answer. Even then, Vladis could see the sadness of loss on Vojislav's face.

"He had my two knights and companions killed. He would have killed me too if I had not negotiated with him." This of course was only half true.

"You negotiated with the Baron?"

"It is long story. I must do something for him. I must leave for Rome to visit some people he wants me to see. I am honor bound to do so. May I offer a suggestion, Prince Vladis?"

"By all means," Vladis replied.

"Let me talk with Princess Illona. After all, it should be no secret to you that we have already discussed our feelings for each other. I am thankful that you had no contention regarding our relationship. Perhaps I can mediate a solution that will be fair for all. What she was proposing is preposterous!"

"I would be grateful," replied Vladis.

Vojislav made his way to her chambers, knocking on the door to the Princess' room. She opened it immediately, thinking it was Prince Vladis come to beg the Princess to reconsider or to give in to her demands. Her surprise was overwhelming when she saw her lover and rescuer standing at the door. After many kisses and an embrace which seemed eternal, they faced each other.

"I have much to tell you, my love!" she said.

"Yes, I know. And I have much to tell you. Please listen…"

*   *   *

When Princess Illona had returned to the castle after her rescue, Annara immediately went to find Peter, her long-time childhood friend. She found him in the village at his home, a modestly thatched hovel at best. She entered after announcing herself.

"Peter, you have always been a good friend to me. I need your help."

As soon as Princess Illona was spotted at the checkpoint at the river, news of her arrival spread like smoke on the wind. Soon, several hamlets had heard the news. There was dismay everywhere. Peter knew why Annara was there.

"Annara, bad news travels like the wind. She is back, is she not? Well, I already know what you wish me to do. I would do the same as you if our roles were reversed. I shall hide your children."

"You were always so clever. It's as if you could read my mind. Yes, hide my children. Do not take them into your home. Hide them…in one of my father's old woodcutter huts. Find one that is not used anymore. Don't tell me where you hide them, but tell the priest, Brother Bartholomew, so if something happens to me or their father, he can find them and take them to safety. It would be dangerous if I know their location. She would torture that information from me. I cannot afford that possibility. When you have done this, bring Brother Bartholomew here to us at the castle.

Peter left the village undetected in an ox-pulled cart and went straight to the villa to find the children. Tayla met him at the door, and allowed him in. He gave them instructions as to what their mother had asked him to do regarding hiding them. They packed enough food for several days along with extra bedding for the nights were sure to be frigid. They hid in the back of his wood cart, pulled by a team of oxen. Peter drove the cart nearly all night to a hut south of the castle, on the southern side of the river. Peter knew of this hut for he had accompanied his father as well as Annara's to this hut long ago. It was the farthest one away of all the huts he knew about.

Annara's children accepted the task to hide out at one of her father's woodcutter huts he had built in the forests when his work would keep him away from the village overnight. They thought of it as an adventure. Annara's instructions told her children to go there and stay until she came for them. They had slept throughout the shivering morning and now, it was nearly noon.

Tayla fixed her siblings breakfast after starting a small fire so each of them could warm themselves. The older sister cared for her charges as if they were her own children. Wishing to keep them occupied, she engaged them in games. This would keep their spirits up and occupy their time.

Tayla watched her brothers begin a game of tag while she and

139

Prieta played another game of hide and seek. Eventually, the brothers decided to join in and play as well. It was Rascha's turn to seek as the other children went off to hide. Tayla set limits as to how far they could go from the hut. There were many old stumps and large trunks of felled trees. Tayla hid out amongst a pile of wood and debris. As she was hiding, she noticed an object that just did not belong there. She pulled back some of the debris only to be astonished by what she found. Lying on the ground under piles of branches and leaves were three chests, two filled with silver and one filled with gold.

*   *   *

Two days had passed since Princess Illona's return. Prince Vladis was distraught. When Annara returned, she stayed at his side. She slept in his chambers, in his bed next to him.

He considered having the former wife arrested, perhaps even flogged, but if he had done that, she would never reveal the location of his fortune. He wondered if his friend, Rekvas had made any concessions with her since her return.

Illona had told him that Rekvas had come to her rescue and sent her back once he had vanquished her captors. Rekvas was the one who told her to return to the castle with the silver and the gold. She told Vladis that Rekvas had never said to hide the treasure and keep it for herself. That was all her own doing. This confirmed what Rekvas had surmised all along.

Peter had done as Annara had told him and brought Brother Bartholomew to the castle. He arrived on the afternoon of the third day of Illona's return. Annara met him in private before he could be seen in the hall.

"Brother Bartholomew, thank you for coming. My husband is in danger. My children are in more danger. Peter has informed you, yes?"

"Yes, Annara. He has informed me of the situation and the location of your children. What may I do for you?"

"I must be able to ensure that I can lay claim to my husband's title and lands should he meet his demise. It must be publicly recorded. I only know that the Bishop of Tarnovo and his office clerks can do such a thing. Otherwise, she will move against us should she eliminate my husband."

"When will she meet again with your husband, the Prince?

"My husband will summon her this evening. He knows things cannot and must not go on like they are now. He is ready to make a deal, but he is not sure what she will accept. I need to be ready should she not accept anything he has to offer."

Her words reminded the friar he still had the letters that the Bishop of Tarnovo had given him before he had come to the Prince's manor. The letter that was addressed to Annara he would give to her soon for it was still hidden.

"Annara, I have letters that state in no uncertain terms that you are the legal and proper wife of Prince Vladis. It also states that the Bishop recognizes this marriage and the children to be of legal status in accordance with the laws of the church. I am prepared to give you those letters should you need them.

*   *   *

Finally, on the evening of the third day of her current stay at the castle, Vladis summoned Illona to stand before him.

She came to him with a flask of wine and a pair of goblets in her hands. "Come to our senses, have we? Well, mercy and tenderness can be found within the walls of this castle. I have decided to allow you to keep what you already have. I will keep what I have and that will be the end of it. Agreed?"

"Why the sudden change of heart? Until I gave in to the Baron's demands, which I presumed included you, I have shown you nothing but mercy." asked Vladis.

"There are plenty of castles in this land. Besides, I prefer the one I grew up in. With my newly acquired fortune, I can perhaps afford to reacquire the home I grew up in and the beautiful land it sets on. This place," she paused as she looked around her, "Well, you can imagine the unpleasant memories it holds for me. I want to be free and happy. Really, that is all I want. If it means that you must be happy as well, then let it be so. There was a time when the thought of you being happy, especially with one such as her," she glanced over at Annara, "was completely intolerant to me. I would rather had been miserable if it meant that you would be as well. As of late, I have had a change of heart. My reputation and diminishing chances of finding a suitor are no longer a concern of mine. If I were you, I would take the olive branch I am offering to you."

Vladis looked over to Annara, still holding his hand. She nodded affirmatively that perhaps this should be the end of their feud and life of discontent with each other. Nothing else had worked. Even giving her away to such a man as the Baron Descondes had not worked out to his favor. Annara thought of her children and the danger she posed if she were around to threaten them. For this reason, she squeezed Vladis' hand and nodded again.

"Very well, even my wife thinks this is good for us to both be rid of each other. Money can be replaced. I cannot reap anything good from what years we spent together. Even you cannot see any reason why we should continue this. I will still honor our agreement to come to each other's aid should war threaten us. I hope that if you are in your land and sit upon the throne of your country, you should do as well. I wish you success and health in your new life."

"Come, dear Vladis! Let us drink to a lasting peace between us. You have pledged to fulfill your end of our bargain. I will fulfill my end of it as well. Come! Drink and seal our bargain."

She poured the wine into the goblets, handing one to him. He did not know where these goblets had come from. He had not seen these upon his table before.

Vladis never trusted his former wife, even when he was married to her. He trusted her even less now that he was not married to her anymore. He always knew there would be a hidden catch to any bargain he would make with her. However, she had him at a disadvantage. She had his fortune, or at least a large part of it. She had hidden it well, so searching for it was futile. He had no other choice but to give in to her demand. He took the goblet and drank from it. The deed was done.

CHAPTER SEVENTEEN

AN UNHOLY THING

Vladis's body was quickly going into a state of shock. Had he been poisoned? Why was he suddenly feeling so ill? He looked at Illona, who was also in a state of surprise, for she had no inkling of what would happen if Vladis drank from the chalice of wine, tainted with the blood of a vampire. "What is happening to me" he stated with a weakened voice, looking at Illona and then to Annara. He fell onto a single knee as the chalice left his hand and fell to the stone floor. His other hand reached out to Annara, who had come to his side.

Annara tried to help him up, but his strength was waning. He was becoming increasingly heavy. "My Lord, what can I do to help you?"

Illona was speechless for a few minutes. She watched as her former husband began to die. Blood began to form at his nostrils, and his lips. It dripped down upon his robes of blue and white. Then his eyes began to turn red causing him to lose his vision.

Brother Bartholomew came into the hall and recognized the crisis immediately. He prepared to give last rites to a man he had come to know as a kind and gentle nobleman.

Vladis lost his strength at a fast rate, such that within a few minutes, he was lying on his back, struggling to breath. As the friar prepared to give last rites, Vladis's heart stopped. His breath left his lungs in an audible hiss. His dark brown eyes, now lifeless and dilated, stared at the ceiling. He was dead.

Annara began to wail in mourning, shaking and hysterical at the loss of her husband. She held his hand, the one with his signet

143

ring upon it. The ring was thick gold with a large red ruby in it. The sides were engraved with the coat of arms of his family. She quickly took the ring off his hand before Illona could stop her. Illona had been looking at the friar and did not notice that the wife had taken it. Illona, dressed in a pale blue and white gown, approached the friar, asking, "Is my former husband beyond salvation? I know he died before you could give last rites. Is he damned?"

Annara cried out, "Are you so eager to make sure he is on his way to Hell? You should follow him! You poisoned him, murderess!"

"I did not. I merely poured wine into the chalice. I just drank from the same wine flask as he did. It cannot be the wine. It must be the chalice."

"And where did you get the chalices from? They bear no resemblance to those found upon my husband's table."

Illona answered, "Vojislav left them in my room after he talked with me, persuading me to give up my demands of Vladis. I merely thought it a gesture of peace between us that we drink upon our agreement."

Bartholomew was surprised that Vladis died so quickly. He had been in many a battle, been wounded several times, even captured, and had survived all of that. Vladis was the kind of man who if you knew of him, his death from drinking wine would come as a shock. As he looked at the dead Prince, lying on the floor, he found himself without an answer. He was just a friar. He only knew what he had been taught by other priests, who were much more educated in the scriptures regarding salvation than he was.

Illona asked again, as if she was were desperate to know the disposition of his soul. Again, Bartholomew could not answer. He could only shrug his shoulders and shake his head.

*   *   *

Annara was glad she had hidden her children from Illona as she trusted her the least. Her certainty that Illona would eliminate them as heirs drove her fears and caused her to constantly be on her guard. She may have been a peasant, but nobility played no role when it came to the politics of women. Vladis's young wife may have not been formally educated but when it came to the safety of her children, Annara was a force to be reckoned with.

Her children, more specifically her oldest daughter, had found the lost ransom chests the Princess Illona had hidden on her way back to the castle. They were waiting for their mother or Peter to come back for them. The food would only last another day before they ran out of rations. Tayla was worried for her siblings. She did not tell them what she had found.

Later in the day, Peter came to them in his cart. He had brought them more food and pelts of fur with which to protect themselves from the nightly cold. His arrival also brought news of their father. It was sad news and because it was, they must stay hidden for an even longer period.

"Peter, tell us of our mother and father. We are alone here and as good as lost for we know not of our way home," complained Tayla. She knew she spoke for her siblings as well.

"Dear child, I bring sad news. Your mother is well, but your father is not. It seems that his former wife is more treacherous than we could have ever expected her to be. She made a bargain with him upon which he drank wine with her to seal it, as most nobles do. It must have been laced with poison for when he drank from it, it seemed as though the life ran from his body. He laid weak and seemed out of his head for a time. Then he went to sleep and did not wake up. His physician came and confirmed that he no longer breathed, and his heart no longer beat. Children, I am burdened with the news of your father's death. I am so sorry." Peter said all this while fighting back tears. At the end, he could not hold back his tears and wept bitterly for Prince Vladis. Peter of course was not there to see the actual death of the Prince. He had heard rumors of how the death had been ghastly but wanted to spare the children the details of it, so he cleaned it up quite a bit. Prince Vladis had been a good lord to his people. He had cared for, protected, and looked after their needs. Now he was gone. His estate and lands were sure to be in turmoil now that Princess Illona survived him. Peter knew that she had no right to his title or lands. He also knew that Illona held all the cards and could have Annara eliminated as well as his children. This would ensure her position and possession of his fortune. He wished he could do something to help Annara secure her position. She needed all the friends and allies she could get. It was then that her daughter stood up and shared with Peter what she had found.

*   *   *

Vladis was confused. He was alone in the darkness, frightened beyond anything he could have ever imagined. He was experiencing the very same circumstances that his predecessors had experienced during the eighteenth dynasty of the Egyptian Pharaohs. He felt around him but could neither feel anything nor could he see anything. It was the same as Akhenaten and Nefertiti had experienced. He wondered how fast he went from speaking to the two women in his life to a world devoid of any stimuli. Nothing visual or auditory was in this world he was in. Was this Heaven? Certainly not, he thought. Perhaps Hell, but where was the fire? Why had the devil not met him yet? He pondered all the things the church had taught him regarding death. More so, he thought about the things he had learned about salvation. Oh, how he wished he had paid more attention to those things. Instead, he had focused more on things like training for war, rutting with women, and managing his estate. His father had told him that these were the things that filled a normal man's life. When he was older, that would be when he could think about the inevitable rendezvous with death. His father had told him, "Death comes to us all." And now, it was here for him.

He had no sense of time so when he began to hear the footsteps of something or someone approaching, he did not know how long he had been in the dark. He could not see, but somehow, he could sense the sound of footsteps.

"Vladis?" a voice called out to him. It was a man's voice which had a familiar ring to it.

Finally, his voice returned to him, so he answered. "I am Prince Vladis. Who calls to me?"

"Ahh! There you are! It's hard to see you in all this blackness," the voice answered. Finally, the light of a torch appeared off in the distance. Soon it found him, and Vladis recognized the hand carrying the torch. It was the hand of Vojislav Rekvas.

"Vladis! So glad to find you. I know what you are going through. Only two others have ever experienced what you are experiencing this moment. Many questions I suspect, so I will begin to give to you answers. This place is the place for those who are dead but not fully dead. By that I mean, you are undead. You are not dead but not alive either. You are in an in-between world. Next answer is the one that tells you how to get out of this world and into either the next one or the one you just left. Which shall it be? Before you answer, consider this. If you are here, it means the door to Heaven is closed to you, or you would already be there. This is about the disposition of your soul. That means there could be only one answer as to what the "next world" could be. So, let us talk about the world you just left. I suspect, that is the place where you would rather be. I can help you get there. So, if you want my help, then you must give to me the answer I desire.

Vladis asked him. "Vojislav! Is this Hell?"

"Oh no!" he replied. "More like the front door of it. The fire comes later. But come it will if you choose to stay here."

"How did you come to this place? Did you die as well? How do you know so much about my situation? I cannot abide in this place. Take me away from here. I wish to go back."

"Wise choice, my friend. As for your other questions, it is a long story. An awfully long story. We will be here a long time if I tell you in its entirety. I will tell you this. I am known as the Dragon. I am the embodiment of the spirit of Set. Set is the Egyptian god for chaos and storms. In short, evil, anarchy and disorder. It is what I thrive on. I created the curse you are now under. In your Christian world, I would be known as the son of the devil, or Satan as your Bible calls me. I am known by many names, but you only need to know me by Vojislav. Later, this body will die and yet another shall take my place.

There is a condition upon your return to the world you left

behind. You will not be the same as you were. You will be as my two knights were. They were creatures of the night, creatures that will become known as vampires. They were the very first ones, in fact. I loved them as though they were my children. They experienced this same experience. Those two were male and female, a king and Queen, of Egypt no less! They too were eager to reclaim the world they left behind. I had the power to enable them to do so. But they were never the same as they were when they returned. They were hated and feared for they were very misunderstood. It was because they were endowed with powers and abilities the world had never seen. Unfortunately, it came with a price. The Baron Descondes, you remember him? He knew about them and knew of their few vulnerabilities. And because he did, he was able to kill them. They served me, faithfully and without question. If you want to return to the next world, you will have to endure what they endured, become what they had become and live the life they lived. If you choose to not accept what I offer, you will stay here, and it will be a long time here in the utter darkness before you meet the fire. Meet it you will, I assure you, for you have no other recourse.

"What must I do to go back?" Vladis asked.

Vojislav stretched out the torch and the light flowed from it.

Vladis looked out as a wave of illumination lit up the darkness, showing a river that flowed in a massive underground cavern. He was standing upon what seemed like a riverbank. He could see the other side and a set of stairs cut out of the rock walls of the cavern. They led upwards until he could no longer see the top for the distance was great.

"If you wish to go back, you have but to cross that river. It separates you from the world you left behind and the world you are now in. I must tell you, Vladis. You shall know me as your master. My word, my orders you will have no choice but to obey. You shall trust only me. I will care for you, protect you when you are vulnerable. I will turn you lose on my enemies, and your thirst will compel you to obey my every command. For this, you will live eternally, and be endowed with gifts that over time will make you so powerful that only one force is stronger than you will be."

148

Solemnly, he turned to look at the face on one whom he had thought to be his friend. "Were you ever my friend?"

"Oh Vladis, I am deeply hurt that you would think such a thing. Of course, I was. I gave you victory over your enemies. I rescued Illona and your ransom from Descondes. I persuaded Illona to agree to leave you alone with the money you had left. By the way, your daughter has found the rest of the money so if Illona had not been so greedy as to make you drink from that chalice, you would have had all returned to you and free to live in peace with Annara and your children. Truthfully, the entire idea was Illona's. I had nothing to do with it. But I could see it happening as soon as I found the chalice missing. It was then I knew what you would become."

Vladis had only one desire. To return to the world of the living and see Annara and his children one more time before serving Vojislav. Finally, he said, "I agree to your terms. How do I cross this river?"

"You simply walk across, along the bottom of the river. The river is of blood. It will cover your entire being but fear not. It is your baptism into your new life. It gives you the new life of power and dominance over the mortals you will face. You will no longer be mortal. When you awaken, I will find you."

The prince stood upon the bank and stared out at the river. Vojislav waited in silence for him to make his first step. Eventually, Vladis turned and walked towards the river. As the boots of the Prince of Wallachia touched the river, he whispered to himself as he thought of his wife and children, "God forgive me for I do an unholy thing!"

* * *

The funeral for Prince Vladis was held in the chapel of the castle. Johannes did the best he could under the circumstances. It was a modest, simple affair for his death had happened so fast, most of those who would have wanted to be there would have to travel great distances to get there. Vladis had not made his final arrangements known. Here, in the chapel, it was as close to God as he had ever gotten. It was the Prince's favorite place for it offered solitude for him to be away from his wife. Now, he was helpless to get away from her. Johannes had knowledge of what Prince Vladis would have wanted.

Vladis was to be buried in his full armor, as he was a warrior and a knight. His sword in his hands, pointed towards his feet and his shield placed upon his breast, was the custom of the day in which noblemen of arms were to be buried. His body would be interred in the family crypt beneath the castle.

His body lay in a coffin with the lid open. His courtiers came by to pay homage and give their last respects to him. He was the last of his family. Aside from his children with Annara, he had no other blood relatives to lay claim to his property. Annara still held the signet ring. Conferring with Brother Bartholomew regarding her marital standing and the legality of it, he reassured her that the letters from the Bishop of Tarnovo would stand for her rights as a widow and her children as his heirs.

Everyone wondered what would happen now after the Prince had died. As far as Illona was concerned, she was not about to move out of the castle. Married or not, it was her home and until she was forced, she was not going anywhere. At least not until Vojislav returned to her and the ransom money was retrieved. It was then she would consider leaving and then, that was only a possibility.

Illona sent men out to retrieve the hidden chests of gold and silver. Her directions, along with one of her attending ladies to go with them, sent them straight to the location where she had hidden them.

On the day Tayla had shown Peter what she had found, he knew the children were in immediate danger. Peter immediately relocated them to another place. He knew no one would leave a fortune behind and not plan to come back for it. He covered his tracks very well afterwards and hid close by to watch for who would come to retrieve the money. Soon, he had his answer. He knew the soldiers who came for the treasure as they were Prince Vladis's guards. He also recognized Portia. They must be under the command of Princess Illona for they looked around thoroughly, as if they knew specifically where to look. They were disappointed for they must have been promised a portion of the treasure should they recover it intact. Soon, they left to return to the castle.

Peter came out from his hiding place and retrieved the children. He took them to another place, in another hamlet. He knew a relative who lived there and left them in her care, promising to come back.

The first place he went to was to the villa of Annara's family. Her father was there. He asked if Annara was coming back soon and Josef could not say for sure. He was grieving for the Prince. "I cannot say when she shall come back. I am afraid that if she leaves the castle, she will not be admitted back inside its doors. The Princess has a mean streak and she will not forget her humiliation at the hands of a new wife, especially the mother of children she could not give to the Prince. That is a wound she will never forget, Peter. She will never forget, nor will she ever forgive. I fear for everyone now."

*   *   *

After the burial of her husband, Annara stayed in her husband's chambers. The castle seemed as cold within its walls as it was outside them. She went through his things, getting to know the intimate and personal side of her now dead husband. Annara had loved Vladis with every fiber of her being. She was still in shock that he was gone. She wondered how she could hold on to what was rightfully hers and her children's birthright. If she left the castle, Illona would probably give orders for her to not be readmitted. In desperation, Annara was at her wits ends trying to figure out what should be done next. This was not her arena. Not even close.

A knock on the door of her husband's chamber door struck terror in Annara's heart. Annara was afraid to answer it. The knock came again and again. Soon, the latch turned, opening the large wooden door. It was Brother Bartholomew.

"My dear lady, I come with greetings and to give comfort. I know this must be difficult for you. You only had him for a while. The time we spend with our spouse is never enough, especially if we really love them. I know you did."

"How could you know of love? You are a monk, a friar, and cannot marry. You cannot give your heart to anyone but God. How could you begin to know of my pain?"

"I was married once, my lady. It was a long time ago. She died quite young and I felt I could no longer give my heart to anyone else."

He sat down on a stool next to a table in the room. She was sitting on his bed. On the walls were tapestries. They told stories of his family and their exploits in battle and the line of successors they placed on the throne. The room had velvet shrouds that hung from windows in the largest turret of his castle. There were several cabinets of clothing with drawers holding letters and records of appointments and grants from the emperor. A fireplace with a nice fire burned brightly in one corner.

"This room should have been ours. I was robbed of my rights as a wife to have been able to stay in this room, sleep with my husband, even bear my children in this bed. What will Illona do now? I have the letter. I cannot read but you can. Can you read it to her and explain my case to her?"

"She will not listen to reason. I have already been to see her. Today, she is particularly enraged. It seems someone has found the ransom chests she had hid prior to coming back to the castle. Now nearly half of the Princes' fortune is gone and she is determined to get it back. If she can't get that money back, she will seize what is left of the money the Prince had. I expect her to keep all of it regardless if the rest of it is found or not. Her true colors are showing now. She will show no mercy to you or your children. I am here to advise you to leave the castle while it is safe for you to do so. Take what small things you can but leave soon for everyday that she cannot retrieve the ransom chests, she will become further unhinged. Her mental state is greatly affected by her sense of any offense towards her."

"I have my husband's rings and I want his sword and armor. I want all his personal things. My children are entitled to them for they belonged to their father. Do you think she will allow that?"

Brother Bartholomew smiled. "I can see. I will ask and if she agrees to those terms, perhaps she will allow you to gather it and leave the castle with safe conduct. Keep the letters and save them for the right moment when you can secure able allies to sue for your rights to your husband's estate. God know she neither has the right nor does she deserve it. I will speak with Princess Illona regarding your wishes. I will return with an answer." He left Annara in the room.

Later, a knock came again, and the friar returned inside the room. "Princess Illona has agreed to your wishes. She wants nothing of Vladis's. She wants only the estate, but you can have anything inside this room. She has agreed to throw in a couple of horses with a cart to transport it from here. You can keep your villa and live out your days there. But there is a caveat to all of this. Neither you nor your children can step foot inside these walls unless summoned. If you agree, you may begin to make ready to leave now. What say you?"

"I think I should agree for the safety of my family and myself. Tell her. I need to secure that wagon to move all of this out of here."

In the afternoon of the next day, Annara left the castle for good. A two wheeled cart used for carrying firewood, pulled by two older horses, carried her and Peter away from the home to which she was entitled. She felt sad that she had been robbed of something she should have kept, knowing all along that Prince Vladis would not have wanted any of this to have happened. But he did die, without having secured his estate for her beforehand. There was nothing she could do now. She had agreed to Illona's demands and offer. At least, she could live without fear of retribution but only if she could trust Illona to live up to her end of the bargain.

After they had left, they traveled the lonely road to Annara's villa. While on the way, Peter told her of finding her children where he had left them. He also included the good news that Tayla had found the ransom money hidden at the same location. Annara marveled at the idea and the irony that Illona had given her the perfect avenue to escape her clutches.

"Peter, I think I should leave this region. With that money, I can go away with Vladis' children and start over, not in poverty. I can afford to give my children a good home and an education.

That is something I never got, but perhaps even I can afford such a thing as that!"

Peter realized then that Annara had not thought any of this out carefully. How could she? She had just learned of the retrieval of the very thing that Illona would kill for to retrieve it. Her motives and intentions were honorable enough. She was still very gullible and naïve when it came to human nature. Not everyone was as sweet as she was.

"I have no idea of what the right move is for you. If you go, I will miss you terribly, but I understand why you would feel the need to leave this place. I do not blame you for such a thing. If you leave right away, Illona will wonder why you left and how you could do so without any money. If you leave, she will know somehow you found the money and are using it to leave the manor."

Annara pondered on his last remark for a few minutes. Then, she replied to his remark. "Yes. You are right. I see that I must wait. I need to have a better reason for leaving the manor. I cannot raise suspicions about the money."

It was late afternoon, and the shadows grew longer. The winds were cold as the autumn grew closer to winter. Soon, the roads would be covered with snow. The horses continued to pull the cart loaded with the Prince's personal effects. A lonely road carried them back to her villa. There was no other traffic along the way. Josef met them when they arrived after sundown. "Please, get inside quickly," he said.

CHAPTER EIGHTEEN

RESURRECTION

Three days had passed since Illona and Annara laid Prince Vladis to rest in the family crypt. It was three days of lying in seclusion…in total darkness, devoid of any light or sense of time. Then, his eyes opened. He took his first breath of life after death. He had been resurrected into his new life. Still, he was in total darkness. He reached up to feel the lid of his sarcophagus. It was cold, rough, and not much room between it and his face. He pushed with all his might and the stone moved. Vladis could feel the rush of cold air in his face. He moved the stone more and felt the insides of the crypt. He smashed the stone lid of the sarcophagus after repeatedly striking it with his fist. After sitting up, he then went to work on the walls of his crypt. Then, his vampire eyes began to see the other side of the walls of the crypt that had not been visible before. Finally, he was able to break free and leave his place of burial. Though he had the strength to smash out of a stone sarcophagus and break through a crypt door, he felt weak, famished, starving. The resurrected man had changed!

Vladis walked around, searching for Vojislav. He had told him he would serve him. Where was he now? Managing to break the seal of the door that led to the underground crypt, he passed through into a darkened corridor. It was pitch black to any mortal but to a vampire, it was as if there were torches every few yards. The gifts Vojislav had promised him arrived as he needed them. His eyes could pierce the darkness at a whim. He could sense people above him. Their blood rushing through their veins reached his ears. The sound of it attracted him so strongly. It was as if it were a hunger he had never experienced. The desire overtook him.

A servant walking alone in a corridor attracted his attention. His legs carried him like the wind until he reached the poor hapless lout. The speed of movement without detection made him the ultimate predator. Without hesitation nor remorse, Vladis sunk his teeth into the man's neck, in a maddening effort to ingest his warm living blood. The life ran from his victim and poured into Vladis's body. The exchange of energy and life was complete in a matter of minutes.

The weakness he felt was his hunger for life. He began to feel power, the kind of power that comes from being refreshed. It was the power of life, life in the form of the blood of the living. After he had tasted it, felt it, he knew he must have it to sustain the power he felt. It was like a drug, so thrilling and so exhilarating. Once he had fed from the living, he knew why he would be so hated and feared. Vladis thought of the words that Vojislav, his new master and creator, had said. The man was right. He represented everything that was not human... everything that was unholy and not part of God's plan.

Vladis knew he must find Vojislav quickly, so he left through an unguarded door out into the courtyard of the keep. He could hear Vojislav's voice calling to him. To get to him, he must get over the walls, so his desire to scale the walls allowed him to change into a creature of flight.

He soared over the walls and his eyes scanned the ground below for Vojislav. He found him, mounted on a horse with the armor that Akhenaten had used when he had existed. Landing in the forest, the new vampire changed back to his human form.

"Welcome to your new life. I trust it will be everything I promised and much, much more." The man on the horse pointed to the armor on the ground. In a wave of his hand, Vladis found himself girded in the armor. It fit as though custom made. The helm covered his face. "You should never show your face in public again for you will be recognized. For that, you will be hunted down, for the superstitions of these people are immense. They will not be happy that you have returned from the dead but see you as evil. And in their way, they would be right. You will be my arm, my sword, my fist. You will protect me from my enemies without question and I will guard over you when the sun is overhead. You will return to your state of death when the sun is visible. Only at night, when it is dark, shall you find the solace of darkness. It is your new world."

*   *   *

Princess Illona was told that Vojislav had been seen in the area. A black knight had also been seen with him. She smiled to herself, knowing that Vojislav was nearby. The black knight was the one responsible for the grisly murder of a servant within the castle. Though she knew he was close by, the princess was dismayed that Vojislav had not come to see her since just before Prince Vladis's death.

Everyone in the castle seemed to know or at the very least, suspected that Princess Illona had played a key role in their lord's death. They viewed her with suspicion and contempt. None of them wanted to be subservient to a murderess. Also, none of them dared to make an accusation. But their eyes did accuse and when one looked at her with accusing eyes, she ordered that one of his eyes be put out with a hot iron. She herself did the deed.

Soon, reports that others were meeting their deaths in a similar fashion, on and off the estate. Young girls were found in their beds, drained of their life force. Men were found, sleeping in woodcutter huts and barns in a likewise manner.

Brother Bartholomew was sent for by Princess Illona. He arrived, reluctantly, and stood before her in the great hall. "I have come to you for you have need of me, Princess?" he stated humbly.

"Yes, I have need of you. This entire manor has need of you. There are murders and murderers about. My magistrate is inept and weak. No one can tell me from whence this comes. What say you about such deeds that are so terrible that even I cannot speak of them?" She was agitated. Her counselors and court advised her to seek out the wisest and most able to tell her of what this terror is and where it may come from. Somehow, his name

157

was mentioned as a possible candidate who could help.

"Princess, there are evils that are loose in this kingdom. They are the enemies of God, enemies of His church. They stand for everything that God is against. Evil has befallen this land. It came before the Prince died…long before he died, dear lady. It walks amongst us. It has walked amongst us for an exceptionally long time."

"And who is this entity you call the enemy of God and His church?"

Bartholomew was nervous and reluctant to reply, for he knew she would surely not want to hear his answer. Finally, after she asked again, he answered. "The man who came to our lands before the wars began against the Byzantines, the same man who brought the black knights with him. You know this man, my lady. It is Vojislav Rekvas."

"Nonsense, Brother Bartholomew! Nonsense I say. You speak of the man I love. He has told me of the one who has slain the black knights. It was Baron Descondes who slayed them. Vojislav told me himself upon his return from rescuing me from being part of the ransom."

"I speak the truth, my lady. Prince Vladis is dead because of something that happened there, I am sure. I cannot prove it. But you have asked what my thoughts are on this. I have told you."

The two were alone in the hall. For she had ordered all courtiers and guards to leave them. "You suspect me to be responsible for my late husband's death, do you not, priest?"

"No, my lady. I suspect you to be responsible for Annara's husband' death. Of that I am certain. I cannot say why or how, but you stood to gain immensely from it. You are not the wife. You have no legal standing here, as either wife or heir or even Princess. Your marriage to the Prince was annulled. I was there when the Bishop told you this. You are a Princess only in your own land of Moldavia. I have studied about you. Your brothers have much to say about you. It would make sense that you do not wish to return to the country of your birth. You were essentially banished from your home and your birthright canceled and given away to ensure a treaty for security between two countries."

"I see. The truth comes to light. I always wondered why you looked so familiar. At that meeting, you were so insignificant. Yet, here you are…As a witness full of testimony regarding such a meeting. Aside from myself, you and Annara are the only living witnesses. Does that strike you as having put yourself in danger?"

"Perhaps, my lady, but know this. The Bishop of Tarnovo is aware of everything here. He knew of your transgressions before I was sent here. He knows of the friar who I came here to replace, his fate being mysterious and unresolved. He knows everything I know and do here. Soon, he will know the truth of you and the things you have done."

Bartholomew knew that he would be put to the test to tell the truth for it was the right thing to do. It was not necessarily the smartest thing, but truth is always the right thing. Because of this, he had given the letters to Annara along with another letter for the Bishop, Janos of Plovdiv. This letter told of the friar's suspicions regarding the activities that had transpired. He hoped and prayed that Annara would send these letters directly to the Bishop, regardless of what might happen to him.

The castle butler, Johannes, still loyal as his counselor to the memory of his Prince Vladis, held his ear to the door of the great hall while Bartholomew endured the icy and cold reception of the Princess Illona. He knew if the Princess could do so, she would have the friar executed, or at the least, his tongue and eyes removed. She had done this earlier that week, to a servant that she overheard talking about his suspicions of Illona's involvement in Vladis' death.

He had talked with Bartholomew prior to his entry into the great hall. The friar had told him of his suspicions regarding the black knights and asked him to go to the crypt and ensure that the Prince's crypt was intact. He was torn whether he should continue to listen or go to the crypt. Johannes had enjoyed a great deal of latitude when dealing with the Prince's affairs. He was certain that he would not be allowed that same kind of relationship with Illona. She had her three handmaidens who would take over that job.

The door to the great hall began to open. Johannes jumped

around the corner to avoid appearing as eavesdropping. It was Brother Bartholomew. He was red-faced, fuming angry and yet seemed satisfied that he had stood up to the Princess Illona.

"Heard the whole story, did we?" asked Bartholomew.

"Yes, I think you are the bravest man I have ever known. I thought about what you said about the crypt. Let us go now to see if your suspicions are true."

"Guide us there, my friend."

They quickly ducked into passageways that no one would enter unless they were headed to the crypt located in the deep cellars of the castle. The entrance was near the chapel, where Bartholomew had presided over the funeral service for the dead Prince. When they arrived at the entrance to the underground crypt, they found it sealed. It would take tools which they did not possess to open it. Opening the door would cause a lot of noise and draw attention. Once discovered, a reasonable and plausible explanation would be required of them by the Princess as to why they were trying to break into the crypt. They were not prepared for that and therefore they abandoned their plans.

Later that night, Johannes met the friar in the tavern just across the river at the checkpoint. They enjoyed some ale together along with a meal. While they talked, Brother Bartholomew calculated in his head the number of days that had passed since the Prince had died and was buried. Then he asked Johannes, "How many bodies have been found since the Prince died?"

*   *   *

Dark days plagued the estate for a time. Winter had come with biting cold and heavy snows. Bodies were turning up everywhere. Sometimes murders would be taking place at other estates while sometimes it would be pilgrims on their way to the Holy Land. Someone or something was killing people at random. No one could come up with a suspect for no evidence or clues were left at the scene of the crime. The only thing that the victims had in common was a wound upon their neck and their blood drained from their body. Where their blood went was as much of a mystery as who did the crime. Brother Bartholomew had his suspicions but needed evidence to confirm them. It seemed there was no pattern to the killing.

Johannes wanted to help Bartholomew get into the crypt. The monk had not told Johannes exactly what he thought he would find but the monk knew if his suspicions were correct, the crypt would provide answers. The friar had not been to the castle in some time. He was too busy ministering to the peasant population. He performed many funerals, so he got to examine the bodies. They were all the same.

Finally, Bartholomew had had enough. He went to see his friend, Johannes to persuade Princess Illona to allow them access to the crypt.

The two stood before her in the great hall. She seemed defiant to their request. "I hear you want to break into my late husband's crypt. And for what purpose? Is this not against the teachings of the church?"

"My Lady, it is against the teachings of the Church, but under certain circumstances it is permissible to determine the evidence of body tampering and theft. If his body is missing, then it may be that whoever stole his body, is also the same who may be committing murders at will. We have no other recourse but to satisfy that evil is not running amok here. We must rule out the supernatural to pursue this tragedy of loss of life. We know these deaths are murders, committed by someone or something that has a fixation for human blood. Cattle and other livestock are not affected."

Princess Illona knew the truth. She hoped her eyes did not give away her complicity in the matter. It would be a disaster for her to allow the monk or her husband's servant the knowledge that Vladis was indeed the one responsible for the mayhem going on. "I forbid it. I will not give in to the superstitions of an ignorant people or a monk who specializes in fanning the flames of suspicions of sorcery and evil to simple minded peasants."

"Lady, if you wish the murders to continue, do nothing. We are trying to understand at the very least the cause and motive for all the murders taking place. Do you not care for the safety of your people? They depend on your protection! They have no

161

other recourse."

"Leave my presence! Come here no more, priest. If you do, you do so at your own peril!" She called for the guards to escort both Bartholomew and Johannes out of the castle.

Once they were on the far side of the bridge at the checkpoint, Johannes looked to the monk, saying, "I am expelled from the castle. What shall I do? The Princess is a cold, bitter woman who knows no bounds of cruelty, no matter how deep she searches."

Bartholomew agreed and said he would help the servant find new employment. They both went to his hovel located behind the makeshift chapel. The monk began to write some letters. One of the letters was to Janos of Plovdiv, the Bishop of Tarnovo and another was to the Emperor.

*   *   *

Time went by, and as usual, the peasantry struggled to survive the notoriously harsh winter. The monk as well as Johannes struggled to survive all the while trying to ensure that as few people suffered from the cold and starvation as possible. Despite the natural hardships, having a vampire running loose amongst the countryside did not help to lessen their suffering. Still, Vojislav was pleased that Vladis was instilling terror in the countryside. The fear he generated could be felt and heard throughout the land. Many would not go out during the hours of darkness. Vladis traveled farther away from the estate to find victims from which he would take their blood.

Vojislav, also the Dragon, knew the Baron would eventually demand that he return to the *Order of the Dragons of Set* in Rome. He wanted to take Vladis to meet the Baron in his own special way, settling the score, but first, he wanted Vladis to grow in power. His thirst for vengeance overrode his better judgement. He wanted Vladis to receive wisdom, as well as the gift of sight. He knew there were many gifts that Set would bestow upon his new companion, but he had to survive in the world of mortals first.

His victim count had increased nightly. Soon, Vojislav and

Vladis would return to the castle. He knew the sight of Vladis alive would alarm Illona. Vladis might turn on Illona out of revenge for giving him the goblet containing the blood of Nefertiti. Though Vojislav loved her, he was torn because he knew she had her own reasons for doing what she did. Vladis reaping revenge on her was a distinct reality.

The first gift that Vladis received was the gift of discernment. He would know if a mortal was lying. Vojislav was worried if Illona would lie to him about anything, and, if so, what would be Vladis' reaction. Discernment had been the vampire's primary method of protecting the Dragon from his mortal enemies. They always knew the true intentions of those the Dragon dealt with.

Vojislav knew that when Illona went into the deep sleep and learned of the world of the Dragon, she learned a lot about the vampires who accompanied him. Perhaps, that is why she gave Vladis the goblet to drink from. Either way, the meeting would be momentous for Illona was still an outsider. Set had forbidden Vojislav from marrying her. She was dark and evil. He knew her heart to be ambitious and selfish. Those were traits reserved only for the Dragon. There could not be two. Set would not allow it and Vojislav knew it.

It was winter and open, white fields of fresh fallen snow easily revealed dark creatures running through the snow. Vojislav's dark horse and Vladis, upon an equally dark mount, would easily be seen from a distance, especially when the sky had a full moon. While approaching the castle, they were careful to ride only through the wooded areas. Vladis could easily get inside the castle without the need for a horse, but Vojislav wanted Vladis to ride with him.

They tied their horses to a tree in the forest, covered them with blankets and left on foot for the castle. They would not go in through the normal, conventional method…the front door. In the dim light of the moon, Vladis flew over the castle walls, with Vojislav in his arms, and landed on the ramparts. They were inside, unnoticed. Soon, they were inside Illona's bedchambers, a place Vojislav could reasonably expect privacy.

It was dark inside her chambers with only the fireplace giving off heat and ambient light. Soon, Illona would arrive to prepare to retire for the night. It would not be an alarming situation should Vojislav be discovered inside the castle. He was not recognized as being a stranger inside the walls of the fortress. However, should Vladis, a man all knew as dead, be discovered out of his tomb, walking and talking, the effects would be disastrous.

It was quite a while before Illona retired to her chambers. The door began to creak while the two intruders waited in the shadows behind a tapestry. The moon cast a soft beam of light through her window. The small group of clouds had cleared so that the moon's light poured into the room through the small window. There was no covering over the small aperture in the stone wall for it was primarily for ventilation due to the fireplace. Thus, it allowed for cold, frigid air to enter the room as well as allowing smoke to be evacuated from it.

Her bed was heavily laden in furs upon a mattress of down feathers. A finely made cabinet of hardwood stood holding her gowns and other personal objects. A chair, with carved arms and upholstered in deer hide over a padding of horsehair, sat in front of a small table. Upon the table sat a candelabra. The candles were not lit. Before Illona would slide into bed, a servant would come to the room and prepare to warm the bed by placing a covered metal dish containing hot coals inside the covers at the foot of her bed.

Many of her servants had already deserted the castle, for the rumors of her murdering her husband had convinced many of them of her guilt. Most likely, she would have to warm her own bed.

As she came into the darkened room, she could sense she was not alone. She knew that only Vojislav would have the ability to slither into her bedchambers unnoticed. "Vojislav? Are you there?" She paused in the darkness, waiting for his confirmation.

"Yes, I am here, my love. And, I brought you a visitor."

Vladis stepped out of the shadows and into the beam of moonlight, revealing his identity. He did not know what to expect, but he knew he was helpless to resist doing anything the Dragon asked or demanded. As Illona looked upon his face, he was pale and expressionless. Her revenge she had always wanted to place upon him was complete. She gasped, partially in unbelief that he walked as if alive but also that he might take revenge upon her for what she had done to him.

Moments passed before anyone spoke. Finally, Vladis made the first contact. "Your revenge is complete. Is your anger and hatred satiated? Is this what you wanted for me?"

"No!" she replied. "I wanted you dead, but not like this." She was lying, for the gift of discernment told Vladis of her deceit.

"I had no idea that this was to happen to you. What are your plans?" she asked.

"Ask my master," Vladis said, glancing over to Vojislav.

Vojislav took this as his turn to speak. "He has replaced my dead companions. He is what they were, a vampire. I control him, and he does only what I say. It is he who is spreading terror over the countryside. This will draw out the Baron so that I may take revenge upon him. As for you, you need not fear Vladis. He may want to take revenge upon you, but I will not let him."

"I do not understand all that has happened here. How? What now?" she asked.

Vojislav answered, "My dear, this is all your efforts, come to fruition. You hated him. You wanted an annulment. He wanted happiness. You hated him the more for that. He had children, heirs to his estate. He gave you away, as part of his ransom. Your hate for him boiled within you. You wanted his death. Your desire for it was granted. He was my friend. This way we both get what we want. You have his death. I have his resurrection."

CHAPTER NINETEEN

A TENDER AGE

Christmas of 1208 came and went. The holiday was celebrated during the day, but at night, everyone stayed indoors. Only a few spent the night alone and anyone who did knew it was dangerous. Everyone dreaded what lay outside their door in the darkness of the night. Brother Bartholomew held services the evening of Christmas Eve, but the service lasted only as necessary. He cautioned them all to consider their faith as their shield and if possible, wear a crucifix outside their garments to ward off evil. Though it was a time of celebration of the birth of Christ, the evil they all feared was very much alive and well in the world they lived in.

Tayla's family rode in the cart to attend that Christmas Eve service. Afterwards, they traveled home as quickly as possible. Once inside, they barricaded the door and placed crucifixes in the windows.

Bartholomew warned all families specifically that should a stranger come to the home, not to let anyone in they did not know.

The winter months of 1209 passed and as they did, Bartholomew worked behind the scenes to get into the crypt of Prince Vladis. Johannes worked alongside him, contacting people inside the castle he felt he could trust. Eventually, Johannes' position was restored to him as near chaos reigned inside the walls. Illona relented to have him back to restore order. Once that happened, Bartholomew worked to procure tools and equipment necessary to inspect the vault. The monk resigned himself that if Vladis was still in the vault, he would give up on the notion that a legend the church talked about but only within

166

its own ranks might be true. The legend of a creature that is dead in the light of day but walks about during the hours of darkness made Bartholomew write a letter to the Bishop.

Nothing could have stopped Vladis from that which he was driven to do. Vojislav knew this, so he insisted that Vladis move his hunting grounds to other areas outside the bounds of the manor of which he was once the proud ruler. The more blood he took, the stronger he grew. The stronger he grew, the more humanity he lost. Human traits such as mercy, kindness and love would erode over time. At some point, he would have none, which was exactly what Vojislav wanted. When he would reach the level where remorse was non-existent, where all human conscience had vacated him, then Vojislav would feel that his beloved vampires would have been replaced. Even if it were only one vampire, it would be enough.

During the winter months, food was scarce. It was not an outright famine, but still, many went hungry. Those were the ones who Vladis targeted. Poor, desperate men who would do anything to fend for their families. The laws against poaching were strictly enforced. Men, who would hunt the forests in the early night in hopes to find game would not return home. Their bodies would be found days later, frozen in the snow, often the target of predators and scavenger who would also be hungry. If they were caught poaching, the punishment was severe.

Johannes told Illona about the hunger of her people, but she cared little for them. It only meant that her labor supply decreased with each victim. Finally, she allowed for some of her grain stocks to be released to the peasantry. The people were grateful and their genuine thanks for the food impressed her. It was then that she knew how to control the people. If she wanted their respect and loyalty, all she had to do was keep them hungry, not starving but dependent upon her generosity and benevolence in times of need. During the spring and summer, she knew that they would have to plant more than they had in the past, for they all knew the shortages could easily return.

Vojislav would stay in the castle at night while Vladis would return to his crypt each morning. The Dragon did not like allowing Vladis out on his own at night but knew it was necessary. His hunting skills had become sharper and he did not require Vojislav's presence. He did not trust Johannes being reinstated as the castle butler but there was no one more familiar with the day to day operations of the castle. While he was gone, things had begun to fall apart. Servants and other staff began to desert. After Johannes returned, many came back to work. Some did not, which meant they probably fell prey to Vladis.

Johannes made sure the crypt door had not been disturbed. He thought about what the monk, now turned friar, had told him. But still, he was not convinced. He personally had never seen anything supernatural and those who might have were dead.

*   *   *

Annara and her family never went out at night. Josef forbid them from going out for any reason. "The stock will be fine," he told them. Tayla and her sister and brothers listened with wide eyes and open ears. They felt fear in their grandfather's voice. Annara knew her children were frightened by their grandfather's words, but she agreed. No one must go out into the darkness.

"Mama?" Tayla asked, "What is out there that is so dangerous? Who is killing the people in our village?"

"I am not sure, my daughter. There are many stories being told in the village. They say it is a man who is killing people. Some think it is a wolf. No one knows for sure. I do not want to take the chance whatever it is. Some say it is your father come back from the dead."

"How is that possible? How can Father come back when he died right in front of you?"

"I think it is all lies. All the people here are just superstitious. Nobody has any proof of what is out there. People say all kinds of things when they are scared. From the looks of it, there are a lot of scared people around us. If it were your father, believe me, you would have nothing to fear from him. Unless, he has changed. I cannot imagine why he would. I know he loved me and even more, he loved you, his children. I believe your father's love could reach across the void of death. If it were possible. But enough of such talk! It is time for you and your brothers and

168

sister to go to bed!" She kissed and hugged them all as if for the last time. They were all such a tender age. Their young ears picked up every word that came out of their mother's and grandfather's mouths. Most of all, they obeyed without question. Their faith in their mother and grandfather was unshakeable.

*   *   *

The people learned to get all the chores done during the daylight hours. If anyone needed to go out to a barn or anywhere during the night, they always did with another person to accompany them.

They did not know that Vladis had moved his hunting grounds farther away from the castle. For a while, there were no victims of murder from a vampire within a hundred miles of the estate. Vojislav let his new pet hunt on his own with the stipulation that he not hunt in the same place more than two nights in a row. After a while, the entire region was in terror. No one had any answers to explain or rid themselves of the murderous phenomenon.

"I have ordered Vladis to hunt elsewhere in this region. The more he hunts, the more he is feared. The more he is feared, the more power he receives," Vojislav explained to Illona.

"Will you ever give me power over Vladis?" she asked of him.

The Dragon was surprised she would ask such a thing. Obviously, she did not know she had that power. If she were aware that she did, she would not have asked the question.

"Set has forbidden it. In fact, Set has forbidden me of several things. For one thing, he has forbidden me of marrying you. I know that does not set well with you," he said when he saw her facial expression change. He continued. "I cannot disobey him. My disobedience has already cost me dearly. My vampires, Akhenaten and Nefertiti paid with their own blood for my disobedience. I learned a lesson that night. It was a very painful lesson, for they were like family to me. Nothing hurts like losing a family member. Would you agree?"

For a moment, she did not answer. She was thinking of what

he had said about losing a member of one's family. It planted the seed of what would become her most devious plot yet.

Vojislav picked up on it immediately. "I see the wheels turning in your heart, Illona. Now, I see why Set said no to marrying you. You want my power, my control over vampires. Now, I see! I can read your mind. You want to use Vladis to hurt your enemy, and by doing so, hurt him so deeply he will live in regret eternally. And you think I am going to go along with this and allow it? I think not."

"I thought you wanted me, for a wife and a partner! Now, I think I was used."

Vojislav raised his voice. "You? Being used? That is quite the statement. To satisfy you cost me more than I dare say. Two dear souls are in Hell right now because I let my feelings for you overrule my better judgement. They trusted me and I, because of my feelings for you, betrayed them, leading them to their deaths. Who was used? Now, you want to use that which belongs to me to further cause pain to the ones you hate. I forbid it. Vladis is mine and you cannot have him."

"Did you ever really love me?" The woman could turn on tears as easily as turning the latch on a door. She held her hands to her face as she sobbed. Vojislav knew it was a ruse. Still, he had feelings for her. The power of love in mortals was strong. And he was in a mortal body. Should he take Vladis and go to Rome? Should he leave the only woman he had ever loved in his whole life because she was very much like him? The longer he stared at her, the more vulnerable to her charms he felt. He decided to leave the castle for the night. He would rather spend the night in the forest than listen to her whine and beg him for the use of Vladis to her own means.

She begged him to stay but he would not listen. "Then do not come back to me! You are not welcome within these walls. Remember, Vladis has to come back here in the day!"

He was getting angrier by the second and stormed out of the castle. He mounted his horse and took Vladis' mount as well. He knew that Vladis would find him in the forest and then, he would tell his vampire of his plans to return to Rome.

Later, in the forest, Vojislav had made camp. A bedroll lay

on the ground with a small fire that seemed to never need wood to give off heat and light. It blazed as if pitch had been poured on it.

As Vojislav sat upon the ground in front of the fire, he became aware he was not alone. He drank wine from a goatskin flask.

"Finding you was easy," said a familiar voice. It was Prince Vladis, who came out of the darkness into the light of the blazing fire.

"Is there trouble between you and my former tormentor?"

Vojislav answered with a sour voice, "Yes. Now I believe she is the evilest of any woman I have ever known. Evil is my profession, but I employ it to further the will of Set. She is all about promoting herself. Even if it means lying to me, using you to get to your family. Stay away from her."

"How can I do that if I must return to the crypt in the castle? Surely, she knows that I must do that. When I am sleeping, I am vulnerable. Who knows what she will do?"

"I must return to Rome to confront the *Order of the Dragons of Set*. I have a lot to answer for and I must set things right. You cannot go with me. Because of how you were transformed, you must stay here. I must leave now, but I will return to you and release you from her. She will no doubt force you to turn on your family. You must resist this at all costs."

"I would never turn on them. I would sooner turn on her than murder any of my family."

"Vladis, you were and are my friend. I promised to protect you and care for you. You, in turn, promised to follow me and do my will. I foresee troubling times coming to us both. There will be risks and threats coming to all of us...You, me, and most of all, your family. I want you to protect your children. That is who stands to lose the most. She will want to have Annara killed. I foresee her doing this to protect her holdings of your estate. I know she is not the legal and proper heir to your estate. I should have stopped her when I had the chance. I was blinded by what I thought was love. She used me and that has caused my relationship with Set to suffer."

Vladis sat down next to him in front of the fire. "Is it true she has power over me such that I cannot turn on her? How long will that be in effect? What can I do to resist her?"

"I am not sure. I have never been faced with such a challenge. You will follow me, but because she gave you wine to drink from Nefertiti's blood in the goblet, she share's in that power. It is as if she knew this. Knowledge is power. I let her inside my realm, and now I am paying for such a mistake."

"It seems as if the goblet is the key. If I gain possession of the goblet, and give it to you, would that change things?"

"I think so. As I said, this has never happened before," replied Vojislav.

"Then it shall be done. While you are in Rome, I will take the goblet, and keep it. Hopefully, it will enable me to leave the castle and the crypt and find solace elsewhere. I will wait for your return."

Morning came, and Vladis had returned to the crypt. Vojislav broke camp and began his journey to Rome. He hoped his friend would be able to deal with Illona while he was away.

*   *   *

Vladis did as he said he would and stole the goblet, still stained with the blood of Nefertiti. He could see the traces of the blood mixed with the wine. It had not been used since then. The church had placed a lot of spiritual importance on relics, particularly those associated with the deaths of apostles and saints. Since the goblet was the key to his transformation, he hoped it would also be the key to his independence from his tormentor. To Vladis, the goblet was an important relic that symbolized his transformation. Perhaps, it was the unholy grail. After all, it had caused his death, not life. And it was death eternal, not an afterlife.

He took the chance one evening that would change everything. Before dawn, he sought shelter in a place that was nearby but not in his vault. It was a cave, high in the mountains above the estate. He had found it while watching wolves seeking shelter from the elements. He followed them into the cave, and established control over the animals. The control over animals was another gift Set bestowed upon him as a vampire. He decided it was here, in this wild and inhospitable place that few if any would dare to seek him, he would stake his lair. The wolves would watch over him by day, and he would bring them his scraps upon which to feed. Here he would stay until Vojislav Rekvas, the Dragon, would return as he promised him.

Bartholomew kept records as to who became casualties of the grisly attacks. He noticed that the attacks had suddenly ceased, suggesting that whoever was behind the attacks may have moved on. He was pleased but always still suspicious.

CHAPTER TWENTY

THE DRAGON RETURNS

In Rome, the *Order of the Dragons of Set*'s membership had dwindled over the last few centuries. Many of the wisest and most influential patriarchs of those who had come from Carthage were unfortunate to have to see their lineage dwindle and die out. It did not matter. It was only important that the lineage of the spirit of Set did not die. It was alive and well in Vojislav Rekvas. He was the current living disciple of Set, the Egyptian god of chaos, storms, and outright evil. No matter what the name used to identify the spirit, it was always the same. Set was the embodiment of what most civilizations and cultures come to know as the Devil. He was crafty and far cleverer than any adversary who would dare take on the daunting task of stopping him from accomplishing his agenda. The Dragon was strong, courageous, determined to succeed, ambitious, and resourceful. He was given every trait necessary to succeed in his mission. This Dragon had a few other traits as well.

When the council of the Order met in Rome, they found that the Dragon seemed to have departed from the established path of fighting the church and trying to suppress Christianity. For centuries now, they had been trying to do so. No earthly adversary was strong enough to stop them. But…a heavenly adversary was more than a match for them. And, if that heavenly adversary were to give aid to an earthly, mortal being, then a true state of alarm would exist within their ranks. Their ranks being few now, due to decades of war, famines, plagues, and political purges, the council decided to recall the Dragon back to Rome to give an account of his actions while he was away. He had been

174

gone for quite a few years without giving so much as a notice as to status of his mission. It was far too unbecoming of one so entrusted with such power to not give account of one's self.

Now, on an overcast and cold morning, Vojislav had returned. Vojislav's family had been in Constantinople when he was born. His father never returned to Rome due to the many wars, but he survived there long enough to indoctrinate Vojislav to Set and his destiny to be the new Dragon upon his father's death. Vojislav had been to Rome only five times in his life. Each time was to visit and confer with the high council of the *Order of the Dragons of Set*. The new Dragon did not like Rome. He preferred the location of Constantinople and wanted to move the Order there. Set had interfered with that decision and ordered that the Order's headquarters be kept in Rome. Later, the Dragon would know the answer as to why and it would be a decision that he would support wholeheartedly. But that was years ahead of them. For now, Vojislav was discontented with the Order and felt they had interfered with his life. Of all the sons of Dragons to have ever held the title of Dragon of Set, Vojislav seemed to be the most willful and rebellious. From time to time, Set had to reign him in like a dog on a leash.

It would be spring in a few weeks but the snows and the biting cold would remain for a bit longer. People in Rome found the cold more agitating than the sporadic snowfall that might beset the ancient city. Still, life went on in the eternal city.

Vojislav went straight to the home of one of the elder council members. He knocked on the large wooden door of the large house. A servant came to answer the door. He did not recognize Vojislav. "I am here to see Matthias. Is your master home?"

"Yes, he is here. I do not think he is awake yet. It is still early."

"Wake him! Wake him now and tell him the Dragon awaits."

The servant, also a member of the Order, had never met the Dragon. He knew of him, and the stories abounded of truth and exaggeration. Nonetheless, he ran to awaken his master.

A few minutes later, an old man, still in the clothing he was fast asleep in, came to the foyer where Vojislav waited for him. "Is it true? You have come back to us? What do they call you these days, master? Are you still called Decentius?"

"No, Matthias. I am not. I am known amongst my current circle of acquaintances as Vojislav Rekvas. I travel throughout Eastern Europe, doing what I do best. I gave up that name when I left Constantinople. My family did not do well there."

The old man smiled. "That is because your family left Rome. Well, that is in the past. Let us have breakfast. Have you traveled all night to get here? Where have you come from?"

They walked into a large dining room. Already, servants were preparing for a gathering around the table. Vojislav had arrived just in time to partake in their breakfast. "I have been traveling for several weeks now from a small kingdom in the east. It is called Wallachia."

"Oh, yes, one of our members has written to us about that. A baron of sorts, I believe."

"Yes, the Baron Regevak Descondes. It is he who is responsible for my travel back to Rome. He killed my two vampires. I should say he murdered them, without provocation."

"Well, Vojislav, you do know who you are talking to, do you not? You cannot lie to us, for we are of the same spirit in Set. Set tells us all. You were there to kill him. We sent him there to watch over you and to try to convince you to come home to us. It worked but I fear your anger will be harder to sooth than your journey will be."

"Just what is your reason for recalling me to Rome? I do not want to waste any more time."

The old man sat down, and others of the council filed in, for they too had been staying there. It was as if they had expected Vojislav to arrive that day and therefore, had already gathered under the roof of Matthias to meet.

"Wasting time? You just arrived. I hardly think you have wasted any time. Sit down and eat something. It looks as though you have traveled all night yet cannot wait to get back to that place in Wallachia and that woman you are bewitched by. Show some patience and some respect!"

Vojislav sat down, as a servant began to load up a plate with food and poured a liquid into a vessel. He had never seen such a liquid as this.

176

"It is something we call tea. You should try it instead of what you have been drinking. It might help you clear your mind. Yes, we know all about this woman, Illona. Set has told us just as he has told you. No!"

"No what?" Vojislav asked.

"No to that woman, and that is Set's final word. Or do you want your new vampire to fall prey to the same fate?"

"Vojislav or Decentius...you have lost your way. You do not seek our master's will and for that, you have paid a heavy price. You have not been seeking to stamp out the church, or to inhibit the Crusaders. Instead, you have been playing politics. Causing wars, finishing wars, starting new ones. You think you are the only one who can do such things? I think not. Man, even left alone, can do all of that. You have a higher purpose and you have not been attending to it. That is the reason why you are here. We are to remind you of it and see to it that you do not stray from it."

Vojislav was surprised at the scolding he was taking from a member of the council. He was not used to being talked down to as if he were a student and his teacher was correcting him. He became indignant very quickly.

"How dare you talk this way to me! I am the chosen one, the reigning Dragon of Set. Who are you to scold me as if I were a schoolboy?"

"We, Dragon, are the High Council of the *Order of the Dragons of Set*. You exist because we support you and the will of Set. Nothing more. It has been this way for millennia."

Vojislav sensed that Set was on their side and he was in danger of being stripped of his status and his power. He felt it was wise for him to be quiet and listen. His thoughts pondered the idea that maybe the council was correct that he had lost his way. It was a dangerous precedent. He was without his vampires, and the newest one was still a work in progress. In fact, he knew because of the method in which Vladis was transformed, he shared power over him with Illona.

Matthias seemed to have read his thoughts. "Yes, you must gain full control over this Prince Vladis before his former wife realizes what power she has in her hands. It could be disastrous to the Order for she will no doubt realize that membership in the

177

Order is denied to her. She can no longer be trusted to keep the secrets of the Order. For that, she must not be allowed to live. It is the price for her silence."

Vojislav knew what Matthias's words meant. Either he would have to do the deed, or Vladis would have to do it. It was breaking his heart. Vladis would love to do such a thing to his nemesis.

"After today, you must return to the land of the Bulgars, take control of this Prince Vladis, eliminate Princess Illona and return here to Rome. The church here is growing more powerful than we ever expected it to. It is as equally as powerful as any king. In fact, there is usually no king unless it has the full support and sanctioning of the highest of the clergy, which means the Pope himself. That is an office which we must infiltrate. You must leave now. Set will give you more instruction when you arrive."

It was a few days later, when Vojislav was traveling north and east to get back to Wallachia. He had stopped to make camp along an ancient Roman road. During the months when the weather was better and more suitable, the road was busy with travelers. Most would attempt to stay at taverns or small towns with inns that might accompany them with supplies and if they were lucky, accommodations that might shelter them from the elements. Vojislav usually avoided these towns for he feared he might be recognized by the any of the multitude of enemies he had made over the years. His powers of survival were intact, and he and his horse never hungered. While he lay upon the ground, wrapped up in several blankets, Set appeared to him. He was hard to see because it was night. Nonetheless, he felt his presence despite the darkness. The light from his campfire did nothing to illuminate his form.

"Have you learned from your travels to Rome, my disciple? Do you know that which I command you to do?"

"Yes, Lord of the Dark. I have been informed by the High Council. I am on my way to perform your will," said the Dragon, wrapped up in the cold of the night.

"When you get there, you will find a challenge waiting for you. There will be many things you will feel you must choose from, but you will know that there is only one choice to make.

The Order must be preserved at all costs. Any threat to the Order must be eliminated, no matter who or what it might be. Is this understood?"

Vojislav knew he was making a reference to the Princess Illona and the death sentence imposed upon her.

"Once you have made this choice and my will is carried out, your next move is to return to Rome. If I cannot attack the church from without, it must be attacked from within. After all, it is the true church that is our enemy. It is the true message of the disciples regarding the teachings of Jesus that is our true enemy."

The next morning found the ground covered with a light blanket of white powdered snow. The campfire had long died out, without so much as a smoldering ember. The Dragon's horse stood tied to a tree, a blanket covering it from its neck to its rump.

The Dragon woke, packed up his bedroll, rekindled the fire and made his breakfast. As he ate, he smiled knowing he had slept no better than his trusty steed had. They shared a common misery…cold and loneliness.

He fed his horse a bucket of oats and prepared to leave for the day's travel. While he rode, there was only one thing on his mind…the look he would find in Illona's face when she saw that he meant for her to die.

*   *   *

Evil comes in many forms. Even in forms we never expect. Since the Dragon had left for Italy life slowly returned to normal. Annara and the village had noticed that the threat had seemed to have subsided. Illona was her usual self. The uneasy peace between her and Annara was kept. Annara wanted nothing to do with Illona and avoided her at all costs. She had hidden the chests of coins in a place where no one could find it, not even accidentally. Josef knew of its location and passed by it often to see if it had been disturbed.

Meanwhile, a stranger began to show up at Annara's home at night. He looked different than his usual self, such that even Annara did not know that the stranger was Vladis in disguise. Changing his appearance was the latest gift given to him. The

179

ability to change one's appearance allowed him a comfortable defense mechanism against his enemies, which, at this time, was everyone not a vampire.

He introduced himself, telling her he was from the crusades and wanted to return home. She allowed him to slowly begin to woo her, wanting to sweep her off her feet. She told him that the last time someone had convinced her to give her heart to a man, it was the most painful experience of her life. Still, he would not give up and continued, even buying her gifts of food and clothing.

He eventually wormed his way into her home by telling her many things about himself without naming himself as her dead husband. Annara became fascinated with him, allowing herself to become infatuated with him. She told him of her marriage to the Prince, which amused Vladis. He was pleased that she still loved her dead husband very much and would never remarry. Still, she was lonely and after a while, in the still of the night, she allowed herself to be taken by the stranger.

This became the reason for the reputation she acquired for letting a stranger come into her home. A short while later, after she became accustomed to allowing him into her home, she began meeting him after hours of daylight in places such as the forest or in the barns. Even out in the fields behind tall haystacks she would meet him and thus became the affair of Annara and her mysterious lover.

Vladis, though changed forever, still found it in his heart to still love his wife. Love was such a powerful force, even to a vampire. He would never harm her as he always made sure he had fed before he came to her. He could not allow himself to be tempted to take from her or the children. It was not every single night he would come. Sometimes, weeks would go by without his making an appearance.

He made sure Annara's needs were met, both emotional, physical and most of all, financially. She had not told him of the recovered ransom chests. Coins were given freely to the woman who managed to capture the heart of the living and the dead. This affair went on for some time, and though she felt it was a secret she was never pressed for details. She was very reluctant to discuss her personal life with even her father. She was incredibly sad when he would have to leave and even cried when he did not show up for a visit on certain nights. He was kind to his children but kept a certain distance. Tayla often looked at him with a curious eye, trying to make the connection between him and the man she knew as her father. If she knew the truth, it would be devastating to her and the others.

Finally, Vladis could not keep his identity to himself any longer. He did not care that Annara might find him revolting, a monster of the most terrifying kind. He only wanted her to know that even in death, through no fault of his own, cursed for all eternity, she still held his heart in her hands.

"Annara, gaze upon the face of your dead Prince, your husband Vladis. Be not afraid. For I am a creature caught between two worlds. I wish to be in the world of the living, but you yourself saw me die, at the hands of one who hates me. She murdered me, but I am not a ghost. I still inhabit my earthly body. I still see with my earthly eyes; speak with my earthly tongue and I still have my earthly hunger. That is my curse."

When he told her, she gasped, held her hands to her face and wept. She did not understand the curse or why he had been chosen. It took some time for Annara to be able to lay eyes on him.

"My darling, I was chosen because of Illona's hatred for me. She is the cause for all the terror, the death, the fear that presides over this land. My will was taken from me. Stolen from me in that I did not wish this for myself. It was the only way I could come back to you and tell you how much I love you, still. My children, they must not know who I am, and most importantly, what I am. I would never hurt them. To do what I do, I am compelled beyond any means to resist. If I had a choice, do you think I would have chosen this life, this false life. It is a living death. I am dead, yet, you see me. I walk, I talk, I think as though I were still alive, but my heart does not beat. It burns with passion for you, my children, and my hatred for Illona."

Annara pleaded, "But we have no future. There can never be a way to go back to what we were, what you were. My children can never come to know what happened to their father."

Vladis's heart ached. "This is true. We must live here in the present tense. One day, you will die. I will live on. I dread that day. The only way for us to be together is for me to change you. I will not do that. Even now, my heart is breaking as the mere thought of you having to do what I do to survive is appalling. I would sooner go straight to Hell than that."

"Are there any more of you? The two black knights that accompanied Vojislav, were they...?"

"Yes, Annara, they were the first two vampires in the world. They were a former king and Queen of a country called Egypt. They were over two thousand years old. But they are dead now. I am the only one in the world."

"My wish is that my children receive an education and I have a way to secure that. I need to show you something. Before I take you to a place where I keep a secret, I have something to give to you. You loved me so much before, and even in death, you still love me. I have your ring. It signifies that you are the Prince of this land. It is a connection to your past life as I am. As you said, one day, I will die but you will go on. Your memory of me will fade over time until I am no more in your memory or your heart. When you wear this ring, you will remember it was me who returned it to you, my husband, my true love."

He took the ring and put it on his finger. "As long as I wear this ring, my memory of you will never die."

She led him to a secluded place some distance from the village. Next to a dead tree stump, she said, "In this spot, under our feet, is the ransom money you paid for your freedom after your capture. Our daughter, Tayla, found this while hiding from Illona. She brought this home with her and I decided when the time is right, we will leave this place and travel to a place where my children can receive an education. They will learn to read and write and know things most people could never come to know. If that means traveling far away from here, so much the better. Even if I cannot go with them, I want them to be educated. I know it is the key to a better life."

Vladis could see through the dirt and saw the three boxes buried about three feet under the soil. The location was in a part of the forest where it was not cleared yet for planting, so the chances of its discovery was nil.

"I agree that they should travel far from this place. I will make sure they receive an education. Starting now, speak with Brother Bartholomew. He can teach them. Tell him, you can pay. Say nothing of me. I am an enemy of the church, for I am unholy. My death is a sacrilege, my existence is a sacrilege. I am caught between worlds and there is only damnation for me. I wish to be with you while you remain in your world. Therefore, I shall come to you when I can. I will not be dangerous to you or our children. I shall look out for you regarding Illona and her vendetta against you and the children. If necessary, I will protect our children from her. I have watched our children. They are growing up so fast. They could not fathom or understand what has happened to their father. Oh, how I wish I could embrace them, especially Tayla. She is so much like you. My sons, they are like me, while our daughters take after you. Still, they are at a tender age, where they are not sure what they will love or what they will grow to hate. One thing is for sure. If they know me for what I truly am, they will hate me for they will fear me. We always hate and fear what we do not understand. I would not blame them. Living without you is hard enough, but without my children, my legacy, is worse. I will watch you die, and worst of all, I will see them die too. It is a pain of which I most certainly will have to bear."

*   *   *

It was a few years later since Vojislav had left Wallachia. Not much had changed and then a lot had changed. The nightly murders in the immediate area had ceased. Everyone was older. Tayla was getting ready for her fourteenth birthday. Her mother promised her she would make her favorite meal. In addition, she had made her oldest daughter a new dress. She had learned the art of weaving from her aunt and had decided to try her hand at making clothing for her children. Each birthday, she would have made something for each of her four children. Tayla's hair was long and dark while her face, with kind and gentle features, was unblemished. She was beginning to fill out in the chest and at the hips, indicating puberty was taking its course.

183

Except for being dirty at times, she was fast becoming a lady. Her femininity was highly influenced by her mother who in turn was influenced by her aunts. She began to show the moodiness and affectations of a teenage girl. Her grandfather Josef knew this would come sooner or later and no matter how you look at it, when a girl is fourteen, beautiful and sweet as Tayla, every boy's head would turn when she came around.

Josef was very protective of his granddaughter in that he did not want her to fall prey to the same heartbreak as her mother had. To have risen above all expectations of one's life and then have it taken away from you so suddenly. That was Annara's story, but he was determined to not have it be Tayla's or Prieta's story. Prieta would soon be of age before anyone would have time to contemplate it and then he would really have his hands full.

He loved Prieta as well as Tayla. He only wanted the best for his grandchildren as would any grandfather. Josef felt the world was stacked against women in general and their chances of happiness seemed to always rest on their choice of a man they would spend their life with. Or worse, who was chosen for them. Josef would have none of that. He wanted Annara, as well as Tayla and Prieta, to have the opportunity to choose who they wanted to marry, or not to marry, if at all. It would seem Josef was quite a visionary for his time, but as he looked around, he saw that most women he knew were dependent solely on a man for support if not for security and happiness. And, he had seen many a woman left out in the cold when their man was taken away either by disease or war. In those days, it was quite common and the life expectancy for peasants was not long.

The birthday arrived and Tayla was excited. Her mother spent the day cooking a venison stew, Tayla's favorite, along with a pie of stewed apples. That night, Annara presented Tayla her gift of a new dress. It was dyed blue and had embroidered designs around the hem, courtesy of her aunt's skills at embroidery. When Tayla tried it on, it fit like a glove. The dress accented Tayla's figure and when she came out wearing it, Annara looked to her father Josef, and the look of worry came over her face. Josef recognized it and smiled. His daughter was experiencing all the anguish and apprehension he had felt when she was that age.

They feasted on the stew that night, each getting their fill. Rascha let it be known that it was he who shot the deer with an arrow. Othar had picked the apples and Prieta had taken them, baking them into a pie.

As they dined well in their home that night, a knock on their door interrupted their merriness. It came again. Everyone remembered the fate of so many who had been found murdered. They still felt the fear of answering the door at night. Finally, Josef got up and answered the door. The door opened to reveal a vast wall of blackness. Finally, a flame from a lantern lit up and a figure in black could be seen.

"Josef, I come in peace. I am a friend, so do not be afraid. I am Vojislav Rekvas, and I was a friend to your wife's husband. May I come in?"

"You come in peace?" asked Josef.

"I do. You need not fear me. But I will tell you who you do need to fear." The Dragon had returned to Wallachia.

CHAPTER TWENTY- ONE

VLADIS RETURNS

Annara's family held a certain degree of apprehension seeing the man who was always seen with the black knights. They wondered if they were nearby. Josef wondered if they were just outside. He had heard only one horse. The entire family were wearing crosses around their necks for if they did not believe in monsters or ghosts, they certainly believed beyond any doubt that evil abounded in these parts, especially after dark. It was widely believed the black knights were responsible for all of it. No one in the village had any knowledge of the knights whereabouts or what had happened to them. They only knew that if the black knights were about, death was just around the corner. The knights would not show up unless they were with Vojislav Rekvas, so where one was, the others was not too far away.

As Vojislav stepped into the villa's main room, he could see Annara pulling her children behind her. Her protective instincts were strong while her apprehension was even higher. Annara had a fearful look upon her face.

Josef managed to acquire the courage to ask, "Where are the knights you are usually seen with?"

Vojislav sighed a heavy sigh. "I am deeply sorry to say they are no longer with me. There is a story behind their departure, but I am not at liberty to tell you. You only need to know there is no need to fear them. My reason for being here is that I need to undo some things I feel responsible for. Annara, your husband, my friend, the Prince, is dead because of something I brought back which his former wife used to kill him. I have come to beg your forgiveness. He is dead because Illona had poisoned him. I brought two chalices from the Baron Descondes' castle. I fought with him and he killed my two knights. It is because of him and those chalices that your husband is dead."

Josef asked, "Everyone subject to the Prince wondered why the killing had stopped. Were they responsible for this plague of death? What became of the Baron? Did you kill him?"

"No, I did not. He is not the one who needs to die. Illona needs to die. If she does not, she will kill all of you. You present a danger to her and her position as long as any of you are alive for you all know the truth about her, her crimes and her plans."

"Those knights! Were they responsible for the killings?"

Vojislav ignored Josef's questions about the murders. He could not tell him without telling the secret about Vladis as well. After all, it was Vladis who had been doing the killing as of late. If Vladis was still hunting in the vicinity, that would have to stop, thought Vojislav.

"Her plans?" asked Annara.

"She plans to take the title of your husband, his fortune and his estate. Because of your legitimate claim, you could contest that and prevent her from doing that. The priest has already notified the Bishop of Tarnovo and he has the ear of the Emperor."

"We always knew this woman was evil. We also know that you both have been seen in the company of each other as lovers would be seen. Is this true?" asked Josef of Vojislav.

Vojislav hung his head and took off his sword belt. He laid it upon the wooden table they usually ate from. His helm he laid next to it. Then he sat down upon a crudely built stool. He took off his gauntlets and warmed his hands over the candles burning upon the table.

"Reluctantly, I confess that the rumors about our relationship are true. Vladis and I talked at length about this. He cared nothing for the woman but I, however, found something attractive about her. Sadly, I feel I have fallen for a woman who cares nothing for me. She seems to be more than my match for manipulating and using people for her own pleasure and gain. I am merely her latest victim. I see that now, and my Order, based in Rome, has thoroughly pointed this out to me. I have been ordered to sever ties with her entirely but before I do, my quest is to right the wrongs that she had done and prevent her from committing more evil deeds. That evil is such that I have already told you about."

After he had told them all this, there was a few moments of awkwardness until Tayla, now fourteen, broke the silence with a question.

"Are you hungry, sir?" asked Tayla. The act of a beautiful child, asking a person like him, in kindness and compassion, if he was hungry seemingly melted his heart.

Vojislav looked at her through his tousled dirty hair. A large dark beard covered his face but his eyes, a greyish blue seemed to be the only soft feature on his face.

"Few people in my life have ever shown me kindness without thought of what gain they may receive. I thank you. Yes, I am hungry."

Tayla took a dish and filled it with the stew her mother had made for her birthday. He relished it and ate it slowly, fighting the desire to devour it rapidly. He was famished but planned on eating again at the tavern later that night.

The Dragon forgot about Illona for the time being and just enjoyed being with good, simple folk who enjoyed the simple things in life. He knew they had no clue as to who and what he was. He had no desire to share any of that with them. The less they knew about him, the better. Better because of the role they would all play later.

Within an hour, he bade them good night and made his way to the tavern. Along the way, he would summon Vladis to meet with him. They had not seen each other in several years, yet he wondered why Illona had not used him to destroy Annara's family. He knew his thoughts alone were enough to summon the creature of the dark to him.

It was quiet as he rode alone. The only sounds were the wind in the trees and the sound of his horse's hooves making its clip clop sounds on the stones and packed earth. As he rode the dark and lonely road, he held a lantern for one who might see him traveling. Soon, a voice came to him, calling from the wood,

"Are you in need of company, old friend?"

The horse he rode stopped abruptly and whinnied. Then a figure dressed in funerary robes of black stepped out of the shadows and walked into the light from the lantern. "I heard you call to me, and I came." It was Vladis, Prince of Wallachia.

"It is comforting to know that you still recognize my voice."

"It is your thoughts I recognize. You have not uttered a sound since you left my family's villa. Yes, I know you told them as much of the truth as you can. I listened while outside. It is more than I can tell them. How could I? I am beyond their ability to believe in such creatures as I."

"Yet they do, my friend. I think they do, for they told me of their fear and the stories that abound regarding my two knights who preceded you. So, since I have returned and if the killings were to begin again, especially around here, I would be the first suspected."

"I understand Master. No blood shall be spilled upon my lands. I should say, 'what used to be my lands'. Now, they are Annara's lands but Illona will never give them up."

"My friend, my creature of the night, that is precisely why I have returned. I have come to make things right. I have visited my Order's headquarters in Rome. The High Council has directed me to clean up this pile of dung I have left behind. The biggest piece of dung is the one who resides in your castle. I want her to be the next victim."

"Master, I thought you would never ask." Vladis prepared to make for the castle.

Vojislav dismounted and walked the rest of the way along the snow-covered road to the tavern by the river, horse in tow, while he plotted and schemed with Vladis.

*   *   *

Illona usually slept alone. For a long while after Vojislav had left, she wondered if she should take another lover into her bed. After learning what she had from him, of the Order, of Set, she did not want to risk any serious relationship for she knew that someday, somehow, Vojislav would come walking back into her life.

Lately, since the winter had been very cold and the amount of firewood to be cut had diminished, Portia and the Princess had been sleeping together for purposes of warmth and comfort. Katerina and Magda adopted the same sleeping arrangements as their beds were very cold when slept in alone.

It would be spring in a few weeks, but one would never know it. This night was like many of the others, bitterly cold with winds. Both women were buried under thick furs, with woolen blankets next to their skin. Their sleeping attire was thick. Fur-lined sleeping caps were on their heads with mittens upon their hands. A fire blazed inside the fireplace, giving off the ambient light which flooded her bedchambers, but its heat quickly dissipated into the frigid air. The windows had no protection against the winds as the heavy fabric drapery did little to keep any heat inside the chamber. Her three hand maidens, though in different rooms, probably thought that if living in the castle provided warmth and comfort, they were at a loss as to tell exactly where it was.

Portia and Illona talked into the night making plans and deciding what to do about Annara's claim to her estate. Both women were childless and equally self-centered. Neither had ever made sacrifices regarding family or relationships. Portia was a beautiful woman who had broken many hearts, having been betrothed several times but backing out at the last minute for construed but nonetheless legitimate reasons. She was a masterful schemer and made a great ally as well as a formidable enemy.

Illona had not told any of her maidens about Vladis. This was her secret. No one knew. Only Vojislav shared that knowledge and she had not seen him since.

"It's been five years since Vojislav left. Annara and her family have lived up to their end of the agreement that the Friar Bartholomew arranged between you and them. Do you still feel that Annara is a threat to you, Princess?"

Portia wanted Illona to move on, since she personally did not feel Annara to be a threat anymore. Years of silence and no act upon Annara's part to break the pact agreed upon was enough to convince Portia that Annara was not a threat to Illona.

Illona, on the other hand, never forgave nor forgot her humiliation at the hands of her husband and his new wife. Though both parties had abided by the agreement, Illona still considered her the greatest threat to her claim on the estate. The estate had begun to prosper in the last few years only because she had kept Johannes on as the butler who should have been promoted as her administrator for Johannes was responsible for the progress of the estate.

Perhaps the most disconcerting thought she had on this cold night was the fact that she had not heard or seen Vladis in the last few years. His tomb was untouched, and there had been no killings as of late in the vicinity of the manor. She wondered what might have happened to him, other than that Vojislav might have returned and took him away, or worse, that the Baron Descondes had hunted Vladis down and disposed of him in the same manner as he had the two black knights. Good riddance she would have said, but the thought stayed with her. The notion that she could not know for sure irritated her.

Finally, she answered Portia's question. "No, I do not feel she is as great a threat as she once was. She has proven that her word is as good as anyone. She is trustworthy, I will agree to that. I have not seen any move on her part that would cause me to think my position is in danger. However, if something were to happen to her or those brats my ex-husband sired with her, I would not shed any tears. I would probably hold a feast to celebrate it. And the others...Brother Bartholomew, Johannes... Neither one is a threat. The friar has been too busy tending to his flock to consider me a danger to him. I suppose that is good. Johannes has done as well, keeping to his business, and staying out of mine. I think I taught them both a lesson when I tossed them both out on their ears. They came crawling back to me for they were destitute without my support. So, it seems I do in fact rule these lands."

"What are your plans now, my lady?" asked Portia.

"I am not sure. I have been thinking about it for quite a while. I wanted to marry Vojislav, but he rejected me for the wrong reasons. I thought I was exactly what he wanted in a wife and lover, but I was wrong. Do not ask me why, but I just know." A tear came to her eye after she had said this. For the first time in her whole life, she had regrets for her actions, for she knew it had cost her more than she ever wanted to pay.

*   *   *

The next night was to be the night that Vladis would confront Illona. Vojislav and Vladis spent the rest of the night planning it down to the last detail. Both were eager to see Illona get her just rewards not just because she was evil, but it was because what Set wanted. Vladis hated Illona for her part in his curse, but Vojislav was the real assassin. Vladis was more than eager to play his part. He was tired of spending his days in the wolf den.

To get an early start on their plan, Vladis returned to the castle, unannounced and undetected. He slipped through the door leading to the crypt and entered his tomb. Johannes had kept vigil over the door to the family crypt. It seemed as if it was never disturbed. He would check it every day, sometimes putting red brick dust on the door and checking for any slight disturbance the next day. There was never any sign that the door had been opened. For the last five years, no one had gone near it. Not even Illona. He knew she found the idea of her dead ex-husband walking around alive after sundown repulsive as well as frightening.

The sun left the sky, and the cold moonlight replaced the sun's last rays. The temperature dropped as Vladis awakened. He arose from his tomb and headed straight to the door leading into the castle interior. He wore his black funerary robes. Annara had also given his armor back to him so he was dressed in a manner such that anyone would have been frightened of him, dead or alive. His armor made the usual clanking sound of metal against metal as he stepped inside the hallway. Vojislav approached the checkpoint gatehouse. The guards recognized him from long ago and permitted him passage. He crossed the bridge over the river and proceeded to the main gate. The signal had been sent by the gatehouse to admit him. His horse made the solitary sounds of hooves hitting the stone flooring of the courtyard in front of the keep. Vojislav dismounted and entered the front door. Johannes met him.

"My lord, it has been a long time since you have entered this castle. It appears you have been traveling a great distance. May I announce your arrival?"

"Yes, by all means, please do so."

Within minutes, Vojislav found himself in the great hall, facing the woman whose last words had forbade him to return. Now, the silence between them was palpable, icy, and tense. Their eyes met while her court of maidens and loyal soldiers looked on, wondering who would speak first.

Vojislav looked worse for wear as his clothing was in near tatters and he looked tired from his travels. Nonetheless, his was a commanding presence as he stood before a woman who could not make up her mind as to how she felt about him.

Then, in the moments that seemed like an eternity to both, Illona's eyes began to tear up, and finally began to run down her cheek. That was when the Dragon knew he had her at a disadvantage. She still loved him, though she would never admit to it.

She smiled through her tears, saying to her cup bearer, "Bring the best wine we have. We have much to celebrate tonight."

Vladis and Vojislav had planned for this moment. After Illona embraced Vojislav, she invited him to sit with her at the feasting table. The steward poured the wine. Illona and Vojislav drank and talked with each other while a musician played quietly. Others of her court dined as well. The doors to the great hall, a place of meeting and feasting, opened quickly and violently, as if a great force was behind their opening. A figure in dark clothing stood alone in the doorway, as if it alone were the very reason for the heavy doors to exist.

Illona looked up and saw Vladis's silhouette against the light of the torches on the walls. He did not show his face yet.

Vojislav turned to look at the man who stood between the heavy doors of the great hall. He said to Illona, "Look, my dear! Behold the Prince of Wallachia, Prince Vladis! I understand you have not seen Vladis for all this time I have been away. It seems he was hiding from you. Why he should hide from you is beyond me. It should have been you hiding from him. I think he was waiting for me to return. We met on the road last night as I was approaching the castle. There was a lot to talk about. It seems that though you lost track of him, he did not lose track of you. The thing about vampires is that they are very patient. They have all the time in the world. They are powerful, patient, and passionate. And all can be used as weapons against their enemies."

"Vojislav, what do you mean? I want this creature away from this place. It is mine now. I have made my peace with Annara and she agreed to relinquish any claim she may have to the estate. He should not be here!" The sight of a vampire in her presence made her extremely uncomfortable, especially this one.

The members of her court whispered amongst themselves. They had not seen the face of him who had opened the doors so violently. The conversation between Illona and Vojislav seemed confusing to them.

The silhouette remained still in the doorway. Torches behind him hid details of his identity. The darkness concealed the details of his face, but Illona's memory did not fail her. She recognized the stance of her former husband. It was Vladis for sure. Vladis had returned.

Guards began to approach Vladis in the doorway. They were shocked to see their former master facing them. They were confused as to what to do. Was Princess Illona being threatened, as a servant had told them? They all knew her capacity for deceit.

Vladis waved them off, entering the room. He commanded the doors to close behind him which they did, by themselves. The guards outside tried to open the doors but could not. Vladis' power as a vampire had grown such that he could command inanimate objects to do his will. These were not the only gifts that he had managed to acquire. He had others as well. He could control weather, had the power to communicate with and to make wild animals do his bidding, could assume the body of an animal, such as a wolf or a bat. Tonight, he was the most frightening enemy of all to a woman…a man.

CHAPTER TWENTY-TWO

THE CONTINGENCY

Vojislav giggled between bites. "Yes, dear princess, your former husband has returned. And everyone here in this room will see he lives. I see so many mouths open, aghast that they are seeing living, sort of, proof that Prince Vladis is alive and therefore, he is the rightful ruler of these lands." Vladis was smiling with glee. He had Illona right where he wanted her.

She had no alternative but to agree that he was still the ruler of the estate. The rage began to burn inside her, as the anger flowed in her veins. Deep in her heart, she plotted to kill both, all of them, to include Annara, Josef and all her children. She wanted nothing more than to be rid of them all.

"Illona, calm yourself down. You are outmatched in every way possible. So, stop plotting against us and enjoy your wine. No one is going to die tonight. Since that subject has come up, let me say this. My Order back in Rome has decreed that you should die. You simply know too much. Anyone who knows of our existence and is not one of us is dangerous to us. We handle our enemies in but one way."

She turned to look at the Dragon. "So, you plan to kill me? When? How?"

Vojislav would not answer her. He continued to dine on the fare in front of him.

Johannes, ever vigilant to know everything going on inside the castle, walked towards the great hall. He knew that Princess Illona was not expecting Vojislav and wanted to see her reaction to seeing him again. Of course, he would report this to Brother

Bartholomew. Brother Bartholomew would report anything worth significance to the Bishop Janos of Plovdiv. He had regular correspondence with the Bishop regarding the status of the estate of the late Prince Vladis because the Emperor felt it vital to the Bulgarian empire to maintain the loyalty of all vassals within his borders.

As Johannes drew near to the entrance of the hall, the door opened slightly to allow him in. He saw a man standing in the doorway, dressed in black. He stopped suddenly and began to tremble. Still able to recognize his former master, he was aghast at seeing him in the flesh, walking, talking, breathing. But he was not breathing. His heart was not beating. For a vampire needs no heartbeat, no breath of air and no warmth to live as the undead. He needed only one thing to survive. Johannes was afraid to approach any closer. The prince turned to look at Johannes, smiling.

"Come closer, Johannes. Cast your eyes upon your master, or I should say, former master. Yes, I live."

Johannes could barely speak. He wanted to scream but nothing would come out. Any courage he had fled away the moment he had seen Vladis. Finally, he was able to utter words. "How, my Lord?"

"It is not important at this moment," Vladis said in a low voice. "Come, join my former wife and her lover. You should witness this historic event to take place. I think you may enjoy this."

Johannes did as he was told and slipped past Vladis into the light of the great hall. Everyone who was inside were also astonished that a man who everyone thought dead was now about to address them.

Finally, Vladis walked into the great hall. "I have no doubt you are surprised to see me, Illona. You cannot hurt me anymore, so do not conjure any evil you have left to persecute me. You already killed me once. I shall not allow you to do so again."

Illona turned to Vojislav, who sat next to her drinking her wine. He continued to eat from her table saying, "This is good. I was famished. I have not had a decent meal in quite a while. As you know, I have been on the road. Rome is far away, but I have returned and as you can see, so has my friend, Vladis. You two have much to discuss. I suggest you have this hall cleared at once. Otherwise, I will not be responsible for the feast he will make of all your guests and courtiers."

She felt threatened. "Yes, I think that would be the wise thing to do." She called for her steward to announce that dinner was over and the hall to be cleared of everyone."

He did so and a few minutes later, the hall was empty except for the four of them. Only Vojislav, Illona, Johannes were left to face Prince Vladis.

Vladis came closer, standing in front of the table. He did not sit, nor did he partake in any food or wine. "It has been very cold lately, has it not, Vojislav?"

Between gulps of food and wine, he answered, "Yes, it has. A tough place to be, out in the cold. Especially at this time of year. Spring is going to be late this year I feel." He continued to feast while Illona sat, staring at Vladis.

Vladis stared back at Illona, with icy eyes. "I do not feel cold. Nor do I feel warmth. In fact, I feel nothing regarding cold or hot. I have forgotten the feel of the sun on my face, or the coldness of mountain streams upon my bare feet. I only know regret. Sadness, loneliness, a sense of loss. That is the pain I have come to live with. That is what I feel. All that and hunger. I should probably say thirst. Yes, thirst. I drink my sustenance, Illona. That is my curse, woman. And you, Illona placed that curse upon me. You poisoned me with a chalice contaminated with another vampire's blood. You knew what effect it would have upon me. There was a price to be paid for that. You did not care that you have taken from me any shred of happiness I might have ever known."

Illona was quick to answer. "Since you acknowledge I did such an act as you say, I have control over you. So, I command you! Cease your existence in these parts and depart into the world, to wander for all eternity! I command you to do so."

"Such a will you possess, such arrogance that you think you can control me. But you have made a mistake. You did not turn me, for I drank from a chalice that contained the blood of Nefertiti, who was turned by the spirit of Set, which dwells inside

197

Vojislav. It is he who is my rightful master, not you. You, my former wife and tormentor, are merely a murderess."

Illona felt fear for the first time in a long time. "Vojislav, is this true?"

Set had informed the Dragon that they would not share power, especially the sharing of power over any vampires. Her former lover gulped down the last of the wine. "I am afraid it is completely true. You see, Vladis is the third vampire to ever exist. Vampires were created to aid the disciple of Set, that is me, and to serve me as their master." He swallowed the last bite. "My other two, Akhenaten and Nefertiti, were of royal blood as well. They were a king and Queen of a powerful kingdom. A vampire creates offspring by having their initiate drink of their blood. Nefertiti's blood runs in Prince Vladis' veins. And I, Illona, created the first two vampires well over two thousand years ago. So, you can see that Vladis is mine to control, not yours."

Illona stood up, ready to run for her life. "So, is this what our love has come down to? You used me! You never loved me!"

Vladis spoke, saying with a harsh voice, "Sit down, Illona. If anyone used anyone, it is you. And you have used everyone in this castle for your personal gain. Without exception, I might add. Even those pretty maidens you have following you around, they do your bidding. And now, justice comes for you."

Illona stood up, saying, "With your permission, I would like to retire to my chambers. You have said that no one will die tonight. I will trust you at your word, Vojislav." With that said, the woman turned and left the hall through an alternate exit. She went straight to her chambers where Portia, Magda and Katerina were waiting.

"Quickly, I need writing paper to get a message to someone. I am in deep trouble. My husband is back, literally from the dead and I fear he will kill me. I have but one option. I need to use his family as leverage."

She wrote down a message and asked that Portia get this to one of her henchmen as soon as possible. Portia dressed for the frigid night air and left the room, intent on completing the task for her mistress.

A guard at the armory was about to nod off when Portia came running in to the room. It was not the place that a woman would normally be found but Portia was adept at being places she was not expected to be.

"Princess Illona's instructions, written in her own hand! I am to give this message to you so that you can deliver it to your captain."

"He nodded and left his post to find the Captain of the Guard. He was the garrison commander who had served Vladis before but as of late, was accustomed to being with Princess Illona during her lonely moments. She also made her maidens available to him as well as a bonus intended to secure his loyalty.

As the guard approached him in the barracks, he held out the message to him. The captain could not read, which irritated him to no end that Illona would write to him. When he received the message in his hand, he unfolded it and saw a symbol. He knew exactly what the symbol meant. Based on a contingency plan that would be enacted upon the receipt of the message, he took steps to put it into action. Now, wheels were in motion that would change the world and history in the future to come.

Princess Illona was a clever one. Far too clever for any mortal ordinary man to conceive her to be. But the Dragon, evil in nature, possessed by an evil spirit, was more than a match. Set's plan, revealed to the Dragon, included many players. Many of those players had no idea of the role they were about to play.

Back in the great hall, Vojislav was smiling to himself as he was quite aware of everything that was happening. He knew the Captain of the Guard had left to arrest Annara's family and bring them to the castle. He also knew what Illona's plans were for them. A great evil was about to befall them. He was content to let it happen.

Within a couple of hours, the group arrived at the castle. Illona was notified of their arrival and hurried down to see them. She also posted guards with crossbows, armed with silver tipped bolts at key posts within the castle. She had the upper hand for the moment.

The group had arrived by cart. It was cold outside. The children were shaking from the weather. Annara demanded to know why they had been taken from their home. The Captain ignored her and when she insisted on answers, he demanded she be silent, after drawing his sword.

Soon, Illona met them. "So, you have arrived. I want you to know your husband is very much alive. I had not seen him for some time after Vojislav left for Rome. Now, he has returned, and I might add, he is not in a particularly good mood. I want to know if you still want to be with him. If so, what price are you willing to pay for that privilege?"

"Privilege?" Annara asked. "I am his wife, or at least I was. I know what he is and what he is not. I know he will not harm his family, but he will certainly harm you. You are evil, Illona! The whole world knows this. You may be assured justice will come to you."

"So, you know what he is, do you? Well, know this, before I am gone, you will know the pain of loss. First your children, then your husband. Every time I see you, I see the gloating look on your face that says you stole my husband from me. Your beauty and charm were as evil as anything I might have used to manipulate the Prince. For that, I want you to pay. I want you to remember the loss every day, all day, without ceasing."

She struck Annara with a hand that bore a large ring. Annara's mouth began to bleed. She turned to the Captain and nodded her head. The children were immediately seized by soldiers and thrown into the dungeon. Josef and Annara were seized as well and placed into different cells from the children.

Back in the great hall, Vladis and Vojislav talked. "Vladis, I have a request for you. You will not like it, but you must perform it. You cannot refuse."

"I am ready to do your bidding, my master."

"Do you have the chalice from which you drank?"

"Yes, master, I have it." He pulled it from behind his cloak.

Vojislav knew the vampire would never refuse to obey him.

"Then, open up your sleeve, and cut yourself, to allow your blood to flow into the cup."

Vladis did as he was ordered to do. He rolled up his sleeve and with a sharp fingernail, sliced open a vein. The vampire blood flowed silently into the cup, nearly filling it. The wound

200

healed immediately.

"Below, in the dungeons, there is a cell that contains the three maidens, Magda, Portia, Katerina who accompany Princess Illona. I have Princess Illona there, also imprisoned. Let us go to them and give your blood unto these four women. They have always been in darkness and tonight, they shall know nothing but the dark."

Vladis followed him to the dungeon cells. Vojislav was a master of deceit. He was able to transform the likeness of the three maidens and Illona upon the four children of Vladis. Vladis was completely unaware of what he was about to do. Instead of seeing his beloved children, he saw only what the Dragon wanted him to see.

The act of betrayal and deceit upon the vampire was a master stroke for Vojislav Rekvas. He had brought everyone together and was about to create four new vampires. Vladis thought he was punishing four evil women. Instead, he was creating four new vampires of his own children. The Dragon knew Illona would be pleased that Annara's children would have been turned but she was completely unaware that the Dragon only plays for his own gain.

The screams of the children begging for mercy and crying from being in absolute terror fell on deaf ears. Vladis could not see his children. He could not hear their cries to their father. They only knew their father forced them to drink of his blood from the same cup that had transformed a good man into one of evil.

A short distance away, Annara and Josef could hear the screams of their children. Both were crying out for someone to help them. When the noise subsided, both Annara and her father fell to their knees, exasperated and helpless to come to the children's aid. They cried for the rest of the night.

PART FOUR

THE CLANS

1216 AD

CHAPTER TWENTY-THREE

MEMORY

"My dearest Malcolm, now I can tell you my story, my real story. When we had talked in front of my fireplace in the library, I told you a story of how I was transformed into what I am now. When you read this, it will be the story of what I was. My gratitude for what you were able to do for me shall not be forgotten. But who is there left to remember, but you, your family, and my familiars? Memories are precious. Hold on to yours for they are your life.

My first memories as a vampire were true. What I told you about the cold dirt, the villager's attitudes, and such, was truth. As I said, my recollections were naïve. I saw and felt what happened but had no reasoning skills to process all that had happened to my brothers and sister and me.

When you are a vampire, memory becomes a gift. We forget much of our life before the darkness. Perhaps that is the real gift. Now, I have gone back, after all these centuries and extracted the memory of what those stones heard and saw. Much of it has fallen into unrecognizable ruin, but some stones still exist intact. They were used to build bridges and other structures. I found them. Again, one of the downfalls of being an immortal is you lose the memories of a mortal. As time goes by, they begin to fade away. The memories of an immortal are immortal.

I saw life through the eyes of a young, naïve, and innocent child. A female caught somewhere between being a girl and nearly a woman. Even back then, a girl was expected to change from being a child to a woman in one night. Usually, that was the night of her wedding. I never saw a night like that, nor had I experienced the joy or the sorrow of being in love.

In the fall of 1216, I died. Then, three days later, I was reborn along with my two brothers, Rascha and Othar, along with my baby sister, Prieta. When we rose from the dead, it was in my father's castle crypt. Other bodies were there, but they were long dead, and decayed. The crypt was sealed, but we managed to break through. My brothers and sister looked to me to explain everything that had happened. I was only fourteen, but I was the oldest and therefore they looked to me for answers. Only, I had none. I was as confused as anyone and my innocence in the matter made all four of us vulnerable.

Illona had lost no time in gathering anything of value and abandoning the castle, warning all others that if they valued their lives, they should do the same. When we arose, the castle was deserted. Almost.

One human had stayed behind in the castle. The only one who would know what had happened and who had no fear of what we had become...Vojislav Rekvas. I suspected he had planned on claiming the throne of Wallachia for himself now that the throne was empty. Perhaps, he would invite Illona back to the castle to marry. There was one problem. He had four new vampires to care for. She had no intentions of occupying the same castle with us. But, for a time, a brief period, she would do just that.

It was from him that we first learned who we were and why all had happened. He lied to us. It is from his lips that my original story was fabricated. He told us that our father had not married our mother. He told us that we were born out of wedlock and therefore could not be buried upon consecrated ground. The truth was that we were all legitimate heirs to the throne of Wallachia. Vojislav did not want us to know that. It would be quite some time before I would find out why the Dragon wanted us naïve to the fact that we were in fact nobility.

He explained our nature, the source of our power and the gifts that we might receive if we would only follow him and do his bidding. He also told me that I was different from any he had ever seen. The Dragon did not tell me why. Neither Akhenaten,

204

nor Nefertiti, not even my father had been like the vampire I had become.

I have mentioned my first memories. As for my first feelings, well, that was something else. It would be exceedingly difficult to describe the feeling of being brought back from the dead. Some things you feel, other things you do not. Sometimes, you can choose to feel something, such as cold or heat, but if you choose not to, you will not. There is an exception to that. Fire. Ice does not hinder us at all. But fire, well, that is a reminder of something to come. It is as you said, Malcolm. Anything that serves to remind us of our damnation comes at us with a fury we find difficult to face.

As a newly "born into darkness" vampire, it was not like learning to walk again. All newborns are eager to seek out their mother and nurse from her breasts. However, there was no mother for us. Adjusting to the continuous hunger for blood seemed to be the biggest challenge. It was a continuous, unrelenting aching to slake that thirst for living blood. I thought it would drive me mad because I held off for the longest time.

I wanted my first victim, my first prey to be Princess Illona. She had left in a hurry, no doubt to return to her home in Moldavia. I wanted to go after her. I wanted to taste and feel the fear she would have in her heart. I knew I would smell it in her skin and hair before I took her. Fear gives the victims a special flavor. As salt gives flavor to mortal food, fear does the same to blood. I knew she would tremble with so great a fear it would fill the air around her. Any living thing would sense it, but an undead thing would find it irresistible.

Alas, the Dragon forbade it. He said it was a courtesy he felt obliged to give to the woman he said he had loved but even he was denied that special joy of someone who would give all they had to be with him. I came to know this all too often to describe the heartbreak I felt when I could not obtain their commitment. I would come to know love, but mostly the heartbreak of it. As you read on, you will come to know my torment regarding that subject.

I was not so inclined to follow the Dragon's every whim and wish. As I said, he was a liar and a thief. He had robbed me of my life, my happiness, and my family. And he had done it through an evil woman, the worst I have ever known. I have known quite a few, but if evil were royalty, she would be a Queen.

The first few months we spent at the castle. It was now deserted for word had gotten out that its occupants and owners were now of the undead and no one would approach it except by day.

The friar, Brother Bartholomew, was a kind man. He was also wise. He confronted us during an evening when he was asked to ward off the evil spirits that inhabited the place. The account of it is as follows."

*   *   *

It was close to winter. The days were growing shorter, making the nights longer. During the day, some of the villagers wanted to go into the castle to see if there were any other items they could take to use. The castle still had tools, weapons, and farming implements as the stables and barns were untouched. The granary was still well stocked. Tayla stayed in her father's chambers while her siblings found rooms of their own. They knew few if any would approach the castle. At least in the light of day, they would have had a fighting chance. At night, when the sun went down, they stood no chance.

The friar agreed to go with some villagers to take items from the castle. He warned them that it was the same as stealing. Their argument was, "Just who are we stealing from?" Bartholomew had no argument against that except that to him, the entire castle was a crypt. And to take from it, was the same as grave robbing.

The rumors abounded about us, our deaths, and our new existence. No one knew the rules by which we existed. The issues about vampires regarding sunlight and the darkness were unknown to them. We had only learned of it recently.

The sun was barely above the horizon when they entered the main hall. There were no torches that would customarily light up the hall, no fire burning in the massive firepit of stone against the wall. Only darkness. And silence.

"Priest, we brought you here for you shall ward off the evil that resides here. Do your work!" The men who came with him were very superstitious. They knew of the creature who had roamed the countryside, taking the blood of victims during the night. They feared the same may inhabit the walls of the very castle they were here to take from.

The villagers were carrying torches and examined all the items inside, including the furniture. All the wall ornaments had been taken save for the velvet draperies that had been used by the grandfather Josef to wrap the bodies of his dead grandchildren down in the castle crypt. No one would touch those. It was not long before Bartholomew realized these men were looking not for what they could use, but what they could sell to profit from.

The sun faded from the sky. Tayla, Rascha, Othar and Prieta awoke from their sleep of the dead. Immediately they sensed that they were not alone in the castle of their father. Their father was no longer with them. Their mother had left the region with a merchant of sorts. Their grandfather had died the day after laying them to rest in the castle crypt. The only two alive who knew the complete story of what had transpired were the Dragon, and Princess Illona. Perhaps Brother Bartholomew knew the story as well, though not as intimately as the two previously mentioned.

Each night, the Dragon would seek out the children to convince them that he was now their new master and that he would take care of them. However, Tayla viewed him with suspicion and would not follow him blindly as other vampires may have done. She was different than them.

On this night, The Dragon had not come to them. Usually, he would bring them someone to feed upon. Their visitors had the potential to be a feast.

As for the villagers and the friar, they knew evil existed within the walls of the castle, but the form of it was unknown to them. Once outside the great hall, they traveled down the hall towards the kitchen. They intended to take as much food as possible.

Tayla stood ready to confront them. The other children stood behind her in the shadows. When the party approached their position, she began to speak. Her voice was strong, with the ring of authority.

"I know who you are. You are the priest of the village, are you not?"

The friar stopped in his tracks, with some villagers behind him. Looking around him in the darkened walls, he could see no one. The young vampire could see him perfectly as well as hear his breathing. She could do so for the others as well. Her brothers and sister were frightened as they hid in the shadows. The young girls voice frightened the priest and his party of men so greatly, some of them drew swords.

Tayla spoke again from the shadows. "Bartholomew, do not fear me, for I am not the evil that resides in this place."

The young vampire told him he was not to come there anymore. "Bartholomew, my brothers and my sister are changed now. We are different in ways we find so hard to understand. Leave us alone. We did not ask to become what we are. We mean no one any harm. The evil you should be frightened of is not here, but I suspect he will return. I have no quarrel with you. Leave this place now. Take what you have in your hands now, and leave, but do not return, for if you do, you do at the peril of your own lives."

For a fourteen-year old, Tayla was well spoken. During the Middle Ages, superstitions ran high, regarding spirits, demons, devils, and the like. In such matters, the young vampire was to find out that she and her siblings would be at the top of the list.

Bartholomew knew the voice of who spoke to him. "Tayla, child of Annara and Vladis, Prince of Wallachia? Is it you who speaks to me?

"It is."

"Child, come out of the shadows so that I can see you!"

"No, friar. I will not, not because I fear you, but I fear what I might do to those who fear a voice in the darkness. Leave this place."

"Child, is there a time or a place where we may speak, on neutral ground, of your choosing? I must speak to you to explain matters of great importance." He was concerned for the souls of these children he had known since their birth.

Tayla sensed his concern. The young vampire replied. "I will let you know. For now, leave at once. For your own safety, do as I ask."

*   *   *

"Dearest Malcolm, the friar, Bartholomew had been kind to my family. I did remember him slightly before my transformation. My mother spoke well of him. When it came to my interacting with mortals, my priority was survival. Instantly, we knew we were feared and despised. When fear and ignorance meet evil, the results are disastrous to one party or the other. I only wanted understanding, and knowledge of whom I had become. That would take quite some time. Since the beginning, I only wanted to live in peace. I had no quarrel with the church, or humanity for that matter. I had not chosen sides in this matter. It was chosen for me. My brothers and sister were seemingly more at a disadvantage. They would never come to understand what I felt. Perhaps even at fourteen, I had maternal instincts. Maybe it was because I loved my family more than anything else that I knew. I wanted to protect them, even in death. How does one protect something that has nothing to fear but those who fear it? Perhaps Brother Bartholomew could help me."

*   *   *

One morning, the friar, Brother Bartholomew awoke to find a hand-written note lying next to his head on a pillow. The room he slept in was as meager as one could get. A small, box-shaped room in the back of the village chapel. A bed of pine-needles covered by the hides of several deer, formed his mattress. A pillow of cloth, stuffed with dried beans served a two-fold purpose, for sleep and for use when soup needed to be made. Blankets of fur and wool covered him while he slept a fitful sleep to stay warm during the cold nights. There was no heat source in the room save for a lamp. The room was for sleeping only. He intended to find a brazier soon to increase the warmth on very cold nights.

He woke to find the crudely written parchment to state "Tonight, meet me at the graveyard where we were refused burial. Come alone."

209

He smiled. It was her way of giving him insurance against attack. He would stand on consecrated ground while she would not. It would be like talking across a backyard fence. They would be able to communicate without trespassing against each other. It was brilliant, he thought. He prepared for the meeting. The need for him to be alone was appropriate since the villagers were highly suspicious and would never tolerate her presence.

The sun went down, as well as the temperature. Both began the journey to the destination. Her brothers and sister wanted to go with her, but she refused, stating that she must meet alone, and they would talk with Vojislav when he came to feed them. They had become vampires with voracious appetites.

On her way, she found an unlucky person who had spent too long at a tavern and now was inebriated such that he passed out on the road. In a few minutes he was likely to freeze where he fell. She made a quick meal of him and continued her journey. The tavern and inn that had been across the river from the castle ceased to do business. Now, people frequented another tavern farther away from the castle. The bridge that had been the main access to the castle was closed and no one dared enter the castle, day, or night. The fields would continue to be farmed in the spring, but the granaries used were far away from the castle. The land needed a ruler. Vojislav was intent on making it his own.

Bartholomew entered the cemetery with his rosary wrapped around the same wrist carrying the torch. Around his neck, a leather thong that held a large wooden crucifix. He was wrapped in a dark, fur-lined cape with a hood to protect his shaved head from the bitter cold. The snow covered the ground, but the markers of the gravesites were visible enough that he would not be standing directly upon one. Soon, Tayla appeared to him at a comfortable distance. She carried a lantern so that he could see her.

"Tayla, thank you child for seeing me. We have much to discuss. I do not think that all can be answered in one night, but we shall try, can we not? I may not have the answers you seek but I can be a liaison between you and the village. I see you understand about the consecrated ground. I have an answer for that."

His torch burned bright in the breezy night air. The cold caused the friar's teeth to chatter such that when he talked, he stuttered.

Tayla was dressed in a black cape, one that belonged to her father. It was large on her. She wore little under it, but the cold did not affect her as it did the priest.

"Bartholomew, I have come to find answers. I know my questions far outnumber the answers I may walk away with tonight. My first question is why us? Why were my brothers and sister and I killed? What did we do that we deserved such a death? And why can we not stay dead? Is this life, or non-life our punishment being who we are?"

"My child, I can only say that a great evil has befallen all the children of Annara and Vladis. I know that there are two forces in this world, light and dark. You have been seduced toward the forces of darkness. I know this was not your choice. I remember you always as a bright and cheerful child, one that I knew would be blessed with a wonderful life. I know this because I knew your parents. They were wonderful people. I did not know that your father had been taken to the dark side. I was there when he was poisoned, for I saw him die. I also know who did it and who she was in league with. The same man who I have seen arrive at the castle late in the day and even at night. I have always thought that Vojislav Rekvas was an evil man."

"Bartholomew, he has told us that we were bastards, that our parents were not married and as such, we have no claim to the throne of Wallachia. Is this true?"

"No child," he said, shivering. "It is not true. I was there when your parents married. It was a real marriage, but there were issues that young children would not understand. Your father had obligations to the Emperor. Illona still resided in the castle as part of an obligation of your father so he could still honor a security pact between his country and Illona's country. The only thing that was not real was the relationship between your father and Princess Illona. He loved your mother very much, just as he loved his children."

Tayla stepped closer. She seemed to know exactly just how far she could approach and not be on consecrated or holy ground. "I want to know where my father is. Why has he left us?"

Bartholomew could barely hold his sadness in. "What has Vojislav told you?"

Tayla answered, "Lies, I suppose. His answer was that my father left because he could not endure the shame of knowing what he had done to his children."

The priest, stamping his feet to stave off frostbite, answered the young vampire, "That is partly true, young lady. Your father came to me while you were yet in the ground. He confessed he did not see you but Illona and her three maidens. He was bewitched into believing he was at last doing some good in the world by ridding it of four evil women. That responsibility falls upon Vojislav Rekvas. He is evil, child. You must not trust him, not for a moment. Nothing good will come of all this."

"Am I damned, priest? Are my brothers and sister beyond hope of salvation? Is there nothing that can be done?"

Bartholomew held his hands to his face, to breathe his warm breath upon them and to protect his face. "Child, I will pray for all of you. All of this is very unfamiliar to me. I cannot believe that our Lord can say 'There is no hope for you' when you have done nothing deserving of such a fate."

Tayla was saddened by his opinion. "So, we are damned. Vojislav said we would never grow old or die. We only require the blood of the living. He told us a lot of things regarding our new existence. I behold an ugly future, Brother Bartholomew. Except, you are no longer my brother. To me, you are prey now. Thank your God that I have dined upon the living already tonight and that you stand on holy ground, where I cannot go. That is your salvation." She turned and walked away into the darkness, leaving the lantern upon the ground.

The friar, full of fear, resolved that he stay in the sanctity of the cemetery for the full night. He used his torch to build a fire so he could keep warm. He also ran out to grab the lantern and ran back as quickly as he could. He spent the freezing night in the graveyard, shivering. The skies were clear and the moon shined upon snow already upon the ground. He was afraid to fall

212

asleep for he feared he may not wake up. Eventually, slumber overtook him.

The next morning, he woke to find himself bundled up in his cape. He was very stiff, but he was alive. He had dressed for the night and was thankful he had done so. The fire had burned down several times so when it did, he went in search of more wood.

As he left, he could see Tayla's footprints in the snow outside the confines of the cemetery. He also could see the footprints of three others there. The prints were small, like those of children. He knew the others had been there as well.

When he had returned to his chapel, he immediately penned a letter to the Bishop of Tarnovo. He wrote, "The evils we talked about, though quite rare yet very real, are here. I have personally spoke with one. She is but a child, of about fourteen years. There are four in all, siblings of each other and children of the late Prince of Wallachia. Our conversation was brief, but lengthy enough to confirm our worst fears. The legends are true. These secrets that the Church holds, will not be secrets for long if something is not done about these creatures. They are controlled by the same entity you and I discussed. This entity is particularly evil and may be more of a threat to the Church than the others. I await instructions as to the matter of dispatching and cleansing of this land. These are truly supernatural creatures. I pray this reaches you without interception. In Our Lord's name, Bartholomew"

*   *   *

Several weeks later, the courier who Brother Bartholomew dispatched to carry his letter arrived in Tarnovo. Going straight to the office of the Bishop, he delivered the letter. The Bishop read the letter to himself in front of the messenger, telling him to wait for he wanted to know if he needed an urgent reply.

He immediately grabbed a quill and a sheet of parchment and quickly scribbled a response to the message. He folded it, and melted the wax upon it, sealing it with the stamp of the office of the Bishop.

He handed it back to the courier, saying, "Make haste for this day is a great day for the Lord's work to be done."

CHAPTER TWENTY-FOUR

THE POWER OF SILVER

"Dearest Malcolm, the Bishop sent a message to the Emperor and one to the Church in Rome. The Church in Rome was wise to the existence of the *Order of the Dragons of Set*. The word was out and the truth of my brothers, sister and myself were no longer a secret. Of all the men I have known, and I have known quite a few, is that Vojislav was the evilest of men. For a woman, Illona gave him fair competition. Make no mistake, the personality of the Dragon is pure evil. Anything he does, is for his own purposes. He cannot be trusted. I learned this in the most difficult of circumstances.

Vojislav began to spend much of his time away from us trying to patch things up between him and Illona. Vojislav was not young in those days. At first, she would have nothing to do with him, but he persisted. Vojislav was determined to get what he wanted...an heir. He needed one for his spirit to live on through his body. Love affects even the most wicked. I think he did have feelings for her, selfish ones. If he decided it would not work out, he would turn us loose upon her. Once he had an heir, he would not need Illona any longer.

He had bedded many women but being who he was, he had not married until he was told to do so. Set had already refused to allow the Dragon to take Illona for a wife, but Vojislav was a rebellious one. Blindly, he did disobey his master when told to do something. Often, he stretched the patience of the Dark Lord. In this matter, he had stretched it too far."

*　　　　*　　　　*

The young vampires had been left alone for nearly a week. They were hungry and went out at night to find victims to take. Tayla had learned where to find people who would most likely be alone and to look for those who would not be missed so easily. These were the days of the Crusades. Travelers, pilgrims and the like who were already far from home were good targets.

During the day, some members of the staff were coming back to the castle. They would notice things that had come back into the castle each day. Supplies were being restored, but there was no one there during the night. The children were gaining in independence. Tayla decided they did not need this man who claimed to have power over them. The only one who would have power over them should be their father since it was his blood they had drank from the chalice. But they could not find their father. Finally, early one evening, just as the sun had gone down on a snow-covered horizon, Vojislav came to the castle.

"Children! Children! Come out and see me!" he shouted. The children came out from the shadows to face him.

"Ahh! There you are. I have news for you! Soon, this castle will be bright and cheerful again. I am going to inhabit this castle and Illona will be my bride. She and I are going to be married. I will be the new prince and she will be the Princess of Wallachia. So, children, what do you have to say about that?"

Tayla, being the oldest, knew this was wrong for him. "By whose authority do you presume to take the throne of Wallachia. There are many noblemen out there who will contest your claim on the throne. You may do so only with the blessing of the Emperor."

Vojislav grew tired of the insolence from the young girl. "Authority? Why, by my own, little one! You question my claim? Do you?"

Tayla, spread her feet and folded her arms in a defiant posture. "My father is still a vampire, is he not?"

"He is! And I have him hidden away where you cannot find him. The throne is lost to him. And to you, his children!" Laughing, he stormed out of the hallway and made his way to the kitchen and to start a fire in the great hall.

215

Tayla looked at her brothers and sister. "Well, we shall see about that! This man has destroyed the family we knew once. He is the cause of our misery, he and that woman." Her brothers and sister looked at her with yearning eyes, knowing that whatever happened, their older sister would take care of them. The maternal instincts she inherited from her mother ran strong in her for she would protect them, teach them, and lead them. They followed her every move now. They knew she looked out for them. Their mother had taught them well to always look up to their beautiful sister.

They spent the rest of the night away from Vojislav and scouring the depths of the castle, top to bottom, to find a trace of their father. Finally, they arrived in the dungeons, to the very cell where it had all taken place. There they found the chalice, lying on the cell floor. Tayla bent over to pick up the vessel of gold and horn. When she did, she received a vision of that event that had turned them. It was as if she relived it. She threw the chalice down and began to cry. The others tried to comfort her. The sight of it brought back the sounds of their screams and their anguish. Most of all, she could hear more screaming coming from down the corridor to another cell. She went to that cell and the others followed her. Able to see in the dark very well, she spied something lying upon the stone floor. Upon the floor, a piece of cloth had been left behind. It had belonged to her mother. It had her mother's blood upon it. Tayla picked it up and kept it close to her. It was the only connection she would ever have with her mother for her mother was now far away.

Still, she wondered where her father was. All the children did. If their father were close by, he could tell them what had happened. She yearned for her father's counsel, but he had not been seen since their transformation. The children wanted to know why he did such a thing to them. Tayla knew that Vojislav could tell them but was not about to tell them.

Several weeks later, Tayla's worst fears came true. The evil former wife had returned to her former home. She arrived during the daylight hours and when the children awoke from their death sleep, they were summoned to Tayla's chambers (formerly the

216

chambers of the Prince of Wallachia). The Dragon was waiting in her room, sitting idly for Tayla to awaken.

She rose from the box lying on the floor of her father's chambers. It was dark in the room, except for the candle that burned on a small table. The window showed a darkened sky with a slightly orange horizon, indicating it was past sundown.

"Sleep well?" He fiddled with beautiful dagger that he kept sheathed on his belt. "Tell the others to come here now."

Reluctant to do any of his bidding, she felt it best that her siblings be included to hear what he had to say. The other children arrived soon afterwards. The Dragon had them lined up such that they looked as though facing a strict disciplinarian. Vojislav set the rules for them concerning the Princess Illona. He forbade any of the children to even approach her.

"As you may have surmised by now, we have a new occupant of the castle. Not new, but a former occupant. You all know her. Your hatred of her is not new either. Therefore, I absolutely forbid any contact with her. You shall not approach her, touch her, talk to her, or attempt to contact her through others. I am the Dragon…the disciple of Set and I have the power over all of you. I can dispense pain and misery the kind that only those of your kind can experience. Do not tempt me to demonstrate my power."

Tayla's hatred for her was nearly uncontrollable. The others were willing to obey Vojislav, but not Tayla. She was different, mainly because she was able to resist Vojislav's will and to think independently.

Earlier that day, Vojislav busied himself with directing new staff in their duties for running the castle. He had letters written to the Emperor declaring himself the new Prince of Wallachia, and his intentions to marry Illona, keeping the security pact alive. He had covered all avenues and all contingencies for anyone who might dispute his claim to the title. Annara's marriage record was confiscated from the chapel, Bartholomew was threatened to keep silent, and the heirs to the throne of Wallachia were dead, to speak of. Bartholomew was not about to keep silent for too long.

Couriers had left the castle enroute to the Imperial capital to deliver the dispatches. Those men had headed west, while another group was coming to the castle from the northeast.

Illona had lunch in the great hall with Vojislav that day. They talked about their plans. Illona was nervous. She knew that the children still inhabited the castle. They would be waking later that day when the sun left the sky. She also knew what they would want to do to her. Vojislav assured her that she had nothing to worry about. He said he had power over them as well.

She had an insurance policy though. It was Vojislav's idea. The most valuable thing to the new, young vampires was their one connection to their past life…their father. Their mother was now gone, certain that she would never see her children again. Fortunately, she would never see them as they are now.

Vojislav had to prove to his new prospect of a bride that he was willing to do anything to win her love, even betray his friend. He had already done so by tricking Vladis into turning his own children into creatures such as he was. She was almost convinced, but not quite. When Vladis realized what he had done, he was overcome with grief. He could not face Annara or Josef. He wanted to kill both Vojislav and Illona, but the Dragon had the power over him. His will was not his own.

Vampires are powerful creatures…far more powerful than humans. The issue of who controls them is simple. The one they can trace their lineage to is their ascendant. The ascendant will usually always be another vampire. But, in the case of the Dragon, he would be the ascendant for Vladis, as Vladis would be the ascendant to the children. Vojislav had been telling the children the lie that he and he alone had this power. If this were true, then the children would have naturally sought out Vojislav. But they did not. They sought out their father.

As the lies began to multiply from Vojislav, he would find fewer and fewer friends to trust him. None of the young vampires trusted him, especially when they learned what he had done to their father. Illona trusted him but within the limits of what she could do to protect herself. The staff whom he had just hired trusted him only if he could pay them. The reputation and honor of the man who had helped defeat the Byzantine army was now greatly damaged. The one who the Dragon was supposed to trust above all else, the Dark Lord, had been disobeyed. Deep in his heart, he could feel the rift between him and the one whose allegiance was sworn to.

The sun had gone down, and Vojislav had told the children about the new arrangement between him and the Princess Illona. He knew it would not set well with them, but he had something they did not know about. He had Vladis as captive, which would dominate the will of the children. He knew the next day, their father, Prince Vladis, would arrive.

He planned on impregnating Illona immediately after marriage. His gift of sight told him when she would be fertile and the most likely time to conceive. Though Set had told him not to marry her, she had a certain magic, a power over him. No one had ever affected him in such a way. It was the kind of power a woman possesses if a man is willing to risk everything for her. Vojislav reasoned that if she turned out to be a good wife, contrary to what Set had told him, he would let her live and raise the child to be the next Dragon. If she turned out to be exactly the kind of woman Set had warned him of, he would dispose of her and by doing so, repair his relationship with Vladis and the children. Then, he would have five vampires at his disposal. Of course, he knew the High Council in Rome would have something to say about this. Vojislav had plans for that time as well.

Finding the cloth with her mother's blood upon it saddened Tayla greatly. Was she hurt? Was she still alive? Where had she gone? All this depressed the young vampire such that all she wanted to do was get away...Away from the castle, Vojislav, and most of all Illona. To have to face Illona would be having to face defeat.

Tayla left the castle to search for blood. She took flight from the courtyard, soaring into the dark sky above the castle. The frigid air did not cause her any discomfort. The loneliness she felt now seemed to freeze her heart. Her mind and spirit called out to her father. She yearned for a connection to him. He had turned her, as well as his other children. Surely, he could hear her cries to him. As she looked to her rear, she could see her siblings were not far behind her.

Though it was dark, they could see easily into the night. They flew over the frozen landscape of forests and fields that were covered in white snow. Within minutes, a road appeared with fresh tracks upon it. They were heading in the direction towards the castle. Changing directions to follow the road, they soon found a group of six soldiers who had just finished making camp, just off the road, while escorting a wagon. The soldiers were of Moldavian origin. Tayla thought perhaps they were escorting property that belonged to Princess Illona. Landing ahead of the wagon, they decided to take the opportunity. They swooped in and took all six soldiers. The soldiers delayed reacting for they saw four children, not four vampires. They were in as much shock as they were in fear. They managed to put up a fight for a while but soon, the vampires were able to overcome them.

Afterwards, they looked around, noticing the wagon and its covered contents. Curiosity got the best of Tayla, so she decided to look inside the wagon, which was covered by a large canvas cloth. The contents revealed boxes and chests of personal items belonging to the princess, but there was also a long box, wrapped with chains. The children looked at each other.

"Why would a box be wrapped in chains?" asked Rascha.

"Probably to keep us out!" said Othar.

"Or, to keep something in!" chimed in Prieta.

"Shall we, my brothers and sister? Shall we break these chains and find out?" asked Tayla.

"Yes, let us find out!" Prieta giggled as she grabbed a section of chain and began to pull.

The children were not strong enough to pull the chains apart, so they looked around for tools. The gift of strength had not fully developed. There were four horses pulling the wagon. They harnessed the chains to the horses in such a way that two horses pulled against the other two in opposite directions. It did not take long for the chains to show their weakest link.

They immediately worked to unwrap the box. It was very heavy and finally, were able to pull against the nails that had been driven into the sides, sealing it.

They could see something moving, as if struggling to get out of the box. The more they could see the struggling, the more zeal they took in tearing the box apart. Finally, the source of the struggle took shape. It was their father, wrapped in a cloak, and secured with a chain of silver around his waist. As they pulled the cloak from his face, they could see his tongue had been removed. This was why he could not speak to them. They quickly realized the chain of silver held a power over him. Illona had been keeping their father as a prisoner and the Dragon had betrayed their father once more by showing her how.

Rascha was shocked at his father's appearance. He had never seen his father in such a way and felt the pain when he touched his father's face. There was a lot of dried, coagulated blood on his face and lips.

Othar was confused as he reached out to touch his father lying in the box. He too felt the pain as his senses detected the pain his father felt. The pain of losing one's tongue was bad enough, but the pain of betrayal was the worst.

Prieta reached out to touch his face as well, and she immediately began to cry. "Oh, Father!" she wailed.'

Tayla reached in to break the chain of silver. The chain was small, and weak, but was strong enough to nullify the powers of a vampire. She hissed as the metal burned her fingers. She wondered why the metal burned her, then cast the chain away. The power of the chain taught Tayla a valuable lesson. Silver was her enemy. It could defeat her and deny her of her powers. It denies vampires of all their powers.

Her father's strength returned to his body upon his release from the chain. He immediately sprang from the box, mounted one of the horses and rode away as if he had an appointment with the devil towards the castle. He had said not one word, but his tongue regenerated before he rode away. As the horse gathered speed, the children heard him saying, 'Tonight it ends!"

CHAPTER TWENTY-FIVE

HIDING

"Dearest Malcolm, when my brothers and sister often quarreled with me over who should reign over the clans, it was times like this that I had to remind them of when the question of who owned their loyalties became an issue. I was surprised how easy they forget, but then, I would find out about things I had forgotten until I had the chance to use the gift of extraction.

I surmised that Vojislav and Illona would sleep together that first night back in the castle. He wanted to bed her in the most determined way, but she was reluctant. As I had mentioned before, he was no longer a young man. After a while, with much foreplay, he lit a fire inside her that had not been lit for a long time, if ever. By my estimate, they were exhausted as they had been making love off and on most of the night. In my experience, a man will say anything when he is in the act of sex. I never confuse sex with love. To continue receiving access to it, a man will say anything and promise you anything you desire, even if it were not in his power to give. Many a maiden has lost her virtue with the promise of a commitment of love and marriage, only to find out they were empty words…Words spoken out of haste, with no thought of the consequences that follow them. Up until the revelation from Bartholomew, I had thought of my brothers and sister, as well as myself, as bastards, born out of wedlock, born with no father or means to support us. Out there, there were others, real women who endured broken hearts and broken souls, desperately seeking to find one whose words are truthful. They always seek one who has compassion and the ability to love. It is a story told all too 223 often. Down through the ages, whether it was expected or not, I suppose all women at one time experience the heartbreak of the dishonesty of men. For some reason, I guess I still believed I would find true love one day. Only I, as a vampire would know for sure if he really wanted me. If he were lying, I would know it. And I would kill him for it."

*   *   *

The vampire children were quite convinced that their father's thirst for revenge had overtaken his thirst for blood. It was evident that they were one and the same. They scrambled to follow their father back to the castle. This was going to be a show to see, they all thought in unison. They flew off in the direction of the castle. Not long afterwards, they found the horse their father rode upon and then abandoned, as he had regained his ability to fly. As they flew, they spoke to each other without talking. Able to read each other's thoughts, Tayla schooled them on how many times the Dragon had lied to them. She reminded them of not just the lies, but the motivation behind them. They were to be used, like tools, weapons in his war against the good things they had always believed in. All the children felt the Dragon had evil purposes for them, of which they did not want any participation. They made the decision not to have him be the one who would choose for them, who would decide their destiny. If they were as powerful as they suspected they were, why could they not choose their own path? They would take from who they wanted, without the care of exposing the Dragon, his mission, and most importantly, the *Order of the Dragons of Set*.

It took a long time to reach the castle. The children had taken an enormous amount of time finding victims and taking them by force. By this time, dawn was beginning to break. They had been far from the castle when they intercepted the Moldavian soldiers. They arrived to find some of the earliest risers of the staff up and preparing to cook breakfast and perform the early morning chores.

The staff had been informed of the nature of the vampires and were assured of their safety if they did not have contact with them. Still, the staff managed to use their superstitious remedies

223

against the vampires, such as charms and talismans to ward them off. Tayla laughed at all of that but still, the children felt compelled to honor Vojislav's agreement and decree that none of the castle's staff were to be touched or harmed in any way. The staff's superstitions and beliefs were only reinforced by the mercy of the children not to attack them.

They rushed to their coffins, compelled by the coming of the sun's rays, eager to sleep the sleep of the dead. Here, in the darkness, covered by the lids of their sleeping boxes and wrapped in their shrouds of different colors of velvet, the children felt safe. They did not fear retribution. After all, they had done nothing wrong according to their new nature. They were hungry, they found prey and took them. The fact that they had uncovered Vojislav and Illona's secret regarding the disposition of their vampire father, Prince Vladis, was irrelevant to them.

*　　　　*　　　　*

It was late morning after the couple's first night in the castle together. The couple's bed was in shambles. He was spent from drink and sex, reeking of the smell of both. She was exhausted as well and neither wanted to come down for breakfast. Both were oblivious to the fact that their secret was out and loose. The coming night would be an interesting one at the very least.

The castle was busy that morning as the weather dictated preparations be made. The weather had turned bad as a blizzard had arrived. Herds of livestock were being shuffled into the many barns inside the castle walls. Firewood was being gathered from all possible sources. The horse that Vladis had rode partially to the castle had found its way to the front gates.

They told the chamber maid to go away and let them sleep. By noon, the maids came with their meals to deliver them to their rooms. In their lifetime, none of the staff who had worked there before had seen such raw intimacy between the master and the mistress of the castle. The moaning coming from behind the thick wooden door of her chambers was annoying to the staff who stood outside during the night. Few if any of them slept that night.

After Vladis had died, the first thing that Illona had done was to remove Annara's name from the door, along with the coat of arms of Prince Vladis. Neither name was now on the door. When she arrived back to claim the castle again, she commissioned the blacksmith to build a mold of her family's coat of arms from iron. Once complete, it would be hung upon the door. She would add Vojislav's name to it when she felt she could completely trust him. As of now, even with all the events of the night before, she still did not feel that she could. She was right. Holding back was something she was accustomed to. She had never given her heart, not one piece of it, to Vladis. She had never met a man whom she despised as much as him. She had considered whether it was a righteous hatred of him or was it because she had been forced to marry someone not of her own choosing. Because these rules were dictated by men, perhaps it was men in general whom she hated.

Illona finally rose, asking for her servants to prepare her a hot bath. Though it was cold outside, the feel and the cleansing of the hot water was soothing to her entire body. Was she pregnant, she wondered? Time would tell. It was her second day back at the castle.

Later, she asked that Vojislav take a bath also. In those days, hygiene was not a priority. Especially for men. The night before, she had smelled odors that she felt few women had ever smelled and was not looking forward to experiencing the same this coming night.

Vampires have a special, yet keen sense of smell. They can smell the usual things but also, they can smell emotions. Emotions such as fear, passion, happiness, and anger. As Tayla and the other children, slept, their gifts of the sense of smell began to refine themselves. When they would waken, they would be able to find many of their senses enhanced.

When the children rose that evening, they could sense their father was still in the castle. He was in the crypt hiding while they were in their rooms. Tayla still kept her father's room, even though Vojislav had his eyes on it and wanted it for his own. The children could hear their father summoning them to the crypt. They would not disappoint him by delaying their appearance.

225

*   *   *

The snow began to pile up outside. Fierce and ferocious gusts of icy cold winds tore through the outside walls and ramparts while those inside huddled around fires or braziers of coals trying to keep warm. Animals were brought inside, to keep them from freezing. The barns became full while any other place of shelter from the cold became highly prized. The most prized were those in the great hall as there was the largest source of heat, the great hearth. Many were spending the night inside its shelter. Meanwhile, down in the crypt, the floor and walls of stone were like ice, and the vampires were safe here from detection as no one would be looking for them here. Vojislav discounted the fact that he had not seen them that evening. He was still working off a hangover as well as napping on and off. His fiancé was exhausted yet sober. She was listening to reports of what had been done to protect the assets of the castle from the blizzard storm coating the grounds with snow. When she was satisfied with the efforts made to protect the animals and such, she dismissed the steward and wrapped herself with a cloak of fur.

Her maidens, all three of them, had traveled back to the castle with her. When one asked if all her belongings had arrived at the castle, it was then that Illona had remembered that the wagon containing the box with Vladis chained inside had not arrived.

She immediately went to Vojislav to report this to him. She found him in the great hall, conferring with stewards about planning for a long drawn out storm. When she mentioned the wagon not arriving, it was as if a bolt of lightning had crossed his brain. He immediately seemed sober, alert, and aware. If the group of soldiers escorting the wagon had not reported in, it could only mean two things. They were still out there, or something had happened to them. It was the last part that worried Vojislav. He knew the children could have easily intercepted them and if so, they would have found the box with Vladis inside. Where were the children now, he wondered?

As his power of perception scanned across a radius that included the entirety of the castle premises, he seemed shocked that he immediately found them. His senses told him they were

226

below in the crypt, hiding with their father. The reunion they were having was bittersweet. The only experience they could now share was that they were kindred creatures. Their father had sired them twice now, once in the mortal world, and again, in the world of the dark. The anger of it dissipated for the fact that they were now with their father again soothed over the anguish of being alone, without a guide in the darkness.

Vojislav's senses told him he should be alarmed. His dreams of living in the castle legitimately as the new prince of Wallachia, holding the throne, marrying Princess Illona, having children with her, were now threatened by four children and their father. Though they were dead yet alive, he was not daunted by their nature or their power. After all, he was the Dragon. The Dragon was the disciple of Set, the very embodiment of the spirit that went to war with the Almighty God Himself! Why should he be afraid? He could see why Illona should be afraid, but he feared nothing. He arose and determined himself to go to the crypt to confront them. They would not hide from him. He would find them.

Find them he did. He went right to them, as if he knew exactly where they were the entire time. With a torch in hand, a sword in the other, he approached the crypt door. He could see it had been opened. Without fear, he pushed it opened. It did not swing easily, as the hinges were old and rusty. They did make an irritating sound as the metal ground upon itself.

"Vladis?" he called out in the dark. "I know you are here, and the children as well. I know you are angry. You have good cause to be. I would like to explain if you will let me."

From the shadows, Vladis spoke. "Come no closer, thou son of the devil! For I shall strike you down if you do! If I strike you now, you shall have no heir. Consider that before you advance. I have demands. If they are not met, woe be unto you, and unto Illona."

Vojislav was startled by the audacity of Vladis, for he was rebelling against his master. Vojislav had never heard of this, for Nefertiti nor Akhenaten had never stood up to him in defiance. Nonetheless, he halted in the darkness. "I will listen to you."

"The children tell me of all you have told them. You are but a liar. But then, Set is the father of lies, is he not? They believe none of what you have told them. You are not to take my throne for it is not yours to take. Even in this life, my children are still my heirs. They will rise to take crowns of their own, to rule in their own kingdoms, and to mete out justice to those such as yourself."

"Vladis, let us reason together. How can they rule when they are dead? Who will follow them when they only have a half-life, the life in the darkness? I can rule in their stead, make their decisions come to pass and let them enjoy at least the half-life they will endure for eternity. Can you not say they should have a life eternal, free from sickness or death?"

"My children shall make their own path, their own decisions and shall carry them out as they see fit. They shall forge a world, even if in the darkness, where they can seek happiness. They shall find a way to redeem themselves and rid themselves of you and of those like you. Vampires shall not be the weapons of war that you will use against the church and its armies. I shall teach them to survive in this world of the dark, not you."

"I believe if you wanted to kill me or Illona, you would have done so last night. We were especially vulnerable then. Why did you not murder us in the bed, in the act then?"

"I wish you to be gone. That is the limit of my courtesy and kindness."

Vojislav knew of the Church's intentions. He was aware that Brother Bartholomew had written the Bishop regarding the existence of the vampires. "Very well, but who shall watch over you and them when the sun rises each day, when the church shall be hunting you and those like you, each day, every day. No matter how many you create like yourself, the church will be hunting you. You may hide, and always be in hiding. But the life you speak of, will never happen. Not for you and not for them."

"The life I speak of is one that has not happened because it has never been attempted. Tayla will find that way. I do not see myself standing in the way, but I will support her and all my children to reach their potential. That means I will not allow

228

those such as yourself and Illona to stand in their way. If that means you die, then you die. It is that simple. If the church deems that it is fitting that we die, then we die as well. We have already died once."

The Dragon was surprised that they were ready to sacrifice their existence of eternal life, though dark, for the ability to exist without the Dragon. "And if I turn my back and walk away from here, then what shall you do?"

"You will leave this castle?"

"Yes, at first light if the weather breaks. I will return to Rome, to the High Council of the *Order of the Dragons of Set.*"

"You will leave Illona here, give no warning or cause for alarm. Remember, we can sense more things now than we could before. You shall leave, saying you are going to look for the wagon that contained me. Take soldiers with you if you like, but do not plan to return here. If you do, I shall forget any kindness or friendship we may have had. And you will die a miserable death full of regret."

Tayla and her siblings were surprised that their father would make a deal with such a scoundrel.

"Then we have an agreement." Vojislav turned, leaving the crypt, and pulling the door closed behind him.

"Father, do you trust him to keep his word?"

Vladis looked down at his daughter. Though it was dark, his vampire eyes told him she was still an unbelievably beautiful young lady. "Daughters, sons, I do not trust him to do anything that is not in his nature to do. He is a liar. Therefore, I trust he will not do what he says he will do. However, he trusts me to be a man of honor and therefore, believes I will do what I have agreed to do. That will be used to our advantage. Come, we must make plans."

CHAPTER TWENTY-SIX

UNTIL THEY BLEED NO MORE

"Dearest Malcolm, by this time, a great amount of pain had been inflicted against my family...Against my father, specifically. The source of that pain was none other than the Dragon. The insult against his authority as the reigning Prince of Wallachia was a wound my father could barely endure. My father was a proud nobleman, a true warrior, and a patriot to his country. He would never willingly or knowingly betray his people or his Emperor. That the Dragon found this so easy to do shook my father's notions of what was good and right to its foundations.

My father concocted a most justifiable, yet equally sinister plan to remove the Dragon from this land, and Illona from this world. I think my father would have made a deal with the devil himself to accomplish such a deed. For the first time since we became what we were, we were afforded the chance to laugh. And laugh we did..."

*   *   *

Bartholomew, the local friar, had been ordered to perform the marriage ceremony within the week. He was reluctant to do so, but his position as the residing cleric would suffer credibility if he did not do the deed. After all, that was his job. Other than that, if he refused, the consequences were more than he was willing to face.

The winter storm had kept most of the people confined within the walls of the castle. Not that records were kept in those days, but it was the longest and fiercest storm in most people's memories. The roofs and battlements were thick with blankets of snow.

While he had been in the castle, he was reminded of many events that he should report to the Bishop of Tarnovo. Bartholomew remembered the scene in which he had witnessed the poisoning, or assassination, of the Prince of Wallachia. He was beginning to see things much clearer. The lines of good and evil were drawn but he was not too sure where they lay in relation to him.

To the friar, there were only two forces at work here, good, and evil. Or, better put, the light and the dark. He knew where he stood. He was on the side of the light. Carefully considering the characters, their natures, and their roles in this drama, he found it hard to decide where to place the others. The Dragon and Illona were on the side of the darkness. That was one of the few things he knew for sure.

But, the Prince, the children, Annara…what role would they play to destroy the forces of the darkness that he could see enveloping the land? He knew he would not feel sadness should Vojislav and Illona meet their demise at the hands of the Prince or his children. In his heart, he would feel justice, and satisfaction. And then, he would feel guilty for desiring such an outcome. Though he knew he was not to be their judge, if absolution were to be given to them, he was not sure if he could perform the rites for them.

If the Prince was plotting revenge, then it must have the Hand of God upon it, he thought. Was this one of those "mysterious ways" the Church had always talked about? Should he be asked, he would lend his assistance to the Prince. After all that had been done to him, he was more a victim here than a villain, it seemed. He conveyed his feelings to Johannes. Johannes thought he had gone mad to say such a thing.

"Are you sure about this? I mean, we could all be executed immediately for such an act! It is conspiracy! Perhaps even treason!" Johannes said to Bartholomew. They were in the chapel of the castle, one of the few places Illona rarely went. Normally it was cold in there, but Bartholomew had brought a brazier into the room.

"We need to be up tonight, all night if need be, for I feel Prince Vladis will attempt to contact us if he can. I think he will do that only if he feels he can trust us."

Johannes was a superstitious old soul who, though good-natured, was still untrusting of something he did not understand. He was afraid, very afraid. "Friar, I will trust a man of God over anyone else in this castle. Let it be known that Johannes followed God during these troubling times."

Bartholomew understood this and gave him an extra crucifix. "Here, wear this around your neck. It will ward off the vampires for it represents holiness. Vampires are unholy so therefore they will be afraid of it. Listen! You must believe in it. If you do not, they will know."

Vladis was plotting for sure but to ensure success, he needed all the allies he could find to put his plan into action. How does a vampire enlist the aid of those he considers prey? He makes deals, or better known as "non-aggression pacts." This was precisely what he wanted to do with the two mortals he had trusted so much in his mortal days.

Vladis was aware that the church would be coming to eradicate vampires soon. They were conferring even now in Tarnovo for the rites necessary to kill what is already dead. He had accepted that. The words of the Dragon still stung Vladis' heart when he was told that the church, the Holy Church he had defended against the enemies of Christ, would be coming for him to ensure his destruction. Because it was Vojislav who had told him of this, it stung, but Vojislav was known for his lies. Therefore, he did not put much stock in such words and threats. He was prepared to give up this existence in return for salvation if it were possible. During the few years he spent in the wolf's den, he tried hard to remember the teachings of the church. As stated before, mortal memories begin to fade away when one becomes undead. The teachings had faded away from him such that he could not remember specifically what he was required to believe in for attaining salvation. Now, the thought of humbling himself before the Almighty God troubled him. It angered him, and he knew it was not himself who rejected the spirit of Christ, but the demon inside him. The fear of damnation was reflected by the demon inside him. That same demon consumed him with hatred toward the church, its teachings, and mortal men. As it was then, it is even now. The demon drives the vampire to do what it does.

Later that evening, Johannes and Bartholomew sat in the great hall, drinking tea while the fire in the hearth burned bright. It was quiet, as nearly all inside the hall were asleep. Johannes was about to fall asleep when he felt a nudge from Bartholomew. The door of the great hall was open. The numbing cold crept inside the hall.

A familiar silhouette of black, with a large cape across its shoulders stood inside the doorway. It seemed to beckon to them, as they could barely hear a familiar voice calling to them, softly and seductively. Soon, four more silhouettes could be seen behind the first one. The Prince and his children had arrived just as Brother Bartholomew had suspected they would. The voice indicated they were seeking friends. Johannes, frightened to nearly paralysis, somehow found his arms and legs, and stood up to approach the Prince and his children. Bartholomew followed him.

They approached and then stood outside the hall, shutting the door behind them. With a torch in one hand, and a crucifix in the other, Johannes greeted the Prince and his children. Vladis was pleased to see them.

"My friends, have no fear. I mean you no harm. We have much to discuss. We can help each other greatly if you will listen to me. Are we agreed?"

Vladis led them to his former chambers. There, they conversed until nearly dawn. Vladis had his plans carefully and methodically thought out. The evil ones would inflict the greatest pain upon each other. This way, when the final blows would come to pass, they would come from a direction that neither would suspect.

Vladis spoke with authority as well as experience when he said, "To take a blow, even a fatal one, from a stranger is one thing. It would be shocking, even brutal to say the least. Painful? Of course. The shock would be particularly numbing though as it would come so viciously quick, the mind would have little to no time to conceive or ponder the source of it."

"And then, there is the one that comes from the one you trust above all else, the one you never suspect. That blow that is the most painful of all, because you least expect it from the one you trust, the one you love. It is so unexpected, even more so than the one from a stranger. The pain is fierce, for it is more than just physical pain. Emotional pain can be the worst of all. The pain of betrayal, killed by a lie and a deed so dastardly, and then the feeling of being laughed at, for now the victim suffers the ultimate defeat, the one at the hands of the one they loved. The wound is mixed with blood and tears. Such is my wound." This was precisely the wound Vladis wanted to create upon his enemies. The children were more than willing to be accomplices in his scheme. So were Bartholomew and Johannes.

*   *   *

Vojislav contemplated the situation he was in. He was cold and lonely in so many ways now. Staying close to Illona was always on his mind for he knew that even Vladis had limits to his self-control. It was evident to him that he had outsmarted himself. Perhaps this was part of Set's plan. He had no vampires for allies anymore. Illona loved him but was she willing to do for him what he wanted? He had played her with such masterful manipulation, such that he wondered how she could ever trust such a man as he was? But then, how could he trust such a woman as she?

Love and trust are inextricably tied together, even to a woman such as she. She expected it, though not willing to reciprocate it, he rationalized. He had to admit, this was Set's doing. Vladis was exerting his will upon the Dragon, letting him know he was not subject to him. He was blocking his thoughts to him, basically giving him the coldest of shoulders. He pondered his priorities. First, he had to have an heir. There was still time. Secondly, he could not risk dying here and now, for the priority of having an heir was not met. There was no one to assume the identity of the Dragon, should he pass. That thought was nearly unthinkable. His only option was to accept Vladis' act of kindness and leave as he had agreed to do. There would be more years to play out this drama, and he resigned himself that another Dragon would have to assume that role. It was not to be his.

At the noon meal, he sat next to the Princess, who seemed in a good mood, though she still wondered where the wagon and her soldier escort was. Vojislav had not told her of his conversation with her late ex-husband.

"After lunch, I will take a detachment of soldiers and will travel down the road to see if the soldiers and the wagon can be found. I may be gone for a day or so. Do not worry."

"My Lord, I will not worry, for you are the Dragon, and soon to be the new Prince of Wallachia. I expect your return by tomorrow evening."

"I may have to backtrack the road all the way to Moldavia. What shall you say then?"

Illona turned to look at him. "If you must go that far, then do so. We both know what is at stake. Return to me, my love. I trust you will find our prize, and all will be well. After all, you and I are soon to be wed. I may be carrying your heir this very moment. That alone should encourage you not to tarry too long in the snow."

Vojislav knew that would be the last conversation with the woman who even now, he wondered if he was truly capable of being in love with.

Despondency set in as he packed food and clothing for the trip. It would be a long way to Rome. He would feign searching, sending troops northeast to Moldavia, while he would scour the countryside with another party of troops. He would then dispose of them, fake his own death, and ride out for Rome. Vladis had other plans for him.

The Prince was waiting for him after the sun had gone down. Vojislav had not ridden too far from the site where the wagon and soldiers were. Vojislav had done exactly what he had planned to do. He had tarried there long enough so that he had left the site by mid-afternoon.

"I thought I would pay you a final visit before you rode away for the last time. I have letters for you to sign. I have even brought your seal with me so that if there is any doubt as to the authenticity of these letters, the seal should put that to rest." The Dragon read the letters, shook his head in disgust and signed them. He was experiencing something he had never felt in his life…defeat. He hated it.

Vladis had Vojislav sign letters informing the Emperor that he has had a change of mind and is abandoning claim to the throne and does not plan to go through with the wedding. He also encouraged the Emperor to fill that vacancy with another nobleman, preferably one that is already married.

"What will you do with Illona?" he asked of Vladis.

Vladis simply smiled, his fangs shown by the light of his lantern. "I plan to do what should have been done a long time ago. I know others will want me to let her go. Is there any humanity in me left? Am I capable of mercy anymore? I cannot answer that."

*   *   *

A week had passed. The weather had cleared. Illona sent another detachment of scouts out looking for the ones who had left earlier. They found the wagon, and a few dead horses who had been ravaged by wolves. All the soldiers had been strung up from trees, on display for whomever would find them. The box had been dismantled but the Princess' personal belongings were still intact. They brought them back, along with the chains that had been torn off the box.

That evening, they brought all of it back to the castle. The wagon was found less than half a day's journey from the castle. The first thing Illona wanted to know was where was Vojislav. The soldiers told her where they found the wagon and the dead soldiers, which indicated to her that Vojislav should have discovered it first and would have returned to the castle. He had not. Nor had any of those who had left with him.

Illona knew what all of this meant. In her mind, she imagined the scene that Vojislav saw, perhaps realizing that a monster was now on the loose, seeking revenge. Perhaps, he fled the area in fear. She had never known him to fear anything. After all, he was the Dragon. He was the one to be feared.

Why would he leave and not come back, unless...Vladis had found him first! Fear struck her heart. Her imagination ran wild, contemplating every possible situation. She was wrought with fear, worry, and sadness. Had something happened to her betrothed? Worst of all, nightfall would be upon her soon. She had little time to prepare. Deep in her heart, she knew she would have to face either Vladis, or the children. Perhaps, both.

She called for her captain. She told him to station crossbowmen at the entrances to the great hall, and her bedchambers. They needed to be cocked with silver tipped bolts she told him. The captain assured her it would be done. He ordered the blacksmith to melt silver so the bolts could be dipped in the molten silver.

Before nightfall, another party of scouts had returned with news that they had found the party of soldiers who had traveled the road northeast towards Moldavia. They had not survived, either by the weather or the children had made short work of them. Their manner of death was not determined. The horses and essential items of equipment were recovered.

Time passed. Illona knew she could not afford to lose any more soldiers. She did not fear attack from without. The real threat was death from within. Now that she knew Vladis was loose, he and the children were surely inside the castle. The only possible place they would be was the crypt. Though Vojislav had been gone for a week, the children and Vladis had kept to themselves. Johannes and Bartholomew had hidden them well. The shock of finding the bodies of men and the wagon was disheartening. What was worse was the feeling of abandonment from her fiancé. Finally, all that, coupled with knowing that supernatural beings were ready to pounce upon her seemed to drive her into despair. The vampires were content to let it destroy her spirit.

Illona was a proud, arrogant, headstrong woman, who though confident to a fault, would be very tough to break. That was exactly what Vladis wanted to do.

237

She had consulted her staff. They sat at the large dining table used at meals and banquets. Much of the staff was in attendance, as well as her maidens, Johannes, Bartholomew, her captain of the guard and commander of the garrison and his aides. It was evident that she was under siege as well as all those who were still inside its walls.

"It is now evident that the master of this castle, Vojislav Rekvas, my fiancé, has either abandoned us or has fallen prey to a monster. It is my guess he has left for Rome. I doubt that he will return. That leaves me the ruling entity in this domain. I will send a dispatch to the Emperor telling him Vojislav has abandoned this castle, his fiancé, and thereby relinquishes all claims to these lands. I will beg the Emperor to appoint a new Prince and I will marry the nobleman of his choosing. The security pact between Wallachia and Moldavia must be preserved."

Bartholomew was pleased. At least the Dragon would not be a problem. Perhaps the church in Rome would deal with him, or better yet, the High Council of the *Order of the Dragons of Set* would address his disobedience against his own Order.

Illona continued. "We have enemies amongst us. The danger is not outside these walls, but within them. What is worse, is that they cannot be defeated. Not without the proper aid and defenses being utilized. They are unholy creatures."

She paused long enough for that to sink in. "You think I am evil. Perhaps I am. I am no saint. I do not expect anyone here to create an abbey or convent in my name. However, I am human. What we face is no longer human. What we face is no longer alive. They are undead creatures, powered by demonic forces that possess their bodies. Day by day, they grow farther from the world of the living and deeper into the world of utter darkness. My former husband is one of them. The others are his children."

The staff gasped, but some of them were there the night Vladis appeared to all in the great hall. They were witness to the fact that he still lived.

While the servants murmured amongst themselves, one stood up, saying, "The Princess speaks the truth. I was there that night

238

when Prince Vladis appeared. He is alive, but I also saw him dead."

Illona thanked the servant for his support. She continued, "We face certain death if we do not support each other. No one is to go anywhere alone in the castle at night. Once that sun goes down, we are in great danger. Your swords will have no effect on them. We must find them during the day and when we do, then we can kill them. Silver is their enemy. Crucifixes repel them. I can only assume the damnation of their souls is now burned into their minds. They will try no doubt to convert as many of you into their world. It is better to be dead than to be undead. Captain, your guards must be armed with silver tipped weapons and blades. Trust me, for it will stop them. Vojislav has informed me the Church in Rome has already been dispatched to come to eradicate these creatures from our lands. We must hold out until then."

Bartholomew looked on in amazement that his letter had somehow informed the Princess of his suspicions and his request of the Bishop to intervene. It seemed she had spies everywhere. He leaned over to Johannes, whispering, "Ask me not how I know, but she knows I have spoken to Tayla. We may be compromised."

The sun went down that night and replaced by a clear night sky full of stars that shone with a diamond-like brilliance. It was calm, with little to no wind. There was still a thick heavy blanket of snow on the ground.

Vladis and his children rose from their hiding place down below in the crypt area. Soldiers thought they had scoured the area well enough, but they had missed some places.

"Father?" asked Tayla. "Shall we dispense justice? I have much to avenge."

"Daughter, not all those who shall sleep tonight in this castle shall rise again to see the sun on the morrow. Our enemies shall pay a price tonight. They shall pay it with their blood. I know who is just and who is not under the roof of my castle. If we are still here when the sun rises, then so be it. But the guilty, they shall bleed until they bleed no more."

The children immediately went to the chambers of Illona's

three maidens. Each one of them had their own rooms, but due to the cold, they had taken to sleeping with each other for warmth.

They slipped into the rooms of each maiden, finding the rooms decorated with crucifixes of all kinds. It made the young vampires apprehensive to approach the pretty women sleeping soundly in their beds. Tayla and Rascha were in the room of Magda. She was sleeping with Portia. Above the headboard hung a wooden crucifix. They left the room and found Johannes. They told him they needed the crucifix removed from the room as well as any other crucifixes that might be in the rooms of their intended victims. He agreed to do the deed. Johannes and Brother Bartholomew had just become the world's first familiars to vampires.

Within an hour, just before midnight, Magda and Portia were dispatched. The young vampires bled them dry. The women were being drained of their life force before they could awaken fully. Suffering such a major loss of blood so quickly prevented them from struggling or calling out for help. Othar and Prieta managed to do the same to Katerina. Katerina had retired before Illona did and Illona was about to find her friend and confidant dead by exsanguination in her own bed.

Illona was escorted to her chambers with a few soldiers who positioned themselves outside her door. Illona saw Katerina's body in the bed, still as if sleeping. She had not noticed the crucifix that normally hung over the headboard missing.

Illona pulled back the covers to slide in without letting Katerina's body heat escape. When she did, she could feel a wetness in the bed linens. She grabbed a candle to see what the feeling was coming from.

She gasped in horror when she could see it was dark red. Her hands grabbed Katerina and shook her to wake her. She did not respond. Then she saw the wounds upon her neck. Immediately, Illona knew it was too late. Her friend was dead. She called for her guards and they came in to find out their worst fears had come to pass.

Illona, barely decent for her bodyguards to see her, grabbed a cloak and told them to follow her to her other maidens' rooms. She went to Magda's room, but no one was there. Magda had gone to sleep with Portia.

Upon entering Portia's room, she noticed immediately the crucifix was gone. Her lamp shown its light upon the occupants of the bed. Their eyes were fixed, looking up at the ceiling. Their bedclothes were soaked with their blood while most of it had been taken by their vampire attackers.

Illona broke down as she held Portia's head in her lap. Her tears were genuine, as she felt the pain of loss. Three of her best friends, women who were like sisters, were now dead, all in one night. Not just dead, but dead due to vampires. Her grief was overpowering.

Meanwhile, four of her most trusted and useful servants met the same demise elsewhere in the castle. To make matters worse, the Captain of her guard had been dispatched by Vladis. The Captain's betrayal against his Prince was unforgivable. This was not only shocking to Illona but demoralizing to the soldiers who were sworn to defend her. It was not yet midnight.

Few if any slept that night. The vampires had struck with a ferociousness few could imagine. Morning came and the carnage became apparent when two of her cooks could not prepare the morning meal as they were now dead.

Those of the kitchen staff who remained, began their early morning ritual as usual. They said nothing about the loss of their cooks, but it was evident to Illona for she could see them crying silent tears while they worked. They were sad and fearful of what the future may bring. There was no happiness nor joy in the castle. Vladis and his brood had seen to that.

After breakfast, Illona and some soldiers went looking for Vladis and the children in the only obvious place they could be hiding…the crypt. The crypt of the castle was used for only one purpose. It was designed to hold nearly fifty tombs of ancestors of the Prince's family, past, present, and future. More tombs could be hewn out of the rock floor underneath the existing crypt if needed. The tomb currently held about thirty remains of ancestors, male and female. Not all of Prince Vladis' relatives were buried here. Many had died on the battlefield as the Dark Ages and the Middle Ages had been very warlike to his family since attaining nobility status.

241

The first place they checked was Vladis' tomb. Vladis' was not about to stay in such a place. He knew he was vulnerable while lying asleep in a coffin. They pushed the heavy stone slab across the top of the stone sarcophagus. There was nothing inside but there was a parchment. It was addressed to Illona who grabbed it from the soldiers' hands. It read:

"Illona, you must be weeping unconsolably at this time. Last night was only the first night of my revenge. I will kill all of you. I shall bleed you until you can bleed no more. None of you shall attain the immortal life I and my children now live. You are undeserving of it. You are trapped. All those with you are trapped. Make your peace now, while you can. I will be coming for you, all of you. You will be last and know that you will be responsible for the death that you will find in this place tomorrow morning."

The parchment dropped to the dark, cold, stone floor. It was as if God himself had just delivered her death warrant into her hands. Sentence had been passed and the executioner would be here after dark. Illona broke down and asked to be escorted to her chambers. It was thought to be best to rest up during the day for the vampires would surely be at their best during the night. They would need to be as well.

CHAPTER TWENTY-SEVEN

NO TRUE VILLAINS AND NO TRUE HEROES

"Dearest Malcolm, the memories are like waves crashing upon the rocks of a beach somewhere, coming at me unceasingly. Here I find a situation not too distant from the one we enjoyed. You have found yourself asking the question, 'who was the true villain here, who was merely a victim and who was a spectator, unwillingly drawn from the seats of the theater, thrust upon the stage and cast into the drama without their consent.' Bartholomew was the victim here, controlled by his beliefs and his desire to do good. Johannes was a spectator, who was fearful of picking the wrong side, chose to follow Bartholomew. Sometimes, there are no true villains and no true heroes. Only deeds performed, left for others to judge.

As I look back, I can judge the Dragon by his deeds. As a vampire, I realized how much a villain Vojislav really was. You could never believe anything he said. I remember when he came to my home on my birthday, he had seemed so nice, so sincere. He had told us that Illona was our true enemy, and that he was there to warn us. It was as if he was constantly changing his shape, his side, his nature. I had no idea of the devil he was. To be that naïve and innocent again…what a blessing it would be to return to that time, that night. Would it have changed anything? I cannot say."

*   *   *

Illona attempted to sleep during the day so she could be up

that night. She wanted to be alert and aware of any threat to her or those she cared about. However, those she cared about had died the night before. Now, only those servants and soldiers who were loyal, or well paid or indebted to her, stayed. Either out of loyalty, or fear, they stayed. How long would this last, she wondered?

Though Vladis had told her she would die, he toyed with her. Knowing she would be on guard against him, for she would not go down without a fight, he decided to play a waiting game. All the people in the castle slept in the great hall. Crucifix's were placed on the outside of the doors as well as any other entrances to the room. The food and the water had been taken into the room in case they had to be there for an extended period. Plenty of firewood stocked the woodbins to keep the fires going for warmth and light. Rarely would anyone need to leave the room during the hours of darkness.

That night, Vladis and the children picked off several soldiers and servants just to let her know that she could not protect anyone, not even herself. Each morning, for nearly a week, there would be a few less people inside the castle. The castle was now turning into a gigantic crypt. It was a place of murder and despair, for the occupants were going nearly mad, out of fear of the vampires and out of fear of Illona. She was completely disagreeable and difficult to be around. Some of the staff left, despite threats from Illona to set her soldiers upon those who were deserting her. Soon, even the soldiers began to desert.

Their commander, Illona's henchman, had been among the first to die. What was left for the soldiers to fight for except their very lives? The answer was nothing. Soon, only a few staff had stayed. Finally, there were no soldiers. There was no one to cock the crossbows, or nock the silver tipped bolts.

Bartholomew and Johannes attempted to talk sense to the desperate noblewoman. They found her hiding within the confines of her quarters so she could sleep during the day. At first, she would not listen to them. Bartholomew asked her to give up any claims to nobility, to give up all claims to any lands that had belonged to Vladis. She refused to submit to any of their demands. "What makes you think my ex-husband will agree to leave me in peace if I make such conciliatory gestures? How would you know? Do you speak to him?"

Vladis still wanted to make sure his children received their inheritance from him. He still believed his children were the rightful heirs to his title and lands.

Both Bartholomew and Johannes looked at each other. This was a 'do or die' moment. Their answer could cost them their life, but who was left to carry out their execution? Illona was essentially powerless. They both answered simultaneously, "Yes, my Lady, he speaks to us."

She was astonished. "Vladis speaks to you? Why?" she asked.

Bartholomew answered, "I believe it is for this reason above all else. He needs someone who is honest to convey his words in such a way that you would completely understand his intended meaning. I believe that is what I am doing even now."

He continued, "The parchment you found in his tomb should have let you know that he moves freely within the confines of this castle. You have no control over your destiny. If you have any hope of leaving this castle alive, you should listen to me. Forget yourself for one moment. You have nothing to bargain with. Who is left but less than a handful of people here? We are not your servants. Soon, you will be cooking your own meals, and how long will that last?"

She recalled the words of her ex-husband from the parchment. It did not paint a good ending to all this madness. She had no friends or allies left. For the first time in recent times, she felt alone and abandoned.

"Why did Vojislav leave and not come back for me?" she asked through tears streaming down her face.

Johannes answered this time. "My lady, Prince Vladis gave him an ultimatum. Leave, without explanation, never to return, or die without an heir."

Bartholomew spoke this time. "My lady, Vojislav is not like most men. He is something far worse than the creature your former husband, Prince Vladis has become. He truly lives forever, changing form after form in this world, for he comes from another world, one we never want to know firsthand. He is

245

a master of manipulation and lies and a champion of deceit. The church is aware of his existence and his compatriots, The *Order of the Dragons of Set*. They have infiltrated our ranks, but we know of them and keep them close to us. The Church in Rome will deal with them, and they will deal with the vampires here. Your real enemy at this moment is time. Those within the church charged with dispatching the vampires will not arrive here in time to save you. Therefore, I beg you to consider your few options."

"Confer with Vladis regarding my options. I do not wish to die such a death. I am agreeable to any terms he proposes." She broke into tears. For the first time in her life, she felt utterly defeated. All that she had desired had crumbled before her, all that she had accomplished now lay in ruins. The despair of complete surrender choked her until she could speak no more.

"We shall do our part in this matter, with respect and every effort to preserve your dignity, Princess." Bartholomew and Johannes bowed before her and quickly exited the chamber.

In the darkness of the night, the vampires are at their strongest. They have full use of their powers and gifts. It is time which grants the wisdom as to how to fully use those gifts to their advantage. Often, it is not physical strength that wins the night for the vampire. It is the cerebral abilities, those which involve the skill of strategy, of insight, of knowing your enemy and his weaknesses and strengths which will win the vampire its victory over its prey. The turmoil between logic and non-logic poses an enemy to the mortal. Determining which one to accept as reality confuses the mortal, but the vampire knows immediately which to embrace. Such was the dilemma facing Illona.

Bartholomew knew it seemed as if he were playing from both sides. He was trying to be neutral, acting as a mediator, but it was becoming increasingly difficult. He had respect for Vladis, though spiritually, they were enemies to the core. Illona was mortal as he was, but he reviled her more than the unholy creature that was Prince Vladis. Vladis showed mercy to those who would destroy him, but Illona had showed none to her enemies. He had seen her cruelty many times over. What she had done to her former husband, his wife, and her father, and most of all, to his children was abominable. As a priest, how could he absolve her of her sins? He wondered how sincere she could be if she was not found with her back to the wall. Her desperation and lack of options had forced her to the point of capitulation. She had little to bargain with. If she were to extricate herself from this predicament, would she accept defeat and never return to Wallachia again? How could anyone trust her? Vladis had trusted her and the priest contemplated what he got in return for his trust. She was a cornered animal at best, wounded as well, making her the more dangerous to contend with.

That night, Vladis appeared to Bartholomew and Johannes. They both relayed the information of Illona's surrender to him and asked for Vladis to have mercy upon her. They told him of her tears. They talked about her wish to not die but live elsewhere. Vladis was cold as a stone.

"I have shown mercy, have I not? I have let her live all this time when I wanted to kill her weeks ago. I gave safe passage to those who wanted to leave the castle. I killed only those who posed a threat to me and my children, or those who were loyal to Illona. I showed mercy when I let the Dragon leave the country without answering for all he has done. He is a liar, and the devil incarnate. He had told many lies, more than all the liars of the world. He used me, used my former wife, and wanted to use my children to pursue his agenda. If it were not for Tayla, we never could have stood up to him. My children released me as I was held prisoner by them both. I cannot and will not serve such a man as he. It is Tayla's will that allows us to refuse to follow."

Bartholomew answered him, saying, "Perhaps Tayla should make the decision as to what to do about the Princess. The Princess has no dominion over Tayla or any of the other children."

In his cold, monotone voice, Vladis replied, "Vojislav told me a long time ago that Set, his master, told him not to marry Illona. He ordered him to have her killed because she knew too much. Vojislav disobeyed, and for that he feels he is being punished for it with his banishment from Wallachia. It would seem I am still serving the Dark Lord when I want to serve no one. I have banished Vojislav and now, about to execute the one he wanted executed."

Johannes spoke this time, "Prince Vladis, you must make a decision whether you will serve the Devil, or yourself. If you kill the Princess, you are performing the will of the Devil. It may seem like justice to you, but you are still serving the Devil. What would God want you to do?"

Vladis turned to him quickly, saying, "I am damned. God has forsaken me! Each day, my memory of what I learned of God grows farther away from my grasp. I slip further into darkness, as if I were falling into an abyss. I cannot say what God would have me do."

Bartholomew stood his ground, confidant that he could redeem the fate of those involved.

"Prince Vladis, to us, you are still the Prince of Wallachia. I remember you in your day of light and life. You were a good man, a noble man with good intentions and a generous nature. No one here will be found saying anything like that about Princess Illona. She is all the things that can be said of Vojislav, the Dragon. I know who he really is and about his Order. The Church is aware of them, and ready themselves to make war upon his kind. If you kill her, little to no good will come of it. All that will happen is that she will no longer be able to wreak misery and evil upon others. You may feel justified, that you will have won. Yes, you will have your vengeance. It will not eliminate misery and evil, for there will always be others that will take her place. We must fight evil with good. I implore you, let her go, send her far away, with no title, no fortune, only with her life and possessions. If she is deserving, she will survive and live out her days. If not, then she will be at the mercy of others."

"Mercy of others?" Vladis asked. "She gave no mercy to those she hated, most of all, me. None to my family. Even the mercy of a peaceful death was not afforded to them. For though they are dead, they walk the earth undead as do I. You have made a convincing argument. I do not want to live the existence I am cursed to endure. If the Church feels I must die, then let my soul find peace. I have faced death many times before. Let me stand before my maker once and for all and be judged. For I am a monster, and I am consumed with my desire for vengeance against her. Tell her to go."

The priest conveyed the words of Vladis to Illona later that evening. He found her curled up on her bed, wrapped up in furs trying to keep warm. She was trembling in fear.

"Princess Illona, I come with good news. I have secured safe passage for you away from here. You must leave at first light. The farther you can get away from here, the better. I have spoken with Prince Vladis and he has agreed to let you go away. You shall have no title, no fortune, and no escort. There is no one to escort you as it is. All the staff have either deserted you or have fallen prey to your husband and his children. You are truly alone. Johannes has agreed to drive you and your belongings in a cart to the next village. I will ride along with you. From there, you will be on your own. At least, you will be alive. To stay here one more night will be your last."

Trembling, she nodded in agreement, and rose to pack some of her things. She said she would be ready in a few hours.

Bartholomew went to write some more letters that Vladis wanted written. He also wanted to write one to his children in hopes that one day, when they had learned to read and write, they could know what he felt about them. Vladis dictated the words to him personally as the priest wrote them down.

Later, Johannes and Bartholomew went to ready a wagon and a team of horses. As the two prepared for the journey in a barn, Johannes asked if the priest trusted that she would not come back. The butler of the castle knew all along that Illona could not be trusted.

He replied, "I expect her to do what we have always suspected she would do. She will lie and probably come back, prepared to make war again on the man she has hated for so long. Her pride will be the death of her."

Johannes said, "I suspect that when she finds that Vladis had Vojislav sign letters abandoning the claim to the title and disavowing of Illona, she will return with a vengeance."

Bartholomew struggled with the horses, getting them to stand still. They were cold as well, even though they had grown enough hair for their winter coats.

Johannes began to help him as he could see the priest struggle. "I suspect she will return with the Moldavian army, all to kill one man."

The priest turned to look at him after tightening the harness around a team horse's body. Though his black frock had a nice hood to it to keep his head warm, his tonsured haircut, typical of a friar of those days, seemed to counter the effort. Shivering, he was chilled in the frosty air. "A lot of good it will do. The armies of the world have no bearing on the fate of the undead. I suspect this cold does not either. They neither have the knowledge nor the weapons to fight them. For that, they need the church. Right now, I need a fire. And something warm to drink!"

*　　　*　　　*

The Princess Illona, along with Bartholomew and Johannes left the castle shortly after morning's light. The three hoped in vain that the day would warm up with the sun's rising. Though the sun did come out, the cold remained a biting constant for the journey. Once they found themselves close enough to another village, the two men reminded Illona that she would be on her own. She wanted to protest but she knew it would be for nothing because Vladis had ordered them to leave her company at the first village they could come to. She knew the two would not disobey Vladis' orders. It was not their loyalty that was the issue, as it was the consideration of the penalty for disobedience.

The two got off the wagon and entered a tavern. Illona simply sat in the wagon, while in the cold, not saying a word. People passed by staring at the noblewoman who sat in a cart drawn by two horses. Two more horses were attached to the rear, for the return trip.

Johannes knew of Vladis' instructions and proceeded to carry them out. Vladis had supplied the priest with more than sufficient funds for the journey. Bartholomew ordered food and drink while Johannes looked around the establishment.

Finally, the butler of the castle gained the courage to speak publicly. Johannes spoke loudly, almost shouting, saying, "I have employment for anyone willing to take someone to

Moldavia. Upon arrival, you will be paid handsomely for the escort of the wagon and its contents to the home of the Moldavian Prince. I have funds to cover the expenses of the trip. Who will perform such a task?"

A few looked around at each other. Finally, one stood up and asked, "Moldavia is three days from here. How much payment? In gold or silver?"

Bartholomew answered, "In gold, and more when you deliver the wagon and the passenger safely, unharmed to the Prince of Moldavia. You have my word you will have your payment, if I have your word that you will perform this task to its end."

Murmuring began in the tavern, as some of its occupants discussed it amongst themselves. "Who is it that sits in the cart outside, freezing while you stand here in the warmth of this tavern. Have you no shame?" asked another occupant.

Bartholomew answered, "It is none other than Princess Illona, of Moldavia. Her brother is the Prince. She is going home. You will be expected to deliver her safely there. Her brother will pay upon the delivery of her and this letter. She sits there of her own accord. Her stubbornness seems to insulate her against the cold. Shall I bring her in if it pleases you?"

The man nodded, "I think it is the right thing to do. Otherwise, she will be frozen by the time you finish that meal."

Bartholomew left the room and went outside to fetch Illona. He knew she would be stubborn, but the shivering of her body and her response between chattering teeth made the decision easy for her. She rose and came down from the wagon with Bartholomew's assistance.

It was silent when she entered the room. It was warm as the hearth blazed brightly with large logs ablaze with warmth and light. The crackling and hissing of the fire calmed Illona as she sat next to the fire to warm herself.

The man who asked about whether to be paid in gold or silver spoke, "It seems as if the fire suits the lady. I will take on the job of getting her to her brother. But I do not think it right to leave just yet. Another blizzard is on the way. Best to wait out the storm. I suggest we get those horses in a barn where they can be fed and watered. Nothing will be moving on the roads pretty soon."

"I want to be clear. No one is to offend the Princess or to ask questions of her status. She is still a Princess of Moldavia. Believe me, she is under the protection of Prince Vladis, her former husband."

"Prince Vladis? We had heard he died a while back. Is he dead or is he not?"

"He still walks. He still talks. He still rules." Bartholomew had not told a lie, but he had not told the entire truth either. He felt is best not to talk about Vladis. The less they knew, the better. He procured lodging for the night for all of them and looked forward to a good night's sleep. Bartholomew and Johannes slept in the same bed for warmth, while Illona slept with an older woman in the same bed. There were many fires in the tavern that night, as woodcutting had continued throughout the daylight hours.

The morning came and the blizzard had not come as expected. A change in the wind had taken the storm away from them. A stroke of fortune had come to them. The man who had agreed to take Illona to her homeland readied the wagon and horses. The tavern owner's wife brought them some food to carry with them. Johannes and Bartholomew had already loaded the cart with food supplies but accepted the wife's donation as it was not frozen. The man took Illona down the road, heading north towards Moldavia.

Bartholomew and Johannes breathed a sigh of relief. Were they finally rid of Illona, the most hateful and spiteful woman either had ever known? They surely hoped so. For her sake, and for Vladis' sake, they hoped dearly that she would not return to take vengeance. They knew it would be a fatal mistake.

Upon returning to the castle, Johannes asked, "What now? Why did we return here? There is no more employment to be had here. This is a place of death and sorrow. Many, many bad memories are here now. It can never be a place of joy, of happiness. Unless another nobleman comes to rule here, by appointment of the Emperor, I see no reason to be here."

Bartholomew answered, his breath steaming from his mouth as he spoke, "I still have a flock here to minister to. You know there will be another nobleman to assume the title of Prince of Wallachia. I think you have only to wait. Prince Vladis likes you. He like both of us. We give him a connection to the world of the living. I believe even his children like us. They have not threatened us, nor have they spoken against us. We learn from them. They learn from us. We both benefit from this relationship. I think the Prince is happy that we took Illona from this place. At least her death will be one he will not be held accountable for.

*   *   *

"Dearest Malcolm, the past comes at me like falling rain, such that I cannot write it down fast enough. I am so surprised that I did not remember all this. Perhaps it was the Dragon cursing my memory, that I would not remember how evil he was. It had to be. It was not just my memory but my brothers and my sister as well. The emotions I feel are sometimes confusing, as I try to remember what I felt when certain events happened. Normally, a vampire remembers everything. The event, the feelings, the details, they remember all of it. But it seems all of this had completely left my memory, like a book with an important chapter missing. Was it a gift or a curse? I do not know, perhaps it was both. I am pleased that I could not have been more wrong about my father. He was a loving man, good to my mother and all of us children. We were robbed not only of our lives, but our futures. Our futures with him, and our mother, and our own families. The more I remember how I felt about it, because I was obsessed with that feeling of loss, I could not forgive. My father was able to forgive, to show mercy, even as a vampire. But I remember I could not forgive what Illona had done to my family. I was determined that she pay for what she had done."

*   *   *

In Tarnovo, the winter was no different than it was in Wallachia. It was early morning, cold with clear skies and little wind. Josef of Planoz, the current Bishop of Tarnovo, was in a foul mood. "I am too old to be doing such things, in the middle of winter, no less!" he said aloud to his aid. The aid looked at him with concerned eyes.

"Yes, I know. It is God's work and it must be done. And soon, I might add," he finished saying as he pulled his heavy cloak about him. The time had come. The old man climbed into the coach with help. The Bishop prepared to leave the monastery with a team of clerics and a detachment of infantry, provided by the Emperor. The soldiers would accompany them and a nobleman, appointed to assume the title of "Prince of the Kingdom of Wallachia.

The new Prince of Wallachia would establish his own garrison upon arrival. There was one problem. Prince Vladis still occupied the castle. Johannes warned him that a new Prince would be arriving any day and would assume the title and throne.

During the evening on the same day, far away, in the castle of Prince Vladis, the castle butler and the vampire formerly the Prince of Wallachia, met in his chambers. The castle was deserted, save for Johannes and occasionally, the Friar Bartholomew. During the day, deliveries of firewood and food were delivered but no one would enter the castle. Goods were left in the courtyard and Johannes would go out and bring all of it into the great hall. The sun had gone down, and creatures of the night stirred within the walls of the castle.

The light was dim, as Vladis preferred the darkness. Johannes held a candelabra of three candles.

"Prince Vladis, I cannot hold off a detachment of soldiers nor a team of priests and the Bishop of Tarnovo no less! What must I do?" he asked the vampire.

Vladis turned to him, saying, "I expect you to do nothing. Tell the truth if you must. Tell them I forced you to do what you have done. We know the truth is I forced no one to do anything other than Vojislav and Illona. If any of my staff, the ones I knew and hired for their service, would have desired, I would have let them go freely on their own accord. You know there were many who were disloyal to me. As for the other two, it was the only way to rid them from my kingdom. Now, they are gone. There is no need for me to resist. I can fly away and be safe, taking my children with me, or I can stay here, and be destroyed as unholy creatures by the church I swore to defend…the church I did defend…many times. I expect them to arrive here within the week. It depends upon the weather. I shall halt all snow so they will not be impeded too much and arrive without undue delay. If possible, I will welcome them. I understand it may be my undoing, but if it must be, then it must be. I want my children to be left out of this, at all costs. They are new to this existence. They have much to learn, from me and from each other. I must do what a father must do…protect his children. I did not protect them from the evil that they faced in life, but I will surely defend them from it in this life!"

"They will want to speak to Friar Bartholomew when they arrive. Shall I warn him of what you have spoken of?"

"Yes, everything I have said to you, applies to him as well. Both of you must know I can foresee disaster coming. Even now, it plots against me and this place."

"Sire, what do you speak of? Is it the Princess?"

"How astute you are, Johannes. You know her as well as I."

"Friar Bartholomew and I discussed it and we both agreed she would return when she felt she had the odds in her favor. Perhaps she is waiting for the Church to do its duty before she plans to return? Could that be her plan all along?"

"I am not surprised that she would want to return. She is not welcome nor desired in her native lands. I should have disposed of her when I had the chance. My mercy will go unnoticed by the Bishop I am sure."

"I have no doubt the Friar will inform the Bishop of your kindness towards her." The butler excused himself from the darkened chamber and went to the main hall. He had quite the roaring fire going. All the children were there, staring into the fire. They were quiet and motionless as if they were statues set in front of the hearth.

Finally, one of them, Rascha asked him a question. "Johannes, how long have you served my father?"

From across the great hall, the butler stopped his work on chopping wood and said, "Well let me see. I think it is close to

255

about twelve, maybe fifteen years, or so. I have not really kept track of time regarding that. Why do you ask?

Rascha answered, "I have not known anyone else in your position. You seem to have always been here."

"It seems like that to me as well. I guess I am supposed to be here. I am but a servant, a peasant and I am owned by my prince to be here. This is where he put me last, and he has not removed me. He has taken care of me all these years."

Tayla spoke this time. "You have cared for my father when he was alive and afterwards. I give you my gratitude. We all do. If vampires can love, we certainly love our father and mother. But can vampires love anyone else? Can vampires grow up to be husbands and wives, fathers and mothers?"

"Oh, children! I wish I knew. Before you were changed, I knew and loved all of you. I love you all still. It breaks my heart to see you all this way. If anyone should have this curse upon them, it is Illona. She would have embraced it for it would mean she would never grow old or sick. She would never die, which she has a great fear of death. This curse has certainly fallen on the wrong souls." He said all of this through tears he thought the children could not see in the dim firelight of the great hall. But vampires see everything in the dark.

That evening, a knock on the large door of the castle could be heard. Johannes was surprised to hear any knock at this time of night. Who would risk their life coming to the castle at this time of night?

He unlocked the door, opening it to see a shivering Friar Bartholomew. "Friar, at this time of night? It must be important. Very important," he said as he allowed the friar in.

"I must speak with Prince Vladis immediately. I have a letter, one from the Bishop who sent me here. I hid it from everyone so it would not be found by the wrong eyes to read. But find it I did after all these years. It was addressed to Annara from the Bishop, my former master, God rest his soul! I think the Prince needs to read this!"

CHAPTER TWENTY-EIGHT

THE LETTER

"Dearest Malcolm, a piece of paper can have the power to protect or condemn. My ignorance and my illiteracy at that time forced me to understand why education is so important. If I could read, then I could do things that most kings and queens could not. My mother could not read her Bishop's letter of protection. Protection was one thing, but legitimacy, well, that is something I have sought after since the beginning."

*   *   *

Bartholomew read the letter by candlelight. It was addressed to Annara. Vladis sat upon his throne in the great hall, accompanied by his children. None of the children could read as they had never been taught. Few in those days could read or write. Even Kings and Queens were rarely taught to read or write. They dictated their letters and thoughts to paper via a scribe.

Bartholomew read aloud, "To Annara, the true wife of Prince Vladis of Wallachia and the legitimate Princess of Wallachia. You are amongst the most unfortunate women I know. The beauty bestowed upon you is a gift, and yet, it is a curse. Your beauty has been the instrument by which you have been ensnared in such a tragedy. I hope it is your innocence that may save you from the evil that stalks your land. Your beloved Prince is in danger. The evil I speak of is the man who had befriended your husband. When this letter is read, you will know his name. Few in our Lord's Holy Church know of the evil I speak of.

Bartholomew, the monk who has been sent to replace the friar now deceased, is aware of his identity. He is charged with watching over you and your young. He is also to watch over your husband. I fear there will come a time when disaster and sorrow will strike out against you, causing you to lose all that you love and cherish. I felt it the moment I saw you, standing alone upon that lonely road. It was my Christian duty to keep you safe, therefore I made sure you arrived safely to your home. Vladis is a good man, naive yet noble in all his ways. Fear not, for when danger comes to you, you may present this letter to those who would do you harm. I place you and those you love under my protection, as the Bishop of Tarnovo, guardian and protector of our Lord's flock in the Bulgarian empire. May the Lord keep thee and yours in the palm of His hand. For those who would do you harm, they do so under the threat of retribution from the Church of our Lord, Jesus Christ. In our Lord's name do I bless thee and those you love, Stanzylch, Bishop of Tarnovo."

Vladis was stunned. Annara had the protection of the Bishop all this time and was unaware of it. He had granted her legitimacy, and therefore, his children had legitimacy as heirs. He gazed at the friar, wondering how this was not made known until now. Yet, he was pleased.

Bartholomew was embarrassed at his oversight. "Prince Vladis, this is my fault. I had hidden this letter and forgot about it. When I was going through some of my other letters, I remembered the one I had hid from the world, to keep it from those who would destroy it. I was afraid that the Dragon would find it. You had the support of the Bishop all along and Illona knew it. To hide that from everyone else, she had my predecessor murdered. Perhaps the Dragon had done the deed, I do not know. All I know, is when the church comes for you, you have this letter of protection. I am a witness to it. I saw him write this letter."

Vladis answered him, "The Holy Church rides in this direction as we speak. At this moment, the current Bishop is on his knees in prayer, asking for divine guidance and strength to face a creature of the night. It is something no one has ever done before. The ones that come have put on the armor of God. They come armed with the Word of God, a stake of wood, a vial of blessed water and an axe to which they will remove my head and a dagger for which they will remove my heart. They will disarm me of my powers with a chain of silver. They may fire on me with silver tipped arrows. All of which is designed to kill me permanently and put me at peace. My instincts are to flee for to save myself. But I consider the eternity I face. I am in the dark, but I desire to look over into the light. In the dark, I find comfort, solace, respite, but I face an eternal hunger, the same hunger my children face. I would prefer we all find ourselves in the light, but I am not convinced that is possible."

"What is your desire, Prince Vladis? How can we help you in your most desperate moment?"

"I have eternity, but I have little time. Ironic is it not? I will require your prayers, no doubt, when the end comes. I shall require last rites be given for me, with absolution if possible. I would make my confession now, but the demon shuts my voice within. I feel the darkness closing in around me, as if the Dark Lord's demons were preparing for battle, and my body is the battleground." He looked around in the darkness. Set hardens my resolution to fight, and if possible, to flee is necessary. My will seems to not be mine any longer. I think it best that you do not see me anymore, for I have no power of will against the hunger that drives me."

He told Bartholomew to keep the letter, find Annara if he could, and give it to her. "This is a letter of protection for Annara, not for me. It is too late."

Bartholomew told Johannes he would return, but that he had to find Annara as Vladis had told him to do. It would be his last act of respect to Vladis and the last time he would ever see him alive, or dead.

*   *   *

By this time, Annara and the peddler had settled in a village about one hundred miles northwest of Vladis' castle. The peddler she had taken up with had secured employment there, while she also worked. It was far enough away that she no longer had to worry about the long, evil fingers of Illona reaching out to bring

259

her back to a painful past. It was not easy for anyone to forget they had lost their entire family to the evil things that had occurred in Wallachia.

Employment consisted of working at a tavern, one which they would eventually become the owners. It was a small establishment when they first came there. Hard work and time afforded them the opportunity to assume ownership when the former proprietor died. He had no family who wished to claim it, so they did. The wages were good, and the customers were steady and constant. Business thrived, especially because the crusades gave them a steady stream of well-paying customers. The tavern was located on a road that was part of the collecting system of roadways that led to the Holy Lands where the men at arms were heading.

It took a few weeks for Bartholomew to find them, for winter had not left the region yet. Finding them was only a matter of time, for the two of them stood out from ordinary people. All one had to do was ask questions. During the winter months travel was slow and sparse. Few managed to move from town to town. If they did, they were remembered.

When he found Annara, it was by accident for he only stopped to get out of the cold and to get himself and his horse fed. Annara saw him first and ran to him. Trying to not make much of a fuss, she held him as if he were family. Perhaps he was the only one left she felt that close to. None of her aunts or uncles had tried to keep her from leaving after she had buried her children and her father.

"Oh, my child, I am so glad I found you. I have been looking for you for several weeks now. How have you been?"

Annara, still strikingly beautiful, yet still sad, replied, "I am here. Sometimes I feel lost, but Stefan tries to fill the void in my heart. He is kind, and gentle. A Vladis he will never be, but he tries desperately to win my affection and my love. I do not think I can feel that way ever again. Thanks to Illona, she has destroyed my heart. In a way, I too, am of the living dead."

"I bring news," Bartholomew said, as if to attempt to cheer her up. "I found this letter. It is a letter of protection and recognition, directly from the former Bishop of Tarnovo. He is the Bishop that gave you the escort back to the castle."

"Yes, I remember. He was a kind and decent man."

"He found favor with Vladis and supported his annulment. This letter states that anyone who brings about harm or intends to do you harm shall be notified that you are under the protection of the office of the Bishop of Tarnovo. Retribution shall come surely and swiftly should harm or the threat of harm come against you."

She took the letter and stared at it. "I see words, but I cannot read them. How shall I use this when harm comes to me, and from who shall it come from? Illona? She is the only enemy I know of who would want to harm me."

Bartholomew understood her anxiety and her frustration of being illiterate. "Exactly, I believe it was because of her that this letter was written. I wish I could have found it earlier. Perhaps much of what has happened could have been avoided. Vladis would be alive, your children would be alive, and you would be a princess. You certainly fill that position with your beauty, my dear."

Annara blushed. "My days of being happy are over, at least for the moment. I would love to see my children again. I know what they are, as they have the same existence as their father. But, to see them that way, well, it would be too much. I would want them to kill me and make me one of them. This way we could all be together."

"Oh no! Absolutely not! You cannot be one of them. They are beyond the grace of God. They are damned! The Holy Church has deemed this to be so. I can tell you that I have spoken at length with Vladis about this. He wants redemption, and his salvation restored. He even offered his confession to me. Listen to me! There is a demon who possesses his body. It blocks him, the real Vladis inside, from making a conscious decision to move to the light of Christ. It is the evil that lurks inside all of us, but in him, it reigns supremely over his power of will. He cannot move towards Christ unless the demon is vanquished. For that, I know of only one remedy and that is already headed to the castle from Tarnovo. They may have already arrived."

When he had said this, it pierced his heart to think that the deed of his execution may have already taken place. And what of the children? They would be subject to the same treatment. The thought of their extermination horrified him, but then he thought, Tayla was not like any other vampire. She was different.

Annara did not want to return to the castle. She was content to start a new life where she was. The site of the castle would only add to her sadness. The Friar bade her farewell and left her in possession of the letter.

When Bartholomew returned to the castle, he found it alive with people. People were moving in, transporting possessions and such, which indicated to him that the business of dealing with Vladis must be over. It had been nearly six weeks.

The new Prince of Wallachia had moved in about a week ago. The friar managed to find Johannes who had stayed on as the castle butler. He could not wait to tell the friar what had happened while he was gone.

They left the castle to go to the chapel where the two could converse privately. The friar's quarters were in such bad shape that Johannes insisted that he take up residence at the castle. At least he could keep warm and be fed there. Johannes would speak to the new prince to ask if it could be arranged and if a new chapel could be built within walking distance of the castle.

"So, is my worst fear now a reality? Is Prince Vladis gone? Is he at rest?"

"Not exactly, dear friar. Vladis asked me to arrange a meeting with the new prince and the Bishop. I was there and saw the whole event. So, after that, Vladis said he was ready to meet his maker but that none of their methods were to work against him. He could not be killed but he could be contained. He offered a solution to their problem. Remember what you told me about the crucifix?"

"Yes, I remember."

"I had to believe in it for it to work. Vladis agreed that the crucifix does have a power of resistance against him. He agreed that the Holy Scriptures would have power over him. But for them to be rid of him, he would have to go somewhere from which he could not escape. Somewhere that no one would dare come to his rescue, for escape for him would be impossible."

"Vladis said all this? He was begging for release from his demonic captor!"

"The Bishop and the Prince both agreed that he should enter into such a tomb, one that would hold him for all time, and no one could arrange his release. Vladis said that on the following night, he would enter such a tomb, with instructions regarding the sealing and care of the tomb.

"And..?" asked Bartholomew.

"He did exactly as he said he would! There is a place in this castle that only he knew about. It was an escape tunnel in case the castle came under siege. I have been here for years and I did not know about it. He took us to it, gave me a letter to give to you, and entered. Soldiers blocked it up with stone and mortar, with a large crucifix on the inside of the sealed wall. This is supposed to keep him away from the door."

"Wait, if that is an escape tunnel, then where is the other end of the passageway?"

"They did the same with that entrance. The entrance was in the crypt. One of the sarcophagus' had a false bottom. It was there that one was supposed to enter and escape the castle. I suppose only the family knew about this tunnel. Now, we all know about it. We also know no one can use it. The crucifix's and blessed water that will be poured upon the tomb doors each evening will keep him from ever coming out of that tunnel. He cannot dig himself out for it is solid rock. He has no tools, no weapons, no one to take for their blood. He is alone."

Bartholomew was astounded. Vladis had sacrificed himself to an eternity in the darkness beneath the castle. For what reason? He knew all he had to do was fly away. What kept him there? It was a question that would haunt him for a long time.

"Why would he not just leave? There is nothing for him to stay close to."

"Perhaps he knows that Illona will try to return to the castle. Is the new prince a married noble?" Bartholomew asked.

"No, he is young and unmarried. But I hear he is betrothed."

"Perhaps this is all just a trap. One final battle for him to fight and win, for all eternity. If he can find a way to escape when she returns, then it will be doom for many who live here. Prince

Vladis' thirst will be uncontrollable. What about the children? Are they in there with him?"

"No, Prince Vladis sent them away. He wrote two letters, one to the Bishop, the other for you. That is why I brought you here, for I hid it amongst your possessions. Now, gather your things. The letter is amongst them. Let us go to the castle, as I am certain it will be your new home.

*   *   *

A few months passed and soon spring was just around the corner. It had been an awfully hard winter. Some of the livestock had not made it through the severe freezes which had taken place. Yet, foals, lambs, kids, and calves were being born despite the hardships of the weather. Food stocks were low, and planting needed to be done as soon as the ground was ready for planting. The castle was ready for some repairs to be made, and people seemed to think the worst was over.

While the land was ready to heal from the worst, in Moldavia, Princess Illona began to get restless. She sent out spies to find out the situation in Wallachia. They did so with the support of her family as they were eager to be rid of her should she move to reclaim her title of Princess of Wallachia. She was still an irritant to her brothers in Moldavia. Her bitterness had grown after her exile from Wallachia.

They reported back to her that a new prince had moved into the castle, and that he was unmarried. Illona knew instantly that she must petition the Emperor to support the marriage of them together. Then, Princess Illona could be the Princess of Wallachia again. The wheels of conspiring and manipulation began to turn as she formulated a plan to worm her way back upon the throne. She had completely forgotten Vladis' threat that she should never again return for it would be her death if she did.

The children were also very much aware that the potential for her return was great. Perhaps, even certain. And, they were anticipating she would do just that.

CHAPTER TWENTY-NINE

ETERNITY OF PAIN

"Dearest Malcolm, this is the destruction and desolation of Illona. She was the catalyst for the destruction of my family. If not for her, the Dragon would never have brought my family such misery. I relish the telling of her demise. I think it important that you are completely aware of the details. I had nearly forgotten about all that happened to her and why. Now, I can tell the story. The stones do not lie."

*   *   *

During the Middle Ages, the Church was completely unsympathetic to the vampire entity. The church hierarchy believed rightfully that they were of the devil. The church leaders did not care whether the undead were cursed through their own doing or the evil doings of others. To them, they were unholy and that was all that mattered. It represented a threat, an unspeakable evil that must be eradicated from the earth, no matter what. The evil of the *Order of the Dragons of Set* was also on their target list. Even now, the Church in Rome began to formulate its campaign to erase them from the earth and from history.

The children had been sent away to avoid the wrath and persecution of the Holy Church. It did not mean to flee for their un-lives but to preserve their new species for they were the only ones who would live on, to thrive in this new world. They were to establish themselves as a dominate species, perhaps as a hybrid of humanity. Tayla and her brothers and sister were eager to do just that. Domination was the key to survival. They had learned early enough that anyone connected to the church, directly or indirectly, was their enemy. The dogma of the church dictated that if it was not of God, then it was of the devil. Tayla did not feel as if the devil, or Set, controlled her. Tayla felt independent. The exercise of her will separated her from the others. They always thought about prey or acquiring prey. They would sit about, after being satiated upon the blood of the living, discussing ways they could seduce, or persuade, or connive to achieve their goal of which was to feed. Simply put, feeding upon the blood of the living was their one and only complete obsession.

Their father sent them away, but Tayla knew she would have to come back to aid him. The children knew their father had set a trap. It had been discussed and carefully thought out, using the gift of sight. She also knew Illona would return too, for a woman like her could not resist the chance to return to the throne. Therefore, they planned for it.

The clerics and the Bishop had returned to Tarnovo, certain that God's work had been done and the issue of vampirism had been resolved. They hoped and expected to never have to return or revisit the issue.

Illona had sent letters to the Emperor, imploring him to sanction a marriage between the new Prince and herself. He consulted with the Bishop of Tarnovo. This was the wisest decision he had made while he had sat upon the Imperial throne.

The Bishop had told him that the woman who was married to Prince Vladis was an evil woman. She had subjected many to ruin and death, and it was believed that she had murdered her husband by poisoning him. The Bishop did not reveal the truth to the Emperor for the secret held by the church regarding the existence of vampires was a closely guarded secret. After hearing the response of the Bishop, the Emperor decided to not sanction a marriage between them. He decided to write a letter warning the new Prince that a marriage between them was forbidden and that the new Prince marry his betrothed as soon as possible.

Tayla had been watching the roads leading south to

266

Wallachia. She and Rascha spied a group of wagons along with some soldiers for escort heading to the castle. The wagons had made camp along the side of the road for the night. She and Rascha wanted to swoop in and take the evil woman right then and there. But patience is something even vampires must learn. Tayla found that the gift of sight was an important tool for acquiring patience. It allowed a vampire to see into the future to determine if their goal would be reached. If they could see the outcome, then they would wait.

Illona's party had arrived at the castle within two days later. The new Prince welcomed her to his home. At dinner that night, a banquet was given in her honor. The great hall had been redecorated, with new tapestries, new furnishings, and, surprisingly, better cooks. She was thrilled that she had been received so graciously but her dreams were about to be crushed.

Illona had arrived at the castle before the letter from the Emperor could arrive. Part of her plan was to entice the Prince to forego his plans for marriage and implore the emperor to consider the security pact between Moldavia and Wallachia. To her, timing was always a key part of her scheming plans.

Deep within the bowels of the castle, Vladis sat in the dark, silent tunnel. He was hungry beyond imagination. Even though he suffered, he never tried to escape or begged for mercy. Tayla knew of her father's suffering and when possible, she would catch a small animal and push it down a ventilation shaft so that her father could have sustenance when possible. When Vladis felt the presence of Illona within the walls of the castle again, he smiled with joy. His hunger would soon be over.

After the banquet, the Prince and Illona met in chambers separate from others. He informed her of his intention to marry.

"Dear Princess, I wanted to inform you in private so as not to cause you any embarrassment or feelings of awkwardness. I am betrothed to another, and that marriage will take place soon enough. I wrote of this to you in answer to your letters. This was done weeks ago."

The young prince was raised properly by a very prominent family in the western part of the empire. He was courteous, kind, skilled at the art of administrating and organizing. Loyalty, education, and the protection of his subjects were his best qualities.

Illona was aware of his intentions to marry another already. She had received the letters in response to his decision but had disregarded them. She lied that she never received them.

"Nonetheless, what is done is done. I am happy to meet you in person. It is much more informal this way. Perhaps, your presence here will enlighten me as to the events which took place here that took your late husband's life."

She sat on a high-backed stool, with a comfortable cushion. A fire warmed the room, as well as lit the walls all around. She noticed new tapestries and the family heraldry upon a large shield above the fireplace. There were fine furnishings about, which made her wonder if Vladis could not have afforded them, or if he did not care for such displays of luxury.

"If you want to know, I will tell you of them. They are sad. My staff deserted me in my time of greatest need, and I was forced to leave for my home in Moldavia. It may be troubling for me to get through it without becoming far too emotional. I hope you will forgive me."

It was then as Illona was speaking that Johannes walked past the door to the room where the new Prince and Illona were conversing. He heard the familiar yet foreboding voice of an evil woman he thought he would never hear of again. However, there it was, speaking as if nothing had happened.

Johannes ran to the quarters of Friar Bartholomew. He was not there, but at the private chapel of the new Prince. Building was going on, as carpenters worked on tables for altars and such. He found Friar Bartholomew busy giving guidance as to how things should be arranged to the workers.

"Friar, we have a problem. I must speak to you now, in private."

They both walked out of the chapel and headed towards a secluded area of the castle. Bartholomew was eager to hear of what news he had, but in his heart, he felt as if he already knew of the answers. It had to be Illona!

"I was walking by a room where the new Prince was speaking to a woman. I did not see her, but I recognized that voice. I know that voice and I know you do as well."

Bartholomew interrupted him before he could speak her name. "Illona!"

Johannes looked at him with watering eyes. "Yes," he whispered. "She is here, now, as we speak. That means if she knows we are here, we are in terrible danger. She will try to silence us from informing the new Prince who and what kind of woman she is!"

"I see. I believe she will do exactly that. Even now, she probably has her henchmen looking for us to kill us. We must hide. Only one thing can help us. Something eviler than she is and hates her more than anything on either side of the grave. He still lives, deep under the castle's foundation."

"It would be an abomination if we released him. We would be excommunicated!" Johannes was trembling after he had said that word. The peasantry had been told many times about the kinds of offenses that if committed, would be grounds for excommunication. In other words, they would be damned and headed for Hell for sure. Nothing struck fear in a serf's heart than the thought that if he thought his lot in life on this side of the grave was tough, try imagining an eternity of pain in Hell.

"No one would have to know," said Friar Bartholomew. "I think this has been Vladis' plan all along. He knew she would come back just as we believed she would all along. And now, she has done just what we expected her to do. She was warned, given the chance of redeeming herself, changing her ways, and to make amends. But she has returned here, and by doing so proves she has not changed her ways. Do you know what they were talking about?"

"Marriage! I heard that word several times," answered Johannes.

"I suspect that is how she plans to remain on the throne as Princess of Wallachia. Regarding that, I am certain Prince Vladis has other plans. We need to speak to Tayla. First, we must leave the castle and hide in the forest. Let us leave a message for Vladis as I am certain he knows how to contact her."

*　　　　　*　　　　　*

Night had fallen. Johannes and Friar Bartholomew were about two miles from the castle, in a wood cutters hut. A small fire kept them warm. It was cold as the wind blew chilling gusts through the trees of the forest. Sometimes, the gusts seemed to echo from hilltop to hilltop. When they did, it reminded Johannes of wolves he had been hearing for the last year or so. Wolves had not been too much of a problem until the children had come into their own as vampires. It struck absolute terror in both of their hearts to know they were capable of transformation into such creatures.

"I hear wolves. You think it could be them?" asked Johannes.

"I think it is just the wind. I do not feel as if we have much to fear from them. We have not wronged them in any way, have we?"

"Are you sure he could hear you? How do you know? Are we out here freezing for nothing?" Johannes was not accustomed to being outside at night, particularly in such weather. Bartholomew was not accustomed to hearing such whining from his friend either.

"Have faith, my friend. We are not releasing him. I think his daughter will do that instead, therefore we will not be responsible for what I fear will happen. We are mere spectators, unable to control what we see. I only wanted to convey a message. I fear that message has been delivered already."

As he said this, his answer came in the form of a figure moving about on the frozen forest floor. Soon, it was joined by another and then two more. Bartholomew reached out with his hand, to get Johannes to notice what he could see. Johannes nearly cried out when he saw the children approaching him.

"Fear not, for we come in peace. You have aided us and given us comfort when no one else would. Therefore, you have protection from our nature. Your angels surround you as well."

Bartholomew answered Tayla back, "I thank you for meeting us here. Your arch enemy is at the castle. I think you know this as well as your father. You must have a plan for dealing with such an evil woman. I will not interfere, nor will I give a hand towards such evil. She was warned, given mercy by your father, and allowed to escape. She came back, against all warnings not to do so. I neither sanction nor favor what is to happen to her. We are here because she needs our silence regarding the truth about her deeds. I ask for your protection against her evil plans which may involve others."

"I grant you safe passage after we have done what must be done. Bartholomew, Johannes, go in peace. Nothing shall befall you as we have already intervened on your behalf."

The two broke camp, eager to get back to the castle, its warmth and comfort. On their way, they found two horses not far from where they had camped. Nearby them, were two soldiers from Moldavia.

"Henchmen from the Princess Illona's escort," Johannes stated when he saw the livery they wore. The uniforms were undeniably Moldavian. Now, they were dead. The two kept onward to the castle.

"I fear tonight is the final night for Illona. The children are aware. Vladis is aware. It is out of our hands," murmured Friar Bartholomew, as they rode on.

*   *   *

At midnight, Illona woke up to a cold hand across her mouth, preventing her from screaming. Her guards were nowhere to be found. She was alone, unprotected, and staring straight into the face of Rascha.

He struck her across her face, knocking her senseless. His brother, Othar helped him carry her to the door, where Prieta had been keeping watch. All was going according to plan. Everyone was asleep or had been dispatched. They carried her to the door that led to the crypt. It had been sealed, but they had to open it so that they could seal the other end of the tunnel. Fortunately, they had not resealed the door because they no longer felt a threat.

Rascha and Othar managed to get her down to the crypt. Tayla and Vladis were waiting at the entrance to the tunnel. Prieta closed the door to the crypt and prepared to guard it from any intruders.

As they lowered an unconscious Illona down into the tunnel leading to a now-sealed exit, she began to regain consciousness.

When she realized she was being passed down to her pending death, she began to struggle and screamed for help. All to no avail. The terror in her heart energized her blood with adrenalin, a powerful aphrodisiac to a vampire. Her eyes grew wide as she realized her fate. She begged for mercy, but they all reminded her that she had been given mercy but had squandered the chance. The vampires were serious in their goal to put an end to the misery and destruction that an evil woman can produce. Vladis had planned to inflict the maximum pain upon the woman. He considered whether she should share the same fate as he, or should he just send her on ahead of him to a world of eternal pain. He chose the latter. Before he did, he made his peace with her, stating, "Illona, can you really say you do not deserve such a fate as I am about to give to you? You caused death to me, to my children, and for what? A throne? A title? For the love of the son of the Devil? You have such limited vision. It matches the shallowness of your love for me, your husband that you hated from our first night together. Do you think that I existed just to make your life so wretched? You must have because you hated me so for your plight. I was not the cause of your wretchedness. But you are the cause of mine. And theirs as well. Now, you must pay for what you have done."

As his children watched, he inflicted the first wound upon her. She fell, and as her life force began to drain from her, the children instantly moved in to finish her off. Even young Prieta, small and frail as she was, quickly managed to get her fill of Illona's blood before she lost consciousness again, and then found herself upon the other side of the grave, staring out into the darkness. There would be no Dragon to find her there, giving her the choice of following him and by doing so, becoming what her husband and his children had become. No, that was not to be her fate. She was instantly cast into the outer darkness, tormented and in eternal pain. It was a fitting end to such a woman.

CHAPTER THIRTY

THE CURSE OF MEMORY

"Dearest Malcolm, the events that are about to take place hold a special place in my memory. My father bestowed upon me the ring I wear, signifying my place in my world. During these times, rings are significant of lineage. My ring bears the same large ruby stone that had been in my father's signet ring. The signet ring indicated his power and position, his rank and station in life. The ring eventually found its way into my hand. I was the oldest child of an established ruling member of a royal household. This technically made me a princess.

That was a position that Princess Illona, a Princess of Moldavia would not tolerate. It was common in medieval times that rivalries between siblings for the throne or birthrights to it were decided in some of the wickedest ways imaginable.

After all, the ascension to power was taught to all young children of aristocrats. Except it was never taught to me. Noble birth usually meant noble entitlement. What was not given to them, was worth fighting for. For many, becoming an aristocrat was a product of birth. For others, by conquest. How one found themselves sitting on a throne or bestowed with a title, was not as important as actually attaining it. There was no set of rules by which one was supposed to ascend to position. In short, the motto of many was "by any means possible."

This is exactly what many nobles and would -be nobles did. Assassinations, blackmail, political maneuvering in and out of the bedroom was a common practice. To have been born into a world of political intrigue, to have enemies from birth simply because you were born under certain circumstances was a detriment to many young children who did not survive the ambition and lust for power a relative in line for the throne might have.

In those times, possession of such a ring means something. It meant, "The wearer of this ring claims rights and privileges over…" whatever lands or peoples they were assuming control over. A ring was like the deed to the land. There was only one like it and whoever wore it, was entitled.

For decades, I simply wore the ring on a chain around my neck. To those I had turned, it signified that I was a royal, by birth, and by birthright. Much later, I fashioned a crown to match the ring left to me by my father, the Prince Vladis of Wallachia along with a scepter. The beginning of my royal treasury were the chests of gold and silver we managed to confiscate from Princess Illona when we hid in the woodcutter's hut. I will tell you now of the well-deserved demise of an evil woman."

*   *   *

The next morning when everyone woke, the Princess Illona was nowhere to be found. None of her escort could be found either. All their baggage, their wagons, every trace that they had been there had vanished. It was as if they had managed to leave the castle in the middle of the night without giving notice or to say farewell, or anything else. They were just gone.

The Prince was amazed, disappointed, and somewhat offended that he had been treated so rudely. He was not accustomed to such rudeness. He wrote a letter to the Moldavian Prince telling him that should she want to return, she would not be welcomed and that any further correspondence between the two should not happen. As far as he was concerned, the matter was concluded.

Illona's body was never found, nor were her escorts. The children had seen to it that any traces of possessions were destroyed or confiscated. Tayla liked her clothing, and therefore, took it for her own. The soldiers had money and weapons which Rascha and Othar managed to take, though they were too big for

274

the boys, they felt they would eventually be able to manage. Prieta took some of the clothing as well as some of Illona's personal items such as comb, brush, and jewelry. The horses were turned loose, the wagons burned along with the bodies of those who had accompanied the princess. They had also dug up the chests of gold and silver and were prepared to leave the region for good.

"No traces..." they all murmured as they watched the flames from the bonfire rise in the night sky. Prince Vladis had accompanied them but had taken nothing for himself. When he threw Illona's lifeless body upon the flames, he turned to look at his children. He took off his ring, which Annara had given back to him before she had left.

"You have all performed brilliantly. You are all vampires. You will remain in this world, and carve out your own kingdoms, fashion your own crowns, titles, and thrones. Become rulers of the night, and rule wisely. Do not trust the Dragon, this one or all those who will follow. For as I was betrayed, surely, they will betray you. I give my ring to my eldest daughter, Tayla for she is the oldest, and therefore, your mentor, your teacher, your guide, for she is the wisest and the strongest. Listen to her, follow her lead, and support her no matter what the conditions are. Your survival in this world depends upon that. I brought you all into this world, twice. The first time, I could not have been prouder to be your father. I had such dreams of wonderful lives for all of you. But then, the Dragon, and this one," he turned to see Illona's body aflame, "came into my life. They created death and ruin, which came to you as well. For that, accept my sorrowful apology, in that I cannot take back that which I have inflicted upon you. Remember, I loved you then, as I love you now. I will not bury you, but you will bury me!"

As he finished saying that, he pulled out a bolt from a soldier's crossbow, one that had a silver tip, and thrust it into his chest. Before he hit the ground, the Prince of Wallachia flung himself upon the flames next to Illona and became consumed by the flames. It happened so quickly the children had no time to react or intervene.

The third vampire to have ever been created had just died the second death. The children were speechless. They cried tears of sadness and of anger that they did not know of what Vladis had planned.

*   *   *

Vojislav was in northern Italy, traveling through some mountainous terrain. He wanted to seek shelter from a storm that was bearing down on him at a monastery but felt he would not be welcome. He came down off the mountains and entered a well-traveled pass. Spring was just around the corner, and cold rains had already come and gone. He was still a few days from Rome when he felt the pain of Vladis' death. He turned to look behind him, as if he hoped to see Vladis' spirit rushing past him in the wind. There was nothing to see, but still, the Dragon felt the pain of loss. It felt the same when he lost Nefertiti and Akhenaten.

He was exhausted, as was his horse. Even his pack mule moved slowly. They had been traveling slowly for several months. He dropped his head while he rode slowly along the lonely road, murmuring to himself, "I should have never left. I should have never betrayed my friend. He was a noble and true man of conscience, of heart and soul. He was the embodiment of all that was chivalrous. And, I destroyed all of that."

He cried out to Set, asking for guidance. Set's voice whispered to his heart, saying, "You disobeyed me. The guilt you feel is of your own making. Now, there are four young vampires out there who seek guidance and protection from a world they know hates them. You must be that one they will seek."

"They will not seek me, for they know I am responsible for that which happened to their father, and ultimately them. They will never trust me."

Set replied to him in an icy whisper, "They do not trust you because they have memory of what you did, in disobedience to me. I will remove those memories of their father. They will no longer remember what happened. Their memories will be the ones I give to them such that they will not see you the way they see you now. Return to Rome. They will seek you out."

276

For the moment, Vojislav would have to be content that Set had not abandoned him. He could have, he thought. Right now, he knew his most important priority was to find a mate and produce an heir. He felt confident that the vampires would seek him out. The climate in Rome was better suited for to raise a child so they would have to come to Rome if they were to seek him.

Vojislav hated Rome for several reasons. The first was he had to deal with the High Council of the Order. Often, he felt contempt for them, disagreeing on policy, which made him feel as if his authority was being questioned, constantly. Secondly, he always felt as if the church in Rome knew of their existence and shadowed them, learning all about them. He had people on the inner circles of the church leadership who were paid well to inform on the church's actions concerning the Order. The information was conveyed to the High Council, which meant if he had to stay current on their activities, he had to remain close to Rome.

Vojislav was a man of action. He liked being out, in the countryside, even on a battlefield. Well, at least close to it. He liked doing his own manipulation, scheming, and implementing his plans. He had become exceptionally good at it over the years. However, he had made mistakes, costly ones, which he lamented over.

When he came to the gates of the city of Rome, he smiled. He was home. Not just his home, but the home of the *Order of the Dragons of Set*. His first task was to visit the baths, to get cleaned up. Then, off to a popular brothel to afford himself some food, drink, and female companionship. Here, he would recharge himself, marry, and re-assert his authority as the Dragon of the *Order of the Dragons of Set*.

*   *   *

Over a hundred years passed by. It was now 1337. Every night had been the same and the one before it, and the one before that. Time passed so uneventful, particularly when it came to the children of a vampire. They did what they did because they had

277

no choice but to follow their evil and terrible nature. Mortal men were the same. The only difference was that mortal men were given the benefit of free will, in that they had a choice as to how they would act. What now seemed natural to them was abhorrent to society. Mundane took on a different meaning. The only changes came in the form of relocation. Careful not to overfeed in one location, they seemed to move around randomly and constantly. They kept a low profile because the threats against them were very real. Therefore, Tayla realized they needed for people to believe they were not real. However, it was the Medieval Ages. People were very superstitious at that time and to any of the people who witnessed the carnage they were leaving behind, there was only one answer for it. It was the work of demonic forces.

In this case, that was exactly true. Demonic forces were at work here. Three of the children did not care what the world they lived in thought of them. They only cared for one thing. That one thing was living blood. As much as they could get seemed to be their priority. Only one of the children seemed to have any sense of control of themselves. Tayla did not like taking lives, though she could and did so with a viciousness that rivaled any of the wolves that were blamed for many of the murders committed.

They left the area of Wallachia after the grandson of the new Prince of Wallachia, Radu Negru became the ruler. The castle they had grew up around had changed so much. Much of it had been rebuilt after siege and combat. A monastery was built close by and thus, a significant presence of the church became a problem. They traveled west into France.

This was the year the Hundred Years War would break out, resulting in many thousands of casualties. Though the first battles would not take place immediately, war was in the air. Here, Tayla would discover the first taste of love in her young, yet old life. As they traveled west, they would see new and unfamiliar things. New places, new peoples, new languages, and customs enticed them. Soon, they began to lose track of their past lives. Just as Set had told Vojislav, who was now deceased but replaced by his heir, he had taken the memories of their parents, and replaced them with false, counterfeit memories. This became the Dragon's curse, in that they forgot the truth, and came to believe a lie. After all, Set, also Satan, was the Father of Lies. They were confused by how they came to be vampires, but then Set is also known as the Author of Confusion. True to his titles, he had done just that to these young and once innocent children. Now, everyone they had known, good or bad, was now in a grave. Their relatives, friends, everyone…was gone. They were alone, save for each other. Tayla did her best to teach them the things they needed to know. Though she could not remember her father's last words to her, she was still carrying out his command to her, to teach, mentor, to guide and to rule. This she did with amazing efficiency.

They always carried the shrouds they were buried in. It was the only tangible thing they brought with them out of Wallachia. The only other item was the ring Tayla's father had given to her. She could not remember him giving it to her, but she knew at some point in time, it had come into her possession, and it entitled her to the title of Princess.

Once they entered France, Tayla tried to blend in with some of the mortal population, careful to not arouse suspicion. No one knew who they were, or where they had come from, but Tayla told her siblings that for them to survive, they must become French. It took a while, but the children learned the language, customs, and culture of the locals, enough to pass as French aristocrats. The money they had brought with them had increased and therefore, they sought to purchase land, but these were medieval times. All the land was owned by the nobility or the King himself or was owned by the Church.

Tayla was confident that there would be another way they could buy an estate for themselves and set down roots. It was naïve for them to think that people would not see them as different at the very least. After all, they would not be seen during the day. If they had staff, or servants, would they not become suspicious in that they did not eat meals, or walk about during the light of day. What if other nobles came calling? They could only receive guests during the day. And most nobles attended chapel services. What would they do when the church clergy asked them why they never attended services?

Tayla thought to herself, "So many pitfalls for us. How are we to survive in this world?" For the time being, they found abandoned and ruined castles that had been fought over and destroyed during the petty wars fought before and during the crusades. They were satisfactory but not accommodating enough for a princess such as Tayla. She was determined to get something better. That something came in the form of a French knight.

CHAPTER THIRTYONE

THE PAIN OF LOSS

"Dearest Malcolm, once again, I turn a corner. For the first time in my existence, I meet a man who completely turns my life upside down. You mortals call this love. I was about to experience the joys of it, and the pain of losing it. I never want to feel that way again, but to not love or to never love again, well, that is a form of death all unto its own, I suppose. Shakespeare said it best when he said, 'Better to have loved and lost than to have never loved at all.' I was about to find out just how right he was."

*   *   *

While strolling the streets of a French village in the early evening, Tayla's beauty attracted many men. It was like picking apples from fruit laden trees. Even to the most chaste of men, one look at Tayla's beauty was like dangling a piece of fresh meat in front of hungry wolves. There was one who demonstrated the virtues of chivalry such that he stopped, dismounted from his large horse, and struck up a conversation with her. Tayla had never been approached by a man willingly since her conversion. She tried to act normal as she wanted no suspicions aroused. She was dressed modestly, in no way giving the indication she was a harlot of any kind.

"Mademoiselle! Permit me to introduce myself, my name is Sir Renard Berenais. Are any of these ruffians mistreating you or bothering you in any way? I shall remove them if you like!" he said as he placed his hand upon the hilt of his sword.

"I thank you sir knight for your protection. I do not think they mean me as much harm as you might think, but I do appreciate a man who is willing to draw his sword to protect a woman's virtue." Though Tayla age in physical years was fourteen. Renard's eyes were fixed upon the ravishing young woman.

"Are you a stranger in these parts? I have not seen such a beautiful woman in this village in a long time. May I walk with you," he asked?

"Oh, please do. My name is Tayla. Tayla Elizabeta Rokosovich."

"That is a beautiful name, but I strongly doubt that it is French."

"You would be correct. I am from Wallachia, far to the east of France, near the Black Sea. My Father was Prince Vladis."

"A prince? That would make you a Princess, yes? I am honored by your presence and ask permission to remain at your side until you take your leave, my lady," he replied to her. "Do you not have an escort? Surely you are not alone on these dirty streets of a common village."

"As a matter of fact, I do not have an escort. I only have two brothers and a sister. We are in exile from our native lands. Due to the Turks we can no longer survive in our homeland. Therefore, we seek shelter amongst the French."

Renard continued to ask questions as they walked. They both seemed to forget the time and before they knew it, it was well after midnight. She gave Renard permission to take his leave of her after assuring him she would be safe without him.

The next night he sought her out, finding her in the same exact spot. This went on for quite some time. Before they knew it, both Renard and Tayla had intense feelings for each other.

The war had started. The English armies had invaded France and the call to arms went out across the French countryside for all and able knights to answer.

Renard invited her to attend a feast honoring the knights who would ride to the French King's army the next day to meet the

English. She panicked at the thought that she might have to eat mortal food, which would give her away instantly. Therefore, she decided to tell him the truth. Love makes one do many things, crazy things, courageous things, and even stupid things. Perhaps telling Renard who she really was fell into that latter category. She was willing to take that chance.

She arrived that night to the village, dressed like a Princess in a brocaded gown, with a ringlet about her head. She was alone, but Renard was used to seeing her alone. He knew she had brothers but had never met them.

"I have to tell you something first before we go any further. I want you to listen to me with an open heart and mind. I have a story to tell you that you may not believe or will find it hard to believe. Rest assured; it is true as for every word is sincere.

Do you believe in the supernatural? Have you ever wondered about things of which there is no explanation? Renard, I am one of those things. I am a monster. I am of the living dead, commonly known as a vampire. Therefore, you see me only at night. By day, I do not exist among the living. My father was a monster and he in turn made me and my family monsters. We survive on the blood of the living. We can only come out at night and must return to our graves by dawn. I have not seen the sun rise or set for over one hundred years."

She told him the complete story, as best as she could remember it. It was a tale of woe, of tragedy, of horror. He could scarcely believe his ears, and if he were not already in love with her, he would have dismissed her as some kind of lunatic. But her words were sincere. His heart knew this.

"The church hates us for they believe we are of the devil. I do not like being what I am. If I could change it, I certainly would. I am doomed to live eternally by night and appear dead by day. My powers are such that you cannot even imagine. I was transformed when I was fourteen and have not aged since then. I will always be young. I will never be sick, but I will always need to drink the blood of the living. A vampire I am doomed to be. Leave now if you wish. I will not blame you. I will never harm you nor will I harm anyone you are close to. I have never loved anyone before, as you are my first. My heart is fragile, regarding this thing called love. It is strange to me, and now, all I know, is that I feel that way about you. I have always wanted to find someone to love. The fire it brings into me is wonderful. All I have known in this existence is loneliness, and hopelessness."

"My lady, you are correct. This is a fantastic story. It is one upon which I must ponder for a while. I do not doubt your sincerity, but I must ponder that should I accept your story as truth, then a decision must be made upon my part. If I accept this as truth, then I must accept or deny my feelings for you, which I assure you are genuine. I too, have a story to tell. But first, I must decide whether to accept your truth. Shall I take my leave of you so that you are not facing any embarrassment? You say you cannot eat food but can drink only blood?"

Tayla's eyes began to swell with tears. The tears of a breaking heart are the most bitter. Renard could see this easily.

"My dearest Tayla, know this. I feel as though I can be completely honest with my feelings as you can be. After all, should anyone else find out your secret, it is a certain death for you and your sister and brothers. My silence is guaranteed to you. I am not pure. I have strayed from the path of the church. I have lain with harlots. My tongue has spoken vile and unclean words, which came from a vile and unclean heart and mind. My first thoughts of you were unclean when I first laid eyes upon you. Then, when I saw your face, my heart melted. It was as if I was spellbound by your beauty instantly. This thing you claim to be, it does not seem to matter to me as I cannot see you as something evil. I do not wish to leave your side for any reason in this world. Even tomorrow's battle seems like something I would much rather put off than have to leave your side."

"Renard, you must do your duty. So, take your leave of me and feast tonight for battle awaits you on the morrow. I will await your return. Think upon what I have told you. If you need proof, then I shall provide it. But always remember, call out to me if you are wounded under a night sky. I shall be there."

In an instant, she was gone, but Renard stood there spellbound, confused, bedazzled, but mostly giddy that his heart was afire for a woman, perhaps the only one like her in the entire world. He finally left to attend the banquet.

Renard rode out the next day to march with King Phillip of France's army to meet the English. They met the English at Crecy and it was a complete disaster for the French. There were many losses on both sides. The French took most of the losses from the deadly fire of the English longbowmen. That evening was spent cleaning up the battlefield, with each side taking what could be used to fight another battle. The English had to learn to live off the land as they were far from their base of supply. The French were on their own territory, making it easier for them. However, they did not have the leadership the English had. This was why they had lost the battle.

Tayla and her family had followed the army in secret for they knew at the end of the battle, there would be a feast to be had on the wounded and missing soldiers that always accompanied the end of a battle.

She found Renard amidst the demoralized men at arms of the French army in their camp. He was happy to see her, yet sad that he had lost so many young men for a cause not many of them understood. Duty was duty, even if it had no reason or rationale behind it. Renard desperately tried to find reason behind their struggle.

"We lost the day, the English won the day, my dear," he said. He embraced her in private yet kept a watchful eye out such that any improprieties may go unnoticed.

"If you left with me, I could assure you that no one will ever find you or charge you with desertion. There is no reason for this war. It is only two men squabbling over their rights to a possession neither will carry pass the grave," she told him.

"I believe you are right. I fought hard today. I killed men who I did not know nor had wronged me in any way. We only did what we did because he was English, and I was French. Nothing more. Neither of us fully understood why we were here."

"Do you still love me, Renard, or is this war more important to you?"

"I am a knight. My honor and duty compel me to fight here. Shall I die and then join you on the other side of the grave?"

"Renard, I am fearful that is not a solution. Death on the battlefield will not guarantee you a place by my side. Should you not return to me, and you are wounded upon the field, I shall find you and give unto you the gift I was given. Of that, you may be assured. But, if you are already dead, then you are beyond my help. I will be heartbroken if you do not return to me."

Renard smiled through a dirty, bloodied face. "Whether in this world or yours, I shall be happy to be by your side."

She smiled as well, hiding her fangs. "Your understanding, your ability to see beyond my affliction as this creature of the night inspires me to be something better. I shall have to learn to live inside your world, though I am no longer part of it."

They parted for the night, as the French army needed to move at first light. Reinforcements would join them before the next engagement. It would be likewise for the English. Tayla and her siblings feasted all night on wounded soldiers.

It was two years later. The English had laid siege to the port of Calais and captured it. Tayla and her family had been following the armies all this time, finding food, and living without fear of discovery or persecution. Meanwhile, another monster was ravaging the continent. The Black Plague had come to Europe. It had already devastated parts of their homeland. Crusaders coming back from the Holy Land had tales of horror as to it effect upon the living population. Rascha and his brother Othar often talked about the plague and its ability to support them better than the carnage left upon the battlefield. They wanted to go to the cities where the plague was ravaging whole populations. Tayla would have none of it. She wanted to be with Renard. They asked her if they could go on their own. She gave them permission to and observe, and then report back to her. They took Prieta with them.

Thus, did the vampires feast upon the near dead of the plague of the Black Death. They missed their sister, but they also found one in whom they could confide while they were in Italy. The Dragon had made his presence known to them. They relished the opportunity to listen to his advice and guidance. He had told them he had been waiting for them to seek him out. Now, they had one who could protect them, ensure they could feed each night, and gave them sanctuary from the church who was very much aware they existed.

Like many a camp follower, Tayla followed the French army to accompany Renard for the next ten years. From campsite to campsite, enduring small engagements and minor skirmishes, she clung to the prospect that he might be mortally wounded and that she could lead him to the crossing over by giving him her blood to pass through his lips.

Renard was a good knight, skilled and efficient as a warrior. He was rarely even wounded. The only wounds he suffered were the emotional ones of seeing such suffering as the result of combat. He had lost his family due to the war. His only comfort was being in the arms of Tayla. Finally, they were together on the eve of the Battle of Poiters.

It was the 18th of September 1356. At a small castle, being used as the headquarters for the French army, they met. Tayla stood upon the battlement of the north wall of the castle, her robes flowing in the gentle night breeze. The moonlight shone upon her, giving her a silvery aura, but casting no shadow beyond her figure. Renard saw her, off in the distance, while in the yard below the wall. He was carrying a torch in his hand but the one in his heart burned even brighter. He was smitten with the seductive Tayla. His conversations with her had become ever more intimate and he had accepted the reality of her being. Yes, she was a vampire, a thing of evil to others, but to him she was different. She made him feel incredibly special and gave him a happiness he had not known for such a long time.

Tayla smiled as he approached her. As the torchlight fell upon her, her beauty warmed Renard as he stepped up on the cold stone of the secluded battlement wall. Here in the shadows, in the darkness of night, they were simply two lovers, embracing each other.

He always asked himself if he was just being seduced. She could have killed him at any time. She could have taken his life force in one complete assault upon his body or persuaded him to

287

give it up to her a piece at a time. But he was in love. Was it genuinely love or infatuation?

She had shared with him her history, the pain of her affliction. She had revealed the loneliness of her existence to him, as he had told her of the pain of his loss. He was now alone as was she. He had told her he could not bear to love and lose another so dear to him. The prospect of loving again and forever appealed to him. It gave him an unspeakable joy—one that made his heart soar!

His embrace and his body's warmth gave her the joy she had been seeking for so long. She sensed his body's core temperature as his blood raced through his veins and arteries. It was warm, flowing and inviting, while hers was yet cold and motionless within her. She took joy in knowing one of the living had discovered that same emotion within the power of her presence. She had found solace in knowing she could be intimate with one of the living and was no longer restricted to the undead. Reaching out to the world of the living, finding a willing, desiring partner was far more than her expectations of love in her world.

"My dearest Tayla, it is with complete commitment that I pledge my love unto you. I place my heart and will in your hands. I know that you could extinguish me, draining me of my life. Or, you can take me completely into your world and accept me as one of your own. And I would not hold you responsible for your actions. After all, it is something you are driven to. You cannot be held responsible. If the "crossing over" is my fate, then so be it. I accept it as my fate, my destiny for which I was born. For to be with you is my happiness. I have never known anyone like you, human or vampire, who could make me lose my need for caution. So, I have thrown it to the wind."

She cupped his face with her long slender fingers. The warmth of his skin exhilarated her. She gazed into his eyes, smiling all the time. She wondered if her coldness would repulse him. Her ability to warm herself had not developed yet. She was still maturing into the vampire Queen she would eventually become. These abilities to perform human functions and partake in them joyfully had not come to pass. But still, she was with

Renard, and that was all that mattered to her on this cold but moonlit night.

"Renard, I have a ring for you. I know we can never marry in a church, nor could we ever be reviewed before a priest. But their condemnation of our union shall not dissuade me from being with you. When the time comes, I shall make it painless so that you may be with me forever. I relish the time we will spend together."

She had asked him for his hand in marriage, declaring she would give him her love and her own immortality as a wedding gift. It was highly irregular, but their relationship was equally as irregular.

He replied to her, "My love, if anything must leave our world, it is time. I am human, and finite. I will eventually die, and you will go on. Therefore, it is necessary that I come into your world now. There must be a redefining of life between us. Whatever power it is that keeps you alive, it must be afforded unto me. I am ready for your mouth to perform its deadly kiss upon my skin. I offer myself unto you."

Tayla had never experienced the joy of one giving themselves to her, especially when such honesty and trust were at stake. He knew what he was asking of her and willing to accept it no matter what the cost.

"My love, I have not known such a willing sacrifice in all my existence. For this I will surrender part of myself unto you, signifying my never-ending love for you. Our lives will mingle as our blood will and the two shall become one. My heart no longer knows the biting cold of loneliness and hopelessness. The word damnation no longer means anything to me. All I know is completeness in my world. I am satiated upon knowing that I am loved. I am needed. And my needs are filled."

"Then fill your needs with me, my blood, and my companionship. We will enjoy our existence together, forever. We will need no priest, no church nor vows to hold us together. For I love thee and no other."

"Then I take thee, Renard, to be my mate and husband!"

Renard echoed her feelings, stating that he was ready to accept her world, as he loved her and could not bear to live only a half-life with her, the half known as the night. She made ready to give her blood for him to drink.

They were interrupted by a call from a soldier at the bottom of the rampart. "Call to arms, Sir Renard! The English have been seen preparing to raid this castle. We must hurry to prepare to defend ourselves. The King must not fall into the hands of the English! The commanders stand ready to issue orders to mount and intercept the English!

Renard turned to Tayla, who was trembling with fear that he would leave her to fight. She had good cause to because that was exactly what he was ready to do.

"My love, I will return. Look for me before the dawn. I shall return to you and will join you in your world. I promise this. Remember my words!" He turned to make ready for battle.

Men were scurrying about, putting on armor, getting horses ready, while others were discussing plans. It seemed as if no one even noticed she was there. A lone woman, amongst so many men, who was noticeable to only one man, who was preparing to leave for battle. Never had she felt so alone as she did at that moment. Even her brothers and sister were not there to comfort her. For the first time since her mother had left, she shed tears because of impending loss. She had the feeling that his words were the last she was to hear. Committing them to memory, she waited upon the battlement walls.

*   *   *

It was near dawn, and not one knight had returned. Tayla, who remained vigilant upon the battlement walls, felt a familiar presence. It was her brother, Rascha, who had come to his sister's aid. He looked different as his appearance was older. He told her of meeting up with the Dragon who had given them the gift of transformation. He offered to share it with her, but she seemed distracted and he knew why. "Come with me, dear sister. I have something to show you."

He took her hand, led her to the top of the tower upon which they glided up to. From this vantage point, he showed her where the battlefield was. It was several miles away, but with her keen, sharp sense of eyesight, she could see very well. The field was strewn with dead bodies, some dismembered from combat. Armor, equipment, dead animals, and personal possessions were littered about the bloodied field. Lances protruded from animals and soldiers alike. She scanned the field, looking for her French knight. At last she found him.

She took off from the top of the tower in the moonlight, capitalizing on her ability to fly swiftly. Within minutes she arrived on the field, accompanied by her brother, Rascha. She glided to the ground as her boots took to the earth in stride. Lying next to his destrier, which was pierced with arrows from the English war bows, was Renard. He too was pierced with several arrows, one of which had struck him in the neck. He had not died immediately, for he had written her name, in his own blood, upon his steed's horse coat. She took little solace in knowing that she was among his last thoughts in this world. Now, he could never be part of hers.

The sadness and sense of loss came like lightning to Tayla. They were powerful and shocking, overwhelming her to her core. Vampires are highly emotional creatures, even those who choose not to love. But to one who does, this was a catastrophic moment. She fell to her knees to embrace her lover's body, sobbing uncontrollably.

Her brother knelt beside her. "My dear sister," Rascha whispered softly into his sister's ear as he held her tightly. "This was not meant to be. He belonged to the world of the light. He was not meant to be one of us. I only brought you here, so you could say goodbye to him. Besides, there may be one or two here who may still live. I thirst for those who may still be in agony. It gives a special flavor to the blood."

Tayla pushed him back slightly to look her brother in the eyes, saying "What would you know of what is meant to be, brother? I have sought for someone to love for years, and finally found someone who accepted me. Loved me! Only to lose him to this thing that the world calls war! This war has been waging itself across this land for years. Where has it gotten anyone? It reeks of death and destruction."

"Yes, it does, and it pleases me that it does so," Rascha quipped back at her, still embracing his sobbing sister. "Look at you. Your eyes are crying rivers of tears when this war is giving us rivers of blood. We can feast at any time and you cry over one dead French knight. This is what we are. Vampires! Not lovers! I for one have given up on the notion of having a partner that I would share my existence with. Besides, we have each other. I am content with only feasting and rutting on the living. You should be too!"

"Rascha," she said, breaking free of his embrace and standing, "I know you mean well for your sister, but you should know I am different than you. I have not been given over to the darker side of this existence as you and the rest of our family have. I still remember the warmer side of our past. The living memories I still carry. You have forgotten all of them."

"This is true, sister. Yes, it is. But because I do not love, I will not be hurt by it. I have not the heart, nor the passion for it. Nor do I have the soul! You of all the undead should know this. This shall become far too familiar because you will go through this again and again till the pain of loss is so unbearable you will avoid it like the plague that runs through this continent. I would spare you the pain of the loss. I speak as your brother, my dear."

"But there was to be only one more day and then the night. Then he would have been mine, and I, his. He carried my ring on his finger! We were betrothed to each other. It is not fair," she said, shaking her fist at the heavens in the moonlight. "It is not fair, not fair, not fair!" she cried repeatedly as she fell to her knees again, sobbing.

Rascha continued, saying, "For creatures such as us, we cannot marry, have children, or love those whom we are damned to consume. My dear sister, you need to accept these laws of our existence. They will not change as the sun will never smile upon us. Never!"

Tayla looked up at him, her eyes flowing with tears. "I suppose you are right, Rascha. We truly are damned. Damned to a life without love! How will we ever survive this world when we do not belong in either? He wrote my name in his own blood.

Do you think he knew I would be here tonight, looking at his body on this field, weeping for him?"

"I think he expected you to come to him before he died, to bring him to the crossing over. That you did not come is sad indeed. I suspect that arrow in his neck prevented him from calling out to you. Otherwise, he may be talking to us at this moment if you had." She wondered why she did not feel his pain from his wounds. If she had, certainly she would have come to him. Nothing would have kept her from him!

Rascha had insulation against this kind of emotional pain. The Dragon had enabled him to build a wall around his heart such that he would not experience the pain of loss that his sister was now experiencing. He did not care to love. He did not believe in it. He had rationalized or at least accepted the fact that he had no capacity for love and that it was not for him to experience. To Rascha, it was the same as dogs and cats never falling in love or mating. It was against their nature. Tayla could not accept that her existence gave her no room or provision for love.

She asked Rascha if this was all there was to this kind of life?

He said he felt as though it was but the best thing to do was to come with him to Rome where she could talk with the Dragon.

Doom seemed to flood her being. Her brothers and perhaps even her sister seemed content to lead this kind of existence. But not Tayla. She had found herself a chance at love. With someone who had accepted her for what she was and despite their differences, still found room in his heart to love the goodness that remained in her.

Her eyes cried tears that burned hot against her cheeks. A mist occurred each time the tears fell from her face to the cold ground in the chilling night air. She asked Rascha if he knew who was responsible for the death of her lover.

He replied that he did not. Rascha knew she would take up the quest of avenging his death by creating another death. And after all, it seemed that this was the cause of her pain. Death for a death, vengeance, and retribution. The cycle would go on and on, through the ages he told her. He had a much more practical approach to the human aspect of war. He was determined to exploit it. As for Tayla, she would have to go on.

CHAPTER THIRTY-TWO

THE HIGH COUNCIL

"Dearest Malcolm, it is now the time of the Clans. Many things have happened by now. I lost my first love, Renard. It was so painful that when I found him, my brother told me this was to be the usual and undeniable result of trying to love a mortal. Mortals and immortals are a very impossible pairing, as you and I both know. The pain of loss, the constant presence of war, the incessant efforts on the part of the Dragon to have me render fealty unto him... It went on and on. Soon, I began to receive gifts that enhanced my abilities. I was not sure if these were from the Dark Lord, or if they were directly from the Dragon.

We found that we could bring others into our world. I started to have my own clan with those I converted. They were loyal only to me and me alone. Being alone was blunted by finding I could have offspring, in a different kind of way. I became as a mother to all those I brought to the crossing over. Those I converted were more like me, not just like me but seemed to have a bit more control over their behavior than those my brothers and sisters begat. I learned how, and what it meant to be a ruler. My brothers and sister did the same. It lent to bickering amongst ourselves. The Dragon saw that he was in danger of losing control and so he stooped to some exceptionally low and heinous things to establish control over us. I would not yield nor would I surrender. This is the account I never told you about..."

*   *   *

It was now decades later, well into the fifteenth century. Tayla never forgot the pain of losing Renard, but she had much bigger things to deal with because of who she was. The Dragon had begun his campaign to woo Tayla to his will. She was having none of it. Rascha had succumbed eagerly as well as Prieta. It took some time for Othar to agree to his protection, but Tayla's instincts told her none of the benefits of the Dragon's protection and tutelage were going to come without a price. Soon, the children began to quarrel.

Rascha, being the first-born male, was always trying to assert himself as the rightful leader and that all four groups of vampires should follow him. The memory of his father's last words had been lost due to the curse. He was good at a lot of things, and particularly good at one thing...taking lives. His appetite for blood was voracious at the very least and he was known for showing no mercy whatsoever when it came to choosing victims. Often, he would enter a thatched house or cottage at night and leave it later with only corpses in their beds. This included men, women, and yes, children. Sometimes infants were taken. Rascha had not a shred of humanity left by this time. This had given him the insulation he felt when tragedy struck. When he saw Renard lying dead upon the battlefield, he felt no loss. He only felt the loss to his sister. It did not affect him personally and he only saw the opportunity it gave him. Soon, Othar and Prieta were following suit. They were learning by Rascha's example and the countryside hummed with supernatural tales of monsters in the night, leaving wakes of death behind them. The church was alarmed and began to send out teams of clergy to determine who was responsible and what could be done about it. The writings of the Bishop in Bulgaria were being examined so that the truth could be revealed. There were vampires at work here!

There would be little they could do for the vampire powers were far beyond what mortal people could understand. Protection for oneself and others grew out of superstitions that were coupled with ideas based upon scriptures. They formed remedies that did not work. Rascha and his brother and sister laughed before the killed. The invincibility they felt was

295

intoxicating.

Tayla thought there must be a better way to survive without becoming gluttons for the one thing that fed them. She was at a loss though for how to control her siblings for the drive for blood was far stronger than she was. The Dragon praised them for their actions and encouraged them, even directing them to those he wanted targeted. If the murders continued at the alarming rate the church had noted, surely some measure of effective response would come against them. Tayla gave her brothers and sister a warning. This was becoming a point of contention between Tayla against her brothers and sister. She was losing control over them because of the influence of the Dragon.

Tayla had gone to Rome to face the Dragon in person. Though she advocated for co-existence, she agreed to address the High Council of the *Order of the Dragons of Set*. Currently, she had quite a clan of vampires loyal to her. She saw no need for the Order to interfere and their interest in vampires had selfish reasons attached to it. Those vampires who were closest to her asked if the issue came to war, who would be their ally? If the Order had the upper hand regarding control of vampires, they would simply be weaponized, much like guard dogs, ready to do their will, even though it went against what Tayla wanted.

The vampire princess wanted the issue settled right away. A guarantee to co-exist, complete with a document signed by members of the High Council would be acceptable to her. What could she do if they did not uphold their end of the agreement? What kind of leverage could she hold over them? She felt that mortals could not be trusted. Since her conversion, apart from Renard, they had brought her only disappointment.

The Middle Age's ending came after the conclusion of the Hundred Years War. It's difficult to put an exact year to it but most use the last battle, the Battle of Castillon in 1453.

The Renaissance had already begun in Italy. Columbus would be making his history-making voyage soon. The plague had already peaked, and Europe was now finding itself decimated of people. Millions of European peoples had died. Young vampires had helped in the carnage, but their efforts were dwarfed by the monumental ability of a species of flea upon a rat to commit genocide. At the time, no one could have known about that. Most everyone who had survived believed that God was punishing the world, for some offense not recognized. If the plague did not kill you, you surely did not want to fall under suspicion from the church as one who had incurred God's wrath to send a plague.

When Tayla arrived in Rome, she did so under the cover of night. Not being able to meet with the High Council during the day, a meeting was arranged at night. Still, the house of Matthias was the usual meeting place. Matthias was long gone, but another member of the Order now possessed the house, which had been handed down for generations to members of the Order, particularly those who were members of the High Council. A room was made available for Tayla to sleep during the day. A bare room, with windows that large opaque tapestries would cover to block out any sunlight. Tayla carried her shroud of red velvet, the same which was originally a window covering of her father's castle. It was necessary for her to do this because it was the only way she could maintain contact with the original grave in which she was buried. All the vampires needed to do this because of the way they were transformed.

Akhenaten and Nefertiti did not need to do this because they were transformed in a different way, directly through the Dragon's power. Prince Vladis' transformation was done through another vampire. This seemed to place him and all other vampires after that under a different set of rules. Those vampires the Dragon transformed were obliged to follow him, but after Vladis, that changed.

The night Tayla arrived, she was greeted with respect and courtesy. The new head of the Order's High Council, a man named Ramone, greeted her, and offered her a young maiden from which to feed if she had not fed already. Tayla refused, as she had already fed from a stranger from the streets of Rome.

"I should like to discuss business now, if possible. Are the members of the High Council available, or do I have to wait until tomorrow night?"

Ramon, a middle-aged overweight fellow with a balding head dressed in high fashion of the day, said, "Oh no! They are here

297

and we can commence with business immediately if you like. We were not sure of what amenities to offer to you. You are very unlike any guest I have had to entertain before. I hope you understand, Tayla."

Tayla was dressed much like a princess, and since she was, she was acting very much like one. She had a commanding presence, spoke eloquently with confidence and refinement. As a princess, she was determined to get the education her mother wanted her to have. She remembered her mother's wishes of attaining herself an education, spending many years learning the basics of self- education. Once she had learned to read, there was no stopping her from teaching herself everything she could. She understood early on that knowledge was a kind of power within itself. When she entered the room with the long wooden table and chairs, she could read the minds of those present and deduced that she was probably the most educated one in the room.

She replied to Ramone, "I am very much unlike any guest you have had before, because I am much unlike any vampire you have met before. You would be wise to remember that."

One by one, each member of the High Council filed in, introducing themselves and taking their seats. Tayla was afforded a seat at the opposite end of the table from Ramone. A servant poured wine into the goblets of each member as they all recited aloud words, they always opened each meeting with. When they finished, they drank from the goblets and sat down. Ramone opened the meeting with an opening statement.

"Members of the High Council, we welcome a highly respected guest tonight. Members, I give you Princess Tayla Elisabeta Rokosovich, eldest daughter of Prince Vladis of Wallachia. We are here to discuss grievances between the *Order of the Dragons of Set* and the clan of Tayla's vampires as well as those of her brothers Rascha, Othar and her sister, Prieta. Princess Tayla, I give you the opportunity to state your position."

Tayla sat down and paused for a moment before she began to speak. "Members of this council, I come here because of my siblings and their behavior. They are out of control, my control, as I am their leader, their mentor, and their sister whose birthright gives me the right to rule over these clans of vampires. The

Dragon has long attempted to woo me into his ring of influence with no success. I see him for what he is. My brothers and sister are blind to his attempts to exploit us. I feel the Dragon does nothing without your knowledge, your approval, and your condonement. I want this to stop. I wish to co-exist, without contact, without interference or influence to challenge my authority as Princess of these clans. I have my father's ring," she said, as she pulled the ring attached to a chain around her neck. "This symbolizes my authority. My father was a nobleman, a Prince of Wallachia, and as his daughter, I carry that authority with me."

She was silent and the council members looked around at each other. Some smirked, noticeably trying not to break out in laughter. Tayla was indignant for she felt as though they were making a fool of her. Finally, Ramone spoke.

"Princess Tayla, where is your kingdom? Where are your subjects? Where are your soldiers, your lands, your castle? What exactly are you the Princess of?"

Tayla sat in silence, knowing they had not listened or understood at all what she had come to say.

He continued, "Your position is weak at best. You have no power here. You certainly have no authority here. You are afforded this courtesy to show you we are not barbarians. Let me state our position. You are a vampire. This Order, the Dragons of Set, created vampires. We have had them for several thousand years. We have the relationship with the Dark Lord that you do not. So, tell me again, why we should have nothing to do with vampires, the very creatures we created? Is it because you want to establish your own order of vampire clans?"

Desperate for an answer to silence the pompous Ramone, she replied in an authoritative voice, "Heed my warning. Do not interfere with vampires, either mine or my sibling's. If you ignore my warning, I will destroy all of you. Your entire *Order of the Dragons of Set* shall disappear from the pages of history. No one shall know of your existence, save that I might write about you one day."

"Tayla, we all die at some point. I foresee even you may die one day. It may be a long way off, but eventually, it will happen."

"That may be true, Ramone. I will be remembered by those who will destroy me. You will not be remembered at all."

"Your words are ones I do not take lightly. They carry serious consequences." He motioned for everyone to stand, as he felt the meeting was over.

Tayla stood up last, and said in response, "Yes, my words do carry consequences. Serious ones. You would be wise to remember that." She turned and left the room. Members of her guard were in the next room. One carried her velvet shroud.

"It is time to leave. We must get far away from here. We are in the camp of the enemy."

As soon as the door was opened, they instantly flew away from the house of Ramone.

Ramone watched them fly away into the darkness of night. He turned to a council member, stating, "Send word to the Dragon."

*   *   *

On a hillside outside the city of Rome, Tayla and her vampire guard found a cave which to spend the day. They arrived long before dawn, so they sat inside discussing what had been said.

Tayla thought hard about what Ramone had said. She spoke to the more senior members of her clan who had accompanied her to Rome. "He asked me where my kingdom was. Where was my castle, my army, my people? I could not answer him, save for those who I have brought to the crossing over. He is right. I need more than a ring. I need to assert my authority by a display of power. They need to recognize I am a force to be reckoned with, not just some ignorant girl who has discovered she can do some amazing things. Then maybe they will recognize me as ruler of all vampires. I will accept nothing less. One day, I will have a crown to wear, and a throne upon which to sit. Perhaps after that, a castle to house that throne. Then, lands to rule over."

The group of vampires were silent. "Do I expect too much? Do I wish for more than I deserve?"

A lone vampire stood up, saying, "Leaders and rulers are worthless unless they have ones to lead and ones to rule over. I believe you are that rightful ruler. I will follow you unto death."

One by one, the others stood up and knelt upon one knee in fealty, and repeated word for word that which the first follower stated. Tayla was pleased. She knew leadership came with responsibilities. Inside, she asked herself if she was up to the task. It did not matter, for she stood on the precipice of something great and there would be no turning back.

Inside a cave on the outskirts of Rome, the *Order of the Clan of the Red Velvet* was born. It was just an idea, but she knew it would have to be organized, recognized, and a claim be made with a charter, declaring its existence. Only that was just the beginning.

Tayla's movement to establish the clans began with the establishment of a headquarters. They had been living in France since before the Hundred Years War. She felt it best to re-locate back to a region where she was not known, nor were any of her clan members to be recognized. She would teach them the survival tools needed, the methods of obtaining victims without fear of suspicion or retribution.

She decided to return to her homeland to see if her father's castle still stood and if inhabited. Many of the castles from the Middle Ages were in ruins. They had fallen into ruin from battle, from the Black Death or the famines that had plagued the lands. Europe was still reeling from the decimation of the population. It would take some two hundred years to recover from it.

Upon the night she arrived in Wallachia, she managed to find landmarks that led to where her father's castle stood. She was disappointed to find it nearly destroyed. The foundation of it was intact but the walls had nearly disappeared except for one of the outer walls. Most of the interior walls were less than three feet tall. She wondered where the stones of her father's castle had gone to. It would be revealed later that they had gone to make bridges and used to build a newer castle some distance away.

A diligent search produced the entrance to the crypt. Surprisingly, it was intact. A large stone had covered the narrow stairway that led down to it. She found her father's sarcophagus intact, with the lid partly moved to allow visualization of the contents. For those responsible for the destruction of the castle, finding the open sarcophagus is most likely what had led to the vampire legends that surrounded the site. It was also one of the reasons it was torn down. Superstition, the Church's dogma regarding such legends, and possibly encouragement by the *Order of the Dragons of Set*. The Order now had listed Tayla's clan of vampires on its list of enemies. The brothers and younger sister had immunity from such wrath, but Tayla was on her own.

They set up their headquarters in the crypt, though it was accepted that it was only temporary.

"We must be careful not to reveal our presence here. There are enough travelers through this region for us to feed upon. No local villagers are to be touched. I command this to be my law. As ruler, I am entitled to make such laws, and my laws will be obeyed."

It was agreed. There were roads well-traveled and rivers by which those travelers who fell victim could be disposed of within. Thus, suspicion would be low, if at all. Tayla wondered often what ever happened to Friar Bartholomew and Johannes. She would not discover their fate until long after. As told before, Tayla and her siblings were transformed in 1216, and now, it was 1453. They were long dead, but the details were not available.

The current Prince of Wallachia was a man known as Vladislav II. It was a turbulent time for Wallachia. Civil wars, Prince against Prince, and for quite a while, whoever was on the throne had the Ottoman Empire to deal with. Vladislav II would not be on the throne for long as the one whom he had deposed would come back for a terrible revenge. That man was none other than Vlad Tepes or Vlad III, also known as Vlad the Impaler.

They existed for a while in the region, organizing, acquiring funds, and converting recruits that were not local. In 1456, in a hand to hand combat challenge to the throne, Vlad III killed Vladislav II and took the throne for a second time. His reputation for being a cruel and sadistic ruler reminded Tayla of Vojislav, the Dragon responsible for the death of her family. She decided to approach him for his reputation had piqued Tayla's curiosity.

It was the summer of 1460. The view from the mountain top of Mount Cetatari was breathtaking. Castle Arges, though damaged and abandoned, sat upon the peak's narrow top. It was probably the most formidable fortress in all of Wallachia. A river flowed through the narrow and deep gorge below. Vlad III had taken the ruined Castle Arges, repaired it and made it his fortress. The castle lay to the far west of where her father's castle was located. It would be difficult to take this castle by force. This was the very castle Tayla wanted, for to reach it, one had to travel by foot. Any mortal who did, did so at his own peril. It was perfect for Tayla's purposes. She was determined to get it if she could.

That summer, she went alone to the Castle Arges. She made her way into the castle easily, bypassing any security apparatus in place. The need for a large garrison was negated by the fact there was such a natural defense of the Castle already in place. Another feature that Tayla liked.

Transforming herself into a mist, she glided down the halls right through pairs of soldiers who stared in amazement of the living mist that approached them, then traversed past them making its way to the chambers of the Prince of Wallachia. Moving under the door, the mist penetrated his room, as he slept. She then reformed herself to her physical completeness. He remained fast asleep.

She sat down in a large chair, ornate with padded upholstery of leather with packed horse's hair underneath. She watched him until he began to stir. She was calling his name in whispers such that he would awaken any moment. When he did, he sat up straight, and saw her sitting in his chair. A young, beautiful woman, barely old enough to bare children staring at him, fearlessly watching him as a hawk would watch a mouse.

"Who are you and why do you dare enter into my presence without permission? Do you know where you are? Who sent you?" He asked so many questions of her she barely could get a word in. When he finally calmed down, she had not spoken.

She continued her stare, with a smirk that said so eloquently, "I know something you do not."

"Speak!" he demanded.

"I am Tayla, Princess of Wallachia. Daughter of Prince Vladis, former Prince of Wallachia. I know who you are, and yes, I do dare enter your presence, Prince Vlad. I like your castle. It is very defensible. Except to creatures like myself. Then, it is the perfect residence for one such as me. it makes me feel like an eagle, perched high aloft on a cliff, where I can spot all my enemies, and my prey as well. And none of them can get to me nor can they attempt to run without my knowledge of it. Enough of the formalities. I know who you are, Vlad Tepes, also known as Vlad III. You will come to be known as Vlad the Impaler. That is your favorite form of execution, is it not?"

"Shall I have one made up for you?" he asked, not having any idea of what she was.

"It would do no good. I am here to talk with you, about your castle, your alliances and how to win against your enemies."

Vlad understood he had enemies. That was mostly due to his political standings. His enemies were Hungary to his north and west while the Ottoman Turks were to his south and east. Fighting a war in two opposite directions is difficult at best, even if you are a great general upon the battlefield.

"Are you here to warn me, or to give aid?" he asked.

"I am here for both reasons. I can warn you of impending troop movements and I can give you immense aid on the battlefield. You need allies, and so do I. I hoped we could strike an agreement, a pact that you and I could support each other."

"If you say you are the daughter of Prince Vladis, I will have to say you lie. Prince Vladis died a long time ago, over two hundred years ago. If you are his daughter, then you must be over two hundred years old. You do not seem to be even twenty years old."

"An astute observation! Just how do you think that could be, Prince Vlad? How could I, who looks so young, who could worm her way past your guards in the night, enter your room such that a seasoned veteran of battle could not awaken to my entering your chambers? How could I do such things?"

He demanded to know, "Are you a witch? A sorceress? What are you?"

"Are you familiar with the legends surrounding my father's castle?"

"I heard they tore it down, to keep certain creatures from making it their home. Only a few stones rise above its foundations."

"You did not answer my question. What are those legends?"

He answered, "The legends are about certain creatures that cannot die. The undead, they rise at night and hunt for living creatures that they might obtain their blood. They are evil, powerful, and nearly invincible."

"Yes. Exactly. I like the word you used, 'invincible'. It has great descriptive power. It is an adjective by which I would like to be known. I am sure you would like to be known as invincible too, would you not?"

"Are you one of the undead, Tayla, daughter of Prince Vladis?"

"Yes, I am. Then, Prince Vlad, answer my question. You would like to be known as invincible too, would you not?"

"Yes, a man who is invincible has few enemies. Most learn from the reputation that precedes him."

"Good. Good answer. A truthful one, for I do not like lies. Now, we are getting somewhere."

*　　　　*　　　　*

Vlad III allowed Tayla and her small clan of vampires to move to the castle. They had struck a bargain. She would only feed off his enemies and protect him against them. Vlad would give sanctuary and protection to them by allowing them to live at the Castle Arges.

Vlad had a wife who lived at another residence. Due to constant wars, he got to spend little time with her. He had no desire to entwine himself with something as unholy as vampires, no matter how seductive they seemed. After all, he was a member of the Order of the Dragon, sworn to defend the Holy Church against the enemies of Christ. Tayla had no interest in him other than the protection bargain she had struck. She still felt the pangs of heartbreak whenever she would see a mounted knight. There were simply too many bad memories to attempt another shot at love. For now, her priority was to survive, for her clan to survive, and to establish herself as a ruler of vampires. To do this, she needed Vlad's protection for she was sure the *Order of the Dragons of Set* were not about to let her go unchecked. She thought it strange that both Orders were "of the Dragon". Similar in names but that was the only thing they had in common.

This arrangement was successful for a while. When they moved in, the workers had just completed the repairs needed to make the fortress nearly impregnable. Vlad had massacred the older ones of the boyar (nobility of the region) families, and the younger ones were marched nearly 50 miles to the castle for repair work. Only a few remained at the end. Many of the older members of the boyar families were impaled. The revenge was terrible and earned Vlad his reputation as the "Impaler".

While under Vlad's roof, Tayla and her vampires had little contact with their mortal hosts. They watched over the castle by night while a small contingent of soldiers stood by during the day. No one could get to the castle by any means other than foot. It was an awfully long climb. Vlad would only leave when it was necessary to join with his armies. Sometimes, at night, Tayla would offer to take him where he needed to go. Often, he could be seen in two different places on the same night miles apart from one destination to another destination. The peasantry as well as nobility wondered how he could accomplish travel across such great distances so easily. Tayla and her vampires were building his reputation for him. He went along with it, for he knew that his people were very suspicious, and they talked. They would embellish stories of his great feats, exaggerate them, perhaps invent them. Vlad knew that these stories would get back to not just those he ruled over but also his enemies. He wanted his reputation to be founded partly on legend and much on fact. News of such feats that could not be explained traveled fast. Tayla was helping him to accomplish this.

Vlad III's enemies included the nobles of many of the neighboring principalities, most of which were small kingdoms. The politics of war, protecting allies and attacking enemies were exhausting to him, but his character was one that refused to yield.

However, the bigger threat to his rule and his people was the Ottoman Empire. The Turks were a constant threat and always demanding of tribute. Tribute was nothing more than extortion. Vlad resented this and refused. He would rather go to war with them, as his reputation for willingness to fight was unsurpassed. Now, he had allies he trusted. He had bodyguards who would protect him. There would be no daggers in the night. He could reach out and destroy his enemies without having to be anywhere near them. Tayla was eager to uphold her part of their bargain.

Turkish blood was good to her and her clan, and they thrived upon it. They would kidnap leaders from the Turkish chain of command and within a few days, Turkish patrols would find the official impaled along a roadside, courtesy of the Wallachian soldiers and Tayla's vampires. The effect it had was frightening.

Before Tayla had come to aid Vlad III, he was already instilling fear in his enemies. Turkish envoys had their turbans nailed to their heads on the pretext they had disrespected him. A much greater official, the Bey of Nicopolis, was sent to make peace with Vlad. They were ambushed, and all were impaled.

When he teamed up with Tayla and her vampires, it became messy. In 1462, they scorched the lands between present day Serbia and the Black Sea. Vlad's armies killed thousands of peasants, not to mention untold numbers of Turks. Vlad's reputation was one which struck fear and desperation to anyone who was in the path of his armies.

Eventually, the Turkish forces prevailed. It was only because of the manpower and the betrayal of the one man who vowed to stop their invasion. The King of Hungary recognized Vlad as the lawful prince of Wallachia, but he did not provide him military assistance to keep his throne.

Mehmed II, the Ottoman Sultan, acknowledged Basarab Laiotă as the lawful ruler of Wallachia. Vlad teamed up with Stephen of Moldavia and set out to go against the forces of the Turks and those of Basarab. Vlad III was killed by the Turks during fighting in 1476. The battle occurred during the day and therefore Tayla was unable to enter the fight. Her benefactor gone, and the land in peril of occupation by an unfriendly ruler, she was forced to leave Eastern Europe for good.

CHAPTER THIRTY-THREE

ELSPETH

"Dearest Malcolm, as you can see from the last chapter, it was I who was responsible for building up the fearsome reputation of a man who has been long thought to be the inspiration for your movie vampire, Count Dracula. Vlad was not a count but a prince. In the 1800's, Mr. Stoker never even traveled to Eastern Europe to learn about Vlad Tepes. In those days, it was convenient to write about something few would ever try to authenticate. So, as you can see, telling a good lie is sometimes more interesting and entertaining than telling the truth. At times, truth is boring. Sometimes, it is painful. Often, we choose lies over truth. As you can see, I affected history. I could not change it, but I had a hand in its development. After my benefactor, Vlad Tepes was killed, I had to find a new home. My ranks had increased such that I would need several places to house them. It was time to get creative. I found that I could have relationships with human mortals. Though I could never marry and have children in the conventional sense you and Rachel have done, I could have friendships based on mutual trust. You and I were not the first of such a relationship. I had several and I enjoyed them immensely. The pain of it is that I will always outlive those I love."

*　　　　　*　　　　　*

It was 1477. The Hundred Years War behind them, Europe still reeled from the chaos of war and disease. The Black Death, known today as the Bubonic Plague, had stripped Europe of over a third of her population. She was weak beyond description in terms of being able to stave off an invasion from the Ottoman Empire. The only thing that really saved them, was a man like Vlad Tepes and the fact that the Plague was non-discriminatory. It affected the Ottoman Turks as well as Christian Europeans. Crusaders returning from the wars passed through empty towns and villages still reeking with the stench of dead bodies not disposed of because there was no one left to bury them. Vultures, crows, ravens, rats, and other creatures that lived off carrion flourished. It seemed they were the only ones who benefited from the terrible disease, having no shortage of food to survive.

Those of the living had a much different tale to tell. Castles considered themselves under siege by something they could not see. No sword, no lance, no arrow could find a target to lash out against to defeat such an invisible foe. This only added to the frustrations and imaginations of an ignorant population.

The Holy Church preached that God was angry with those still living and had dealt with those already dead. They said that witches were everywhere, and Satan walked amongst us, eager to infect us all. Many innocent people were put to death because of this childish belief that all affected were being punished. Sometimes, sick people are sick through no fault of their own. But these were the Medieval Times, on the cusp of the Renaissance, the age of enlightenment. The only enlightenment that Tayla and her clan saw was the lightening of the purses of the masses and the coffers of the church becoming weighted down with the same coins.

Money meant nothing to Tayla. Unlike many mortals, she did not obsess over it. She could easily take that which she wanted, though she could not own it outright. Dead people do not own things. When people are deceased, all their property is divided up amongst those who are relatives and such. However, none of the conventions of wealth and inheritance affected Tayla as she did have gold and silver. Much of it still left over from the chests that Illona had hidden.

The decades of war and disease had also brought about famine in certain areas. This resulted in many changes in the levels of population, political power, and land ownership. Tayla found several castles that were in various states of ruin and uninhabited. The locals had looted them, taking anything of value with them. Many of them were left in soot-filled ruins after they had lit the premises thinking that fire would rid the place of evil and the disease.

She also found one with only a few remaining inhabitants left. They located this castle in Eastern France. The method of discovery was by accident. The vampires were good at locating anything that was living. It was as if the heartbeat of a living person sent out a signal. It made it nearly impossible for the living to hide from them.

One night, after a cold rain had just ceased, the overcast sky began to clear and a moon shone through light clouds, giving off some light. A lit candle near a window caught Tayla's eye as she flew overhead. Some of her clansmen were with her. They saw it too, as they turned to investigate. What they saw, shocked even Tayla. It did not seem to startle her other vampires, but it shocked her, to her core. Why did she always get emotional about such as she was seeing? She was just beginning to understand her emotional makeup.

In a tower, there was a room containing a family of seven, huddled together next to a fire. The fire was low, barely enough to keep the room warm. The windows in the tower were no more than firing ports for crossbows and long bows in case of attack. No mortal could fit through such an opening. But, a vampire capable of turning themselves into mists, could easily enter such an opening. Tayla had come into the tower through a window to another room and taken the stairs up to the door. At the same time, she turned the latch on the door, several vampires entered the room through the open windows. Keep in mind, in those days, there were no glass panes to keep out the cold winds or creatures such as vampires.

The room was dark. If not for the light of the fire in a brazier, there would have been no visibility. Tayla sensed fear. As usual, she was drawn to it. As the door latch turned, she entered. Her feet made no sound upon the floor made of heavy wooden beams. The family did not see her, but they heard the door creak open.

"Who is there?" asked the woman in a voice full of fear.

Tayla stopped, saying, "Who asks of me?"

A child cried out, "Mother, it is a lady! It is not him!"

Tayla telepathed her other vampires to stay in the shadows. It was obvious they were hiding, and she was curious to know why and from who they hid themselves from.

Tayla, with gifts of control of the elements which included fire, made the fire brighter so that the room was illuminated. The family of two women and five children huddled around the brazier to bath in its warmth. No one dared to question how she was able to perform such a feat.

The young girl who had cried out looked at Tayla, dressed in noble finery, "Look mother, it is a lady, a very pretty lady! She must be a princess."

Tayla was taken back. The words of the child revealed that she saw Tayla as a potential rescuer, a possible hero. The innocence of the child went straight to her heart. Tayla was hungry but she was in control. Always in control. She told her vampires to seek elsewhere for their sustenance. She would stay the night here.

"Again, who asks of me, who I am?"

The woman struggled to rise to her feet. She was weak, dirty, unkempt, and fearful but protective of her children. "Forgive me, and my appearance, but I am Countess Elspeth DeVacquerie, widow of the late Count DeVacquerie. We are all that is left of his family."

"What has happened here? I sense great fear and mistrust. You are hiding here, no? And, who does the child refer to?"

"Many questions," replied Countess Elspeth.

Tayla interrupted her. "Princess Tayla Elisabeta Rokosovich, eldest daughter of the late Prince Vlad of Wallachia."

The child sitting in front of the brazier leaned over and told her sister, "See, I told you she was a princess."

"Fear not, for no harm shall come to you, not this night. Let us talk. Have you enough food?"

They had nearly exhausted their food. They were cold, tired, and discouraged. Their fear was because the man who had made her a widow was out to destroy the entire family. If there was an heir, his plans for taking the Count's estate were in peril.

The castle they were in had been the result of a siege and subject to the plague. The plague had affected the Count's forces as well as the other nobleman's forces. The Count's retinue had been decimated, but oddly enough, his family had been unaffected.

The contest had come down to the act of one man's efforts to search for and eliminate the surviving members of his enemy's family. Tayla wondered why had he not come directly to the castle?

Elspeth continued to explain to Tayla her plight. Elspeth was English. She had been given to the late Count as part of payment of a debt. Her father had been taken prisoner during combat at the Battle of Formigny. He was held for ransom which was paid but also part of that ransom was the promise that should he have a daughter, she would marry the son of his captor. It was agreed, for the English nobleman had no daughters, only sons. That was to change later in the years to come. Elspeth was that first daughter and her existence was found out by the French nobleman. When she came of age, the son of the Count DeVacquerie came for his prize. True to his word, he gave his daughter in marriage to the son of his captor. Payment was due and payment was made. In time, she came to love the son of the Count. The Count died and her husband became the new Count of DeVacquerie, and she became Countess. She gave him five children, who still lived. They had three other sons, who had died earlier in life. All in all, she had borne eight children. Of the five left, there were three daughters and two sons.

After the English had left, there was a great deal of lawlessness. Bands of mercenaries for hire replaced garrisons of troops that had been loyal to noblemen. They answered to only a few if any. They raided and pillaged, much like the Norsemen had done hundreds of years ago. The Church struggled to maintain a sense of social structure. The French monarchy was still trying to establish itself as the sole authority of the land.

In this world, in this time, it was as it had always been, war and disease responsible for the plight of the peasant. She thought of her nature and wondered why the evil in this world knew no bounds. It was strange that these thoughts should cross the mind of a vampire. To be a first-row spectator of the chaos that follows disasters such as war, plague, and the famines that accompany them afterwards made her see the world of the mortal much more clearly.

"This war has taken all that you have loved, has it not?"

"Yes, Princess, it has. Have you lost as well?"

"Oh, yes. I was to be married to a French Knight. His name was Renard. He was killed by the English."

"Who did you support in the war, French or English?"

Tayla responded, "I supported no one. I hated this war, but for different reasons than you might expect. I hate this plague, but it has served a purpose." She had not let on about her true nature. She pondered if she should divulge her nature and identity. To do so would be certain death for this family, who had suffered so much already.

"What will you do now?"

Elspeth responded, "I have no idea. I have no one to fight for me, yet I am responsible for my children. I know I am responsible for those charged unto my care, but I cannot fight for them. I know not where they might be, but if there are others loyal to my husband, they will be loyal to me. Hopefully."

"The night is long. Does this man, who seeks your death, is he nearby?"

"He is afraid to enter here, for below, at the front door, are the bodies of those infected with the plague. He dares not to pass that doorway for fear of contracting the plague. I hear his camp is near the river. I cannot be sure, as we have not left this tower for days."

"You will remain here. I will take care of everything. After tonight, you will be and remain forever more, the Countess Elspeth of DeVacquerie. You have my word as a Princess."

The land was desolate. Tayla knew her vampires would have to search probably the entire night to find victims. It was the first time she had ever considered rationing of victims. She telepathed to them to search for a camp near the river. She would be joining them soon. She would bring food and water back to the castle if they found any. Tayla had a secondary motive for being kind.

313

This castle was a possible home if she could gain the friendship of Elspeth.

She met up with her fellow vampires at a camp on the banks of a river. The vampires had already attacked the mercenaries and their leader who had coveted the castle of the Count DeVacquerie. Their bodies were laid out except for two. They had kept them alive for their leader, Princess Tayla.

Upon arriving, she entered the camp as one with authority. "Where is the leader of this group of corpses?" she asked.

A young man, still in his armor, pointed his arm towards a large burly fellow, lying on the ground. The man had tried to fight off his attackers but to no avail. He was doomed the second the vampires had hit the ground. The vampires had sensed this man was the strongest threat to fight back and he was the first to die. The others died in a complete panic upon learning that their weapons had no effect upon the supernatural creatures of the night.

"Gather all their food, ale, weapons, horses. Take that wagon too. Search their bodies for any coins. Whatever you find, I want it taken to the castle of the Countess DeVacquerie."

The vampires immediately set to work, completing their tasks as given by Tayla. The two surviving men watched in disbelief as the vampires worked at breakneck speed. Tayla watched them as they watched her clansmen. "What do you see?" she asked.

"I see things I do not understand," one said. "Our weapons had no effect. I know I struck true into the bellies of at least three of your men, and nothing happened. There should be at least three of your men on this ground next to my comrades. But there are none."

The other one, who had pointed out the leader said, "I have heard the priests talk about those like you. They have told certain ones about some who walk amongst us that should have died a long time ago. I know a priest who spoke of ones like these who attacked us. They said there is hardly a defense against these creatures. But there is a defense that never fails."

"Who is this priest?" Tayla asked.

"Father Joachim, of the Dominican Order. He has been sent all over, searching for ones like them. He has had success in destroying those creatures."

"I do not know this priest. Perhaps, someday I will meet him. For now, I am your judge. I find you guilty of the offense of searching out to kill, without justification, the family of the Count DeVacquerie. Your actions possess no justification other than to illegally obtain rights to the estate of the late Count. You are in the company of those who conspired and carried out the murder of the Count, and those who willingly conspired to do such illegal acts. I sentence you to death. Kneel!"

The two men did as they were told. They whispered silently to themselves. Tayla was not sure if they were praying, for they did not "cross" themselves as members of the Holy Church usually did. She heard confessions of the two, their past sins, and their remorse. It was then she attacked.

The vampiress took one man by his head and tilted it to the side, exposing the neck to the fatal bite she was so ready to make. The time it took to drain his blood and life force was short. When she let the head go, the man slumped over, falling forward upon his face. She immediately repeated her actions upon the second man, who also did not make a sound. Within minutes, Tayla was satiated.

The clansmen reported that everything they had found was ready for transport. She ordered that all the bodies be burned beyond recognition so that no one would know who they were or why or how they died. Once the bonfire had been lit, and the bodies piled upon it, they set out to return to the castle.

Tayla flew ahead to clear away the bodies that lie in the doorway. She cleared all the corpses, along with another vampire. Once this was done, she returned to the tower. The brazier was almost at the point of dying out. She immediately re-lit the fire, noticing that the family had gone to sleep.

Dawn was approaching in a few hours. Knowing that, she wanted to speak with Elspeth, so she woke the woman. Taking her outside the tower room, she told her that she needed shelter for the night and if she had her permission to take shelter in her castle. She stated she would need to sleep for the day and would speak to her after sundown the next day. She informed her that food and other supplies were in the great hall. Letting her know that her tormentors were no longer a threat alleviated the greatest of her worries. She could recover, rebuild, and raise her children without fear, at least fear from that brigand.

Elspeth granted Tayla's request as she felt it was the least, she could do for her benefactor. Though she knew there was many questions that needed to be answered, she held off for the right time to inquire them. The few servants she had were ordered to make available the quarters that Tayla said she required.

Before she retired, she told Elspeth, "I know you have many questions about me, why I have helped you, and most importantly, how I was able to do such things. I will answer your questions tonight. Say nothing to no one about what has happened here. For now, all you need to know is that you and your family are safe."

The evening came and Elspeth anxiously waited for the sun to set in the west. As Tayla had surmised, she did have questions. Questions that she was afraid of the answers. Her obligations to her family and her staff demanded that she find courage and stand to receive those answers.

Superstitions as well as rumors abounded in the region. Across Europe, the curse of the undead ran amok. Tayla's siblings had not been as careful as Tayla had instructed them to be. The Dragon had met with them and had them firmly under his control. Murders, assassinations, executions abounded, as well as other lawlessness. Tayla had no doubts that the Dragon was involved and probably her brothers or sister were involved as well. The more they killed, the larger their footprint became. Soon, much of Europe, at least those who still survived the plague, were whispering about it.

This also meant that the Church would have to act as well. Only a few monks had taken the pains and time to write about such instances of vampirism. To preach publicly about it was considered heresy, for the Church wanted no validity to be given to such tales. If the Holy Church were going to act, it would have to be done quietly, privately and without the official sanction of the Church in Rome.

Earlier that morning, Elspeth's staff got busy trying to clean up the mess from the battles and the siege. There were not many of them left. There was enough wood from the shattered siege engines for firewood to hold them for a while. Some peasants had fled the estate, but others from other estates had come looking for the protection of a nobleman. Elspeth was eager to take on anybody for an estate with less than an adequate labor force would not survive.

Finally, the sun disappeared from the sky. The light of dusk quickly faded with it and soon, it was dark. As expected, Tayla appeared with her escort in the great hall of the castle. Elspeth sat in the chair she had always sat, next to her husband's.

"Good evening, Countess. I am ready to answer your questions. You may be alarmed at some of my answers. I will be as honest as I can. I sense a great deal of apprehension on your part. I am not your enemy. I eliminated your enemies. Your sanctuary is returned to you. Your children shall have their birthright. I too, was in great danger of being robbed of my birthright. It is something that all nobles must face, rivals to their position of authority."

Elspeth said nothing for a few minutes. She wondered about the rumors, the superstitions that she had heard about for the last few years. Finally, she found the courage to ask the questions to which she needed an answer.

"You say you are a princess. I have no reason to doubt you. Wallachia is your home, you say. I have not heard of this kingdom."

"Wallachia is no longer recognized. The Ottoman Empire took it from the Hungarian Empire. It was once part of the Bulgarian Empire. And, sadly, this all took place many years ago, long before you were born. I know you will be trying to understand that if this took place many years ago, how could I be here? Why do I appear as young as I do? The questions you want to ask, please ask them."

"Alright. I will ask those questions. First, are you friend or foe? I have seen your kindness. I have heard of your ferocity. Which do you mean to give unto me??"

"I believe my kindness and protection to you, defending your family against an armed attack upon your family would be proof that I mean you no harm."

"Very well, then. Your statement of where you come from would mean that you are much older than you look. How can this be? I would prefer that you start from the beginning and leave no details untold."

"I shall do so. But...remember it was you who wanted to know." Tayla began the long story of who she was and how she came to be that creature of the night. She was a refined woman. Though of the undead, she was not without emotion, nor reason, nor logic. If anything, she was much wiser than most mortals, having had many years to acquire and understand that which many mortals take a lifetime to learn but seldom practice. Plainly speaking, she said she was acutely more aware of the world than her mortal counterparts, and even more aware than her vampire brethren. She spoke at length of her family, their struggles to survive, her love of her mother and father and the dangers the world faced due to the manipulation of world events by the *Order of the Dragons of Set*. By the time she was finished, Tayla had told her everything. Elspeth was amazed, and frightened.

"The legends are true. It is your kind that feeds off the diseased, the wounded on the battlefield, and robs those of their life blood in the middle of the night."

"I stand accused of such crimes and I am guilty. Guilty of being a victim, and of repeating the crime done unto me. What will you do with such information?"

"Information like this can get one killed," said Elspeth. "However, I think if you wanted to kill me or my family, I would already be dead."

"I could do exactly that. The soldiers we killed yesterday, they wanted to kill you. Today, you live. They do not."

"You are capable of mercy?"

"Yes, and of kindness. And courage, and rage, and love. I see your family and I am envious. I saw your needs, and I felt compassion. I saw my love, Renard lying on the battlefield, with my name written upon his horse's coat in his own blood, and I felt sadness. I am a Princess, and I have my father's ring. The *Order of the Dragons of Set* asked me where my kingdom was. They said I had no power or authority. I wanted to show them that I do. My brethren, my clan you see here, will follow me and obey me, no matter what."

She gestured with her hands, showing all the ones who followed her. This was only some of them. She had many more.

"What is it that you seek?" asked Elspeth. She was less apprehensive.

"I seek sanctuary from persecution. I seek for others to understand me, and my brethren, my brood if you please. I seek the solace of refuge in a place such as this. In return, I shall protect you, defend you, and this castle. You shall not want for anything. I shall obtain whatever you need. I ask in return for your discretion, your silence of who we are, and your protection during the daylight hours. It is then we are powerless."

"If I refuse, what then?"

"Then, we shall move on, leaving you and your home intact. We will not harm you. I have compassion, and honor. I am not the monster who continues to ravage this land. That honor goes to my brothers and sister. They too are of my kind and are hugely different than I am. I should say, I am different than they are. They follow the darkness, the Lord of Darkness. The Dragon, the disciple of Set, has set his influence upon them and they do his bidding. I will not follow them. The last Dragon I dealt with was very evil. I suspect the one who lives now is no different."

Elspeth thought about all Tayla said. "Do you need an answer now?"

"Though I have all the time in the world, I have only the hours of darkness to live in. By day, I am dead. By night, I live. I shall await your decision before dawn. Then, I shall either retire here, in the chambers below this castle, or I shall leave you and you will remember me no more."

319

CHAPTER THIRTY-FOUR

A VELVET CORONATION

"Dearest Malcolm, I had learned to love another man, such as Renard, and in so doing, I learned the pain of love, or I should say loss of love. Moreover, I learned a lesson about my nature and that of mortal men. We are not the same. Co-existing with mortals is not easy, but it can be done. Living in the castle of the Countess Elspeth was much easier than I thought. That was because I spent as little time there as possible. She and I were in a relationship based on trust and mutual respect. The Countess became my friend. She never broke our agreement and I never harmed her or her family or staff. She prospered as did her children. I saw to it they never wanted for the things they needed. I traveled often, staying at pre-arranged places, where I learned that I needed familiars for more reasons than I had ever hoped to know. This co-existence was vital for the survival of the clans and I taught it to my siblings as well. Another survival tool I equipped them with.

Upon our first gathering, I learned the significance of my ring, and the rings of my siblings. This was due to the Dragon. As for my familiars, sometimes I found uses for them other than what you might think."

*   *   *

Tayla had a contingency if Elspeth refused her offer. She knew she had undertaken a risky proposal but hoped Elspeth would remember that she owed her life to the vampire princess. Perhaps she might think that she could learn to trust her, and that the relationship might be beneficial for her. On the other hand, Tayla also thought she might be deluding herself and should be cautious should she send word to the local priest that the very monsters that terrorized the land were at her castle that very moment. Her dilemma was that she could not be sure. She would have to learn to trust Elspeth much in the same way she hoped Elspeth would trust her.

Elspeth wrestled with the decision the entire night. She was much too uneasy to get any sleep. The other lady they found with the family was her trusted maiden. She had been with Elspeth since she was a child and Elspeth considered her nearly a sister. To the children, she was an aunt. The two talked about it the entire night. The maiden was mostly concerned for the children. Logic and emotion made a strange bedtime concoction by which neither would sleep. It was a life and death decision, for both, and perhaps even the vampires.

Elspeth's position was that they were indeed better off than the day before. Surely, today would have been their last day on this earth had it not been for Tayla's interference. To allow them sanctuary, even for a short time was not too much to ask if their safety could be guaranteed.

The maiden, Anna, was not so sure. She felt gratitude for such measures the vampires provided, but how could they guarantee safety when it was one of their kind, their siblings no less, who were the very monsters of whom they should be afraid? What if the siblings were to find their sister's place of refuge and desired to stay also? Would one vampire protect them from the hunger of their siblings? What kind of loyalty should they expect if it were tested? Neither one could be sure. To trust the vampires at their word was trust in its purest form. They had no assumptions or facts upon which to base their trust. They had only their fears and stories.

The rumors and exaggerated accounts of the murders that had taken place, not just locally but across the countryside, had been told a thousand times. There was no doubt each time it was passed on by mouth, it became more vicious and murderous than the last time the incident was told.

321

Elspeth interjected another possibility. Would there be more usurpers to come, hoping to take the castle, its lands, and the title? Who would stop them from doing what their predecessors could not do? Anna had no answer for that other than the idea that Tayla could take the castle for herself and leave their murdered bodies out in the fields to rot.

Elspeth replied, "But she did not do that. She saved us, offered us mercy and kindness. That is not the trademark of a monster. She is willing to forego our refusal if we choose not to entertain her as our guest. I think we need to keep her here with us until a better solution is found by all parties."

Anna bowed to her saying, "It is your decision to make, Countess."

An hour before dawn, Tayla came to the Countess Elspeth's chambers. A simple knock on the door startled Anna. Elspeth had already fallen into slumber. She was exhausted for the week's events had drained the noblewoman of her strength.

"My lady, the Countess Elspeth wants me to inform you that your request is granted. She is asleep, completely tapped of her strength. I am to inform you that the North Tower is intact, and empty. You may stay there, make improvements as you see fit and make it your home. You will be safe there as I will inform all staff that it is not to be entered unless for a reason agreeable to you and your clansmen. I understand that you will abide by her wishes as we will abide by yours, Princess Tayla?"

"I will abide most graciously by the Countess' wishes and my deepest thanks to her for her hospitality. Please convey this to the Countess when she awakens."

Tayla walked away with a smile upon her face. She informed the clan that their new home was to be the northern tower. The tower had three levels. It was intact and it was the most fortified. Why the Countess put them there was a mystery. One would think that the Countess would secure that for herself. But she stayed in the manor hall, in the upper chambers. It was away from the walls and therefore, most likely the last to be breached in case of attack.

The vampiress was determined there would be no attack. Not now, not soon, not ever! She would see to it that the Countess would not regret her decision to allow them to stay. For Tayla, she would come to know that not all threats come in the form of armed mortal men. The Dragon and the Order were still out there. She knew she was not free of their wrath nor their sphere of influence. Her brothers and sister would need to be free of them as well. That would be her new mission. The *Order of the Clan of the Red Velvet* could not be truly established until all threats to it were extinguished.

*   *   *

While Tayla wanted to maintain contact with her siblings, her current location could not be revealed. Therefore, when she traveled, she would travel with a limited entourage and seek shelter in only familiar places she knew to be safe during the day. This involved securing the services of mortal familiars. Familiars became the term used to describe a mortal individual who was either seduced into service to a vampire or put under a spell of loyalty and service because of their special talents or skills. Many of her clan members brought specially selected people who either possessed castles for refuge or others with ownership of business interests who could be of great value to the *Order of the Clan of the Red Velvet*. It had taken her a while to secure "safe places" all over Europe. She and her clan used them often when they traveled. She surmised her brothers and sister did the same as she found similar support systems being developed by them.

She sought out the brothers first. Finding them in northern Italy, she met with them. The meeting was amicable but still an air of tension could be detected among them.

"My dear brothers, I have missed you all these years. Often, I hear of you, but not from you. Why is that? Do you not wish to speak with me? Do you not care for your older sister as you once did?"

Rascha, the oldest male, spoke. Othar, shy when he was mortal, still held the same trait, even as a vampire. "Dear sister. I still hold you as dear to me. I have merely followed a different path. Othar's existence as well as mine are easier and more manageable while in the service of the Dragon. We worry not of being discovered, nor do we fear the church's efforts to persecute and hunt us down. While it is merely a matter of time for you, we do not fret about such things. Everything is taken care of. It is the same for our younger sister. It could be afforded to you as well if you would only submit to the Order."

"No. I will not submit. The Dragon is the one responsible for our current and everlasting condition. I will not betray my father's memory by allying myself with such an evil entity."

"Very well. I suspected your decision would not change. I wish you well. The church will close in on you, and they have the means to destroy you. I shall regret the loss of my sister. I shall weep, perhaps for the first time, much like you lamented over the loss of your Renard that night on the battlefield."

"Yes, that was very painful. It made me feel alive for the first time in many years. Pain, joy, any emotion... is part of the human condition."

"As I said on that night, I have no use for emotion."

"And you Othar, you have said little. What say you as to emotions?"

"I can only feel rage. I feel it when I attack. I feel it when I think of how people do not understand me."

"A slight thread of humanity perhaps left," she said. "Nonetheless, I hear you have organized much in the same way I have."

"True, sister. We have named our lineages after your fashion. After the colors of our burial shrouds. We still carry those with us," declared Rascha.

Othar said, "We watch you, learn from you, though this makes the Dragon angry. Prieta does as well. She is not as close to the Dragon as we are. Yet, she is not independent like you. She is still within the circle of influence as we are. Prieta resides currently in the northeastern part of Europe. She does well, when necessary to carry out the Dragon's wishes.

"As you are a princess, we have declared ourselves princes," said Rascha as he held out his hand along with Othar. "We have even fashioned rings, which symbolize our power. They have been sanctioned by the Dark Lord. Our authority is tied to the rings, as is yours."

On their hands were rings, like the ring that their father had worn. The major difference was that the stone upon each one matched the color of the burial shroud. A black onyx stone adorned Rascha's ring as an amethyst was set in Othar's ring.

"Mine is secured by birthright," she replied.

"True, sister. Perhaps, we should elevate you to the position of Queen. The Dragon would be infuriated that we would think of such a thing. We hear all kinds of things about you from the Dragon."

"I suspect you would. He has nothing but contempt for me, only because I reject him. He shall not lead me, and because of that, he will seek to destroy me. Think of that. That is his price of loyalty. Follow or die."

"Sister," Othar said, "We will not ever take up arms against you. Our loyalty must never be tested against our family. All four of us, must remain family. Though we are separate, we must still be united."

Tayla spread her arms, embracing both her brothers. It felt good for them to still have the one bond of family blood between them. She knew she would cherish it always, as she hoped they would feel the same. They embraced for a long time.

"We are united by blood, by fate, by purpose and nature. We could not change our fate, but now we must embrace it. We should set aside a time, each year, for us to come together, to gather as vampires, to celebrate our existence. The mortal world commemorates times on the calendar to remember events of the past. I think we should do the same. The time of our conversion, our birth into darkness," said Othar.

"No," replied Tayla. "I think it best that we commemorate the coming of our clans together as one kingdom, four colors, united under the blood of one family. Our coat of arms is the same. This is the month of June. Each year, at this time, we will agree to meet in a place of secrecy, of safety from persecution, and celebrate our existence."

"Yes, I agree," said Rascha. Othar agreed as well, stating that Tayla's idea was a better one, and that she should be the Queen of the clans. They would travel to Prague where Prieta had established her clan and inform her of this development. Prieta received all of them well and was in full agreement that their clans should be united as a kingdom. Their first gathering was in June of 1485. It served a dual purpose for the clans for they also held the coronation of Queen Tayla. The ceremony was held in the forests east of Prague. It was an ancient forest, far removed from any village or town. A perfect place for privacy as the throng of vampires was massive. It seemed as if a great army had gathered around their leader, just before an attack. Tayla had no crown or scepter fashioned at this point. She did not have a castle, nor a throne. However, she had thousands of vampires who were loyal to her.

She wore a gown of red damask, with a cape of white ermine. Damask fabrics were created in Damascus, Syria. This cloth rose to prominence in the 12th century for its unmatched beauty and flawless production. She held a bouquet of red roses for a scepter, mingled with white ones. Rascha had a ringlet of gold fashioned as the first gift given to a Queen. A great and beautiful crown would follow later.

As the eldest son, Rascha crowned his sister with the golden ringlet. She spoke her oath of devotion to all the clans, to lead them, to protect them, and to progress them. She declared it before all who were present. Afterwards, many mortals were taken for their blood as the coronation of their first and only Queen was cause for celebration. It was a great success.

The Dragon, even though uninvited, appeared. Rascha wanted him to be received in a civil and formal way. Being preoccupied, the Queen did not see this coming, but agreed. Her first edict was to declare the kingdom of vampires to be independent of the Order and would always be so. The amount of influence the Dragon had begun to wane after this gathering and this sparked a vicious response later from the *Order of the Dragons of Set*.

They finally met in the forest, immediately after her coronation. The Dragon, dressed out in his finest clothing, holding the reigns to a large black steed, whose horse coat reminded Tayla of the one which her lover, Renard rode upon the night he was killed.

"You recognized this horse coat do you not, Queen Tayla?" he asked. It was as if he knew she would and that it would bring a tear of sorrow to her.

"Yes, it belonged to Sir Renard Berenais, someone I knew and loved long ago."

"I brought it to you as a gift, to remind you of the price you have paid for the position you now hold. It has been an expensive journey for you, has it not?"

Tayla remained still, quiet and reserved. Finally, she spoke. "Yes, it has been awfully expensive, and I am not sure of the worthiness of it. It has cost me dearly."

"However, you are now a queen, the first queen of a newly founded kingdom. Prince Vladis would be so proud of you, all of his children."

"Do not speak of my father! You have no right to utter his name."

He took the horse coat off the stallion and gave it to Tayla, placing it in her arms. The blood of her lover still stained part of it with her name written in it.

The Dragon stated, "Yes, I know. I know the truth, but I will not tell you. You have severed all ties with the *Order of the Dragons of Set*. Set bestowed upon you many gifts, gifts that will help you survive the upcoming trials and persecutions. You will need them. The Order wanted to help you, protect you from all that which is to come. You have refused us, rejecting our authority over the vampires. We made the first ones, and therefore our control over them was legitimate and sanctioned by the source of their power. Now, you have come along and taken that legitimacy and authority away from the Order. Therefore, I have a message from Set for you. It is as follows. You and your siblings shall create rings and crowns and thrones for each of yourselves. You shall give yourselves royal titles. But know this lacks the sanctioning of the body who has created the race of vampire. From this day forward, your authority and power will be based upon the rings you wear that shall bear your royal stone and seal. That which happens to those rings shall happen to you

327

and those you will create. Set has decreed this shall be your blessing and your curse."

He mounted his horse minus the horse coat and rode away. They did not see him again for many years afterwards.

The divisions between Tayla and her siblings were kept to a minimum. Laws were put into place prohibiting any conflict, armed or otherwise, against each other. An attack on one clan was an attack on the others. It was forbidden for any vampire to assault another vampire. Policies and procedures for many concerns were put into place. Each clan had an ambassador assigned to provide diplomacy and communications to each of the other clans, so each clan had three ambassadors. A scribe from each clan was appointed to write these laws down such that there was no question as to the judgement to be handed down. The scribe also kept records of events and decisions made, and the history of the clans was thereby kept intact.

This was how the Orders of Velvet were established in 1485. Tayla's wish had come to fruition. She had established a vampire kingdom and she was its Queen.

*   *   *

Queen Tayla returned to her new home at the castle of the Countess DeVacquerie in eastern France. The household of DeVacquerie were thrilled that they had a new Queen living amongst them. They celebrated privately, and this was when Queen Tayla received some new gifts. She was able to eat and drink as mortals did. It made it much easier to blend in with the mortal world. This would soon come in to play as her nature would soon be tested.

Countess Elspeth had three small villages upon her estate. They were thriving as the harvests of the last few years had been bountiful. This was due in part to Queen Tayla's gift of power of the elements. She could blight the land or make it fruitful. She was making it the latter so the Countess would have abundancy for herself and her people she was obliged to protect and care for. Some others had noticed her good fortune as well.

A herald from a nobleman knocked on their door one day. He gave a letter from a Baron Phillipe Sauvienne who intended to visit within the next few days. The letter was designed such that preparations could be made for his arrival.

When Tayla was allowed to read the letter, she said, "Such arrogance he has to presume you would go to the efforts of preparing to entertain him when you have not invited such a visit by him or anyone else for that matter. What do you intend to do?"

"I suppose I will hear him speak. I expect he is here on a mission to see if I am open to his pursuit of matrimony. If I refuse him, I doubt that he will spend any time under my roof as I do not invite strangers into my house. I have not had time to come to know this man nor do I have the escorts needed to ensure my safety…at least during the day. The night is a completely different issue, is it not?"

Queen Tayla answered, "Most assuredly, the night is completely different. I have familiars who can watch over you during the daylight if you wish it. If he comes, perhaps he can stay over for one night. I would like to know what his purpose is for seeing you. I fear his intentions may be less than honorable. On the other hand, I may find something redeemable in his visit."

The day came when an entourage of brightly covered wagons drawn by handsome teams of horses, escorted by soldiers dressed in fancy livery. The Baron Phillipe Sauvienne had arrived.

He was received by Elspeth's staff and given quarters to stay in. A dinner would be given shortly after dark when he would finally meet the Countess. He had no idea he would also be meeting with a Queen as well.

The hall of the Countess was well lit, decorated and stocked with plenty of food, as well as wine and ale. Her estate had some of the best wineries around with herds of top bred cattle. In the region, she had one of the most successful estates.

Baron Sauvienne and his entourage came into the hall expectant of food and entertainment. The Baron was seated next to the Countess at the head table. The spectacle was full of merriment and gaiety, marked with laughter and music.

Musicians from a traveling troupe had been in the area and were hired to play for the evening.

The castles of those days lacked any consistent heat source and each room had to have its own independent hearth. The one in the great hall was no different. The hearth blazed brightly. Braziers close to the table served the same purpose.

"Baron, your letter stated your purpose for arriving here at my castle. Can you tell me why I should consider marriage to a man whom I have never met, much less know? My first husband was a man whom I had never met but was promised to before I was ever born. The fact that I managed to come to love him despite the way our marriage was arranged is an extraordinary feature of my marriage. Now, I am widowed. I bore eight of his children, of which five have survived. My son will be the next Count DeVacquerie. So, tell me, for what reasons are you seeing me as a potential bride?"

"I am here for proposal of marriage, yes, but I have other advantages of being married as well. I offer my castle, my estate, and farms as well. The union of our fortunes benefits us both. Do you not see this?"

The Baron was slightly older than Elspeth, distinguished in appearance and was well spoken. He had also fought in the war with the English where much of his fortune had been spent.

Elspeth replied to the Baron, "I have been learning as much about you as I could prior to your arrival. It is wise that one study about their potential mate as much as one should study about their enemy as well. Do you not think so?"

"Oh, of course! Countess, I have not been able to learn as much about you as you have of me. Enlighten me in your own words. Why should we not marry? You are widowed, as am I. You are of nobility, as am I. You have your estates, which you would retain title to, as do I. Together, we could make a good match."

"Very well, Baron. First, I am widowed, but I am not lonely. I have my children. I am independent, in wealth, in title, in lands and castle. I want for little if anything at all. If I could wish myself into happiness, I would only wish my husband were still alive to see what I have been able to do with his castle. I think he would be proud. You offer me nothing that I do not already possess. On the other hand, I can offer you much that you do not possess now because you may have lost it, through mismanagement, or through bad decisions. But, at this time, I see no reason I should desire a companion."

The Baron was dismayed for he thought in a chauvinistic way that she needed him more than he did her. Elspeth had made him realize that she did not.

Elspeth smiled for she had not only put him in his place as a guest and not master of this castle, but she had asserted herself against a man of nobility. Until Tayla had come into her life, she had been very meek and mild, submissive to a fault to her husband, yet a very loyal wife and dedicated mother. Her title as Countess was just that. It did not define her. Now, she was showing strength, independence, and assertiveness. Tayla had taught her these things. It was something nearly unheard of in those days of the late fifteenth century.

Queen Tayla entered the banquet hall, escorted by several of her guard. The rest of her clan were stationed about the region, for it had grown, requiring more than just one place of sanctuary for their protection. She was dressed in her concept of royal finery. A gown of several colors of velvet, with a fur cape. Her slippers were of the finest leather, while her hair was pulled up off her shoulders. A tiara crowned the top of her head such that only a blind man could not see that she was majestic.

Before she could sit, the staff butler announced her arrival. When he had pronounced her name and title, the Baron was astonished. He had no idea that there would be another guest of nobility at the banquet table.

Baron Sauvienne leaned over and spoke discreetly to Elspeth. "A Queen here at your table. No wonder you have no interest in me. I am a lowly baron compared to a queen. And to what land or kingdom is this beautiful woman the Queen of?"

"She is a Queen of Wallachia, a land that is no longer recognized. She is my permanent guest here and my protector and my friend."

Elspeth asked many questions of the Baron. She wanted to know all about him, not because she had romantic intentions, but more out of curiosity. Besides, she considered the need for allies when times might become bad.

Queen Tayla sat on the opposite side of Elspeth. Though there were many conversations, the vampire's ability to overhear conversations from any point in the room made it possible to hear the one between her friend and the Baron. The Countess and the Baron talked for a great deal of the night. Soon, after midnight, the people in the hall began to retire, either drunk or so full that they could no longer fight the urge to sleep.

On the way to the Countess' sleeping quarters, Tayla accompanied her. Tayla had heard nearly every word of their conversation, which Countess Elspeth was fully aware. She sought Tayla's advice.'

The vampire told her that if she was even remotely considering his offer to consider that it might be good for her.

"Elspeth, you have only to say the word. I can make him a familiar to me. You would benefit greatly, as I would from his service. I could guarantee his loyalty to you, as I can guarantee it to myself. Your lands and estates would be secure. Your legitimacy as a noble would be strengthened. No one would be coming around to attempt to marry your fortune to theirs as I know that is the motivation for these widowed noblemen coming to your door. This is all being done out of safety and security, both militarily and financial. I can benefit to as his castle would be accessible for me to increase the sanctuaries available to the *Order of the Red Velvet*. Again, I give you the choice. I only wanted to point out the benefits to an arrangement."

Elspeth asked of the Queen, "You have stated the benefits but what are the disadvantages to such an arrangement?"

"Other than the changes to our existing arrangement, I cannot think of any. If he has family, which he said he did not, that might be the only consequence to a marriage between the two."

"I just do not know or think I am ready to have another in my bed. I have grown content to sleeping alone. After all, I am not a young woman anymore. I have aged, unlike you."

"If you do not want him in your bed, I can tell him as a familiar to me that sex with you is not to be. A consummation shall not take place. My father had such a relationship with his

332

first wife. It was one of the reasons an annulment was possible. If you want only companionship, without the intimacy, I can make that happen as well. Again, your choice."

Elspeth giggled. The thought of getting married again intrigued her. She planned to ask the Baron to go for a ride with her in the morning.

In the morning, fog lingered around until just before noon. The Countess and the Baron had gone out, with a small retainer of groomsmen and soldiers, to converse about the Baron's proposal.

Elspeth laid out her desires and terms of such a marriage should she decide that it take place. The Baron had few objections. Even though Elspeth made some highly selfish demands, she only wanted to see his reaction to such ridiculousness. He stated his positions well, being reasonable and fair. She thought she could not expect more than that, having accepted his answers.

The Baron stated his expectations. They were not out of the ordinary, in fact, they were quite reasonable. His request that she live in his castle was the one she would not agree to. She insisted that he would have to move into her castle. Her loyalty to Tayla was the reason for it.

After a few days, she accepted his proposal for marriage. Her family was apprehensive at first, but Tayla assured them their family would lose nothing. Plans were made and soon afterwards, the day of bliss came. Tayla decided to make him a familiar after the marriage would take place. Then, Elspeth, Tayla, the Baron would all have what they wanted.

Tayla made him the familiar that would support Elspeth, and Tayla's will. All that Tayla hoped for was coming to pass. She added more familiars to both castles, ensuring more security and sanctuary capabilities for the *Order of the Clan of the Red Velvet*. It was a good time for the Clans, but she knew the Clans had enemies, formidable ones. Before they could rest easy, those enemies would have to be confronted.

CHAPTER THIRTY-FIVE

INQUISITION

"Dearest Malcolm, at this time, my plans for establishing the clans are now a reality. I finally have my kingdom. All my labors were beginning to pay off. I met some darling people along the way who helped me, despite of what I was. I repaid them in kind, with as much as I could afford in kindness and protection. I missed my brothers and sister such that I traveled frequently, meeting with them, assisting them in whatever capacity I could. I received more gifts from the Dark Lord, more powers of intuition, of sight, of abilities I never knew were possible. It was fortunate that I did because I needed those gifts. I found myself often intervening on behalf of my siblings, their clan members and the familiars to shield them from what would become known as the Inquisition."

*   *   *

By 1490, the Inquisition had become something of a thing of the past. At least that is what it seemed. In private, a reign of terror was still very much alive. Any heresy, no matter how slight, no matter what the challenge to church teachings were, was treated harshly. The Holy Church was happy to assign such challenges or noted heresies to the attention of an established monastic order known as the Dominicans.

If the *Order of the Dragons of Set* had infiltrated the Holy Church, then it was certain that some of those who had infiltrated it were members of this order of priests. The current Dragon was a man named Diego San Carlos, a Spaniard raised in Rome, who had been appointed to join the Order of the Dominicans priesthood. He was personally tasked, unknowingly by the Pope, to seek out and destroy the vampire plague that raged against the continent of Europe.

Tayla began to lose clan members to the efforts of Diego. He had teams trained to deal with vampires. Diego knew specifically how to destroy them and used every tool at his disposal. His arsenal was vast as the Dominicans seemed to be everywhere.

The *Order of the Dragons of Set* had their long tentacles of influence and power reaching across Europe. From the highest seats of government, to the high positions within the Holy Church, they controlled events of the day through power-manipulation of people, of currency, of trade and politics. The message of the Church was tainted enough and though some were able to see through much of the charade, a large part of the people believed in a more twisted form of the gospel. Some monasteries had monks who were enlightened enough to read for themselves the gospel. In this way, the true church determined that much of what they believed was manmade. They kept the trappings of rituals and ties to paganistic faith that had blended with the church over the centuries only because of the fear of being accused of heresy if they spoke out. The true Christian church had already gone underground.

The Dominican Order at this time was attacking anyone who challenged the teachings of the church with the vicious smear of the brush that denotes heresy. Heresy was a sin, a major sin. As it was, heresy was an adjective, describing a plethora of sins and sinful natures that were subject to punishment by the law as prescribed by a panel of clergy. Essentially, it was whatever they said it was. You could be burned or hung, tortured to depths not seen before, just for being accused, with no proof nor any recourse under any law as do many who benefit from today's judiciary. It was an extremely hard time for one to be an independent thinker.

There was one Dominican who seemed to be very adept at waging a war against vampires and familiars alike. It was the same name as Tayla had heard thirteen years before. Father

Joachim was a true Dominican. He adhered to the doctrine of stamping out heresy to the letter of the law. The law stated he could use any means necessary to obtain a confession if it did not involve the spilling of blood.

For nearly two decades, Joachim had traveled across Europe, mostly in France and Flanders, but he had also traveled into Germany and Poland. He had found and attacked the network of familiars and vampires belonging to Prieta. Prieta asked her sister for help in ridding her of this man. Tayla traveled to Prague where Prieta had staked her claim of Europe for the *Order of the Clan of the Blue Velvet.*

Arriving in Prague by coach, Tayla was received by her sister in an underground cellar. The two conversed over what seemed to be a crisis for Prieta's clan.

"I have lost nearly a third of my brood to this man. He attacks the familiars, obtaining confessions and information regarding my clansmen. Then, during the daylight hours, he, and his minions attack, wiping out whoever shall be taking refuge in that house. The familiar is forced to reveal the next house that is safe for vampires to stay at. The process is repeated. Where he stays at night is not known. If I knew, I would be on the attack right now."

"Prieta, dear sister, you must be ever so careful. We must fight back in a careful and precise manner. To make war against the church itself is exactly what the Dragon would want us to do. It is the *Order of the Dragons of Set* who is our real enemy. Diego San Carlos has gotten the church to set their power against us for the Order knows we no longer do their bidding. This is their revenge, their punishment for you and your brothers leaving their circle. They offered protection, yet, you have need of protection against them."

"What shall we do, dear sister?"

"I shall have to lure this Father Joachim into a trap, get what information I can and then, proceed from there. I must find a way to tie them to the *Order of the Dragons of Set*. I will fight fire with fire, the very same fire they have tried to burn us with, shall be their undoing."

Tayla left the next evening, but before she did, she wrote a letter with her own hand to the priest, Joachim. She detailed that she was wary of him and that she was the leader, the Queen of a kingdom hidden from mortal eyes. If she were to be killed, then the plague of vampires upon Europe would be over, and that he would take credit for it. She taunted him that it would never happen because she was wiser than he, more cunning and more deadly than any vampire he may have encountered so far. To take her head, would indeed be a prize. Her last words before she signed it were, "Come take your prize if your faith allows you!"

She ordered Prieta to have it placed conspicuously so Father Joachim was sure to find it. Tayla then left for home in France.

Prieta, feeling particularly aggressive that night, flew to an area where she knew Joachim was scouting for vampires. She found a safe house a familiar owned and had prepared for the reception of her vampires. She gave the letter to the familiar, ordered him to set fire to the house and place the letter atop a pole outside the blazing residence. Then, the familiar was to escape to France and find Tayla. The familiar did as he was told.

Prieta flew away and was particularly thirsty of her usual fare to dine upon. She found three villagers and quickly disposed of them. Flying off, she carried all three to the site of the blazing house. The vampire left the three bodies at the foot of the pole upon which the letter read its deadly challenge to Father Joachim. Sure enough, the next morning found many peasants standing around the smoldering ruins staring at the bodies, not burned but no less dead, at the foot of the pole.

Tayla had laid a tempting trail for the Dominican to follow. It was one that would have made any friar think that Tayla was spoiling for a fight. In truth, she was doing exactly that, but this fight was to be on her terms, the terrain of her choosing and with the odds stacked in her favor. She had vowed she would never enter a conflict that she did not already see victory.

*   *   *

A location was the first thing Tayla needed. She had already decided on her method. The timing was inconsequential, for as long as he was tracking her, she could track him. The old saying about "Go hunting for vampires and they will go hunting for you" probably got its start right here. A castle would be the best place. Preferably, one in ruins would be more suitable as it would be the most likely place Joachim would assume was the actual place for vampires to call home. As it was, Tayla lived in the Countess Elspeth's castle. She was now much older, and their relationship had been one of utmost trust. Time had proven to the Countess that Queen Tayla could be trusted at her word.

An ancient ruin, dating back to the Dark Ages, was not too far from the Countess Elspeth's castle. It was a simple fortification, consisting of one tower, with walls less than ten feet high at the highest point. There was no moat, and the gate had been torn off and used as metal for other things. The largest building or structure had only walls, most of which were decreased in height by either ruin or assault. There were no other permanent structures that could be utilized. Even the tower had only a partial floor on the top. The timbers were old and not safe to be used by men at arms. In short, the site was barely usable against the elements and completely useless against an assault. Less than a night's flight away from Tayla's true refuge, it was perfect.

By giving an informant a message to give to the priest, she could be sure he would show up in exactly the right place of her choosing. She also knew the priest would not come alone nor would he come unarmed. What weapons would he use against her?

She stationed her minions about the place, out in the forests to act as lookouts, and to give her early warning of Joachim's approach. The vampire scouts were to notify her where they were always and how many. If possible, they were to dispatch as many as possible, all of them if need be. She wanted none to escape.

She had explored it prior and found there was a basement below. She made sure the priest would find it by lighting a torch upon the battlement of the tower. Her silhouette would surely lure him in.

After the sun had disappeared, she waited. Within the hour, a column of soldiers and clergy appeared, each carrying a brightly burning torch. Father Joachim rode at the head of the column along with the soldiers' captain.

They came into view of the torch and surmised they would have found the exact spot. Tayla had led them here, so naturally, they were cautious. The captain told his men to spread out, to be watchful for familiars and vampires alike. They did so and with each group, a Dominican friar accompanied them. It was the friar who was the weapon. The friar had the shield of faith, and the sword of scripture, ready to recite against any assault by a vampire. They too seemed to be laying a trap for the vampires. They planned on waiting until after dawn. Their mode of operation was exactly like Prieta had said.

When the scouts informed Tayla of this, she called off the attack, saying that the target was Joachim, not the soldiers or the other friars. They would wait until tomorrow night.

When morning came, the soldiers and clergy seemed to storm the ruins, looking for any sign that the vampire Queen Tayla had been there.

She left clues that she knew they were watching her and therefore, she was watching them. This frustrated Joachim. He withdrew his forces for the day and retreated to a monastery to regroup. The captain of the soldiers scolded him for being a coward.

"You do not know what you are up against, captain. Your swords shall have no effect upon these creatures. Only your faith shall save you."

Night came and there was no column coming from the monastery to the ruins for a second night. The priest was afraid for he had lost the element of surprise. He went to the ruins during the daylight hours only and found only letters addressed to him, taunting him. This made him angry and he lost control. He decided to assault the position during the night. When she would leave her letters to him, then he would pounce upon her.

The same column came to the ruins in the same fashion as before. Only this time, Tayla was waiting for him. Her vampires, along with some of her most trusted familiars, were waiting in ambush some distance from the ruins. They were not expecting to be ambushed so far away from the ruins. He had lost the battle when he made the fateful decision to come to the ruins at night. She had caught him off guard, for she had the patience to wait, whereas he did not. That was his mistake.

Out of the forest, from trees and bushes and up from the ground it seemed, the road became full of vampires. Men were pulled from their horses and killed with a ferociousness not seen by most. It was as if bears with claws and fangs had set upon them. They never seemed to see them in the darkness until their attackers were already upon them, biting and clawing them, releasing their blood into the air and upon the ground. Man, and beast died together. The clan enjoyed a feast of man while the familiars dispatched the clergy with longbow and crossbow. All died except for one. He fell with a blow to his head, rendering him unconscious.

The dimly lit chamber was deep within the lower levels of the castle. It was the deepest one could go. The castle, long abandoned by the former occupants, now belonged to the undead, the rightful heirs to it. The dungeon was old, the air stale and dank. The smell of mold mixed with the smell of charcoal left a malodourous smell in the room. The only light was that of the torches and the brazier full of branding irons. Without that light, they would have been in utter darkness, without any sound.

The vampiress had waited for a long time for this moment. Her victory was in the making. The priest, Father Joachim, had followed her carefully laid out trail and fell into her trap. He alone survived her ambush. She had taken him captive to extract information from him. She wanted to know why this war between the siblings and the church had gotten to this point. The vampires wanted no war. They only wanted to survive. The church would not tolerate their existence. She had to know why.

The priest who had been unconscious began to stir, showing signs of coming back into awareness. When he opened his eyes, he got the shock of his life.

She tightened the noose around the priest's neck as his labored respirations became even louder and more strained. No matter how much she had tried to give the church a wide berth, it had not worked. The enemy she had not wanted had placed her and her kind at the top of its enemies list. She had the priest just where she wanted him: On a rack, bound and naked. The look in her vampire eyes inspired fear into the priest that he had never known or had even seen in his parishioners. He could see into the brazier sitting next to the rack. The firebrands glowed red as they sat in the fire. The heat in the chamber caused the priest to sweat profusely.

Tayla hissed and spat out her feelings. "My anger has had years in which to build its foundation upon. The endless cavalcade of persecution, with the shadow of damnation hanging over my head has tested my patience long enough. Now, you will pay, as will your family and their offspring as well. I shall wipe out your name from the earth, as you and yours planned to extinguish mine."

She had all the instruments of torture that he had come to know and use to extract information from her familiars to track down and kill her spawn. The vampire Queen, Queen Tayla of the *Order of the Clan of the Red Velvet* told him what she had planned for him. She planned to separate not only his connection to this world, but that no one would ever know he had ever been born. "This blade shall sever you and all that you have done from the history of this world. The world shall remember you no more. Only I, Tayla, Queen of the *Clan of the Order of the Red Velvet* will know of your fate. No one will know of where your remains will lie, or the fate that put them there. To kill a mother's children is to bring out maternal instincts of anger and revenge that many think not possible. You know the tears of a mother who has lost children. If you do that to a vampire's children, you invite retribution more terrible than you could imagine. Dominican, you have done exactly that."

"Not true, thou foulest of creatures," cried out the priest. "I know your ways, your propensity for evil. I also knew you would eventually find out who is at the source of your torment. Yes! I have killed your spawn. I tracked them down and slew them in the name of the Almighty God. It is His commands I obey, and He commands that you all be put to the stake, to the flame for purging, and delivered up to eternal damnation!"

The priest, though a rope was about his neck, taut and constricting his airway, was defiant though he knew he was damned to his fate. He told her of his mission, as it was his crusade to extinguish her kind from the earth. "Your soul is beyond hope, and it is damned, do you hear? Damned! You may kill me, and you may be able to make me cry out pitifully, but you will never persuade me to betray my faith in Christ. You are the devil's agent, Tayla. The devil's agent! He uses you, and through you he multiplies his legions of agents. His army is being born through you and your wickedness. To save the earth from you and those like you, I was compelled by the will of God to destroy you!"

Ahhhhh!" he cried out in pain.

No family of his would survive this world. They were all marked. Marked with the edict of death that the undead monarch could give, and all vampires were bound to fulfill. His family, his existence would not even be a memory. It would be as if neither he nor his family had ever existed. He would be forgotten.

"I have done no harm to you. I left you and the church alone. What did that reward me? It rewarded me not. And from whom do you take these orders to murder and persecute, priest?"

"The Dominican Order has orders from Rome," he panted as his pain increased and his airway was compromised, "to expunge all heresy from the church and any agents of Satan who encourage and preach it. You and your kind are placed at the top of the order in which we must do this. Any of your familiars whom you have placed under your spell are targets and their confessions have led us to the colonies of your evil spawn. It is my mission in life to destroy you and your kind. From the beginning, your kind has been the enemy of my God!"

The vampire Queen had suffered the loss of too many faithful and obedient servants. The Dominicans and their inquisition had also murdered many innocent believers in their endeavors to stamp out the heresy of vampyria. It was not as if she had had a choice. This madness of persecution and the pursuit of survival had forced her and her brothers and sister to react.

Tayla knew of the Dominican's policy for torture. They could use any means necessary that did not draw blood. Therefore, the use of the rack, the firebrand, and crushing weights and water to inflict pain, done with such skill that any mortal would sing like a bird allowed them to obtain confessions, most of which were doubtful. The Vatican had told the order that she and her kind were as a plague upon the earth, and that they were to destroy them. The Vatican along with all the cardinals and bishops of Europe were convinced she was the agent of the devil and her spawn was to be Satan's army. From what source did the church receive this information?

"You fool! You cannot even abide by your own edicts of blood. You torture my familiars and then draw the blood of my kind. Which is it? Blood or no Blood? Well, I can think of many endless ways of exacting the most pain from a miserable creature such as yourself, but I think I will just give you what you give us. What was it you said? The stake, the flame and damnation? Tell me how the stake feels!"

"No, wait! Please!! Aaaaahhhhhhhhhhhhh! Oh, forgive me Father!"

Tayla had decided to give the same fate to him that he had given to her kind: the stake into the chest, piercing the heart. As she drove the stake into his heart, he cried out in utter terror. As she finished him, cutting off his head, she raised his head to look him in the face. His blood poured out upon the stony floor.

"Since you told me your orders were from Rome, then to Rome I will have to go," she said softly, with a gleam in her now violet eyes. She intended to confront the Pope himself.

*   *   *

It was now 1492. Pope Innocent VIII had died just days before Queen Tayla had arrived in Rome. She was sad that she could not confront him directly. The Cardinals were all in conclave to elect a new Pope. While this was occurring, Tayla decided to look up some old "acquaintances". The house where she had confronted the High Council was still there. Of course, Ramone was long dead, and a new leader of the High Council served in that position. She asked his servant for a face to face meeting with his master. He went to waken his master who came to the door, still drowsy from too much wine and not enough sleep.

"Who are you and whom do you seek?"

"If you are the High Council leader, I am surprised that you do not know me? Do you always question royalty when they summon you?"

"Royalty? Then I assume you are Tayla, the vampire Queen, come to give me a piece of your mind. Come in, sit for a while." He looked at his servant telling him to bring him wine.

"A bit late for wine, do you think?" she asked.

"Yes. But having to deal with you demands it."

"Quite insolent you are, especially in my presence. Do you still think of me as an outlaw? A thorn in the side of the Order? I am more powerful and much wiser than when you last saw me."

"The truth is I have never seen you. When was the last time you were here?"

"I believe it was 1453. At the end of the wars in France. Ramone held your position. He was an insolent man also. I suspect he is dead, no?"

"Oh, yes. Some twenty years now. Came down with the plague I believe. In fact, the plague reduced our numbers significantly. Even we were not immune to this dreadful disease. We understood it to be a manifestation of God. The question is whose god?"

"I am not interested in your problems. Did Ramone suffer?"

"I was a young man when this occurred. I believe he did suffer but not for long. The plague kills quickly. That is the only mercy it carries."

Tayla continued. "The Pope has died. They are busy electing a new one. Did you know Innocent VIII?"

"Yes. I did know him. I had many dealings with him. And, I know what you are about to ask of me. The answer is yes. He acted upon information that the Dragon gave to him. The Pope was not one of us. That is not an office we have been able to infiltrate. But, I suspect, one day we will. I remember Ramone saying at a meeting, after a failed attempt to take the Papal Office,

'We will never ascend to a throne, but will stand next to it.' I did not know what he meant by that but over time, his meaning became clear. The Pope acts upon the advice of his advisors, his counselors, his cardinals, and bishops. I now know what he meant for those words to say."

"How do I get this Papal Edict against vampires rescinded?"

"I do not know if it can. We would have to go back and change history. The Holy Church and you are set against each other because of the Dragon's failure to keep you and your brothers and sister in our fold. Because you, Tayla, have taken them away from us, we had no choice but to declare war against you. That which we do not control, is hostile to us. I do recall that day that Ramone allowed you to speak to the High Council. I was a servant then. Today, I am its leader."

She quickly turned and looked into his face with fierce eyes, "Then you remember what I said to him, do you not?"

"Oh, yes. I remember your words as if you had just spoken them. Especially the part about words having consequences. Those words spoken by you. You threatened Master Ramone. He did not take kindly to that or to your meddling against the Dragon. You have been reaping his wrath and the wrath of the Dragon these years of late."

Tayla got remarkably close, almost nose to nose with the Councilman. "I want that edict rescinded, or the world is going to know about you, the High Council, and the Dragon. Mark my words and mark them well," Tayla threatened. "I am in no mood to be trifled with. I say what I mean and mean what I say. Lies are not part of my character. I tell the truth for I am not afraid to say it, especially if I am angry."

"You would not dare! We have resources that you cannot imagine! We have power over nearly everything we see!"

"Do you see me? Take a good look, my friend, because you do not have power over me. I am your worst enemy. Be sure of that! What is your name?" she asked.

"My name is Caminus Sergio Perginas! I am the leader of the High Council of the *Order of the Dragons of Set*. Do not threaten me!"

When Tayla would become angry, her eyes would turn to a violet color. Tayla's eyes were as purple as the robes of the ancient emperors. "You get that edict rescinded or face my wrath. That is all I have to say!" She stormed out of the room.

Caminus finished off the wine. He called for his servant. "Send for the Dragon. We have a problem," he told the servant. The servant left the house to do his master's bidding.

CHAPTER THIRTY-SIX

DEATH OF THE ORDER

"Dearest Malcolm, surely the question has crossed your mind about why there is no more *Order of the Dragons of Set*. All you ever knew about was the *Order of the Jackal*. This chapter answers that question. As I have noted before, in my times I have met people, been a lot of places, and saw a lot of history unfold. This event is not famous, nor would it seem important. But, to me, it was a significant if not a great event that would finally set the kingdom free of the *Order of the Dragons of Set*."

*   *   *

Tayla was a creature of action. She would implement her plans quickly and decisively when necessary. Inversely, she might hold back with extreme patience for the right time to strike. In this case, her plans for action had been set into motion when she left the house where the High Council always met.

Somehow, she would meet the new Pope personally, hoping he would do the right thing if the information were presented in a carefully laid out manner. The Pope, if he was a good man, must be made to see that the real enemy to the Church was the *Order of the Dragons of Set*. The church with its dogma based upon the Holy Scriptures would always be adverse with the supernatural and what they had to do to survive. No attempt at reconciliation or redemption had ever been attempted.

A few days later, the city of Rome was alive with the announcement of a newly elected Pope. Queen Tayla was determined to speak with him.

The new Pope's servants prepared him for the night's slumber. He said his prayers while on his knees, took off his large golden crucifix and crawled into his bed. Another large cross of ornately carved wood hung over his bed. All but one of the candles had been extinguished but a fire still burned in the hearth. His room was spacious and elegantly furnished. A large doorway led out onto a balcony. During the winter months, the large heavy wooden doors would be closed.

The air outside was warm as it was summer, so the doors were open. Tayla appeared on the balcony on a moonless night. Silence is a deadly trait as it gives no warning. Most of all, the advantage belongs to the one who is silent and has stealth. They can see you, but you cannot see them, unless they want to be seen. A vampire cannot enter a sanctified place nor upon holy ground. The Pope's chambers were not sanctified. His windows to the side of the large doorway were small, but not so small it would be a problem for the vampire Queen.

In the darkness, Tayla entered the new Pope's chambers. She picked up the lit candle, holding it to her face. She was silent, but as she whispered his name into his subconscious, he began to wake. As he opened his eyes, he was startled to see her, but terrified was a more apt description. Few knew that he was plagued with nightmares from deeds long ago. Before he could speak or call out for guards, Tayla began to speak.

"Fear not, sir. I am not sure of how to address you, but I needed to see you. I chose this time of night for it is the only time you can receive me. There is a matter of great urgency, one that you should know about, and I am the only one who can tell you about it."

The newly elected Pope, Alexander VI, was able to say, "the title of 'Your Eminence' is sufficient. I am listening."

"Your Eminence, the church has a great and powerful enemy that is unseen and unheard, yet it is in the shadows, invisible and silent, yet still there. This enemy tells the church that it is my kind that seeks to destroy the church, but it is not me that you should be afraid of, for the enemy of the church is a group that has been working against it from its inception. The church has been infiltrated with those who speak with tongues as snakes, and as we speak, they scheme to twist your message with half-truths, such that they pervert the teachings that were original. I know my warning is difficult to comprehend, at least at this time of night. Make no mistake! I speak the truth. I may be of an evil nature, but I am not like my kind I have produced. The night is not long enough to explain. I am the only one of my kind. I have siblings that are far different than I am. They may be deserving of your wrath, but I am not. A Dominican priest has told me there is a Papal edict against me and those of my clan. I wish it to be rescinded. If you grant my wish, I will fight against those who wish to destroy your church from within. I will be an unlikely ally, yet an ally I shall be. If you refuse my help, I will leave Christendom as far as I can go. Please, I beg you, stop the persecution against the *Order of the Clan of the Red Velvet.*"

The Pope's name was Rodrigo de Borja only days ago. He was to become one of the most controversial and infamous Popes of the Renaissance Period. He knew all about corruption, about not being worthy, and most of all, how to use his new office for the gain of his family. He also knew about the *Order of the Dragons of Set.* They had already gotten to him. He was not a member but the opportunities that were presented to him were too much for him to ignore or to have adverse sentiments against the *Order of the Dragons of Set.* Deep inside, Tayla knew her efforts to achieve a peace or an agreement to stay at arms-length from each other were to no avail.

"You are the one they spoke of! And you dare enter my presence, unannounced and uninvited."

Queen Tayla was amazed, shocked, and dismayed that her efforts were to be fruitless. She paused, taking her time to regain her composure. "I had hoped for a better outcome from this meeting. But now, I see, your 'eminence'. I see that I have been announced already, by the very ones I have come to warn you about. You are as corrupt as they are. I have wasted my time here. But then, I have all the time in the world, 'Rodrigo'. I would never call you by your Papal name. You are a fraud, a

349

cheat, and a hypocrite, not worthy of your title. I was ready to give you the respect of your office, but I can see you for who you really are. If you will not rescind the edict against me and my kind, then it shall be war against you and those like you. I shall not wage war against the people I find pity for. If I must use them to survive, that is one thing. I am honest about my use of them. You, well, you must lie, cheat, and deceive them to get what you want. Power is a drug, Rodrigo. I can see you are addicted to it. It makes a man do evil things. I, too, have power. You will see it firsthand. Remember my words." She disappeared in a flash, out the window like a wind escaping through the large opening.

The Pope got out of bed immediately, taking pen and parchment out from a drawer at a desk. Dipping the quill into the ink, he wrote a message out in a hurry. "Guard!" he called out. He instructed the guard to have a messenger deliver it to Caminus immediately.

It was obvious that the Pope was shaken as he had just been threatened by the Queen of the *Order of the Clan of the Red Velvet*. When Tayla had left the room, she had not gone far. In fact, she was just outside on the balcony, listening to everything the new Pope had said to his guard. The vampire Queen knew that she had to act and soon.

She predicted his reaction the moment she knew he was in the pocket of the Order. His first move was to notify the Dragon and the Order that she was in Rome and if they were to move against her, now was the time to act. Tayla was not just a creature of action but also one of survival and part of that nature was to have moves of counteraction. It was very much like chess. You anticipate your opponent's move, not one but at least two or three moves ahead if possible. Moving against the Order, especially moving against the Dragon, was a dangerous one. Tayla knew it and had preplanned for her clan to act once the signal was given. Rodrigo was about to learn the meaning of the word, 'alone'.

A senior member of the *Red Clan*, Henri Delacroix, was given command of the group to attack the residences of the Order of the High Council members upon receiving the signal. That signal was given by telepathic powers that only a few of the clansmen had received. The receiving of a gift of ability was the equivalent of a promotion in the vampire world. Only Tayla had received more gifts than any of the others. Her siblings were not far behind her, but because she was the oldest and possessed the birthright, she possessed the most. The night was still young, not having reached the midnight hour.

Henri received the message from Queen Tayla, and immediately moved to attack the residences of all the members of the High Council. They would also gain information regarding the locations of other members.

Each house of the Council members had several vampires assigned to it. They moved as beings of living darkness, like snakes of black smoke creeping into the openings of the houses. No permission was needed to accept them. The council had already received Queen Tayla before them. Now, they were essentially disarmed from keeping them at bay.

Into the rooms of the sleeping council members they slithered, taking form of their natural selves just before they would strike. Some woke just as they took their final breath while others, never gained the consciousness to realize they had seconds to meet death. Many who woke before they died, tried to call out, but their voices were snuffed out as a cold and clawed hand covered their mouths. A few struggled but their efforts were futile. The vampires were supernatural predators and as they murdered their enemies, they smiled. They delighted in their bloody deed. Their victim's blood, mixed with fear, made a particularly delightful taste in that these victims were deserving of their fate. These were not victims of necessity. They were targeted for their actions for being the enemies of vampires. The haughtiness and pride of this group had set them up to fall before a group that would be more direct in dealing with its enemies.

The High Council was the governing body of the *Order of the Dragons of Set*. They set policy as to the goals for which the Order would commit its resources. The assets of the Order were under their control. It was they who would choose the successor to the Dragon should he not produce an heir. It was a situation that had not ever occurred. In short, they were the head of the snake that Queen Tayla reviled so much and had made the decision to eliminate.

351

It was a bloody night. Within hours, the deed of eliminating the head of the Order was accomplished. Their deaths were violent. They died the way they feared the most, at the hands of a vampire, the very creature they had brought into the world. Entire families were wiped out. The Council members and their wives and children were gone. The only ones that may be left were the relatives who were not in the household at the time of the attack.

Queen Tayla wanted Caminus to be her victim. She had given him the warning that he ignored, citing he had stood up to her, boasting of their power and that she was not deserving of their respect. She would show him in the worst way, that to respect one is to fear them. He found the fear when she stood at his bedside, fangs drawn, and claws outstretched. The mere sight of her caused his heart to nearly jump from his chest. He had no time to react as she sunk her jaws into his neck, sucking the very life from him. When she finished, she looked into his lifeless eyes saying, "I warned you. You did not listen. The Pope did not listen either so I will let you deliver my message."

The next morning, many households were filled with screams of terror from finding many bodies in many homes, dead from the vicious attacks from supernatural creatures. The wounds were simple puncture wounds to the necks of each victim, which confounded the magistrates of the city. They knew what these puncture wounds meant, as Rome was full of superstitious people and remaining members of the Order. The knowledge that all this occurred in one night shook the remaining members of the Order to the core. They were paralyzed with fear as they dreaded the coming night.

At the Pope's palace, the sun had rose and with it, so did Pope Alexander VI. As he wandered out onto the balcony, he was shocked to find Caminus Sergio Perginas sitting in a chair. Queen Tayla had posed his body such that he appeared as if a messenger of death. His nightshirt was stained with blood and a parchment was attached to his chest. It read, "Rodrigo, I warned you. I warned Caminus. The Order is dead. Neither of you listened. This is what happens when you do not listen to a Queen. Rescind the edict against me, or the war continues."

352

The Pope was visibly shaken, as he called for his guard to take the body away. He had taken the parchment from the chest so no one could see the warning written upon it. He sat in private chambers the rest of the day, contemplating his next move. He wondered, "Where was the Dragon in all of this?"

Later that afternoon, a message was given to the Pope as he sat in silence. "I am coming to meet with you tonight. Be ready to receive me. We are in crisis."

After the sun had left the sky, the Dragon was announced to be received by the Holy See. Pope Alexander VI sat on his Papal throne ready to receive the Dragon. He had never actually met the man, so he was not sure what to expect.

A handsome young man of dark, shoulder length hair walked into the hall, presenting with a tall stature and a confidant gait. He was dressed smartly, in the garb of a man of means, with a robe of black. His boots were high, and a gilded sword hung at his waist, along with a dagger in a gilded sheath. A medallion on a gold chain hung from shoulder to shoulder. His black cap, with a pheasant feather completed his stylish fashion.

"Allow me to introduce myself, your Eminence, I am Francisco Antonio Cessario. It was I who wrote to you asking for an audience."

Rodrigo de Borja appeared pale and disturbed. He knew he would not sleep tonight. Francisco could see this and assured him all would be dealt with in good time.

"You said we are in crisis. Explain yourself."

"Yes, I did. I was in Florence when I received a message from Caminus. He said Tayla was in the city. I came as soon as I could. I am sorrowful that I could not prevent this from happening. Again, we are thwarted. I thought that the Dark Lord had his hand on this, capable of preventing such a catastrophe. I was wrong. It is not the Dark Lord who is behind this. I am afraid that it is the God that you are supposed to represent who has put His hand against us. Do you know that centuries of work, painstakingly done to infiltrate your Church, has now been stopped? My brethren have been wiped out in a single night. And it is all because of a decision you would not make."

"She asked me to rescind the edict against the heresy of vampirism, of the supernatural. I am the Holy See, the head of the Church on this earth. How can I do such a thing? To do so would be a heresy! You must remember it was the High Council's request that an edict be made against your enemy by my predecessor. I did not make the edict, and I would not rescind it either. Even now, I would not do so. I must consider the office to which I have been elected, not just by the College of Cardinals, but by God as well. You want me to believe these creatures are the enemy of the church and God as well. I do. I have considered the fact that you and the organization you are affiliated with are also the enemies of the church and of Christ. Did you not say that it was your mission to pervert and destroy the message of Christ? These were your own words, Francisco! I cannot serve two masters. Christ Himself addressed this in the Holy Scriptures. I have considered my actions regarding this. I have caused the deaths of many last night by standing by my convictions. I have returned to my true allegiance, and my own faith."

Francisco, frustrated with the Pope, exclaimed, "There is essentially no more *Order of the Dragons of Set*! We have been in existence since the days of Sahure, Pharaoh of Egypt. We made these creatures! The first Dragon was there when the first two vampires burst through the doors of their tomb. My ancestors cared for, protected, and used the vampires to carry out the will of Set. Do you not care for what such power can do to you? Do you think that your God will protect you from me? I am what remains of the Order."

Rodrigo had spent most of the day to contemplate what his greed had done. It had brought about a bloody night where a lot of evil men and their families had been sent to their deaths. Finally, he answered Francisco's rant.

"You, Francisco, represent the death of the Order. You represent death and evil. Nothing more. There has always been evil in this world. Since the beginning, the spirit of Set was there, tempting the first man and woman. In the scriptures, it is written about his being here on the earth. The scriptures give him another name, Satan. He has many names, of which I am sure you know

354

all of them, for he resides in you. My sins I will answer for. Even now, I repent of my actions to continue my alliance with you. Depart from my presence, depart from Rome, depart from this earth. There is no place for you or the vampires in God's kingdom."

Francisco turned his back on the man who had found his conscience and walked out, angry, sullen, and vowing for revenge on the church and the Queen of the *Order of the Red Velvet*.

Rodrigo went to his chambers, fell to his knees, and looked up in solemn prayer to ask forgiveness for his sins. The coming night would allow for no peace nor mercy.

CHAPTER THIRTY-SEVEN

BUILDING THE KINGDOM

"Dearest Malcolm, this is a short chapter. I only included it so you would know how I managed my affairs during this period. I had a castle, an army, servants, and I had wealth, lots of wealth. My father's ring I wore around my neck, but my own ring came much later. Of course, the wealth was confiscated from my enemy, but as mortals always say, all is fair in love and war. This was certainly a war. I did not know at the time that the war would continue for a long time. I had won a great battle, but my enemy still walked the earth. Mortals have this saying, "Fight fire with fire." It took me a long time to fully understand that. Evil was at war with evil. All I knew at the time was I was doing what was necessary to survive. I learned what it was like to lose a friend. I had already lost a lover. These emotional experiences were difficult to say the least and I struggled to find meaning to all of it. My brothers and sisters have emotions that are dull and blunted. When you are the kind of vampire that I am, your emotions are charged and very explosive. At this time of my life, I had to learn the hard way to keep my emotions in check. Sometimes that is good, sometimes it is not, especially if it is a negative one."

*   *   *

As expected, the next night was indeed bloody. Tayla had obtained a roster of names and residences and her clan poised themselves to strike out against them with masterful efficiency.

She visited the Pope personally for only she was willing to give him a last chance to correct an error. He expected she would show up and he prepared a document, renouncing the inquisition, and the edict against the heresy that was vampirism. She listened to the Pope tell her he had told the Dragon to begone from his sight. His words "Depart from my presence, depart from Rome, depart from this earth. There is no place for you or the vampires in God's kingdom," brought a smile from her lips when she confronted him that second night of retribution.

"Rodrigo, you have done well. You have stood up against that which many, many have failed to do. The Dragon is not one to be trifled with, but, neither am I. I commend you acting upon your convictions. You say vampires have no place in God's Kingdom. I believe you are right. My powers come from the same source as does the Dragon's. But know this, my kind wants no war with you or the church you represent. If we can live in peace, so be it. For that, I will spare your life. I only ask that you find and root out those who have been corrupted in your church. That is the only way to fight against the evil that is the Dragon."

That night, hundreds more members of the Order were visited by angels of death during the darkness, leading to more screams of terror in the early morning hours. Her plan to purge the *Order of the Dragons of Set* from the city of Rome was successful.

Those who had escaped the second night of terror busied themselves in a frantic effort to escape the city. Some had fled on foot with only what they could carry while others arranged for transportation for a quick escape from Rome. They had no time to plan for their escape, resulting in much of their wealth left behind. There were many times in history, Roman citizens had panicked in front of their enemies who had breached the gates. From the Etruscans, to those who lived during the Republic, to those who lived during the Imperial golden age of the Caesars, there were many times blood was spilled in the streets. This was now the time of the Renaissance. Yet, the city of Rome did indeed bleed on this night. She had turned her entire clan upon the citizenry of Rome, mainly to seek out and destroy every living member of the *Order of the Dragons of Set*.

357

As she stood outside the house that had been the meeting place of the High Council, she thought about all the evil planning that had taken place there. Specific examples included the edict against vampires by the Pope. The house was thoroughly searched for wealth, for information and specifically, the location of the Dragon. She wanted him if he had not left Rome. If the High Council was the brains of the Order, he was the heart of it.

"Burn this house down, so that the memories of it will lie in ashes as well." Her vampires did as she ordered.

Queen Tayla ordered all confiscated wealth to be taken to their stronghold in France. Caravans of wagons moved during the next few nights, north out of Italy toward France. Now, she was rich beyond any measure she had thought possible.

Queen Tayla had plans for building the vampire empire into something that would last. It would take money and now she had it. The confiscated wealth would first be used to repair and enlarge the castle of the Countess Elspeth DeVacquerie. It would be Queen Tayla's first palace and in that palace, her royal crown and the scepter would reside.

The task of improving the castle of her benefactor and friend took over ten years. During that time, Elspeth took ill and died. The Baron, consumed with grief, died soon after. Tayla believed that Elspeth had indeed grown to love the Baron. The rest of her days were spent in comfort and a hidden joy, one that she showed only to the Baron in their most intimate moments. The Baron, already a familiar to the Queen, revealed that he had indeed fallen in love with the woman he had married, and that the marriage was no longer one of convenience but of love and adoration. The Queen, already astute to the feelings of the mortals she was around, knew this to be genuine. It made her smile that she had a hand in giving them both the joy they desired.

Countess Elspeth had contracted a fever and was confined to her bed for some time before she died. Tayla visited her during the nocturnal hours, talking with her, attempting to comfort her, and reassuring her that her family would be taken care of should the worst outcome be realized. She died in Tayla's arms and the entire family saw the Queen weep uncontrollably. Tayla had loved her like a sister.

On that day, Elspeth's son, Thomas became the new Count DeVacquerie. The Baron relinquished all claims to the title but continued to live at the castle, in the service of the Queen Tayla. The son continued the tradition that his mother had started. He was but a child when Queen Tayla had arrived at the ruined castle that dark and fearful night. The vampire Queen had watched the lad grow up and now he was a young man, standing in the shadow of adulthood. He had a well- built castle, he had a lot of wealth, and would be a desirable suitor for many noblemen's daughters. The vampire Queen saw many problems facing the young man. Often, she would sit with the young count during the night, counseling him on what he should do and not do. He thought of the vampire Queen as an "aunt" who he sincerely believed only wanted the best for him. His upbringing in the Christian church sometimes collided with the reality that his family had given shelter and sanctuary to the very thing that had been branded as evil heresy in its most tangible form. He and the Queen had many talks about this. She did not pretend she had the answers. She suggested he get an education so he could read and then he could delve into the scriptures and find out himself that which was the right Christian stance to take concerning these creatures.

Tayla never pretended to be something she was not. She never told him that they were good and all else was evil. Quite the contrary, for she told him though her nature was evil, she surmised that all men were evil. Some were worse than others. The right to judge men as to their righteousness was given to no man, for she had seen men for what they truly were, even the Pope. She told the young count all about her encounter with the Pope Alexander VI.

He was amazed and wanted to know all about the Order and their demise. Telling him these stories, though they were truthful, was akin to telling a child tales of adventure, or even a fairy tale. The young count was interested in the things, though they were completely fantastic, that Queen Tayla would tell him. As he grew, he became very fond of Tayla and her closest circle of vampires. He and his family were all much older than when they first met Tayla. Because they had grown up knowing about Tayla, her clansmen and what they were, they seemed to accept all of it and thought nothing of the fact that they were indeed predators, only that they were not in the food chain.

The Queen counseled him on his choice of a wife someday. It was inevitable as well as expected that he would marry and start a family of his own. His children would inherit his castle and his wealth one day. How would he explain his "Aunt Tayla" to his new wife? Tayla suggested that the castle be split into two joined but separate structures. This way, no one who was not privy to the arrangement the family had made, would unknowingly wander into a forbidden area and subject themselves to danger. The young man eagerly accepted this arrangement and the hallways and passages to each castle were walled up permanently.

Sometimes, Tayla had to travel. It was sometimes for days, other times for weeks. When she came home, the family seemed happy to see her, for they felt safe when she was around. There were no soldiers and the staff were picked for their discretion. To ensure they could be trusted, Tayla made them familiars except for family members. The term 'familiar' means a trusted one, a faithful servant who would always be reliable. To ensure this, she had to place them under her control. She could see what they saw, hear what they heard. Even when she was in her 'death sleep', she could stay aware of what went on during the day. The family of the staff member was unaware that they served Queen Tayla, not the family. The Queen was not about to divulge this secret, and neither were the familiars.

As a Queen, she had to hold her composure, careful not to let emotional matters cause her to lose control. This happened when Elspeth became ill and died in Tayla's arms. She wanted to bring her to the crossing over but could not because Elspeth was a Christian. This was when she learned of just one of the many limitations of her powers. Elspeth's many virtues included she was a kind, understanding, accepting, and forgiving woman. Tayla realized that her children needed a protector. They looked to Tayla for such a person. As mentioned before, Thomas became the new Count DeVacquerie.

Often, her patience was tested, with the family and with the vampires of her clan. The vampires had to be watched closely, so that boundaries were never breached. There was only a small inner circle of these creatures that she trusted to be around the family and staff. Her rules regarding conduct between the two, vampire and mortals at the castle were extremely strict. Any breach of the rules was dealt with harshly.

There was a time when a child of one of the familiars wandered near an area that was strictly off limits to any mortals. The child was reprimanded, and though too young to understand the nature of the Queen, the child never repeated the offense. Tales were told to the children, mostly to instill fear and respect to those who would challenge the rules. It worked.

The Dragon for the most part, had disappeared from the vampire world for the time being. He would not go too far away but kept watch upon the vampire kingdom. For the first time in history, this evil entity had to start over, reinventing himself and the Order as well, but that is another chapter.

CHAPTER THIRTY-EIGHT

RENASSAINCE

"Dearest Malcolm, at this time, I reflect upon my travels and times. I have seen many wonderful things. Most of them were small wonders, but a lot of them were important, world changing events. I have been through many wars, in Eastern Europe and Western Europe. I traveled extensively throughout the land, learning languages, cultures, meeting heads of state. I have seen the Hundred Years War, watched Henry V fight at Agincourt, at Crecy, while the Holy Church tried and burned Joan of Arc at the stake. Many good men fought and died for pride and ego. Such a waste! I have been through the Black Plague, seeing entire towns, families and regions scoured clean by the disease. For my kind, it was a time of feasting. For the mortal world, it was as if the judgement day had already arrived. The inquisition was a particular difficult time as I had already written about, but nonetheless, my kind survived all that too. I saw the Ottoman Turks capture Constantinople and reclaim the Holy Lands back unto the Moslem world. I remember reading a proclamation stating that Christopher Columbus had returned, discovering a new world across the sea. Oh, how I wished I could have traveled with him! I vowed someday I would cross that sea and see for myself the wonderful places he had found. And, I had seen the Renaissance, watching the masters create their renowned works. I would ask when you read this, look up and see my picture on the wall above the fireplace where we use to sit. This chapter is dedicated to them."

* * *

The year was 1500 AD. It became the passion of Queen Tayla to learn how the master painters in Florence and Milan developed their expertise on creating the likeness of humanity upon canvas. Her favorite paintings were those of scenes in the daylight. She could not see the sun and had not for hundreds of years. It was a glimpse into being normal. Having her memories of times when she was mortal thrilled her, as she could see green hills, mountains, and towns, with people doing all sorts of things. She left France for a while to seek out these painters.

Her benefactor, the Count Thomas DeVacquerie was informed of her plans. Knowing she would be away for a while, he assured her that the palace and castle would be just as she had left it. He would ensure its security and her vampires would still inhabit the residence in her absence. The Queen left for Florence, to meet with some other students of a painter, Leonardo DaVinci. He was considered one of the best, especially amongst the painters that came from Florence. History reveals that the greatest of these 'rebirth artists' came from Florence. This painter, DaVinci, was not just a painter. He was a master of what seemed to be all the mediums known at that time. He could do everything and most of all, she wanted to know his secrets, if they were, and how she could do that as well. Her thirst for human blood was the only thing that outmatched her thirst for knowledge.

Queen Tayla had to adapt to Florentine life in an unusual way. She had to learn to paint only at night. She was asked quite often why she did not paint during the day. It was known that she preferred the canvasses that revealed life during the daylight hours. Tayla could only tell them that she had a skin condition that reviled the sunlight, not just on her skin but her eyes as well. Because she could not venture into the daylight, she missed the brightness of the day. Her reasons were not questioned but thought very unusual that someone wanted to enjoy looking at pictures that should be enjoyed personally.

Leonardo questioned Tayla about it constantly, not to pry open her secrets, but wanted to find a way to help her. It was

363

because he was also interested in medicine. As he thought it to be a medical condition, such as something today known as xeroderma, he recommended to her various people to see. Of course, Tayla had no use for any referrals to other people for she knew her condition to be beyond anything medicine, modern or otherwise could offer to her. Medicine in those days would not have even imagined such a thing.

The master painter developed a friendly relationship with her. For a woman to paint in those days was rare, for most of the artists of the day were men. Tayla broke all the molds which Leonardo found refreshing. She was such a quick study, for her learning appeared to be accelerated above any pupils he had encountered before. Before long, she had begun to master his techniques, imitating him stroke for brush stroke.

Leonardo wondered what other gifts his protégé might have. He asked her about music. It was not too long before she was standing before musicians to the court of the Doge of Venice, the King of Florence, and other rulers of the many states of the Italian peninsula. Music seemed to be something that came natural to her. When she was taught to read music, it was like a second language to her. It was discovered the vampire also had a voice, a beautiful voice which flowed like water from a spring to a thirsty ear.

Soon, Tayla put down the brushes and the canvas, and began to sit in front of a harpsichord. The notes flowed like blood in the veins, a natural phenomenon of beauty, with purpose and direction. Her ability to play it beautifully developed into a phenomenon. She was asked to perform in front of nobility, royalty and did so with style. When she would be asked to perform in public, she made sure the event was one scheduled at night. Leonardo, always the gentleman, made sure it was understood his protégé would perform only during the hours of darkness.

Tayla was not known to make many mistakes, but with all the pleasantries of living a life as close to normal as possible, mistakes were bound to be made. The artists of the day made their living by having patrons to support their artistic endeavors. Patrons were rich families of means, and usually commissioned the artists to paint or sculpt works of art for them. Sometimes, the church itself was a great patron of the arts. Whenever Tayla would perform, everyone wanted to know who her patrons or sponsors were. This part she had not figured out yet as she had not given it much thought. This was the mistake.

One night, she performed on the harpsicord all the while singing a song written by an Italian composer. After an applause by those in the room, an official with the Florentine government asked who her patron was. He wanted to congratulate them and her for such a grand display of talent. The moment the question was asked, she knew she was caught off guard and so she blurted out a name, which was the mistake. That name was the name of one of the guests who was in attendance.

When they went to him, he denied ever knowing Tayla and wondered why she had used his name. Queen Tayla was embarrassed such that she left the room promptly and hid for the rest of the night. Just before dawn, Leonardo found her in a garden, gazing up at the moon over Florence. She was tearful, for she knew she could not keep this façade up for too much longer.

"I suppose I should ask why you used the name of Medici as your patron, but I think you want to tell me without me asking." He was a wise man.

"Leonardo, I have secrets that beg to be told, but I cannot without risking much. Everything about me is a lie."

"Risky for you or for me?"

"Both of us," she said. "I am not what you think I am."

"Well, let us see." He sat down on a bench in the garden. "I can see you only at night. That is the beginning of this, is it not?"

Tayla, still dressed in her noble gown, replied, "Yes, it is."

"Is that the secret or is there more?" he asked.

"Oh, there is more, much more. You are a man of science, a man of invention and new ideas. You have an open mind, yet I am afraid what I must tell you may close it forever. You have been so kind to me, and a wonderful teacher. You have made these last month's nights so wonderful for me. I have not felt this normal for a long time."

"And how long is that, my child?"

"Three hundred years. I know, it is difficult to explain."

"Did I ask you to explain?" he asked.

"No, but your mind is telling me you want to tell me something."

"My mind is always at work. It seems to never stop. I have used my intellect to study you, as you have studied me. I have come to this conclusion. You are not like anyone I have ever known or will ever know. Your secrets are yours and yours alone. I have no right to pry or to even ask you about them. You have not done anything to me that I should ask you to explain yourself. All I know is that you are different."

"I am afraid I will have to leave Florence. Perhaps even tonight. Should I be found out who and what I am, my life is in danger. Perhaps, even your life as well. The world is a much better place with you in it, than for ignorant and superstitious people to remove you. I must bid you farewell, Leonardo, my dear friend. Continue to paint, to sculpt, to invent! I am certain you will do well."

With those last words from her mouth, she sprouted her wings and flew off in plain view of him. She regretted leaving him but felt with what he just saw with his own eyes, he would know the truth.

*   *   *

Queen Tayla returned to her palace in France. It was as she expected. Everything was still intact. Thomas, the Count of DeVacquerie had done as he said he would. She told her benefactor of her times in Florence, Milan, and Venice. She did not want to return to Rome for any reason. For her, there were too many bad memories there. After hearing of her experiences, Thomas was anxious to go there to study and get the education she recommended he seek. He was deeply interested in arts and sciences.

She wished that she could speak with Leonardo again. She had written a letter to him, stating how he had impacted her life. When Thomas left for Florence, she gave him the letter with a vague explanation for her sudden leaving of Florence. It included an apology for her deserting him, especially when the local population were excited to hear her play and sing again.

Meanwhile, other things needed her attention. Elspeth's children were all grown by now. They all sought after Queen Tayla's advice and company. Tayla knew they were of age to be married and to start families. Her better judgement told her that should any of that begin to take place, it would be complicated to maintain the relationship with Elspeth's children when they had husbands and wives who would no doubt move into the castle. The castle was large enough and the staff big enough to accommodate them, but it all made Tayla uneasy. The gift of sight made it clear that she would have to seek out another sanctuary soon, one that she would not have to share.

Thomas wrote a letter back to Queen Tayla. It was accompanied by another letter from Leonardo DaVinci. Thomas said his education was coming along beautifully, stating that he loved learning. He had found Leonardo and told him that he was her actual patron. Leonardo had begged him to bring Tayla back to Florence, but he made no promises. Leonardo did not care to have Tayla play again but wanted to paint her portrait. She was moved by such a request, for in those days, royalty or nobility was the usual subject of most portraits. Thomas said Leonardo wanted to paint a portrait of a woman who was born to be a Queen. Tayla was moved by the last statement.

She then opened the letter that Leonardo had given to Thomas' courier. She read, "To Tayla, the woman who fascinates me and inspires me to do better than I ever imagined, I write this letter to inform you that I have thought about you every day since you left so quickly. I watched in amazement in the manner how you left and then I knew who you were. I have traveled the country, listened to the most intelligent men of our time. I have surrounded myself with the most brilliant men of our time and kept their secrets unto myself. You are known amongst the circles of these men I have spoken of, the enlightened. I have heard the superstitions, the rumors, and the ignorance of my time, only to have the courage to make up my own mind and judge for myself. Perhaps I am one of the few. Your words to me that night, accompanied by the manner of which you left, could only leave me with one impression. You are of a supernatural nature. You have been able to do what no other has ever done. Do I wish that you would return that I could study you? Any man would do just that. But I would like to paint your portrait, for I know who you are and what you are. You should be able to see how beautiful you are, without wondering, taking others word for it that you are beautiful. I will paint only in the hours of darkness, until it is complete. And when it is, you may be able to keep it, to appreciate its beauty, for that beauty is yours."

When she finished the letter, she smiled. "He wants to paint me. I will finally be able to see what I look like!" she exclaimed to her other vampires. They applauded her, wishing her well in this experience.

She let the younger brother of Thomas know of her intentions and he too gave the same guarantee that all would be the same when she returned. The night she left for Florence she was as excited as one could be. This would be a life changing experience for her. She had never seen herself in a reflection, not in a mirror nor in a pool of still water. Now, the greatest painter of the Renaissance era was going to paint her portrait. She knew she would treasure it for all time.

Her gift of sight, though usually shortsighted, told her this portrait would be special and she should dress appropriately for the sitting. A portrait of a queen demands all the royal trappings. Thus, she wanted to wear a crown and hold a scepter. The problem was that they did not exist yet. She wrote another letter stating she wanted the portrait to be painted but she had to delay the sitting. The reason for the delay was not given.

She went to Paris where the best goldsmiths were. Usually, they were in Italy, but she did not want to get too far from their source of creation. The best of these were commissioned to make a crown of her design, and a scepter to match it. The payment was lavish, part for the expense of the items, and part for the discreetness of the patron. No one was to know of the contract for the work. Familiars were assigned to watch over the craftsmen. Before too long, the craftsmen became familiars to the Queen. This way, her siblings could have their own royal devices made without fear of indiscretions made.

Within six months, the work was completed on the items. The crown held large rubies and diamonds inside a feminine-designed crown of gold. There were also large rubies and diamonds upon a gilded scepter. When they were presented, Tayla nearly gasped at their sheer splendor. The Queen was so impressed, she gave an extra amount of gold for their work.

Now, she was ready to sit for her portrait. She went to Florence to meet with Thomas, Count of DeVacquerie.

Thomas met with her the evening she arrived. His living quarters was a villa just outside the city of Florence. He had arranged for her to stay with him for the duration of her stay. She also brought an entourage of vampires with her. Thomas said he had a surprise waiting for her.

When she met with Thomas in his dining room, her brothers and sister were there, eager to meet with her. She had not seen them since the establishment of the clans. That was over two years ago.

"Sister!" said Prince Rascha, "We have not met each year as we have said we would. Perhaps this can suffice if we see you here. Count DeVacquerie has given us his welcome and his consent for us to abide with you during your stay here."

"Oh, Thomas! This is a surprise! To see you, my brothers and sister! I am overjoyed."

She sat down and they began a conversation that lasted well into the night. Their glasses were filled with the blood of a fresh kill, thanks to Prieta. They shared the blood, while everything was discussed. Thomas, of course, drank wine.

Tayla told the siblings of her castle in France, of her arrangement with Thomas' mother, how they had met, and how she had cared for them and they had cared for her. Rascha was impressed as well as his brother and sister.

"Perhaps we should have a similar arrangement for ourselves. It would certainly help us where security and protection were concerned." All agreed that such an arrangement should be sought.

The next night, Thomas agreed to escort Tayla to Leonardo's studio. He told all his students to leave for he had important work to do. She walked into his special room just for portraits. He had this room for portraits because of the lighting. Those were usually done during the daylight hours. This was to be different. Leonardo had reservations about how he could do such a painting without his usual lighting.

Tayla noticed he had torches in sconces upon the walls. She had them lit, and turned them up to their brightest, as well as having a brazier brought in, which she had burning bright as well.

"Will this lighting suffice, Leonardo?"

She was wearing a gown of fine silk, with a sash. Around her neck, she wore pearls, diamonds, and rubies. Then her vampire retainer opened two boxes. One contained the crown she had made special and the other contained the scepter to match.

Leonardo gasped and then smiled. "Oh, my! I have no words that can describe the majesty that my eyes behold. Such beauty accompanied by objects of such beauty! A sight that I am honored to paint. I shall do my utmost to be worthy of such!"

He had prepared his canvas, his easel, and his paints and brushes prior to her arrival. The lighting was perfect, and he began to sketch his basic lines.

As he did so, he was silent. Tayla, sitting upon a stool perfectly still, was busy reading his thoughts. Finally, she said, "We could converse while you work, can we not?"

He paused, and then said, "Yes, we can. I just am not sure of where to start. I read your letter and it did not answer the questions I still have."

"Ask them, Leonardo. You are deserving of my answers."

"You flew away from me when I last saw you. Only one creature can do such a thing. Are you such a creature?"

She smiled. "How do you know of such creatures?"

"Ahh! Answer a question with a question!" He continued to sketch.

"Some of my associates, those men who are enlightened I spoke of earlier, have told me of their experiences and their studies of such things. Your ability to fly away matches their accounts exactly."

"And what exactly did they tell you about those like me?"

"They said those creatures are very dangerous, and few have ever seen them and lived to tell about it."

"Well, my friend, I can tell you that their accounts are true, and people like me are extremely dangerous. But I am different, as you might have guessed. What did they call those who are like me?

He put down his brush. He was trembling when he said the word, "Vampire. They call you vampire."

It was silent for several minutes. He was not sure if he should continue to paint or wait for a reaction from a woman he just identified as a vampire, the most dangerous creature he had ever encountered.

"Are you afraid of me, Leonardo?"

"I am not, for I think if you wanted to do me harm, you would have done so already."

"Good. You can continue without fear of me or any of those who are with me. You are correct. I am vampire. I am the Queen of Vampires. My name is Queen Tayla Elisabeta Rokosovich, Sovereign of the *Clan of the Order of the Red Velvet*. And you are painting her royal portrait."

He picked up his brush and pallet, replying, "Your majesty, I am honored to do so."

"Tell me more of the enlightened men you associate with. I am curious to know what you know."

Leonardo DaVinci began to tell her of the group of men who had become the most learned men of their time. He said they had been in existence for quite some time. The more he spoke, the more he alluded to knowledge of the *Order of the Dragons of Set*.

"The *Order of the Dragons of Set*...what exactly do you know? This is a secret order, of which membership is severely restricted. Is there one in your group who is referred to as Dragon?"

"No, but there is one who calls himself the Dragon who has asked for membership into our circle."

It turned out that the Dragon was recruiting for members into a new order that he would create, using the wisest and most

371

learned men of the day. He wanted to recreate the Order that she had destroyed.

She smiled. Fate had turned in her favor. She now knew what the Dragon was planning. Warning Leonardo DaVinci not to allow him membership into their group, she told him who he was and what had happened to his group she called the "Order". They talked for quite a while, and then, it was not long before dawn would be approaching.

"Leonardo, if you know what I am, then you know I must depart before the dawn. We shall continue after I return here tonight just after sunset. Remember, say nothing to no one. I remember everything, and I forget nothing."

She left soon after and DaVinci found himself exhausted. He was painting the portrait of a Queen! He locked the door to his studio and walked his way back to his place of residence. He had met a vampire, a vampire queen no less, and he had lived to talk about it. Only, he could not talk about it. He would have to keep this to himself for the moment. Perhaps he could talk about it someday to the group of enlightened men. At the time, they were only a few but these men would establish a fraternity of wisdom, of learning and later would become known as the men of the Illuminati.

The next night, Queen Tayla appeared before Leonardo, ready to sit for her portrait again. She had seen the basic sketch lines, and was satisfied, though she could not realize the finished picture at this time. Never mind, she thought. His reputation for producing such fine work assured her that this was worth her time. She was wearing her crown and held her scepter in her hand while sitting upon the same stool. With a glance of her violet eyes, she turned the fire up on the torches and brazier.

Leonardo came in, ready to paint. He was smiling as he was in a particularly good mood. "Good Evening, your majesty. Are you well this evening?"

"I am always well, Leonardo. I have little to worry about and I never get sick. My needs are…well, you know what my needs are."

"Yes, your majesty. I do know, which makes me a liability. Something we are both aware of."

"Leonardo, I have no intention of harming you. I may be a monster, a thief, a murderer. I am all those things. I may be considered the worst of all creation. However, I will not be guilty of robbing the world the greatest of its creative geniuses. The world is much better off with you in it."

"Your majesty, my curiosity about you and your nature is simply one based upon my need to discover that which is unknown, or undiscovered. My associates have discussed that which has never been proven but discussed about in circles of rumor and superstition. Now, I am in the presence of the very creature that my associates want to study, learn about, perhaps even to unlock the secrets you might hold within yourself. How old are you if I may ask?"

Queen Tayla cracked a smile. "If I tell you, you may laugh at the preposterousness of my answer."

"Laugh at a queen? I should think not."

"I was born in 1202, in Wallachia. I died in 1216 at the hands of my father, Prince Vladis, who was duped by a man known as the Dragon to his followers, but locally, he was called Vojislav Rekvas."

"Your majesty, is this the same man you asked about yesterday who was known amongst my associates?"

"The very one! I can tell you of my history, but I think it will cause you to wonder more about me. I am as much a victim of this terrible curse as those upon whom my thirst and nature are directed against. Shall I start at the beginning? Or will my story take so much time to tell that you may have to paint several portraits of me?"

"Your majesty, I will gladly listen to you for as long as you wish."

"Very well, Leonardo…," as she began to tell a most fantastic story. By the time the dawn was approaching, the Queen noticed that Leonardo seemed sad, almost to the point of tears.

"Do not be sad, Leonardo. What is done was done over three hundred years ago. I have learned to accept such a fate. There was no choice for me to make. It was made for me. Until tomorrow, I hope you find rest."

On the third night, much was the same. The Queen arrived first and gazed upon the face on the canvas for the first time. The image upon the canvas was stunningly beautiful, as was the subject. She had already set the lighting.

The latch on the door turned and Leonardo Da Vinci walked in, finding her standing in front of the canvas. He carried a flask of wine, along with bread and cheese. He watched her admire his work in silence.

Finally, he asked, "Do I have your temporary approval for my work?"

She turned quickly to face him. "This is how you see me?"

"Your majesty, I paint what my eyes see. I see a most beautiful woman, young, vibrant, radiant who though she says she is dead, I see life, beautiful life."

"I am a fourteen-year old girl, who is dead and has been for nearly three hundred years. And yet, this is what you see?"

"Your majesty, you cannot see yourself. Not in a mirror, or in a pool of water. But my eyes can see you. My eyes do not lie. And I would not lie to you. If you were a monster, I would paint a monster. But all men are monsters, for we all are imperfect. The church teaches us we are all sinners, that we have no righteousness amongst any of us. I can only paint what my eyes see. May I finish your portrait?"

"I am nearly speechless for I see myself for the first time in three centuries. I had no idea. You brought food. I hope that is for you for I have no need in any of that which you brought with you."

"This is a time of beginnings for you and for me. You are seeing yourself for the first time. You have learned to do those things that you promised you would do. You have established your kingdom. You have achieved your education. You defeated your enemies of the *Order of the Dragons of Set*. You spoke last night about gifts you receive that enable you to maintain your position as Queen. What other gifts are possible to attain that would make you even more powerful? Do you think that you have received them all? I do not think so. The gift of sight, strength, of control of elements, of wisdom, intuition, heightened senses, and so on and on, is there no more? You said that a vampire is all about survival. Surely there are more gifts that enable you to survive, such as being able to pass yourself as a mortal."

"You are very persuasive in that I do believe there may be more gifts I will be given. Perhaps they will be powers I will develop over time. But for now, go ahead and eat your supper. I have already dined. I make sure I do so that I am not tempted by the sound of blood coursing through your veins."

He sat down, opened the bottle, and poured himself a glass. He broke the loaf of bread, cut a slice of cheese, and began to eat. While he did, Queen Tayla began where she had left off the night before regarding her story. When he had finished, she sat upon the stool, and assumed the same exact position as before so that he could continue to paint.

Every now and then, he would ask a question regarding her story. She was glad to answer any question and did so truthfully for she was averse to telling falsehoods. She hated liars, for it was a lie that was told to her father that caused her and her siblings their demise and their ultimate conversion. Finally, Leonardo asked her a question that intrigued her very much.

"Your majesty, would you ever consider entertaining my associates and colleagues in person if I could guarantee your safety, and their discreetness, swearing all to secrecy?"

"Such an interesting proposition. I might consider it if it were to take place on my terms. Remember, I and my clan have survived only because of secrecy and our defensive capabilities. We have never given ourselves to any forum of discussion, or examination. We are not specimens to be studied. If I meet with anyone, it will be only a few if any. Consider yourself fortunate that you and you alone can be in my presence without fear of harm. I respect you but I fear I do not know any of your associates who profess to be the most learned men of their time enough to trust my survival based upon their desire to know for sure if I exist."

"Yes, your majesty. I will bring up the matter no further."

The portrait was finished within a few weeks. The Queen was enamored with it. She stared at it for great lengths of time and often. Soon, she was ready to leave Florence. Within a few years, she would hear of the great master painter's death. The audience he had asked for his enlightened associates would never happen. She did not know their identities, nor did they know of hers. They only knew her kind existed, but they had no proof. True to his word, he had never mentioned her to anyone.

CHAPTER THIRTY-NINE

THE BOX OF LETTERS

"Dearest Malcolm, the kingdom of vampires was established in 1485. I had come to know firsthand the greatest personality of the Italian Renaissance. When he proposed that he paint my portrait, I was elated that he would even consider it. He painted my portrait, in all my royal regalia. When I consider all my memories, this was perhaps one of my finest and most cherished. This portrait was painted for me in full scale. I had no need to show it off. I was singularly impressed with his work as this portrait became my mirror. Its preservation would require diligent efforts on my part over the years so I wondered where I could store it, or even display it. My kingdom was now realized with a crown, a scepter, a ring, a castle, and an army. I often thought of the High Council member, Ramone, and his words to me. Perhaps I should have thanked him for he gave me the drive and ambition to do exactly what he thought I could not do. He asked me where my kingdom was, and the trappings of that office. Unfortunately, he did not live long enough to see me realize my dreams.

When I returned to France, I was faced with a new challenge. A vampire's most important priority is survival. Our tools are secrecy, deception, wisdom, and good use of the gifts we are given. If we remain secret, silent, and hold the smallest footprint, we stand the best chance of living amongst mortals. If all mortals were like you, perhaps that would not be necessary. Most mortals are not like you."

It was June of 1519. While holding court in her palace at the castle she shared with the DeVacquerie family, Queen Tayla received a message of parchment, rolled, and tied with a ribbon of silk, lying in a long slender box of crafted wood. The wooden box was constructed of different colored pieces in a masterful mosaic pattern. It was from a clan ambassador that resided in the city of Florence where Leonardo Da Vinci had lived… and now most recently died.

She was sorely grieved to read this news. Strangely, the message was written in Da Vinci's own handwriting. How could this be, she wondered, unless he knew he was dying and wanted to send his last words to her. Finding out the details of his death may be easy, but why did he send her this letter stating that his death was eminent. It was one of life's mysteries she would never gain an answer to. But then, Leonardo Da Vinci, had many secrets he took with him to the grave.

"My friend Leonardo is dead," she said in a near whisper as the parchment fell from her hands. Standing up from her chair, she declared that all should be in mourning for a great mind had left the world in a better but in a still needful state. She asked that her ambassador find the location of his burial so she could go to pay her respects. Bringing him to the crossing over would have been impossible for he was reportedly to be a Christian. She had already found out that conversions of those of that faith was not possible. The loss of her friend affected her severely.

Her ambassador, Henri, a young but highly intelligent man who had held administrative positions in his mortal life, had foresight enough to know to use familiar mortals as a conduit to speak and inquire of the living to get information. He said he would put his assets upon the task immediately. His familiars went to work on the task, drafting a letter to inquire upon the disposition of his final resting place.

Many of her advisors to include her ambassador cautioned her against visiting the tomb. No doubt it would be on sanctified ground, making it inaccessible for her to approach. She declared, "He knew me. He knew about me and held my very survival in

378

his hands. Yet, he remained silent, trusting not even his closest confidants. He told me that even his closest associates knew of our existence but refused to utter out loud the reality that we exist. Yet, all these years, he remained trustworthy… and silent. He was a good friend, though I knew he was afraid, he trusted me to cause him no harm. Few mortals are that trusting. To not visit him would be to show disrespect."

She visited his tomb site but was not able to get too close for as advised, he was buried on sanctified ground. His tomb was in the Collegiate Church of Saint Florentin at the Château d'Amboise. The Chateau was now the royal residency for the French Monarchy. She stood upon the opposite banks of the Loire River, staring at the building she could not set foot near.

The vampire queen spoke aloud, as if she thought he might only be lying in his tomb, waiting to hear her familiar voice. "Oh, Leonardo, why could you not have called on me sooner? I would have come to you. I would have given anything to have kept you in this world, even risk bringing you into mine. There was no price I would not have paid to do so." She fought back tears as she relived each and seemingly every moment that she had spent with him. He was her friend, her teacher, her mentor who had taught her more about humans, the world, and the possibilities it might hold than anyone she had ever known. She talked and listened for a reply, but none came.

The vampire did this for several hours before she went hunting for blood. That did not take long. In the town where the Chateau was located, local markets had not closed for the evening yet. She waited for vendors to start putting their wares away and closing shop for the night. Carts began to pull away from the marketplace, heading home. Taverns were still full of patrons who were filling themselves of locally made ale, and wine. Sooner or later, a patron who had drank his or her fill would come out. Then, she would strike at the precise time.

Queen Tayla hid in the shadows, waiting patiently for her intended target to enter the 'kill' zone. When the young maiden did so, the vampire queen moved with such precision and speed that any observer would have missed a great deal of the movement necessary to have performed the kill. Within seconds, the maiden lost consciousness and then went limp in Tayla's arms. When Tayla was finished, she took the corpse of the victim up into the air and flying above the river, dropped her into the dark waters of the Loire, such that the current would take her down river before she would be found. Then, she went to find another. Emotionally traumatized, she lost control. Her anger that Leonardo was dead drove her to excess. She was on a killing spree. That night, eight more victims met their doom.

Her anger was directed at her victims because she could not enter upon holy ground. The entire church premises were considered sacred and therefore, she could not approach. The next day, she confessed that her emotions had gotten the best of her. The fact that it was nine people that died that night stirred up the local populace. The rumors about vampires abounded afterwards and the local churches were in an uproar. Investigations were launched and again, the Holy Church let loose the Inquisition. This time, with a great vengeance.

Local magistrates met together along with many witnesses to provide leads as to who or what was committing these murders. Many people relied on superstitions, but the magistrates and local clergy wanted facts. Had anyone seen what was committing these murders? Actually, no one could say they had seen anything. Only the aftermath of such carnage was available for examination. All the victims had the same type wounds, all had died the same death, and no one could say they had seen anything.

Few vampires would ever, if any, take a victim in the presence of another mortal unless that mortal was to be taken as well. Vampires were particularly good at leaving few if any clues. When they would take a victim, there was no witness, or the attack could be accomplished in such a manner that no one would notice it had happened.

Because Queen Tayla's attacks had occurred near the French Royal residence, the monarchy got involved. They sent envoys to Pope Leo X in Rome, imploring him to get involved. Leo had a box of letters that Popes before him had written. Few if any knew of these letters, for they were meant only for the eyes of those elected to the office of Pope. A letter from Pope Alexander VI, also known as Rodrigo Borgia, was addressed to any Pope who would be serving in times of dire crisis. Leo was no fool. One of the first things he had done was read the letters of his former office holders. This was the way that Popes talked to one another, even from the grave. Lessons were taught, wisdom passed on, and secrets were revealed. When he had read Alexander VI's letter to future Popes, he was astonished. He had heard of the heresy, but had refused to believe it, as all the officers of the Church were.

Now, his eyes were opened. He was ready to stamp out what many of the church had thought but had refused to verbalize their opinions. Leo called a meeting of the Cardinals. The meeting was a closed meeting and no assistants were allowed, only the Cardinals. In a private chamber, a long room with a long, fine table and chairs to match its grandeur, a meeting of the highest level of clergy of the Church took place in secret.

"We must do something, for doing nothing demonstrates we have no power against this evil. I have read a letter from one of my predecessors. He has given me enlightenment as to what we are up against. For decades, perhaps even a century, a theory has been covered up. It was forbidden to talk about, even mention in careless conversation. To have done so was considered heresy. Now, the time has come to face this evil head on. With the help of God Almighty, we will prevail. The word we have been afraid to say is the one I will say now. Vampire. Vampire!" He screamed out the last word. The Cardinals murmured amongst themselves.

"Years before, one of our own had actually had a conversation with one. He had conversed with the leader of these vile creatures. But did nothing. He says the vampire wanted to exist without persecution and wanted no war with the church. Yet, it is making war against us because it makes war against humanity. These were God fearing creatures that were murdered. They went to mass, prayed, confessed, gave tithes. Yet they paid with their lives for no other reason than the nature of the vampires demands the blood of the living."

He let all that he had said sink into the minds of the Cardinals. He looked out at the long room which each side had the high-ranking clergy seated in two rows facing each other. "I am open

381

to suggestions as to how to proceed. This is to be a war, a war that the public must not know about. It is not about the silencing of ideas that are contrary to our faith. It is about the extinction of creatures that are contrary to our faith and it must be done quickly, thoroughly, and discreetly. I feel that if the public knew about this, it might open the door to other challenges to the Church and its authority."

Several Cardinals made suggestions as the Pope listened. He dismissed some as ridiculous and gave serious consideration to others. Finally, one Cardinal from Germany suggested that the Dominican Order had experience in such matters and should be assigned to deal with such.

"What experience has this Order had regarding vampires?" the Pope asked.

"Years back, one of our most experienced priests had gotten close to the source of such incidents...a Father Joachim. He discovered a way to get close to the vampires by identifying their helpers. He wrote down all his notes in a book. This book is kept in the abbey where this priest lived. Perhaps, we should obtain it and then learn about our enemy."

"Now, that is the best suggestion I have heard today. Let it be done. Is this priest available to come before me?"

"Your excellency, no he is not. He was eventually killed by the vampire. His body was found tortured and finally killed by a stake through his heart, the same preferred and prescribed method of execution of a vampire."

"Is there another priest who has this kind of experience?" asked the Pope.

"There was," replied the Cardinal. "His name was Heinrich Kramer. He died a few years ago, in 1505 I believe, your eminence."

"Oh yes. I have been reading his book, "Malleus Maleficarum." Does he have any apprentices, proteges possibly? If so, then bring them, and the notes by his predecessor, this Father Joachim and any of that Order who has had experience with this, to meet with me. I shall assign them as a special inquisition against this evil."

Members of Tayla's clan noticed immediately that she had lost control of her emotions because of the news of her friend's death. They were keenly aware when they woke from their sleeping places the next evening. A sense of doom came over them. Up until now, she had maintained control over her highly charged emotional character. The wake of this incident would cause a strong reaction from the mortal world, particularly the Holy Church. They were determined to talk to their queen about it.

"Your majesty, it has come to our attention that last night's hunting on your part was particularly, well," he knew he needed to tread lightly, "it creates a problem."

The Queen had risen and met the clan in the throne room as she always did. Clothed in a scarlet red gown with ermine fur collar, and crown upon her head, she sat upon a large chair that served as the physical throne of her kingdom. The Queen, still reeling from being barred from Da Vinci's tomb, replied, "Yes, I know. What I have done will bring consequences. My actions were my fault. I lost control and have put you all at risk. Now, it is my leadership that you look to for resisting against the retributions that are sure to come. My emotions won the battle between good judgement and bad. It brings judgment on my entire clan, not to mention upon the kingdom. Retribution by the Holy Church will come upon us hard and heavy, as if we were the iron pressed against the anvil. The Holy Church's hammer is coming down upon us."

Her ambassador to the clans spoke up and asked if a conference should be arranged between the royals and their ambassadors. He felt she would agree to a consensus that whatever plans were made, they all needed to agree to that plan.

"Yes, by all means. Get the word out now, that the Princes and Princess should come to me or I will go to them. We must devise a strategy.

She replied that she would accept possible courses of action and confessed that her gift of sight had not given her a clear picture of what was surely to come. "When I have been given a view of the future, I will inform you and then we will act accordingly. I fear a war with the church, a war I never wanted, is being declared upon us. We must be ready to act.

CHAPTER FORTY

THE HAMMER OF THE INQUISITION

"Dearest Malcolm, through the years, much of my journey was spent learning about myself, the new self which I found to be strange, exhilarating, and cursed all at the same time. Upon my transformation, I received the basic traits, powers, gifts etc., that all vampires would receive. Often, I wondered if Akhenaten and Nefertiti had received these powers all at the same time or if over time, they found they could do things they could not do before.

Of all the basic characteristics of the vampire nature, the one power most are familiar with is immortality. We are not subject to injury, disease, or the normal effects of aging. We will live until the criteria that will cause the destruction of us are met. That is a rare event because most mortals are not familiar with vampires enough to know that criteria.

The next basic characteristic is our constant hunger of living blood. The blood of humans is preferred by vampires. However, animal blood will suffice when our choice is not available. It just must be that of a living organism.

The power of superhuman strength is another basic trait. This power is such that as a predator, I can overpower my victims. The gift of sight, or ability to see into the future, sometimes short range, sometimes long range is a gift that comes soon after conversion but not immediately. I did not receive it until several years later after my conversion.

The ability of manifestation came even later. That gift is the ability to manifest themselves in many forms. We can disguise ourselves as a mist, or fog, or a wind. We can manifest ourselves as animals, or different people. Only I would be the one, the only one, in history to achieve the ability to manifest myself as different people. This gift did not manifest itself until centuries later. Eventually, my journey would lead me to the point where I would be able to have mortals see me as a completely different identity. I would eventually do this in three different personalities and faces.

The ability to adapt to our environment comes almost immediately. Vampires will find themselves immune to such extremes such as hot or cold temperatures. We can see through fog, and smoke and through other solid objects. We can also see far away. Remember when I found my lover, Renard on a battlefield far away? That was nearly a mile away.

There are many other gifts that vampires will receive. It is not known if they are bestowed because of maturity, or the need for them is outstanding, or if they have curried favor with Set (Satan). As for my case, I think it was because Set felt that if I succeed, then it would ensure the survival for all vampires. Either that or the devil had other plans for me.

Other abilities followed with maturity, such as my ability to retract my fangs and claws. It coincides with the ability to adapt to our environment, tying in with camouflage. My ability to partake of human habits was a true gift, for I had long forgotten what it was like to taste mortal food and drink. Having sex was also a wonderful ability to blend in. I particularly enjoyed that when I was being with Sir Renard Berenais. I still miss that experience.

Being able to read the thoughts of mortal's minds was a particularly useful gift. All my powers are used to ensure my survival as well as the survival of my race. When the Pope issued a special inquisition against me, I had to use all these gifts. They essentially became my arsenal of weapons I would use to outsmart, outmaneuver, and outgun their messengers of evil and hypocrisy.

*   *   *

From inside his sparsely furnished room, the occupant heard a knock at the door. The room was clean, small almost like a cell of a prison. It was poorly lit for there was only one small window on the wall opposite from the door.

This occupant was a resident of the monastery of the Dominican Order. His white habit, covered by a black robe, was the standard wear of this order, which caused its wearers to become known as the "Black Friars." He opened the door to see a fellow monk at the door with a rolled-up parchment sealed with a wax seal from the Archbishop of Cologne. Father Karl lit another candle so he could read in the dim light. He smiled when he read the letter addressed specifically to him. It was a summons, but he treated it as an invitation to join the Archbishop the next day at his office for lunch. A summons from such a well-placed clergyman did not lend itself to refusal. He would go immediately at first light. The trip would take a couple of hours which would give him time to reflect upon what matter this involved. When he read the part of the letter which asked that he bring specific documents with him, his smile was even broader. Those documents were the diaries and notes of the work of Father Joachim who was also a member of the Dominican Order along with Father Karl. Father Karl knew Joachim when he was campaigning against the heresy of witchcraft and vampirism. Though it was against church policy to talk about it, all the Dominican members knew about it and that it was a real issue. Another close associate, Heinrich Kramer, was also a campaigner against such things. But now, Karl reflected, they were both dead.

"Finally," he said under his breath, "Somebody is going to listen to us. Maybe this time will be different."

He went to the scriptorium, the library of the monastery, to retrieve all the materials the Archbishop had asked for. Finding them was not difficult because he had hidden them. He did this for they dealt with such a forbidden subject. When he was able to get them, he left for the Archbishop's office at the Cologne Cathedral and abbey.

He came into the office, giving the usual grouped salutations and rituals of meeting such a highly ranked church official. Once seated, the Archbishop did not speak directly of what the issue was that he wanted to speak with Father Karl about.

"Any trouble on your journey over here?"

Father Karl merely nodded no. He was a man of few words and preferred that opinions of him be based on his deeds and not his words. The Archbishop's assistant began to bring in lunch for the two to have while they conversed. Once the table was set, the doors were closed as the servers exited the room. The Archbishop blessed the meal, saying grace over the table. Then, he spoke to Father Karl in a direct tone.

"The Pope has asked me to enlist your aid in dealing with a subject that has been forbidden for such a long time. Hardly anyone knows how to deal with it. Suggestions were made, and Father Joachim's name came up. Since we all know that he is dead, the next best solution was to enlist any of his associates that might have experienced the same things he might have. I know that you and Father Joachim had discussions, some of which I might imagine were said in confidence regarding this subject. What have you to say about this?"

"Your eminence, I wish you would just come out and say what you want. Or, should I do it for you?"

A few moments passed by. Father Karl continued, "Very well! You want me to use Father Joachim's notes regarding vampyria to help the church and its agents to fight against them for the church has absolutely no idea of how to combat these unholy creatures. Since Father Joachim is dead, as is Father Heinrich, there is only me left to carry the burden of carrying the battle to these agents of Satan. Something has happened that now forces the Church to adopt a new stance on the subject that was once considered heresy. Probably some vampire has gone off on a killing spree and now someone important has appealed to the Holy See in Rome. Now, have I missed anything?" Father Karl was one of few words, but he had just said more words than he usually would have said in a day.

The Archbishop was taken aback. He was not used to being talked to so bluntly. The red-robed man was silent for a few moments, trying to regain his composure as well as trying to come up with something to say for rebuttal. But all he could say was "Yes. That is exactly why I am here."

Father Karl smiled. "Good. It is about time we got around to dealing with this. It is not heresy to deny the existence of something so evil and so dangerous when all of Christendom is in danger. Not because of what they can do to any mortal, but how they can aid the enemies of the Church is even more alarming. The Ottomans, are they still at the front door of the Holy Roman Empire? Suppose they went to them and offered their services to them? It is not such a fantasy to consider the possibility of our enemies enlisting the closest thing to the devil walking amongst the living. Listen to me, your eminence. I have read every word of Father Joachim's writing and his diaries too. He left them to me, for he knew I was the only one who listened to him, believed him. I went along on his quests at times and heard the inquisitions of their familiars. I heard their confessions, how they support their undead masters, how they hide during the day and prey at night. I am the only living man who knows the most about the vampire creature. I want to get to know it, understand it, and learn about it. Then, I can truly learn how it can be banished from this earth, this life, and put on the correct side of the grave. I feel their soul is immortal in this world, but their body is not. If we can destroy the body, the soul will have nowhere to reside but in the next life, the life reserved for such an evil creature. Let God deal with them on that side of the grave. We are charged with putting them there. Let loose the hounds of God."

This time, it was the Archbishop smiling. He poured himself a cup of wine, and Father Karl's cup was filled. "I have not seen anyone possessing such passion to carry out the wishes of the Church in such a long time. Perhaps Father Joachim's life was too short. We could use such a man at this time. Coupling his knowledge with your fervor for carrying out this mission, I would consider this a winning combination. At least we have his writings. And we have you. Let us drink to a successful endeavor, such that you will be victorious in eradicating God's enemies from this world. It is His will!" They toasted by touching cups lightly and began to eat of the bounty of the table.

389

When they arrived at the Church's headquarters in Rome, Father Karl was amazed. He had never seen such an extravagant display of wealth other than in some of the royal palaces in Germany. Stunned did not even come close to describing his sense of overwhelming.

It was just after Christmas of 1519, when the two finally rode into Rome. Upon meeting Pope Leo X, he did so with only the Pope, the Cardinal and himself. The Pope began, saying, "I can only assume that you know everything we know and much more if you are the one, we have been looking for. We are in a crisis at this moment. Many of our so-called experts are in full agreement that Europe is overrun with vampires. Do you think this is true?"

Father Karl tried to hide a smile when he heard this consensus of other church members. "No, your eminence, I do not. I think there is probably less than a thousand of them in all of Europe. I know you will ask me why I believe this so I will tell you. If Europe were overrun with them, there would be very few mortals left. I do not see that from my view. I see a lot of frightened men and women who want to believe it is the end of the world and we should be expecting judgement at any time. I believe that each vampire is required to take a victim each night, at least one. But there is a controlling force that exercises restraint on their part. Most vampires are mindless bloodsucking creatures, constantly searching for victims and disposing of them when they have fed on them. I do not see as much of that as your experts have said. If they did, we would see no less than several thousand murdered victims each morning when we would wake. I feel that for us to be able to get our hands around the neck of this problem, we must learn about our enemy. Every soldier knows that to defeat your enemy, you must first know him. How many generals have made this mistake by not knowing their enemy? Plenty. So, I believe that is the first thing we must do. Their behavior is dictated to them but not on their own accord. Their habits are predictable, but not understood. They do what they do because they are driven to do it. What is it that drives them? Is it will, or instinct?"

"You have this information in your writings?" the Pope asked.

"I have Father Joachim's and Father Heinrich's writings both here in my arms. I added my own to them as well. We all collaborated on this subject before their demise. They fully expected the vampires to come hunting for them."

The Cardinal interrupted him, asking, "Why did they expect them to come after them?"

Father Karl replied, "Because they told us so. They wrote it upon a wall of a victim's house in his own blood, 'Come hunting for us and we will go hunting for you!' That was a message that came true for Joachim and Heinrich."

"All the resources of the Church are at your disposal. Do what you must do. Go where you must go and take with you what you need to be successful. Send dispatches back to me or to the Cardinal of your endeavors. I always want to be fully informed. We have already gone through a period of history when we would find empty towns and villages. I do not wish to repeat those days. Hire all the people you need even if it is to be an army. But it must be an army of men devoted to the purpose of eradicating the vampire, once and for all."

Father Karl left the office of the Pope and felt his first step was to visit the nearest Dominican Order to begin to recruit 'soldiers' by which to fulfill his mission. He did this with fervor, finding no shortage of men who feared the creature known as the vampire, or nosferatu. When he found these men in numbers, they were men of courage willing to do what they believed was the right thing to do. In great numbers, they would be strong.

Each night, he read and reread all the notes written down in the journals. He read about habits, their deeds, how bodies were found, common characteristics about murder scenes, times and situations that were common amongst the victims. It was exhausting for he was looking for a pattern or patterns. Like a sleuth of the supernatural, Father Karl was approaching this problem in a very professional, methodical way. He was not wanting to make the same mistake his colleagues had made. When he would find something interesting, he would share it, for he knew the only reason he was there was because his two deceased friends had shared their knowledge with him.

Father Karl instructed all the monasteries, convents, and abbeys to give up any knowledge or testimony of experience of encounters to any Dominican priest. They were to instruct all parishioners to do likewise. The priests were not bound by the sacrament of confession if they were to hear of any information about vampirism. Father Karl loved to fish as a boy. He found that the more hooks you baited, the more fish you would catch. The same was true in this instance. Soon, reports started coming in about people who had seen or heard things. Father Karl would send someone to investigate or go there himself.

Upon one of those instances he did investigate, or conduct an "inquisition", it was on a tavern owner who had been known to entertain guests who would show up only during hours of darkness. This piqued the interest to Father Karl for he knew that vampires only traveled after sundown.

The tavern was at a village crossroads in northern Italy, near the base of the Italian Alp passes. The most notable village in the immediate area was the town of Bergamo. The priest knew when he agreed to take on this mission, there would be a lot of traveling involved.

He took with him a company of armed men along with a detachment of priests, all fully aware of what the dangers might be. If they were chasing after a suspicion and none of it being fact, then they had no worries. However, if this tavern was an establishment ran by a familiar, hosting vampires as they traveled on their way across the European countryside, there was great danger.

The priest and his company arrived during the day to the tavern. They had dropped by the local church where the local friars had told them of their account, heard about third or fourth hand, but still worthy of checking out for veracity. Father Karl knew how local peasants and travelers were superstitious to the core. He was in search of facts, not fears or fantasies.

It was winter. Snow covered the ground and the vegetation from the woods was now sparse. Only evergreen trees provided any cover. The priest asked for everyone to surround the area, with no one being allowed to leave until all those who were inside were able to be questioned. When Father Karl walked inside, it seemed business as usual. People were eating, drinking, conversing while some loose women were conducting business transactions that would take place either out in the barn or upstairs in a warm bed. Others could be seen in the back through a large doorway, cooking and preparing meals. Nothing seemed out of the ordinary. A large hearth kept the inside quite warm.

He inquired of the proprietor's location and identity. He was identified as the fat man who stood behind the bar, filling steins of beer or cups of wine. He was also taking orders for lunch or early dinners. His wife, also a stout woman could be seen through the door to the kitchen, preparing some food that smelled very appetizing. The owner was friendly to talk to.

Then, the inquisition began its first phase. Easy to answer questions were asked, and answers were obtained. Father Karl had his ways. He did not want to be mean or cruel. He did not even like to intimidate people. However, he had the full support of the Roman Catholic Church and its Holy See, Pope Leo X. He could do no wrong, for he had the official sanction of the Church, per the Pope's own words. Officially, what he was up to would never be written down as church history. There would be no Papal edict mentioning anything of this activity.

Karl told the man who he was and why he was there. He also told him he had nothing to fear if he told the truth. "I have heard, on good sources, that there are people who come here during the night and leave during the night. Do you not think that to be strange? Do you conduct business during the hours of darkness all the time or just recently?"

"Sometimes I have guests that come at night. Is that a crime?"

"No, that is not a crime. Harboring fugitives, or enemies of the church, well, that is a crime. A serious crime. I have heard from witnesses that certain men come here often, for lodging, and are never seen again until the next night. Do they sleep during the day only to rise during the evening?"

The owner, getting irritated with the line of questioning from the priest answered, "People do what they want to do, when they want to do it. I do not ask questions. It is none of my business. I have four rooms upstairs. What goes on up there is none of my business. Even those harlots there," he said pointing to the two women laughing in the corner talking to a well-dressed merchant, "I never ask them who or what they are doing. They pay the rent on the room upstairs and I am richer for it. I do not think the church cares as much where its money comes from either as long as it comes, do you?"

Father Karl smiled. He thought of the many priests who though they had forsaken marriage, they had not forsaken sex and indulged themselves as much as any whoremonger. Many of them had left the priesthood in shame and dishonor. They claimed they had said no to marriage when it was chastity they were supposed to have embraced.

Though this was the time of the Renaissance, the world was an evil place, full of temptations and snares to entangle mankind's faith. Karl understood this, accepted this, but did not partake of this. He did not like his world. A perfect world, one without sin, he knew was beyond his realization, but he was determined to remain pure to at least one vow he had made. Heresy was his enemy. It was the manifestation of Satan upon the earth to him. He had taken a vow against heresy, to stamp it out, wherever he found it. That vow included killing vampires…in God's name. He knew this was to be a true Holy War. That is why he was now the hammer of the inquisition.

"Proprietor, I will ask you to show me where they rest. I do not care if it is the barn, or the rooms upstairs. I only need to see a complete inspection of your establishment. If I find everything satisfactory, then my men and I will leave. Will you allow me to inspect?"

"Of course. I have nothing to hide. I only ask that you look and not destroy or harm my stock. Look inside, as priests, not soldiers for loot. Understood?"

A nod from the priest gave the signal for the clergy to begin a search. A group went upstairs, while another group went outside to the barns. The entire tavern was really a farm with a large farmhouse and other associated buildings.

There were two barns, one full of livestock because it was winter, and another was for storage of grain and other foodstuffs. There was also a brewery across the yard where the smell of brewing ale could be taken into the nostrils. A bakery house was attached to the back of the tavern, so freshly baked bread sent its aroma across the breeze. Nothing seemed ordinary. Chickens roamed free across the cold and snow-strewn ground, while an occasional bellow from a cow could be heard while a milking maid tugged on its udders.

For the next few hours, the priests, aided by some of the soldiers, searched every cranny of the place, looking for anything that would suggest something out of the ordinary. Even Father Karl was not sure of what he was looking for, but he was sure when he saw it, he would know it was the proof he needed.

Nothing was found out of the ordinary, and the priest thanked the fat man, and his wife for their hospitality and cooperation, and then left. As soon as they got out of sight of the tavern, Father Karl and a contingent of his men left the group, to hide out in the woods, within sight of the tavern.

"If the owner was telling the truth, we shall see for ourselves. I know that if they are familiars, they will lie unto their deaths to protect their masters. We need someone to watch the back and the front. Arm yourselves with your crossbows. I know that silver is your only defense against them. Getting closer than that is extremely dangerous, even foolhardy. Use your crucifix as a shield. Vampires are afraid of holy things."

They spread out and waited. The sun would be gone within the hour. As they waited, the sun dipped lower as well as the temperature following it. Soon it was dark, and because Karl had ordered no torches lit, he and his men were shivering in the cold. They did not have to shiver for long.

Not long after the sun had disappeared from the horizon, a figure could be seen coming out of the granary. No one had seen anyone go into the granary during the daylight nor in the darkness. That meant that the person who had come out must have been in there all day. Father Karl was now suspicious but also giddy for he felt he may be on the brink of discovery. Tomorrow, when it was light, he would reinspect the granary. For if the figure who had emerged from the granary was of the undead, most likely, his bed for day-sleeping would be in there, hidden from any prying eyes. Eyes that Father Karl had.

*   *   *

From her throne room at the Castle De Vacquery, Queen Tayla felt an uneasiness as she sat upon her large and ornate wooden chair, She still had not had her official throne constructed because she knew if she had to move, it would be too difficult to move. The feeling of uneasiness and tension was so strong, it made Tayla mention it to her clan members. Some of them said they could feel it as well. It was a feeling none of them, including Tayla had ever felt before. It could only be described as foreboding, like a dark cloud on the horizon about to break into a storm.

Queen Tayla asked, "I want to know if there are any of our clan who are not accounted for?"

No one responded.

"Do we have emissaries about who have not been heard from as of late?"

Her ambassador and right hand, Henri, stated that there were emissaries as well as familiars escorting them that had traveled to Florence to meet with likewise members of the Black and Blue Clans. They were last reported to be on their return trip. Vampires can travel extremely fast, but if they have familiars traveling with them, they only move as fast as the familiars can travel.

"I sense something wrong, something disastrous about to happen if they are not warned in time. I can send messages to them, but I cannot tell if I am already too late."

"Your Highness, I sense it too," replied Henri, "for I sense the Inquisition may be involved in this." Others who felt the same sensation, agreed by nodding their heads. They murmured amongst themselves that something was wrong or about to be wrong.

Queen Tayla felt that if anything happened to those of her clan of vampires, she would be personally responsible for it was her actions of disregard that would have brought this down upon them. But now was not the time for guilt. It was the time of intervention and how to intervene was the question unanswered.

396

Henri suggested they send a vampire patrol to check out the return path, to find out the status of the vampires. Tayla agreed and wished them good fortune. She wanted to go herself, but Henri objected stating they could not afford to lose the Queen. They all knew that their existence depended on hers. If she died, they would do likewise. Such was the price to pay for the rejection of the Order and the Dragon's power. Tayla felt she was a much better alternative to being slaves of the Order and the Dragon. She had made sure of it with the elimination of the Order's hierarchy.

Tayla felt that much of her reign would be centered around the elimination of her enemies or efforts to keep them at bay. She was to be proven correct over this time and time again. Now, she was sending a group out to assess the threat against her and her kind and then decide what to do about it.

A group of ten left the castle just after the decision was made. Her vampires could cover over two hundred miles in a night. By telepathic messaging, Tayla was able to contact her brother Rascha in Italy. She notified him of her plans and that he should do as well.

He confided in her that he and Othar had felt the same feeling of doom and that they also were busy conferring what to do about it. They confirmed that a party of familiars and vampires had left a few days ago and would be somewhere in northern Italy about this time. That would be the best place to zero in on to locate and determine the disposition of the group. They sent out a patrol as well.

Now, the vampires had two patrols heading towards northern Italy, one from the north, and the other from the south. Within two days, the parties met each other on a dark and lonely road just a few miles outside Bergamo. Because vampires have heightened sensibilities, they can track each other. Their efforts led them to a tavern-inn just outside Bergamo.

*   *   *

It was two days later. A winter's evening came upon the place with the wind howling through barren forests, piling up snow drifts against the tavern inn. The granary was a known location of sanctuary amongst the vampires as it secretly had an underground room. A *Red Velvet* vampire named Saumbier headed the patrol that arrived first. They had set up surveillance of the farmhouse and tavern. They had familiars who were miles down the road to the north prepared to give shelter. When the *Black and Purple Velvet* vampires arrived, they did so in force such that if this were a trap, they would have enough force to do a lot of damage.

Saumbier had already sent for familiars to enter the farmhouse. They were still nearly an hour away. Observation revealed no one going inside or ever coming out the entire evening. When the familiars arrived, they were given a cover story and told to go inside. The vampires would be able to see through their eyes the interior of the tavern.

The familiars, three men, entered the tavern with the story they were merchants on their way to Bergamo but were traveling long and required shelter for the evening. The proprietor, also a familiar, had been replaced by a priest disguising himself as the owner. The familiars who lived a few miles down the road, knew the owner and immediately knew it was a trap. They kept to their story and paid for rooms in gold. They went to their rooms, immediately giving signals from a lamp that this was indeed a trap. Saumbier zeroed in on their thoughts and determined that the vampires and familiars here were either dead or were being held somewhere else. He alerted everyone else.

He telepathed to the familiars to go downstairs and order food, to start a conversation with the pretending owner and ask why the place seemed deserted on such a dreary night. They did this but found the place empty. No guests, no proprietors, no one could be found. The familiars asked if they should go to the granary. Saumbier said for only one to go there. Other vampires took positions close by to aid the familiar should he be attacked. The other two familiars would stay behind.

The granary on the outside appeared empty, but when the trap door was pulled back, it seemed all hell broke loose. Below, a contingent of soldiers and priests were exposed. The owner and his wife were also there, tied up and gagged. Saumbier saw the same image through the familiar's eyes and quickly moved in. The vampires moved like lightning to intercept the inquisition persons. The priest who pretended to be the owner, produced a crucifix, which he knew would have held the vampires at bay. Then, he produced a vial of blessed water, "Holy Water" which he prepared to sprinkle over any vampire who might enter the underground room. The crucifix did hold the vampires. The familiar ran back to the tavern. As he entered the tavern, he told the others, saying, "There are people inside the granary, priests and soldiers. I think I saw the owner and his wife being held in there."

The other one responded by pulling his sword and the other one produced a crossbow. He cracked the window that faced towards the granary. He was prepared to kill any one of the soldiers or priests that would emerge from the building.

Saumbier ordered a full assault upon the building. They did not have time to waste until sunrise. What needed to be done needed to be done now. They had no idea of how many were in the granary cellar. At least two of them were familiars. If there were any vampires, he surmised they were probably destroyed.

Yelling and threatening, the priest with the crucifix came out of the cellar. He was accompanied with soldiers and they held the owner and his wife at sword point. They threatened to kill them if anyone made a move against them. Saumbier readied his vampires for a quick and massive strike. All would die at the same time. The familiar who held the crossbow waited for the signal to fire.

The first one to emerge from the granary was a soldier. The priest was hiding behind him. The soldier held a sword and a shield. The priest held a torch, and the vial of Holy Water. He had more of such vials in a bag slung over his shoulder. Inside that bag was also a half dozen sharpened stakes of wood. The priest had come prepared. He was a Dominican priest who had been schooled by Father Karl and thus, had come prepared to do battle with a vampire. He did not realize he would have to face nearly forty of them. The priest was obviously full of fear and his senses were tingling with adrenalin. He was not alone as were all the others as well.

Their fear did not go unnoticed. Saumbier could smell their fear from the wood line. He smiled. "A feast awaits us if we are careful. Their blood reeks with fear. They have no idea of who they face," he telepathed to all the other vampires. The cold wind continued to blow, but it was blowing in the direction of the vampires, such that the smell of fear running through their veins was unmistakable.

They had set a trap for the vampires and familiars but now it would seem they were the ones who were trapped.

The priest yelled out, as if he knew there were more than just a familiar who had discovered them in the cellar, "I have more on the way. More soldiers, and more priests! We have come to destroy you and your minions." The proprietor and his wife were pushed out to the front, as if they would be the first to be executed. The soldier in front of the priest prepared to thrust his sword.

Saumbier gave the order to the familiar in the window. A simple pull of the trigger on the crude crossbow energized a bolt with an armor piercing tip. The bolt flew to its intended target, striking the soldier in the chest. The bolt pierced the thin armor causing the soldier to drop his sword on his way to the snow-covered ground.

The priest looked on in horror. He was not invincible, not against his mortal enemies. A simple yet crude weapon as a crossbow, (actually, advanced for that period) took down the soldier who the priest had placed faith for his protection upon. The other soldiers drew their swords as well as their shields which were painted with the sign of the cross. The soldiers formed a circle around the priests and in the core of that circle were the proprietor and his wife, still bound and gagged. The crucifix image painted upon the shield held the vampires off. The soldiers and the priests tried to move as a formation.

The proprietor, a large overweight man, struggled with his bonds. He finally managed to run towards the soldiers, hitting them in their backs and knocking a few down. He got up and ran towards the tavern. Some soldiers chased after him, breaking up the formation. The circle was broken. Saumbier gave the order to move in and take them down.

It was over within a few minutes. The sounds of dying men, struggling against fangs and claws ripping at their armor and woolen robes was terrible. Blood was spilled all over the barnyard, of soldiers and priests alike. It stained the snow with a crimson blot. When the snow would melt, no one would know what had happened here. The proprietor and his wife were released from their bonds. They were told they could not stay here but would need to return to the Castle DeVacquerie. The other familiars would need to return to their homes farther away. They did not need to be reminded of their oath of silence regarding the subject of vampires. All traces of the priests' and soldiers' presence were scrubbed clean. The tavern, and all its buildings surrounding it and the farmhouse, were set ablaze along with the bodies of the dead. The livestock were let loose to wander about. By morning, only ashes and smoke were left of the tavern.

Within two days, the vampires were back at the Castle DeVacquerie, standing before the Queen. They had managed to carry the tavern owner and his wife with them. The two looked very poorly for traveling so far in such a small amount of time.

"I am ready to hear your report, Saumbier. State your account."

"Your majesty, I have determined the fate of our vampires who were in the vicinity of Bergamo. They were ambushed by priests of the Dominican Order as well as their armed escort of soldiers. As you had surmised, they were killed with a stake through their hearts. The tavern owner and his wife were witness to this event and saw it all through their own eyes. They gave us a detailed account. They were taken hostage and were told they were to be bait for the next vampires who would seek refuge there. The other member of the inquisition team from the Dominicans left to seek other targets in the area. When we got to the tavern, it was deserted and indeed they had laid a trap for us. If it were not for our trusted familiars, they might have been successful. But, fortunately, they were not. They were killed, and our familiars were rescued, as we have brought them here. We laid waste to the soldiers, the priests, and to the location itself. Then, we made haste to come here to report to you, my Queen."

"Is it known how they knew we might frequent this establishment. I am asking the familiar this question."

The proprietor of the tavern, his voice trembling with nervous anxiety, said, "They came in as though they had been watching my place for quite some time. They asked a lot of questions but kept their eyes out the windows, as if to scout out my property. Two *Red Clan* vampires came to us that evening. All customary procedures were followed. The signals were given. The customary rules were followed. Somehow, they knew my place was a stopover for those of the undead. All was fine until morning. Then, they went to the cellar and killed the vampires. I could not stop them. When I went to check on them, they took me and my wife hostage. They questioned us all day. We told them nothing."

Henri interjected, "They waited for more to show up, is that correct? How did they know more of us would show up?"

"Master, I can only guess that they had seen a pattern of people coming and going and this was the only thing different about it. They did mention something about, 'not fitting the pattern'. I do not know what they were referring to."

Somberly, Henri looked at the Queen, saying, "Your majesty, this was not an isolated incident. No one gets that fortunate. This was a hunt. We are being hunted by none other than the Inquisition. The war you never wanted…is upon us."

CHAPTER FORTY-ONE

A KINDNESS GIVEN

"Dearest Malcolm, my actions had brought about the second death of two of my creations. I was very distraught over such a loss. I know it may be hard for you to understand how I could be so emotional over losing two vampires, as you may think I could go and bring to the crossing over any two or four or eight at a whim, to replace my losses. I do not see it as that simple. I choose very carefully those who I would include in my brood. I see them as my children, my own blood. After all, they have literally partaken of my blood and therefore, they have allegiance to me and me only. It would be the same for my brothers and sister.

Now, the Holy Church had declared war upon my race. I tried to avoid this at all costs, but my loss of control brought about expected consequences. The account of what you read in the last chapter was a typical one. But the outcomes were not always the same. For the next hundred years, my clan, along with those of my siblings, fought with the Holy Church and its Inquisition for the purpose of survival. The church wanted to see our extinction. My first impulse was to go so far underground that the church would believe that we no longer existed. Our very existence challenged their authority to control the peasantry, the monarchies of the continent, and the ability to continue their stance as the sole authority of all things spiritual. We did not care to challenge any of what they stood for or their power over the people. I only wanted to be left to do what we were forced to do, while coexisting with them. But they would not allow us to do that. So...we fought against the Inquisition. Sometimes we won, sometimes we lost. It seemed to be a stalemate for a while. Then, I decided to try something different…"

*   *   *

The *Clan of the Order of the Red Velvet* had fought for nearly a century against the Inquisition. The other clans, black, purple, and blue, also had fought a good fight against the Holy Church's Inquisition. The Dominican Order had suffered losses, as well as other Orders of Clergy who had been enlisted to aid the cause. Priests, nuns, soldiers, and constables had been slaughtered to an extent that no one would talk about it. Records of the deaths if any were kept at all, were attributed to other reasons such as wars, plagues, and such.

It was not just the Church that suffered losses, but the clans of vampires also racked up its own casualty lists. The Church thought it was doing well against such super predators. Both sides considered how long this would go on. The Church was pledged to nothing less than the complete eradication of the vampire race. The war went on for several generations. For the vampires, they were the same ones that the generations before had made war upon.

In 1550, Father Karl had taken ill while on his campaign against her in Germany. Now, he was being cared for at a farm by peasant farmers and members of his entourage. He was not fit to travel to his Dominican abbey in Cologne. The couple gave up their bed for the ailing priest to receive his last rites. In the dark room, only a single candle gave off light. It was enough for one to find their way inside the room. It smelled of old and unclean linen, stretched over a mattress of hay and sheared wool left over from the shearing of the flock. It was soft enough, if you could get past the smell but it was the best the farmer and his family could offer. It had rained a lot in the past few weeks and the leaky roof had created a smell of mildew. The sound of leaking water falling into pots below on the floor broke the silence of the night. To say the least, the room was not conducive for the health of a sickly man. Even now, a soft rain was coming down outside.

It was well into the middle of the night. It was likely he would die that night and his fellow priests were already sure of it. They had no physician to attend him and their knowledge of medical science, like everyone else's, was minimal. He was sickly, running intermittent fevers, causing him to shiver, drifting in and out of delirium.

Queen Tayla did a most unusual thing. She visited him on his deathbed. Regally dressed, she appeared in the room of the house where he was being sheltered. If it were a monastery or abbey, she would not have been able to get this close to him. His attendants had fallen fast asleep, due to the much wine they had drank which Tayla had laced discreetly with a sedative. They would not wake until the sun had risen to the highest point in the sky. Tayla, with the powers to control the elements of weather, made the rain stop.

The Queen had many powers by this time. She could inflict pain, and she could instill comfort. She took pity upon her long-time enemy. His helplessness caused her sadness. The war with him would soon be over, but she knew the war with the church would go on and on. She whispered his name aloud, barely audible, drawing him into consciousness.

The Queen's keen sense of smell detected the oppressive odor when she slipped into his room. The vampiress quickly projected her own scent into the room, such that the terrible smell of uncleanliness was taken away from the priest's nostrils and replace with the scent of a seductive and attractive Queen. She watched him, listened to him breathe while hearing his blood coursing through his veins. Strangely, she was not tempted in the slightest to feed upon him. It was not the reason for her coming. Her whispers continued.

"Karl, wake up. See me, your enemy! I am Queen Tayla, Queen of the *Order of the Clan of the Red Velvet*, your immortal enemy who you have sought to vanquish. I am the one who has eluded you for all these years." She placed another blanket over him to keep him warm. She gave him some water, and touched him, taking some of his pain away, placing it upon herself. Aware of the amount of pain and discomfort he felt, she realized his time was growing short.

405

Her presence and touch appeared to give him clarity of mind and the energy to sit up and look upon her face. His expression was one of surprise and fascination. She could read his mind and knew the answers he sought.

"I have sought you out for decades," his old and feeble voice said. "Why do you come now to torment me?"

"I have not come to do you harm. I have come to converse with you before you die. I thought it a kindness and courtesy if we were to meet before you pass on. I know you are dying so I am here to answer all your questions you never received answers to."

He replied, "I often wondered what a monster would look like. I am surprised that one would look as you do, so evil, yet so beautiful and I must say, compassionate. And then, you have been kind enough to visit me in my hour of agony and soon to be of glory."

"Your description of me is accurate. I am capable of compassion. I exercise that trait every chance I am offered. I once saved a family in France from extinction by murdering those who would have killed innocent women and children. It is men who are evil in this world, Karl. People, sinful and willful people. They choose to do the evil they do. I on the other hand, have no choice. I want you to know that I could have killed you at any time. I could either have commanded it or done it myself. I chose not for I knew we would have an opportunity one night to talk. That time is now. Karl, I cannot die, unless done so by your prescribed methods. My desire for self-preservation is extraordinarily strong. It is why I fought you so hard. You were a very worthy adversary."

She could see his eyes watering from sadness.

"I failed to rid the world of your kind. I shall pay for my failures."

"Oh, no!" she assured him. "On the contrary, you fought well. But you fight against the devil, and his minions. As do I. They are far more powerful than you would think. I did not ask for this existence. I hate what I am. If I could, I would allow you that victory that has eluded you. But my nature will not allow it. No vampire will willingly allow itself to be taken by the forces of light. That is what you have been. A force of light. A light I cannot dwell in, that I cannot partake of. I miss seeing the sunlight. I have been alive for over three hundred years. The blessings of mortality are denied to me. I go on night after night, doomed to the same existence. At least you can pass on to another world."

"Is this your confession? Someday you will face my Lord. You will see him standing at the right hand of the Father. You will suffer the judgement for your sins here upon this earth."

"Yes, Karl. I know I will someday. I have no idea of when that day will be. I struggle against myself nightly. I do not want to do what I must do, but the urge is the same as the urge to draw your next breath. Can you resist that kind of urge?"

"Killing is not the same as breathing," he replied.

"Not to you but to someone like me, it is the same. I cannot stop myself. I cannot stop being what I am. Therefore, I am at war with myself. I wanted no war with you. Or the Church."

"War is what you got for your trouble. I hated you. Hated you and your kind for what you do. My people were like sheep in the fields while you and yours were like wolves. And you came at us like wolves. We had no defense." he whispered, falling back upon his pillow. He seemed to be fading.

"Karl, you have hated me, and I do not blame you. I want you to know that I never hated you. I barely knew you. You also barely knew me. Perhaps not at all. You did not understand me or my kind. I suppose that will never happen."

His breathing was labored, and his voice struggled to be heard. "I am dying. I fear I will not last the night. I have received the sacrament and given my confession to one of my priests. The angels are coming for me, even now. This is the end of my war and my life. But you know it will go on. I am thankful that before I die, I could at least meet you, face to face. Are you going to kill me, or let God have His way with me?"

She smiled, and answered, "Karl, who am I to deny you the peace of death that God is prepared to give you?"

"May God have mercy upon you, Queen Tayla." He closed his eyes and she heard his last breath escape his lungs. Father Karl had died in her presence of natural causes while doing what he felt was his life's calling, persecuting that which he could not understand. He did not die alone, but in the presence of his enemy who did not rejoice at his passing.

"Yes, I hope He will have mercy upon me." She felt a sadness and relief at the same time. Perhaps now she could feel some respite from the persecution of the Inquisition.

*   *   *

It was now1620, years after Father Karl had died. The *Clan of the Order of the Red Velvet* had already left the Castle DeVacquerie for reasons of protecting the family of DeVacquerie from the liability of supporting the vampires. Their best option was trying to burrow deeper underground to get away from the Inquisition. It was with great reluctance that she departed ways with the DeVacquerie family. They had enjoyed a fruitful relationship. For now, the estate of the DeVacquerie family prospered well but to stay there would eventually place the family in great peril. Her gift of sight was not such that she could see disaster later in their future. She would not be able to protect them from the reign of terror brought on by the French Revolution of 1789 that would take place more than a century and a half later.

In Germany, familiars operating safe houses had found the ideal hiding place for a large gathering of *Red Clansmen.* Children had found a cave complex that turned out to be extensively large. Several of the locals had gone exploring and were unable to explore it to its entirety, because of the many small and impassable passages. This was no problem for a creature who could turn itself into a mist and blow right through the small openings. The rooms went back for miles but were inaccessible to mortals. It contained many ideal chambers to give the vampires sanctuary yet still enabled them to strike out specifically against those of the Inquisition.

The Pope who had initiated the war against the heresy of vampirism had long since died. Many other Popes had come and gone since then. Some had long reigns while others had but a month in office. The current Pope, Paul V, was reputed to be a stern and strict leader of the Church. He was unyielding in his beliefs as well as his opinions. Queen Tayla actively sought an end to the conflict but was as unyielding as was the Pope. To do this, she knew she must speak with the head of the Inquisition, or in other words, the Pope. She had done this before, as she remembered Pope Alexander VI.

The Queen began to study him, to find out if he could be reasoned with. She decided he could not. Therefore, she would have to make sure he would be replaced soon for a more cooperative subject. There was but one way for that to happen. The Pope would have to die. The planning of his death commenced.

Familiars were sent to Rome to contact Pope Paul V. He refused to see any of them, sending spies to watch them, to determine their affiliation and who had sent them. The familiars knew they were being watched and therefore left the city of Rome. Before leaving, they managed to pass their mission and resources on to others, ensuring that the spies would report that the strangers no longer posed a threat.

The spies could not have been more wrong.

A familiar managed to get inside the Holy See's private apartments. Posing as a steward, he pretended to re-stock some of the wine in the personal kitchen of the Pope. It was there the blow was struck. The familiar managed to get out before being discovered.

In the month of October 1620, the entire city had heard that he had taken ill. His symptoms were indicative of what today is called a cerebral vascular accident, or more commonly known as a "stroke". The first ones were mild, but he continued to hold the office as they were not incapacitating. Then, in January of 1621, a massive stroke occurred, whereby killing him within hours of having the incident.

The Roman Catholic Church was plunged into mourning. Couriers were sent out all over the continent to all the dioceses that the Cardinals needed to come back to Rome for Conclave to select another Pope. When the word reached the familiars of Queen Tayla and her royal brothers and sister, they immediately informed their masters.

In a fashion, another kindness had been given by her in that a gruesome death had been spared, but still, his death was no accident. Deep inside a well-hidden chamber of the cave complex of the *Red Velvet* Clan, Queen Tayla's court was in session. The subject of conversation was the death of the Pope, Paul V.

"Yes, Henri, your advice went well. I would have personally administered the potion myself if I could have. Reward the familiar who carried out his mission with such courage and nerve. Thank your physician friend for his recipe. I am happy I did not have to demonstrate to the entire Vatican my message of will and resolve to do what needed to be done."

"Your Majesty, my physician friend has been long dead. He is not amongst the living dead either, but he did write down much of his knowledge of medicine and chemistry. I found it useful when you want someone to die but it looks as if it were of natural causes. I am glad you found it satisfactory."

"I found Father Karl a worthy enemy. He was at least honest in his method of warfare. He did his own fighting, commanding his troops in battle. Popes sit on a throne, writing out laws and edicts for others to carry out. They never see the consequences of their actions. They fight wars from afar, never seeing the battlefield, or the enemy. Nonetheless, we have eliminated an enemy. Now, a new Pope will be selected. Let us hope he is of a good nature, perhaps pragmatic enough to realize that we can live in peace if he desires it as well. We can be reasonable if they are."

Henri asked, "Your Majesty, who do we think will be the one to take his place upon the Papal throne? What does your gift of sight reveal unto you?"

"Henri, my gift of sight reveals that the one who will take his place shall be one who will prove to be ever more formidable than his predecessor. We shall have to fight even harder, endure a more severe persecution than ever before. And, of course, we may have to resort to what we have done before."

It turned out to be true, for Pope Gregory XV issued a "Declaration against Magicians and Witchcraft" which reformed the way the Church viewed the subject. Some punishments were lessened but the death penalty was held in place, especially where homicide occurred because of making a pact with the devil. That charge sounded uncannily familiar to the Queen, describing what vampires usually do. As she predicted, the war went on, the persecution remained in place.

Then, disaster struck. News of the vast cavern complex drew the attention of the forces of the Inquisition. They found the cave complex to be the probable place of sanctuary for the vampires. They knew they could not enter, so they resorted to fire. Incendiary devices were made and prepared to be inserted into the small apertures of the caverns. Once lit, they destroyed multitudes of the undead. Many barrels of Greek fire were poured into the multiple openings at the same time the undead began to make their way from the caverns.

Screams of pain from the undead, lit ablaze by the flames echoed through the caverns. Only one thing saved the clan. Before they would all be set on fire, Queen Tayla managed to get around them through an unknown passage they had not considered to block with fire. Tayla had taken a dozen of her best and managed to get behind them, setting the barrels of liquid flame upon those who were busy pouring the liquid into the small openings. Before they realized their predicament, they too were roasting in their own entrapment of flame. The remaining vampires were directed to take the route that Tayla had taken. They immediately sought out safe houses for refuge.

Most of the remaining Inquisition members thought the vampires must have perished in the flames, unfortunately along with their many gallant priests and soldiers who had tracked them down, trapping them in a living, hellish fire. The Vatican declared them destroyed and the war won. Tayla was fine with the verdict, for it afforded them to be thought of as destroyed, even though they were not. For her and her clan, it was a kindness given to her.

*   *   *

Queen Tayla began to hear more about the New World. She remembered the news of when Christopher Columbus had

411

returned from a voyage to the west. His report of a strange and beautiful new world of unimaginable things piqued her interest. She remembered her promise to herself that one day she would go there. Perhaps now was the time to pull up stakes and move to the west. Getting there would require some doing for it was not just herself that would have to travel. The journey would be long and logistically, it would be a nightmare. How would they survive the trip? How would they feed? The crew would be needed to sail the ship. Many questions to answer, and none to give. It would be much later that a way would be determined, but that is not to tell just yet. There were many events that would see Tayla's hand before they would come to pass.

The many wars of the Colonial Age were only matched by those of the Medieval Ages. However, those wars made it possible for all the clans to survive without the constant discovery of murdered civilians drained of their precious blood. The Dutch, the French, the Italian states, not to mention the British, Scots and the Irish all competed against each other for power, wealth, land and resources. In the east, small conflicts most people had never heard of erupted in Prussia, Poland, Russia and even back to the childhood lands of the Queen. Eastern Europe had many small conflicts that eluded many historians. Much fighting, much bloodshed, much death...it served a purpose. It lowered the awareness of the vampire's presence as there were far more important things to deal with, than chase after beings many were not sure even existed. War has always been a good friend to the vampire.

CHAPTER FORTY-TWO

BLOOD AND STEEL

"Dearest Malcolm, it is true. I was sad when Karl died. His goal in life was to end mine. He failed and he felt immense guilt for it. He knew many would die because I had not. I do not think he ever thought about the impact of the other vampires on humanity. He compared us to wolves and the people as sheep. The two together produce expected results.

Currently, a new church was coming up in Europe. By the early 1600's, the Protestant movement was growing and the conflict with the established Catholic church began to grow like a weed. It led to a series of small wars that became known as the Thirty Years War. Most of it took place in Germany, where my cave complex was located. But in truth, war was everywhere. Small scale though, but the casualties were horrible, even on my scale. As I said, war has been a good friend to vampires. When war, politics and religion meet at the crossroads of history, disaster is there directing the traffic. It does a poor job of it. When people are passionate about what they believe, such that they are willing to murder over it, it gets very ugly. Even for me. I often wondered how two factions who worshipped the same God, could hate each other so badly. Even today, people ask that same question, pertaining to Jews, Christians, and Muslims. They all make the claim they believe in the same God, but their ways are at odds with each other. Such is the phenomenon of hate. Sometimes they hated each other more, perhaps because each side knew the other and each believed they were right.

Rarely is there love amongst the faithful. All of them hated us, that is for sure."

*   *   *

In 1620, while Queen Tayla was manipulating the Papacy for a better deal regarding the Inquisition against the vampire kingdom, her sister, Princess Prieta was involved in a bloodletting of immense proportions in a location just outside Prague. Prague was the home of the *Order of the Blue Velvet Clan.* They had fared far better than most of the clans regarding the Inquisition's second attempt under Father Karl. Her familiars were disciplined, unbending and loyal as iron.

She had her own diplomatic corps of vampires represented by familiars for legitimacy. All was done in a most clandestine way. Many officials were bribed, blackmailed, and extorted to get what the Princess wanted.

At the time, Prague was in a kingdom known as Bohemia. Later it would become known as the Czech lands and eventually the Czech Republic of modern times. In 1620, the Bohemians were Protestant and an army of Bohemians along with units of mercenaries were arrayed against the forces of the Holy Roman Emperor, Ferdinand II. They were outnumbered, outflanked, and beaten badly.

Night fell on the battlefield. The sounds of the wind sweeping across the ground sounded like the Norse angels of death, known as the Valkyries coming for the heroes fallen in battle. It must have seemed like that but the sounds that were heard were the moans and cries of pain and anguish from mortally wounded men. Members of the *Blue Velvet Clan* feasted in the darkness on those who were left dying on the battlefield.

In the camps of the men who had survived, their fires gave off light only to those gathered around them, but they could hear the cries of the wounded. The wounded and dead lie upon the wet, bloody ground in the dark. There were no medical personnel of any skills capable of helping these poor and unfortunate souls. Soon, the sounds of the wounded began to subside. In the morning, scavenger parties would come out to search for those still alive, and for anything of value that could be used for future combat.

The next morning when the usual cleaning up of the battlefield took place to remove the dead and surviving wounded along with equipment, the victors were surprised. So many casualties were taken away already. What had happened? For Prieta, it was a recruitment day. She wanted her own army and what better way to recruit them, but on the battlefield, where the only choice was between eternal life, and certain death. What she found was that for many, she could not convert them for these were Christian soldiers. The mercenaries were fighting for money. They did not mind selling their soul for eternal life. But the true believers, chose death over a cursed existence.

Later, Prieta would relay this information to Tayla. At the gathering of that year, the four siblings met in a tent in the ancient forest in the far eastern border of Europe. They were miles away from any settlements or roads. They had complete privacy.

In the tent where they held court, Tayla sat on a makeshift throne. It was at the head of a long, rough-hewn table which had been hastily built for the occasion of the gathering. Familiar ambassadors along with vampire ambassadors sat alongside each other while the royals sat at four corners of the table.

As they gathered, conferred, fellowshipped with each other, Prieta made an announcement to the other siblings. "At the Battle of White Mountain, the Bohemians lost to the Holy Roman Emperor. It was a blood bath as they lost many fine soldiers. We feasted and I took many to the crossing over and now my ranks are swollen such that I have my own army to defend my clan against the Inquisition. As I went from each wounded soldier, I found that those who are true believers are not susceptible for bringing to the crossing over. Their soul is not theirs to give, as it belongs to God, the one they believe in. Their faith is so strong that they cannot succumb to our seduction. So, my brothers and sister, in the future, be wary of those who cannot be seduced. They are immune to our powers of stealing their souls."

Rascha spoke aloud, "You gave them a choice? Yet they refused? And then you took their blood? We still win."

"Yes," Prieta replied. "I took their blood or left them to be taken by my clansmen. I wondered about that the whole night. It happened many times, almost as many times as those I brought to the crossing over. There was one soldier, I remember he was a true believer for I specifically asked him why he would not choose to be immortal. He said his eternal life waited for him in Heaven. For some reason, I flew into a murderous rage and I killed him and that was that. It was a glorious night of feasting on those who refused me and a rebirth into our world for those who accepted me."

Queen Tayla sat quietly, listening to her brother's and sister's relishing. Finally, she spoke. "The ground…it was wet, no? With rain or blood? The sounds were the same, the crying of pain, of torment, of hopelessness?"

"Oh, yes, very wet. Wet with the blood of soldiers. Alas, it had rained that day. The ground was soft with mud, mixed with the blood of the dead and dying. The armor, weapons were of such you could have walked across the entire battlefield on steel left by the fallen. Everywhere it was blood and steel." Prieta answered.

Tayla continued, "I am always amazed by this thing called war. We do not make war upon each other. Yet man has always sought to settle disagreements and challenges by this thing called war. I lost my Renard to it. Women, whether wives, mothers, daughters or, sisters are left to clean up the mess left behind. To mourn, to bury, to carry on, to start over. To find some meaning to all of it. Yet, I cannot."

Rascha chimed in, "As I told you when Renard was killed, you still believe in the emotional aspects of relationships. You hang on to this silly thing about pairing up, sharing times with the one who you are attached to. This only sets you up for sadness. I know you are different. You have always been different from the three of us, but you will feel pain all the time if you do not let your emotions fall away from you. Shed it like a snake sheds its skin. The snake does not lament over it. It grows another skin and continues to do what it does. It is the same with us. The biggest difference between them and us, other than the obvious, is that they shed blood. We take it."

416

His cup was filled with blood as was all of those which belonged to vampires. He stood up, made ready to toast to the success of the gathering. Queen Tayla was the only one who kept her seat. Still, she pondered about why she could not be so cold and unfeeling as her brothers and sister. They were so unfeeling about the taking of lives.

The gathering broke up and each went back to their strongholds. Prieta was the only one who did not occupy the cave complex in Germany. Her fortress of sanctuary was below the city of Prague. Prague had been built, destroyed, and rebuilt many times. Some of the city's structures were built upon remnants of structures still in existence. This allowed for many underground spaces not known to exist. This was where Prieta lived for many centuries.

*   *   *

Not much mention has been made regarding the Dragon of late. Truth is, Queen Tayla established a group of vampires and their familiars to keep watch on the whereabouts and the activities of the one whose evil far surpassed the combined evil of all the vampire clans. After all, he was the source of it. The Dragon and his ancestors, all being the embodiment of the devil of Biblical scriptures, had been behind the scenes regarding most wars, particularly those of religious causes. The Thirty Years War proved to be no different.

The Dragon had had some success in trying to restore the *Order of the Dragons of Set* but now it had a different name. He had created the *Order of the Jackal*. Set was not mentioned in the name. The Dragon was the supreme leader of the Order. Only the Dragon took his direction from Set. There was no High Council.

This group of observers became the eyes and ears of the Queen. Together with specific familiars, they made up the foundation of her intelligence network. The Queen had no mental link with the Dragon. It was good they did not for the Dragon would have known every move she made, as well as her siblings clans. He could have notified the Inquisition and had

417

them wiped from the earth like a bad stain. The Queen foresaw this and for this reason alone, she had broken all ties with the Dragon and the Order. It was the primary reason she had them eliminated. They were the bigger threat to her and the vampire kingdom other than the Holy Church. They understood the true power of vampires and considered them not only a threat but a challenge to their plans.

Queen Tayla hated the Dragon for several reasons. Those have been covered previously, but her conscience bade her to block and thwart him at every move for she cared for the innocents that would fall prey to his evil plans. She could not do much regarding her nature and her need to feed upon them. However, she foresaw a much greater calamity to befall the continent if she did not intervene wherever she could.

She knew there was a message she could not hear, for it was forbidden for her ears to hear it. It was a message she felt compelled to listen to, but her nature violently blocked any attempt for it to be revealed to her. This carried on for centuries. A thirst for blood, for knowledge, for truth. These were the things she sought after. Blood was easy to find, knowledge a bit more difficult, but truth always eluded her. She felt this was a curse put upon all vampires.

The continent of Europe was in turmoil, covered in blood and steel. The war took place upon battlegrounds and in places one would not think of as a place to settle a difference of belief. On battlefields, Queen Tayla walked with her royal entourage of vampires amongst the dead and dying. She earnestly sought for one who was not dead yet but perhaps could tell her why he was willing to die for his belief. Each time, the results were the same, for their words caused such a violent and rage-filled reaction from her. Her vampire attendants saw this side of her and thus were filled with fear, seeing her in such a fierce way. Queen Tayla was angry, yet sad that she was denied access to answers to her questions. She blamed it all on the Dragon.

She was to find out that these battlefields were the direct result of the Dragon's meddling, pitting two factions of Christianity against each other.

The Holy Roman Emperor, Ferdinand II, descended from a long line of ancestors of the House of Hapsburg. Being so, he was designated a king of many states which comprised the Holy Roman Empire. This empire would last nearly a thousand years. She had taken the time to study her enemies, such as the popes who had instituted and supported the inquisitions against her. Now, she wanted to know why and how this war had come to pass. A feeling of destiny came upon her to seek out the truth of why this war continued.

She found many interesting details of Ferdinand's past, his education, his parents, and their familial history. When she investigated his education, it was then she found the clue as to why he made war upon his own people of which he ruled. He had studied at the Jesuit's college in Ingolstadt. His parents had sent him there, to keep him away from the Lutheran influences emanating from the nobles of smaller provinces. As a zealous Catholic, Ferdinand wanted to restore the Catholic Church as the only religion in the Empire and to wipe out any form of religious dissent.

While there, he met a man who began to have a great influence upon him. A man named Jerome Kruger was also a student there. He befriended Ferdinand immediately and soon, the two were as close as two could be. Jerome was not of a noble house and therefore Ferdinand's relationship with him was kept to a minimal profile. He did not talk about his relationship with Kruger with his parents nor his attendants. He knew his parents would intervene as they only wanted him to associate with the members of noble families. The Hapsburgs motives were always about relationships that could be used later for gain.

Kruger had come from a family that had originated from Rome. His father had been the Dragon, which meant only one thing. He either was or was being groomed to be the next Dragon! The vampires reported this to Queen Tayla.

"I see now. This is a snake that never dies. He will haunt me all the rest of my life, no matter how long that may be. Perhaps, forever. So, the son of the Dragon has befriended the man who would become the Emperor of the Holy Roman Empire. And, in doing so, has been able to start a war against the Protestants, because they challenge the Holy Church of Rome. They have a message that the Church of Rome does not want the world to hear. Even I cannot hear this message for its power is such that the nature of the vampire cannot stand it. Perhaps, they have a message of truth. I know the Dragon has always supported the Catholics for they infiltrated it, perverted its message to control the masses. So, this is what the Dragon has been up to all these years. Thank you, my children. This is valuable information you have brought me. You have done well."

Henri, her advisor and ambassador, spoke up, saying, "So, we have now determined why our feeding stocks are so plentiful! Is this a bad thing, Your Majesty?"

"Henri, it depends upon how we look at it. If all I wanted was blood, I would be dancing upon their corpses. But I also seek truth and knowledge. They are sources of power and understanding. Truth and knowledge go hand in hand. One speaks of the other. Knowledge is the key to understanding. Understanding is the key to tolerance and acceptance. Acceptance, freeing one from the shackles of ignorance, is a form of freedom. It allows you to discover without fear of what you discover. Alas, it escapes me."

"And you will continue to search for it, my Queen?"

"Oh yes, I will continue. It drives me."

"As for the Dragon, what are your orders, my Queen?"

"Continue to watch him. From afar. Use your familiars as much as you can. He will detect vampires quicker than you can imagine. In this case, the familiar is the best camouflage. Do not interfere but report back to me his movements and his associations."

"You shall be obeyed, my Queen."

CHAPTER FORTY-THREE

DEVIL ON THE LOOSE

"Dearest Malcolm, it is the beginning of a bloodletting, known as the Thirty Years War. The Dragon has reared his ugly head like the snake in the grass he is, for he started the war with his lies and scheming. He has used the church, the church that you Christians have always believed in, the church that uses the scriptures to teach the message that I find I am not privy to. His Order infiltrated the early church centuries ago, subtly changing the message and teaching it as doctrine. This has led so many down a path to lose their way.

As a vampire, I continue to make my journey through time, feeding off living humans while watching my enemy prey upon the ignorance of people. I often wonder who is the bigger villain? My deeds are for personal survival, while his are done at the behest of the Dark Lord. Now, in Europe, he is on the loose. The war was fought initially over the issue of how does one worship, as Catholic or Protestant? Meanwhile, we watch and observe the human cattle upon which we feed, and the Dragon who feeds upon their souls."

*   *   *

In July of 1618, Jerome Kruger, the current Dragon, and leader of the newly founded *Order of the Jackal*, stepped outside the palace of the Emperor. It was a warm day, with a gentle breeze blowing. The smells of freshly baked bread coming from the bakers of the palace mixed with the smells of the marketplace nearby made a delicious aroma that would stimulate the appetite of anyone.

The young man, newly graduated from the Jesuit University, was confident the newly crowned Emperor of the Holy Roman Empire would appoint him to associate with a highly placed clergyman. He did not know who exactly this person was to be, but it was a sure thing as his gift of sight had all but guaranteed it. It fit in with his agenda concerning the church and the challenge of the Reformation. He was not sure what the position would be nor in what capacity he would function.

As usual, he would be working behind the shadows, involving himself in the multitude of events only when he needed to. Maintaining a small profile, was all within the framework of his agenda. By being a nobody, but being the one who would light the fuse, he would provide the very spark that would start a war.

Within a day or so, he received his orders. He was informed he would accompany a Jesuit priest, Lorenz Sonnabenter to an area where the population was predominately Lutheran. Lorenz was also a graduate of the Jesuit University. The new Emperor's uncle was instrumental in helping the Emperor in making the choice of sending Sonnabenter and Jerome together. Ferdinand had to hide his relationship with Jerome from his uncle for he knew he would never approve of his association with one whose family ties had no value to the Hapsburg's. He packed and made ready to travel to Graz.

In Graz, there was a sizable Protestant population. Lorenz was sent there to preside over the Catholic congregation in that parish. Upon arrival, Lorenz would meet opposition from the Lutherans there that would cause the beginning of the Thirty Years War. The match to light that fuse traveled with him as another Jesuit, sent by the Emperor. As Jerome rode the horse on the way to Graz, he was smiling. Lorenz noticed him smiling and asked if he was smiling with optimism.

Jerome answered him back, saying, "I am smiling as I see us doing God's work. I feel we are on the precipice of something great."

"I wished I shared your optimism, my friend. The Emperor said you were the person who could be trusted to do great things. I expect you to know the high standard you are held by."

"I was befriended by a great man. I am not from a noble family, but he trusts me to do great things for the Church. I shall not disappoint him. He is a devout believer."

Lorenz said, "Yes, the Emperor believes all the world should not be just Christian, but Catholic. He believes it is the only way to be Christian."

"Well," said Jerome, "We have our work cut out for ourselves. I expect there to be some resentment towards us. The priests in Graz have reported a lot of resentment towards the Holy Church."

"We shall have to show them whose side God is on!"

Jerome thought to himself how successful his masquerade had been so far. He knew what he was going to do. His friend Ferdinand would not tolerate for too much longer his lands where his subjects did not all have the same religious beliefs.

In 1609, the Holy Roman Emperor Rudolf II had signed a letter, commonly known as "The Letter of Majesty". The letter essentially granted religious tolerance and freedoms to both Protestant and Catholic worshippers in the state of Bohemia. The letter helped forge a peace, but it would not last long. Barely a decade into the peace, fighting would break out again. Jerome Kruger was going to make sure it would.

As soon as the two arrived in Graz, Jerome took an assessment of the parish, and their counterparts. The following week, he met with all the priests as well as some of the Lutheran clergy. None of those meetings went well. In fact, shouting matches broke out, drawing crowds from all around. If there were any Christian love to be shared, it was not to be shared at any of those meetings. Jerome was in the center of all of it, inciting anger and reciting Papal bulls, as well as opinions of the Emperor Ferdinand. Within a month, blood was spilled. Jerome did it himself but made it look as though Lutherans had killed a priest. When the Emperor was informed, his anger could only be satiated by the spilling of more blood.

One would think that Queen Tayla and her brothers and sister would have been overjoyed at the opportunity of having an abundance of victims to indulge themselves upon. They were overjoyed, excessively giddy but not Queen Tayla herself. She saw this as an ominous sign of impending doom. To her, it was as if the world was ending. Her human half agonized at the needless killing of so many people. Her vampire half eagerly followed up after most battles, eagerly playing the part of the grim reaper. Some she would take to the crossing over, for she was not without pity. Others, she attempted to discern why they were willing to pay with their lives for something they believed in, but she did not understand.

The civility between neighbors, countrymen, had disintegrated. Entire societies and cultures were being torn apart. The cruelty and barbarism seemed to have no limits.

It did not stop the vampires from doing what they do. Jerome was ecstatic for it seemed as if hell had been unleashed on earth. To be honest, the devil was on the loose, and his name was Jerome Kruger. Once the fighting began, Jerome left the scene, and headed back to Rome. When he did, many of the states of the Holy Roman Empire were in flames.

To Jerome, the Dragon, he did not care who won. He only wanted chaos to reign. He served the Dark Lord, Set, and Set wanted death and destruction to spread across Europe. A few centuries from now, most of the world would be engulfed in wars that seemed to spread as if it were a form of the plague.

Queen Tayla's detail assigned to the surveillance of the Dragon reported him having left for Italy. "Henri, my vampires report that the Dragon is on the move. He is traveling south towards Italy. I suspect he is going to meet with his new *Order of the Jackal*. No doubt, he will meet with the Pope as well. I wonder if he will also meet with the Holy Roman Emperor as well. I want him followed and I personally want to confront him when the opportunity presents itself. I want a full battalion of vampires with me when that happens."

The Queen intended to confront the Dragon once and for all. He must have known this for he avoided a direct confrontation with her. He was not at every battle, but he had the ear of the

Emperor and of the Pope. He influenced them heavily, as the Catholic forces waged war against the Protestant armies. It would take a long time for the Protestant armies to afford to undertake the Peace of Westphalia, a new political order.

Tayla considered it her duty to confront, thwart, or stymie every attempt the Dragon undertook to influence people. She always knew he was up to no good, and because he had tried to control the vampires, not to mention creating them in the first place, she hated him. He was the only real enemy she had. The church would not even know about the heresy of vampires if it had not been for him. The wars raged on. Finally, Tayla found that she could play his game as well. She influenced familiars to act independently to negotiate peace accords to end this silly but terrible war. In 1648, her familiars negotiated the Treaty of Munster and the Treaty of Osnabruck. This led to the overall Peace of Westphalia, which ended the Thirty Years War. By this time, the Dominicans had abandoned the Inquisition against the vampires.

Jerome Kruger disappeared from the scene once again only to reappear in another identity. Jerome's purpose, to start the Thirty Years War, had been fulfilled. His evil resulted in the violent deaths of approximately eight million people. It would take nearly a century to replenish the population that was extinguished. But, as vampires rarely give up on a quest they undertake, they could not pinpoint the Dragon's location or identity. He knew to stay in the shadows and would only strike when it suited him.

Tayla and her clan still inhabited the cavern complex in Germany, only much deeper with secret exits. Once the Dragon had found the hiding place in the cave complex, he came in during the daylight hours, and stole something of Tayla's that was valuable. He managed to get her father's ring off the chain which she kept hung around her neck. While she slept, there were no familiars close by for she slept where they could not follow. He did it not only to anger her, but as a final way of trying to control her. It did not work. It only infuriated her.

She noticed immediately it was gone when she rose that evening. The Dragon was not able to travel as far as he should have. When you have an infuriated vampire on your heels, you should never stop running. It was imperative that she reacquire the ring back. He had it covered such that the sunlight did not fall upon it. It was easy to track. Her familiars retrieved it when he left it upon holy ground (inside a church building) while he made his escape. Though he himself could enter upon sanctified ground, he instead chose to give it to a young boy to place for the price of a few coins. It was the last time the Dragon would be able to infiltrate the vampire's sanctuary while they slept. Familiars retrieved the ring, but forever afterward, there would be a guard assigned to protect it. Namely, it would never leave the possession of the Queen.

"For one day, the ring that symbolizes my power was out of my possession. Why were there not any consequences when the Dragon had my ring?"

Henri answered, "Perhaps it was because it never felt the sun's rays upon it. I believe he had it in a bag, inside a box, and it was in a building. Out of your possession must mean something. Perhaps it is about whoever wears the ring, not just you. I fear to think of anyone else leading our Order. There is no one capable of carrying such a responsibility."

"Henri, your loyalty is admirable. On this day, a most serious breach of security has occurred. We are vulnerable and we must take steps to shore up our weakest areas. I need a security familiar and a security vampire. The need to organize my staff is obvious. A vampire's priority is and has always been survival. This was the closest we have ever come to disaster. It seems difficult to even imagine how close we came to it today. It must never happen again."

*　　　　*　　　　*

It was 1649. The Parisian night was young, although the thick fog made it seem as though it were late. A tall, stunningly beautiful woman dressed very elegantly walked into a small shop which made and sold jewelry to some of the highest nobility of France. It was on a less traveled street. She was accompanied by a couple of gentlemen dressed equally of refinement.

426

Reflecting wealth and elegance at every turn, they were as smartly dressed as she.

The jeweler was an older, short, rotund man whose blue eyes sparkled. The artisan's hands were gnarled because of years of using tools and shaping metals. His face was covered with a white beard. His reputation for being such a skilled artisan and craftsman was renowned for he was the personal jeweler to the French crown. The jeweler knew these potential customers were prepared to spend money. A lot of it.

"Yes, madam, what can I do for you on such a night as this?"

Her commanding presence demanded his attention.

"I wish a ring to be made. I have a sketch for you to follow and the jewel I wish to have placed in the setting."

"Of course, may I see the sketch?"

Tayla gave the sketch to the accomplished craftsman of sculpting precious metals and the cutting of precious gems. He had been highly recommended by her high counselor for he had crafted pieces for the French monarchy. The Queen had no doubt that she had come to the right place.

"This is a unique design. Who may I ask drew this sketch?"

Tayla replied, "I did. Can you make the ring to match the sketch?"

"I most certainly can but it will take some time. What type of gold would you prefer? I can provide several different concentrations of gold, everything from twelve to eighteen carats. Of course, the higher the carat weight, the softer the gold."

"For a ring such as this, I prefer something in the midrange, say perhaps sixteen carats?"

"Very well, I can do that. And the setting, I can sink the stone in a closed setting, or do you wish it to be held with prongs? Prongs are much more delicate, but the stone's size will be better expressed."

"Just like the sketch shows. Prongs are fine."

"Very good, madam. This may take a week or so. Is there a specific time you would like to take possession of it?"

"Take your time. Do your best. I will know when you are finished. My companions will come to take possession of it. I will pay a high price for high quality. A down payment as a gesture of good faith, for you come highly recommended," she said, looking at one of her companions.

The man took her finger size while one of her companions gave a small bag of gold coins for a down payment. She took out a small leather pouch containing a large ruby and some diamonds to accent the setting.

"I shall get started on this immediately. A lady such as you should not be kept waiting." He smiled, taking the pouch of coins and the pouch of stones, bidding her good night and closed his shop to begin work.

Her father's ring had been recently stolen and then retrieved within a 24-hour period. She wanted to make sure it would never be stolen again. She took the jewel out of the ring to make a ring with the same ruby. It symbolized her power because it came from her father. In short, it was a ring that was inherited, much like her claim to royalty. She was a princess and now a Queen. She had the ring that authorized her reign. She did not need the Pope's approval.

Up to this point, the ring of her father had been kept on a gold chain. Now, it would be worn on her finger. She was now without the ring, but she had familiars that were within the proximity of it, waiting for its creation. When the jeweler's task was completed, she would take possession of it, placing it upon her finger. The ring would not leave her finger after that.

CHAPTER FORTY-FOUR

THE SCARLET RAIDER

"Dearest Malcolm, I managed to get through the seventeenth century without much fanfare only because I decided to create as low of a profile as possible. There were challenges to my kingdom, mostly from the church, but we went as far underground and clandestine as possible. We wanted them to think we were no longer a threat. In fact, as far as Europe was concerned, the black plague, the Thirty Years War, the invasion of the Ottoman Empire to eastern Europe were far greater threats than we were. We never wanted to be considered a threat, the greatest or the least. I struggled for a long time to find ways to coexist with mortals. It was of no use. It was like the deer coexisting with the hunter. One would always be prey and the other would always be the predator. I decided the best thing was to leave the continent. This way, the church would no longer consider us a threat for there would be no victims showing up the next morning, drained of their precious blood. I had always wanted to go to the Americas, as I had promised myself when Christopher Columbus had returned to Isabella's Spain. Now was the time to go since America had just won its independence from England. It was an exciting time. Also, the French Revolution was just around the corner. To be of nobility was a certain death sentence. Unfortunately, I could not intervene on behalf of my mortal benefactors, the House of De Vacquery. I grieved greatly when I heard they were wiped out via the guillotine in Paris. It was then I knew my decision to leave was the right one."

*   *   *

It was 1787. In a port in southern France, a familiar of the *Order of the Clan of the Red Velvet* sat in a tavern. In the cold and dampness that lurked outside, a thick fog enveloped the waterfront establishments sitting close together across from the seawall and the wharfs. If one walked along the timbers stretching to the seawall, they would see lanterns hanging from wooden posts at equal intervals to let you know where to walk so you would not inadvertently walk off into the water. The tavern was frequently visited by sailors or French Naval personnel.

The familiar, known only as Petri, was dressed in a thick, heavy, brown peacoat. His boots rose nearly to his knees, and his trousers were tucked into them. He wore a tricornered hat, plain and black. If he wore a cutlass, he could have passed as a pirate or privateer. He was not anything of the sort. His employer was far more dangerous than any pirate currently sailing the seas.

The temperature outside was cold, but not freezing. The dew from the fog made it seem as if it had just rained. Inside, the temperature was warmer, the light dim but enough to see what you might be drinking or eating, and better yet, to see who you might be sitting with. The smells were of rum, beer, and tobacco. Probably no one had had a bath of late, and those who smelled better than the sailors were the harlots who patrolled the establishment, looking for customers desiring to sample their feminine charms.

Who had Petri come to see? Petri would not know him if he saw him. He was looking for one known as the Scarlet Raider. He had no clue as to how he would recognize him, or if it would be him and not just a representative for him. Amongst those who participated in the illegal trade of smuggling and piracy, there was much talk of a mysterious captain of a ship known as "The Phantom." Most people would say the ship had changed its name, maybe several times, to keep the Royal Navy at bay. All navies were looking for the Phantom. She was rumored to be a fast ship, heavily armed, with a ruthless crew of seasoned and

430

brave men. Petri did not know much about piracy, or naval affairs of any sort for that matter. He only knew that Queen Tayla had arranged through mysterious means for him to meet with a representative or the captain himself.

He watched the barmaid serving those seated at tables. He finished his drink and ordered another mug of ale. The barmaid asked which ship he was from. She only drew a blank stare from him.

"You a sailor? You do not have the look or the manner of a sailor. Do not even drink like a sailor! What is your business here?" she asked in a heavy French accent. She spoke English only because the British navy frequented this port as well.

"I am looking for someone who comes from a ship of red sails." This was the bona fides for letting the barmaid know who he was looking for. Soon, the Scarlet Raider would make themselves known. He placed several gold coins down on the table, to signify he was willing to make a financial transaction.

"This should cover my fare for the evening," he said, hiding the coins with his hands. The barmaid could see the coins between his dirty fingers.

"Yes, it will cover tonight's fare. Help yourself to one of my girls if you like while you wait. Should I call for one to come over?"

"That will not be necessary," he said.

"We will see about that. You look like you could use some company." She walked away and raised her hand with the coins in them. It was a signal.

He sat there for a while, but no one approached him. He was beginning to think no one was going to show. Frustration was beginning to set in. He kept his eyes on the door expecting some mysterious man, perhaps a pirate captain, to walk in. He was not too sure what to expect. All he had been told was that someone representing a ship with red sails would meet with him. The familiar was there to negotiate passage for the *Red Clan* to go to the New World, most notably, the recently established United States of America.

The winning of the thirteen British colonies' independence from England had been the talk of the decade. The American

431

Revolution had inspired many to go to America to start a new life. It also had inspired many French thinkers that if the English colonists could do such a thing with their king, perhaps they could too. France was to find out the answer to that question within two years,

Soon, one of the harlots who had been turned down by one of the patrons because he had no money to spare for her company came over to Petri. Without asking, she pulled up a chair and sat down.

"Need some company, sailor?" the pretty woman asked.

"No thank you, I am here on business. I am meeting someone," after taking a drink from his mug.

"Yes, I know. You are looking for one who sails under a ship with red sails, no?"

This caught Petri's attention immediately. He noticed her accent was not French but Irish. He mentioned that her accent was strange for being in a French port.

"I am not usually in a French port though I have been in many ports, in fact, most ports."

"My, you get around some, yes?" He noticed she had deep red hair, dazzling blue eyes, and fair and flawless complexion except for one small scar on her left cheek. An ample bosom was nearly cascading over her low-cut dress. In short, her appearance was very seductive.

"State your business!"

"I am to meet someone who goes by the moniker of 'The Scarlett Raider'. Do you know where I might find him?"

"Yes," she replied. "You are staring straight into the Scarlett Raider's eyes. State your business or risk getting your throat cut before you can make it to the door!"

"You? You are the Scarlet Raider?" He was exasperated that the one he was looking for was a woman, an exceptionally beautiful woman.

"Aye, the one and only. Now, one more time, state your business!"

"I seek passage to the Americas. Most specifically, New York or Massachusetts. Either one will do."

"Why not book passage on a legitimate cargo ship that is used to taking passengers to the Americas? Why do you want a pirate ship?"

"My employer is of a special class. They cannot risk discovery by any authorities. We know that you, as a pirate, have ways of sailing without being seen, and can slip in and out of ports without detection. We pay well, in fact, better than well, and I have been sent to negotiate terms for passages. In short, a contract that will prove to be very lucrative for you and your crew."

The woman relaxed, sat back in the chair, and lit up a pipe of a very aromatic blend of tobacco. The smoke billowed from the pipe, as she puffed away on it. It was not usual for women of the day to smoke anything, but this one was not a usual woman. She sat for a few moments, enjoying her smoke, then leaned over and took a long drink from Petri's mug. She drew her arm across her mouth to wipe away the excess ale and said, "How many passengers are we talking about?"

Petri answered, "I am authorized to offer up to fifty pieces of gold per passenger."

She sat up straight. "No one has that kind of money except maybe the King or Queen!"

He smiled, saying, "That is right. Only my employer is a queen and as I said, will pay up to fifty pieces of gold per passenger."

"The Queen of France?" she asked.

"No, a different kind of Queen. More beautiful, intelligent and far more powerful than any queen you might know."

"Well, my ship is anchored off the coast at this moment, hidden in some offshore islands. I can handle about 25 people per trip. The trip will take about four to six weeks, depending on weather and wind. I would sail to the West Indies, then go north to the eastern coastline. We would arrive in New York first. I expect payment up front, and then again for the next trip. Ever travel at sea before?"

"No, but I assure you we will have no problems with the weather or the British or French navies. We do have special needs though which my employer will address in person with you. We will need to meet again, with her in attendance."

"Of course. Bring your Queen. But bring the gold as well. Talk to the barmaid for details on how to reach me." She got up and walked away.

Before, he had not really noticed her. The last thing he would have assumed was that she was a pirate captain, or that she was a pirate at all.

*   *   *

Within the month, Queen Tayla accompanied Petri to the same tavern along the waterfront. The weather was much fairer this time. The barmaid recognized Petri sitting alone at a table in the corner of the large room. He stared at the hearth while he waited to be served.

The barmaid, an older buxom lady who had seen her better days go by, walked up to him, saying, "You been here before, yes? I recognize you. What will you have?"

"Red Sails," was his quiet reply.

"I think we can find some of that," she said, turning away. The two harlots in the room were different than before. The number of patrons were far less than before as well. It was as if the Scarlett Raider knew who was coming and the less eyes and ears to see and hear the transaction made the better and safer it was for everyone.

Soon, a man came to the table, saying, "You seek the ship of the red sails?"

Petri looked at him, seeing it was not the beautiful woman as before. "Yes, I do."

"Be along shortly, so do not move from this table. If any soldiers or naval officers come in here, do not make a move to speak to them. We all have to be careful, now do we not?"

"Yes, of course. My employer is here already, so I advise you to do the same. In fact, my employer has already found your guards, even disarmed them. So, I advise you to bring me the Scarlett Raider and quit this fooling around. My employer will know if there are British or French Navy people anywhere close

434

to us. If a woman comes in here and sits with me, you had better produce the Scarlett Raider. Or, it will not be good for you or anyone else here for that matter."

The man, a salty sailor with years of experience at his trade, said, "You know this? How do you know this? Your employer speaks to you?"

"Yes, she does. She is about to walk through that door within seconds, so I advise you to give up your seat now." The ability of Tayla to speak telepathically to other vampires as well as familiars was in play. He had no longer finished speaking when Queen Tayla walked in. She was alone but there were other vampires in the area. No guards were killed or injured, merely incapacitated. Their positions were then occupied by vampires.

Queen Tayla was enveloped in a black cloak, which covered a more elegant ensemble of clothing. One look from her and the sailor across from Petri immediately stood up to give her the chair. She took the chair and sat without saying a word.

No one said any words at all for about a half a minute. Finally, the Queen said, "Bring me the Scarlett Raider. I wish to converse about a very private matter. When she arrives, no one can enter this room. I shall not repeat this again."

The sailor spoke humbly, "Yes, Mademoiselle, she shall come to you at once." He left and was not seen again that night.

Within minutes, the woman who Petri had spoken with before, came into the room. She was dressed in red breeches, black leather boots up past her knees, with a red vest, and white blouse still showing her bosom. Her cuffs were of lacy ruffles as was her collar. A black cape draped across her shoulders. Defiantly dressed as a swashbuckler, a cutlass hung on her side as did two daggers were sheathed in her baldric. A flintlock pistol was tucked into her wide black belt.

She took a mug of ale from the barmaid and a chair from another table. She then motioned for the barmaid to leave. They were officially closed for the time being.

"I am the Scarlett Raider. We are here to discuss a business deal, are we not?"

Petri spoke first, "Allow me to introduce to you, my employer, Queen Tayla, Sovereign of the *Clan of the Order of*

435

the Red Velvet. I am called Petri, and you go by the name of the Scarlett Raider. What is your real name if I may ask?"

Queen Tayla spoke before the pretty woman of the sea had a chance to speak. "She is Kerry Brown, from a small fishing village on the northern coast of Ireland. A pirate like her father before her. Your ships are anchored four miles due southeast of here. Your crew numbers one hundred fifty-six. Your ship, the Phantom, carries forty guns, and can master up to thirteen knots if the wind is right. You also have two sloops that can also master the same speed, each with ten cannons on board. Shall I go on?"

Kerry Brown was dumbfounded. How did she know all these things?

Tayla was now reading the thoughts of the Scarlett Raider. "I know about you because it is in my best interests to know such things. Especially if one is going to enter a business contract with them. You said to bring the money as well as myself. Well, I am here and here is what I offer. The door opened and two vampires came in carrying a large chest by the handles attached to its sides. They set the chest down, opened it and left.

Kerry brown stared at the contents of it. The chest was full of gold coins... French and Spanish coins. Her eyes wide as saucers, and her mouth open, she was stunned at the sight of such riches.

"So much for payment!" Queen Tayla knew how to negotiate from a position of power and strength. She knew the pirate needed the finances to make another voyage to a more secure sanctuary and this was the very thing to make that happen.

"You seek sanctuary in the West Indies. I seek sanctuary in the Americas. It is that simple. You transport me and my entourage to the New World and you get the gold. In that chest contains enough gold to transport twenty-five passengers at the rate of fifty coins per person. Do we have a deal?"

Kerry Brown could not take her eyes off the chest's contents. Tayla repeated herself, knowing that Kerry's attention was diverted. "Yes, I would say so. Shall we seal this with a signature or in blood?"

Petri said, "Oh, do not mention that word to her. You may regret that. I have a contract here. It is a mere formality. Not legal or binding but merely a reminder that here, two parties with honorable intentions do hereby enter into an agreement forthwith."

They signed, and afterwards, Tayla spoke with Brown about her special needs. "I need to acquire a slave ship. I am not talking about the kind of slaves you may think. I will fill it with people of my choosing. You only need to crew it for the voyage. Do not worry about the weather for no storm, no lack of wind shall befall us. You will make top speed to the west. I will see to that. I will only be seen at night as will all my entourage. Only my servants will be available during the day. My only condition is for your crew and you not to ask any questions and do not disturb us during the day. All my people are day sleepers. Obedience on your part will be rewarded greatly."

Kerry Brown answered, "Getting a slave ship will not be difficult. I can intercept one on their way to pick up their cargo. Have your people ready to fill it, waiting at a place we agree upon. We will have all your needs fulfilled." She said this while staring at the chest.

Queen Tayla was pleased. "Petri shall be in contact with you and all arrangements shall be made through him. I trust that you have enough people to help you get the gold to your ship." The Queen stood up and left the room.

Kerry Brown looked at Petri across the table from her. "She reads minds?"

"Yes, she does. She can do a lot of things that you may never understand. It might be better if you do not understand. Only that you keep your end of the bargain."

"I have heard of people like that. My travels have taught me a lot of things, seen a lot of things, heard about a lot of things. Like I said, I have heard about people like her. That is why I had a silver ball in my pistol."

Petri smiled. "You have done your homework. Tell me, what else do you think, what do you know?"

"Long ago, when I was in Ireland, the priest there told us about a heresy called vampirism. He described these creatures as being the most dangerous creatures on earth. I laughed when I heard this, as I did not believe anything the priest said, either

437

about the devil or even about God. I do not have a fear of the devil nor of the Christian God. For a pirate, it would be an occupational hazard. I only fear the gallows. It turned out no vampires were ever found in Ireland, but the stories and rumors abounded in mainland Europe...France, Germanic kingdoms, even in Italy. I still hear stories, but no one can say they have direct proof they even exist."

Petri replied, "I would keep what you think you know about the Queen to yourself. I suspect you and the Queen will have many private conversations before we reach the New World. If you prove to be loyal, discreet, and supportive, I have no doubt that you will benefit from a good relationship with her."

"I am always looking for allies. I can tell that she can be a great ally to me. I will start getting that slaver ship on the morrow. My ship was a slave ship at one time. We modified her to be a ship capable of good speed, good firepower, and our home on the water. I can do that again. First, I must get to that ship. I will let you know when that happens by my barmaid, and we can go from there. Agreed?"

Petri nodded as she got up from the table and headed for the door. The barmaid got her attention and received a nod of approval from Kerry. Then, the pirate stepped through the door and out into the darkness of the night.

*   *   *

The Scarlett Raider, also captain of the Phantom, a converted slaver ship, was a careful and cautious pirate. Shrewd, cunning, ruthless to her enemies, she trusted few people in the world. Her history of relationships was dismal at best. Men had abused her since she was young. Her father, also a pirate, had left her mother to go to sea. She grew up longing for a relationship with him, eventually going to sea to find him. She did. In a prison in Port Royal, Jamaica, she came to see him, and was there long enough to see him hang for the crime of piracy. It was there she had made up her mind to do something that she felt he would have wanted her to do...be like him. In fact, it was the opposite of what he wanted her to do. Her mother had told her when she came back to visit her to tell her of her father's fate that being a pirate was the last thing her father wanted of her or any of her siblings.

Being a rebellious and headstrong child, she was convinced that she could do a better job of being a pirate than he or anyone else could. She was determined to make being a woman an asset for being a pirate. In those days, as well as any other time prior to modern times, it was not advantageous to be a woman, unless the woman was clever, confident, and knew to draw her strength from those other than herself. Being meaner and tougher than most male pirates was essential for her to be accepted as a pirate but being smarter and showing leadership was what had made her a pirate captain.

PART FIVE

THE NEW WORLD

1787 AD

CHAPTER FORTY-FIVE

NEW ORLEANS

"Dearest Malcolm, to finally be in the New World was amazing. The Scarlett Raider, Kerry Brown, was true to her word. She carried every single member of my clan to the shores of America without losing one single vampire. My gifts of power brought the wind that carried my clan to the New World at a sustained speed of 18 knots. As gratitude, I gave the Scarlett Raider the power to race all her ships at a speed of 18 knots so she could catch her prey and escape from her enemies. She became a good friend, but that is another story.

We landed in New York, then moved on to Philadelphia. Once the numbers of victims began to rise, we moved on. We did this several times. While there in Philadelphia, it was a sightseeing tour to be sure, for I knew that many of the places there would eventually become national monuments or landmarks, for the history that made this nation was founded in Philadelphia. The signing of the Declaration of Independence and the meeting of the founding fathers there at that building was historic. The feeling of excitement was great in those early days. I too was an immigrant to this land. A vastly different kind of immigrant, but no less, I had come from the old country to a new one. I adopted this country as my own.

Soon, the British wanted the country back, and thus the War of 1812 came along. I went to Washington to see if I could do something to prevent the destruction of the White House for the British were closing in on the capitol. I tried awfully hard to intervene in the burning of the White House and other government buildings.

Later, I would be in New Orleans. Large cities are where I can blend in the best. My clan always went everywhere I went but we were always looking for a home, a place where we would make our final home. I was tired of moving for it felt as though I were running from something. I knew it was a big world out there, and the Pacific was all the way on the other side of the country. That was where I wanted to be."

*   *   *

The scene in Washington was chaotic. The President, James Madison along with his government and many other officials had already fled the city because the British army were coming, and they were not feeling very merciful. The British were vengeful for the American victory on Port Dover in Canada.

The British general had already laid down the orders of engagement regarding the destruction of buildings and the treatment of non-combatants. As far as buildings were concerned, they all were fair game, especially government buildings to include the White House and the Capitol building.

The Queen was near Washington on her way to the southern United States. The Battle of Bladensburg proved disastrous for the Americans and that night, any wounded or dying left on the field, British or American, were feasted upon. The Queen knew the British had left the field enroute towards the young capitol city of Washington. There were not enough American troops on hand to repel the British. The enemy army relied on their fleet in the Chesapeake Bay for support. Soon, they would attack the port of Baltimore.

When the Queen arrived in Washington, the city was already on fire. The British army, a professional and seasoned army having defeated the French emperor, Napoléon was efficient at destruction. She saw the Presidential Mansion (White House) on fire and went immediately to aid in putting the fires out. Torches were being thrown into the windows. The staff had already taken as much as they could out of the structure before the British arrived to set it afire. One British soldier could see a woman inside the house, with a torch in her hand as she tried to gather more torches. The next thing he knew, she was standing behind him, torches upon the ground, with her arms around his neck. She fed immediately upon him, and when finished, saw three more soldiers watching her feed upon him. Several of her clansmen dispatched them as fast as the Queen had taken her fill.

Soon it became evident that the burning of buildings was out of control and only the weather could put the fires out. One of the basic gifts of vampires is the ability to control the weather. The day had been long and unbearably humid. It was August and therefore it was not uncommon to be so hot. The conditions for creating rain were perfect and Queen Tayla knew this. She stood outside on the lawn of the Presidential Mansion, raised her hands, and called for the sky to open its clouds and deliver the rain needed to douse the fires. Within minutes, the rain came down in torrents. A tornado passed through the center of the capitol, when it tore down on a street. Two cannons were located there. The tornado lifted the cannons and dropped them a few yards away, killing their crews.

By morning, the rain was still falling. Her efforts to save Washington had put out the fires but the effects of the rain caused cracks on the walls of buildings that might have been salvageable. The Queen and her clan had retired for the day, but the rains had left Washington in a smoking quagmire. The British army made their way back to their fleet in the Chesapeake Bay. The Queen left Washington sad because she was not able to prevent its destruction.

Making their way southwestward, the clan eventually found itself in Atlanta. After rattling the nerves of the people of Atlanta because of murders that went unanswered, they left that town for the same reason they left all towns, to prevent discovery of themselves. They were in slave country. Slaves, though uneducated, were particularly superstitious and were terribly frightened for they were the principal targets of the vampires. Afraid of most things considered supernatural, they appealed to their masters for protection, but none could be found. The owners were first in disbelief, then the proof would be present itself in the form of corpses found drained of their blood. Everyone was subject to suspicion, but no arrests could be made based on no evidence to tie to any suspects. After a few weeks of such terror, the clan moved on.

By the time they reached New Orleans, a calamity was in progress. The Battle of New Orleans was about to begin. The Americans were outgunned, and outmatched because the British troops were well equipped and well trained. A fleet of sixty ships with almost fifteen thousand troops had sailed into the Gulf of Mexico. From a garrison on Pea Island, they embarked a vanguard force of 1800 troops which landed on the east bank of the Mississippi River. They encamped at a plantation to wait for reinforcements. Little did they know that this plantation was the very one where the *Red Clan* of Queen Tayla had just descended upon for victims to feed upon. Once there, they decided to leave the slaves alone and take victims from the ranks of the British soldiers. The plantation was very rural, so the chances of causing anyone to notice something was going on was not among the Clansmen's concerns. Many died that night, and the bodies were thrown into the river. The alligator population in the area was plentiful and disposed of many bodies.

When the troops approached the home of the plantation owner, a Major Gabriel Villere was there. He was an American officer who escaped and was heading to the city to warn General Jackson of the approaching contingent of soldiers and where they were now. As he was on the road, the *Red Clan* was determined that no one would escape before dawn. He was intercepted and brought before Queen Tayla.

"You are an American officer? What are you doing here? Among so many British?"

The man, not even in uniform for he had to escape through a window, stated, "I must get to General Jackson to warn him! I have no horse by which to travel and it is imperative that I reach him. Within a few days, the British shall be marching on New Orleans. We cannot afford to lose the city!" He was desperate when he stated his case.

"The British are on the attack? The war is still on?" The Queen did not know that the war had spread all the way to the

444

city of New Orleans. It made sense that it would because of the economic impact on the young nation.

The Queen had not wanted to take sides in this war, but she did not come to a new land to only have the same persecutions and societal norms put upon her that she had just left. To her, if freedom was to be preserved, all ties with Europe…British, French, or Spanish, had to be severed.

"I will take you to him. Otherwise, you will be running until you drop, and no one will hear your message." She took him, looked him in the eye and said, "I am taking you to the General. Do not ask questions how you managed to get there or tell anyone what you see. If you do, you will not see another night. Do you understand?"

The disheveled Major nodded he did. The Queen sprouted wings and took his hand and carried him through the humid night all the way to New Orleans. She spotted some defensive works just outside the city along a canal and landed there, allowing the Major to walk away, completely befuddled as to what had just happened. Queen Tayla did not stick around to find out what he was going to say, but she did not want the Americans to be taken by surprise.

As it turned out, the British defeat was not because they failed to surprise the Americans. It was because of a poorly executed assault by the British accompanied by other factors that led to their defeat.

Queen Tayla remained around New Orleans for more than just a few years. She preyed upon the rural population while enjoying an entertaining life in the city. Renting several large houses in the city, she harbored only a small part of her clan there. The rest of the clan spread out across the marshy swamps to other towns, also preying upon transient populations and slaves. It may seem racist that these super predators would choose slaves to feed upon, but they were highly regarded by the vampires because their blood would fill with adrenalin so quickly when they knew they were about to die. The adrenalin in the blood was quickly sensed by the vampire. It gave the blood a certain flavor that seemed delicious to the predator.

Before too long, the swamps were becoming full of bodies, ready for consumption by the alligators. Even the city became a cruel, evil, and heartless place to live after a while. There was talk, particularly amongst the slave quarters at night. They would huddle with each other, praying in their Catholic ways, and when that did not stop the murders, they turned to their old religion, the one known as voodoo. All kinds of evidence of spells and curses could be found in the woods, swamps, and the like. High priestesses of the religion would cast spells that would grant protections against vampires and demons, along with curses that would single out one's enemies for retribution.

On certain plantations, aristocratic families prayed for deliverance and protection against the evil that lurked in the darkness of the Louisiana night. Night after night, bodies would turn up. Even in the port, the sailors were not safe in their ships. One such plantation was the Acadia Plantation in Thibodaux, Louisiana. There was considerable history about the plantation. It was started in 1828 by the Bowie brothers. It was the culmination of several smaller plantations which eventually became as large as 2100 acres. Their original business involved the slave trade, both buying and selling. Then, came the sugar business. There were a lot of slaves on the property as the need for their labor was obvious.

Many of these slaves were first generation people from West Africa. The religion of these newly arrived slaves was anything but Christianity. They practiced their own religion, regardless what the Catholic priests did to change their pagan ways. These slaves recognized the method of murder of their compatriots when they were forced to retrieve their bodies from swamps, woodlands, and even from the corners of their houses of quarter. Anguished family members shedding tears prompted the plantation owners, and the Sheriff of LaFourche Parrish, Stephen Bowie to investigate. These were murders to be sure, and he was determined to find the source of the evil, as he had a financial stake in all of this.

One night, he was sitting on his veranda, smoking a cigar, and enjoying an after-dinner brandy. He could hear singing coming from the slave's quarters some distance from the house. It was

446

loud, and every now and then, a scream could be heard above the noisy din of their revelry. Finding it very annoying, as it interrupted the quite of the young southern night, he called for his house butler.

"What is that infernal racket? It is not Sunday night, so I know they are not in Church. And that screaming! What is all that about?"

The butler, an older, black gentlemen who had performed house duties for years, answered, "Sir, I believe they are in the middle of some 'voodooing'. It is a religion they had over in Africa."

"You mean they are carrying on with that religion they brought with them?"

"Yes sir! I believe so. I have nothing to do with that. I am scared of that."

"I am going to look into this. I want this noise to stop!" Stephen Bowie put his brandy down, got up and went to investigate the raucous behavior occurring in the slave quarters.

He entered the room and immediately the noise and celebration stopped. "What's going on here?" he asked.

No one moved or spoke for several minutes. A slave woman with her Christian name being Rebecca, who had been in Stephen Bowie's service for quite a while stood up. "Master Stephen, I think you should hear what this woman has to say. It may help you."

The woman who had nearly arrived only a few weeks ago was told by Rebecca to stand up and speak in her native tongue. Rebecca translated her words into English.

"Master Stephen, we have an evil here. It is taking blood and life from your slaves. I am trying to ward off these spirits of evil, to tell them to seek blood from other places. I know these creatures, and they cannot be reasoned with. They must be driven away!"

He replied, "You are new here. What are you called?"

She replied through Rebecca, "I am Toomba, and I am new, just arrived three weeks ago. Sir, I know what I am seeing. They are here. They are killing us."

He asked, "Who is killing you?"

447

"They are the undead, sir. They come out at night, they prey upon the living and they leave death wherever they go. The priests have called them vampires. We had another name for them."

What would vampires be doing in Africa, other than their usual nocturnal activities? It would be because of Othar's *Clan of the Purple Velvet*. He was migrating southward through Africa for all the clans had decided to leave Europe to Prieta's clan. Too many hunters competing for the same prey was detrimental to all the Clans' survival. So, Rascha was in the process of moving his clan to the Southern Americas, as Queen Tayla had moved hers to the North American continent.

The Catholic priests finally remembered the heresy of vampirism when the Sheriff approached the priest of the parish and consulted other higher, ranking clergy. They were convinced that the plague of death that invaded every facet of society could be attributed to one thing. The heresy had returned.

CHAPTER FORTY-SIX

GO WEST

"Dearest Malcolm, my clan is once again in danger. The church and its persecutorial practices that I thought I had escaped from had been waiting for me here in this new land. The Holy Church which had been so dominate of Europe accompanied its colonists to the New World and so had permeated the society and culture of each colony. I was foolish to think that I could outrun its reach. The dogma of the Church now dominated the societies of the colonies. The only thing more dominating was its desire to maintain its hard-won freedom."

*   *   *

"Sheriff Bowie, we have seen these things throughout history. I am glad you have come to consult with us, but no one here has had any experience with this. I have heard of such a heresy, but this ranks right up there with witchcraft, demonic possession, and such. The supernatural is not something we relish having to deal with. We all know it is dangerous and requires the utmost of faith on those who intervene against it."

"Father Jonathan, I am the Sheriff. Everyone here is depending on me to do my job to keep them safe. How can I do that when I am blind and impotent against such things I do not understand. How can I fight against an opponent I know little to nothing about? What weapons do I have? None!"

"This may take some time. I can advise you to tell all your citizens to keep all doors and windows locked. Allow no strangers to cross the threshold into your homes. If you invite them in, you may be inviting death to your homes. If you have a crucifix, then wear it. But I tell you, it will do you no good if you do not believe with your heart and soul that the sign of the cross shall repel the vampire. They can only come out at night. During the day, they are vulnerable. They seek the blood of the living. They are driven to do this."

"That is exactly what Toomba said. She said they have these things back in Africa. Now, they are here. We have a serious problem, Father. I suggest you speak of this during Mass on Sunday."

The large framed plantation owner and Sheriff turned and left the Priest's office. He was frustrated yet hopeful that he had done the right thing by consulting with the priest. After all, Toomba had said these 'things' are of the undead. That fell into the priest's arena. Stephen Bowie knew he was far outclassed and outgunned on this matter. His first matter was to tell his entire plantation, and all associated with it to lock their doors and windows, stay inside and not to venture out in the darkness. He would also tell them not to allow any unknown visitors into their homes after dark. It was a start, but not to be considered their only defense. He also had some of his slaves start to whittle small crucifixes for the other slaves to wear. He wanted all of them to have one, with no exception. Even those who followed the old religion of voodoo were required to wear them. He forgot about the priest's warning that one had to believe with their heart and soul that the cross had power over the vampire. That would be to his detriment.

It was afternoon when Sheriff Bowie returned to Acadia Plantation. The slaves were still out in the sugar cane fields while others were attending their usual duties. He called for his foreman to assemble the slaves of the plantation. This took a while and it was just about dusk before he had a chance to speak to them. Finally, they assembled at the slave quarters.

Bowie rode up on a horse so all could see him. He shouted out, "I know of your fears. I have consulted with the priest here and he told me that such a creature was known to exist long ago, but it seems now they have returned. Toomba has told me of

450

them and knew about them in the old country. The priest told me to tell you to lock the doors and windows, allow no visitors in after dark, especially ones you do not know, and to wear your crosses around your necks. Even if you are not a Christian, wear them. They have protected others. These creatures are called vampires. They are of the devil. If we do not allow them to feed upon us, perhaps they will move on."

The priest had not told Bowie of the ways that a vampire can be killed. The information given was limited to defense and not offense. Father Jonathan had written to the Bishop of the Archdiocese to inquire of any more information that might be helpful to combatting these creatures. It would be some time before that could be known. Much of it would be found out by accident, by trial and error, and by a Baptist minister who used scripture to determine that what vampires can do and not do was related to scripture.

That night, the slaves huddled like frightened children in their houses. The doors were locked, and the windows closed. Being the summer, the heat was unbearable. The heat was such that the temptation to opening a window to catch the ventilation from the evening breezes was almost too much to resist. Kerosene lanterns and candles lit the rooms so that the residents could see if door handles were turning or if latches were being tested. Every sound of every insect and every lizard or snake that crawled over every dry leaf on the ground kept the slaves awake. They knew that death crept just outside their walls, seeking a way to get in.

Tayla's vampire were doing exactly that. There were four that had visited the plantation that night. They stood in the shadows waiting patiently for a slave or occupant of the big house to have to come out to the small structure that stood away from all the others for them to relieve themselves. One of those was a house slave. He wore his crucifix around his neck and took another slave with him. One stood guard outside while the other relieved himself. When he came out, the other slave was in a slump, against the wall of the outhouse.

He screamed, running for the plantation house, calling for his master. His lantern in his hand, he fumbled with the key to open

451

the main door. Turning to look behind him, he could see the shapes of four vampires, black and cruel, moving silently across the lawn, coming for him. He was able to turn the key and enter the house, closing the door and locking it before they could get to him. The butler, the same one who had told Bowie about the voodoo rituals, backed away from the door, watching the knob being tested. He was frightened and the vampires could smell his fear through the door. Their whispers, "Let me in!" could be heard through the heavy doors.

Finally, they went away, but not before Bowie came down the stair with a candelabra of six candles to witness himself the sound of them whispering to his butler. "James, I thought I told you to keep this door locked. What happened? Tell me what you saw?"

James was so frightened he could barely speak. When he was able to compose himself, he could only speak with a stutter. "Sir, I had to go make water and I took George with me 'because I was afraid, and he had to go too. So, I went first and when I came out, George was on the ground, not moving. I heard nothing but came out and he was on the ground." He started crying for he and George were close friends.

"And then what?" asked Bowie.

"I started screaming for you, and I ran to the door. I had locked the door behind me, so I had to unlock it. I turned around behind me and I saw four of them, moving slowly towards me. I got inside just in time, locked the door and as soon as I had locked it, they were trying to get in. I could see the knob turning but they could not turn it all the way. They were whispering real loudly for me to let them in. That was when you came down."

Tayla heard later that night the report of the incidents at the Acadia Plantation. She also heard reports of the same at several others around New Orleans. She knew that sooner or later, the mortals of the area, with the help of clergy, would be able to drive them out. It would be by finding ways to repel them, or eventually to combat them by destroying them. It would be a matter of time. But still, the temptation to prey upon beings whose fear was so great and stirred in the blood was too much to resist. The killings went on for quite a while.

452

Sheriff Stephen Bowie made his rounds to all the other plantation owners to inquire if they were experiencing the same calamity he had on his hands. This took several days as not every plantation bordered upon the next. There were vast areas of undeveloped land, between the large farms. Every owner said they were but were at a loss as to how to describe it and even less how to report it.

Bowie called for a citizen's meeting at the courthouse in Thibodaux. It was several days after George had met his demise that the meeting took place. George had been at the voodoo ritual that Toomba had led, telling the attendees that the devil was on the loose, and out for their blood and their souls. Eternal damnation awaited any victim of the vampires. It was no wonder that every slave in the region was scared to death. Toomba was not the only voodoo practitioner in the area. The Bowies had several on their plantation alone.

In the courthouse, the audience was full and the smell of tobacco from cigars and pipes was in the air. Most of those in attendance were males. Clergy, council members and the mayor were there as well as other prominent citizens. Nearly all the plantation owners were in attendance as well. The point was made that it seemed only the slaves were affected by this dreadful epidemic of murder. Everyone's contingent of slaves were frightened to the point of not wanting to venture out of their quarters, day, or night. While on his rounds, Sheriff Bowie told some of the foremen of the plantations present at the meeting the same things he had told his own slaves.

In the courtroom, he repeated himself. "Since the beginning of Acadia Plantation ten years ago, I have tried to set the example for how we as owners and masters should treat our people. Look out after them! They look to us for everything. Not just survival but comfort as well. Part of that comfort is security. They need to know you care for them, willing to protect them if need be. If you do that, they will work for you, willingly, in exchange for that sense of belonging. Everyone here works together for one purpose, the plantation. Everyone benefits from everyone's labor. You need to believe that, and they need to see that in you."

One cigar-smoking plantation owner spoke out, saying, "Your compassion for these people is admirable, morally uplifting, but be careful they see a weakness in your character. They might take advantage of it."

Bowie answered, "There is no weakness in trying to protect the weak. You would do the same for your cattle, your flock, would you not? Especially if your livelihood depended upon it?"

The judge interjected, "Point well taken, Sherriff Bowie."

He turned to address the group. "I am charged with keeping the peace here. I cannot do that if there are those who do not take this threat seriously. We have the bodies to prove this is a serious matter. Pragmatically speaking, for every slave lost, it is a threat to the functioning of our enterprises. Morally, it is the loss of human life. Some of us do not equate them as human as much as others, but I am sure our Lord will disagree with them!"

Father Jonathan spoke out, "The Sheriff is completely and justifiably correct. This is a menace that will affect us all. Does it mean that we will not consider this a serious threat until one of us, our families or members of our community is taken by one of these undead creatures? I pray to God not!"

Bowie turned to the priest and asked, "Father, what other things can we do to protect ours and those we have charge over?"

The priest answered, "I have written for instructions and details of when the Church had an inquisition regarding such creatures. Those records must come from Rome, where they were stored. Centuries ago, a papal bull was issued declaring this heresy forbidden to even talk about. Then, the threat became so evident, a special inquisition was formed to seek out and destroy them. What became of it, I do not know. I do know if there were any records of what to do, they would have been recorded and stored in the archives of the Vatican."

Pastor Duquesne, a minister of the local Baptist Church stood up, with a Bible in his hand. His head was bowed, and his lips were moving, as if saying a silent prayer. Finally, he opened his eyes. "May I have the pleasure of addressing this body without interruption?" There was no objection from anyone in the room.

454

"Sirs, I suggest we rely on the Word of God for instruction. After all, most of us in this room have no doubt that the answers to all our cares and problems can be found somewhere in the scriptures. I have been listening carefully to some of the instructions given by the Catholic priest. He states that the vampires cannot pass into a dwelling without being invited or obtaining the owner's permission. There is a scripture regarding something to that phenomenon. Christ cannot enter your heart without your permission, so why should the devil be able to? You say these creatures cannot exist during the day? Perhaps it is because they are of the devil and the Bible says the light has no fellowship with the darkness. Does anyone see a pattern here?"

Murmuring of the crowd in the room became an audible roar, as they all knew the minister had discovered something that few if any had even considered. This was truly a holy matter. Pastor Duquesne sat down.

The only witness who could give testimony as to what these creatures looked like was James, Bowie's house butler. Bowie was reluctant to let him testify of his experience for few would take a slave at his word.

Sheriff Bowie stood up once again, saying, "Until we can come to an agreed manner upon which to deal with this, I declare that there be a curfew effective at dusk, that all doors and windows of every building, residence and such be locked with no entry granted to any stranger. If necessary, place a crucifix upon the door or window, wear one around your neck if you have one, carry your Bible if you have one. Please, my fellow members of our community, if we stand together, perhaps we may deter them. If they cannot feed here, they must move on."

There was more bickering, more discussion, more disbelief amongst the citizens attending the meeting. Bowie walked out the door in a hurry to reach his plantation before dusk. He advised others to do the same while mounting his horse. The horse carried him at top speed all the way back to Acadia Plantation. Upon arrival, the sun was low in the sky. It would be dark soon, and the creatures of the night would be loose. A stable hand took his horse and led him into the barn.

"Take care of that horse and get back inside before it gets dark!" he yelled back to the slave as he walked up towards the house. There was about an hour of daylight left.

*   *   *

Queen Tayla had given instructions that all caution be taken for she knew the mortal population had been warned. Her familiars had been outside the courthouse for there were no seats available. They were quick to report back to the clan.

It was always her strategy to use stealth and people's beliefs to hide amongst the mortal population. The vampires never left clues as to who had done these murders. The only connecting clue was the method of death, which was exsanguination by a wound to the neck. There would be no signs of forced entry, no signs of struggle, and no signs of any get away. No horses, no carriages seemed to have been there. No witness had ever come forward to say they had seen something. She wanted no battle and no confrontation, only the quick, merciful death that their kind could deliver. They would strike only as wolves upon sheep in the night. On this night, vampires would travel far distances in the night to make their kill. They did so, but now half the state was aware that something was not right in the bayou country. There were many funerals that week.

The Queen wished there were some other way, but she knew that there was not. Vampires needed to feed, and humans were what they fed upon. Up until this point, Queen Tayla had never considered any other type of living blood. It was assumed that only the blood of humans was to be consumed. She considered the possibility of a substitute.

At a meeting in the house where Tayla rented in New Orleans, the subject was brought up. It was suggested that cattle be attacked instead of humans for a while. The court of Queen Tayla agreed that it might take some of the attention away from them for a while but nonetheless, farmers would be alarmed when their herds started to face depletion. Either way, the vampires could not feed without coming under fire from the mortal world.

Queen Tayla said, "If animal blood could be added to our diets, it would lessen the threat to the mortals. I suggest, no, I order all those of my clan to alternate their feeding with those of animals, either wild or not. I believe this will help. I also suggest that we learn to cultivate our own feeding stock. The mortals, since time was recorded, have always raised flocks. They raised flocks of sheep, of goats, of cattle, of horses. If we had a planation of our own, we could raise our own food, in the form of animals, or perhaps even our own human stock. We need only a location. In France, we had a palace, a castle from where we based our home, our sanctuary. Here, in America, we must do the same. Otherwise, we will always be wandering the land, like nomads. I suggest we set that as part of our plan, to find a place where we could settle down, to make our permanent home."

That night, at several locations, vampires were seen and at one location, were repelled with slaves using the already implemented measures. The vampires returned to their lairs hungry.

At the next meeting, it was reported and discussed to the Queen. Tayla considered all things and made her decision. They would move westward. Most of the western part of the continent was undiscovered. Surely, there must be more opportunity to establish her kingdom out there. There were far fewer white settlers westward, even though a lot of Americans were flooding into Texas. There were native Americans, also mistakenly known as Indians then, and herds of millions of animals that roamed the plains. The lure of all this tempted Queen Tayla to move westward, but the comfort and style of New Orleans tempted her to stay.

In 1838, Queen Tayla formed an expedition of her own, mirroring that of the Lewis and Clarke expedition. They would travel light, fast and live off the land of which was more than able to support them. San Francisco was a fledgling town on the west coast of California. It was as far west as she could go without having to learn how to swim. Vampires could not do such a thing, even if they knew how in their mortal life. The reason? Water that supports life is considered living water, which Jesus said he would give to all those who thirst, and they would never

457

thirst again. Vampires are always thirsty, thirsty for the one thing that is symbolic of life, but they can never quench that thirst.

In the winter of 1838, Queen Tayla left New Orleans. They took no wagons, no horses, no weapons. They had no need of them. Queen Tayla took a compass, a satchel of maps that existed at that time. She estimated they could make about two hundred miles each day, flying through the night. If they flew over the herds of buffalo, they would feast upon them. She had no doubt they would not go hungry. Though it was winter, the buffalo were still there. They flew northward out of Louisiana into the Ozarks and northward till they reached the city of St. Louis on the Mississippi River.

They feasted for a week or so while in St. Louis, getting updated maps and listening to wagon masters who had led trains of prairie schooners across the Rocky Mountains to the west coast. Everyone told her that the trip would be so hard and treacherous that she was crazy for wanting to travel there. All that she talked to, told her she should catch a ship from New Orleans and travel southward around the Cape Horn of South Anmerica. They all claimed it was safer and more comfortable. Few if any knew about the storms that accompanied such a trip.

Tayla and her vampires only smiled at their concern. She wanted information, not sympathy or concern for their safety. Naivety on their part made her feel pity for them. They departed St. Louis in January of 1839, heading westwards through the areas of what would become the states of Kansas, Colorado, Utah, Nevada and into the California territory.

On the way, they preyed on buffalo, elk, and indigenous peoples of Ute, Blackfoot, Cheyenne, and Crow tribes. The winter was hard, as these were temperatures that though cold, they would never be recorded. The tribes were courteous when they met the vampires. They were amazed at the powers of the creatures of the undead and feared them greatly. The tribal elders would tell the stories of the gods of the night for many winters to come. Eventually, it would become forgotten as the tribes were reduced to their lowest numbers.

In the summer of 1839, Queen Tayla arrived at the California coast to enter the settlement of San Francisco. Here she set up shop on the street of many storefronts as the madam of a brothel. She kept a few vampires with her, but she sent the others back to begin the process of moving the clan out west, a few at a time. Eventually, by 1849, much of the clan would have arrived in San Francisco. The rest were spread-out all-over America.

CHAPTER FORTY-SEVEN

A NEW LIFE, AN OLD ENEMY

"Dearest Malcolm, I have finally arrived in the land in which I would make my final home. I have crossed many borders, those of countries and kingdoms of Europe, the Atlantic Ocean and the states and territories of the United States. The most important borders I have crossed are those of life and death. One day, I will make a border crossing from which I shall not return from.

Arriving in California was the epitome of my excitement. Such wonderful opportunities awaited me here. The ability to feast on prey here was easy and prey was abundant, but I wanted more. I wanted to be able to live and prosper as any mortal would have. I suppose it was because I always felt as if my father were watching over me. Though for so many centuries I thought him to be a cruel man, I invented a kinder, gentler father in my own mind who I imagined would be cheering me on in my endeavors to make him proud. As of this writing, I now know I did not have to invent such a man, for such a man as I had envisioned was my father.

My nature prevented me from fully realizing that dream of living as a mortal, but nonetheless, I was determined to make a lifestyle fitting of a queen that I could live under, passing as much as a mortal as I could so I and my clansmen would not have to live in fear. I found land north of San Francisco I would eventually save enough money to buy. It would take years of hard work, finding familiars of specific talents that would work the land, above and below, that would eventually become my estate and palace."

*   *   *

It started in a wooden storefront, a building consisting of several large rooms with even more smaller rooms. Several of Tayla's clansmen were females. All of which were equipped with the standard charms plus the added charm of irresistible seduction. If a man found his pleasure with them, he might find that his death would be equally pleasurable. Many men found their end would be just that. However, Queen Tayla did not start the business of running a brothel for the sole purpose of preying on men at the height of their weaknesses. She did it because she could make a lot of money doing so. The range of occupations for an independent woman was narrow in those days. This was perhaps the best route. Even so, she had not had many lovers she felt romantic about. At this point, it was just about sex, sex for money. Her girls, some familiars, some vampire, were keen on making money. The familiars knew that at some point they would be offered the life of a vampire if they had served well enough. It was the highest reward she could give and was most sought after by all the familiars.

Regarding the life of a familiar, one must know that they are changed in such a way that they are no longer the person they once were. Their memory of their past lives is wiped clean. This is to insure they have nothing to want to return to. They know they once had a life before the spell of becoming a familiar is put upon them. Their names are changed. They do not know the name they were born with, but only the code name, or nickname they go by forever afterwards. The Queen talks to them through mental telepathy, such that even during the day, while the Queen sleeps, her voice echoes in their heads, telling them what she wanted them to do. The Queen picks her familiars based on specific criteria. It is not enough that they just want to be a familiar, as in one day they may incur enough favor that she will bring them to the crossing over. No, it is because they possess certain skills and talents, or because they are in such a position that they might serve the *Order of the Red Velvet* in such a way that might be a valuable service. The strongest ties to the Queen

461

are held by the personal staff, such as the butler, her foreman of the ranch, her cook, her wrangler, or her maid. Over the years, the personal staff would grow and as each grew older, if they wanted to be taken to the crossing over, the Queen would consider it. Becoming a vampire was never a guarantee. The vampires looked after the familiars, protecting them, as the familiars protected their masters.

The brothel was not too fancy, but its reputation for the finest entertainment for gentlemen was beyond compare. Tayla invested the entire first year's profits into the business. Until that happened, the rooms were semi-private and private. Girls were purchased for a night's pleasure, either in house or out call. Whiskey and other spirits were purchased along with the other pleasures the gentlemen came for.

Gentlemen who paid and tipped well were spared the title of victim while those who were new in town and would not be missed often found themselves in a bad way. The first years went by fast as the town of San Francisco began to grow. Then, in 1849, at a place called Sutter's Mill, gold was discovered. The California Gold Rush was not just a national event. It was a global event as it drew people in from not just all over the United States but all over the world. To get to the gold fields, they had to go through San Francisco. That meant, Queen Tayla and her clan got a first look at them. People from all over came through the town as it was growing by leaps and bounds. Many of them would not be missed and became food for the vampires, who not only took their gold but their life blood as well.

Queen Tayla and her clan grew rich. Her business prospered and she began to grow her profits by investing in shipping firms and real estate. Eventually, she was able to purchase her own ship which led to the purchase of another and another. By 1851, she had her own fleet. Profits from shipping were big. All equipment for mining had to be imported. It was manufactured in the east, so ships were busy transporting all the goods to the west coast. The competition was fierce at first but when the gold rush came in, many ships found their crews deserting to rush to the gold fields to find their fortunes.

In 1846, at the end of the Mexican American War, Commodore John D. Sloat had claimed California for the United States. Soon after, Tayla acquired a large tract of land in the north, in what would eventually become the county of Glenn. There was no town close by, and she bought the land from the US territorial government of California. The price of the land was cheap as she quickly homesteaded it. There were no conditions attached. She and her clansmen sowed the creek on the northeastern boundary with raw gold, in nuggets and some of it in dust. The value of it was of no consequence to the Queen as she knew eventually it would be discovered. The miners would find it and begin the foundation of what would eventually become her Lower Estate.

That same year, Tayla was given the gift of maturity. This meant that she would appear as an adult version of her younger self, the one that she never was able to grow into naturally. Thanks to her gifts of sight and keen intellect, Queen Tayla had found the way to quickly build the foundation to making a fortune that would sustain her empire for over a century. She had her shipping business, her real estate holdings, and her brothels inside the port of San Francisco. Outside that busy port city, north of the quick sprawl the city would undergo, she built her plantation. Beginning with a homestead, it quickly grew. After the tents came down, and as the small cabin and other structures that housed her employees began to fall into disrepair, she rebuilt. It started with a large home, built from timbers cut from her property. It would become the home she never had for decades until she was ready to build what she really wanted, her own castle. In America, castles did not exist, but she wanted to build a new version of the great and grand structures she knew during the centuries before. Her wisdom told her that to build too quickly would draw too much unwanted attention. After all, she was more interested in what could be built underground.

She quickly planted grapes in the region, as well as vegetables and raised large herds of cattle. She established a winery, one of the first in northern California and supplied much of the domestic wines for several decades. Farther south, in the Napa Valley's future, she would also have vineyards planted. As for where she was now, there was plenty of free range in those days that would support a large herd.

Tayla had a large following of familiars in those days. It was needed to man the large sprawling estate as well as her other ventures. She needed persons to man the businesses, especially in the executive and administrative positions. More than enough money came in to pay the bills. She paid her employees and familiars well, so that she incurred loyalty amongst those who were not familiars and reinforced the loyalty of those who were.

Many of these men and women were people she would come to rely on and regard them fondly. She prized loyalty and devotion to a purpose more than anything else. When she saw a familiar who envisioned the reward of being a vampire by working to great lengths to please her, she was eager to reward. It also served as a reminder to others that if one is deserving, one is rewarded.

During the decade of 1850 to 1860, not only was there an explosion of gold mining but silver as well. The Comstock Lode in Nevada in 1859, drew hordes of fortune seekers to San Francisco, eager to get to the silver fields of Nevada. As with any high-density population areas, crime and vice grow like weeds in the summer. Lawlessness was common, and an area of the town known as the Barbary Coast became known as a haven for criminals, prostitution, and gambling. Queen Tayla's vampires visited this area frequently. Many a drunken sailor or gambler who was down and out found themselves at the mercy of the vampire, of which there was usually none. This decade was extremely prosperous for the *Clan of the Order of the Red Velvet.*

Queen Tayla had a master plan for her California estate. Though it did not look like some of the plantations she had seen back east, especially along the Mississippi River frontage, she could see its potential. What she planned to build would last for centuries beyond what mortal man had already deemed the epitome of luxury.

When the gold was discovered on her property and the miners flocked to the northern parcel of her property, she met with each one at her homestead, now a ranch house. No one ever seemed

464

to think anything strange about her. It was not unusual for anyone to see her only after sundown. They were all working hard during the daylight hours.

One miner, a tall muscular youth in his late teens who had come from back east, was invited to her house to discuss the terms of his lease of her property to mine. He was of Scandinavian descent, a second-generation Swede. He had received an education back east, but his family had met with a tragic accident and were all wiped out. The only relatives he had were those still left in Sweden. He had never met them.

Eric Petersen was greeted by her butler. "Come in, Mr. Petersen. Miss Tayla is expecting you." He was led into a parlor, the usual place for meetings and socializing. Tayla sat behind a beautiful desk of walnut. A chair in front of the desk awaited the Swede.

"As in my usual custom, I want to meet all those miners who have come to mine on my land. I have an agreement prepared for you to sign if you agree to my terms." She pushed a single page document towards him across the desk.

Tayla was dressed in the high fashion of the day. She looked every bit the part of a sophisticated and wealthy socialite presenting the image of wealth and power. In those days, those terms were usually synonymous.

In contrast, Eric Petersen was dressed in a clean pair of overalls and shirt which other than what he usually worked in was half of his entire wardrobe. He had taken care to clean the dirt and caked mud from his boots that went up to just below his knees. He had taken his wide brim hat off as he had come through the door.

The young man was literate and read the terms, which were liberal. The conditions read that you as a miner pay no money up front, bring your own tools, mine as much as you can, but pay a percentage of your lease in gold which was usually ten per cent. He instantly signed his name.

He held out his hand to shake hers, something she was not accustomed to, but she took his hand, feeling the warmth of his blood in his hand. It stirred something in her. By her touch upon his skin, she sensed his innocence, his nobleness and courage. It reminded her of Renard in some respects. Though by his own admission, he was not so innocent. He had done his share of whoring and killing, for that was part of the lifestyle. Either get rich or die trying summed up his profession. Eric Petersen had not lived long enough to know the evils that roamed the world, both day and night. She looked into his eyes and could see that no one had ever captured his heart. No woman had ever captured his heart nor had broken it. Naivety abounded in this young but strong specimen of a miner. It attracted her though she did not know why.

He noticed her hand was cold, but he thought nothing of it.

She was determined to keep her hands and her fangs off her miners, particularly this one. After all, they were more valuable to her as miners, digging the tunnels she would need later.

Things were going very well until one day, a stranger from her past caught up with her.

*   *   *

"I would like to see the mistress of the house if I may?" the stranger asked the butler from outside the front door of the ranch house.

"Whom shall I say is inquiring at this time of night?" asked the butler. The butler, a familiar since Tayla's arrival in San Francisco, went by the name of Scratch. Tayla had discovered that giving the familiars new code names, completed the erasure of memory of past lives. This was done only for personal staff of the estate and hired help. It ensured loyalty and discretion.

"An old friend of her past... her distant past. She will know me very well."

Scratch welcomed him into the foyer and bid him to wait. It was late, near midnight, which made Scratch wonder who would want an audience with the Queen at this time of night.

Within minutes, the Queen appeared. Though she did not recognize him, she still introduced herself, "I do not believe we have been introduced. I am Tayla, the owner of this house and estate. You are...?"

466

The stranger reached out his hand to take Tayla's hand. He politely bowed his head low and bent at the waist. Immediately upon touching her skin, she felt a familiar presence.

"I am Ricardo Draco, the current form of the Dragon. My, you are hard to find these days. I have been searching for a long time."

Tayla was stunned as the smile ran away from her face. The Dragon had come back. She regained her composure after a few seconds. "I see, you have returned to find me. For what purpose is this visit?"

"We have much to discuss. Can we do this over a glass of your own wine. I have heard they are quite good."

"Your flattery is of no use, devil. Very well, Scratch?"

"Yes, your highness?" Scratch replied.

"A bottle of my best for my guest, in the parlor. Come, Ricardo, I want to know more of why you are here."

They went to the parlor where Tayla sat behind her desk and Ricardo sat in the chair before it.

Scratch came into the room with a service set for wine. Only he brought two glasses as well. Ricardo noticed it for she normally would not drink anything other than the blood of her victims and her service set was not silver but glass.

Scratch poured the two glasses with a dark red wine, of which Ricardo picked his up, sniffing its bouquet, and commented, "I am no wine connoisseur, but I think I am going to enjoy this. He held it up to Tayla who picked up her glass and together they drank.

"Drinking these days?" he asked.

"When it is called for," she answered. "Another gift I have been given. It is part of my ability to camouflage myself and blend in with the mortal population. Part of my long-time desire to be as mortal as possible."

"Yes, I know. You have always wanted the best of both worlds. But in your case, eventually you will have to make a choice as to which side you will be loyal to, your vampire nature or your human nature. Even in the scriptures it says that no man can serve two masters."

"I have been doing so for nearly six hundred years."

"Yes, and the Dark Lord wants you to choose. He has been generous in your case. And most tolerant, I might add," Ricardo stated.

"Is this why you are here? To remind me that I am a vampire and that I must take my orders from the Dark Lord through you? I am fully aware who I am and most emphatically who you are. Your ancestor is the reason for all of it."

"That was not me. My ancestor you speak of was something of a rebel, even against the Dark Lord."

"Well, I am doing fine here. I came here to get away from all that reminded me of who you are, the church's ceaseless persecution, and to find a place I can call my home. I own this property, this house, and all the businesses that support it. I bought it, legally and with good money. I intend to keep it. I want no war with anyone, church, or you. Is that understood? If so, why else are you here?"

"I have come to give you a friendly warning. We both have enemies. Sometimes they are the same enemy. The Franciscans, the Jesuits, and the Dominican Orders all have ties to Rome and thus to the Pope. Your sister has been sloppy as of late, and currently, her activities have been made known to the Pope. They in turn have dispatched a special task force to find her and eliminate her. They also have knowledge of my existence. That means I have had to change my venue as well. I am now down in the Spanish colonies in South America. You will come to know us as the *Order of the Jackal*."

"For you, that is a fitting name for any organization you might head up. The Jackal is a dog, a scavenger of some type? Anyway, you are still up to your neck in Catholic country."

"I can understand your disdain for me. After all, I represent everything that you have come to hate. The jackal is also a creature for what the Egyptian god, Anubis is personified as, so, as you can see, even the Egyptians respected our namesake."

"Regarding our disdain, well at least you are telling the truth!"

"We still have hope that you will join in our cause. That is why I am here. A gesture of good will," he said.

"I will never join your cause. Your cause is pure evil, as its plans have been written by the author of evil. Finish your wine and get out."

Ricardo was a lot more refined that his predecessors. Educated, experienced in matters of administration and law, he was what most people would consider a gentleman. A handsome, well-dressed man of fancy tastes and well-traveled exploits, he was not used to being spoken to in such abrupt ways. He gulped down his wine and set the glass down. He stood up, saying, "I had hoped this meeting would have resulted in a better outcome, an act of cooperation between the two of us. I am sad that it did not. If you should ever have need of me.... I bid you good night." He turned and Scratch handed him his coat and hat as he left through the front door.

Tayla called for Scratch. "He is never to be admitted across that threshold again. I forbid it! I am placing a spell that will forbid his entry, the same one that is on my entry into places that I am not invited into."

Tayla continued telling her butler the story about the Dragon. It was better if Scratch, one of her most trusted familiars, knew everything he needed to know. She had to admit, this version of the Dragon was much more amenable than those she had dealt with previously.

The Queen was aware of what she could do and not do, though she had no idea of why. If it worked on her, it had to work on the Dragon as well, she thought. She would find that some of those "laws" did not always apply to the Dragon. The Dragon could do things she could not. She could do things he could not. Together, they would make for a formidable enemy to mortal man. Tayla, however, was determined that alliance would never be made between her and the Dragon.

Scratch complied with her command and promised that he would never admit Ricardo Draco through any door of the house. Tayla stormed out of the room, went out the back door and flew off, eager to kill someone. She was angry and her next victim was about to know that wrath.

Flying through the darkness, she could see men camped around their fires from her height in the air. They were the miners

469

who had leased the land they worked from her. Her enhanced senses included acute hearing. The men were singing around their fires, seemingly happy, for they had worked hard all day, having scraped some of the gold out of the ground. Their voices were optimistic, and their singing was for those they left behind in hopes of striking it rich.

She did not want to harm those miners. Orders had already been issued to her clansmen that none of those who worked for her were to be touched. Also, the young miner, Eric Petersen was down there, probably thinking about her while he sang songs with his fellow miners. She could sense it. A mortal caring for her again? The thought of that cooled her anger. It subsided after seeing their contentment after working hard and productively.

She flew on until she was over a herd of cattle. It was there she came to realize that she should never kill out of anger and that feeding was only for survival. The idea of having human cattle to feed upon as the mortals fed upon herds of bovine, appealed to her. Eventually, she would utilize this idea when her underground tunnel complex would become the home for the *Order of the Clan of the Red Velvet*. She would begin to acquire mortals, to be used like cattle, keeping them alive in cells that would become titled "The *Stables of the Damned*." A policy of controlled and limited feeding would follow later.

A year later after the Dragon had paid Queen Tayla a visit, his words came to fruition. The cooperation of the different monastic orders resulted in the blessing of a task force created for the sole purpose of seeking out and eliminating Queen Tayla. They identified her by name! Across America, in private, different monasteries and convents were cooperating, reporting strange cases of mortalities and homicides. Detectives were hired by the church and their orders to seek out and investigate the murders and report back.

There were bands of *Red Clan* vampires all over the country. All the vampires were not physically near the Queen. The footprint it would create would be far too large to keep hidden. It was better that they be spread out evenly so their feeding would not be concentrated in one geographical area. Those groups would also adopt her policy of feeding stables.

As the years started to go by, the mines began to steadily decrease their yield to the miners. Soon, the miners began to give up on some of the mines in that they felt they had worked all they were going to get out of them short term without having to do major excavations to go deeper where Tayla knew the real veins of gold were.

Sometimes, the miners were within a few feet of hitting a major vein. She could see this when she would travel inside the mines to inspect how deep and far in the miners had dug. She would lay nuggets of gold to tease the miners the next day so they would dig at a spot she had picked out. The men would refer to whoever was leaving the gold nuggets as signs as the gold fairy. They had no idea nor were they trying awfully hard to find out. Once the word had gotten out that if you saw a nugget on the floor of the mine next to the wall, that was a place to dig. They did not share that with any of the other miners in the area. If they had, there would have been a lot of "claim jumping" which would have resulted in violence and ultimately someone's death. Tayla did not want that. She wanted the miners to be successful and to continue to dig her tunnel complex. Soon, some of the mines were extremely long and few if any were straight and level. After a while, they went deep, with their tracks being laid down at a steep grade which would require mules to haul out the ore cars on the tracks. Everyone prospered, but soon enough, the miners would relinquish their leases and another miner would soon take over the back-breaking work of gold mining. Soon, they built shafts and put in elevators that would be lowered using mules and pulleys to lower cars down into the deep mines of the darkness. Timbers cut from trees on her property would be used to shore up the mines, preventing cave-ins.

One night, while all was quiet, and everyone was asleep but for the vampires, she ventured into the mines. Though the mines were as dark as midnight during the day, it seemed as if the mines were shrouded in a special kind of darkness at night. The vampire felt comfortable in such darkness. Having a natural night vision, it gave her a sense of power and domination over the darkness as she was not hindered by it.

Her vision allowed her to not only see through the darkness but also the rock as well. Deep through the layers of rock she could see. Her eyes revealed how close some of the miner's tunnels opened into other tunnels from different claims. Should one intercept another due to unknowingly crossing paths, a problem would erupt. She knew she would have to address that issue. She walked on, her feet not making any sound in the eternal silence that invaded every particle of space there. Soon, the sounds of dripping water broke the silence.

She felt the need to explore. Like a child, she followed every foot of mined passages. Soon, she had gone as deep as any miner had been before. The depth was near four hundred feet deep. The special powers of vision allowed her to see where the gold veins were inside the walls of rock. The vampiress could see far off into the darkness, visualizing all the passageways, piles of debris, the connecting tracks, and at the blind end of one passage, there was a small hole.

It was a passage that was still too small for any human to pass through. The miners had not finished punching their way through this yet. She peered through the small opening to see what structures were on the other side. It opened into a seemingly bottomless pit. Its depth was several hundred feet, straight down.

She would not be able to pass unless she changed her form, something she could do but did not like doing. She had the ability to change into such creatures as the bat, the snake, or the wolf. She had reluctance to do any of that for they were all abhorred by mortals. However, a mist was not so threatening and could go anywhere, no matter how small the opening was. Moving as a mist, with gravity playing no role in slowing her down, she swooped down to the bottom in a dizzying dive.

At the bottom of the abyss, she found a roaring underground river with a powerful current. The water and air were very cold, but it had no effect upon her. The river appeared from one side of a rock wall, churning as it passed her at the bottom of the pit, and disappeared again at the opposite side. The sound of the water speeding past the bottom of the pit produced a deafening roar. Around the walls of the deep pit she found that there were other passages, some small while others were larger, but none of them were mined by human hands. They formed over the course of thousands if not millions of years. Small but steady streams of water poured from these passages into the main river at the bottom. These passages were conduits that fed water to the main underground river. And all of this had been unseen and untouched by any human alive.

Tayla was amazed. It took a lot to take away the breath of a vampire, not that they have one, but this…was amazing. This place was what she had been waiting for, a place where no one had ever ventured before. It was here that she visualized the location for her tomb. The site was perfect. It was safe, secure, unknown, and most likely, unreachable by any mortals. She determined that this was to be her home.

She could sense the underground river below her, as there were many areas where the tunnel walls leaked water. But more than that, she could see below to a large underground lake. A single overly large stalagmite rose out of the center of the lake. It was not completely up to the ceiling but was well on its way for it rose nearly thirty feet above the waterline of the lake. The water of the lake was still.

There was another large underground cavern at an elevation higher but directly underneath her. It would become her *Coliseum* and another cavernous room not far off from that would become her palace. She had visualized what would become known as the Lower Estate.

When she exited the mines that early morning, ready to retire, she was euphoric. She left word with Scratch she needed to have a meeting with the miners, for she did not want them punching through to the abyss where the river was. Perhaps it was time to end the lease and have the miners leave. She would show them where the remaining gold deposits were so they could leave with something for their trouble. It was fair, she thought, especially for Eric. Her affection for him needed to be kept in check for she knew she could not keep him unless she made him a familiar. She and Eric Petersen had become friends, as she often invited him to dine with her. He remained polite and his boyish charm fascinated the Queen. He talked about his home back east and his family who was now gone, but he remained optimistic about

473

making something out his life. He wanted to earn enough money to go back and finish his education, perhaps even going on to college. A few more years and he would have enough to afford to be able to do both. Tayla kept that in mind when she would visit his claim. To her, pointing out where to dig was just a way for her to show her appreciation and her affection towards him. She knew falling in love was not possible for the pain of it still made her heart ache. How soon would it be before he would desire to go back east and continue his education? Would he ever return to the west? No answers were available to her currently. She enjoyed spending time with Eric and for now, that was all that mattered. When it was time for him to leave, she would say goodbye and leave it at that. At least she would not have broken his heart.

Turning her attention back to her plans for her tunnels and caverns under her estate helped her to not fret too much over the potential loss of a new lover. She began to draw up plans of a grand design. Next, she wanted a meeting with the elders of the *Red Clan*. She could not wait to tell them the news and scope of her plans. After all, it would be their new home as well.

CHAPTER FORTY-EIGHT

MAJOR ERIC PETERSEN

"Dearest Malcolm, the years roll by me like the days roll by for you. Before you know it, time has moved on so quickly, so quietly, you hardly notice how it just flew past you. Time to me does not mean the same as it does to you. I am a prisoner of eternity. Your dealings with time will come soon enough for you and those of your kind. But not for me, or those of my kind either.

The mines gave me enough wealth as did my other businesses, that everything I wanted was attainable simply by my signature on a piece of paper. What I wanted, money could not buy, but here in my prison cell, so lavishly decorated, I found that if I had to suffer the endless cavalcade of days and years rolling by like the trains traveling east to west, this was the way to do it.

I began to build on my mansion after the War between the States. It was such a tragedy. During the war, much of the gold mined was sent back to the US Government to support the war effort. Some of the gold financed the laying of the foundation of my home.

Eventually the homestead ranch house that I lived in was torn down to make way for the extravagant mansion you now live in. Bringing in the best architects and craftsmen did not daunt me when I determined the cost of the mansion I intended to build.

I built it to last for a long time, which now you see it already has. With all the repairs and modifications that seem constant, the house has perpetually been rebuilt several times over. That is the house you live in. As for the underground, the Lower Estate, that has been intact since it was formed.

475

When I focused on the Lower Estate's building, it too cost me a lot. Not so much in gold, but in lives. I could not afford for those engineers and miners who knew of its existence to be able to talk about it. I kept some of them on as familiars. The others, well, they became my first occupants of the *Stables of the Damned*.

This caused me some problems in that because they were not familiars and could not be accounted for by those who knew them, people came searching for them. It was an experience I learned from, and one that others could not.

*   *   *

For some years now, people had been working on the mines, connecting tunnels and shafts to existing caverns. Tayla had many engineers working on the project in secret. They had become her most valuable familiars such that she treated them as valuable property. She ensured they were afforded the best treatment, having the best living accommodations and food available. There were accidents along the way, as some were maimed while others were killed outright. Those who were maimed, she brought to the crossing over as then they would become whole. They could continue to work at night when all others would be resting. She wanted no waste of life or talent. It took several decades for the workforce to accomplish what she wanted and when they had accomplished the work to her satisfaction, it was 1880.

Surely, people who knew her might wonder why someone like Tayla could live with longevity as she did and not age like the other people did. Normally, that would have been the case, had not Tayla been given the gift of being able to change her appearance. For one generation, she was a quiet, reserved, and mysterious brunette, tall and slender, beautiful with dark eyes and long dark brown hair. She would drop out of sight for a while and then reappear as a redhead, petite, perky, athletic with green eyes. This Tayla was full of energy, bold, confidant and full of personality. Then, again, when this version of herself had entertained the generation of acquaintances and associates, she

476

would reinvent herself again, as a blonde, demure, maternal, kind, and sweet with a good nature that was pleasant to be around. All three were passed off as cousins to the same fortune that the Queen had amassed over the forty years she had already been in California.

Tayla saved her best engineers for the last part of her project of the Lower Estate. This was the tomb she wanted built that would last an eternity. It had already been there since the earth was formed it seemed and probably would last that much longer, she thought. It was perfect as it was far better than any of her brothers or sister were resting in during the daylight hours. Why should it not be? She was the Queen!

In the year of 1869, a former US Army Major engineer by the name of Petersen arrived one day, answering the call for experienced engineers. He had learned his craft at West Point, had served with distinction during the war and now wanted to apply his vocation according to the ad that had been placed in papers back east. When he was to meet the prospective employer, the reaction of hers was complete surprisal.

Tayla was now masquerading as the redhead version of herself. The Major Petersen was none other than the Eric Petersen who had worked a claim that was leased from her years ago. He did not recognize her, but she recognized him immediately. She did not let on that she knew him but asked many questions as to his qualifications and how he came by them.

"Well, madam, I had been a miner long before the war on these grounds no less. Although, this magnificent house was not here, I admit. I was a young man, who was fortunate enough to have met the most beautiful and charming woman who was kind enough to have leased to me, a claim alongside the creek north of here for mining. It seemed as if there was gold everywhere. In those days, people were happy to mine a mud puddle if they thought it would give up some gold.

I was fortunate to have been given a claim from which I managed to extract a small but ample sum of gold by which I used to get an education. I was accepted by West Point for my secondary education and in turn I served in the Union Army as an engineer officer. They put me in charge of fortifications at

477

one of the harbor forts. I saw little action but the experience of it all gave an insight of all the things possible through engineering. I found employment with the railroad that connected the east with the west. Now, that it is completed, I was no longer needed. When I read the ad about excavation here on this site, my curiosity was piqued. The lady I knew before, is she still here?"

Tayla wanted to change right before his eyes, but her restraint took hold. "No, I am afraid she is not. She was my cousin, but now she is gone. I have taken over her holdings in the family, and of course things have changed very much since you were here, Major Petersen."

"Oh, please Madame! Address me as Eric. Mostly I came back for I thought it would be a pleasure working for such a wonderful lady as she was. Might I inquire of her demise?"

"Eric," she paused, then began again, "My cousin was a woman of extreme passion. She had found someone whom she thought there might have been a chance of a more permanent relationship, but alas, she had to break it off. It broke her heart, and she pined away so hard I believe she died of it. But that was a long time ago. Now, you are here, looking for employment, I assume?"

The conversation went on for an hour. She told him of what she wanted to do, how it fit into her business plans regarding the storage of perishable items. He was a delight to talk with until Tayla finally asked the man if he was still interested in the job of overseeing the excavations still going on in the old mines, connecting the tunnels and such. He agreed to at least have a look and then to give an answer if such a task could be performed.

Tayla was delighted, for if Eric agreed, perhaps she could make him a familiar to her. But she knew that one day, that relationship would have to end, either by his death, or by his being brought to the crossing over. Eventually he would not be the same young man for whom she had fallen as a mortal. Another impossible dream she thought, much like the heartbreak she had felt when her French knight had fallen in battle. She asked herself if she was willing to go through that again. Her answer to herself was no. If she really loved someone, she would let them go on, to live the life they were meant to live. Though she had been denied that privilege, she felt she should not deny it to someone she cared about. It was painful, but necessary.

The next day, Eric Petersen went to where his old mining claim had been. The main shaft was very much in need of repair but still open. He asked one of her familiars if anyone had been inside the shaft in a while.

"No one in years, Mr. Petersen," was the reply.

"Which shaft have you been using to get inside?"

"Follow me, sir. Prepare to be amazed," was the reply from the familiar miner. He had been working there for over a decade for Tayla. It was his assessment that some parts of the mine complex were safe while others were mere death traps, waiting to be sprung on unsuspecting victims.

Eric Petersen came to the same conclusion about most of what he saw. He spent the entire day, walking about the mines, noticing that all the intersections had been marked so people would not get lost inside. His observations told him that would be easy to do. The familiar produced a crude map of the first level and an incomplete map of the second level. Eric had no idea that there was a third and fourth level waiting to be finished as well.

Later that night, he and Tayla dined together, along with some of the familiars. This was the beginning of the house staff dining with their Queen, a tradition that would carry on into the 21st century. He noticed that she called them by their "nicknames", a practice he had never seen before. Usually the wealthy do not dine with their staff, much less call them by their first name, let alone nicknames. But here, there were a lot of unconventional practices going on.

"You find this strange that my staff joins me at dinner?"

Eric was chewing when she said that and was befuddled as to how he should reply. Finally, he swallowed, saying, "Well...Why, yes! I do find it strange. I have dined with very high-ranking officers, and very wealthy men and their families in my time. I have never seen such a practice as this. However, I find it refreshing and interesting as those who put their hands into such projects as you have going on here, have the most interesting input into the topic of such conversations that will dominate during the meal. Bravo!" He continued to eat.

Tayla smiled. He had experienced many a hard day's work in his life. He was not pampered, nor was he privileged. Nothing had been given to him, that he had not already earned. Such a man should not be single she thought. "What a husband he would make! If only it could be..." she telepathed to her staff, particularly the females. They giggled and smiled in agreement to the Queen.

The next day, he went to the second level and down to part of the third. Again, he took all day to do so. He was so amazed at the scope of such a work. He was thinking of the possibilities of such a complex, particularly the ability to store things for refrigeration, like the chilling of wine, the storage of meat and such. It seemed the deeper they went, the colder it got.

At dinner that night, he announced that he was ready to give an assessment of her mine complex. And, that if the position of chief engineer were available, he would accept the position. Tayla was pleased, both with his assessment and his acceptance of the job. She insisted that he stay in the mansion as her guest so that he could give daily updates on the progress.

His stay at the mansion turned into quiet a lengthy one. Tayla kept him employed for quite some time, not just because she was fond of him, but also because he proved to be an incredibly good engineer. The first and second levels of the tunnel complex was completed by 1880, using a lot of cheap labor, most notably former workers of the railroad. A lot of them were Irish and Chinese. Many were accustomed to mining tunnels for the transcontinental railroad to pass through. This experience was valuable to the vampire queen and she took in every out of work former railroad worker that came to her.

When the third level of the Lower Estate was completed in 1882, she let go many of her workers. At least that was what they thought. At the first darkness, her familiars and her *Red Clansmen* rounded many of them up. They found them on the roads, camped for the night. Some were going south while others were heading north. Some were headed towards Nevada for the silver mines. No matter where they went, they were captured and

480

brought back. Down in the mines, a temporary holding pen was established. This was the beginning of the *Stables of the Damned*. It was a good thing she did for her clansmen examined the belongings of some of these men and found they had been keeping journals, describing the Lower Estate in detail. This was information that could not be afforded to get out into the public.

The fourth level of the Lower Estate still had to be completed and would take much longer. When you are a vampire, you are not known for being in a hurry. Patience is your strength.

The ones she kept on for work were the healthiest and the most loyal. The numbers were about fifty. They were the ones who never asked why they kept digging and connecting tunnels. When they were asked to continue to mine for gold in the tunnels, they found it easy for Tayla had directed the miners to dig in the direction of the gold veins. They mined for her interests, not theirs. One day, she asked them to come visit her at the mansion for a feast. It was to celebrate their collective good fortune. It also meant she had plans for them for she meant to enslave them as familiars. They were about to go where no one had ever been. They were about to begin the final level of Tayla's Lower Estate. The first to be brought into the fold was Major Eric Petersen.

The ritual of bringing in a human mortal to the level of familiar was complex yet simple. It required one drop of the monarch's blood and a kiss upon the lips for a mortal to become a familiar. They could have no other claim upon their soul. If they were a Christian, they were not a candidate. All these men were chosen for that one unique qualifier…there was not a true Christian amongst them. Of the hundreds that had been let go and were currently being rounded up, some of them were Christian. Being human cattle for the purpose of feeding vampires was not affected by their faith. Being transformed into a vampire certainly was but the vampires could never understand why.

Tayla nearly burst into tears when she made Eric a familiar. She wanted that kiss to last the entire night. When her lips finally separated from his, he saw her as the dark haired Tayla he had known years ago.

"Now, you understand, do you, my love?" she asked of him.

481

"I understand, you have come back to me. I loved you years ago, but I was just a miner. You would not have looked at me the same way you do now."

"On the contrary, dear Eric, I looked at you this way when I first saw you."

They talked more and then she explained she needed to perform the same ritual on the other men. Eric understood and was compliant and helpful. He brought the next man inside the room where the men were to fall under her spell. It went on until the last man was firmly under her control.

*   *   *

It was the fall of 1882. The first three levels of the Lower Estate were complete. The fourth and final level would be an engineering feat that would require some outside resources. As her chief engineer, Eric Petersen knew where to find them. This he did with the utmost efficiency. He managed to get the ear of the most accomplished excavators and spelunkers in the country. Tayla gave him a nearly inexhaustible budget with which to work with and the train of supplies and equipment came without delay.

He was able to do more without the huge numbers of men by focusing on one area of the complex and leaving the rest of the mined tunnels alone. In fact, he ordered at her request that all the rest of the open entrances to the mines be sealed up permanently. This meant one way in…and one way out.

The fourth level started out by digging a shaft directly under the house. She wanted an entrance that she could enter the Lower Estate directly from inside the house. The digging started and within two years, it was complete. They had dug a round, vertical shaft straight down of about five hundred feet, complete with a mechanical elevator run by a steam engine at the top. The shaft was about fifteen feet diameter across. The top portion was lined with stones and mortared in to form a wall that would prevent the soil from caving in. Eric Petersen, now a familiar with the code name of Hammer, did this to prevent the foundation of the house from eroding due to the soft soil above the bedrock. Hammer planned for every calculation and possible contingency. Tayla also had two side chambers built in for contingencies as well.

The excavation was dug down to where Tayla knew there was a natural cavern formation with passages already leading out away from the base of the shaft. This would be the only entrance used for entry into the Lower Estate for many decades, until someone would come along and give it the name of "Gates of Hell". Tayla had other escape routes made but they would require knowledge of which ones were only slightly sealed and those which were permanently sealed.

After the shaft was completed, the tunnels were connected to the third levels where most of the equipment for excavating had been pre-positioned. Once that took place, the real construction of the Lower Estate took off. It would last well into the Twentieth Century.

Hammer would work on this for Tayla until one day, he could not get out of bed. It was the fall of 1900. The weather had turned cool, with the leaves changing as usual. The harvests were in, the cattle herds had been taken to market back east. The mansion was in its most elegant state to date. All was good except for one thing. Tayla's chief engineer was ill. At the age of 69, arthritis had so debilitated him, that he could not stand without help. Hammer could no longer serve Tayla in his usual capacity. She had benefitted greatly from the thirty-one years of hard work from him. Now, she would have to make a choice as to what to do with him. That night, when she rose from her tomb on the underground lake, she already knew of his condition. He was in great pain. His knees and hips were of such he could not stand without pain, much less walk. He had hidden it well as he had been getting worse for quite a while, but Tayla knew he felt pain. He had worn himself out for her. She was grateful, but the choice needed to be made.

She came to his room and sat at his bedside. "Hammer?" she asked, "What can I do for you? I know you are in pain. You know there is a choice to be made here. Perhaps right now if you are ready. When we started, I told you how I felt about you. I still feel that way. I can make you as you once were, or I can take that pain away from you and let you go on to the next world. I cannot guarantee what that world will be. The known, or the unknown. That is the choice, and only you can make it. If you need time to think about it, I will understand. No need to rush such an important decision."

At 69, Hammer, aka Eric Petersen, was a well-worn man. The lines and wrinkles on his face of leathery skin, the grey beard and his silver hair told the story of a man who had worked awfully hard all his life. His hands and fingers showed his arthritis and now trembled when he tried to use them to write. It seemed as if his youth and strength had disappeared all in one night. Even the sparkle of his eyes had left.

His life was one of service, to his country as an army officer, and his Queen, as her chief engineer. He had performed well for her and now was ready to receive his reward. He received some pain medication from the physician who was also a resident familiar. Soon, he was resting peacefully.

She asked the doctor about his condition as a mortal. The physician said he might last a week. It was not just the arthritis that plagued his body, but his lungs were congested, and his heart was failing him. In short, the man who she had come to love was dying.

She went away that night, weeping for Eric. Depending on his answer, she was ready to bring him to the "crossing over". Would he change for the worst, as her brothers and sister had? Would he manage to hold on to some of his goodness as she had been able to do? So many unanswerable questions? If she let him go peacefully, she would mourn him, much like she had mourned Renard. The pain of the loss of the knight was as if it had happened last week. To go through all of that once more was not something she wanted to do.

She knew what she wanted to do. She wanted to bring Eric into her fold, as one of her brood. After all, the familiars all knew the reward for years of service was immortality. They had all talked about receiving that gift when Tayla said it was time. Many looked forward to it, seeing it as a great and most worthy reward.

Many familiars had come to see him but were turned away by the doctor who insisted he needed his rest. Many had known of

484

his debilitating condition and were now sad that he was not going to be with them much longer, at least not as a familiar.

Though Hammer was medicated for pain, his pain had not allowed him the comfort of sleep. His end was coming quicker than he had anticipated. In the weeks preceding this day, he had a lot of time to think of what he wanted Queen Tayla to do. It was true that he felt very fond of his Queen. So much so, that it was no secret that he was her favorite of familiars. And therefore, she had entertained him as no other woman could.

He wondered about the "unknown" she had mentioned and decided to ask questions about her death experience before giving her his answer. He told the doctor he wanted to talk to her at the first chance.

When she came to see him, he sat up as best as he could and had a conversation with her. He was feeling somewhat better for he had thought about his questions to ask. Time to prepare for what may come is hard to do when what may come is such an unknown.

"Hammer, my dear, I came as soon as the sun left the sky. You have questions. Perhaps I have answers. I know the first question you have. You want to know what dying is like, what my experience with death was about. I will tell you. At first, I was in a world of complete and utter darkness. I could not see, or feel, or hear. All my senses were of no use to me. I stood alone for what seemed an eternity, but there is no sense of time in that darkness. You have an awareness, but that is all. For me, the Dragon came to me in the darkness, and offered me and my siblings a choice. He illuminated some of the darkness which showed a river inside a large cavern. The river was of blood. I had to swim across it and by doing so I was transformed into a vampire. There were stairs leading up and out. I do not remember coming out of the cave, or even reaching the top step, for in an instant, I was forever changed. The next thing I knew was I was awake inside a box, a crude form of coffin, wrapped up in a tapestry of red velvet. Until I crawled out of that box, I was in complete and total darkness. It seems as if I have been descending into darkness ever since. It has been eight centuries since I saw a sunrise or sunset. My brothers and sister have said their experience has been exactly like mine. My father told me his experience was remarkably similar. So, there you have your answer. At least my answer. I do not know if your experience would be the same as mine. The origin of my death was at the hands of the Dragon. He has not been around here in quite some time. I know he is out there for he has always been with us, usually in the dark of the shadows, hidden away, waiting to take advantage of opportunities. Enough of him!

Have you decided yet? Once you pass, I cannot help you."

In a weak and raspy voice, he managed to say with clarity, "I want to live. I prefer to live a long time, like you. I fear the unknown, as I am sure you did. You were but a child, as were all of you when the Dragon put his evil against you. I have lived a full life as a man. I have enjoyed my life, hard as it was. I have seen great things, done great things. Now, I feel as if I have been running like a train, full speed ahead, hauling a great cargo, rushing to meet my deadline. Alas, I have run out of track. So much to do, so much more to see. I want to finish what I started, but I cannot like this. I can only do that if you take me."

A sigh of relief came from his lips as he exhaled. He had reached over and placed his hand upon hers. She remembered the last time when a man had touched her out of affection and trust. That man was Renard. She reminisced about when his lips touched hers, when his arms were wrapped around her waist as he had held her. If Eric became a vampire, of his own choice, perhaps they could have the love she so deeply craved. However, she worried about the effect of becoming forever changed. At least it would not be immediate change, but perhaps a gradual one, like her brothers and sister had. Alas, her brothers and sister had been so greatly influenced by the Dragon. Eric was hers.

"My dear, I shall make it as painless as I possibly can."

CHAPTER FORTY-NINE

CROSSING OVER

"Dearest Malcolm, it was with great joy and sadness that I brought Eric Petersen into the *Order of the Clan of the Red Velvet*. I did so out of love and, I must admit, out of selfishness. I loved him, and I was too selfish to let him go into the ground. I could not bear to be alone again, though I was surrounded by those of my kind, they were still vastly different than I was. I needed the companionship.

I was surprised to see that Eric came back to me not changed very much at all. I asked Eric if his experience was the same as mine. He said it was exactly as I had said mine was. The Dragon came to him and told him that if he went to the other side, he would be given immortality. If he stayed on the bank of that river of blood, he would be there until the judgement. Eric said that he was damned either way, so he swam over to the other side of the river, climbed up the stairs and on the third night, he awoke a new creature. I was delighted that he was much like me. He had much to learn and at first, I treated him as a child of mine, essentially a newborn. He eventually became my consort and lover. For the first time in my existence as a vampire, I was happy. And happiness, as we all know, comes and goes."

*   *   *

The word went out that the next day, Hammer would be taken to the "crossing over". It was a ritual that was seldom seen by familiars. Hence, there was a lot of mystery about it. Tayla had

487

decided that all of Hammer's friends could attend for they wanted to be able to say goodbye to their friend, the ingenuous engineer who had helped make all that they saw possible.

One by one, they came into his room, with letters of farewell from those who could write, and letters from those who could not write but written by those who could. It was a very touching moment, much like a farewell, but also a "congratulations, you made it!"

Eric, aka Hammer, told all of them he would remember them for as long as he could, and that he would see them again, soon. He had tears in his eyes, for he was joyful, yet fearful of what he still considered the "unknown". This was his last night on earth as a mortal.

Vampires and familiars both carried Hammer down to the large cavern which would eventually become the *Coliseum*. There, before a nearly packed cavern, Hammer would be taken to the crossover.

Tayla's throne was there. She was dressed in her robes of red, with her crown and scepter in her hand. She also carried a box with her. She addressed her clan, vampire and familiar alike.

"Brethren of the *Red Clan*, we are gathered here tonight to pay homage to a great man, familiar, engineer, and someone I have come to know and love very much. He has earned the right to be here, and I have offered what all my familiars have been promised for a lifetime of service. He is to become one of us, vampire. He shall be afforded all rights and privileges to which all my brood are entitled."

Tayla asked him if there were any words he wanted to express before he went through the process. He said he did.

Sitting in a chair to which he had been assisted, he addressed the cavern full of vampires and familiars alike. "My Queen, vampires of the *Red Clan*, my familiar brethren, I want to thank everyone for their support for all these years of service. My only regret is that I could not finish my work in this life. I look forward to the change that I am about to undergo. I understand I am doing this on my own will. It has been my decision to do so. I have not been coerced in any way. In fact, I was offered a choice, in that I am dying in this life. I made my choice and took

488

our gracious Queen's offer. These are my final moments of mortality. I have seen the sun for the last time and made my peace with this life. Let this life end as another one begins."

A vampire's nails are sharp. Nails can quickly turn into claws when necessary. But this time, the vampire's claws would not touch the mortal's skin. Instead, Tayla used her sharp appendage to lance her own skin. From the wound upon her arm, her blood flowed into a remarkably familiar cup. It was the same chalice from which she had drank from, centuries ago.

Long ago, when she had returned to visit the site of her death, she kept the cup she had found. The cycle was repeating itself. Only this time, the only blood that entered the vessel was Queen Tayla's. There was no trace of the first two vampire's blood there, nor was there any trace of her father's. The only tie between the vampires was the vessel, the ornate and antiquated chalice of gold and horn. Tayla knew the Dragon had possession of the other chalice for there had been two matching vessels, connected by the blood of vampires.

"Eric Petersen, this is the last time you as a mortal shall hear your given name. It is the name you were born with, and the only thing you shall return with when you come back to me as a transformed creature. You shall be a creature of the night. Time will no longer hold you prisoner, no longer subject to sickness, age, and infirmity. You shall fear nothing of the trappings of the mortal world. Power shall be given unto you, as gifts of abilities will be added to you. You shall be a blood member of the *Order of the Clan of the Red Velvet*, and I, Queen Tayla, Sovereign ruler of this clan, shall be your queen forever more. Drink of my blood from this cup, in love and in submission to me, and I shall give unto you my gift of immortality."

She gave him the chalice. He took it and raised it to his lips, closed his eyes, and drank it down. Within seconds she took the cup before he would drop it. Death came quickly to him.

His face became ashen, as the life began to leave his body. His expression became one of discomfort and then quickly became expressionless as he passed from life to death. As she had promised, it was quick. She had the doctor administer a pain killer prior to his transformation.

He was taken to a place in the cavern and laid out where he would lie in a state of death for three days. Then, on the evening of the third day, he would arise as a new creature.

When that time came, Queen Tayla was waiting for him to open his eyes. She wanted to be the first thing he saw as a newly created vampire. This was a special moment.

"Welcome to my world, my love. You can now fully understand my nature, my world that I have wanted to share with you for so long. Now, it has come to pass. All the wonderful things that I know of, am capable of, can be yours in time. Perhaps you at some time, may surpass even my powers. Come, we must feed. This may take some getting used to, but trust me, it will happen. I will tell you now, the first thing you must learn is discipline, self-control, and self-preservation. Literally speaking, you must learn to survive. Though you are now at the top of the food chain, it does not mean you have no enemies. Trust me, you have many."

Eric was a quick study. It did not take very much time for him to find his place amongst the *Red Clan*. Other clan members taught him things, many things, many secrets only a vampire knows, and remember, a vampire remembers everything. At first, Eric was eager to learn. The more he learned, the more he secretly questioned his choice. He did things he regretted, such as murder. His regret was quenched by his hunger being satiated. He wondered if it was the same for Tayla.

One night, while walking amongst the tunnels, he asked Tayla some important questions. She already knew of his feelings. "My Queen, these feelings I have, sometimes they make me feel as if I am at war with myself. Did you go through such feelings of confusion as this?"

"I still do, my love. Eric, when you crossed over the river, did you walk across on the bottom, or did you swim across?

He replied, "I swam, as you said you did. I believed you wanted me to do such a thing as well."

"That is curious, I must say. I swam for I knew how to swim, but my brothers and sister did not. Most of my clansmen do not as well. Perhaps they did but the Dragon must have told them to submerge themselves. Perhaps, that is what makes me different.

If so, perhaps you are to be different as well. I do not know. He did not tell me to immerse myself, but I instinctively kept my head above the blood. And you say you did as well?"

"Yes, my Queen, I did as well."

"Then, my love, we have something in common no other vampires have…a conscience."

Eric replied, "Sometimes I would rather not have one. It interferes with everything I do as a vampire. Now, I feel like I am two beings, always at war with each other."

"Yes," she replied, taking him, and putting her arms around him. She held him for the longest time, as he held her in a tight embrace. They kissed, long and passionately, as it was rare for Tayla to express herself romantically as she was usually accompanied by others. When their lips parted, she looked deep into his eyes, and said, "Yes, I know exactly how you feel. I am the same way."

"I am new at this, but you, well, you have had a long time to deal with this. How do you do it?"

"My love, seven centuries of this existence has taught me that there is nothing I can do to change my nature. You cannot change your nature either. You have heard me speak of the Dragon often, usually in a very disdainful way. It is because he is my enemy. He is your enemy as well. His name is Alejandro Valenzuela. Know him by his name. The Dragon will approach you at some point. He will try to woo you over to his side. Do not listen to him. He is evil and you will recognize it immediately. It will be because of your dual nature. You regret the sins of your vampire nature and your human nature reminds you of what you do and that it is wrong. My brothers and sister of which you will meet one day, have no problem murdering for a cup of blood. For them, it is as easy and natural as breathing was for us when we were mortal. I am grateful that part of your humanity is still intact. I tell you now, there is nothing in this world you can do about it. You simply must learn to exist in this world for here we are damned to stay. Do the good that you can, and only the evil that you must. I have always strived to do this, but it is difficult at times. The Dragon is your worst enemy. He will try to seduce you but know him for what he is. He is the Dark Lord's disciple

on this earth. His ambassador, his emissary, his messenger...
Beware of him and listen not to him, trust not in him. He will try
to take you away from me. He will do it to hurt me. I will not
let him, as I will do whatever it takes to keep him from you."

*   *   *

The crossing over of Eric Petersen dealt the Dragon a blow
which made him display anger few of his Jackal followers had
ever seen. From his headquarters in the jungles of Colombian
backcountry, he howled like a wounded animal. His forest
temple had been under construction for a while and was almost
completed. It was not an elaborate temple, but what was amazing
about it was that you could be standing right in front of it and not
know it was there. Made of the materials all around the
jungle...wood, vine, stones, mud...the camouflage was superior.
The only thing that seemed to be manmade was the altar. This
Dragon was very much a supporter of human sacrifice.

His grandfather was Ricardo Draco. Ricardo pretty much left
the *Red Clan* alone after he was told to leave the estate on the
night he visited. His son, a Dragon who was more of a builder
than a destroyer, built up the *Order of the Jackal*, organizing its
ranks, its logistical makeup and refining its doctrine. He had
recruited more than a thousand people of all types and
backgrounds into their organization. In short, he had created a
clandestine army. They kept their operations limited to the South
and Central Americas, but the Dragon never took his eye off the
vampire clans. He vowed that one day he would bring all of them
back into his fold, no matter what it would take.

This current Dragon would prove to be one of Tayla's most
worthy adversaries. Over the millennia, the Dragons of Set
always had one purpose in mind; to do the will of the devil, or
Satan, or Set as the Egyptians referred to the Dark Lord as. The
will of the devil has always been to thwart the will of God. It has
been said by many people that there is no God, but it is true that
even the devil believes He exists. This current Dragon, grandson
of Ricardo was determined to be the cleverest of all the Dragons.

The *Order of the Jackal* was well organized. They had established a library of their history, complete with a librarian and a historian. The historian was charged with the keeping of the history of the *Order of the Dragons of Set* which included the accounts of the high priestess Abinosekhat, and then the history of the *Order of the Jackal*. The Dragon who created the *Order of the Jackal* no longer had included a High Council. There was a council, but the Dragon no longer answered to them. Contrarily, they answered to him. The Jackal soldiers were accomplished criminals of all types. Some were just thugs while others were criminal masterminds. These high-level soldiers were experienced terrorists, assassins, saboteurs, and spies.

The Dragon and his Order had relocated to the jungles of Colombia but like any organization, they were chaptered all over the South American continent. By the mid 1930's, they numbered in the tens of thousands. Their greatest weapon of all was their secrecy. If one were to describe the rumors and the accounts of their rituals, they were usually dismissed as being far too fantastic to be real. Usually, they were considered fairy tales and the results of many who had let their imaginations run away. The next greatest weapon they had was they did not need to seek the support of the poor countryside. Instead, they were the ones most terrified of them, particularly when the local constabulary would not take them seriously regarding what they saw. The Dragon ruled through fear, his trademark, and savagery was the price paid for those who did not submit.

The Dragon had placed spies all over Tayla's business dealings as well as her estate. He was impressed at how well she had prospered when all she had to do was find victims, drink their blood while they still lived, and obey his commands as the emissary of the Dark Lord, master of the demons who resided in their dead bodies. It frustrated him to great discomfort that she would not submit herself or her kingdom to him. He knew the Dark Lord was growing impatient as they had entered the 20th century. What Tayla was up to did not fit into his or the Dark Lord's plans. Something would have to be done to bring her to her knees and submit her to the Dark Lord's will. Though he had not contacted her or her siblings, he needed to let them know who

493

he was and what his agenda was. It was time he reasserted his will over the race his ancestors created. As for the brothers, Rascha and Othar, he would appeal to their greed and thirst for power. As for Prieta, her weakness was the need for security. He would offer his protection for her loyalty. When it came to Tayla, greed and power would have no effect. She needed no security from him either. But he always believed that everyone had a weakness. As for her, he knew just where her weakness was.

CHAPTER FIFTY

BIRDSEYE'S VIEW

"Dearest Malcolm, Now, we are entering the century in which you would be born. Many fascinating things are happening. Inventions of things I never could imagine are coming about. Automobiles, airplanes, telephones, electric lights, all sorts of new and marvelous things. If my parents could have been able to see all the wonderful things…I do not think they could have comprehended it all. Alas, just when one thinks everything is doing well, a disaster happens. It always seems that way. Nothing good or great lasts forever. The Great War came along and with it, death, and misery. The maps of Europe were changed forever. From your view, I might think nothing good comes from war. Perhaps the only things might be the preservation of your ways and to not be subject to the ways of another. My brothers told me about the depravations of the Great War. It was robust with unspeakable horrors, but I would imagine the worst for a soldier was to be wounded, left for dead on the battlefield, only to open your eyes and find one of my kind about to finish you off. They delighted in putting an end to their misery. They said it was better to die in minutes than to suffer for hours or even days before death would take them.

I found ways to prosper despite the war. But my happiness was in being with Eric. Eric and I traveled everywhere together. Of course, we could only be seen at night, but we danced, and sailed, and flew. We went to parties, attended plays, concerts, and any event that was held at night, we managed to attend. Such great times together. I was never happier than when I was with Eric because I was in love. And, I know he loved me.

As before, I told you happiness comes and goes. In my case, it was about to be stolen from me. I saw it coming from afar, and I knew its source. I should have been able to stop it, but I could not. Even the first vampires had each other. In their previous life and in their afterlife, they had each other. They suffered the first death together as well as the second death. I know they must have loved each other so much.

Hatred and happiness are such opposites. My old adversary haunts me for breaking away from the grasp of the old Order. He let me know just how much he hated me for it."

*   *   *

The world had been through many crisis' since Eric Petersen had crossed over the line of life and living death. A world war, a disease pandemic, massive unemployment, and political/social unrest, and then the Great Depression which came about after the stock market crashed in 1929.

World War I proved to be a boom time for Prieta's clan. War was happening again all around her and her clansmen were feasting away on the wounded and the deserting soldiers, particularly on the Eastern Front. Othar's Purple Clan took over the same business on the Western Front. To Prieta's Blue Clan, it did not matter who they were, be they Russian or German, or any other nationality. When that sun left the sky, they fed on them easily. The *Red Clan* all but sat this conflict out.

When the Spanish Influenza pandemic came along at the end of the war, all the clans were able to take full advantage. The trick was to get to the dying before death took them. This was easy enough to do. The flu strain took tens of millions of lives. The world only thought it had seen enough death and misery for a while. It could not have been more wrong.

During the war years, thanks to Tayla's business managers, her shipping business flourished. The war did reach her interests. She lost many ships due to enemy submarines. Her ship line business eventually branched out to the shipbuilding business, for the demand of seaworthy vessels was high. This would again be proved years later during the fight against the Nazi Navy, the dreaded Kriegsmarine.

In the period between Eric's crossing-over, and the Great Depression, Tayla continued to build her Lower Estate, while refining and decorating her Upper Estate, notably the mansion, the carriage house, and the servant's quarters. These structures came after Eric's arrival into the clan, for he helped to design them along with the tunnels that provided access to them. Tayla wanted all the buildings of the Upper Estate to be accessible via tunnel for security purposes. Later, this decision would prove greatly beneficial for she felt that at some point in the future, be it near or distant, there would be an open conflict with the *Order of the Jackal.*

Because Prieta's clan had entered the arts and antiquities business, Tayla was able to acquire a lot of art treasures by which to decorate her mansion. Of course, her favorite treasure of all was the portrait by Da Vinci in her library above her fireplace. Tayla spent a lot of money acquiring art treasures and priceless furnishings to decorate her finished mansion. She also commissioned an artist to create the great stained-glass window of the large library-study. By 1920, the mansion looked like the residence of a Queen, though she never considered it her palace, for she did not conduct clan business there. Her brood were welcome to come into the mansion, but they never considered it their home as did Tayla. The mansion was hers and hers alone.

During the Great Depression, Tayla, like many wealthy Americans, lost a great deal of money. Fortunately for her, she knew the meaning of the word "diversify". She had stocks and bonds and other various financial products in her possession, but she also was sitting on a rich deposit of gold ore. When times became tough for other Americans, she was not worried in the slightest. She did not worry about losing her home, her property or her business'. Most of what she already had was paid for. There would be no foreclosures on her properties. Most wealthy people spend their lives acquiring wealth, possessions, titles, and such. Only to find at the end of their days, they cannot take any of it with them. As for Tayla and Eric, most of the time, they were either in each other's presence or tied telepathically to each other's minds. It seemed they never tired of each other.

Tayla's gift of sight told her bad times were coming for the entire world. She would turn some of her vacant properties into shelters for those out of work, or soup kitchens for the hungry. However, there was a dual purpose in this. From these sources, she could procure stock for her *Stables of the Damned*. Yes, she resorted to such things, for she felt that without her, many of these people would have starved. She only took the neediest or the unhealthy, those without any family to look after, anyone who would not be missed. When she had them, she fed them, cared for them, and kept them alive for purposes of feeding the clan.

Tayla considered this an act of benevolence. She was not without mercy or compassion, as would have been her brothers and sister. If they could have, they would have swooped down upon the crowd in misery and fed upon them without the slightest shred of pity.

But the world would survive all of this. The world was evolving fast because technology was exploding. It was advancing so fast. Travel, communications…it all made the world a much smaller place. A smaller place indeed.

After the war, the *Order of the Jackal* began infiltrating parts of North America. Now, it seemed as if the Dragon was preparing to make a move against the *Clan of the Red Velvet*. Queen Tayla needed a chief of security to head off the perceived threat. She found one. In 1922, she came across an out of work former soldier who had served during the Great War on the Western Front. He was a major, who had worked at the staff level of an Army Corps. Planning and Intelligence were his specialties. Queen Tayla brought him into the fold and he became the predecessor to what Dread would become decades later. His familiar name was to be "Birdseye" and he became exceptionally good at what she wanted him to do.

Birdseye had set up a headquarters in the same room that would one day be known as the "War Room". Whatever he wanted, he had Tayla's approval and budget for it. He had even asked for the authority to order vampires at his disposal for surveillance and intelligence collecting.

Birdseye found that the infiltration was far more serious than what was once thought. He began to set up the security and intelligence network that Anubis would later perfect. Instead of having an apparatus that would be expensive and costly to operate, he decided to tap into existing networks and use them clandestinely for their own gains.

Parts of his network included an elaborate spy network. He had familiars posted in jobs where they could keep tabs on a lot of people. He had them at train stations, at the airport, bus lines, on the docks and in the police departments. Each week, he would receive letters or if it were urgent, a phone call from anyone who had information they thought he might need to know about.

In September of 1927, just 2 years before the stock market crashed and the Great Depression was to begin, she met with Birdseye inside his headquarters one night. He had a staff of four, all familiars of course, who contributed to the operation of collecting and analyzing data to finding answers to questions that would affect the security of the estate.

"You have something to tell me, my chief of security?" she glided into the room with the ease and grace of a cloud. Then, she sat down in a comfortable chair, ready for her intelligence briefing, as if she did not know what he was about to tell her.

"My Queen, I have news. Since you have made me your chief of security, I have taken steps to keep you aware of any threat. There are many signs that tell us the *Order of the Jackal* seem to be encircling us. I think they are up to something big, but this encirclement seems to be for surveillance for the time being. We detect outposts or observation posts here, here, and here, with others being built here, here and here," he said, while using a pointer to show locations on a map of the county of Glenn, California.

"And what might you say draws this conclusion?" she asked.

"I sent out a team of security as well as a scout team of clansmen. What they came back with were pictures of this. I have more photos I am ready to develop but these were what drew my attention to think they have us under surveillance."

He placed photos in front of her on the table. She viewed them with a keen eye as her hands moved them. "I see cameras,

499

radio equipment, binoculars, and something else. I do not know what that is. How long has this been going on?"

"We discovered this in the last year. As to this device, neither do I know it's purpose, but I think it is a device for tracking the flight path of our vampires. If this is true, then they will know the entrance to our Lower Estate. If so, then they can come into the tunnels to find the Cavern of Crypts and destroy you and your clan while they sleep. If you will notice, they have a direct line of sight over the ground where the shaft entrance and exit is. If they find it, we are compromised."

"I believe you are right, Birdseye. Good work. We shall have to work fast if we are to remedy this."

"My Queen, I also have information that confirms each one of these outposts are equipped with weapons specifically designed for combatting an assault by vampires. We must proceed with extreme caution."

"I think everyone in my brood usually flies in a straight line. Even I have never thought to fly in any other pattern. We need to get this information to the other groups of the clan."

"I have already done so, my Queen. They are linked in with us via telephone and their familiars are taking steps as well."

"Someday, Birdseye, we will be able to keep in touch minute by minute, around the clock, to tell everyone if there is a threat. I can see this in the future, but it is off in the distant limit of my vision. For now, we have to rely on what we have."

*   *   *

As it turned out, the *Order of the Jackal* was planning something. Birdseye had accurately predicted their plan. The Dragon wanted it known that submission to the Dark Lord and his disciple was not a choice. It was mandatory that they all be brought under the power of the Dragon or face the consequence. That consequence was simple; the destruction of all those who would not submit.

At the end of the war, the Dragon was frustrated that he felt he had to do what his predecessors were not willing to do. The *Red Clan* needed to be eliminated and the best way to do it was to kill the Queen. To do it, they would have to find her at her most vulnerable time. Laying a trap for a vampire is a tricky thing to do. It would require bait and there was only one bait that could draw Tayla out of her fortress...Eric Petersen.

This Dragon was determined to leave nothing to chance. He knew that his adversary was up to the task of thwarting his primary move of eliminating the Queen. Her fortress was built for that purpose alone. Survival of the vampire Queen and her *Clan of the Order of the Red Velvet*. To the Dragon, it seemed she was still attached to the old world in many ways. Traditions, heritage, and such were very much a part of the vampire's organization. Even the idea of a monarchial system seemed archaic. But not to her or her vampires. All of it explained why some things were and other things were not. If he were to succeed, he most likely would get only one chance if any.

The Dragon had been watching the estate for quite some time. He also had teams watching the other bands of vampires across America. There were quite a few of them, usually in groups of twenty-five or less. Nonetheless, his focus was on the estate. He knew that if he could kill the Queen, the rest of the clan would die the moment the sun came up. He knew the rest of the clan drew its life from the life of the Queen. If the Queen were to be terminated, so would the rest of the clan follow her. To the Dragon, the only worse threat than a vampire was one that was not under his power.

For the *Order of the Jackal*, they too had employed certain systems for clandestine operations that were like the ones the vampires used. In short, they were copying a lot of their ways. The Order needed to stay underground and could not afford the knowledge of their existence to become known. Oaths of loyalty and secrecy contained words that were spells that ensured obedience and secrecy amongst its members. Violence and the threat of violence kept most of its members adhering to its policies. Most of all, an indoctrination of the deepest kind took place amongst all its new members, to ensure that they would become old members.

The Dragon and the Order were in full support of blood sacrifice. Whether it be animal or human, they practiced it for they believed it demonstrate to the Dark Lord that they were devoted and dedicated to his cause. Every full moon, blood was shed on the altar of the Forest Temple located in the Colombian jungle. Not everyone was required to attend, but the knowledge of it was observed by all members.

In 1925, the Dragon began to study his target. Tayla was not the target just yet. His intended target was the bait, Eric Petersen. He wanted to know everything about him, for he already knew that Eric was a creature very much like Tayla. It would take four years for him to get into position to strike.

He learned that Eric had a benevolent side to him as did Tayla. His malevolent side could be brought about if one worked hard at it. Mostly, he was not much different than he was when he was mortal. It was easy to understand why Tayla had fallen in love with him. He had the capability of returning that love with his own. As a vampire, he had matured. He was happy…something that did not sit well with the Dragon. He was happy he felt none of the pain he had before he had crossed over. His newfound strength and youth enabled him to work harder and faster than he had ever been able to before. His work ethic had built the self-esteem that lingered upon the character of Eric.

In the early years, Eric was eager to learn everything. Learning survival was easy when your companions are all veterans. At night, when Eric would go out, he was schooled on how to get along in public, the use of social camouflage, and basically just blending in with mortals. He was taught what worked and what did not work. Sometimes he went out with other vampires and sometimes he was with Tayla when she had no other duties that required her attention.

The Dragon was looking for a pattern. When he would find one, that would be the point for which he would start planning his attack. It is not a good thing to be predictable. When it comes to vampires, they are predictable only on several points. First, they sleep during the day, and roam at night. Secondly, the must feed upon the living. Other than that, it is difficult to know exactly what they will do. In the case of Eric and Tayla, the Dragon knew they retained their human souls. Because emotion is derived from the character of the human soul, it can be either weakness or strength. That was what the Dragon intended to use to his advantage.

As Queen Tayla had familiars and vampire lieutenants, the Dragon followed suite with his own. One of them was a particularly mean and wicked one whose Jackal name was Scimitar. He was a blade waiting to be released, an assassin who is a weapon. It was to be his task, to take out Eric Petersen, even if it meant that it would lead to his death. Scimitar accepted the task as if it were meant to be an honor. Scimitar was of Arab descent. His father was also a Jackal. Scimitar had been groomed in the arts of death and murder since he could read and write. His entire life was about how to kill without remorse. To say that Scimitar was something of a sociopath would have been an understatement. He did not fit the description of psychopath, for he had good judgement. His grasp of reality was surprisingly clear and rational. He lacked any resemblance of a conscience so therefore, in terms of DNA, he was the perfect human killing machine.

A master of martial arts, he was skilled in several styles of lethal hand to hand combat. He was also a master of the sword, particularly the Samurai and the Scimitar. He was the equivalent of the Japanese Ninja, only he did not look evil, mask or not. He could be standing next to you with a completely nonchalant appearance, the epitome of "normal" and all the while, he has figured the many vulnerable points about you. He looked about thirty, dressed very normal, with dark hair, and trimmed beard of black. His dark eyes and olive complexion suggested either Hispanic or Middle Eastern. With an IQ of 175, he had many non-lethal talents, to include a photographic memory and speaking several languages. As charming as he was ruthless, if you were the intended target, he would get to you. His ability to charm, to blend in, to assimilate was unparalleled. Scimitar was a chameleon. At the same time, he was a ghost, difficult to defend against, impossible to study, and devoid of emotion. He was as close to a vampire himself without crossing over the line.

Educated with several degrees to include chemistry and engineering that enabled him to accomplish his missions, he was a master of improvisation. Able to make split second decisions as if he had all the time in the world to study and analyze before devising a plan was one of his strongpoints. To the Dragon, Scimitar was his weapon of choice.

CHAPTER FIFTY-ONE

SCIMITAR

"Dearest Malcolm, it is autumn of 1925. Your kind called this the "Roaring Twenties." This was a time that was particularly difficult for Eric and me. I knew the nature of the Dragon better than anyone else on earth...perhaps even better than those in the *Order of the Jackal*. What the Dragon is capable of and what methods he will employ to get his way are the same. To put it mildly, whatever it would take to subdue me, bring me to my knees and acknowledge him as master, that was what he was perfectly willing to do. There were no limits to the evil he would commit.

I should have sent Eric away or better yet, gone after the Dragon. As for Eric, he would see the end of his days. I knew that the Dragon would come after him and no matter what the cost, he was willing to pay it to take Eric away from me. At first, I thought he might try to seduce my lover and use Eric to betray me. The evil one had other plans. He knew how much I loved Eric and how much Eric loved me. To the Dragon, happiness and contentment were not to be tolerated amongst vampires. Our lives, if you can call them that, were to be devoid of hope, happiness, and fulfillment. He wanted us to only have despair, loneliness, and darkness. That was his rule. He had never specifically told us that, not even when we were young vampires, but over the centuries, it was not hard to discern that this was the existence the Dark Lord intended for us. The gifts were to be used for his purpose and given only for our appeasement.

I had tried to be happy in my state of existence, and with Eric, I found that I could be. I would have gladly laid down my life for him. I believe he would have for me as well. That made the Dragon so angry, so hateful, he declared war on me and the *Order of the Clan of the Red Velvet*. Therefore, I had to organize my Clan into an army, ready and able to defend itself. I had already decreed that the vampire clans should never war against each other. My brothers and sister had promised me they would never raise a hand against any members of any other clan. They were to discipline and punish only members of their own. Up until nearly the end, I was able to hold them to their word of honor. Again, the Dragon…"

*   *   *

It was autumn of 1925. The assassin Scimitar visited the observation post regularly, at least every few days. The post had been established for nearly two weeks. He read all the notes about the comings and goings of every winged creature seen in flight over the suspected opening to the Lower Estate. Today, he arrived early just after dawn at the outpost. It was on the opposite side of the creek that ran across the northern boundary of the estate. After giving the bona fides to the Jackal lookouts, he was granted permission to approach.

In a quiet voice, just above a whisper, he asked, "Good morning, my friends. How are we? Brought you both something!" He produced two thermoses of hot coffee along with a bag of donuts from a local bakery in town. The two Jackal observers devoured the delicious treat and relished the coffee. The two lookouts knew of Scimitar, the dashing young man dressed in hunting clothes. His reputation preceded him everywhere in the world of the Jackal.

"I know it is difficult to stay awake when you are bored looking at the darkness turn to sunrise. This should help a lot."

"Thank you, Scimitar," one said. "What we saw last night was more of the same. We can usually see details only in the light of a full moon. We cannot take photographs of them because of the darkness and because they are vampires. Not too long ago, just before the first light of dawn, the last of them returned to go below."

"That is why we must rely on your eyes, my friends," Scimitar replied.

"The path they seem to fly is one that lines up with that slight bend in the creek. We can show you the direct azimuth from where we first see them fly, and if one is there at the bend, you can work backwards. The two lines will cross and there I believe you will find the shaft entrance."

"He is correct, Scimitar," the other answered. "We have watched for two weeks and it is the same, without change. We have established a pattern."

"No!" Scimitar interrupted. "They have established a pattern. You have merely discovered it. Good for you. It gets cold here at night, windy too. I will keep the coffee coming. When is your relief due?"

"Soon, I expect. We will complete our report and send it up the chain."

"No need! You have already done so. I want to have a look around. Anyone patrolling around that hidden shaft?"

"We have seen nobody."

Scimitar made good use of the early morning light, for it was dim, and a mist made visibility difficult. He walked as silently as a deer in the forest, making little if any sounds at all. He found the bend in the creek, and then, forded it with great care. The current was not too strong, but the temperature of the water was bitterly cold.

He came out of the water on the other side of the creek and continued in a straight line. He was using a compass to keep his bearing on the point where the points of observation should cross. It was an easy task to find the shaft though it was a small opening, barely wide enough for a man to lower himself down into. The camouflage was well done, appearing as natural as could be.

He had brought a camera with him to take photos. First, he had to clean off the lens for the change in temperature caused condensation to immediately cloud the lens. There was no need for a flash. He took many pictures of the shaft, from every direction along with the compass showing the azimuths from the

507

hole to landmarks so anyone with the photos could find the shaft. He had not discussed anything else with the two lookouts but wanted to get the camera back to the lookouts who were about to be relieved. The photos were important to get developed in case his plan did not work.

He brought the camera and the lens back to the lookout. Then, he took one of them with him along with some climbing equipment to the shaft. The lookout tied the rope to a tree while Scimitar fashioned a Swiss seat (climbing harness) out of another piece of rope. He put on some gloves, taking a flashlight and a .45 caliber M1911 pistol with him.

The lookout asked him if his ammo was of silver. Scimitar replied, "Of course. I did not get this mission because I am careless. I just hope I do not have to use it."

"That is good, senor Scimitar. Because I do not think you have enough bullets that you are going to need."

Scimitar smiled. He understood the lookout did not understand his methods. That was fine with him. He had no time to explain. He prepared himself to descend into the darkness.

The opening was small but had just enough room for a man of slender build to descend into a deep, dark hole. The assassin had no idea of how deep this shaft might be. He knew that miners always dug back shafts for air, in case of cave-ins and such.

This was the vampire's entrance to the Lower Estate. From a distance, the lookouts had watched the shaft personally and observed the vampires coming out in a mist, transforming into winged creatures, half human, half something else. The opening would glow as the mist would reach the top of the shaft. Then, the glowing greenish-white mist spewed out across the ground, almost like a ground fog that hugged the surface surrounding the opening and the creatures would appear out of it.

While some appeared like humans with the wings of a bat, others were a bit more frightening. Whether by choice or by nature, these were creatures with the appearance of the gargoyles that sometimes were perched atop cathedrals built during the middle ages and the Renaissance. Some looked like deformed birds of prey, buzzard-like or dragon-like. Either one was frightening enough for anyone to meet in the dark of night.

508

Vampires do not usually attack in the form of the creature they fly as. The normal modus operandi is to transform back into the human form before taking a victim.

Meanwhile, Scimitar was thinking this was the most difficult assignment he had ever had. The Dragon was bold to send him into such a dangerous place, but the Dragon was the leader, the one with the power. Scimitar also knew that refusing was not an option. He took pride in knowing that the Dragon trusted him and him only to be able to accomplish this task.

The Dragon had always considered the possibility that Eric Petersen might have been sent away for his own protection. This was why the *Order of the Jackal* had surveillance on all the other bands of *Red Clan* vampires across the United States. He concluded that Tayla and Eric had the relationship that would make them want to be with each other all the time. In short, they were essentially married, happy and content. The Dragon hated all of that. Vampires were not created for any of that. They were created to serve the Dark Lord and that was the only reason they existed. If they did not serve the Dark Lord, they were to be eliminated or replaced with vampires who would submit and serve.

All the intelligence collected pointed out that Eric Petersen was down here, somewhere, along with an unknown number of super-predators who, when the sun left the sky, would begin hunting him. This meant only one thing to him, find Eric Petersen before anyone else found him.

Due to their heightened senses, the vampires would detect the scent of a human inside the shaft, and they would know who it was. Then, they would go hunting. Scimitar had no doubt they would find him for it was what he wanted them to do. If he could not penetrate the Lower Estate, then he would draw them out.

The two lookouts he had been so nice to did not pretend to know his plan. They knew his mission, but they were not privy to his method. They knew when the vampires were released from the Lower Estate, they would pick up the scent of a mortal intruder and immediately go into the defensive posture. If they determined that the penetration was not deep enough to look for the intruder in the Lower Estate, then they would seek him on the

509

surface during the hours of darkness. The first mortals they might encounter were the two lookouts at the observation post. This did not set too well with them.

The two lookouts discussed what they would do after darkness. "It is not our problem. The two that are on duty have this problem. We will be sleeping, safely away from here."

"Should we tell our relief when they come on duty?"

"Yes, of course. But we are not staying here. We need to get this film developed. They can take care of themselves. They have weapons to defend with. Probably not enough, but they will take some with them."

Their weapons consisted of sawed-off shotguns with plenty of shells that the shot was of pure silver. This would enable them to defend themselves well without the necessity of having to aim at the living dead. Each weapon could carry six shots each due to not having a plug. The shortened barrels enabled them to have a wider spray pattern.

Their relief, consisting of two other Jackal soldiers arrived within minutes. They were given a report of the situation and that Scimitar was in the shaft, working his way down into the Lower Estate.

"Scimitar is here. He is eager to get started so he is down in the shaft we found. You need to be vigilant in case he needs to come out. We have film that needs to be developed. I suspect you might have encounters tonight before we relieve you. Stay strong, stay alert! Good luck!"

Scimitar managed to get about twenty feet or so down the shaft before it became impossible for him to descend any further. He would have to find another way into the Lower Estate. He managed to get himself out, with the help of the two lookouts who knew he was going down the shaft. He managed to get out within a few hours of sunset. Those remaining hours of daylight passed by slowly. Scimitar remained at the post for a while, telling the two lookouts what they must do.

"Staying on sight is essential to this mission's success. To draw the vampires out, they had to have a point to gather towards. My scent will lead them to here. I have no doubt the vampires are aware of our presence already. It is not like we have been

510

trying to hide it too well. Why have they not attacked this outpost already? Probably because we have not tried to probe into their territory yet. Today, that has changed. Now, the scent of a mortal is inside the shaft leading to their stronghold. This will provoke them to give a response. They may come in an aggressive manner, willing to kill without question. If so, I want you to be prepared for them. I have this straight from the Dragon. He tells me these weapons will stop them. Silver is their enemy, as is sunlight. We cannot use the sunlight, but we have silver. Each of those shells contains silver shot. A crucifix will repel them but not kill them. We cannot use crucifix's because we are not Christian. We cannot use holy water for the same reason. We also have crossbows, which have silver tipped bolts. These will kill also. When you see them, if you are lucky enough to see them first, I suggest you not ask questions but strike first, take as many of them as you can. There is one named Eric. Take him out if you can. He will be one who asserts authority. If he makes his presence known, I will make my move on him but if you can take him out first, then do so. I will not be angry if you do before I can get to him."

"Will we get any reinforcements or are we just bait?" asked one of the lookouts.

"Tonight, we are on our own. At best, you might be decoys. Tomorrow, there will be reinforcements that will descend upon the entire estate. This is to be a minor skirmish. If you must fight, make every shot count. If you run out of ammunition get to your car, and drive as fast as you can. There is more ammunition in your car. I will be in hiding so they will be focused on you two and will not realize I am waiting in the shadows, ready to strike. Steel yourselves well, gather your courage. For this will be the fight of your lives."

The assassin disappeared into the woods to find a choice spot from which to attack from. The two lookouts grabbed the shotguns, which were already loaded, and cocked the crossbows.

As the sun began its descent below the horizon, the lookouts wondered if they would ever see it again. The match had been struck, the fuse had been lit. Now, they waited for the response of the *Red Clan*.

CHAPTER FIFTY-TWO

WAR IS UPON US

"Dearest Malcolm, I had destroyed the *Order of the Dragons of Set* in one night. I was merciless and cruel, but so was my enemy. I felt that was the way to meet them, on their own terms in their own ways. Knowing the Dragon as I do, I am sure he never forgot that.

I and my clan would be able to meet them head on. There were disadvantages though. I was only alive during the hours of darkness. The autumn was affording me more time for nighttime activities than during the summer. The *Order of the Jackal* could operate day or night.

Eric had foreseen this and knew that the deeper my lair was, the safer I would be, for they would not find me in one period of dawn to dusk. If they were in the Lower Estate, at some point, I would awake and then they were mine. This happened several times. Therefore, I made the Lower Estate essentially a labyrinth. I also had many pits and booby traps built so that if they did get deep and I did not get to them first, perhaps the traps would slow their advance against me.

My familiars had to be trained to defend against them during the daylight hours. Birdseye hired and trained a force of mercenary soldiers whose loyalty was to me and me only. He equipped them well, and they trained for the fight I knew was coming. Most of them were veterans of the Great War and found this was what they did better than anything.

I half-desired a message from the Dragon to have a meeting or something with me, but I received nothing. His silence was a message itself that war was upon us, and that we should prepare. I knew the Dragon would be after Eric so when my clan moved through the shaft that night, I ordered Eric to stay behind. I picked up on the scent immediately when I got close to the exit of the shaft. I knew I was on the threshold of a war I did not want. Perhaps I was too cautious."

*   *   *

The sun was nowhere to be seen and the only light was from a fading twilight of pink and purple hues in the cloudless sky. The wind was blowing from the west as a gentle breeze. Some of the stars had already come out and twinkled faintly in the darkening blue. Scimitar had taken a position some distance from the bend of the Stony Creek. He lined himself up the azimuth of the shaft opening, so when the flock of flying creatures came out, his blasts of shot would strike them in the air, causing them to burst into flames. He wore two bandoliers of shells, crisscrossing his chest along with extra clips of ammunition for his .45 pistol at his side.

Soon, as expected, a glow could be seen from across the creek on the southern side. In a few minutes, all hell would break loose, for the vampires would know something was not right. A greenish-white fog, came billowing out of the opening in the ground, spilling onto the brush around it. Within moments, ten human figures could be seen silhouetted against the mist. The first one to be seen was a woman. She wore no wings and did not fly up into the air. It was the Queen herself!

Tayla had detected the scent, just as Scimitar had expected. He had hoped she was not accompanying the group. That might have given him the chance to take out Eric before things got out of hand. It did not go as he had planned. Now that someone had penetrated the shaft, he hoped it would put her and the clan on the defensive, making them think twice about leaving the caverns below at night. He wanted them to feel hunted. If Tayla was here, surely Eric would not be too far away.

From his position, using the light from the glow of the fog, he could count only ten vampires who had come out. He was not

513

afraid, and therefore he was not giving off the scent of fear. He wished his lookouts could do the same.

When the fog cleared, the vampires stood in a circle, staring outwards as if setting up a perimeter. Queen Tayla had been the first one to come out of the shaft. Standing motionless like statues in a garden, their heightened senses would detect anything living within a short distance.

Scimitar knew they could detect his presence almost immediately. However, he was not like the rabbit who would run when the fox appears. He was the fox, who lay waiting for the rabbit to make a mistake. His prey was Eric, but he did not see Eric anywhere amongst those of the undead. A slight smile ran across his face as he knew he was in a battle of wits with the Queen herself. She was his ultimate target. If he could take her out with his silver ammunition, so much the better. He could take down the entire *Red Clan* and that would be fine with him as he knew the Dragon would be so pleased.

He would lay there, silent, still. His only movement was his chest rising and falling with each slow and cautious breath. After a while, more vampires came out to feed, flying off in several general directions. Tayla and her original ten stayed at the entrance to the shaft, guarding it against whoever the scent belonged to.

Tayla had never met Scimitar before but she had heard of him and his fearsome reputation. He of course had never met her either. Neither looked forward to that meeting, for Tayla understood the meaning of immortal, which was not the same as invincible. She knew vampires had limitations.

If it were just her that the assassin was after, it would be different. She knew she could find him within minutes, but she knew she was not the target. She already knew her enemy's strategy. It was not to destroy her, but to hurt her, to cause misery, to remind her who was to rule the shadows and who she should be subject to. Tayla would never kneel to the Dragon, nor would she ever let anyone she loved to be taken from her.

If she had to guard the entrance all night, she would. Vampires have the last word on patience. It is innate to them.

514

She called out to the assassin, "Scimitar, I know you are out there. I know where you and your Jackal compatriots are. Come out! Let us face each other! I will give you safe passage from here. No harm has been done yet, so I can forgive your trespass. Should you persist, I may have to change my mind about that. Come out!

One of the Jackals broke silence and called out, "We are ready for you! Come and get us!"

Scimitar knew one of them would break silence easily and give away their position. He watched two vampires in red robes disappear swiftly and silently as they came up behind them. They took the weapons from their quarry before they had a chance to react. The Jackal soldiers looked into the eyes of the creatures who opened their jaws revealing the fangs by which they would die. The fear they exerted made them a tasty meal for their killers.

Soon, he heard them cry out in terror as the vampire's fangs sung into their necks and drained the life from them. He had anticipated the fear and instability of the two Jackal observers, predicting they would act as they just had. They had not failed him. He preferred to work alone but this time he needed the distraction.

Tayla shouted out to Scimitar again. "Your compatriots told us to come to them. We obliged. As you might have guessed, they have regretted giving their position away. They were prepared to do us harm. Is that your intent as well? If you leave your weapons where you are, I will guarantee you safe passage. You know how we feel about self-preservation. This is your only chance. Come to me, let us talk."

The assassin knew he would never get off a clean shot at the vampire Queen. She would be anticipating it for she had already locked into his mind, anticipating his every move. Scimitar had no choice but to trust her at her word. He stood up and left his weapons at his feet, then began to walk to the creek. It was a little bit of a walk, but he crossed the creek and walked to the figures dressed in red robes.

When he walked up to them, he was impressed by their appearance. It was the first time he had seen any *Red Clansmen*

515

up close. Their clothing was odd for the day, but they looked like regular mortal people, at least for the moment.

"Good evening, Scimitar. We finally meet. I know the reason, but I want to hear it from your own voice. Why are you here?"

"I am sent by the Dragon, for the purpose you already suspect."

"That purpose is to destroy my love, Eric?"

"Yes, to destroy Eric."

"And me as well, I assume?" she asked.

He nodded that it was so. She knew he had no choice but to do the will of the Dragon.

Quietly, but firmly, she said, "I cannot allow that, Scimitar. Tell your master you have failed, tell him that it will serve no purpose. For if you are successful against Eric, you will certainly die, and the Dragon will never see me on my knees before him. We will be at war, and many Jackals will die. If I could kill the Dragon, I would have done so a long time ago. I wish for no war. Only to be left alone to be who and what I am. Why can your master not allow that? Can he not create another vampire who will be subservient to him, as he did long, long ago?"

"Queen Tayla, my master wants you to serve him. He already has the alliance of your brothers and sister. They have an uneasy peace with him. But it is you…, you are the prize he is after. I have been given the assignment to do that which will bring you to your knees."

"Killing Eric? Well, at least you have been honest with me. I guaranteed you safe passage. Leave this place. If you come back, I will not guarantee the same again. If your master wants war, then he shall have it. Tell him to be careful of what he wishes. I bid you farewell."

As she watched him walk away, she tried to see into the future. The reputation the assassin had made her feel uneasy for he was accustomed to working within the realm of the supernatural. Terminating mortals of any kind, straight up civilians or even members of other cults was a specialty of his.

Her gift of sight did not see any foreboding event coming soon. But then, she thought, it could be the Dragon was blocking

516

it by consulting with the Dark Lord to limit some of her powers. If that were true, then the Dark Lord could just simply summon the demon that resided in Eric's body to leave it and Eric would drop like a stone to the cavern floor. Either way, her heart would be broken. The Dragon would have his way after all. Still, she was resolved to never serve the Dragon in any capacity, willingly or unwillingly.

When Scimitar left the area, he breathed a sigh of relief. He was thankful that Queen Tayla had a sense of honor about her. If she promised something, she would deliver. It was a characteristic he considered a weakness, but then, there is no honor among those of his profession. Honor is something that makes one predictable to their enemies. He felt he could not afford such a trait. Neither could he afford a conscience. It did make him wonder at times who was the most dangerous, an assassin such as himself and others he knew of his profession or the vampires themselves. Even vampires had to play by the rules. He had declared that he did not.

The fact that he had to sacrifice two loyal Jackal soldiers to perform his mission did not bother him in the least. As far as he was concerned, the end justifies the means. It was necessary for him to get close to the clan members and to lay eyes on the Queen. She was every bit as beautiful as he had heard.

He had gotten exactly what he had gone there for, which was information. He had considered Tayla might already know what he was up to. Now, he knew for sure. It meant they would take defensive steps and be waiting for any offensive action. Waiting for Eric to come outside the fortress was highly unlikely, making his assignment more difficult. He knew the only way he would be able to terminate Eric Petersen was to go into the Lower Estate itself and find him. That was a suicide mission at best, he thought to himself. Those were the kind of missions he was best suited for.

CHAPTER FIFTY-THREE

FIRST WAVE

"Dearest Malcolm, these last few years of the 1920's were busy ones. My estate, both upper and lower, were getting their finishing touches. The *Coliseum* construction had begun and would continue all the way up until just before I would meet you. The *Hall of Skulls* was also being worked on. As for my tomb, it had been finished before any of the other specialized caverns were started, thanks to Eric.

The shaft we used to exit the Lower Estate nightly was modified so that it was made to serve as a vent shaft, too small for any human to climb down in. Of course, the Upper Estate mansion was continuously being upgraded with the modern conveniences of the times.

The assassin Scimitar was about to find out that neither I nor my vampires had been idle, thinking we were invincible. We had taken steps to protect ourselves, for we all knew that once the Dragon had set the wheels in motion, there was no stopping him without some great effort on our part."

*   *   *

For several years, Scimitar had planned for the termination of Eric, but he wanted to do it in such a way that fit in with his master's desires. Then, the chance of a lifetime came to him in which if he had planned better, he could have taken the Queen at the shaft close to the creek. The Dragon heard of his missed opportunity and was angry, disappointed, and growing impatient.

He continued to access information that would lead to a successful end to his mission but Queen Tayla was more than a match for the assassin. She would block most attempts of the assassin to access entry to the Lower Estate. She really did not think he would attempt to assault the vampires in their own lair.

He managed to get blueprints of the house from the property appraiser of the county along with the information about the property from the county tax collector. All the old mines were found to have all been sealed at the entrances.

He spoke with the company that had installed the elevator. They still had copies of the plans of the house, the dimensions of the shaft and the plan of the car, and the winch that would lower and raise the car.

He was recalled to Colombia to meet with the Dragon to give a progress report. The Dragon was not pleased that so much time had already gone by without results. The Dragon lived on a plantation, dominated by a large main house. The signature of wealth was everywhere. The two met in the Dragon's private office.

"Scimitar, it has been three years since I gave you this task. Yet, Eric Petersen is still alive. Tayla is not under my influence. I am not pleased. What have you to say for your lack of results?"

"My master, the task you have given to me is one of which there may be only one chance to succeed. Therefore, I am taking such steps that must be carefully planned, so that success is attainable. Timing is critical. All factors must be favorable. This is no ordinary task of my profession. Any mortal would have been terminated long ago. But this target is one that is not alone. How can I kill one without killing them both? They can read my thoughts, analyze my actions and with a higher than usual intellect, predict my next move. It will be difficult to meet your demands without incurring failure. A full assault would seem out of the question, but it could serve as a distraction for the main attack I would inflict upon the Lower Estate." He had already decided that was the way he would attack. He could not let the force of Jackal soldiers know that they were merely a decoy force and not the main threat.

He continued, "Of course, the main force would be vulnerable once the sun goes down. The vampires would be immediately drawn to them. The force that would rise to meet them would surely destroy them outright. I can guarantee you will have many Jackal casualties if not all of them."

"I am prepared to accept that if it will buy you the time to get to Eric Petersen. Tell me how many you will need and when you need them. I will take care of the rest."

"Yes, Master!" Scimitar turned and left to prepare to return to the US. The master assassin was pleased in obtaining the permission to use a large force of Jackal soldiers as the decoy he needed to cover his penetration into the Lower Estate.

"Just one more thing, Master. If the opportunity arises that I may dispatch both vampires, should I, even in the interest of self-preservation?"

The Dragon chuckled to himself. "If that situation presents itself, then by all means, you may destroy both. She has been a thorn in my side for centuries. It will destroy the entire clan if you do but that is fine with me. Just do not fail."

"In this case, it is easier to get permission than forgiveness." Scimitar left the office to return to the US.

Using both boat and plane, he arrived a few weeks later in California. He consulted with the Jackal commander for that region and told him of his plan. The Jackal leader was enthusiastic to set the plan into motion for he and his subordinates were bored with the same usual routines of collecting information on the comings and goings at the Upper Estate and at the shaft by the creek.

The Jackal commander managed to array a force of 250 men. Most of these men were hardened by either military service or time spent in prison. All were accustomed to violence, either issuing it or receiving it. The Jackal organization had taught them discipline. Now, the time was coming when they would use all their skills. They would need them.

It was the dawn of a July morning in 1928 when they all met at a pre-arranged location. Their objective was to storm the mansion, find the elevator shaft to the Lower Estate, and descend into the vampire's lair to destroy all vampires found. This would allow Scimitar to diverge from the main body and hunt for Eric Petersen.

Tayla knew the safest place for Eric would be with her, even during the daylight hours. So, she told Eric she would share her tomb for the time being with him. He had designed the tomb and helped build it. The familiars who had constructed it were dead, per her orders to ensure secrecy. He was the only vampire to ever have set foot in her well-hidden tomb on the underground lake. He was sworn to secrecy for he understood the importance of keeping the secret of the location of her tomb.

Scimitar had pondered the possibility that the two might be together. If that were true, he would destroy them both. But he had to find them before the sun went down. This was why they were beginning so early, to allow maximum time to find the vampires. Scimitar and his company did not want to face the vampires after sunset. It was July which ensured the longest daylight time.

The front door burst open and Jackal soldiers rushed through the door. The butler had been knocked down and was slow to get up. The mansion was caught by total surprise. All the familiars were either held at gunpoint or killed outright. Birdseye was already up when the front door was breached. While in the planning room, he had access to firearms. His staff was able to get to the gun cabinet, loading while running to defend the elevator shaft.

Most of the Jackals had been trying to find the elevator on the first floor. They found the elevator but could not get the doors to open or call the car down. Birdseye had already disabled the car, so that they could not run it from the first floor. It could only run from the second floor which Birdseye and four others were prepared to defend. Within minutes, a group of them came charging down the hallway, past the planning room to the elevator. They were met with shotgun blasts and pistols firing.

The Jackals went down in a heap. More Jackals came down the hall, followed by many more. Soon, the familiars of Tayla were taken down by heavy fire from the Jackals. A key was found on the body of Birdseye and unlocked the car. They piled in and began the long descent into the darkness of the Lower

Estate. Car after car took loads of the Jackal soldiers down. They gathered at the base, in an area that would later become known as the Gates of Hell.

This area had large wrought iron gates stretched across the large entrance to the Lower Estate. Torches burned in the sconces on the gates. The air was cold, and the scent of death in the air was foreboding. Before they would breach the gates, the Jackal commander wanted everyone down below. While waiting, some of them found the back passage that Malcolm would use decades later to exit with a girl named Julie. It was sheer luck they found it for it could not be seen unless one knew it was there.

The Jackal force split up, half taking the back passage while the others worked on opening the iron gates. After nearly 45 minutes, the gates were breached and over 150 Jackals flooded the passages leading to places like *Stables of the Damned*, the Crypt Cavern, the arena (*Coliseum*) and the *Hall of Skulls*. They made a lot of noise while going there, so that anyone in those passages could hear them, even if they were far away.

Soon afterwards, when the groups would come to an intersection, some would continue while others would branch off and take the other tunnels. They were automatically diminishing the size of their groups. After a while, it seemed that each group numbered no more than 15-20 Jackals per group. By noon, no one had made it down to the third level yet. Only a few had breached the second level and were thoroughly lost. Now, they were not just losing time, but even if they decided to leave, they could not for they were lost in the darkness. The blackness was consuming because Tayla had put a curse upon the Lower Estate that the torches would not burn bright during the daylight hours. They would burn very bright during the night hours. Soon, death traps would begin to claim many of the intruders. Doubt and fear would set in amongst them, causing the uneasiness that would lead to panic.

Meanwhile Scimitar managed to push on alone. Finding a vertical shaft would be his key to successfully penetrating the Lower Estate. He managed to find the *Stables of the Damned* all on his own. Some of the human feeding stock called out to him, for they knew he was not a vampire. He told them he was trying to rescue them. He needed information from the captured mortals. Those he talked with were only too happy to supply it. He broke open the chambers they were kept in, asking everyone where the vampires slept. No one could tell him. They did not know for that information had never been shared with them.

They did tell him what their purpose for being there was, which explained why there was not a great number of people in the area turning up as victims. He asked which direction they came from and what direction they left in. The answer was almost always the same.

He wasted no time, heading off in that direction. His weapons were a Thompson submachine gun, with many clips of silver tipped ammunition and a Colt M1911 pistol. A fully automatic weapon in this place was required and a pistol with the same ammo was a great backup. A silver-plated blade in a sheath on his belt was for a "just in case" scenario.

As he went down the mined corridor, he found it opening into a larger room. He had anticipated that the corridor would be mined or booby-trapped with devices designed to stop or slow down intruders, so he carefully looked for trip wires. This room contained a makeshift cabin which was used for taking care of the victims of the *Stables of the Damned*. It was empty when he examined it. He continued, hoping that the Jackals above were having success in finding some of the places where the vampires slept. If so, then, perhaps his job would be easier. He had not told them to keep going downward. The maze up on the upper levels were mere traps, designed to get the intruders lost and to waste their time until the vampires would rise in the evening. He looked at his watch. It was 1:30 in the afternoon.

If successful, he had not really given too much thought to how he would exit these caverns. He just knew he would probably have to leave the same way he came in. If he could find the *Stables of the Damned*, he could find that vertical shaft. That would get him off the third level. The second and first levels would be more difficult. There were no landmarks.

He found that some of the passages went up and then went back down. Soon, he found himself in the arena. He could see the construction of a larger, grander place than what it was originally. It was lit up, even in the daytime. As he walked into the center of the large room, he looked around for exits. He could see exits leading away from the room in several places. This would take time to explore. He had to pick one and he really could not afford to pick the wrong one.

Tayla had built these exits away from the Coliseum as an addition to the mazes above. These exits would lead away from the Crypt Cavern and ultimately lead to her death traps. As he walked towards one, he heard yelling from a distance back from where he had come from. Soon, a group of Jackal soldiers entered the arena cavern. He was glad to see them, for he was not sure which exit to pick. There were twenty Jackals who had found him. He asked them to split up into three groups, each taking an exit and exploring it. This way, someone was exploring the exits all at the same time.

One of these exits led to the Crypt Cavern and the *Hall of Skulls*. The other three led to death traps. He took the one that led to the *Hall of Skulls*. It seemed to be well traveled, as the walls had more decorative motifs carved into the walls. Because of these special markings, he felt this would not lead to the death traps everyone was trying to avoid. The *Hall of Skulls* was not far from the room currently known as the "Arena."

Eventually, his torch cast light upon an open area which forked again, one towards a massive wooden door, the other to someplace unknown. The door caught his attention foremost, which made him think that this led to someplace important, perhaps where the vampires were sleeping. If so, then he had time to get in, destroy as many, specifically Eric Petersen, and then get out as fast as possible. If he managed to get out alive, he had two contingency plans in place. If he only succeeded in killing Eric Petersen, he had a place that would make him safe until the vampires had to retire again. If he succeeded in killing Eric and Tayla, then he would not need the second plan. The clan would be destroyed.

Scimitar expected the doors to be sealed during the daylight hours. They were not. They opened with his pushing against them. His torch added to the light that came from many flaming torches and braziers burning brightly in the darkness. He was surprised that he had just walked into the throne room of the *Order of the Clan of the Red Velvet*. Her royal banners adorned each wall, which was decorated from floor to ceiling with the skulls of past victims. There were thousands of them. Directly opposite the door was an elevated platform which contained her throne. A massive throne, carved from a block of black granite, was where she sat and held court. Her scepter stood in a stand next to the throne. A foot stool covered in red velvet was at the base in front of the seat.

There were no familiar guards around to stop him as the *Hall of Skulls* was empty, for now. A passage ran back from the Throne room which led to her private chambers, but that area was small. He needed to find a large cavern that could hold many of the undead.

He left the throne room, hoping to find the other Jackals he had met in the arena. It was too late, for they had fell into the death traps. These traps were like the "tiger traps" used in India to hunt the big cats. Large holes disguised with false surfaces that would give way under the weight of the targeted. Their weight would cause them to become impaled on sharpened spikes below. If they survived the fall and the stakes, climbing out was impossible. The pits were deep, nearly thirty feet and the walls were smooth, making climbing extremely difficult.

He ran from the arena back to the area that faced the door. The passage that led away from the door and the arena must be the way to go. He followed it, alone until he found the entrance leading into the *Cavern of the Crypts*. His watch told him it was now 3:30pm.

It was a scary place, for it was dark, with no torches lit. He could not see far, for the torch light was too weak to carry all the way across the large cavern. Eventually, he was able to use a large flashlight he had brought along. His eyes began to make out the holes in the walls, which contained the coffins of the vampires. He prepared to light a few of the coffins on fire after dragging a few out into the open. The vampires were still asleep and could not wake. They were helpless.

The wood of the coffins was old and dry, which made them akin to kindling. They lit easily and burned brightly. He did this over and over, destroying as many as he could. After a while, he just lit the coffins afire while still inside their crypts. He knew what Eric Petersen looked like from a photo that was taken before he had "crossed over". That was who he was looking for, but he had no time to examine each one.

The light from the blazing coffins began to illuminate the entire *Cavern of the Crypts*. He was surprised to see how large the cavern was. It would take him longer than he had expected to destroy them. He looked at his watch, noticing it was 4:30pm. If he was going to exit this place, he had to start now. That was only a maybe that he might be able to find his way out.

He turned away and started to back track his route out of the Lower Estate. If he had known, he would have taken the shortest way out, which was to travel to the other side of the *Cavern of the Crypts* and head straight for the Gates of Hell.

By 5:45pm he arrived at the large iron gate. On the other side was the elevator shaft. There were no other Jackals around, but he knew he had no time to wait. He had inflicted damage, but to what extent? Was Eric Petersen in one of those coffins? As it turned out, he was not in the *Cavern of the Crypts* at all. Tayla was right to have him retire with her in her tomb.

By 6pm, Scimitar reached the second floor. When the door opened, there were familiars waiting for him. They knew it the minute he started to ascend, that the intruders were in the car. As protocol amongst the familiars, a call would always be placed to notify those up top that the car was coming up.

Scimitar knew he would have to fight, especially if he made it to the top. When the doors opened, he opened fire with full auto, killing several familiars outright. He managed to fight his way out of the house and get to a vehicle with barely an hour of daylight left. Speeding down the highway, he managed to get to his pre-arranged shelter which consisted of a mausoleum in a cemetery. Why there? It was because he knew it was considered Holy ground, and therefore sanctified. Vampires would not be able to go there. He intended to stay there during the hours of darkness.

526

When he arrived there, much to his surprise, the Dragon was waiting for him. "Greetings Scimitar! I trust you penetrated the Lower Estate?"

"Yes, Master, I did just that. I do not know if I found Eric Petersen or not. I did not see Queen Tayla either. But I did find the vampires. They will come looking for me or anyone they think might be involved, such as you."

"Let them come. I am ready for that. Nice touch, picking this place...sanctified ground. It works against them, but not against me. Get some rest. I brought food for you. It is inside, along with extra ammunition. You might need it. Meanwhile, I also brought reinforcements. They will be here by tomorrow morning and will make up the second wave of the assault. You are going to go back in there and finish what you started. I also brought along a friend of yours."

"Who might that be?"

"Scorpio! He will be here by morning. I have briefed him on all he needs to know. I do not think we need to waste time tomorrow in the *Cavern of the Crypts*. I think if Tayla intended to protect him, he is lying right beside her somewhere down there. She would not lie in the *Cavern of the Crypts*. As a Queen, she would have a special place, a place fitting for a Queen."

CHAPTER FIFTY-FOUR

SECOND WAVE

"Dearest Malcolm, I knew the Dragon was the main force behind this. Yet I was powerless to do anything against him personally. He could not do too much to me either. He could hurt me only by taking that which I loved. I could not even do that to him for he had no one that he cared about other than himself and his precious *Order of the Jackal*. When I rose from my tomb that evening, I immediately felt the feelings I felt when my father had thrown himself upon the funeral pyre so many centuries ago. Perhaps the Dragon was behind all that as well. I will never know. What I did know was that I had intruders and the contingencies I had planned for were about to come into play."

*   *   *

When the Dragon told him to finish what he had started, Scimitar knew the meaning of the Dragon's words. The damage he had caused would have consequences. The Dragon knew the vampires would be out in force looking for those responsible. Those who were still in the Lower Estate would have to be written off as lost, casualties of the war the Dragon had wanted.

"You, Scimitar, have lit the fuse to the charge I have attached to the vampire's lair. Now, it is only a matter of time. The sun will drop from the sky soon so it will be a short time before they will hover upon us like a plague of locust. They cannot touch us for we are protected. As the Dragon, I can use the tools of the holy and the unholy. That will make the Queen and her host of undead furious, like a swarm. They will probe us all night, searching for a way to enter but they cannot. She will summon all her familiars she will have left to defend them during the day. Tomorrow morning, we will overcome them and find her resting place. She will be the top target for if we get her, we get them all."

*   *   *

It was as the Dragon had said it would be. The moment Queen Tayla rose, she knew something was wrong. The pain and sadness of loss filled her, as she screamed out into the darkness. Eric awoke beside her. He felt it too.

She summoned her familiars but found them to be dead or incapacitated. She visited the *Cavern of the Crypts* first. The smoldering coffins revealed the remains of vampires burnt while they slept. The number of them was staggering. Scimitar had done his work efficiently. Nearly a fifth of her clan of vampires were gone. They could be replaced she thought, but they were close to her. She considered them family, so she cared for them deeply. The other vampires circled around the coffins, some of which were still smoking with glowing embers.

They were sad, and angry at the same time. "My children, I sense the intruders are still within our grasp to exact our revenge. Seek them out and destroy them!"

In the blink of an eye, the *Cavern of the Crypts* emptied, as vampires became bodies of mist and vapor, fanning out to all the levels of the Lower Estate. They would find them and take them for every drop they could get.

Eric took charge of those who stayed within the confines of the Lower Estate, while the Queen flew out the shaft with a contingent of her vampires, looking for anyone who might have found their way out. Another contingent went topside to the Upper Estate to assess the damage done there.

Finding Scimitar was not hard. When she found his trail leading to a cemetery, she thought him to be very clever. Who else would have known to take such defensive measures? She

529

was surprised when she sensed that the Dragon was also there as well. The Dragon was laughing at her and she could feel the anger and hatred for him rising inside her.

The vampires covered all four sides of the cemetery, with the Queen at the front gates. She knew they would stay inside the boundaries of the graveyard the entire night.

Meanwhile, back at the mansion, the vampires found that many of the familiars had been killed. Her butler had been knocked unconscious when they burst through the door. Her maids and cooks hid themselves as part of the protocol should intruders enter. Birdseye and all his staff were dead, shot down in a hail of gunfire. There were also a group of Jackals found killed just outside the elevator on the second floor not far from where Birdseye and others were found. Fortunately, there was little damage done to the mansion except for the front door off its hinges. Bullet holes adorned the walls of the hallway on the second floor but other than that, nothing seemed destroyed. There were less than a dozen familiars left to defend the mansion or the elevator. All her other familiars were in the city of San Francisco. She had them notified by phone to come to the mansion immediately, without delay, and to be there before daylight came again.

Those distant familiars obeyed the Queen, arriving before midnight. She sent a group to the cemetery to get into position so when Scimitar emerged, he could be eliminated. Wounded was what she wanted for she wanted to kill him herself. She needed a way to neutralize the Dragon's abilities but could not think of any way other than use the same abilities he had. If he were gunned down, he always had a second person who would assume the mantle by allowing the demon to possess them, thereby perpetuating the persona of the Dragon.

Tayla was very tired of dealing with the Dragon. She wanted to be rid of him once and for all. Destroying the *Order of the Jackal* would not do it. She had to find a way. She would eventually but it would take decades to do it. Meanwhile, she had a battle to fight.

Eric was sending a message to her, stating that the mansion had been secured, as well as the Lower Estate. There was no threat left to fight there. He asked her if he could come to the cemetery to fight alongside his love. She considered it, but said no, for she felt it would be a trap, especially if the Dragon was on sight.

Eric said he understood but he felt he could fight his own battles, especially if she were at his side. At this time, she was unaware of the second wave that would attack at dawn the next morning. The Dragon was blocking her gift of sight. It was one of the advantages he had over her. He could not rescind any of her powers but could temporarily block the use of them.

One thing he could not block was Tayla's good judgment. She felt at this time, Eric was right in wanting to be by her side. But she felt it was better if she was at the mansion for him to be next to her, not here at the cemetery. When the familiars arrived, they were heavily armed. One team had a machine gun, while another team carried grenades, procured from a military warehouse.

Tayla flew back to the mansion, which was only a few miles away. While on her way back, she scanned the nearby town. She noticed a lot of cars and trucks parked on the streets that were usually empty at this time of night. Suspecting them to be reinforcements for the Jackals, she swooped down to investigate.

Her suspicions proved correct, for she saw armed men, sleeping inside the vehicles parked on the street. She notified her vampires to come immediately to dispatch the second wave. Over 150 vampires descended upon the parked vehicles and tore into them, ripping the thinly covered roofs off to get at the victims. Eric was one of those vampires who came. He did so only because he knew that Tayla was already there. As they mauled the few armed men, it turned out they had been drawn out by the decoy of the appearance of more Jackal soldiers. Tayla could not understand why they were drawn out, but not attacked as in an ambush. How does one ambush a group of vampires? Perhaps it was not their intentions to ambush but to distract? Tayla ordered everyone back to the sanctuary of the Lower Estate. There were enough familiars to defend the Upper Estate, or so she thought. Come dawn, she would know for sure. They

531

were busy preparing defenses all night for a fight they were sure was coming.

Tayla left the estate again for the cemetery. If she had to, she would hover over the mausoleum all night, but she was not going to let the assassin live nor was she going to allow the Dragon to overrun her estate. The familiars would kill him as well, even if only temporarily. What she wanted to do was to find his second, his heir to the mantle of power, and kill him, therefore ending his ability to pass on the demon, but there was no time. It was after 3am. She had two priorities, her vampires, and her estate. She would defend them to the death.

*   *   *

Scorpio was in command of the second wave of Jackal soldiers who had consolidated from many small groups located throughout the county. The group located in town that Tayla had just destroyed was a distraction for them while they began to stage just across Stony Creek. At first light, they would attack.

These were men that Scorpio had trained. Scorpio understood the Dragon had not told Scimitar everything and he felt that the Dragon was willing to sacrifice him for Scorpio's force to succeed. As it would turn out, he was right. The Dragon anticipated that Tayla would come after Scimitar with a vengeance, hoping it would cloud her judgement. It had not, but it made her question some of her own decisions.

Scorpio, another of the Dragon's premier assassins, was a Hispanic of Colombia origins. He had been with the Dragon for a long time. He too, like Scimitar had been trained since he was a young boy, indoctrinated into the *Order of the Jackal* after he had proved he was no stranger to murder and violence. The Dragon became his master teacher and Scimitar his mentor. He had learned much from both. The Dragon had ensured he was educated in all the necessary subjects to make him as well rounded a tool as was Scimitar. He had not disappointed the Dragon as he too had never failed.

As his forces were completing their staging on the creek, the light of dawn began to show in the eastern sky. That meant the vampires were having to retire and only the familiars were left to defend both Upper and Lower Estates. He was confident his force would overpower the familiars like the day before and make their way to the *Cavern of the Crypts* as had Scimitar. They wanted to wait for Scimitar to arrive so he could lead them straight to it, but a messenger arrived to tell them the Dragon and Scimitar were holed up in the cemetery as familiars waited for them to exit. They were to go alone.

What they did not know was that Tayla had left orders for her familiars to assault the mausoleum and kill Scimitar at all costs. The Dragon would probably escape, but she did not care. The Dragon had been forbidden to enter her estate. Four familiars watched the mausoleum, waiting for any sign they were to exit or come out shooting. It was 3:30am and nothing was happening.

Inside the Dragon woke the assassin up, saying "You have company, my friend. I think you better prepare yourself for a fight. I am summoning my second to come to this place as soon as he can. He is here just as a precaution should I meet my demise along with you. You have been in situations like this before, so I trust you know what to do to extricate yourself from this position. I will merely follow your example."

Scimitar stood up and peered out the small aperture in the thick wooden door. A small stained-glass window was higher up on the back wall that would allow some light to pass through the darkened chamber when dawn broke. The crypt containing the occupants of the mausoleum were below the stained-glass window. The safe space he had found had turned into a trap. He wondered if he could push out the walls of the back of the crypt, but he knew the rear was probably guarded as well by the familiars outside. If by some chance he made it out, his only defense was the cover of darkness, but he could not leave the cemetery for he knew that Tayla was out there waiting for him.

Along with Tayla, there were four familiars, Decadent and Reaper in the front, along with Requiem and Sinister watching the back. Decadent and Reaper manned the .30 caliber machine gun set up directly facing the door, while the other two had rifles and grenades. The front team also had grenades. Sinister, a brave soul, managed to creep up to the rear of the mausoleum. He had

533

several grenades with him and wanted to shoot out the stained-glass window and drop the grenades down into the interior of the burial chamber. Tayla communicated via telepathy that she wanted to throw the grenade into the room. She only needed for Sinister to break the thick stain glass with a rifle shot. Hovering above the tomb she would catch the grenade thrown to her and toss it into the window.

Sinister thought it to be brilliant and did exactly that. He climbed up the back wall, onto the split-level roof and fired a bullet into the glass, shattering it. Then he picked up a grenade, pulled the pin and tossed it to Tayla hovering just above and watched her throw the device in. Sinister jumped off the roof onto the ground below just in time to hear the explosion. The well-built structure contained the explosion, damaging the inside of the front door. The other familiars rushed the front door to find both the bodies of Scimitar and the Dragon lying on the floor with multiple wounds. They dragged the bodies out so Tayla could see them.

Ricardo Draco was out of commission for a time and could not aid the Jackals until his second could assume the role of the dead Dragon. Killing him had bought her some time. It also freed up her gift of sight he was blocking. She brought back the bodies to the Lower Estate while the familiars went to the aid of those already in position to defend the Upper Estate.

It was 4am when Sinister, Decadent, Reaper and Requiem arrived. They had enough time to set up their machine gun off to the side of the front entrance but were oblivious that the Jackals would approach from the north, coming from the creek.

Sinister and Requiem set up on the roof on the back side, prepared to drop grenades down on any sizable force attempting to enter from there. Other familiars were also up on the roof.

While up on the roof, they could see dawn approaching. Tayla and her vampires were ready to retire. She had taken the bodies of Scimitar and the Dragon to the *Cavern of the Crypts*. Tayla said, "Here are the bodies of those who would invade our realm as we sleep. Here are the bodies of those who would do to you as they did to your brethren. You know what to do."

The vampires tore the bodies apart and fed them to the creatures that were in some of the death traps. They enjoyed watching the hungry animals devour their flesh. Pythons, anacondas, alligators, and crocodiles seized the pieces of flesh and devoured them as they had not been fed recently.

Normally, Tayla would have thought it to be all over with, but her gift of sight told her that a second wave was about to strike, and she would be helpless to aid her familiars in repelling them. She did warn her defenders topside that another assault was eminent. The vampires prepared to retire, but Tayla had two familiars in hidden positions to take out any Jackal who might be able to penetrate the crypts. The familiars above in the Upper Estate were ready. People were on the roof, inside the mansion, and below in the *Cavern of the Crypts*. Tayla would be safe in her tomb, but unable to help.

The defenders knew they could not hold the Jackals off for a long period of time. Reinforcing familiars were still coming in from great distances. They would be arriving at various times during the day. They could only hope they could defend until the sun set later that day. The maids and the cooks had decided to help by transporting ammunition to various positions.

Within a half hour of dawn breaking, the Jackals moved out of their staging area, crossed the Stony Creek, and moved up to the rear of the mansion. Spotters on the roof saw them and notified everyone. The battle had begun.

When they had reached the gardens in the back, they sprinted towards the back doors, of which there were three. The maze was still in construction and the shrubbery was not high or thick enough to provide cover or concealment to the Jackal soldiers. The force came in stages. The first stage was about twenty men whose job was to secure the rear entrances. Once that was accomplished, then, others would follow along and take out all the defenses of the Upper Estate. This way, they would not be caught in between two opposing forces. The truth was that the Upper Estate defenders were the main opposing force.

When the Jackals made the effort to reach the rear doors, the spotters on the roof began to drop grenades. The effects were devastating. The defenders dropped two grenades apiece, then

535

within a minute, another two. All the attackers were killed outright. However, the doors were also damaged. Inside, some familiars began to reinforce the doors with boards and barricades. Getting inside the mansion was going to be costly. This went on for an hour. By 8am, over fifty Jackals were lying dead in the rear of the mansion due to gunfire and grenades.

The Jackal commander, Scorpio, had sent a group around to the front. He knew they had lost the element of surprise and therefore, it was a set-piece battle, siege style. He had no heavy weapons such as artillery, nor heavy machine guns to counter the effects of the grenades. The open lawn of the mansion provided little cover and no concealment. To maneuver to the front would take some time. The wood line along the creek was the only concealment. However, they were still in range of rifle fire.

Scouts told him there was a machine gun covering the entrance to the front. Scorpio was aware that Scimitar and the Dragon had been killed at the cemetery. He decided to call off the attack until the new Dragon could be instated and supply them with the proper weapons to resume the attack. He had already lost his leader, the element of surprise, and a lot of men.

CHAPTER FIFTY-FIVE

THE ENEMY OF THE VAMPIRE

"Dearest Malcolm, writing this chapter is like opening an old wound. Even now, writing about it brings me such pain and misery. The anguish and regret of my losses were almost more than I could bear. I did not want to write about it, but the events were part of my story that demanded me to tell of them with great sadness and sorrow."

*   *   *

The offensive continued against the *Red Clan*. Within a week, the Dragon had been reinstated. For the first time in history, a Dragon had been killed without transferring his mantle of power over to the chosen one to receive it. A ritual, one of striking similarities as the one used for "the Crossing Over" to the world of the immortal, was used for such cases. Tayla had destroyed the Dragon's body. There was no way possible for the Chosen One to be able to ingest his blood. However, the Dragon, always the clever one, had set aside a vial of his blood prior to his killing. Should the Dragon be killed, his second would be able to take part in the ritual and thereby establish himself as the new Dragon.

The new Dragon arrived soon after and the campaign against the *Order of the Clan of the Red Velvet* resumed. This time, they came prepared. They brought Browning Automatic Rifles (BAR), Thompson SMG's, explosives, and a machine gun to counter the one Tayla had watching the front of the mansion. As usual, they took advantage of the daylight, thereby eliminating the vampires from taking part.

By noon, the familiars had been driven back, and retreated down into the Lower Estate. Once they had arrived at the Lower Estate, they disabled the car of the elevator so that the Jackals could not descend. It was brilliant for it bought a large amount of time for them to wait for sundown. It also meant they were trapped below.

Above, the Jackals searched the entire mansion, seeking an alternative way to descend. There was only one elevator. Tayla had sealed all the mine entrances, thereby preventing them from entering. However, only those entrances were sealed, not the entire tunnel. It would be possible to dig out if needed. There were tools available nearby.

A few of the familiars assigned themselves the task of digging out should the Jackals penetrate the first level. That left only twelve familiars to fight off over one hundred Jackal soldiers. They retreated to the *Hall of Skulls* and the *Stables of the Damned*. By 3pm, the familiars were in place. There, they would wait.

Meanwhile, above the surface, the Jackals could not find a way to bring up the elevator car. They managed to open the doors and peer down the shaft into complete darkness. They dropped torches down the shaft to determine its depth. The depth was over 800ft down. That brought them to the first level. After that, there were vertical passages that would take them lower, but they had to find them and that would take time. It was time they did not have. For their assault to be successful, they needed to be inside the Lower Estate first thing in the morning.

Scorpio decided he would have no part in attacking the near-impregnable fortress she had down below. The odds were stacked against him there. He knew Tayla had designed her estate to be unassailable in just one day. She was wise to do this for no one yet had devised a plan that would take them in, accomplish her destruction and get out all in a single period of daylight.

The Jackal commander, Scorpio, had planned for this, a battle on his terms. They would stay the night on the premises drawing

538

the vampires to them. It would be the level playing field he had wanted.

The Jackals were armed with silver tipped ammunition. The vampires had no familiars topside to fight for them in a conventional fight. It was now a case of vampire versus well-armed soldiers who could fight and kill at a distance. The vampire had to get in close to kill, the Jackal did not. Here was the advantage the assassin had sought after.

When the sun disappeared from the western sky, Tayla and her vampires were up and out in force. Escaping from the airshaft where Tayla had first met Scimitar, the greenish white fog spewed like a thick gas onto the brush covered landscape. They took to the sky by the dozens, in intervals heading toward many directions. They intended to feed first, then return to fight the Jackals.

When the vampires returned, they would take up positions above and below the ground. Tayla knew there were more familiars enroute, but they would not arrive until sometime after daylight. It was paramount that the vampires try to establish control during the hours of darkness when they would be strong. She and Eric would lead the assault together to retake the Upper Estate. The vampires could enter through many entrances the Jackals had never bothered to think about. They started at the top and began to work down. They came in through chimneys, through heating conduits, and any other way inside they could find. The vampires cut the power off to the house. The Jackals were in the dark. Due to their ability to see in the dark, they found the Jackals hidden all over the house, behind obstacles. The Jackals must have thought the obstacles would draw the vampires to close in so they could kill the Jackal behind it. The Jackals would be waiting with a sting made of silver.

Tayla's rage got the best of her and because of it, she made a mistake. She allowed herself to be separated from Eric. It was thought that since Scorpio was after Eric, if they were together, the assassin Scorpio would declare victory with a single blow against Tayla. After that, it would be all over. It was also considered that if Tayla was with Eric, they could protect each other.

539

Eric led a band of clansmen from the top of the mansion, seeking and destroying Jackals wherever they could be found. The Jackals had other ideas about that and defended themselves well. The *Red Clan* began taking casualties. Eric saw this and cautioned his fellow undead. The vampires moved fast, faster than the Jackals could aim and managed to take many of them out. Eric was adept at this, and once he had killed one, he examined his weapon and saw it was loaded with silver-tipped ammunition. These bullets were killers to a vampire.

He notified all his vampire brethren as well as Tayla. They became acutely aware of the dangers they faced. Eric telepathed to all they should pick up a weapon laid down by a Jackal and use it against them. This way, they could use their own weapons against them. If they ran out of ammunition, they could turn to shapeshifting to approach their enemy and get in close. Bullets went through the mists without doing any damage. When the opportunity presented itself, this allowed the vampires to get close enough to take down the Jackal soldiers. After a while, the vampires were making progress, obtaining the upper hand.

Scorpio was watching this fight, carefully not disclosing himself before the chance to make his move against Eric. He could hear Eric moving down the hallway of the fourth floor. The assassin wished he could also hear the voice of Tayla calling out to her fellow vampires to change forms but that was a gift that mortals were not granted.

Scorpio hid himself in a closet, pistol loaded and drawn. In his other hand, a silver-plated knife blade. He could hear Eric's approach getting closer. He steeled himself to give the deathblow, either a fatal shot or a plunging of the knife into the chest, or both.

Tayla arrived on the floor underneath the one Eric and Scorpio were on, only yards away from each other. She wondered if Eric could sense the assassin inside the closet, with pistol and blade drawn. Eric messaged her back that he could indeed sense him inside the closet. She told him not to make a move until she arrived. Tayla had been distracted while on the floor below, when a group of Jackals began firing silver at her and those who accompanied her. While her attention was diverted towards the Jackals at hand, Eric grew impatient.

Scorpio, waiting in the closet, saw the doorknob of the door begun to turn. He fired the shot through the door, hearing the roaring of the vampire turning to flame. The smell of burning flesh filled the hallway outside. He opened the door to see it was not Eric but another vampire he had shot. The hallway began to fill with the greenish white mist that Scimitar had told him about. The mist in the hallway became so thick, he thought it must be full of vampires.

Indeed, it was full of vampires, in the form of a mist, that obscured his vision of Eric coming down the hall to kill him. Panic took hold of the assassin. He knew his demise was coming. He had given his position away and now they knew where he was. Eric had found him and was directly behind him, unknown to Scorpio.

Eric had told a vampire to try the doorknob, and that was when the first shot was fired. That unfortunate vampire caught the bullet and went up in flames.

Scorpio wanted to retreat to the closet and when he turned, he stared directly into the vampire eyes of Eric. The mouth of Eric opened to reveal his fangs, which were about to sink themselves into the neck of the assassin. In a split second, Eric's fangs penetrated his neck and when they did, the .45 pistol went off, striking Eric across his abdomen. He did not immediately catch fire but stumbled backwards and fell on the hallway floor.

Scorpio fell back, bleeding profusely from the wound Eric inflicted, but another vampire finished the job that Eric had started. Scorpio was dead within a minute.

Tayla appeared in the hallway within seconds, knowing immediately what had happened. Though the knowledge was with her, she could not help but deny the inevitable. It had happened again. Her beloved was about to leave her and with only seconds to act, what could she say? What was she supposed to say? What could be done to prevent what she knew was about to happen all over again?

In a split second, her memory took her back to the ramparts of the French castle, where she could see far off, her lover's body

541

lying under his dead horse, having written her name upon the horse coat in his own blood. She had meant that much to someone, and now she found the chance for someone to love her as much if not more. The perfect situation for one such as she. They were equally yoked in this existence. His death was voluntary, for he chose to be with her. It was something that Renard did not get the chance to do, to choose willingly. Being prepared to commit is one thing but doing so is quite another.

Tayla picked up Eric's head, holding it into her lap. Tears began to flow as her heart was breaking. "I wanted you to wait for me. You should have waited!"

Eric, dying from his wound, said, "I have loved you since I first met you so long ago. You should have taken me even then. We would have had more time together. My wound is superficial but, nonetheless, the silver has infected me. Though it is a slight wound, it will still be fatal, my darling. My greatest pain of death is leaving you. We have won, though it has cost us dearly." Then, Eric burst into flames upon the floor.

Her screams of agony were deafening. Her rage of feeling robbed again made her dangerous, especially to her enemies. Her Eric was gone, and nothing could replace him. Only a pile of smoldering ash remained.

The vampire queen tore through the rest of the Jackals singlehandedly, finishing them off before dawn. The Dragon cowardly shrank from this fight. It was as if he had seen the outcome of this fight. He considered the loss of Eric as his victory over Queen Tayla. He had already left for Colombia before this fight having seen the damage inflicted and the punishment delivered.

It was over. All that was left to do was cleanup and repair of damage done. The losses were catastrophic to Tayla. Many of her brood had perished. The Jackal soldier's bodies would feed the animals in the death traps. The weapons were collected and added to her arsenal. If not for Tayla, all would have been lost. She had saved her clan but was not able to save her precious Eric. Her tears seemed ceaseless, as she would spend many a night crying for him. She swore off any more romantic notions about having a permanent consort or lover. At least no one to love with

542

her heart! She knew the Dragon would not let her rest if she ever found happiness. The pain was like that of a knife in her chest.

In the days following the death of her beloved, Queen Tayla was inconsolable. The loss had nearly paralyzed her. The remnants of the Clan looked to the Queen for leadership. She had to rebuild and resurrect her Clan. She received no words of consolation from her brothers or sister.

They had not come to her aid or made any effort to communicate with her. The Dragon had poisoned their mind that she had seized the throne without due course. The Dragon had convinced Rascha that it was he who should have taken the throne. She felt anger towards her brothers and sister, but never mentioned it nor showed her resentment. Because of their actions, Tayla canceled the gatherings for quite a few years until she was ready to commence holding them again. The Queen simply taught them to never listen to the Dragon or there would be consequences when they held their gatherings in later years.

The monumental task of replacing her familiars with equally skilled and talented people not to mention the replenishing of her clan of vampires would be difficult. After the battle, she had less than a hundred vampires.

The mansion was damaged but not too much. Repairs were easily done. The familiars were the hardest to replace. It would take nearly a decade rebuilding her *Clan of the Order of the Red Velvet*. By the end of the Great Depression, she had managed to rebuild her ranks and her cadre of familiars to exceed what she had before the great battle that took Eric away from her.

The Dragon had thought that losing her beloved would bring her back into his sphere of influence, perhaps forging an alliance or at least a pact of cooperation. It only forged a deep hatred for the man whose real personality was the personification of evil. He had cost the vampire queen her family, her adulthood, her future, her heart, and all that she had ever cared about. She could not name all the names of those she had lost in her lifetime. But they all pointed to one name, the Dragon.

Now, it was determination and drive that fed her hatred of the Dragon. She would attack and annihilate the *Order of the Jackal*. If she could, she would kill the Dragon repeatedly. She would search him out, search out the Jackals for they were the enemy of the vampire and always would be.

CHAPTER FIFTY-SIX

FAMILIARITY

"Dearest Malcolm, we are getting close to contemporary times. As you already know something of the familiars you came to know and trust with you and your family's lives. It was important to include them, for you need to understand my side of the story and why I picked them. Each one had to pass certain criteria. Their talents and skills were peculiar only to them. I chose these people for I knew I would need such a special team that would work together as a unit for the conflict I saw in the distant future. I also saw you coming into the picture, later than the staff you would meet. It seems that I often live in the past and the future. By that I mean, I am often thinking of the past, where I was and what I was doing. The same goes for the future, as I constantly look to the near future. My present consists of learning from the past and preparing for the future." Often, when I thought of my familiars and how important they were to me, it seemed that the very least I could do for them was to record their stories, their backgrounds and such. It was to that end that I planned for them to go back to their lives, or what might be left of them, so that life as they once knew could return to them."

*   *   *

In 1950, the predecessor to Mortis, the butler of the Upper Estate was a man who was born Roger Hastings. He was a true gentleman's gentleman. Born and raised in Winchester, England, he was educated at the boarding school known as Winchester

College, one of the oldest secondary education institutions in England. He attended Christ Church College afterwards and received a degree in world literature. For a while he taught English in public schools, then emigrated to the US after becoming dissatisfied with the current school politics of the day. He became even more dissatisfied with trying to teach in the American school system and became a gentleman's gentleman, otherwise known as a butler. He was immensely proud for his first job was not only as a butler but also a tutor to his employer's children. When the children got older, the opportunity to teach went away, and he was left with only the job of being the butler. His employer was very wealthy and paid him well, but he always wanted to teach. He decided to become a novelist on the side, and in his spare time, he wrote a story about himself, using a fictitious name.

Tayla met him at a bookstore because she wanted to add some selections to her already astounding library. He was there, signing some books. His eye met hers that evening, and the rest is history. He sold all his books that night and he and Tayla went for a drink later afterwards. She convinced him that she needed a butler, and a librarian. The idea of being both appealed to him. He asked also if he could find opportunities to teach on the side, and she said most definitely he could, should he find the time available.

She brought him to her mansion, showed him her library of rare books and documents. It intrigued him that his potential new employer had such a collection. He accepted the position as butler and librarian, but truthfully, he had become a historian. After he became a familiar, he started keeping records that has become part of the body of this manuscript.

Roger Hastings' familiar name became Anvil. She named him that because he was part of the forge rebuilding her estate, helping to shape what is in existence today. He held that position for twenty years. He never looked back.

He became ill in 1970 and died after a short illness. Tayla was heartbroken and buried him in a plot of a cemetery that contained all the familiars who had passed by natural means while in her service.

She knew she would need another butler and soon. Fortunately, Anvil had brought his work up to date regarding keeping records and such. She met another man, Winston MacKenzie, at a theater one night. Having been widowed and childless, an early retirement had not set well with him. He had taken a job as a "Gentlemen's gentleman" for another prominent San Franciscan family. It was his night off and he decided to take in a play. He seemed sad for he had no other family. That is one of the basic requirements Tayla looked for in a familiar. She saw opportunity so she befriended him. He had all the qualities she sought after in a butler, true devotion, no questions, and a perfect gentleman. When he first met Tayla, he told her that if he had had a daughter, she would be exactly what he would envision. Of course, Mortis had no idea of just who she really was. Tayla was touched deeply by his statement. He was so kind to her. Tayla convinced herself on that night; she needed Mortis in her Clan, to be that special confidant, that special "maker of wishes come true." So, she brought him in in 1970 and he stayed long after she met her end.

*   *   *

As far as domestic staff were concerned, every house the size of Tayla's estate needed a cook. After all, there were a lot of people to cook for. Up to this point, Tayla had two and sometimes three cooks. But that was because the availability of modern conveniences saving time and work had not occurred yet. Now, it was 1975. The number of cooks had dwindled to one. Her name was Glynis Jamison. Glynis had been with Tayla for several decades but was getting old and wanted to retire. So, Tayla began looking for another cook or chef to take her place. She found one in a restaurant in the city. She and Falcon were dining together at a posh dinner club when the chef came out of the kitchen to ask how well they were enjoying the meal. The food was so delicious, that Falcon was the one who asked her if she was happy working there. She said she was but was always interested in moving upwards. He asked how she would like to be her own boss in her own kitchen, cooking for royalty.

The chef, aka Sally Kensington had prepared dishes for tables of which royalty sat at before. Born the daughter of a Scottish farmer in Stirling, Scotland, she had attended a prestigious culinary arts school in France. Her former employers were a wealthy family who had now moved back east, releasing her to seek employment elsewhere. She found herself working for another chef who owned this restaurant, creating dishes of her own creation which the other chef took credit for. As a professionally trained chef, she delighted in preparing and serving for those who really appreciated good food. After being offered a job by Falcon, she accepted. Her familiar name became Shade. She has been with the Queen ever since. She even stayed on after the Queen's demise and married a good friend of Malcolm's, Paul Vetter.

*   *   *

Harvest, aka Emil Worcester was an exceptional gardener. It was he who completed and kept up the shrubbery maze. Amongst his accomplishments, it is the most notable on the grounds of the Upper Estate. Often, he used outside help to complete some projects. The paver bricks which make up the maze are granite. All the corridors converge at the center where one will find a fountain and a sundial in the middle of the fountain. It is here that the rings of power are kept after the demise of the clans.

Emil was found working at a golf course in Augusta, Ga. In 1955. He was not the one who oversaw the same course that the Masters Tournament is played on annually, but another one of lesser importance. After the attack on the Estate in the early 1930's, the need to clear up the external battle damage was great. It would require some cosmetic repairs to the outside of the mansion and also the grounds surrounding the massive home.

Tayla had seen golf courses before and though she did not understand the need for mortals to play such a game, she did enjoy the pastoral scenery they presented. She desired that her back-yard look as such. For that, she would need a landscaper who had experience in such matters.

An ad was placed in such publications that a landscaper would read. Few if any wanted to leave the golf course and tend to someone's back yard. But Emil was different. He liked the challenge of turning what was once a rough, unkempt, and undeveloped piece of terrain into something beautiful, something that no other man of his profession had attempted to do. He would be the first and only man to have put the land under his hand's touch. Quite a few were interviewed, but when they saw what lie before them, they backed away. They preferred to improve instead of create something new. This was why Emil was different.

So, Emil was brought on board, given the familiar name of Harvest, and was given free reign over the grounds of the Upper Estate. Emil was the Queen's chief gardener and landscaper for many years. The landscaper had done wonders with the grounds. Often, at night, Tayla and he would walk the grounds together in the moonlight and he would show her his latest project's progress or its completion. Tayla delighted in such walks, knowing her home was meticulously cared for, both inside and out.

One day, Emil took ill. Tayla's physician told her that Emil had terminal cancer. When Emil found out, he told Tayla he was afraid. She gave him the same choice she had given Eric Petersen when Eric found that he was dying. Emil chose the immortality Eric had chosen. Before that would happen, Emil wanted to find and interview someone he felt would be a good successor to his achievements. The Queen allowed this. It would be 6 months before he would find Moon. He thought of him as the best prospect because he had known Moon professionally and met him at a convention of landscapers in England. The two were great friends and communicated often.

Ben Watson, aka Moon, had worked in England developing large estate grounds and golf courses. He had worked on the grounds of colleges and universities as well. His resume of completed projects convinced Emil that he was the man to succeed him. Emil asked Ben to come and visit him at Tayla's estate. When he did, he was impressed at the length of time it took to complete such an accomplishment. He was particularly excited at the size of the shrubbery maze. Emil told him it was a difficult thing to keep up the appearance of it and everything else. Then, he told him about his condition and that he needed someone he could trust to continue his work and dream.

Out of loyalty to his friend, Ben took the position. As a familiar, he was equally enthralled to be working for Queen Tayla and was grateful that his friend would not die but pass into immortality as a creature of the night. He would see him again, as Emil remained a part of the *Red Clan* up until the demise of the Queen. After the Queen's demise, which also meant the demise of Emil, Moon stayed on with the Harris', continuing to keep up the grounds up until the present. He could never go back home to England for he had outlived his family.

*   *   *

After the battle for the Lower Estate, Queen Tayla began to organize the tasks of the familiars by installing a command structure. There were tasks that needed to be assigned and ensured that they were performed. There were tasks to be performed in the *Stables of the Damned, Cavern of the Crypts* and the *Hall of Skulls.* Maintenance and repairs had fallen to anyone who was available, but she could see that a structured organization was needed to ensure efficiency. In 1956, she began to look for an executive type who could fill that role as overseer of the familiars of the Lower Estate. She had Anvil looking after the Upper Estate, who did an excellent job. She needed another who could do such a job below. Within a few months she found such a man, John Scotti.

He was a Korean War veteran, who had been disfigured for his trouble. He was a decorated veteran, awarded three Purple Hearts, a Bronze Star, and a Silver Star, both for gallantry upon the field of battle. He was unemployed. Finding employment was difficult for him due to his disfigurement.

She found him walking along a street in the city during the wee hours of the morning. He looked lost and full of despair. She asked her driver to stop and ask if he needed help.

He said, without looking at the open window of the limousine, "Unless you've got a paying job for me, keep driving." The tone of his voice indicated his determination to keep his dignity without sounding like he was at the end of his rope. What he really needed at that moment was hope, along with a shower and a hot meal. Tayla commanded the car to stop and threw the door open. She stepped out, dressed ever so elegantly for 1956, and said, "Mister, if you want a job, I have one for you. I promise that you will have your dignity, hope, and all your needs met. If you are interested, get in my car."

He looked at her, smiling, and said, "Seriously? No kidding?"

She replied, "You are serious, are you not?"

"Yes Ma'am! I'm serious."

"Get in the car," she said.

While they rode, she asked questions and he answered, truthfully. He had been discharged after he was released by the military hospital. The VA had done all they could for him. He received a monthly check, but he wanted to work. It was the only way he could feel whole, complete, and put the past behind him.

She asked if he was afraid of the dark. It was an odd question to him.

"No, he said, "I'm from the Pennsylvania coal country. My whole family mined coal, but I don't want the black lung disease. Being underground doesn't bother me. What kind of job are you offering?"

Without answering the question, she asked another, "What was your rank in the army?"

"I was an NCO, Master Sergeant to be exact. I was a platoon sergeant, in charge of a bunch of good men. Lost many of them though. That's how I got all these scars."

"Would you like to be in charge of some more men?" she asked.

He smiled, and through all the scarred tissue on his face, she could tell she had struck a chord. That is how the first Chief of the Lower Estate came into the service of the Queen. She named him Scourge because he who would crack the whip and get the Lower Estate into the shape she wanted.

In 1974, an accident in the tunnels of the Lower Estate took Scourge's life. Tayla was very saddened by the loss of her Lower

Estate Chief. He had been a well-respected and trusted ranking member of her team. Mortis told her that he would be difficult to replace. She tasked Falcon to find the replacement for Scourge. Falcon had known Scourge well and knew the kind of person she wanted to replace him with. It took well into the next year to find such a person. Falcon had an ad put in the want ads of the paper. The ad noted the qualifications needed and a brief description of the position. Of course, the ad was misleading as it did not say you would spend most of your time hundreds of feet below the surface of the earth. And that you would be working for a vampire. But a man who had been a corrections officer, Franco Banzetti, answered the ad. Falcon interviewed him, then introduced him to Tayla.

Franco had been in an "accident" while working as a guard on a cell block at a NY state prison. Franco had a habit of abusing some of the prisoners who gave him a lot of verbal abuse because he was a very ugly man. They called him "Bonzai". His teeth needed a lot of work, which he absolutely refused to have fixed. He had no family and wanted to return to similar work after his face had healed.

The prisoners who had abused him verbally wound up on the receiving end of his physical abuse. It got out of hand and the prisoners set his head on fire. It burned a good portion of his scalp such that it did not grow back again. The healthy part of his scalp was growing fine. He had let it grow such that a ponytail was growing on the side of his head instead of the rear. It added to the shock value of his appearance. His personality was that he was a humble man, takes orders well, and works well in an overseer position.

Falcon recommended that Tayla give him an opportunity for the position. She said yes and Franco Banzetti became Shock, the new Chief of the Lower Estate. Later Shock would be killed at the Battle of the Gathering.

*   *   *

The same year they recruited John Scotti, aka Scourge, the *Red Clan* also acquired a new engineer. Eric Petersen had been gone a long time, and rarely would you ever hear his name mentioned. It brought such terrible memories of his death and how it had hurt Queen Tayla to lose such an important person in her life. Anvil, acting as her confidante and informal counselor, suggested it was time to get a new engineer while things were still in good shape above and below. This way, the new engineer could be making small repairs instead of having to make big ones when the smaller problems had grown into larger ones.

Orson Talbot was an engineer who was employed at one of Tayla's business'. He worked as an engineering consultant for large construction projects. He was asked who he would recommend for a position as an engineer for smaller construction jobs. As it turned out, Orson had a man in his consulting firm who was good but did not get along well with the others in the group. He was competitive, well-educated with experience. His only problem was that he did not get along too well with Orson. His name was Franklin Weber. Franklin was also a skilled and talented architect. He was a "take-charge" type of guy who liked to have his hands in everything. Orson did not like him because he liked to micromanage. He was more than happy to have him transferred out of his section.

When Franklin was told he was being transferred, he was angry and wanted to quit the firm altogether. Orson told him not to think of this as punitive but as an opportunity. He was told Tayla, the top of the ladder, wanted to speak with him personally. A meeting was arranged in the city of San Francisco, over dinner.

She told him that she had a secret project that needed a special person and one that could be trusted to not let information leak out. He asked how his name came up. Tayla had a shrewd method of convincing him that he was special. She told him that his boss not getting along with him and transferring him out of that section was a ruse to hide the fact that he had been chosen for a special job that required secrecy. A special assignment required a special candidate for the job, and he had been selected to be her personal chief of engineering at her estate. Still, he was not too convinced and requested to come to her estate to see this special project. She obliged him and took him directly to her home and showed him the elevator. In those days, not too many people had a personal elevator. He got in with her, and they traveled all the way to the Gates of Hell. By the time they had arrived, she had already kissed him, placing him under her spell.

Tayla had already screened him, knowing he would not be missed for he had been flown from a location that was outside the country. The plane was reported missing on its return trip and he along with other passengers were not to be found. Of course, that too was a ruse. It was not the usual way for her to obtain a familiar with a special talent. Franklin was never heard of again in his hometown of Houston, Texas nor any other place. From that moment on, he was known as Worm.

He turned out to be an engineer of extraordinary capability, up to date on the latest technology. He was shown the "special project", the unfinished construction of the *Coliseum*. He would continue it, making it 90% complete before he died in 1976. When he died, another engineer was needed and that was when Leech, aka Dan O'Reilly came into the picture in 1978. He was a former Special Forces soldier who was trained as a combat engineer, therefore making him an expert at destroying things as well as building them. The training he received from the US Army enabled him to further his education. He was a graduate of Duke University with a degree in structural engineering. He was found at a conference for engineers. After approaching him in the bar of the hotel where the conference was located, he was offered a job at the mansion to finish a "special project". Once he was told what it was, he was eager to finish such a project. After meeting with Tayla, she convinced him to stay on and finish it. There was not much left to do but finish it. When it was finished, she made Dan a familiar with the kiss that enslaves mortals. Leech proved to be a great asset to Malcolm's team, as his military training provided valuable assistance in their missions. He was with her all the way to the end. Malcolm Harris returned his memory to him at the end.

*   *   *

During the time of the construction of the *Coliseum*, there were many accidents. Accidents seemed to always accompany the operations at a construction site. She had a personal physician, but he was more concerned with the healthcare of the *Stables of the Damned* victims. He was kept busy during those days for the Stables were packed with human feeding stock.

To alleviate the strain on both operations, she recruited more medical staff. In 1992, she found two physicians at a medical conference. One of them, an emergency medicine specialist from New Jersey, Don Kulovski had ventured into the bar of the hotel hosting the conference. Tayla's physician met with him and struck up a conversation. The two were talking when Tayla walked up and sat down with them. Don was surprised that a woman of such striking beauty would sit down with strangers. When he was convinced that she was not a hooker or up to no good activity, he agreed to have dinner with the two.

After dinner, they sat, and she seduced him into going to his room. Once there, she kissed him and enslaved him into being the familiar from which he would be known as Scabs. She told him to depart, the next day, go home to New Jersey, resign his position, sell his home, get his affairs in order, and return to San Francisco forthwith. He could not resist her will, and so, he did exactly what she told him to do.

He returned to San Francisco, and Windsong picked him up at the airport and drove him to the mansion. The rest is history.

While in the service of Tayla, he performed many emergency procedures on victims of accidents during the construction of the *Coliseum* and other smaller projects.

Her physician for the *Stables of the Damned* was getting old and wanted to retire, as his health was fading. She gave him the option of retiring or bringing him to the "crossing over". He chose the crossing over, for he had nowhere else to go. He had no memory of his past life and decided there was no turning back.

After this, she decided she needed more medical staff and brought Walter Sorenson into the fold. She also brought his two nurses, Jennifer Walston and Michelle Pratt. They would all become known by their familiar names of Bones, Medusa and Cadusa, respectively. Walter Sorenson was a general surgeon and his nurses were trained as surgical nurses. They made a good team. Strangely, they remembered each other, but they did not know why. They knew all about each other but could not recall too many memories of past experiences that they had shared. They remained with the Queen until her end and stayed on with Malcolm and his team until the final battle was over. In the end, they all received their memory back and returned to the lives they had known before service with the queen.

*   *   *

In 1968, Tayla's limousine was a large Lincoln Town Car, designed in the most luxurious manner. She had considered a Rolls Royce but decided to stay with American brands. A Rolls Royce would be equipped with every known touch of elegance and class available, drawing attention everywhere it went. Few people of wealth had such a car.

Her Lincoln was driven by a man who had been a chauffeur much of his life. He had never had an accident in all his years of driving. He had never been cited for a traffic violation either. Such a qualifying feature is difficult to find. His familiar name became Rambler, after the car maker which is no longer in existence. The reason? Such drivers, like the car, do not exist anymore. He was one of a kind. They never broke down, nor did they ever run out of fuel. Her car was always in spotless condition and he took care of it like it was his own. The car was getting old and Tayla asked him about trading it in for a newer model.

The look on his face was one of betrayal and sadness. How could he let that car go? How could the Queen ask him to give it up for another? She had no idea of what he would do next. The next day, he told the Queen he was taking the car for one last drive. He made it to the gatehouse, parked the car in the middle of the road and set it and himself on fire. The loss of his most favorite thing he could not endure. Queen Tayla was shocked and saddened that he would do such a thing to himself, let alone the car. The loss of the car was nothing to her, but to him, it was like taking a piece of himself, the best piece, and throwing it away like it was nothing.

Queen Tayla for one of the few times in her existence, had been blindsided. She had no idea of the value he had placed upon that car. It was an inanimate object, but nonetheless, the object of his affection. His funeral was attended by all and he is buried in the cemetery the Queen has reserved for all those who die in her service.

Perhaps, it was because Tayla had not asked his opinion, or maybe he just wanted to keep the car. It was too late to ask him. The man was in his sixties already. Anvil knew he had not been feeling well and acting strangely of late. The butler was curious to know if he had been seen by any doctors. Later, Tayla was to find out that he had been to see a doctor, outside her knowledge, which was unusual. The doctor suspected cancer but test results had not come back. That was the reason he decided to commit suicide, for he felt he could not take the news of a terminal illness. Tayla said to all she could have offered him the option of immortality, or a quick, painless death. Instead, he chose a different path altogether, one that haunted her and the familiars.

Regardless of what happened, now she needed another driver…And a new limousine. As usual, Anvil put an ad in the local paper advertising a position for a chauffeur for a wealthy client on a permanent basis.

A man of Chinese origins, Teng Xu Ling answered the ad. He was of small stature, but his ability to recall locations on maps was astounding. Originally, he had learned to drive with professional ability while working as a cabbie in London. In London, to work as a cabbie is a difficult job to get, for the requirements are so demanding. It was quite possibly the most perfect qualification for a chauffeur anywhere around.

He was hired immediately, and soon afterwards, became the familiar known as Windsong. It fit in with his Asiatic appearance and many people thought that Windsong was his real name, as it sounded like an Asian name. He fit in well. It turned out he did not have any family he was close to. Many of his family were still in China. He had left China on a work permit to emigrate to Great Britain, and there he learned that being a cabbie was a well-respected and well-paid position.

In 1995, Windsong celebrated his 78th birthday. To him, it was the anniversary of almost 30 years of driving for Tayla. When asked what he would like, he said he wanted to join the *Clan of the Red Velvet*. He said his hands hurt, and his eyes did not see as well. He was afraid he could not drive for her as well as he used to. Tayla wanted to oblige him, and only asked that he train another driver before he left her service. So, he said to find a driver, one must go where drivers go to. Events! So, Tayla began to be more sociable, having her driver take her to places that would require valet parking and that other limousines might show up at. They started going to car shows, charitable benefits, premier moving showings, etc. to gain access to some of the younger, but still experienced drivers. They did this for nearly two months before they finally found somebody who not only met the driver's characteristics but also the other criteria that were needed to become a familiar.

Sandy Dawson had been in and out of trouble most of her teen and young adult life. She was parking cars at an event, when Tayla scanned her mind. She was behind a Ferrari sports car when she could see that Sandy was there as a plant for looking out for cars to steal. There was a long list of specific cars that were to be stolen, delivered to a ship docked in the port and to be taken overseas, and resold. The Ferrari had just made the list. The owner got out of his vehicle and gave the keys up to the valet, who called for a driver to come and park it. Sandy ran to be the one who would secure the car. Tayla urged Windsong to drive forward bumping into the Ferrari before Sandy could drive off in it.

Having intercepted the theft of the expensive car, Tayla insisted they call the police to report the accident. Windsong knew what Tayla was doing. Windsong came up to Sandy and told her he knew she was going to steal the car. He asked her if she wanted a legitimate job and alibi before the cops got there. Sandy was in a jam as everyone had seen her as the driver of the Ferrari when it was hit. The cops would want to talk with her. Though she was not at fault, her identity would be known and as she was on parole for grand theft auto, she could not afford to be seen at the accident.

Without giving it too much thought, she said, "Okay, what do I have to do?"

Windsong, replied, "Get into my employer's car, now."

Sandy did so, and Tayla made her disappear inside the car. The owner of the Ferrari returned immediately after learning what had happened to his car. He was irate and wanted to know where the driver was who took possession of his car. The valet said that his driver had gotten out of the car and fled away.

Police interviewed Windsong, who admitted it was his fault, and that his insurance would pay for the damages to the car. Tayla never had to get out of the car and Sandy was never discovered hiding in the back seat with Tayla and Anubis.

When they drove away, Tayla began asking questions of Sandy. She was hesitant to give up any information regarding her past. She knew information about people in the wrong hands could be dangerous. But Tayla knew the answers to the questions before she asked them.

"Sandy, my name is Tayla. My driver offered you a job as well as an alibi for attempting to steal the Ferrari. I already know a lot about you. I can read your thoughts."

"Oh, cut the crap, lady! I needed to get out of there for sure, and you provided the perfect way to do it. Just let me out and we can call it even, okay?"

Windsong did not slow down. He was headed straight back to the mansion. Tayla continued to talk.

"I do not think so. You are a car thief. I know what you were planning to do. You were not so successful earlier which is why you served some time in prison and are now out on parole. You have returned to your bad habits. Would you not rather have a real job driving expensive cars?"

"What are getting at?" Sandy asked.

"As my personal driver, you would have access to my limousine and any of my other cars that might join my fleet. It pays well and there will never be any police action against you."

"Okay, I'm listening."

"First, you have to believe in what I am and who I am." She leaned forward, taking Sandy by the head. and kissed her fully on the lips. From that moment on, Sandy was in full devotion to the

Queen. It was a kiss of knowledge and absolute proof that Tayla was a vampire, and that she had power over her. Her orders were to be obeyed without question and only full devotion to her was acceptable.

Sandy could hear a rushing of wind, of waves like the sea crashing on the rocks of the shore, washing away the memories of her life. Every familiar that Tayla ever had experienced the same feeling. Within seconds, all that Sandy Dawson had ever known, including her name, was erased.

"Now, you shall be known as Talon, my chauffer. Windsong is the driver you will be replacing. Now is the time for you to ask all the questions you want. I warn you there are answers that will be forbidden to you."

Talon proved to be more than a good driver. She was adept at procuring and managing the auto fleet that Malcolm would need to employ against the other Clans of Vampires in their mission. She also proved to be a good soldier once dismounted from any vehicle. She had her memory returned to her at the end and found that she had a family waiting for her. Her legal troubles were arranged to go away so she could finish out her parole, and stay with her family, raising a young daughter.

*   *   *

In 1980, Tayla had procured a large and valuable piece of property inside the city of San Francisco. She had taken it as part of a payment on a loan that had defaulted. Once she had come into possession of it, she wondered what to do with it. She sat on it for a couple of years until she had the idea of turning it into a night club. It was to be a special kind of night club, one with a theme. Seeing how at this time, there were many "strange" people who sought out the exotic and surreal night life, she thought it might be a nice idea if she could incorporate that with a restaurant and a dance floor, complete with live talent, and a bar. It would be a full-service bar, one that would cater to celebrity and young sophisticated clientele as well. The live talent would be top shelf, the food as well, and the clientele would never stop talking about their visit to the club that made them forget their troubles.

The club opened in 1982, and at Anubis' suggestion, its name would be Club Halloween. It promised to be different from any club the city had ever seen, and it would be a place where Tayla could perform from time to time. The club employees would dress in costume of the classic horror movies genre. The club was a collection of movie sets in which one would be overwhelmed by the visual experience. When it opened, a lot of critics predicted it would not last. But it not only lasted, it thrived. It seemed to be packed with patrons nearly every night.

In 1983, a man who went by the name of Richard Gaines wanted a job there. He got a job as a bouncer, first manning the front door, deciding who would get in and who did not. When Tayal found out that some people were being screened at the front door, she asked him personally why he did that.

He replied, "Some people do not belong here. Those are the tourists. The ones who say, 'Oh yeah, been there, done that." Then they go back home and brag about it. I think you want patrons who can really appreciate what you are doing here. I see some who are really into the gothic thing and they add to the atmosphere, by dressing up in costume and playing right along. Then those others, like the tourists, they seem so out of place here. I can tell who will be good for this club and who will not. That is why I screen them at the door. This club is for those who are in the spirit of Halloween all year long, not just because they are too old to go trick or treating."

"I see, Mr. Gaines. Are you always on the front door?"

"Well, that is where the manager usually puts me. I would rather be inside enjoying the shows and the clientele. Maybe like a guide, so to speak. I love this job."

"As you wish, Mr. Gaines. I shall speak with my manager."

Tayla did exactly that, and before the night was over, she invited him back to her mansion for a dinner she usually had with her employees to engage with their outlook on their jobs. Several of the Club's employees came along. She found that Gaines had never been too long at any job. The job at the Club seemed to be the one he would call his favorite. She found out from him that he had minor offenses against the law that he had served small sentences for. Those offenses were in other states. He was not on parole, but he did have a record. There was a felony charge against him at one time, but the charges were dropped. Most of all, he had no family, at least none that would claim him. He had been kicked out of his home while still a teenager and had never looked back. He was street smart and knew his way around in a fight.

Tayla liked him. She asked him if he would stay on permanently. He said he thought he already had a job with the club.

"You do have that job, Mr. Gaines, and another one if you like. You are most qualified for it," she told him.

He accepted and he was brought into the fold of the *Red Velvet Clan's* familiars as the Captain of the Hunt. His familiar name was Necro.

At the end, he stayed loyal to Malcolm. His talents proved especially useful in the team's missions. When the final battle was over, his memory was returned to him. He found he had no family to claim him. He elected to stay on as manager of Club Halloween. Gaines went on to finish his education, receiving degrees in business and hospitality management.

*   *   *

In 1979, Whitman Baur had completed his doctorate degree from Oxford University. It was his third doctorate degree, which made him one of the most highly educated people one might ever meet. At times, he was aloof, seemingly there but not there, as his mind was on something else which at times made him forget all else around him. It was a bad habit that irritated others who were trying to have a conversation with him. His mind seemed to never stop.

It was his third doctorate, accompanied by degrees from Yale University and King's College in England. His majors had been computer science, business administration and political science. With such an impressive educational background, the employment opportunities would seem endless. He wanted to work someplace exciting, exotic with interesting people. That is how Queen Tayla came to find him in San Francisco.

His education had cost quite a bit of money, as doctorate degrees were not cheap. He was heavily in debt, much of it due to student loans. When he met Tayla, she immediately saw the leverage she could use to convince him to come work for her.

In 1981, he had come to San Francisco for a Mensa convention. Mensa is a society for certified geniuses, the brightest minds of our time. Whitman certainly fit in with these people. Mensa was also holding a job fair at this convention and many firms had set up booths hoping to lure the cream of the crop to their camps.

The Bently Reserve center served as the venue of this conference and job fair. Mensa is a small organization, due to its criteria for membership. The location had served as the former San Francisco Federal Reserve building in 1924, which gave its main event space, The Banking Hall, its name. The sophisticated and elegant atmosphere was impressive as Whitman entered the room. Mensa held its job fair in this room while in some of the getaway rooms held conferences for Mensa members.

Queen Tayla needed a special person to act as her high counselor. That duty required the talents of someone who could handle the complex and difficult day to day details of her business world during the daylight hours. She would rather concern herself with the affairs of being the Queen of the clans of vampires, ensuring they would survive and prosper. Each clan managed its own affairs, those being specific to each clan, but it was the Queen's job to ensure the security and proliferation of the vampire race.

Her current counselor, Falcon, had recommended that she find someone more qualified than he was for that purpose. Falcon was good at what he did, but he was not skilled in the legal aspects of things such as corporate law, taxes, and accounting. Falcon was formerly a planner with a security firm. The position Tayla needed to fill was above his ability to perform.

Anubis had business experience. As a graduate with an MBA he had served at a corporation as a junior vice-president. Not very satisfied with the corporate world, he had decided to go back to school, and go as far as possible to show his business model was superior to the conventional thinking of the time.

Falcon had been tasked for finding a man for the position he had suggested to Tayla. Fate found him at the Bently Reserve that day. If you want the best and the brightest, look for where they would meet, Tayla told him. So, there he was, sitting in a booth at the job fair, along with many others looking for the same type of person. That was how he met Whitman Bauer.

When they met, Falcon tried to seem indifferent, but he was drawn to Whitman Bauer as soon as he saw him. There was an air of distinction, of nobility and of arrogance about him. He managed to start up a conversation with him and learned about what kind of employment the man was looking. Falcon told him what he could offer and surprisingly, Whitman accepted an appointment for a job interview with Tayla at the earliest convenience.

The next night, he would be having dinner at the estate and meeting with Queen Tayla. His life would never be the same afterwards. He arrived via her limousine, dressed in business attire. The butler took his overcoat and showed him up to the library on the second floor. "Mr. Falcon should be in to meet with you shortly. May I bring you something to drink, sir? Coffee, tea or whiskey?"

"Coffee would be fine."

The fire in the library's hearth was burning brightly. Its warmth flooded the oak-paneled room. He looked around, even examined a few books off the shelves. The large oversized stained-glass windows were spectacular, as they took up the whole outer wall of the room. Most of all, he was drawn to the portrait of a beautiful woman hanging above the fireplace.

The butler brought him his coffee into the library. Whitman asked, "Who is this beautiful woman? I have never seen such a painting. Who is the artist?" Whitman could hardly take his eyes from the painting.

Knowing he could not divulge the answer to the question, the butler responded, "I will let the mistress of the house answer those questions, sir." He turned and left the room.

Falcon entered the room just seconds after the butler left the library. "Good evening, Whitman. I trust your ride here was not too uncomfortable."

"Oh, no. It was fine. I enjoy riding in limousines through the countryside." Bauer continued to look at the painting.

Falcon noticed it and said, "You are admiring the portrait?"

Whitman quickly replied, "Yessir, I am. Admiring this portrait is exactly what I am doing. Who is this person? I studied the Renaissance in college, and I thought I had seen every masterpiece from that period, but this…this I have never seen before."

Falcon chuckled to himself. "When we go to dinner, you may ask that question again. As you can see, this is the library of Tayla Rokosovich. There are many rare books here, as she is a collector of fine and rare art. This mansion is full of such fine things. The estate here is about 75 acres. This house is a fifty-room mansion, complete with stables, carriage house and a barracks for the hired help. This is one of the best kept secrets of American architecture for this building is over 130 years old."

A shocked expression came over Whitman's face. "Oh, my! It is well kept. I would never have guessed its age."

They continued to talk about the estate, its history until the butler came into the library, stating, "Gentlemen, dinner is served!"

Whitman followed Falcon down marbled tile floors to an elevator which went down one floor and opened into a hallway which connected to a large dining room.

Normally, Queen Tayla dined with her familiars each night, but tonight it would be just the three of them.

Falcon introduced Whitman Bauer to a beautiful woman sitting at the end of a long dining table. A gourmet meal had been prepared by her chef, served with wine from her own vineyard. There was beef from her own herd, vegetables from her own farms, as every part of the meal was designed to impress the young man from Chicago.

When he laid eyes upon Tayla, sitting at her usual place at the end of the table, he was speechless. She was dressed in an elegant ensemble of red and black. Her dark hair was coiffed while her makeup was perfect. Tayla was struck by his ice-blue eyes and height. His hair was dark, straight, and he was clean-shaven. He smelled masculine, and his demeanor was appealing to her.

Whitman had not had too much experience with the opposite sex. In fact, he was quite awkward when meeting women, but he knew class when he saw it and to him, Tayla was elegance personified. After he got over his usual shyness of speaking with a woman, particularly one like Tayla, he finally realized the woman in the portrait was the very woman he now sat next to at the table.

Before he could ask the question, she said, "Yes, that is me. But it is incredibly old."

"How old is it?" he asked, thinking it had to be a joke.

"Older than you would think."

"I have heard of doppelgangers, but…"

Tayla smiled at him, saying, "Yes, I understand all about that. I will explain later. Now, we must dine before it gets cold. Everything on this table came from my estate. I hope you will enjoy tonight's meal."

He and Tayla had quite a conversation that lasted well into the evening. Many sorts of subjects were covered, particularly his business experience. He said he had come up with a new business model which he wanted to introduce but did not have the capital by which to bring it to bear. This interested Tayla very much, as she knew that wealth had its own form of power…a power to control, power without the attachment of force, power to persuade without consequences. This was the kind of power she preferred.

She learned that Whitman had a family, in Chicago. He was the oldest of four children, with living parents who had spent their life savings and then some to put their eldest through school. He was the only one who had attended post graduate school. In college, Whitman was not an athlete, but could have been for he was tall and slender. He never saw the point of team sports other than personal enjoyment. He preferred swimming, and cerebral games such as chess. It seemed he knew a lot about any subject that came up.

He explained his business theories to Tayla and Falcon. They were truly radical for they had not been tried successfully. Whitman pointed out where others had gone wrong trying to do so. He had a working knowledge of corporate tax structure, even without a law degree, stating he felt that any corporate executive should have a basic knowledge of it before trying to expand any business. It continued to amaze Tayla that he knew so much with limited business experience. By the late evening, she was convinced this was the man she would pick as her High Counselor. It would prove to be a good choice.

She told him, "Mr. Bauer, I would like to offer this position to you. Falcon and I believe you are the only candidate for this job. There are great things in your future should you take this opportunity. I can see you are a cautious man, one who does not step without knowing where his foot will touch. Therefore, you would like to see on paper the assets and holdings of which I want you to oversee. Mr. Falcon can have that ready for you by the end of the week. I invite you to look things over, take time to make up your mind and call us if you decide to accept. I promise you; nothing will be the same afterwards."

Whitman Bauer left the mansion in the same limousine that brought him. On his way back to his hotel, he pondered the opportunity that lay before him. More than that, he could not get the painting out of his thoughts. "That woman," he asked Windsong, the driver, "the one in the portrait, it is the same woman I just interviewed with, is it not?"

Windsong already had permission to answer questions Tayla knew he would ask. This was one of those questions. "Truthfully, sir, it is the same woman. There are many secrets about Tayla Rokosovich you will be privy to if you take this position. By the way, I am Windsong. I drive for her."

The limousine came to a stop at a nice hotel in the city. He had Falcon's card to call. He had already decided to accept the position before the doorman could open the door. He walked through with a smile on his face. Good things were happening for him. He would become the one known as Anubis.

*   *   *

567

Richard Vandemere, aka Valkyrie, was the Chief of Security for Tayla's ever growing empire. He had built a security apparatus which was in use throughout all her businesses. She was not there to personally oversee the affairs of the many companies she owned. It did not mean employees were not tempted to put their hands into the profits gained. He was also head of security of the estate itself. He had come into her service in 1960. He was a former law enforcement officer and a military veteran of the cold war era. Both of those backgrounds made him qualified to do what he did for her.

Now, it was 1990. Valkyrie was getting older. He was already in his late thirties when he became a familiar so that put him in his seventies when Tayla decided to retire him at his request. He wanted to "cross-over" when his time came.

So, the Queen decided to start looking for another Chief of Security to take his place. She was not sure where to even start looking. One night, she visited one of her usual haunts. It was a bar near the port, a seedy, low-end bar where if you were looking for trouble, here is where you might find it.

By 1990's standards, it would be considered a dive bar. In the 40's and 50's, it was known as a waterfront bar, an establishment that was near or on the waterfront that catered to sailors who had just come into port or getting ready to sail. Either way, these were men who needed a drink and did not care too much about the class of the joint or the clientele. The real question is what would a beautiful, classy, well-dressed woman be doing in such a place? Every now and then, Tayla would visit some of these bars because she knew most of the clientele were not locals. As said before, they were either coming or going. Many were sailors from other parts of the world and would not have written home about where they were on the night they would disappear.

She especially liked this bar. It was dark, intimate, and most people kept to themselves, particularly if they were alone. If there were "working girls" cruising, sometimes a fight would breakout over one of them, but usually, it was quiet. It was easy pickings for the vampire queen. One of those nights she indulged herself by visiting the waterfront bar "Macs" named for the owner. The "owner", a familiar to her for nearly 30 years, was not the true owner. Tayla was the owner. He ran it for her, like the one who he had replaced before. If he saw her in his bar, it meant she was on the hunt for fresh blood and he knew she would find it there. He would call her when one of the freighters or tankers came into port.

The door opened and someone dressed to kill entered. The heads turned, the jaws fell, and the silence came over the place. The jukebox was the only sound that could be heard. Using a seductive walk, she took a seat at the bar. She appeared as elegant as anyone who had just walked the red carpet in Hollywood. She would order a double scotch on the rocks, light up a cigarette and turn on the bar stool, to scan the patrons, and read their thoughts.

Usually, within a few minutes or so, an adventurous sailor would come over to start a conversation with her. She rarely would brush anyone off, as she was more intent on his ability to feed her than impress her. If she liked the man, she would leave with him. And like so many of them, he was never seen again.

A sailor, one of those adventurous types, walked over and took the bar stool next to hers and asked if she minded if he sat next to her.

She smiled and said she did not mind. "I like meeting new people," she said. Her clutch style purse was on the bar. She moved it closer to herself so to provide room for the man's drink.

He started by introducing himself, but the information went in one ear and out the other for she was focused only on one thing, his blood rushing through his veins with each heartbeat. The sailor, a man from somewhere in Europe, continued to speak with clichés of how he was attracted to her, of how beautiful she was, and hinting of the things he would like to do with her. She just sat there and took it all in. Vampires miss little details when it comes to sleight of hand maneuvers and that was exactly what this sailor was doing. He was slowly and methodically trying to get closer and closer to her purse. She knew of his plans and decided to see how bold he could get.

Another patron in the bar, a man from Great Britain, was also watching. Soon, before the man could make his move, the British man came over and throttled the sailor by his collar and threw him to the floor. The sailor was stunned and pulled a knife out to defend himself. The Briton was a trained soldier, an ex-SAS soldier in fact, and was going to have none of this man's nonsense with the knife. He kicked the knife from the man's hand, assumed a full mounted position, and began pummeling the man mercilessly. Other patrons had to break it up or surely, the sailor would have been beaten to death.

The British man turned around to look at Tayla, who had not moved the entire time, and said, "I am very sorry to have made such a fuss and all, but this man was about to steal your purse. I could not sit by and watch that happen."

Mac, the bartender, told the other patrons to throw the other man out of the bar. He thanked the Briton and offered him a free drink. He accepted and took a stool at the bar a few seats away from Tayla.

Tayla knew what impressed most ladies and what did not. She also knew that this man did what he did not to impress her but because he felt she needed his assistance. That had not happened very often. In fact, the last time that had happened, it was with Renard, her French knight. Chivalry was something she admired, and this man obviously had it.

"Thank you," she said to him. "Might I have the name of whom I owe my gratitude?

"Sean McAllister, my lady. From England." He held out his hand to her.

She took his hand, grasped it gently, and said, "That man was about to attempt to steal my purse?"

"Yes, madam, he was. I noticed it all the way across the bar. It seemed to be the right thing to do. He needed to be taught a lesson."

"Do you do this kind of thing often or just when you think it might impress a lady?"

"Madam, I did not almost kill a man to impress you. I was trying to protect you. If you think I planned for that to happen so I could sit here and get a free drink, you are mistaken."

"It was very observant of you to watch him make his move on me. I could see it too, but I did not say anything because I wanted to see how far he would go."

"You knew?" Sean McAllister asked.

"Oh, yes. But I do appreciate what you did. And with such efficiency! I take it you have some training in hand to hand combat?"

"Yes madam, you could say that. I am former British Special Air Service."

"Oh, I have heard of them. Exceptionally good at what they do. Now, I am impressed."

"As I said before, madam, I did not do it to impress you."

"Perhaps so, but nonetheless, I am. Would you mind waiting for me. I will be right back."

"I am not going anywhere for a while," he replied.

Tayla left the bar and when she got outside, she found the sailor who was beaten badly sitting on a bench. He held his head in one hand, while wiping the blood from his mouth and nose with a rag in his other. McAllister had done quite a job on him.

He looked up to see the woman he had just try to rob staring at him. "Come to rub it in, lady?"

"No, but I will tell you something else. No one robs from me, ever. I do have need of you, though." Before he could ask what those remarks might refer to, she was on him before he could scream. She took all his blood, for it was full of adrenalin from the fight. Satiated, she took his body, flew up into the night sky and dropped him into the chilly waters of the San Francisco Bay.

Within minutes, she was back inside the bar, ready to converse with her newfound friend, McAllister.

As she talked with him, she found him interesting, if not intriguing. As she read his mind, she found answers to questions he would have never answered truthfully. He had a past. He also had no place to go and few who would miss him, except for the SAS.

Her previous chiefs of security and intelligence had died. All of them had died natural deaths except Birdseye. He died with Eric, trying to protect him. She wanted to ask him why he had left the SAS so she did, knowing he would not answer the truth.

As soon as the words left her mouth, the painful and bitter memories of his exploits in the legendary organization came to light. He had lost many friends, suffered some life-threatening wounds but the most painful of all was the betrayal he felt when he was left for dead on the battlefield. It was during the Gulf War. His teammates begged to go back and retrieve him. When permission was granted to do so, they found him alive. He was evacuated to a hospital. Sworn to secrecy, he could not even tell the medical staff the details of his wounds. He went on medical leave for quite a while before he was deemed fit to return to duty. When he was able to return, the fire in his spirit just did not seem to be there. He did not trust his superiors for what had happened to him. At the first chance, he resigned from the SAS, and left to wander. Due to his resignation, the SAS had officially classified him as KIA for security reasons. Tonight, he had wandered into Mac's bar.

"May I call you Sean?" she asked.

"Of course, may I have your name as well?" he asked in return.

"I am Tayla. Sean, I have a proposition for you. I can tell that you are not employed right now. Asking me how I know is not important. What is important is I need a man of your qualifications. You might think, I did not come in here tonight for a job interview. That is true. You did not. But, by your actions here tonight, I would say that was the most concise job interview I ever conducted. I am a businesswoman, and I own quite a few enterprises. That means I am very wealthy and as such, I must be careful that nefarious creatures such as the man who tried to steal from me do not attempt something much more sinister. It means I have need of one who can be trusted, loyal to a fault, and can run a security apparatus already in place, improving it such that I can monitor all threats against me worldwide. You, Sean McAllister, meet those requirements. I would like you to come to my estate, look the place over and then make up your mind. You are under no obligation to come and work for me, but I think you will feel right at home should you decide to."

He finished his drink. "Well, no harm in checking your place out, I suppose. When is a good time to call?"

She reached into her clutch purse and drew a business card out. "Call this number and set up an appointment. I look forward to your visit."

He took the card and left the bar. As she read his thoughts while he was leaving, she learned he was quite impressed with her. His distrust of strangers was still evident, but she had planted a seed of curiosity in him that told her he would indeed call her. She would let Anubis know to expect a call from him. She would arrange for transportation to her estate for him. Smiling, she knew she had found the right man for the job of Chief of Security.

When she arrived home that early morning, Anubis met her. He had received her message regarding Sean McAllister and the job interview.

"This man, Sean McAllister, you are sure he is the right man for the job vacated by Valkyrie? I know we need someone for that. I cannot do both jobs at the same time. At least not as good as someone whose sole duty is that job."

"Anubis, your fears and concerns regarding being double-tasked are heard and well-founded. That is why I think I have indeed found the right person for this job. He is former SAS, a combat veteran, wounded and decorated for his exploits on the battlefield. He is highly intelligent, fit, adept at many non-lethal skills, and most of all, he is a gentleman. I admire that the most. Tonight, for the first time since Renard, someone felt that I needed help and he rose to the occasion to defend me. It was quite a sight, Anubis. He thrashed a would-be thief right in front of the entire bar at Mac's. He was so modest about it. Mac gave him a free drink and we sat and talked. I could read his mind, and saw he was in a lot of mental anguish. His problem was he felt torn between two worlds, the world he is in and the world he left behind. He has been a soldier nearly his entire life and feels that is all he knows. The team he was with came under direct and indirect fire incurring some casualties. He tried to rescue them and was wounded for his trouble. When the team was exfiltrated, they left him on the battlefield with the other wounded and dead

573

because the fire was so intense. That is why he has an attitude toward military superior officers. Betrayal. It is the worst offense a leader can do to his men. I think he needs this job and I intend to give it to him."

"Very well, my Queen. I look forward to meeting with him."

Two days later, Anubis received the phone call from McAllister. The meeting was set up, and McAllister was told where a limousine would pick him up. The soldier of fortune or in this case "misfortune" was wearing the same clothes he was seen in while in the bar. He was used to traveling "light".

Talon had only been working for a short time when she picked up McAllister. "My, you are as pretty as the lady I met in the bar the other night. Does everybody look this good where we're going?"

Talon replied, "No. Quite the contrary. I think Miss Tayla and I are as good as it gets, soldier. However, I do not think you will be disappointed in this job. There may not be very much time for romance or relationships. Do you have luggage?"

"No, not really. I travel with the least I need. Other than that, the best part of that is there's not much to lose."

Talon thought about what he said. She put her hand to her abdomen, thinking of the stretch marks on her belly she could not account for. She had not talked to anyone about it, but still it told her of a possible past she could not see.

The limousine drove out of the city and continued to head north. In a few hours, Sean McAllister would be known from there on as Dread. He would be with the Queen until the end as well, performing a great service for her and for Malcolm's team. In the end, his memory was returned, and he found his happiness in the Egyptologist, Martha Rivera.

CHAPTER FIFTY-SEVEN

MALCOLM HARRIS

"Dearest Malcolm, you are about to enter into the final phase of my life. The familiars are in place, my estate, both Upper and Lower, are complete. Yet, with all the wealth, and all my vampires and familiars to keep me company, I still feel empty. It is the curse of being a vampire. I will always be a stranger to satisfaction, to completeness, to fulfillment. It is in these times that being a Queen, does not mean as much to me as it once did. I know there is so much more to life, even as I live in death. I have tried to partake of the life mortals know, though I am limited as to the extent that I can. I live a lie, never being able to be accepted as who and what I am. If I were to tell the whole world what I am, I would be considered a monster, and a dangerous one at that. I would deserve it for I am guilty of all the crimes for which I would be accused. My confession is of no use, as I cannot atone for any of it. I suffer from its guilt, which makes me feel empty and sorrowful.

I am the only one of my kind who can possibly feel that way. When I wrote of this, I knew you would come into my life. For what reason, what purpose you would serve, I did not know. My gift of sight did not reveal that until later after I had already met you. It made my death so much easier, in that it meant something."

*   *   *

575

In 1990, Tayla took up the habit of reading the newspapers, and keeping up to date on the news of the living but mortal world. She wanted to stay informed for she knew the *Order of the Jackal* had never rescinded their declaration of war upon the *Order of the Clan of the Red Velvet*. She would hear of many things, both ordinary and the strange and bizarre. When she would read of such things, like events of the paranormal, she would struggle to keep from laughing. Often, she could be found in the library laughing out loud. When Mortis or any other familiar would ask what was so amusing, she would point to an article she had read and state that it was so strange that they wanted to witness a real supernatural event. It seemed the mortal world was always seeking something that would link them to a world they could only imagine.

The familiars thought it was amusing as well for they lived in a world where supernatural was ordinary and common place. It was the mundane and boring world of the mortals that was absent at the mansion. Every night, the familiars would witness the sudden appearance of vampires in the house, doing things only a vampire could do. Many of them did not have all the gifts the Queen possessed, such as the ability to sit at a dining table and enjoying a feast of superbly prepared food. They knew her sustenance did not come from any of it but the blood of the living. The fact that she sat and dined with many of her familiar staff was because she enjoyed the activity. It made her closer to them and drew them closer to her. For the most part, all her familiars loved her. All of them feared her as well, but knew they had nothing to fear if their loyalty to her remained intact.

For Dread, if she were to ask him if he wanted to be transformed as a vampire, he would have done so without a second thought. He loved her, as a man would love a woman. He was that devoted, and she knew it. But, after Eric, she swore off relationships with mortals or vampires.

All the others were loyal, for they were treated well, much like employees were. She paid them a generous salary, with benefits, taking good care of them. She allowed them a type of freedom that was in place if they were to perform as needed for her.

Anubis was nearly like an older brother to her. She respected him, listened well to his counsel, and often pointed out that his decisions were to be treated as though they were her choices. He enjoyed an immense amount of respect and authority. Mortis, she treated as a father figure. When she wanted the wisdom of a father, she consulted with him.

The interactions of the familiars with her seemed like those of any large family. But it was not Walton's Mountain. Often, the familiars were assigned to dispose of victims, clean up messes made and the sights of some of it were ugly. This was the original role of the familiar, to cover, to conceal and to protect the identity, the location, and the vampire itself from all harm. This was how a familiar served their master.

As Tayla began to stay informed of the current events of the world around her, she came across an article about a man who was fast becoming an expert in the field of the occult. She read about him, noting he was not a practitioner of the dark arts but an expert regarding the fallacies portrayed by those who would use it to defraud, and manipulate others. He never said it did not exist, but that many of that day were claiming they could read people's fortunes, etc.

She read that he had exposed many of their schemes and fraudulent enterprises. This same man was also a consultant with many law enforcement agencies. The man was Malcolm Harris.

For reasons she could not quite explain, she felt drawn to him. Months went by, and she heard about him again. Another month went by, and another article about him. He was becoming nationally recognized as an expert on cults, covens, strange beliefs, and Christianity as well as other religions of the world.

She began to follow him in the media. He had published an article in some magazines, which she read over and over. Then, she saw him on a talk show where the subject was about Satanic cults and other forms of "black magic."

His occupation was a journalist. He investigated many stories about the supernatural. She noted that he did not seem on a crusade designed to rid the world of vampires. He was not affiliated with the Holy Church of the Catholics. There was no order telling him to destroy her. He was completely unaware she existed. Eventually, that would change.

He was from south Florida, the Miami area, working for a local news station. Eventually, her curiosity got the best of her. She knew there was a band of *Red Clan* vampires in Florida. She ordered him to be surveilled. Everywhere he went, she could find out about it. Notes were gathered on him, and finally, a dossier on him compiled. Why she was driven to this was a question she could not answer. Not to her vampires, familiars or even herself. She just knew something about him was significant and she was drawn to him, either out of curiosity or his recent accomplishments made her sit up and take notice.

She ordered that he nor his family were to be touched. In 1992, when his notoriety began to take on momentum, she decided to come to Florida and see for herself that which she felt drawn to. When she saw him one night, dining with his wife, she listened to his voice, his conversation with his attractive wife.

Anubis was with her. He said, "I really do not see the reason we are here in this humidity and stifling heat. I much prefer the climate of northern California as I know you do too."

She replied, "I cannot seem to understand what it is about him that attracts me. It would seem he has some purpose to fulfill regarding me. He is mortal, he is married, he is religious. What is it that seems so special about him?"

"Does he serve a purpose for you? Other than being a potential victim?" Anubis asked.

"Perhaps he does, Anubis. Perhaps. I have many questions about this world, this life, and such. Perhaps, he has answers. Perhaps not."

"I think the latter is much more likely the truth. I do not like this. We know the Jackals are active in this area. Perhaps it is because of him. Perhaps, they are laying a trap for you and using him as bait. And it seems as if it might be working." He continued to eat his Latin food.

"And he is oblivious that I exist! Here, a man who is regarded nationally as an expert on the supernatural sitting less than ten feet away from a vampire, a Queen of vampires, no less, and has no clue of it."

"I find it strange that you are interested in him infinitely more than he is in you," said Anubis.

"Well, yes, for now," she replied.

At that moment, Malcolm looked over at her table and saw her looking directly at him. The instant their eyes met, something happened. She knew he could not know who she was or what she was, but the look in Malcolm's eyes said as if he did.

She wondered if she had just given herself away. Then, a waitress who was behind her, brought her dessert. It was the dessert that Malcolm had been looking at and it gave him the inspiration to order the same when he was finished with his main entrée.

Malcolm had not given her the look she was afraid of. Only a few had ever done that, and they were the ones who wanted to destroy her. She relaxed, and finished her meal, conversing with Anubis.

When Malcolm looked again at them, he was looking at Anubis. She read his thoughts again and they told her he was surprised that a beautiful woman would be with a man who looked like Anubis. The two just did not look like a couple.

"Let us depart from here. I do not want him to remember me or that I had noticed him. I should be completely unknown to him." The two left while Malcolm and his wife continued to discuss the growth of their two-year-old twins.

Tayla departed Miami that night and would meet with Anubis again in California. Still, she felt that she must be introduced to him, for reasons still unknown to her.

*   *   *

Malcolm and his wife readied themselves for bed that night after getting home in time to keep from paying their babysitter overtime charges. As they checked in on their children, Malcolm asked his wife, "You know, I felt as if someone was watching us tonight."

Rachel responded, asking, "Really? How?"

"I don't really know. Just a feeling, I guess. As if every move I made, I was being watched."

579

"Don't be silly. If someone was watching us, I would have known. I have a sense about such things. Remember that time…"

He interrupted, "Yes, I remember that time. This time was different, though. It was as if someone was trying to speak to me, saying 'look this way, look at me'."

"I think your imagination is running away with you. I suppose you will dream about it all night long."

They crawled into bed and soon, they were fast asleep. He did not dream for outside their window, a figure stood in their backyard, telling his subconscious to forget what he had seen or felt that night.

As Tayla flew on towards the dawn and a safe house that awaited her, the night's events were heavy on her mind. She knew this was not an accident. She was supposed to meet with him. She did not want to on this night for she had seen his wife. She felt she was beautiful, and that he was devoted to her. She had no idea of how right she was to assume that this man would be able to resist her, able to see in her what others would never be able to see, and provide her with answers to questions she had been asking for almost eight hundred years.

CHAPTER FIFTY-EIGHT

A PURPOSE TO FULFILL

"Dearest Malcolm, there is no feeling like the feeling of betrayal. The betrayal of a lover, of a friend, cannot match that of betrayal from a family member. I experienced that at the gathering of 1993. I began to prepare for what I knew would eventually happen...A coup of sorts, one that would shake the foundation of my race, instigated by my brother. I learned one thing from that experience. Once a vampire is completely in the service of the Dragon, there is no turning back. Family does not mean anything at that point. All I knew was my father would have been so ashamed of what his children were doing.

I was about to turn a corner, as some people say. A significant event was about to happen. I was about to become aware of something important. When I thought of my past, particularly my struggle against the Holy Church, I always wondered why they hated me so much. They hated me, what I was, what I stood for. I could never understand that. All I did know was that I had to survive. There was a purpose in my life that needed to be fulfilled, and a discovery made during surveillance of your home was the key to it."

*   *   *

The *Red Clan* that resided in Miami continued its surveillance of Malcolm and his family. They questioned amongst themselves the reasons for it, but the Queen had ordered it so therefore, they obeyed. Now, it was 1993 and Jackal activity was beginning to increase. Francisco Cordero, a Colombian national had just arrived in Miami. His arrival was immediately noted by the *Red Clan*. What was more alarming about it was that he arrived with a contingent of *Black Clan* vampires. It was immediately reported to the mansion in California.

The Queen was dismayed when she heard this news. Her brother had gone over to the side of her enemy. At the gathering of that year, she confronted him. He was very frank about it.

"Yes, I have an alliance with the Dragon. I told you a long time ago, he was your enemy, not mine. I have never had a quarrel with him. You, on the other hand, have never stopped hating him."

"Rascha, you have such a short memory. Have you forgotten completely what he did to our family? Our father?"

"I know what our father did to me, giving you his ring, completely cutting his eldest son out of his birthright. He made you the leader when it should have been me all along."

"Your mind is poisoned, brother. The Dragon has infected you with his lies. Our father did so because his heart told him it was the right thing to do. I know this to be true. Who taught you how to survive? It was me, not the Dragon. He would have done nothing more than enslave you. You think you have power. You only have what he allows you to have!"

"Dear sister, one day I shall wear your crown. I shall be king and enjoy that which was given away to someone who does not deserve it. We were created by the Dark Lord. It is from him by which we are given our power. I remain loyal to him and his disciple here on earth, the Dragon. You, have chosen to rebel against him."

"Because I have chosen to not follow the lies of the Dragon, you think that disqualifies me from my royal position? You just said it was because I was a woman that I did not deserve the crown. Your lies and flawed reasoning betray you, brother. Stay away from him, come back into our family."

"Our family? You mean Othar and Prieta, who have also embraced the Dragon's will? My dear sister, it is you who is on the outside of the fold of the Dark Lord. There are consequences to that. Are you prepared to endure them?"

"If I must, then yes!"

The Gathering of that year ended in bitterness between the *Red and Black Clans*. The Purple and the Blue Clans seemed to adopt a neutral stance, siding with whoever would come out on top. For the moment, it was a bitter stalemate. At least, Rascha had been honest about his discontent with the status quo. She knew he would continue to plot against her. If it were any other vampire, she would have known immediately what to do. However, it was her brother, who had come to disdain her as a rival, jealous of the birthright that was bestowed upon her and not himself. He felt that the eldest son, the male, should have gotten the lion's share of the inheritance, which in this case was the ring of power and authority of his father. He had been denied and was fuming about it ever since.

Since they had gathered in the *Coliseum*, it meant that they knew of the layout of the Lower Estate. That was something the Jackals had been trying to learn about since 1929. If they were allied with the *Black Clan*, they could easily relay this information to the *Order of the Jackal*, thereby allowing another invasion of the Lower Estate. Tayla's gift of sight predicted this was exactly what would happen within less than a decade. The Dragon could enter also, via the *Black Clan's* treachery. Then, it would be a disaster. Tayla needed to come up with a plan, a proverbial secret weapon that could counter the Dragon's and the Jackal's efforts to destroy her and her clan. She did not know it at the time, but she had already seen this weapon, Malcolm Harris.

*   *   *

The *Red Clan* continued the surveillance of Malcolm. Finally, her gift of sight told her that this man would come dangerously close to encountering the Dragon, the *Order of the Jackal*, even entering his realm. Her sight was not clear how or when this would happen, but as time went by, things began to fall into place.

She returned to Miami in 1995, which by this time, was under vast reconstruction from the damage inflicted by Hurricane

Andrew. Malcolm and his family sought shelter from the storm, but when he resumed his position as a reporter, he found himself all over the Miami-Dade area. From Key West to Fort Lauderdale, he was everywhere in between. He reported on all kinds of scandals, scams from reconstruction to the emergence of Santeria covens, Voodoo practitioners, and such. It was interesting to the public, but it also meant that a growing number of the population were becoming duplicitous in their belief systems.

Malcolm noted that one religion, Santeria, was becoming popular amongst the highly concentrated Hispanic population. Santeria is a religion wherein the devil receives worship from people. For those who practice Santeria, they believe it is an extension of their Catholic religion. Santeria means 'Way of the Saints.' It is an Afro-Caribbean religion based on Yoruba beliefs and traditions, with some Roman Catholic elements added. Yoruba is from Nigeria and is the basis for many religions that have spread to the New World, most notably in the Southern Americas. It is primarily the religion of the *Order of the Jackal*.

Malcolm began to study about it, and because he lived in Miami, he had a vast opportunity to speak to many practitioners of it. He learned of it, studying its methods and how to recognize some of its rituals, particularly of sacrifice.

His expertise in this enabled him to begin to assist the Miami Dade Sheriff's Office as a consultant on crime scenes. This was how he became close with Luis Martinez. As all this was happening, it was being reported to Queen Tayla.

Tayla began to study Malcolm. She felt an irresistible force about him. One night, a *Red Clan* vampire, assigned to watch over his home, reported he could hear Malcolm and his wife praying together. An overwhelming force seemed to surround them, so much that the vampire had to leave their vicinity. He felt repelled, though he was sure it had nothing to do with the Jackals, the Dragon and perhaps even with the Dark Lord. It was quite the opposite, as it was a force of light, not of darkness.

The vampire reported that night after night, this phenomenon occurred when he and his wife prayed. None of the vampires could stay on watch when this happened. They had to conduct surveillance from quite a distance away.

This information intrigued Tayla. He had power that repelled even some of her strongest vampires. If he could do this, imagine what he could do against vampires of the *Black Clan*. She decided she would keep tabs on him, no matter how long it took to discover what kind of power this was that protected him, even against vampires.

She dispatched a team of familiars to watch over him during the hours of daylight while the vampires kept watch at night. The familiars noted they did not feel this kind of power during the day. They did notice that he went to church services faithfully, every Sunday. The vampires could see during the night, that soon after he rose from his sleep, he would engage in what Christians would call 'quiet time'. It consisted of prayer and study from a book that no vampire could get near. When he read from that book, the power that was mentioned in earlier reports again, was overwhelming.

The Queen decided she wanted that book, the one he read from each morning. If it had that kind of power, surely, she could use it to fight against the Dragon and his minions. Every attempt on the *Red Clan*'s part to obtain it failed. A team of familiars broke into his house when it was vacant and took it. No vampire could pick it up but a familiar could. They brought it to the Queen. It was packed in a box. She too, could not pick it up. When she realized its power was too much even for her, she asked Anubis about it.

Anubis leaned over and pulled it from the box. "Oh, my. Do you have any idea of what this is in the box, my Queen? It is a copy of the Holy Bible. Most, well, many Americans have a copy or have had a copy at one point in their lives."

"It is scripture? Well, that explains why my vampires, nor I could touch it. It is indeed holy. This book is the antithesis of the Dragon, the truest of all holy relics."

"Christians believe it to be the word of God. When they read the scriptures, they believe it to be God talking to them. There is much to be learned from it, especially if you believe in it," Anubis

585

added. "To hear its message would drive you away, my Queen. It is power, but a power that is toxic to one such as you."

"Then I am truly damned," she said solemnly. "I cannot hear its message. Is there any way I could hear it without it hurting me?"

"I can think of only one way. If this Malcolm Harris believes in its words, he believes in its message. Only he can tell you about it. I suggest you approach him to hear what it says. This is the reason why you are so interested in him. It is not him, but the message he can give to you."

A wave of hope came over her, flooding her with emotions. Perhaps it was a glimpse of hope, a glimmer of salvation from her lonely existence. Perhaps this was not the only world for her. She remembered hearing of it, people talking about it at the Church services. She had never understood what they were talking about. She only knew that they had talked about a God who was loving, about a God that would send some to Hell and others to Heaven, but she never knew how this was done. No one had ever told her about God. She only knew it had to do with good and evil. When she thought about herself, she saw only evil. The amount of murder and evil she had committed over the centuries were sure to send her straight to Hell if she were to die the second death. Was there another way? This was the question she wanted to ask Malcolm. Maybe he could tell her how to make amends with God, to come to a reconciliation with the Creator, to come to know and understand Him. At least she would not be in the darkness, without knowledge as to why. She knew the other vampires were different than her. Sometimes she did good things, but much of the time, she had to perform evil things. What was worse, she did not delight in doing evil things as her siblings did. They had no remorse, no guilt, no conscience.

*　　　　　*　　　　　*

By the year of 1994, Francisco Cordero had established a large coven of Jackal followers. They began to hold meetings and sacrificial rites in his home located in an upper middle-class neighborhood. It was the kind of residential area one would never think of such things occurring. This went on for several years before the police would find out that his blood sacrifice rituals involved animals...animals that belonged to other people.

Francisco's neighbors were oblivious to the events happening right under their noses. It was not the usual kind of activity that one would think of in suburban America. Because the neighbors were not picking up on any of the signs that were obvious to the *Red Clan* vampires who were also assigned to surveil the home of Francisco Cordero, Tayla decided that someone should place that call to the local authorities. She took the initiative and told her band leader to make the call herself. The female vampire did as she was told, disguising her voice to sound like an elderly woman. A familiar to that clan was there when the police came out and was interviewed by the police. She told a very convincing story to the investigating detectives. She complained aggressively that she could hear animal's screaming in fear and pain. She could not stand it anymore, so she picked up the phone and called the police.

The familiar was eventually interviewed by none other than Malcolm Harris himself. By this time, all the *Red Clan* vampires and familiars of that area knew of Malcolm Harris. He was a celebrity of sorts amongst them, but he had no idea of his notoriety.

The vampires later reported to the Queen that Malcolm was on the case along with his police friend, Luis Martinez. The band of vampires down in Miami knew that with these two on the case, Cordero was soon to be out of business.

Tayla's gift of sight told her that things were starting to fall into place. Malcolm would soon be the sworn enemy of the *Order of the Jackal* and anyone who was their enemy was to be her friend. She had found her secret weapon.

CHAPTER FIFTY-NINE

COLLISION COURSE

"Dearest Malcolm, we are getting close to the moment that we acknowledge that I am what I am, and you are what you are. I am evil, living in the darkness. My two natures fight against each other, leaving me exhausted. You are good, but you too have two natures. Yet, you live in the light. And you feel blessed and loved.

How you would feel about me I did not know. My feelings were ambivalent up to that point. I knew you had treated all proposed supernatural events with a healthy dose of skepticism. I could not blame you. You had seen a lot of fakes and frauds that had turned out to not be what they claimed.

But you were willing to listen and consider what you saw in that room, looking out the large windows on that stormy night. I considered the possibility that I might fail to convince you. There was no time for that. You had to believe right away that I was serious, and that you were in the home of a real vampire. There was no other way to convince you but to demonstrate my power.

I watched you and Luis take off for Colombia. My gift of sight told me you were in far more danger than you ever thought possible. The Dragon saw you as a threat, the most serious threat he had ever encountered of late. Not since people like Joseph of Arimathea had the Dragon felt defeated by a man of faith. That was what I admired the most about you. You had something I desired, and I was not about to waste any time or effort to find out what it was, and if possible, attain it for myself."

*　　　　　*　　　　　*

Malcolm and Lou Martinez had just taken off from Miami enroute to Bogota, Colombia. Both were hesitant, nervous, uncertain if they would find out anything at all about Cordero and his religious affiliations. Most of all, Lou was concerned about Malcolm for he was the one who would have the most trouble blending in. He was right, for Malcolm stuck out like a sore thumb that just got hit twice by a hammer.

Familiars who were stationed at the airport relayed back that they were seen boarding an aircraft, but also that the Dragon had boarded the same plane. The Dragon was playing with Malcolm's head as he would appear, disappear, and then reappear out of nowhere just to confuse the Caucasian male. 90% of the passengers were Hispanic.

Anubis' intelligence network extended all the way around the world, specifically those places where there were known Jackal covens. The largest was in the backcountry of Colombia where they operated with the maximum of freedom without fear of retribution or interference from authorities. The hacienda ranch of the Dragon was located there.

There were familiars all along the way. The cab driver was a familiar, working for the band of vampires in Bogota. He also followed the two Americans around Bogota, reporting on the activities of them. When he reported on the Americans riding out to the backcountry of Colombia to visit a place known as the Forest Temple, Tayla was concerned. They were getting far too close.

When the two Americans arrived at the mission of Paul Vetter, they explained the reasons for being there. When Paul saw the photo of Eduardo Arrellano, he was stunned. He warned them about him, imploring them to stay away from him. He told them of his connections with the *FARC* and the *ELN* (*Revolutionary Armed Forces of Colombia, National Liberation Army*). They were out of the range of the familiars and the *Red Clan* Vampires. Tayla knew she had to intervene personally, so she had her own jet fly her to Bogota.

"I want to fly at top speed to Bogota airport. No stops, no slowing down, nothing to impede us. Understand?" she asked the pilot at the darkened airport close by her estate. She got on board, sat in her seat and place her head in her hands, as she sought to see the outcome of this event. Anubis and Dread were both with her. They too were worried, worried that she may be making a mistake. Dread especially was worried for he knew that the Dragon, should he find out she was on her way there, would set a trap for her and try his utmost to destroy her. She knew it too.

She arrived that evening of when Malcolm would return from his encounter with the Dragon and the *Order of the Jackal* soldiers at the Forest Temple. He had already taken Lou, who was wounded at the Temple to Paul Vetter's compound for medical treatment. She changed her appearance to the persona of the red headed woman. Nervously, she waited for his appearance back at his hotel. Malcolm had returned only a short while before she had arrived. He had gone up to pack, take a quick shower and brought Lou's luggage down for the clerk to place in storage.

As Dread and Anubis had their scouts out, observing everywhere Tayla and Malcolm were, so did the Dragon also have his scouts out. One of them spotted Tayla. Dread spotted him and dispatched him but not before he was able to get a text message off to the Dragon.

In the lobby of the hotel, Tayla said her first words directly to Malcolm. She introduced herself and they began to converse, even though she was aware the Jackals had already tracked Malcolm back to his hotel. Because of her focus on Malcolm, she was unaware that she had been spotted as well by a Jackal scout.

Malcolm was torn as to where to continue their conversation, Lou's or his room, or the hotel lobby. They stayed in the lobby, drinking the beverage for which Colombia is famous for. They sat and talked for hours. Though Malcolm was so enchanted by her, he failed to notice the time. He was very tired, dismissing himself to retire to his room.

Tayla was aware the Jackals were making their move against him. Malcolm could see them approaching the front doors and gallantly, tried to warn her that she was in danger from the

Jackals. The clerk was killed in a hail of gunfire after he came around from behind the desk to see what the yelling was all about. Malcolm ran for the elevator as the Jackals moved through the broken glass front doors. He hit the floor of the elevator to avoid the gunfire. Tayla knew the next spray of gunfire would be directed at him, which she knew would finish him off. There was only one thing to do. She had to take those bullets for herself.

Less than five minutes before they had attacked, the Dragon was notified that Tayla had been spotted in Bogota. His orders to his Jackal soldiers to re-arm themselves with silver tipped ammo did not reach them in time. The ammunition they were loaded with was not silver, but ball ammunition. If they had been silver, this story would not be written.

Tayla feigned an award-winning death scene that any actress would have been proud to have performed. It convinced Malcolm that his newly made acquaintance had just been killed by those who were bent on killing him. It bought Malcolm enough time to get to cover before Tayla could intervene on his behalf.

Tayla wanted Malcolm to get to cover, obtain his weapon which he had already proven proficiency, and prepare himself to use again. Meanwhile, the Queen moved to dispatch a dozen or so Jackal soldiers. She did so within about a minute and prepared to remove Malcolm from the country, not to capture him, but to protect him. Otherwise, he was set on a collision course with the Dragon, courtesy of the Jackals.

Malcolm came out of the room within a few minutes of the end of Tayla's complete destruction of the Jackal contingent. Their deaths were swift, complete, and efficient. No blood, no weapons, only broken necks, and bodies on the floor.

When the door opened, a frightened but cautious man stepped out into the hallway, ready to fire on anything that moved inside the darkened hall. Tayla was already in his room, waiting for him. She did not want to alarm him, so she waited for the precise moment to incapacitate him with a cloth soaked in chloroform. The drug was so overpowering that it dropped Malcolm Harris in only a few seconds.

The next thing Malcolm was aware of was riding in an airplane at 30,000 feet, with nothing but the roaring of jet engines to bring him to semi-consciousness. Then, he was out again.

CHAPTER SIXTY

NIGHT AFTER NIGHT AFTER NIGHT

"Dearest Malcolm, I could have ended my story right there. Anyone who has read your story would know the rest of the tale you told so well in your memoirs. However, a biography is intended to take the reader to the end, or at least up to date currently. In my case, it must end with my death. It must tell the where, the why and the how of my final moments on this earth and in this life. You did it very well. Now, my words must tell that story."

*   *   *

Malcolm and Queen Tayla spent nearly a year preparing for what would seem to be a turning point in the history of the race of vampires. She knew all along how this was going to end. Night after night after night, her gift of sight would remind her of all that she had been through, and all that was to happen eventually. Often, she would wake, in the complete darkness of her tomb, and sit wondering if there was another way to avoid what was becoming inevitable.

She was tired...tired of living the life of a vampire when she felt her world about to collapse on top of her. Her brother Rascha had betrayed her. Her other two siblings were trying to stay neutral, but that was not enough for her. They should have been supportive of her. Instead, they would sit and watch their brother conspire with their immortal enemy, and support whoever came out victorious. It hurt her so to see this happening.

She had begun to prepare her vampires and her familiars for the upcoming battle she knew she would not survive. She did not tell them that she would not survive. They had to believe they still could come out victorious. A lot of preparation had to go into her plans. The only ones who knew anything of what she foresaw coming could only be told a little of it at a time. Too much information could spoil everything.

Rascha had the Dragon in his corner. She needed someone of equal value to be in her corner. That person could only be Malcolm. Malcolm's faith was his shield, and his Bible was his sword. Only Malcolm could wield that sword. It would be fear versus faith, truth versus lies, and above all, good versus evil. All that resided in the pages of Malcolm's Bible. When they brought Malcolm out of Colombia, they took special care in making sure the Bible was brought to the mansion as well as the owner.

As expected, Malcolm used his knowledge of scripture to inform Tayla that all was not lost. That hope of salvation was within her grasp. Still, there was one thing she needed to do before she left the world to the other clans. She had to prevent Rascha from taking the throne. He could not be allowed to rule. Blood would run like it had never ran before. She envisioned an apocalyptic event should it occur. Malcolm was her weapon. At first, she did not envision his wife becoming part of the team, but she did, and she performed beautifully. The Dragon stirred a fire in Rachel's heart by threatening her family. She would defend them to the death if necessary.

Much of Tayla's actions were directed towards that end, the destruction of the *Black Velvet Clan* and the destruction of the Jackals that accompanied them into the Lower Estate. Malcolm and his wife put their heads together and came up with the plan, with the added input from Dread and Anubis. They trained for it, using the known methods and weapons proven to kill vampires.

During the gathering, Malcolm and his wife, Rachel, accompanied the Queen's entourage when coming into the *Coliseum*. They sat next to the Queen. When Rascha approached Queen Tayla as she sat upon her throne, he sneered at them, insulting her and them both. He was walking directly into the

594

trap set for him. Tayla kept up the argument she and he were having, while Malcolm and Rachel prepared to strike. The signal was to be when Queen Tayla's hand reached out to take Rascha's ring bearing hand. When that happened, the two mortals struck, one severing the hand from the wrist while the other severing the head from the body.

At that moment, the *Black Velvet Clan* vampires were rendered powerless. They would be as mortals until the sun shone upon the land above. Those that would have survived the battle at that time would die then. Queen Tayla had decreed that the vampires of Rascha's clan were now enemies of the Queen and they were to be destroyed. The battle ensued, *Red Clan* versus *Black Clan* and *Jackals*. The Queen took Malcolm with her while Rachel was escorted to the Upper Estate to place Rascha's ring on the sundial.

Queen Tayla's battle plan was multi-fold. The first part was to destroy Rascha and his clan. That was the easy part. Rascha was never known to be overly clever. He was overly evil. Tayla used that to her advantage. Evil is because of greed. Rascha wanted the throne, for the Dragon had convinced him that it was rightfully his and that it had been a mistake that Tayla had become Queen.

Rascha was bold, and trusted that his sister was afraid of him, because he had the Dragon's support. She used that to her advantage as well. Rascha had never felt the need to be cautious. It was his undoing. Rascha had failed to understand the purpose of Malcolm and his wife, and therefore had ignored it as his pride dismissed them as mere mortals, incapable of inflicting harm upon him. Eventually, Tayla's other siblings would repeat the same mistake, underestimating the couple. They failed to see the power they had through their faith. Also, the cause of their undoing.

The second part of Tayla's plan was to destroy Jackals who would invade the Lower Estate shortly after the death of Rascha. Her familiars, particularly her engineer, had prepared charges that would destroy many of the Jackals before they would ever reach them. The rest were to be destroyed by the *Red Clan* vampires and the familiars.

595

The next part of Tayla's plan was her own exorcism, to free herself of the demon that inhabited her body, fighting with her own conscience night after night after night. Once that had been completed, then and only then could she hear the message that she knew awaited her while in a mortal state. She wanted this one opportunity, this one moment in time, to hear the message of salvation from one who possessed it. It was her dying wish, but it was not to be her only wish.

She had left instructions with her vampires that upon her death, their deaths eminent, they were to pledge loyalty to Malcolm and Rachel until the sun rose once more. They were to follow every order and every instruction, aiding them in their quest to reach the surface and to avoid the Jackal soldiers at all costs. Her familiars had received the same exact instructions, with the only exception that their loyalty was to remain until all the clans were destroyed. The familiars were well on their way topside when they felt the death of their Queen.

Meanwhile, down below, in the lowest part of the estate, the Queen had taken Malcolm to her most closely guarded secret, the location of her tomb. She showed him the vault, her mausoleum, and her heart. She told him how she felt about him, that she wanted to love him in such a way he could love her back but knowing he could not. More specifically, she could not stand to lose another like Eric Petersen. She did not tell him of all her lovers, because she did not want Malcolm to be tempted to be like Eric, and therefore, become a vampire like her. She had brought him there for one reason, to help her die.

Tayla told Malcolm of her journals and papers she had written. She had given them to him, along with a massive amount of treasure. What she had not told him that all her writings would be compiled into one document after she had left. It was to be her final spell.

Tayla fought her demon, while Malcolm fought it as well, reciting the scripture that reveals the truth, projecting the power with his faith in the King of Kings, the Lord of Lords. It was a struggle, but she knew it would be, for she had foreseen it all. And because of that, she had prepared for it. The Queen had told him his angels were with him. He had no fear for he knew he was not alone.

Before the demon left her body, it told Malcolm that it would destroy the woman that Malcolm had come to love. Malcolm saw it as the lie that has plagued man since the beginning of time. He would not suffer the demon to have its way. He continued the slashing and parrying with his sword of truth, until the demon was vanquished and left the body of the vampire Queen.

When it had done so, the body of Tayla collapsed upon her tomb's floor of marble. As Tayla began to return to her mortal body, the leathery wings, the sharp talons, from around her mouth began to fade away. She was now the one that was fourteen years old at the time of her death.

It was there, in that deep, dark recess of the earth's darkness, a chard of light in the form of hope, came piercing through. Malcolm knew that time was short, as her body was aging at a rapid rate. He only had a few minutes. He gave her the message of salvation, that she was redeemable, that her life and soul were not worthless. Her sins could be forgiven, and her soul restored, if she would only accept as truth the gift the Son of God had given her by believing. This she did willingly, and without hesitation. Her mind was clear though her body was fading. She passed into eternity, a true eternity, with a true immortality.

Malcolm was exhausted. He was saddened for he wanted to tell her more. However, he had told her enough, in that she was saved in the last few moments of her life. He tidied up her tomb, so it would not look as if a struggle had taken place. To him, the struggle she had fought was over. There should be no reminders of the battle that was fought there in the dark. He placed her body, wrapped up in the red velvet shroud she had slept in for nearly eight centuries, back into the coffin surrounded by the dirt of her native land. Torches gave off light enough for him to see.

When he went down to the vault, he decided to leave everything alone, for his mission was not over. He had quite a bit more to do. He had a long journey to get back to the part of the lower estate he was familiar with and then to get past any enemy Jackal soldiers he might encounter. Next, he had to get the ring upon the sundial and make sure it was there before the sun would set.

Malcolm would cry tears. They were tears he would not write about. He did love Tayla. For all the right reasons. The women in his life were all important to him. If he could have, he would have tried to find some way that this Queen of vampires could have lived a normal, productive life on this earth, in this century. He would have been the greatest friend the Queen would have ever had. Malcolm put the torches out and set out to finish his mission.

CHAPTER SIXTY-ONE

A FINAL WORD

"Dearest Malcolm, we have now come to the end of this story, and the beginning of the one that you will write. I have tied the ends of the two together. I have had an exceedingly long and eventful life. Most of it, I lived in darkness. My story was a tale of sorrow, of survival, of triumph, and victory. For nearly eight centuries, I witnessed history in the making, even helped to shape it.

The history of Europe is so closely interwoven with the history of the clans. Medieval life was tediously hard, cruel, as well as dangerous. As mortals living in those days, we fought disease, the weather, the superstitions of ignorance and the dogma of religion. It seemed there was always a war, struggling for power and the right to rule over others less fortunate as ourselves. As a result, the life span of ordinary people seemed far too short. Far too often, the peasant was caught in the middle between duty to king and duty to family. The struggle to advance beyond all that was even more difficult. And yet, my kind used it to our advantage.

I often wondered what the purpose of all of it was as I wrote about my life and those events which took place before I was born. The Order of Dragons of Set had created and shaped the destiny of my race before I came to exist. I was the one they never expected and for my entire existence as a vampire, I fought against the Dragons and the Orders they formed. I now know the answer why. It was to illustrate to me my final destiny, the one you participated in. Vampires were not meant to exist in this world. If we were, I believe they would have been created by the same who created you and all the other people in this world. It would not have been the Dark Lord.

The Dark Lord, Set, or Satan as you may call him, is enormously powerful. However, he is not as powerful as the Lord I now reside with. His gifts to me were his undoing of the power over me. He had made my memory void of the loving father I once knew. My ability to extract memory from inanimate objects undid the curse he had placed upon me and my siblings. My memories of my father came to me like a shower of fresh rain, inundating me with drops of memories, each more enjoyable than before. I also came to know the painful memory of what the Dragon did to him just before our transformation. I hated the Dragon long before I learned the full story of how he had betrayed my father, and ultimately my mother. Before I died the second death, my eyes were opened. Like the blind man in your scriptures, I finally did see. Becoming a vampire is descending from light into darkness. Because of you, I was able to come into the light again.

I saw the purpose and intent of the *Order of the Dragons of Set*. I came to know the origin and purpose of the *Order of the Jackal*. It all made sense to me that this was a history of the battle for the soul of humanity. It seems to me that it was like a play that God was watching, knowing the ending for it was He who wrote the play, but let mankind make his own decisions, for He knew the direction mankind would take.

The gifts the Dark Lord gave to me enabled me to have learned many things. My most precious gift was the gift of sight. Without that, I would not have been able to write this account of my life. Because of it, I can write about things that needed to be told, even after I was gone. The story and the people who played a role in it is quite long. I wish I could go back in time and give thanks to those who helped me, ask forgiveness for those who I had transgressed against, change some things, and most of all, make restitution. But time travel is not possible, because if it were, atonement would be possible I suppose. Nothing I can do will ever wash clean the blood on my hands.

I gave myself an education which enabled me to help shape history, help others, and ensure the survival of my race up to this moment. I learned to sing, performing before some of the great families of Florence during the Renaissance. One of the greatest masters of all time taught me to paint. I conversed with the Kings and Queens of medieval Europe, all the while, feigning mortality. All the experiences, the adventures, the thrills of exhilaration and victory, along with the despair of defeats and losses have shaped my view of the world. The ordinary citizen, the lowly peasant, the courageous soldier, the arrogant aristocrat and monarch, the pious Pope, and the visionary that was the artist of the Renaissance; I have met them all.

The outcome of my story was possible through your loving kindness and courage to help me. None of any of this would have been possible without you and your family. You once said that you thought I 'invaded' the Napa Valley at the turn of the century. The truth is I had already purchased that land prior to that. It remained dormant until after 1906, right after the San Francisco earthquake. That was because I knew that much of what was already established would be destroyed or damaged. I had concentrated most of my fortune in shipping and gold mining. I had purchased ships and they sailed everywhere for me. My ships, my familiar crews, that was how most vampires got around intercontinentally in those days.

As you know, you are the sole beneficiary of my estate. That means both upper and lower estates. Do with the Lower Estate as you will. If nothing else, let it be a memorial to the race that was never meant to be. As for the artworks I have collected over the centuries, they are yours now as well. Most of them are extremely valuable, because as you read this, if you look up, you will see a Da Vinci original of me. I treasured this painting above all the works I collected. It was my mirror. I only wish I could have had more done of me in my other identities. If it requires some loving care, be careful who you let do the work. It truly is one of a kind.

You, like me, have lived a wonderful life, full of rich and enlightening experiences, but yours, unlike mine, has been blessed by relationships. Rachel is the most fortunate woman I know for she found her true love and was not denied it. She is fortunate to know the role of wife and mother and she must cherish each day of it. Many women have been denied both.

Now comes the time I must prepare you for. I have given you the gifts I promised. You received all the tools needed to accomplish your mission. Yet, the dangers you faced are still out there. All things will not be right when you have reached this point. My gift of sight tells me that one clan, the *Order of the Blue Velvet* will have survived. It survives because a familiar has enacted a contingency that will ensure the species will go on. You have made a pact of mutual exclusion that will ensure no interference shall be made against either party until you have passed from this world. It was an honorable thing to do under the circumstances.

This agreement is binding while both of you are alive. However, your children are not bound under oath to this pact. One day, you and Rachel will pass on from this world. Pass on to your children your legacy, for they will share it with the world.

There are still three more contingency vials of vampire blood, enough to resurrect all the clans. This must not happen, under any circumstances. The *Order of the Blue Velvet* and the three remaining vials of vampire blood must be destroyed. Therefore, you must prepare your children for the task that you could not finish. They will find it much easier than you did because you will have taught them well. You know the location of the lair of the vampires and how to attack them. You must prepare them for this. They must be able to read these manuscripts, to prepare them. Most of all, the Dragon must never be set free. The angels will see to that.

I leave you now. These are my final words to you and my final farewell. Remember me fondly until we meet again, in that eternity we both have sought after,

Your friend, Tayla.

THE END

GLOSSARY OF CHARACTERS

Akhenaten and Nefertiti: The first two vampires ever created, King and Queen of the 18th Dynasty of the New Kingdom, ancient Egypt. Their tomb has been discovered, but no bodies were ever found, due to their rising and leaving Egypt.

Anna: A trusted maiden of Countess Elspeth. She had been with Elspeth since she was a child and Elspeth considered her nearly a sister. To the children of the countess, she was an aunt.

Annara Rokosovich: The mother of Tayla, the mistress of Prince Vladis and eventually his second wife, mother of his children.

Anubis: Counselor to Queen Tayla, a genius and the most intelligent of all familiars. He is the right-hand familiar, serving as the "Chief Counselor" to Tayla, her most trusted advisor. He was tall, impressive and his appearance would intimidate even the most confident of humans. Tayla met Anubis as an applicant from a job fair in San Francisco in 1981. His high intellect and analytical abilities had served both Queen Tayla and Malcolm Harris well. Their close working relationship had forged a friendship that would last a lifetime. Anubis, aka Whitman Bauer, had doctorate degrees from Yale, Oxford Universities, and King's College in England. His degrees ranged from computer science, business administration and political science. He was a certified member of the Mensa Society. Anubis was also a member of the Mensa Society. He was the most intelligent and analytical of all the familiars. Tayla considered Anubis more intelligent than some of her vampire brood. Even with all their powers, Anubis could confound some of them. The concept of vampires challenged Anubis. This intrigued her and for this and his other talents, she brought him into the familiar fold. She knew he was right for the job because of his analytical manner, his great organizational skills, and his communication skills, not to mention his interpersonal relationship ability. He was the puppet CEO for Tayla's corporate empire. At the end, he became Malcolm's business manager.

Anvil: Aka Roger Hastings, served as Queen Tayla's butler from 1950-1970. Mortis replaced him in 1970. Born and Raised in Winchester, England, he was educated at the boarding school known as Winchester College, one of the oldest secondary education institutions in England. He attended Christ Church College afterwards and received a degree in world literature. For a while he taught English in public schools, then emigrated to the US after becoming dissatisfied with the current school politics of the day. He became even more dissatisfied with trying to teach in the American school system and became a gentleman's gentleman, otherwise known as a butler. He is immensely proud for his first job was not only as a butler but also a tutor to his employer's children, which he was proud of. When the children got older, the opportunity to teach went away, and he was left with only the job of being the butler. His employer was very wealthy and paid him well, but he always wanted to teach as well. He decided to become a novelist on the side, and in his spare time, he wrote a story about himself, using a fictitious name. She brought him to her mansion, showed him her library of rare books and documents. It intrigued him that his potential new employer had such a collection. He accepted the position as butler and librarian, but truthfully, he had become a historian. After he became a familiar, he started keeping records that has become part of the body of this manuscript. Roger Hastings' familiar name became Anvil. She named him that because he was part of the forge rebuilding her estate, helping to shape what is in existence today. He held that position for twenty years. He never looked back.

Archbishop of Cologne: The Archbishop who knew of the Dominican friars who had been combatting Vampyria all along and enlisted Father Karl as the special inquisitor against them.

Baron Phillipe Sauvienne: A French nobleman who desired to marry Countess Elspeth. Queen Tayla gave her some points to consider before marrying him. She did marry the Baron, living in her castle, combining their fortunes and lands. It was an unconsummated marriage. Tayla made him a familiar so to keep him obedient with her plans.

Baron Regevaks Descondes: Prince Vladis' captor after the Battle of Phillippopolis. He wanted to take Princess Illona prisoner and as part of the ransom payment, but her armed escort was intercepted by Vojislav Rekvas.

Bartholomew: Monk at Tarnovo monastery, clerk to old and new Bishop of Tarnovo. Assigned to Wallachian parish, eventually becomes a friar. Aids the children and Prince Vladis even after their conversion to being vampires.

Birdseye: The familiar name of Major Phillip Terwin, a former army officer who had worked at the staff level of an Army Corps. Intelligence and Plans was his specialty. Queen Tayla brought him into the fold and he became predecessor to what Anubis would become decades later. He was able to do what Anubis did without the advantage of computers. He was killed defending the mansion from the first wave attack in 1928.

Bishop of Tarnovo: Name is Stanzylch, gives aid to Annara, recognizes her as legitimate wife of Prince Vladis, writes letter of protection for her.

Caminus Sergio Perginas: A member of the High Council of the *Order of the Dragons of Set* during the 15th century (1492). It is he who is the last leader of the High Council before the Order is extinguished in a single night at the hands of the *Order of the Clan of the Red Velvet*.

Count Thomas DeVacquerie: Son of Elspeth, Countess DeVacquerie who inherits the title of Count after his mother dies.

Countess Elspeth DeVacquerie: A noblewoman, of English birth, widowed to a French nobleman who was under attack from her husband's murderers, befriended and protected by Queen Tayla in return for support and sanctuary.

Decadent, Reaper, Requiem, Sinister: Four familiars of the *Order of the Clan of the Red Velvet* assigned to watch the mausoleum where Scimitar and the Dragon were hiding at after the first wave assaulted the Upper and Lower Estates in 1929.

Dread: Familiar to the Red Clan, aka Sergeant Sean McAllister, Chief of Security of Upper Estate. He is a faithful and devoted servant of Tayla. He is originally from Liverpool, England. Dread was a former British SAS soldier who was out of work and just wandering. He was considering joining the French Foreign Legion. Tayla met him in a bar in the waterfront district of San Francisco. Some guy was conversing with Tayla, telling her his life story but it was she who was playing the pick-up artist. Dread, who was sitting at the bar, noticed that the man was trying to take her purse. Dread then came over, grabbed the would-be-thief, and almost destroyed him to the point that the bartender and several others had to intervene. He told Tayla what the man was doing, and the others took the would-be-thief and ran him out of the bar. Tayla was impressed that someone had thought that she needed help. She met with Dread the next night, and he too came under her spell. She said he was perfect to watch over her during the day as she slept. She had already noticed that he had a keen eye. He was the kind of man she could trust not to let his guard down. He loves Tayla, mistrusts and very jealous of Malcolm. After Tayla brought Dread in, he built a security force (with the sanctioning of the Clan) that guards the estate and acts as bodyguards for other familiars when meeting vampires outside the clan. His exploits were near legendary in the special operations world, and he had disappeared years ago, now officially listed as dead. His family still lived in Liverpool. He had never married nor had children. At the end, his memory was given back to him and within the year, he married Martha Rivera, leaving the estate, and joining her on more archaeological excavations in Egypt.

Eduardo Arrellano: aka as the "Dragon", leads the Order of the Jackal in the western hemisphere in modern times. He is extremely powerful, very clever, and very evil.

Emperor Boril: The successor to Emperor Kaloyan, whom it is suspected that he murdered him to usurp the crown.

Emperor Kaloyan: Current ruler of Bulgarian Empire, lays siege to Varna, lays waste to Byzantine garrison there.

Falcon: Familiar to the Red Clan, Richard Vandemere, aka Falcon was the first to hold the title of High Counselor and served starting in 1965 and continued his service until 1981. Replaced by Anubis 1981.

Father Joachim: A member of the Dominican Order of Priests who personally led the inquisition against all vampires and their familiars. Queen Tayla lured him into a trap, extracted information from him and executed him.

Father Karl: A Dominican "Black Friar", former associate of Father Joachim and Father Heinrich Kramer. He is a man who currently possesses more knowledge than any mortal alive.

Ferdinand II: Holy Roman Emperor during the time of the Thirty Years War.

Francisco Cordero: a Colombian national who starts the whole mystery off by getting caught running a local cult chapter in the Miami-Dade area, and charged with pet-knapping, cruelty to animals and drug charges. He is assassinated while in custody, under very mysterious circumstances.

Harmony: Familiar to the Red Clan, 1954, aka Glynis Jamison, Cook. She was replaced by Sally Kensington, aka Shade 1975.

Harvest: Familiar to the Red Clan, 1955, aka Emil Worcester, Estate Gardener. He was replaced by Ben Watson, aka Moon, 1978.

Henri: Ambassador of the *Order of the Red Clan*. He is a young but highly intelligent man who had held administrative positions in his mortal life.

Illona: Princess of Moldavia, married to Prince Vladis to seal a security pact, arranged by both their parents. She hates Vladis because she had to leave her homeland to marry him. She never loved him and cannot stand the sight of him, but mostly, does not want him to be happy, either with her or anyone else. She hopes to see him killed during battle but that does not happen. He instead comes home with the willingness to have their sham marriage annulled so he can marry a commoner he truly loves. She is enraged beyond reason and conspires in all kinds of ways to destroy him.

Janos of Plovdiv: New bishop who replaced the one after his death.

Jerome Krueger: Current Dragon during 1618, the spark that started the Thirty Years War.

Johannes: Trusted counselor and castle butler to Prince Vladis

John Scotti: 1956, aka Scourge, Chief of Lower Estate, succeeded by Shock in 1975.

Josef Rokosovich: The father of Annara, the mother of Tayla, the grandfather of Tayla.

Kajil: Bulgarian nobleman, warrior, and friend of Prince Vladis.

Katarina, Magda, and Portia: Handmaidens and confidants to Princess Illona.

Kerry Brown: A female pirate captain of the ship, Phantom, also known as the Scarlett Raider.

Leech: Familiar to the Red Clan, Aka Dan O' Reilly, originally from North Carolina, he was a former Special Forces soldier who was trained as a combat engineer, therefore making him an expert at destroying things as well as building them. A graduate of Duke University with a degree in structural engineering, he had demonstrated invaluable skills and worth to the team. Engineer for upper estate, and sometimes for lower estate. He engineered the final construction of the *Coliseum*. He also helps to install the defenses and traps for Malcolm. He is thin and pale, speaks with a southern accent. As the engineer whose ingenious ability to perform feats of design to ensure victory as well as survival for the team, he survived the battles against the clans and at the end, had his past returned to him. He had family who still farmed back in North Carolina. They welcomed him home with open arms. He had been gone nearly fifteen years.

Leonardo Da Vinci: Master painter, inventor, sculptor, musician, who befriends Queen Tayla, teaches her the arts, and paints her first portrait. Suspects he knows of her secret identity and is cautious about pressing her for details. She confides in him and reveals the secret of her past.

Lorenz Sonnabenter: A Jesuit priest assigned to the parish of Graz, where the Thirty Years War started.

Luis (Lou) Martinez: A detective with Miami-Dade County Sheriff's Office, friend of Malcolm's, eventually part of Malcolm's organization against vampires. He is captured by vampires twice, survives and plays a key role on Malcolm's team. He is a long-time trusted friend of Malcolm's, who reconciles with his wife and family. He brought them out to San Francisco where he began to work as a private investigator for the law firm of Barclay, Feinstein, and Associates. He and Malcolm remained life-long friends.

Major Eric Petersen: A Swedish-American army engineer officer who at one time had leased a claim on Tayla's estate. He left and came back nearly 20 years later to become her chief engineer for building the Lower Estate. Eventually he becomes "Hammer", a familiar to the *Red Clan*. He is brought to the "Crossing Over" by Tayla for she had loved him since he was a young miner digging for gold on her land.

Major Gabriel Villere: An American army officer, who was at a plantation that the British came upon and occupied. He barely escaped unnoticed and was taken by Tayla to General Andrew Jackson to warn him of the British approach from the plantation.

Malcolm Harris: One of two co-main characters, he is husband to Rachel, father to Jennifer and Jonathan. He is the reluctant hero and leader of the vampire hunter-killer team, charged with the annihilation of all the clans of vampires. Malcolm is a mortal, a Christian, and an investigative journalist, who has been recruited by a Miami-Dade County Sheriffs Dept detective to investigate a cult which has resurfaced after a few years in seclusion. It starts with Malcolm reporting the story of a pet knapping ring being busted, but then it is learned that these pets were being sacrificed for a cult that believes in blood sacrifices. The lone suspect is taken into custody by the detective. The detective knows of Malcolm's unique knowledge of cults, especially those prevalent to Latin America. He recruits Malcolm as a consultant at first, but then begins to trust Malcolm with all his dirty little secrets. Malcolm doesn't know if he should be working this story or not. He agrees to keep all of it under wraps until all the story is found out. Malcolm's investigation leads into Colombia, where he meets other characters. His investigation takes him into the back country looking for an altar identical to the one found at the scene of the crime in Miami. Through a series of events, Malcolm is guided to meeting up with Tayla, Queen of the Order of the Clan of the Red Velvet. Such a long name for a character! It's more title than name. Malcolm learns all about the vampire world, after being reassured in a most unusual way that he is not imagining anything. He accepts this reality, and then he accepts the mission given him by Tayla.

Matthias: A member of the High Council of the *Order of the Dragons of Set*. It is he who resets the path of Vojislav and directs him to kill Illona.

Medical Staff: Bones 1992, Scabs 1992, Medusa 1992, Cadusa 1992, Dementia 1992:

Bones aka Walter Sorenson, 1992. Queen Tayla's physician to the Stables of the Damned. He alternates duty with Scabs. At the end, Dr. Walter Sorenson, stayed on for a while to help take care of Mortis. At the time, he knew that Mortis was in declining health and the end would come soon. After Mortis' death, he returned to a surgical practice in San Diego, California.

Scabs aka Don Kulovski MD, 1992 Queen Tayla's physician to the Stables of the Damned. He was an emergency medicine specialist and returned to practice at a hospital in his native New Jersey. He had family there.

Cadusa aka Michelle Pratt, 1992, assistant to Bones and Scabs in the infirmary near the Stables of the Damned. Registered Nurse, she left with Bones, (Walter Sorenson) as she had been one of his nurses in his practice before coming into the service of Queen Tayla.

Dementia, a Registered Nurse, assistant to Scabs and Bones in the infirmary near the Stables of the Damned. Found murdered in the Infirmary after the Black Clan raided the Stables of the Damned. No one knew her real name.

Medusa: Registered Nurse, assistant to Scabs in the infirmary near the Stables of the Damned. Aka Jennifer Walston left with Bones, (Walter Sorenson) as she had been one of his nurses in his practice before coming into the service of Queen Tayla.

Moon: Ben Watson, aka Moon, had worked in England developing large estate ground and golf courses. He had worked on the grounds of colleges and universities as well. His resume of completed projects convinced Emil that he was the man to succeed him. Emil asked Ben to come and visit him at Tayla's estate. When he did, he was impressed at the length of time it took complete such an accomplishment. He was particularly excited at the size of the shrubbery maze. Emil told him it was a difficult thing to do to keep up the appearance of it and everything else. Then, he told him about his condition and that he needed someone he could trust to continue his work and dream. Out of loyalty to his friend, Ben took the position. As a familiar, he was equally enthralled to be working for Queen Tayla and was grateful that his friend would not die but pass into immortality as a creature of the night. He would see him again, as Emil remained a part of the *Red Clan* up until the demise of the Queen. After the Queen's demise, which also meant the demise of Emil, Moon stayed on with the Harris', continuing to keep up the grounds up until the present. He could never go back home to England for he had outlived his family.

Mortis: Butler, and confidant to Queen Tayla. He is a middle-aged man who is the stereotype of a butler. A pale and thin man, standing straight and tall, wears a flawless, navy-blue suit, wire rim glasses and shined black shoes. He has graying hair, neat, slicked back with a light amount of mousse. He is very polite, kind and devoted to the Queen. He's happy to carry out any of her requests. Very trusted. Mortis also got his life back. Having been widowed and childless, an early retirement had not set well with him. He had taken a job as a "Gentlemen's gentleman" for a prominent family in the San Francisco Bay area, mastering the art of the profession. Mortis, now Winston Jamison, remembered the family he had once served. He made a visit to them to explain what had happened. It was so long ago, as the children had grown and become the masters of the house. His employers had died. However, the children did remember him, much to his satisfaction of not being forgotten. However, his age prevented much of his memory coming back. He elected to stay on as Malcolm's butler, and after two years, he died in his sleep while in his room. His funeral service was a grand one, as all the familiars, without exception, attended.

Necro: aka Richard Gaines 1983, Captain of the Hunt, runs the club "Halloween". He was a ne'er-do-well, who met Tayla while at a club. Generally, those people have someone paying attention if they just disappeared. Careful selection was the general rule. Necro is like a wolf eyeing a flock of sheep selecting targets who fit specific criteria. He keeps the Stables of the Damned full and supplies replacements when one dies. She noticed how observant he was of patrons, as he knew how to pick them for their vulnerability and ease of approach. For this reason, she picked him as the "Captain of the Hunt". He served Queen Tayla well for this position, also exhibiting many more talents she found useful. He had no family to come to claim him. Because of this, he elected to stay on as manager of Club Halloween. Gaines went on to finish his education, receiving degrees in business and hospitality management.

Nefertiti and Akhenaten: The first two vampires ever created.

Othar Rokosovich: The second and younger brother of Tayla.

Paul Vetter: Missionary/Priest in Columbia, South America, and friend of Malcolm's from college days, eventually a part of Malcolm's organization against vampires. Paul is a valuable member of Malcolm's team, and eventually marries Sally Kensington, aka Shade.

Peter: A boy who had been a childhood friend of Annara's when she was young.

Petri: A familiar of the *Red Clan*, designated by Queen Tayla to negotiate passage for the *Red Clan* of vampires to cross the ocean to the Americas.

Pope Alexander VI: Rodrigo De Borja, the successor to Pope Innocent VIII. Queen Tayla asked and was refused by him to rescind the edict against vampires.

Pope Leo X: The Pope who read the box of letters from previous Popes and became aware that Pope Alexander VI had met Queen Tayla. He calls a meeting of the Cardinals and issues a special inquisition against the vampires.

Prieta Rokosovich: The younger sister of Tayla.

Prince Vladis: Wallachian prince, with castle and lands just north of the Danube River. Proud father to four children who eventually become vampires, and husband to Annara.

Ramone: A member of the High Council of the *Order of the Dragons of Set* during the 15th century. It is he who shames Tayla into establishing her own *Order of the Clan of the Red Velvet*.

Rascha Rokosovich: The oldest but younger brother of Tayla.

Ricardo Draco: Dragon at the time of Tayla's mansion being completed. He approached her to tell her of the Church's new inquisition against not only the vampire clans but also against his group, the *Order of the Jackal*. He wanted cooperation and a last chance for an alliance between him and her, but she refuses. He is not greeted cordially but is instead told to leave, not to come back, and a spell guarding against his reentry put on the Upper Estate.

Saumbier: A Red Velvet vampire, Saumbier headed a patrol that arrived first at a familiar's farmhouse and tavern. Ensuing combat between a priest with his escort of clergy and soldiers and the Red Clan vampires resulted in death for the mortals who attempted to lay a trap for the familiars but were rescued by their vampire masters.

Scimitar: Jackal name for the Dragon's most talented assassin. He is the one assigned the mission to terminate Eric Petersen. Scimitar was of Arab descent. Scimitar has been groomed in the arts of death and murder since he could read and write. He lacks any resemblance of a conscience so therefore, in terms of DNA, he is the perfect human killing machine. A master of martial arts, he is skilled in several styles of lethal hand to hand combat. He is also a master of the sword, particularly the Samurai and the Scimitar. His dark eyes and olive complexion suggest either Hispanic or Middle Eastern. With an IQ of 175, he has many non-lethal talents, to include a photographic memory and speaking several languages. As charming as he is ruthless, if you were the intended target, he will get to you. His ability to charm, to blend in, to assimilate is unparalleled.

Scorpio: Another of the Dragon's premier assassins. A Colombian national, he has been with the Dragon for a long time. He too, like Scimitar has been trained since he was a young boy, indoctrinated into the *Order of the Jackal* after he proved he was no stranger to murder and violence. The Dragon became his master teacher and Scimitar his mentor. He had learned much from both. The Dragon had ensured he was educated in all the necessary subjects to make him as well rounded a tool as was Scimitar.

Scourge: A former Chief of the Lower Estate. Aka John Scotti, he was a Korean War veteran, who had been disfigured for his trouble. He was a decorated veteran, winner of three Purple

Hearts, a Bronze Star, and a Silver Star, both for gallantry upon the field of battle. He was unemployed as finding employment was difficult for him due to his disfigurement. She found him walking along a street in the city during the wee hours of the morning. He looked lost and full of despair. She asked her driver to stop and ask if he needed help. John had mined coal back in PA and was not afraid of the dark. He had been a platoon sergeant during the war and was used to organizing and leading men. Tayla decided he was perfect for the job of Chief of the Lower Estate.

Shade: Aka Sally Kensington, Cook of Scottish origin. She was born Sally Kensington, the daughter of a Scottish farmer. Formally trained as a chef at a very prestigious culinary arts school in Europe, Shade met Tayla while was dining at her restaurant in Frisco with Anubis. Impressed with the menu and the quality of the cuisine, Falcon suggested that Tayla hire the chef as the cook for the estate. Tayla trusted Anubis' judgment on these matters so that was that. Tayla arranged an interview with Shade and brought her into the fold. She is in her fifties, slightly plump, very jovial, and very maternal. After professing faith in Christ, she had taken quite a liking to Paul Vetter, who taught her more about Christ and scripture each day. Their affection between them grew. Within the year, they too were married. They elected to stay on at the mansion, much to the satisfaction and delight of the Harris'.

Shock: Aka Franco Banzetti, Chief of the Lower Estate. Tall, and slender, he resembles something from the Rocky Horror Picture Show! A physically ugly character of a man, he looked more like a corpse. Shock's scalp looked partly disfigured, as hair only grew from part of it. The rest of it was bald perhaps from what appeared to be burn scars. When he smiles, he shows that he is in dire need of dental care. His personality was that he was a humble man, takes orders well, and works well in an overseer position. Arranges for Malcolm to set his trap for the Black Velvet Clan. The Black Clan also murders him during the gathering of the clans.

Sir Renard Berenais: A French Knight during the Hundred Years War, who was Tayla's first lover. He was killed just prior to the Battle of Poiters.

Stephen Bowie: Co-owner of the Louisiana plantation "Acadia". He is the brother of the famous Jim Bowie, of the famous knife design. He is also the sheriff of the county. It is his efforts that prompted Tayla and her clan to head west from New Orleans.

Talon: 1995. Chauffer to Queen Tayla. Talon's real name was Sandy Dawson, who had a felony record for grand theft auto. She had served time in the Oregon state corrections system, was paroled, and shortly after, met up with Queen Tayla. A former member of a professional car theft ring, she was a "wheel man". Tayla had noticed her working as a valet parking attendant at a corporate holiday ball. Tayla had read her thoughts that Talon had decided to steal the Ferrari that had just drove up behind her limousine. Tayla did not want any crimes happening on that night, at least not there so, she sent Dread out to intercept Talon. He held her for Tayla to do with what she wanted. Tayla sensed that this girl was a professional driver, one who could replace Mortis, so he would be free to look after just the estate. She decided that Talon would be perfect for the role as Tayla's driver, so Talon became Chief of Transport. To clear up any loose ends with the police, Tayla had Anubis clear the records of Talons entire existence. Talon is a non-person so officially she does not exist. She is very seductive, and beautiful. Talon had one of the most important reasons to want to regain her old life. She was a mother. Talon had always suspected she had given birth to a child as she felt a feeling of emptiness, an unresolved emotional attachment to something. Her stretch marks across her lower abdomen gave a good clue that at one time, she had been pregnant. She longed for the answers to that question. Now, she knew. She had a daughter, who would be about ten years old now. At the end, she departed the estate to search for her daughter. Because of her being on parole, and then disappearing, it was difficult for her to find her daughter. She was in violation of her parole. Lou Martinez was able to help her. It turned out that the child's father had custody of her daughter and eventually reconciled with Talon.   Talon was able to get her parole reinstated and began life as a full-time mother and wife.

Tayla Elizabeta Rokosovich: Firstborn child of Annara and Prince Vladis, transformed into a vampire at age 14, led her siblings down a path of existence as vampires, ultimately becoming the reigning monarch of a race of creatures whose presence the world has denied. Born in 1202, transformed 1216. She is the co-main character of the first novel, "Fear No Evil" and the main character of the novel "Descent into Darkness: Biography of a Vampire."

Tayla is without a doubt an immensely powerful vampire. She is not a mindless, evil, bloodsucking carcass shell of a once human being that comes out at night, to feed off the living. She is a beautiful creature, who has the unique ability to change forms, just as the old legends and myths state that vampires can do. She refuses to be a bat, or snake or any other vile and loathed creature that are often associated with vampires.   Tayla is a beautiful female vampire who usually manifests herself in one of three identities. She is a tall European; a slim, dark haired woman with a flawless complexion, with sexy curves, and more than ample sexual charm that seems to exude from her as steam does from boiling water. She has dark eyes, soft features, and a demure look that suggests abundant femininity. Her voice comes out of her throat in a smoky whisper that is very sensual. It is smoky, smooth and resonates with a light echo as if someone else were whispering her words as she spoke them. It's an eerie voice, but one that is very seductive. She can throw her voice anywhere and make it appear as if inanimate objects were speaking to you. Her hands are small, long and with slender fingers, accentuated by perfectly kept nails.   These nails can quickly turn in to retractable claws when attacking a victim. She wears impressive jewelry, but only while in her royal attire. Her hair is black, straight, kept, and shiny. She is the tall woman with dark hair, eyes, and soft features.

The second identity is that of a voluptuous, seductive blonde. This lady has extremely long blonde hair, all the way to her hips. She too has soft features, eyes that are Mediterranean blue, full red lips, with a curvaceous smile. She has a more than ample bust line which has a cleavage that she likes to show off. She is of medium height. The voice is pretty much of the same smoky quality but without the echo. She too is very seductive.

The third identity is that of a petite redhead. This lady is brimming with sexual allure. She has bright green eyes, soft medium length red hair, with a freckle-less complexion. She is pale, but so is the European Tayla. This woman's voice is seductive enough without the echo, or accent. She is petite, and always seems to be dressed scantily, or at least dressed to get attention.

Tayla was only fourteen at the time she was brought into the vampire realm. And she was the oldest of four. She was only a child at the time, never having been allowed the chance to grow up, to love a man, to marry, to have children, to have had a life. Her emotional makeup was and still is that of a teenage girl. Her human half has desired to make up for the things that she was denied in life, such as a father's love, a husband's protection, a lover's desire, and attention from men. She does things upon impulse at times, while at others she shows the cunning and shrewdness of a veteran schemer. She treats her vampire brood as though they were her children, the children that she could not have in mortal life.

Teng Xu Ling: 1968, aka Windsong, limousine driver. He was succeeded by Talon in 1995 He was of small stature, but his ability to recall locations on maps was astounding. Originally, he had learned to drive with professional ability while working as a cabbie in London.

Toomba: A recently arrived slave on the Acadia Plantation, who told Stephen Bowie that she had encountered vampires in Africa before coming to the US. These vampires were affiliated with the Purple Clan of Othar.

Valkyrie: Carl Prager, aka Valkyrie, was the Chief of Security for Tayla's growing empire. He had built a security apparatus which was in use all throughout her businesses. Just because she was not there to personally oversee the affairs of the many companies she owned; did not mean they were not tempted to put their hands into the profits gained. He was also head of security of the estate itself. He had come into her service in 1960.

He was a former law enforcement officer and a military veteran of the cold war era. Both of those backgrounds made him qualified to do what he did for her. He was replaced by Sean McCallister, aka Dread in 1990.

Vojislav Rekvas: The current embodiment of the Dragon, the vessel in which the evil entity Set dwells within.

Worm: Familiar to the Red Clan, 1956, aka Franklin Weber, Engineer. He was replaced by Dan O'Reilly aka Leech 1978.

Made in the USA
Columbia, SC
23 September 2020